SIXTY YEARS OF GREAT FICTION
FROM
PARTISAN REVIEW

Edited by William Phillips

Partisan Review Press

ISBN 0-9644377-5-9

Foreword

In my early twenties I went off to Madison, Wisconsin to do an advanced degree in cultural anthropology. My late friend Isaac Rosenfeld, still an undergraduate studying philosophy, had arrived a few weeks earlier and was living near the campus. The first days of the term were warm and hazy. We went canoeing on Lake Mendota. I capsized the canoe – Isaac luckily was still on the dock and helped me up the wooden ladder. We went to his room where I stripped and hung my wet chinos to dry on the windowsill.

It was Indian Summer, the room was filled with sunlight. I wrapped myself in a towel and we began to talk. What the subject of our conversation was I cannot be expected to remember, some sixty years later. But we never discussed anthropology at all and had little to say to each other about philosophy. Novels and poems, poets and novelists were what we eagerly and continually talked about. We went from Shakespeare to Dickens, from Dickens to Kafka, from Tolstoy to Isaac Babel, from Balzac to Proust to Malraux. We were big on Theodore Dreiser, Hemingway, Dos Passos, Thomas Wolfe and Faulkner. Delmore Schwartz's "In Dreams Begin Responsibilities" I considered then to be a masterpiece, and Schwartz was now – today, at this very moment – looking out of his window in Manhattan or walking by the Charles in Cambridge!

Schwartz's story had appeared in *Partisan Review*. *The Dial* had perished long ago, and so had *transition*. There were other literary reviews of course – the *Southern*, the *Hudson*, the *Kenyon* – those were all very well and good. We considered them a bit academic. They did not offer what we longed for, namely, deep relevance, contemporary high culture, left-wing politics, avant-garde painting, Freudian mining of the unconscious or Marxist views of past and future revolutions. In *Partisan Review* you could read George Orwell, André Gide, Ignazio Silone – during the Civil War in Spain, I remember, *Partisan Review* printed a curious piece by Picasso, "The Dreams and Lies of General Franco." These were *Partisan Review*'s European heavyweights. On our own side of the Atlantic *Partisan Review*'s contributors included Edmund Wilson, Sidney Hook, James Burnham, Paul Goodman, Lionel Trilling, Clement Greenberg, James Agee, and Harold Rosenberg.

The editors were William Phillips, Philip Rahv, Dwight Macdonald and, from time to time, F. W. Dupee. There was more dissonance than harmony among them and the closest of their outside supporters. Meyer Schapiro was the guru of one group; Sidney Hook of another. Hook records that when the war broke out the Leninist insiders insisted that it was a rerun of the imperialism of 1914-1915 and held to an orthodox Marxist position: "The main enemy is at home." The editors were preoccupied with European Marxism and especially with the Soviet Union. Edmund Wilson was said to have referred to *Partisan Review* as the *Partizanski Review*.

At the time of the magazine's founding, Leon Trotsky who was still alive in Mexico City took a considerable interest in it. His assassination in 1940 and the fall of Paris in that same year dealt the high culture left a double blow. It would be untrue to say that *Partisan Review* was a Trotskyist journal. Certain of the editors were of course sympathetic to Trotsky but only Stalinists would have described them as his followers. The left majority, at this time, came disguised as the Popular Front. We have learned in recent years that this supposed union of left-wing groups – including socialists and even anarchists – formed to resist fascism was organized by a Communist conspirator named Willi Münzenburg, an expert seducer of European and American intellectuals, journalists, academics, and artists – types referred to by Lenin in his day as "useful idiots." Much of the cultural life of the West was indeed in the hands of "useful idiots," unaware in their foolish innocence that they were being manipulated by Münzenburg and his skilled specialists. Moscow itself taught the world to laugh at the very thought of "Moscow Gold."

Partisan Review was a left-wing magazine, certainly. We, the literary radicals of the late thirties, would not have looked twice at it if it had been centrist. We were young and we wanted action, change, transformation. We had faithfully studied Marx, who told us that history was the history of class wars. We were living through a great, seemingly endless depression and maybe a rousing revolution would bring us out of it. But there was not the slightest evidence that the American working class had a revolutionary temper. It dearly loved FDR.

That neither Communism nor fascism tempted America's proletariat was seen by some of us as a sign of its immaturity and backwardness. Revolution was European and we seemed to believe at that time that this was a sign of superior development – revolutionary politics appeared to make possible a higher intellectual and artistic development. *Partisan Review*'s version of Europe was tremendously, enviably attractive. *Partisan Review* in those days imported intellectual goods from Europe. It suggested to its young readers that in New York, in Boston, even in Chicago, they could combine radical politics, philosophy, poetry as intellectuals did in Paris and live as bohemians and free artists. To be an artist, to write novels was infinitely more satisfying, more serious, more glorious than the study of savages. Persuaded that I should become a novelist, I gave up my Wisconsin stipend and returned to Chicago. Inevitably, I became for a time a New Yorker, I moved my shop – my confused mind – from Hyde Park in Chicago to Greenwich Village.

In New York I was encouraged by Dwight Macdonald, helped by William Phillips, taken seriously by Philip Rahv, befriended by Delmore Schwartz and William Barrett.

I was very briefly a protégé of Clement Greenberg. He told me what he believed every young writer should know. It was important, he said, to come under the influence of an older woman. She would prepare him for the world, teach him about sex, cure him of brashness – she would civilize you, French-style. These notions of his came directly from Balzac, whose novels I had read in Chicago. I could never be a *jeune ambitieux*, French-style. I agreed with Clem that I was unformed. I listened to him willingly. But no mature woman ever came forward to sponsor and instruct me.

Clem was respected by *Partisan Review*'s editors and taken seriously by certain of the 10th Street painters. Late in the thirties *Partisan Review* published his famous essay "Avant-garde and Kitsch." The editors did not say this was a declaration of their ideological principles. But clearly it formulated and justified their quest of "the new." What they detested and resisted was popular culture or kitsch. It is best here to let Greenberg speak for himself: "Commercial art and literature with their chromeo-types, magazine covers, illustrations, ads, slick and pulp fiction, comics, Tin Pan Alley music, tap dancing, Hollywood movies, etc. . . . Kitsch is a product of the industrial revolution which urbanized the masses of Western Europe and America and established what is called universal literacy. . . ."

To literary Americans of my generation Greenberg made clear the relations between the majority in our industrial capitalistic American mass democracy and the intellectual artistic minority. I shall refrain here from outlining the whole of his position. He was of course a Marxist. He was a Leninist. There were no illusions about Stalin. Stalin was loathed; Lenin was idolized. Lenin was hard, was strict, pure and stern – merciless as a revolutionist must be when he takes power. Clem was himself strict, doctrinaire, pure and hard and believed that he was doing in art what Ilyitch had done in politics.

"True, the first settlers in bohemia – which was identical with the avant-garde – turned out to be demonstratively uninterested in politics," Clem wrote. "Nevertheless, without the circulation of revolutionary ideas in the air about them, they would never have been able to isolate their concept of the 'bourgeois' in order to define what they were not. Nor, without the moral aid of revolutionary political attitudes would they have had the courage to assert themselves. . . ."

Artistic patronage had fallen away, Clem argued, artists had been thrown upon the markets of capitalism. The avant-garde searched for an absolute in art itself – in "the disciplines and processes of art and literature. This is the genesis of the 'abstract.' "

On these premises Clem planted his flag and claimed the 'abstract' in the name of revolution. He gave historical reasons for this and told us that without a correct view of history our efforts would be barren.

There was no room for the likes of me in this historical picture. I was obviously stuck between kitsch and avant-garde owing to my concern with persons and with the external world. Because of my unwillingness to yield to historical necessities I was struck from Clem's list of the elect.

Many years later at the Arts Club in Chicago I saw him in the dining room. He, the honored guest of the evening, had passed me by, had cut me and sat down at the next table with the high-look of the justified cutter. As there was a dish of fruit within reach I threw green grapes at his bald head, and after I had scored a couple of hits he decided to acknowledge me. He turned and said, "I never *did* like you."

Clem had in his young days been something of a street fighter. Even at seventy, he may have felt like throwing a punch at me. This would have been a godsend to the Chicago newspapermen who had come to cover his lecture. He *might* have found it funny to be pelted with grapes. Perhaps there was one comic particle that he had never expelled from that tigerish Leninist heart.

That he had never liked me was not true. He had liked me. We had liked each other. I still liked the old fool. He was after all the Lenin – or a Lenin – of our art revolution. We had had two or three of those.

It is not irrelevant to speak of him here. I am trying to give you the flavor of *Partisan Review* in the old days. For some years I had thought of him as the soul of the magazine, but he could not associate himself with any group. No editorial board could ever be pure enough to suit him. He was and remained a revolutionist. The editors of *Partisan Review* did not form a coterie, though some believed that they did. They were eclectic, willing to be heterogeneous, open to new talent in every form. Though they frequently and violently disagreed they knew real writing when they saw it. Readers of this collection, if they are not too captious, will agree.

SAUL BELLOW

August 18, 1996
Brattleboro, Vermont

Contents

Acknowledgements

"Two Syllables" by Ignazio Silone. Reprinted with permission of Darina Silone.

"In Dreams Begin Responsibilities" by Delmore Schwartz. Copyright © 1941, 1961 by Delmore Schwartz. Reprinted with permission of New Directions Publishing Corporation.

"Hurry, Hurry" by Eleanor Clark. Reprinted with permission of Eleanor Clark.

"Red, White and Blue Thanksgiving" by John Dos Passos. Reprinted with permission of W. Tayloe Murphy, Jr.

"The Autobiography of Rose" by Gertrude Stein. Reprinted with permission of Partisan Review, Inc.

"The Only Son" by James T. Farrell. Reprinted with permission of the Estate of James T. Farrell.

"A Goat for Azazel (A.D. 1688)" by Katherine Anne Porter. Reprinted with permission of the Literary Estate of Katherine Anne Porter.

"The Man in the Brooks Brothers Shirt" by Mary McCarthy. Reprinted with permission of the Mary McCarthy Literary Trust.

Clement Greenberg's translation of "Josephine, the Songstress or, The Mice Nation" by Franz Kafka. Reprinted with permission of Janice Greenberg.

"Of This Time, of That Place" by Lionel Trilling. Reprinted with permission of Diana Trilling.

"The Hand That Fed Me," copyright © 1944 by Isaac Rosenfeld, renewed © 1972 by the Estate of Isaac Rosenfeld. First published in *Partisan Review*, from *Alpha and Omega* by Isaac Rosenfeld. Used by permission of Viking Penguin, a division of Penguin Books USA, Inc.

"Cass Mastern's Wedding Ring" from *All the King's Men*, copyright © 1946 and renewed 1974 by Robert Penn Warren, reprinted by permission of Harcourt Brace and Company.

Eleanor Clark's translation of "The Prison" by André Malraux. Reprinted with permission of Rosanna Warren.

"The Interior Castle," *The Collected Stories of Jean Stafford*, by Jean Stafford. Copyright © 1969 by Jean Stafford. Reprinted with permission of Farrar, Straus & Giroux, Inc.

"Two Prostitutes" by Alberto Moravia. Reprinted with permission of Casa Editrice Valentino Bompiani.

"The Jail" from *Requiem for a Nun* by William Faulkner. Copyright © 1950, 1951 by William Faulkner. Reprinted by permission of Random House.

"Gimpel the Fool" by Isaac Bashevis Singer, translated by Saul Bellow, copyright © 1953 by Partisan Review, Inc., renewed © 1981 by Isaac Bashevis Singer, from *A Treasury of Yiddish Stories* by Irving Howe and Eliezer Greenberg. Used by permission of Viking Penguin, a division of Penguin Books USA Inc.

"The Magic Barrel" from *The Magic Barrel* by Bernard Malamud. Copyright © 1958 by Bernard Malamud. Renewed © 1986 by Bernard Malamud. Reprinted with permission of Farrar, Straus & Giroux, Inc.

"Seize the Day" by Saul Bellow. Reprinted with permission of Saul Bellow.

"The Renegade" from *Exile and the Kingdom* by Albert Camus, translated by Justin O'Brien. Copyright © 1957, 1958 by Alfred A. Knopf, Inc. Reprinted by permission of the publisher.

"Any Day Now" was originally published in *Partisan Review* in 1960. It is excerpted from *Another Country*. Copyright © 1960, 1962 by James Baldwin. Copyright renewed. Reprinted by arrangement with the James Baldwin Estate.

"From the Black Notebook" reprinted with permission of Simon & Schuster from *The Golden Notebook* by Doris Lessing. Copyright © 1962 by Doris Lessing.

"It Always Breaks Out" by Ralph Ellison. Reprinted by permission of the William Morris Agency, Inc. on behalf of the author. Copyright © 1963 by Ralph Ellison.

"The Will and the Way" by Susan Sontag. Copyright © 1965 by Susan Sontag, reprinted with permission of Wylie, Aitken & Stone, Inc.

"Runaway" by William Styron. Reprinted with permission of William Styron.

"Whacking Off" from *Portnoy's Complaint* by Philip Roth. Reprinted with permission of Philip Roth.

"Mercier and Camier" from *Mercier and Camier* by Samuel Beckett. Copyright © 1974 by Samuel Beckett. Used by permission of Grove/Atlantic, Inc.

"Levitation" by Cynthia Ozick. From *Levitation: Five Fictions* by Cynthia Ozick. Copyright © 1982 by Cynthia Ozick. Reprinted by permission of Alfred A. Knopf, Inc.

"The Idea of Switzerland" from *How German Is It* by Walter Abish. Reprinted with permission of Walter Abish.

Introduction

BY WILLIAM PHILLIPS

Am I too immodest if I state flatly that the stories printed in *Partisan Review* since its beginning sixty years ago represent the best modern writing in this country – and to some extent abroad? In any event, a reader of this collection will find it a valuable, selected history of American literature since the 1930s. It is difficult to characterize this fiction; perhaps it might be said that it is intelligent narrative and that it explores the range of modern experience. It is not minimalist. It is not narrowly personal. It is not limited to sex. It is not what might be called "he said, she said" fiction.

Although we had no programmatic idea of fiction – indeed each story was judged simply on what we thought were its merits, one at a time – the composite picture has turned out to be a collection of a good deal of the best modern fiction. Some writers had reputations; many were young men and women, relatively unknown, submitting their early work.

What were our criteria? As I have said, each piece of fiction was judged on its own. But when we started out, we were reacting against the fashionable current of proletarian, realistic fiction. More specifically, we were rejecting the prevailing radical – mostly Communist – notion of fiction that represented the lives – and struggles – of the working class, the poor, the disadvantaged. The air was full of strike novels, and the mode was a version of Soviet-infused social realism. We, ourselves, were still faintly Marxist, but we felt that a truly advanced literature had to be not only radical in some fundamental, implicit manner, but also had to be in the vein of the modern sensibility. But we did not go in for vacuous, anti-narrative experimentation, though that too was being touted. The closest thing to so-called experimental writing we published was Susan Sontag's "The Will and the Way," and then later Samuel Beckett's "Mercier and Camier," but both of these pieces of fiction have a narrative line and structure. Beckett's story is in fact a somewhat fictionalized version of his play *Waiting for Godot*, and Sontag's is not anti-narrative in the manner of the French at the time. The only "realistic" story is by Farrell, whose memory and ear for talk and the expressed experience of the lower class gave his fiction its essence of mundane reality. To be sure, as we moved into the forties and fifties, our views changed considerably, and we were concerned with fiction that expressed the range of modern consciousness. In fact, this was evident in the very first issues of *Partisan Review*, in Delmore Schwartz's "In Dreams Begin Responsibilities," which sounded a new note in American writing, and in "Two Syllables," Ignazio Silone's striking insight into mass politics.

There followed a succession of talented stories: Eleanor Clark's distinctive combination of irony and evil in "Hurry, Hurry." "Red, White and Blue Thanksgiving" by John Dos Passos, in which his sharp eye for social contradictions and nuances is evident; Gertrude Stein's polished experimentation; Katherine Ann Porter's reinvention of an early incident of supposed witchcraft; Mary McCarthy's bold, personal account, "The Man in the Brooks Brothers Shirt"; Kafka's superbly symbolic

"Josephine the Songstress," a story of an artist in the guise of a mouse; Lionel Trilling's little masterpiece, "Of This Time, of That Place," a story of academic-style madness; "The Hand That Fed Me," by Isaac Rosenfeld, which shows a narrative gift that was cut short by his early death; Isaac Bashevis Singer's charming story of a wise fool, superbly translated by Saul Bellow; Albert Camus's subtle Algerian narrative; Robert Penn Warren's masterful recreation of an earlier period in Southern history; Faulkner's evocative tale of a Southern town and its jailhouse, in a quasi-Joycean style; André Malraux's elegant prose; Jean Stafford's stylization of intense physical experience, "In the Interior Castle"; Alberto Moravia's unsparing portrait of two sisters.

In 1954, the warm and moving story, "The Magic Barrel" by Bernard Malamud, which marked the beginning of his expansive literary career, appeared. There followed, in 1956, Saul Bellow's early masterpiece, "Seize the Day,"an outstanding example of his future ironic tone and sophisticated range of expression.

James Baldwin's noctural interracial drama; a section of Doris Lessing's groundbreaking *The Golden Notebook*; a sad and funny piece from Ralph Ellison's work-in-progress on a new novel; William Styron's grim story of a runaway slave; a section from Philip Roth's famous *Portnoy's Complaint*; Cynthia Ozick's dazzling story about two writers and their tenuous domesticity; and Walter Abish's memorable reconstruction of mood and place were other high points in the magazine's history.

More recent decades are represented by excerpts from one of Italo Calvino's elusive, fabulistic novels; Amos Oz's short sketches of Israeli life; Michel Tournier's brilliant account of a dwarf that just verges on the symbolic; Daphne Merkin's bitter family saga; Tatyana Tolstaya's allegorized character sketch; and Norman Manea's intimate memories of life in a totalitarian society. Unfortunately, we could not include André Gide's story, "Theseus," because of its length. And too, we had to leave out Aharon Appelfeld's folk story, "A Visit to His Married Granddaughter."

This formidable array of great talent and range of cultural awareness reveals another aspect of *Partisan Review*'s history. It bears out our conviction that the magazine, unlike most other publications, has been contiguous with the literary history of the country. We have both influenced its cultural development and have been influenced by it. Thus each story, though separately chosen, was affected by earlier fiction and, in turn, affected the further growth of the genre.

It is said that we are now in a postmodern era. Whether that means that the standards and accomplishments of literary modernism will no longer guide the direction of contemporary writing remains to be seen. If literary modernism does continue in some form, the fiction represented in this collection will be seen as a kind of model and legacy.

SIXTY YEARS OF GREAT FICTION

FROM

PARTISAN REVIEW

Two Syllables

BY IGNAZIO SILONE

In the banquet hall and on the steps of the inn, men and youths are going ceaselessly back and forth. One group, wearing the Fascist Party emblem, is seated at a table and discussing, in voices that are already hoarse from too much talking, the details of the spontaneous and enthusiastic demonstration which is to take place this afternoon. It is a question, through stern and strict measures, of assuring the spontaneous and enthusiastic participation of the entire population of Fossa and vicinity.

"Should we send trucks to Pietrasecca, too?" someone asks.

"Sure, to Pietrasecca, too," someone answers him. "And we must send *carabinieri* along with them, so that the population will understand that they are to come in spontaneously."

At another table, a group of pot-bellies, under the artistic direction of Lawyer Zabaglione, are unctuously going over the bill of fare for the banquet this evening. Zabaglione is so flurried that he does not notice Don Paolo's presence. A strenuous and basic difference of opinion has arisen, and Zabaglione finally and impulsively brings it down to a personal issue.

"On my word of honor," he shouts, "on the honor of my wife and the stainless honor of my daughter, I swear to you that I will have nothing to do with the banquet, if the white wine is to be served before the red."

"That's blackmail!" shout the other members of the committee, in high dudgeon. Zabaglione folds his arms and remains unshaken in his contention.

"Principles are principles!" is the only answer he will give.

Up on the second floor, in the landlady's bedroom, the recruiting commitee is meeting. Those who have not been able to find chairs are seated or lying on the widow's bed. The pillow slips are neatly embroidered in cross-stitch with the words, "Pleasant Dreams!" Over the bed hangs a colored print showing a guardian angel in the act of caressing a dove.

In Fossa, the mobilization of the hungry bums has been followed by that of the bankrupts. The directors of the Bank of Fossa, who are facing a suit for fraudulent bankruptcy, have volunteered to go to Africa. Their patriotic example has had its effect on all sides. The hardware merchant, who has a little shop on Town Hall Square opposite the Girasole Inn, and who has had to close it for insolvency, has opened it again this morning, has put Gelsomina, his wife, in charge, and has pasted on the door a sign reading: "Creditors are hereby informed that the owner of this business has enlisted as a volunteer!" And no constituted authority would venture to order the seizure of a war hero's wares. . . .

The registration official, having read through the list of recruits, is led to exclaim: "This seems to be a mortgagors' war!"

The nearer the hour draws for the radio announcement of the declaration of war, the denser becomes the jostling crowd in the street. From the righthand side come the authorities, from the left the *cafoni*. From the right come motorcycles and autos, bearing police, *carabinieri* and militiamen, with officials of the Fascist Party and the

Corporations on trucks. From the left, donkeys, bicycles and more trucks, bringing the peasants. Two blaring bands go up and down the street, playing the same hymn over and over again. The musicians are for the most part artisans, and are clad in the uniforms of circus animal trainers and hotel porters, with fancy stripes and a double row of brass buttons down the front. Outside a barber shop is a picture of Abyssinian women with long breasts dangling to their knees. Gathered around this picture is a large cluster of young lads, who eye it laughingly and covetously. From the left, the *cafoni* keep pouring in: small landowners, charcoal-burners and shepherds from round about. From the right hand side, the stream of Fascist Party representatives is likewise an uninterrupted one.

In back of the small square, between the Party headquarters and the colonnade of Town Hall, a radio loudspeaker, decked with an array of small flags, has been set up. Down beneath the diminutive but miraculous object upon which the fate of a nation depends, the poor people take their places as they arrive. The women squat down as they do in church, while the men in the marketplace are seated upon sacks or upon the pack-saddles of their donkeys. All know why it is they have come together here, and they now sit blinking at the little mechanical object which is soon to resound with the call to arms; but they all feel rather out of place in its presence; they feel downcast and distrustful. The square and the neighboring streets are soon packed and jammed with humanity, as the silent, unbroken influx shows no signs of letting up.

This is the general mobilization of the hungry populace. There come the lame from the stone quarries, the blind from the blast furnaces, the bent and emaciated tillers of the soil, men from the hills with hands reddened by sulphur and lime, mountaineers with legs crooked from the mowing. Inasmuch as his neighbor was coming, every man has had to come. If war brings misfortune, it will be a misfortune for all, and not just for a few. If it brings luck, then one must go after it, so as to be in on it. And so, they have all set out; they have let the treading of the grapes, the cleaning of the vats and the preparation of the seed corn go, and have made their way to the provincial seat. The inhabitants of Pietrasecca also arrive, and dismount in front of the Girasole Inn. The school teacher explains to each one, repeatedly, just how he is to behave, just when he is to shout and when he is to sing; but her voice is lost in the universal hubbub.

From the left hand side, more *cafoni* are to be seen coming from the outlying villages. Shepherds in goatskin breeches, with sandals on their feet and gold earrings. From the right comes Don Concettino Ragù in a militia officer's uniform.

Don Paolo sees him and steps back into the room, in order not to run the risk of being recognized by his former school fellow. He takes up a position behind the window curtain on the second floor of the inn, so that he may be able to observe the throng and the progress of the ceremony. He is reminded of the time when he was a child and had similarly stood at a window while the street down below swarmed with a long procession of ragged pilgrims singing litanies in honor of the Virgin Mary. The pilgrims came from far and were bound for far; most of them were barefoot and bore the stains of dust and perspiration. He remembers yet the feeling of oppression and of horror which this saddening spectacle inspired in his childish heart. Viewed from a second-storey window, the throng below, gathered about the loudspeaker, reminds him of a concourse of weary and oppressed pilgrims about a wonder-working idol.

From his hiding place, over the roofs of the houses below, Don Paolo can glimpse two or three bell towers as thickly dotted with young lads as a dovecote with doves.

All of a sudden, the bells begin to peal. Through the crowd go members of the Fascist Party, bedecking the loudspeaker with patriotic fetishes in the form of tricolored flags, black pennants and a picture of the great Duce with the strong protruding lower jaw. Barbaric cries of "Eja! Eja!" devoid of all understandable meaning are now raised by Party members, while the throng maintains a persistent silence.

In front of the loudspeaker room is made for the "Mothers of the Fallen," poor old ladies who for fifteen years have been wearing mourning set off with medals, and who in return for their small gratuity are required, whenever the Department of Propaganda calls upon them to do so, to place themselves at the disposition of the Sergeant of Carabinieri. Behind the "Mothers" the priests of nearby parishes take their places, jolly-looking old priests, gloomy-looking priests, athletic and respect-inspiring priests, and a canon as fat and rosy as a well-fed wet nurse – he is conversing with Don Girasole, the owner of the inn. Under the loggia of Town Hall, a few proprietors appear, with bristling beards, unprepossessing eyebrows and clad in velvet hunting jackets. The authorities, that is to say, the members of the Fascist Party, are standing in the middle of the square. In their midst is a solitary woman, Donna Evangelina, with her husband, the carpenter, whom she has compelled to volunteer.

"She has not only found a father for her child," one of the girls remarks, "but what a father! A hero!"

"Donna Evangelina is a born war widow," coments one of the men. "When she's able to wear mourning and a medal on her bosom, she'll be happy."

The bells peal forth as the lads tug on the ropes. A sign is given them to stop, that they may not drown out the impending radio broadcast; but they either do not understand, or pretend that they do not. There must be a dozen of them altogether, ringing the bells with all their might and filling the streets below with a lusty din. Militiamen appear upon the neighboring belfry and order the youths to cease; but as soon as they have gone down again and the lads perceive that the other bells are still pealing, they, not wishing to be outdone, start up once more.

The first raucous tones from the loudspeaker got out over the heads of the crowd, unheard. From the groups of *carabinieri*, militiamen and Party members there goes up a mighty cry, a rhythmic cry, a passionate exorcism addressed to the great Duce:

Ce du! Ce du! Ce du! Ce du! Ce du!

The cry spreads, is taken up by the women and answered by the children and then by the entire multitude, even by those standing on the outskirts of the throng and by the onlookers in the windows, a solemn rhythmic chorus:

Ce du! Ce du! Ce du! Ce du! Ce du! Ce du! Ce du! That name which no one in private life would presume to utter, either by way of praise or imprecation, lest it bring bad luck, is now in the presence of his picture which they view with timidity, in the presence of this fetish of the fatherland, taken up and shouted time and time again, at the tops of their lungs, like a formula for warding off evil, in a religious frenzy:

Ce du! Ce du! Ce du! Ce du! Ce du!

In the vicinity of the loudspeaker, an effort is made to get the crowd to be silent so that the speech coming from Rome may be heard; but those in the adjoining streets still go on scanning the mystic formula, continuing to call upon the great Duce, the Sorcerer, the Wizard, in whose hands lie the future and the very life-blood of the poor.

The shouts of the throng together with the pealing of the bells make it impossible for Don Paolo to catch any of the radio address. Down below, at one corner of the inn, he sees the women from Pietrasecca squatting on the ground and the men grouped about a cart; they with the rest of the crowd are shouting those conjuror's syllables:

Ce du! Ce du! Ce du! Ce du! Ce du!

Upon the cart, towering above the throng, sits a witch staring up at the sky. Her lips move back and forth and her gloom-laden face holds mysterious presentiments. The exorcism grows louder and louder until it becomes a deafening roar, a fanatic ecstasy, an oppressive obsession:

Ce du! Ce du! Ce du! Ce du! Ce du!

The multitude is chanting now, including those up near the loudspeaker, the *carabinieri* and officials. The latter have become convinced that it is out of the question to hear anything of the broadcast from Rome. The cry, *Ce du! Ce du!,* goes on hammering the air with its measured beat, with the continuity and the verbal intonations of a mass of sinners beseeching an angry god for grace and forgiveness. The two syllables end by losing all normal and comprehensible significance and become no more than a mysterious formula, mingling with the holy chime of the bells.

From his post of observation behind the window curtain, Don Paolo gazes down mournfully. He remembers the feeling of anxiety he had when as a boy he once witnessed certain experiments in mass hypnotism. He remembers having the same feeling whenever he has viewed demonstrations of those primitive and irrational psychic forces which lie slumbering in the individual and in the masses. How can one ever hope to talk reasonably to these poor creatures who have come under the influence of a hypnotizing wizard?

Those standing near the radio now give the sign that the broadcast is at an end.

"War has been declared!" shouts Lawyer Zabaglione, and raises a hand to indicate that he has something to say. But his voice, hoarse like the rest, is lost in the rhythmic chant the wailing echoes of which are still to be heard:

Ce du! Ce du! Ce du! Ce du!

The radio is silent, and no one has understood so much as three words of what has come over it. No one has taken the trouble to understand. No one is sorry at not having understood. For it is not necessary to understand; and what is more, there is nothing to be understood.

Translated from the Italian by Samuel Putnam

In Dreams Begin Responsibilities

BY DELMORE SCHWARTZ

I think it is the year 1909. I feel as if I were in a moving-picture theater, the long arm of light crossing the darkness and spinning, my eyes fixed upon the screen. It is a silent picture, as if an old Biograph one, in which the actors are dressed in ridiculously old-fashioned clothes, and one flash succeeds another with sudden jumps, and the actors, too, seem to jump about, walking too fast. The shots are full of rays and dots, as if it had been raining when the picture was photographed. The light is bad.

It is Sunday afternoon, June 12th, 1909, and my father is walking down the quiet streets of Brooklyn on his way to visit my mother. His clothes are newly pressed, and his tie is too tight in his high collar. He jingles the coins in his pocket, thinking of the witty things he will say. I feel as if I had by now relaxed entirely in the soft darkness of the theater; the organist peals out the obvious approximate emotions on which the audience rocks unknowingly. I am anonymous. I have forgotten myself: it is always so when one goes to a movie, it is, as they say, a drug.

My father walks from street to street of trees, lawns and houses, once in a while coming to an avenue on which a streetcar skates and gnaws, progressing slowly. The motorman, who has a handle-bar mustache, helps a young lady wearing a hat like a feathered bowl onto the car. He leisurely makes change and rings his bell as the passengers mount the car. It is obviously Sunday, for everyone is wearing Sunday clothes and the streetcar's noises emphasize the quiet of the holiday (for Brooklyn is said to be the city of churches). The shops are closed and their shades drawn but for an occasional stationery store or drugstore with great green balls in the window.

My father has chosen to take this long walk because he likes to walk and think. He thinks about himself in the future and so arrives at the place he is to visit in a mild state of exaltation. He pays no attention to the houses he is passing, in which the Sunday dinner is being eaten, nor to the many trees which line each street, now coming to their full green and the time when they will enclose the whole street in leafy shadow. An occasional carriage passes, the horses' hooves falling like stones in the quiet afternoon, and once in a while an automobile, looking like an enormous upholstered sofa, puffs and passes.

My father thinks of my mother, of how ladylike she is, and of the pride which will be his when he introduces her to his family. They are not yet engaged and he is not yet sure that he loves my mother, so that, once in a while, he becomes panicky about the bond already established. But then he reassures himself by thinking of the big men he admires who are married: William Randolph Hearst and William Howard Taft, who has just become the President of the United States.

My fathers arrives at my mother's house. He has come too early and so is suddenly embarrassed. My aunt, my mother's younger sister, answers the loud bell with her napkin in her hand, for the family is still at dinner. As my father enters, my grandfather rises from the table and shakes hands with him. My mother has run upstairs to tidy herself. My grandmother asks my father if he has had dinner and tells him that my mother will be down soon. My grandfather opens the conversation by remarking about the mild June weather. My father sits uncomfortably near the table, holding his hat in his hand. My grandmother tells my aunt to take my father's hat. My uncle, twelve years old, runs into the house, his hair touseled. He shouts a greeting to my father, who has often given him nickels, and then runs upstairs, as my grandmother shouts after him. It is evident that the respect in which my father is held in this house is tempered by a good deal of mirth. He is impressive, but also very awkward.

II

Finally my mother comes downstairs and my father, being at the moment engaged in conversation with my grandfather, is made uneasy by her entrance, for he does not know whether to greet my mother or to continue the conversation. He gets up from his chair clumsily and says "Hello" gruffly. My grandfather watches this, examining their congruence, such as it is, with a critical eye, and meanwhile rubbing his bearded check roughly, as he always does when he reasons. He is worried; he is afraid that my father will not make a good husband for his oldest daughter. At this point something happens to the film, just as my father says something funny to my mother: I am awakened to myself and my unhappiness just as my interest has become most intense. The audience begins to clap impatiently. Then the trouble is attended to, but the film has been returned to a portion just shown, and once more I see my grandfather rubbing his bearded cheek, pondering my father's character. It is difficult to get back into the picture once more and forget myself, but as my mother giggles at my father's words, the darkness drowns me.

My father and mother depart from the house, my father shaking hands with my grandfather once more, out of some unknown uneasiness. I stir uneasily also, slouched in the hard chair of the theater.

Where is the older uncle, my mother's older brother? He is studying in his bedroom upstairs, studying for his final examinations at the College of the City of New York, having been dead of lobar pneumonia for the last twenty-one years. My mother and father walk down the same quiet streets once more. My mother is holding my father's arm and telling him of the novel she has been reading and my father utters judgments of the characters as the plot is made clear to him. This is a habit which he very much enjoys, for he feels the utmost superiority and confidence when he is approving or condemning the behavior of other people. At times he feels moved to utter a brief "Ugh," whenever the story becomes what he would call sugary. My mother feels satisfied by the interest she has awakened; and she is showing my father how intelligent she is and how interesting.

They reach the avenue, and the streetcar leisurely arrives. They are going to Coney Island this afternoon, although my mother really considers such pleasures inferior. She has made up her mind to indulge only in a walk on the boardwalk and a pleasant dinner, avoiding the riotous amusements as being beneath the dignity of so dignified a couple.

My father tells my mother how much money he has made in the week just past, exaggerating an amount which need not have been exaggerated. But my father has always felt that actualities somehow fall short, no matter how fine they are. Suddenly I begin to weep. The determined old lady who sits next to me in the theater is annoyed and looks at me with an angry face, and being intimidated, I stop. I drag out my handkerchief and dry my face, licking the drop which has fallen near my lips. Meanwhile I have missed something, for here are my father and mother alighting from the streetcar at the last stop, Coney Island.

III

They walk toward the boardwalk and my mother commands my father to inhale the pungent air from the sea. They both breathe in deeply, both of them laughing as they do so. They have in common a great interest in health, although my father is strong and husky, and my mother is frail. They are both full of theories about what is good to eat and not good to eat, and sometimes have heated discussions about it, the whole matter ending in my father's announcement, made with a scornful bluster, that you have to die sooner or later anyway. On the boardwalk's flagpole, the American flag is pulsing in an intermittent wind from the sea.

My father and mother go to the rail of the boardwalk and look down on the beach where a good many bathers are casually walking about. A few are in the surf. A peanut-whistle pierces the air with its pleasant and active whine, and my father goes to buy peanuts. My mother remains at the rail and stares at the ocean. The ocean seems merry to her; it pointedly sparkles and again and again the pony waves are released. She notices the children digging in the wet sand, and the bathing costumes of the girls who are her own age. My father returns with the peanuts. Overhead the sun's lightning strikes and strikes, but neither of them are at all aware of it. The boardwalk is full of people dressed in their Sunday clothes and casually strolling. The tide does not reach as far as the boardwalk, and the strollers would feel no danger if it did. My father and mother lean on the rail of the boardwalk and absently stare at the ocean. The ocean is becoming rough; the waves come in slowly, tugging strength from far back. The moment before they somersault, the moment when they arch their backs so beautifully, showing white veins in the green and black, that moment is intolerable. They finally crack, dashing fiercely upon the sand, actually driving, full force downward, against it, bouncing upward and forward, and at last petering out into a small stream of bubbles which slides up the beach and then is recalled. The sun overhead does not disturb my father and my mother. They gaze idly at the ocean, scarcely interested in its harshness. But I stare at the terrible sun which breaks up sight, and the fatal merciless passionate ocean. I forget my parents. I stare fascinated, and finally, shocked by their indifference, I burst out weeping once more. The old lady next to me pats my shoulder and says "There, there, young man, all of this is only a movie, only a movie," but I look up once more at the terrifying sun and the terrifying ocean, and being unable to control my tears I get up and go to the men's room, stumbling over the feet of the other people seated in my row.

IV

When I return, feeling as if I had just awakened in the morning sick for lack of sleep, several hours have apparently passed and my parents are riding on the merry-go-round. My father is on a black horse, my mother on a white one, and they seem to be making an eternal circuit for the single purpose of snatching the nickel rings which are attached to an arm of one of the posts. A hand organ is playing; it is inseparable from the ceaseless circling of the merry-go-round.

For a moment it seems that they will never get off the carousel, for it will never stop, and I feel as if I were looking down from the fiftieth story of a building. But at length they do get off; even the hand-organ has ceased for a moment. There is a sudden and sweet stillness, as if the achievement of so much motion. My mother has acquired only two rings, my father, however, ten of them, although it was my mother who really wanted them.

They walk on along the boardwalk as the afternoon descends by imperceptible degrees into the incredible violet of dusk. Everything fades into a relaxed glow, even the ceaseless murmuring from the beach. They look for a place to have dinner. My father suggests the best restaurant on the boardwalk and my mother demurs, according to her principles of economy and housewifeliness.

However they do go to the best place, asking for a table near the window so that they look out upon the boardwalk and the mobile ocean. My father feels omnipotent as he places a quarter in the waiter's hand in asking for a table. The place is crowded and here too there is music, this time from a kind of string-trio. My father orders with a fine confidence.

As their dinner goes on, my father tells of his plans for the future and my mother shows with expressive face how interested she is, and how impressed. My father becomes exultant, lifted up by the waltz that is being played, and his own future begins to intoxicate him. My father tells my mother that he is going to expand his business, for there is a great deal of money to be made. He wants to settle down. After all, he is twenty-nine, he has lived by himself since his thirteenth year, he is making more and more money, and he is envious of his friends when he visits them in the security of their homes, surrounded, it seems, by the calm domestic pleasures, and by delightful children, and then as the waltz reaches the moment when the dancers all swing madly, then, then with awful daring, then he asks my mother to marry him, although awkwardly enough and puzzled as to how he had arrived at the question, and she, to make the whole business worse, begins to cry, and my father looks nervously about, not knowing at all what to do now, and my mother says: "It's all I've wanted from the first moment I saw you," sobbing, and he finds all of this very difficult, scarcely to his taste, scarcely as he thought it would be, on his long walks over Brooklyn Bridge in the revery of a fine cigar; and it was then, at that point, that I stood up in the theater and shouted: "Don't do it! It's not too late to change your minds, both of you. Nothing good will come of it, only remorse, hatred, scandal, and two children whose characters are monstrous." The whole audience turned to look at me, annoyed, the usher came hurrying down the aisle flashing his searchlight, and the old lady next to me tugged me down into my seat, saying: "Be quiet. You'll be put out, and you paid thirty-five cents to come in." And so I shut my eyes because I could not bear to see what was happening. I sat there quietly.

V

But after awhile I begin to take brief glimpses and at length I watch again with thirsty interest, like a child who tries to maintain his sulk when he is offered the bribe of candy. My parents are now having their picture taken in a photographer's booth along the boardwalk. The place is shadowed in the mauve light which is apparently necessary. The camera is set to the side on its tripod and looks like a Martian man. The photographer is instructing my parents in how to pose. My father has his arm over my mother's shoulder, and both of them smile emphatically. The photographer brings my mother a bouquet of flowers to hold in her hand, but she holds it at the wrong angle. Then the photographer covers himself with the black cloth which drapes the camera, and all that one sees of him is one protruding arm and the hand with which he holds tightly to the rubber ball which he squeezes when the picture is taken. But he is not satisfied with their appearance. He feels that somehow there is something wrong in their pose. Again and again he comes out from his hiding place with new directions. Each suggestion merely makes matters worse. My father is becoming impatient. They try a seated pose. The photographer explains that he has his pride, he wants to make beautiful pictures, he is not merely interested in all of this for the money. My father says: "Hurry up, will you? We haven't got all night." But the photographer only scurries about apologetically, issuing new directions. The photographer charms me, and I approve of him with all my heart, for I know exactly how he feels, and as he criticizes each revised pose according to some obscure idea of rightness, I become quite hopeful. But then my father says angrily: "Come on, you've had enough time, we're not going to wait any longer." And the photographer, sighing unhappily, goes back into the black covering, and holds out his hand, saying: "One, two, three. Now!", and the picture is taken, with my father's smile turned to a grimace and my mother's bright and false. It takes a few minutes for the picture to be developed and as my parents sit in the curious light they become depressed.

VI

They have passed a fortuneteller's booth and my mother wishes to go in, but my father does not. They begin to argue about it. My mother becomes stubborn, my father once more impatient. What my father would like to do now is walk off and leave my mother there, but he knows that that would never do. My mother refuses to budge. She is near tears, but she feels an uncontrollable desire to hear what the palm-reader will say. My father consents angrily and they both go into the booth which is, in a way, like the photographer's, since it is draped in black cloth and its light is colored and shadowed. The place is too warm; and my father keeps saying that this is all nonsense, pointing to the crystal ball on the table. The fortune-teller, a short, fat woman garbed in robes supposedly exotic, comes into the room and greets them, speaking with an accent. But suddenly my father feels that the whole thing is intolerable; he tugs at my mother's arm but my mother refuses to budge. And then, in terrible anger, my father lets go of my mother's arm and strides out, leaving my mother stunned. She makes a movement as if to go after him, but the fortuneteller holds her and begs her not to do so, and I in my seat in the darkness am shocked and horrified. I feel as if I were walking a tightrope one hundred feet over a circus audience and suddenly the rope is showing signs of breaking, and I get up from my seat and begin to shout once more the first words I can think of to communicate my terrible fear, and once more the usher comes hurrying down the aisle flashing his searchlight, and the old lady pleads with me, and the shocked audience has turned to stare at me, and I keep shouting: "What are they doing? Don't they know what they are doing? Why doesn't my mother go after my father and beg him not to be angry?

If she does not do that, what will she do? Doesn't my father know what he is doing?" But the usher has seized my arm and is dragging me away, and as he does so, he says: "What are *you* doing? Don't you know you can't do things like this, you can't do whatever you want to do, even if other people aren't about? You will be sorry if you do not do what you should do. You can't carry on like this, it is not right, you will find that out soon enough, everything you do matters too much," and as he said that, dragging me through the lobby of the theater, into the cold light, I woke up into the bleak winter morning of my twenty-first birthday, the windowsill shining with its lip of snow, and the morning already begun.

Hurry, Hurry

BY ELEANOR CLARK

No one was there when the house began to fall. It was a beautiful June day, warmer than it had been. I remember that people had been particularly expansive that morning as after a thunderstorm. They had gathered on the porch steps at mail-time, exclaiming over and over on the warmth of the sun and the color of the tiger-lilies that had just sprung out all over town. One of the ladies, receiving a long-awaited letter from her nephew, had suddenly become very witty and had kissed everyone in the store, and this could never have happened on an ordinary day. Naturally it occurred to no one that a disaster was about to take place.

The only creature that might have given some warning was the French poodle, de Maupassant, who had been locked in the house and should have sensed that everything was not quite right, but he gave no sign of life until the end. Probably my mother had spoiled him too much by that time. Certainly she loved the dog, especially since the accident that paralyzed one of his paws, so that it was hard for her to deny him anything. People laughed at her for this, and she laughed at herself, but she could always find something in him to excuse her behavior. She loved the aristocracy of him, the way he tossed his luxurious black mane – Louis Quatorze she called it – or drew his shoulders a little together and pointed up his slender glossy snout. In the evening he snuggled at her feet, and then, though in the daytime her profile was too sharp and her green-flecked eyes leapt too quickly to the defense, there was something almost of a madonna in my mother's face. But she had spoiled the dog. In the end he was incapable of serious thought and must have played or slept through the whole catastrophe. The servant spent most of his time writing love letters to the village saxophonist.

I too was of no use, partly because I was walking on the hill about half a mile from the house. The other reason is simply that I was not interested. Later when I saw all my mother's property tumbling to ruin I did try to concentrate on the tragedy of it: shook myself, rubbed my arms and legs, even kicked my shins and jumped up and down as if my feet were asleep, but with no effect. I spent the entire time – two or three hours it must have been – under a maple tree, and rescued nothing but one silver-backed hand mirror which fell out of an upper window and happened to land in my lap. I think that I was also the last person in the village to be aware that the house, where I was born and spent most of my childhood, was beginning to collapse. I noticed it quite by accident from the hill. The house was swaying very gently, the top of the cobblestone chimney with a graceful and independent motion, rather like the tail of a fish, and the foundations with a more irregular ebb and swell as if the stones were offering a futile resistance to their downfall. The kitchen ell and the woodshed had already gone down, tearing an ugly wound in the north wall and leaving the servants' quarters exposed.

Naturally I made my way back as quickly as possible, but the lane had become so overgrown with sumach and brambles that it was almost half an hour before I reached the road. By that time the whole town was present and the lawn was already clotted with little groups of people (in one place the ladies of the Altar Guild, in an-other the three families that lived off the town, and so on) debating the causes of the collapse and the possibilities of doing something about it. My mother was running from one group to another, shaking hands with everyone, receiving advice and expressions of sympathy: She had been at a cocktail party and cut an especially charming figure, with her white picture hat and her flowered print. So much so that for some time – until the front wall actually began to bulge out over the lawn, like a paper bag slowly surcharged with water – most of the people were unable to keep their minds on the disaster and acted as if they were attending an ordinary funeral or tea.

Now and then my mother paused in her rounds as hostess, tucking the minister's arm under hers, and while appearing to cast down her eyes, with one of her green calculating upward Victorian glances managed to caress his face. "Ah Padre," she sighed, plucking at the black cloth under her fingers, "what a good friend you are," and added, turning to the church ladies, "He's the best Democrat any of us has ever seen." The minister, who had also been at the cocktail party and whose cheeks were somewhat flushed, gazed with sly benevolence over his flock, laughed his deep-bellied indifferent laugh, and kissed my mother's hand. "Ha ha ha," rattled the church ladies, and with one motion, as from a released spring, began to run in tiny circles around him, pointing delightedly at his full chest and the rather uncouth vigor of his jaw. "Always joking," said the minister, "here her house is on the verge of collapse and she talks about democracy! What a woman." At this the church ladies could no longer control themselves, they rolled and pivoted with laughter, poking each other's corsets and smacking their lips enviously toward my mother. "It's true, upon my word it's true!" she cried, one arm to the sky. "He treats us all the same, rich and poor alike! Here's to Padre!" and she raised her empty hand still higher in a toast. "The best friend this community has ever had!"

In the meantime the disintegration of the house was becoming more and more apparent. From the upstairs bedrooms, and even in the pantry and dining-room, beams could be heard falling, and already a wide crack was beginning to open diago-nally across the front living-room wall, exposing the dust-covered leaves of books, first the historical works and later the vellum-bound editions of Dante, Baudelaire and Racine. It was this, I think, that first awoke my mother to a real awareness of what was happening. It was not only that the books were threatened with destruc-tion: it was also obvious to everyone that their pages had not been cut. Even the town servants noticed it, even Myrtle who was hired for the lowest and heaviest form of cleaning, but Myrtle was a poor half-deformed creature and she would not have dared to smile behind her fingers as the others did.

One by one the books fell among the barberry bushes, raising a cloud of greyish powder so stifling that the people nearest were forced to stumble back over the flowerbeds, holding handkerchiefs to their mouths. "Oh good Lord! the books! the books!" my mother gasped. She ran up under the crack in the wall, and holding her white hat with one hand, with the other attempted to catch the volumes as they toppled from their shelves. But they were coming too fast. Many of them, too, fell apart immediately against the outer air, leaving only something like silica dust mid-way to the ground, so that my mother was soon taken with a violent fit of coughing. At last, reeling and choking under the rain of classics that were now striking her head and breasts and shoulders, she was obliged to stagger back toward the road. "A wonderful woman," the ladies said, and they began to scamper to and fro, picking little bunches of sweet william, wild roses and delphinium for my mother's hair. Gratefully she closed her eyes and was nestling her grey curls more warmly against the Padre's ample lap, when the cobblestone chimney tore itself loose from the main beams of the house and crashed through the lower branches of the elms and across the lawn.

Immediately my mother sprang up.

"George! Burt! Albert!" she called. "Somebody's got to save my things! Where's the Fire Department? Fire Department!" The Fire Department was not really a department at all, but a group of farmers who no longer farmed, so they had nothing better to do than to jump on the fire engine as it went by. They were now lying on the grass passing around a bottle of beer and laughing at some story or joke. "George!" my mother wheedled. "Albert! Burt!" and she ran from one to another, prodding and kicking them with her white pointed toe. The firemen looked up slowly at the waving roof and the colonial columns which were beginning to bend like wax candles in the sun, then hoisting their quids all together to the other side of their faces they announced, "It ain't a fire," and lay down again, covering their necks against the afternoon sun. "But the highboy!" my mother cried. "The highboy! It belonged to my grandfather, it's been in my family for two hundred years, my little old Aunt Mary left it to me in her will. She was so weak she could hardly hold up her head, and she whispered to me" – here my mother's voice broke – "she said, 'I want you to have it, because it's the loveliest thing I have, and you're the only one that's stood by me all these years.' "

This recital so moved my mother that for a full minute she stood with her face in her hands, sobbing, but perceiving that she had still had no effect on the Fire Department she whipped away the last traces of her grief and turned to hunt out Cedric the servant. Cedric, however, was in no condition to be called upon. The collapse of the kitchen ell, taking with it the entire outer wall of his room, had revealed him stark naked playing pinochle with one of the summer residents, an incident that he was now trying to explain to the saxophonist. "Cedric!" my mother shouted. "Come here at once!" But just then a shutter fell on Cedric from the attic window and with a moan he dropped to the ground, followed by his friend. Fortunately my mother was spared this scene. She had just remembered de Maupassant and was threatening to run into the house for him when she was assured that someone had seen someone taking him away.

In the end it was Myrtle who went in for the highboy. She was not at all anxious to go, even cried a little when it was first suggested, which was rather a surprise because everyone knew that her life was not worth anything. She had lost four fingers in a meat-chopper, so perhaps it was the pain she was afraid of, or the noise: it was hard to tell. At any rate, as soon as she heard that the Selectmen had chosen her for the job she began to whimper and for several minutes stood twisting her fingers in her apron, made out of an old pair of bloomers my mother had given her, and chewing her hair. "Oh no," she muttered to herself, "you don't see *me* going in there" – she had the habit of talking to herself while she worked, even told herself long stories sometimes as she cleaned out the toilets – "Not me, nossir! They come up to me all together and they says, 'Now Myrtle,' they says, 'you just run along in there and bring out that hairloom. 'Tain't as heavy as it looks,' they says, kind of coaxing-like, 'and mind you don't smash it on the way out.' I like that! Mind you don't smash it, they says, on the way out! And there was the whole house rolling around and a crack in the front big enough to drive a Ford through. Why you could watch the ceiling come down in the parlor, and all the upstairs furniture coming down too, bang! bang! bang! Mind you don't smash it, they says, on the way out! And do you want to know what I said?" Myrtle placed her crippled hands on her hips and with her eyes fiercely lit up she went on, raising her voice to a scream in order to hear herself above the splintering and crashing of the house. "I says to them, 'No!' I stood right up to them and I says, 'I ain't going into that house, not if you give me a million dollars I ain't! And as for what I think of *you* . . . Yes,' " her lower lip began to twitch and her voice dropped suddenly, "as for what I think of you. . . ." But she was now surrounded by all the important people in town, including my mother, the minister, and the schoolteacher – a tiny knifish man with a cone-shaped head and glasses – and realizing that she had been overheard she was taken by a fit of trembling and was unable to go on. "I just got the habit of talking to myself," she apologized, letting out a choked laugh, and then she began to cry again, with her head hanging and her red stubs pressed into the hair over her eyes.

"I have no sympathy with any of them," said the schoolteacher. "They ought to be horse-whipped, they don't want to work." He strode through the crowd, receiving with a wrinkling of his beagle's nose their murmurs of agreement, tore off a stout black cherry switch and with little nasal shouts, like a cheerleader, began to slash at Myrtle's ankles. "Oh mercy," said Cedric. He giggled a little, then with a sob turned back to hide his face. "Oh darling," he moaned, waving his fingers in the direction of Myrtle who was now hobbling toward the doorway, "It has such dreadful feet!"

My mother was not wholly in sympathy with the schoolteacher's tactics. She pushed her arm under Myrtle's, and half dragging, half comforting her, pressed a dollar bill between her thumb and what was left of her forefinger. "I want you to take this, my dear, and get yourself something pretty." Without raising her eyes Myrtle took the money and poked it in her shoe.

In the doorway a new difficulty arose, the columns and the door-frame itself having already collapsed, leaving only an irregular space no bigger than the entrance to a small kennel for Myrtle to pass through. However several white-flanneled husbands now sprang into action, lifted Myrtle over the debris on the stoop, and twisted and heaved her head first into the hall. In less than a minute there was nothing to be seen of her but one soleless shoe with the crisp corner of a dollar bill sticking out at the side. "It seems rather a pity," the minister murmured, looking at my mother. "Yes," she hesitated. "Poor dear Myrtle, she's such a pitiful little creature really and she has so little. . . . But of course I can make it up to her." She smiled, grabbed the dollar, and with a hidden ladylike gesture forced it into the Padre's reluctant hand. "For the new altar cloths," she whispered. "I have so little these days, but this much I *can* do for the community."

For almost half an hour Myrtle fought her way through the wreckage inside the house, trying to reach the highboy in the downstairs guest-room. From time to time we could see her face in an upstairs window, perspiration dropping from her hair, or her arm through one of the cracks that were now widening on every wall. "Hurry!" my mother shouted, with increasing anger as one by one her treasures – a Russian ikon, the Dresden china coffee cups, the Renaissance desk brought so tenderly from Florence – fell and were crushed. "Hurry up, Myrtle! Hurry up! Hurry up!" And every time a part of Myrtle came into view the schoolteacher's eyes brightened and he danced back and forth cracking the black cherry whip above his head. "She's a good worker but terribly slow," the ladies agreed, twisting their handkerchiefs and criticizing Myrtle's progress through the house. Some of them, the old New England stock, filled the time more usefully: dusted the grass and bushes where the books had fallen and arranged those that had remained intact in neat piles along the flagstone walk.

During this time the front of the house had been bellying more and more out toward the lawn so that it was no longer possible to see into the guest-room. "It's gone!" my mother cried. "Ah, Padre!" and she leaned against the minister. But a moment later Myrtle appeared again, this time on all fours, crawling up the circular staircase with the highboy on her back. "Bring it down! *Down*, Myrtle!" All the downstairs exits, however, were blocked: the lower half of the staircase too was caving in, leaving Myrtle hanging by two fingers while with the other hand she struggled to keep the massive piece of furniture from slipping back into the pit. Now and then over the sounds of falling timber we could hear her groaning and crying out, "Oh Holy Virgin, help. . . . Oh blessed mother of God. . . ." Then the whole front of the house squeezed down slowly, and we heard nothing more but the breaking of beams and an underground commotion of water as heavy objects fell through to the cellar.

The next and last time that we saw Myrtle she was trying to reach one of the attic windows, still struggling under what must have been a part of the highboy, though it was bashed to a skeleton. Her face was dreadfully distorted, as if she had been pinned under some heavy weight and in freeing herself had pulled her features half off.

Of her nose there was nothing left but a bloody splinter of bone, and her chin, which had been rather underhung, now stuck out in sharp diagonal, forcing her mouth into an enormous grin. Yet in spite of this it seemed as if she were trying to smile, perhaps out of pride in having salvaged as much as she had. She kept pointing at the mahogany ruin on her back, nodding continually and working her mangled features in an effort at communication. "I can't bear it," Cedric said, "they oughtn't to allow such things," and he turned yellow and vomited in a patch of lilies. Everyone else was shouting at Myrtle – "Don't throw it!" "Wrap it in a blanket!" "Let it down here!" – but she had suddenly let go her load. Even from the ground one could see the wild look that came into her eyes, a brilliant hatred aimed down at the crowd. Yet perhaps there was some confusion in it too, for before the wall crashed her face changed again – for a moment she resembled a small wounded animal crying for its life – and she fell with her torn-off wrists lifted up in prayer.

The rest of what happened was so sudden that I have no clear recollection of it. I remember that shortly after Myrtle's death the ladies set to gathering flowers again and made a kind of tiny monument of them on the grass, with POOR MYRTLE written in English daisies across the top. The schoolteacher scoffed at this, saying there might have been some sense to it if she had done what she was sent for, but the general opinion was that the ladies had been very kind to think of such a thing. "She was very bitter," the minister said, "but a good soul too," and he took the carnation from his buttonhole and tossed it on the mound.

I think it was at about that time that the French poodle suddenly clawed its way up to the window of my mother's bedroom, the only part of the house that was still standing. Yapping and rolling his eyes he perched on the swaying sill, his bandaged paw held up and a large drop of yellow liquid rolling down his aristocratic nose. "Moppy! Moppy!" my mother cried, running up under the wall. "Did you think your mummy had forgotten you? Oh Moppy you did, you're crying! he's crying," she repeated, almost crying herself. "He thought I was going to leave him there all by himself. Come to me, my darling, come to your mummy, jump!" I remember the two of them that way: the dog afraid to jump, tossing his ruff and his long silken ears, and my mother in a new flowered print and a picture hat, holding up her arms, with an expression of love, almost – I thought at that moment but I am not sure now – almost a look of fulfillment in her face, which at times made one think of a madonna though the profile was too sharp. And then the last of the house fell and buried them.

Red, White, and Blue Thanksgiving

BY JOHN DOS PASSOS

There was the time Uncle Glenn and Aunt Harriet had come to Thanksgiving Dinner. The sizzly smell of the turkey and the spices in the stuffing filled the kitchen every time Mother had opened the oven door to baste. Glenn had helped lay the table in the cramped dining room of the little apartment and had filled the two china swans with red, white, and blue candies and, carefully, with only one or two smudges, had printed out the names on the placecards.

Dad had been around the house all morning getting into Mother's way in the kitchen and frowning as he sat bent almost double reading with his green eyeshade on at his desk in the corner of the living room. A letter had come from Tyler overseas that morning that had upset Dad a good deal. The letter had said that Tyler wasn't coming home with his outfit but that he had just gotten under the line with his commission at Saumur before the armistice and was going to be sent to Koblenz in the Army of Occupation. Glenn was too excited about Thanksgiving and everybody coming to dinner to pay much attention. He and Mother were attending to everything and Dad was just mooning around now and then pulling at his sandy mustache with that worried look and taking down first one big book and then another from the top of his desk and setting them down on chairs and forgetting to put them back.

Mother in her pink apron with her hair in curlers was leaning over the oven of the gas stove basting the turkey. Glenn was standing beside her with his mouth watering as he watched the little splashes of juice sizzle as they trickled off the kitchen-spoon onto the brown tight skin of the turkey. Mother was out of breath. He said couldn't he do that because she'd promised him and Dad she wouldn't do too much. She said never mind darling for him to run around the corner to get the ice cream at Etienne's. It was all ordered but she was afraid they wouldn't bring it in time, and twenty-five cents worth of salted almonds, and to be sure to wear his muffler because it was a terribly raw day.

Glenn had run down the three flights of steps two at a time and almost fallen on his neck in the lower hall. Outside in the broad streets behind the trees rusty with fall, the waving flags and the bunting showed up bright and candystriped under the gray blustery sky. Down at the end of the street there must have been a parade or something because a marching band was playing "Over There."

In the French candy store on Connecticut Avenue it was warm and smelt of chocolate and baking cake. The fat lady behind the counter gave Glenn the ice cream and the salted nuts in a little fancy pink carton tied with ribbons at the top and first thing he knew he'd bought a plaster turkey with little tiny gum-drops in it for seventy-five cents out of his own money. That sort of thing helped to garnish the table, the fat lady agreed in her wheedling French accent. When he got home he ran up the three steep flights of the back stairs and broke breathless into the apartment through the back kitchen door.

Dad was in his shirtsleeves mashing the potatoes and saying Ada he couldn't help feeling bad about the thought of our boy in a uniform strutting around lording it over those miserable defeated Germans. "I'm afraid he'll never be good for anything again." Mother was whispering she could only feel thankful that he was safe. Yes indeed Dad said, when he caught sight of Glenn, in a loud false voice that made nothing seem fun any more, it was a real Thanksgiving day for the Spotswood family all right wasn't it my boy; and then he said for him to help his mother beat the potatoes because he had to change his clothes because the family would soon be coming and it would never do for them to find him like this, they had a poor enough opinion of him as it was. And Glenn set to beating the mashed potatoes with all his might with a big fork while Mother poured in a little milk from a cup. She'd put the mashed potatoes on the stove in a double boiler to keep hot.

My they looked good he'd said, he was so hungry he could eat an elephant, and Mother told him to run along now and brush his hair and wash his hands because they'd soon be there and to tell his father to come and open the oysters.

He'd hardly gotten into his bedroom when the bell rang and he ran to the door and there they were, Uncle Glenn and Aunt Harriet and Lorna. Aunt Harriet and Lorna smelt of perfume and furs and Uncle Glenn smelt of bay rum like a barbershop. They had so many coats and mufflers and furs to hang up that Glenn was still in the coatcloset when cousin Jane and Miss Jenks arrived in tweedy out-of-doors looking overcoats, and everybody was crying out about my dear what a wonderful Thanksgiving it was and the news about Tyler, imagine his coming back an officer and going to the Army of Occupation and maybe he'd have a career in the regular army, and when Mother came out of the kitchen in her new silky-ruffly dress and with her hair all curls, there was such squealing and kissing and my dear you look like a schoolgirl and to think that Tyler's a second lieutenant at twenty; and out of it came Uncle Glenn's voice grumbling that Tyler had ought to have gotten his commission before he went over like the other college boys did, but Miss Jenks screeched that Herbert hadn't wanted him to, he'd wanted him to rise from the ranks it was so much more democratic, and she thought it was splendid.

Mother said for Glenn to go help Dad bring in the oysters and Uncle Glenn followed into the kitchen where Dad was standing by the sink. Dad had a couple of plates of oysters ready but he'd jabbed himself in the palm of the hand with the oysterknife and was standing there looking down with that slow puzzled look he had at a little drop of dark blood swelling up in the palm of his hand.

Uncle Glenn roared that it was too bad Herbert and that he'd ought to use a leather mitt, and grabbed the oysterknife out of Dad's hand, and started to open the oysters at a great rate while Dad and Glenn carried the plates into the dining room, where the table had every leaf in it and they'd hung paper festoons round the electric light fixture that Mother always said was so ugly. Glenn went around straightening the old linen tablecloth with its stiff creases and Mother's best silver spoons and forks that had belonged to Grandmama Carroll. Uncle Glenn caught him at it and slapped him on the back so hard it hurt, and said he was darned if they hadn't turned little Glenn into a regular parlor maid, so that Glenn blushed and went out in the back hall and stood looking out the window at the garbage cans and the spilt ashes in the yard where there was still an oak all golden with fall and a scraggly privet bush with green leaves on it. Somebody had stuck a faded paper American flag at the top of the privet bush.

When Glenn got back they were all at their places and Dad was standing still with his eyes drooping waiting to say grace. As soon as they'd sat down Aunt Harriet said now dear Ada mustn't do another thing she was afraid she'd overdone. Mother shook her head, but she did look pale instead of looking flushed like she had in the kitchen. Her voice sounded tired when she said she'd so looked forward to having everybody at her house this Thanksgiving so that they could be happy with her because she was so happy and tears began to run down her cheeks.

Well now the Huns would get what was coming to them, Uncle Glenn said. He was lifting an oyster dripping with cocktail sauce into his fat mouth. He smacked his lips and said he for one hoped they'd hang the Kaiser and burn Berlin to the ground, teach 'em a lesson, that was all they understood.

Two wrongs didn't make a right; Dad was speaking his carefully pronounced words from the end of the table, when Lorna began to kick up a row because she'd found an oyster crab in her oyster. Uncle Glenn roared that she must eat it and Glenn said he thought they were cute and Lorna screeched that they were horrid and Glenn said nothing in nature was horrid, they were just cute little pink crabs that lived in the oysters. Lorna dared him and double-dared him to eat it and poked it across the table at him on her spoon. The tiny crab crawled a little on his tongue but he crunched it up and swallowed it. Then Lorna kicked him in the shins under the table and said now she thought he was horrid.

Uncle Glenn got red in the face laughing and spilt cocktail sauce on his chin gulping down his oysters so that it looked like he'd cut himself shaving. He said he didn't think the younger generation appreciated oysters, so he distributed Lorna's oysters among the grownups and Glenn lost some of his oysters too though he liked them fine. When Uncle Glenn had eaten his last oyster, he pushed back his chair a little and Aunt Harriet made him wipe the cocktail sauce off his chin and he declared that nothing in the world could beat a Potomac oyster. But now that we'd won the war the Huns would have to pay for it, he said looking straight at Dad. Mother and Cousin Jane were fluttering around taking away the plates.

Dad got that cornered look on his face. He took off his glasses and rubbed his grey bulging eyes and leaned forward across his plate before he spoke. He hoped that those really responsible for the war would be made to pay for it instead of the poor people of Germany who were its first victims, he said, his voice trembling a little; he had confidence that the President . . . Cousin Jane came to the door and said in her businesslike way that Herbert must come help them with the turkey, they were afraid they'd drop it; it was so heavy and wasn't little Glenn coming to act as headwaiter so that his poor mother could sit down and entertain her guests a little.

When Glenn was through passing the vegetables with a napkin on his arm like a real waiter, he sat down and began to eat. Oh, she hoped the turkey wasn't dry, Mother kept saying as she watched Dad shakily carving. Everybody was eating the turkey and saying how good the stuffing was and please pass the cranberry sauce or the piccalilli and it wasn't until the second helping had gone around that Uncle Glenn started to argue with Dad some more. Of course Uncle Glenn said, he was for backing the President, but he thought the leniency shown to conscientious objectors and disloyal elements in this country was a scandal. Dad flared up and said did he call twenty years in jail lenient when the Constitution . . . Uncle Glenn interrupted that that kind of talk was disloyal at a time like this when our boys were giving their lives to defend the very principles . . . "After all, Brother Glenn, Tyler's our son," Mother said with a shy smile, "and we ought to know about sacrifice." Then she told little Glenn to clear the table and bring in the ice cream. She said for Lorna to help him but Lorna didn't move.

When he brought back the ice cream it slithered back and forth on the platter. Cousin Jane who was following with a silver sauceboat of chocolate fudge sauce cried, "Whoops my boy," in her jolly way that made him feel good again. But Uncle Glenn was still talking about how pacifism was giving aid and comfort to the enemy and at a time like this . . . Dad looked very pale and stern and was spacing his words slowly and saying that after all that he'd spent his life in the study of the gospels and the teachings of the Master and had done his best to apply them to modern conditions, not through the dogmas of any particular church, he realized that a great deal of dogma was out of date and rather obscured the gospels than clarified them . . . Then he said his voice shaking again that he could find no justification for a Christian to take part in war and that he thought the application of Christianity to war was not only spiritual but practical.

Uncle Glenn pushed back his chair and got very red and said he hadn't come to listen to a sermon but in his opinion all pacifists were yellow. "Glenn, Glenn, now you promised me you wouldn't," Aunt Harriet was whining in a singsong voice. Cousin Jane added in her snappy cheerful tone that this was Thanksgiving dinner and that arguing at meals gave people indigestion.

"Herbert, don't argue with him, please," Mother whispered down the table, and made Glenn get Uncle Glenn's plate and gave him another helping of ice cream. It made Glenn feel awful to see how her hand was trembling when she poured out the chocolate sauce. "I should think his own sons would be ashamed," Uncle Glenn muttered as he helped himself to another piece of fruitcake.

Lorna started giggling as Aunt Harriet kept hissing hush across the table. Uncle Glenn went on rumbling in his throat that it was a surprise to him Herbert hadn't been arrested before this for his disloyal utterances and us with him for listening to 'em.

Dad had gotten to his feet leaving his ice cream with the bitter fudge sauce untouched on his plate. "After all Glenn you are my guest and Ada's." He walked over to the window and stood there looking out with his thin hands clasped behind his back.

"Mercy," broke out Miss Jenks who hadn't said much during dinner because her new set of false teeth bothered her, but had sat there with her little bright lined face munching fast like a rabbit. "You wouldn't think the war was over would you?"

Then Aunt Harriet suggested Glenn take his little cousin Lorna for a walk around the zoo. Lorna pushed her face out in a big pout and said she hated the old zoo but all the aunts and cousins thought it was a lovely idea and Uncle Glenn gave them a half dollar to buy peanuts for the elephant with and they were bundled up and shooed out of the house into the chilly twilight of the streets.

The Autobiography of Rose

BY GERTRUDE STEIN

How does she know her name is Rose. She knows her name is Rose because they call her Rose. If they did not call her Rose would her name be Rose. Oh yes she knows her name is Rose.

That is the Autobiography of Rose.

The Autobiography of Rose.

Rose knew about afraid and when it happened she knew about afraid. This is what happened.

Grass that is cut is hay.

There there is sunshine

Here there is snow

There there is a little boy

Here there is a little girl

There his name is Allan

Here her name is Rose

Is it interesting.

Rose has an autobiography even if her name was not Rose.

Let us make believe that her name is not Rose. And if her name is not Rose what would be her autobiography. It would not be the autobiography of Rose because her name would not be Rose. But it is the autobiography of Rose even if her name is not Rose oh yes indeed it is the autobiography of Rose.

The Autobiography of Rose.

What happened.

Hay is grass when it is cut.

Hay has nothing to do with water.

Marshes have to do with water but not hay.

But when hay is on a hillside and there is water. Hay can damn the water. And Rose, Rose with her father and her mother can be caught by all that water but Rose and her mother and her father were caught by all that water. That is the water went away.

The Autobiography of Rose.

Nobody did not remember that her name was Rose. And if her name was Rose did that have anything to do with playing checkers and being beaten by her grandmother, oh no that had nothing to do with her name being Rose.

Rose does know the difference between summer and winter and this has something to do with her name being Rose. It has something to do with her name being Rose.

The Autobiography of Rose.

Rose could look at herself and when she saw herself and she knew her name was Rose she could look at herself and not see that her name is Rose. Oh yes she could. She could see that perhaps her name was not Rose.

If Rose was her name was Rose her nature.

She did not know the difference between Rose and Rose at least she said she did not know the difference between Rose and Rose.

Nobody said.

Nobody does not make any difference in her name not being Rose.

Rose is her name that is what she said.

The Autobiography of Rose.

It is taller to be taller.

Is it older to be older.

Is it younger to be younger.

Is it older to be older.

Is it taller to be taller.

The Autobiography of Rose.

A glass pen oh yes a glass pen.

Would Rose prefer a little dog named Pépé or a glass pen. A glass pen does not write very well and a little dog named Pépé does not allow himself to be caressed very well, so after all there is no choice there is no choice between a little dog named Pépé and a glass pen there is no choice for Rose because neither one she has not been offered either oh no she has not been offered either one.

The autobiography of Rose who has not been offered either one. If she has not been offered either one what is her autobiography. Her autobiography is not that she has not been offered either one. Indeed not. Even if she has not.

And now everybody prepare.

Rose is to be offered one.

Which one.

Which one is Rose to be offered the glass pen or a little dog named Pépé. Which one. This one. And which is this one. Ah which is this one. That is the autobiography of Rose, which is this one.

The Autobiography of Rose.

When Rose was young she is young now but when Rose was young. How young does Rose have to be to be young. She was young she is young, she was very young she is young enough to be very young, and she knows all about being young enough to be young. How young do you have to be to be young. Seven years is old for a dog but not old for Rose. Seven is not old for Rose but is it young.

The autobiography of Rose is that she was young. And when she was young oh yes when she was young she said she had been young and that is quite certain she had been young. Was she regretting that she had been young so young, was she regretting anything. If she was regretting anything she was not young, how young can you be to be young. Every time Rose was young she was young. Every time and every time was every time. And now. Every time is every time. And Rose is young. Has Rose an autobiography. Rose has an autobiography. Has she an autobiography of when she was young. Rose has an autobiography of when she was young.

A garden and a gardener are two things to Rose.

And then one thing follows another.

A school succeeds a garden.

And a garden succeeds a school.

And later later succeeds a garden.

Later never sounds younger.

Oh no oh dear no

Later never sounds younger.

Older as yet.

There is 110 older and no as yet.

And so there is no older as yet.

Therefore older does not follow later. And not as yet.

The Autobiography of Rose.

Outside now there is no Rose although in winter yes in winter often in winter quite as often as in winter there is a Rose. And as autumn does not follow winter, autumn comes first and as spring very often does not follow autumn winter comes first and as summer very often comes after what is the matter with Rose knowing it most. She does know it most. That is the autobiography of Rose not that she knows it the most. If she knew the difference between summer and winter and spring and autumn she would know it at first, which she most often does and which she much the most often does. Generally not.

Rose has only one autobiography.

This is the autobiography of Rose.

Any little while she does not neglect being taller not older. Any little while she does not neglect. Being taller. Not older.

The Autobiography of Rose.

Rose. What can she remember. Can she remember Rose. Can she. I am wondering.

October, 1936
Bilignin par Belley, Ain

To Rose. *When they said if she would be good, she said she would know all about it all the same, and all the same she can know all about it. Which is a pleasure to her friend,* Gertrude Stein.

The Only Son

BY JAMES T. FARRELL

It was Patrick McMurtrie's twenty-first birthday. Father, mother, and son sat down to supper. Mrs. McMurtrie was a lean woman with tannish, rough skin. Her face seemed always drawn, her expression changelessly tight and sad, her bony hands work-worn. The father was a gruff looking little man with a weather-beaten and wind-roughened face, the result of his years of work in the building trades. He was now working as a foreman on a building that was going up. The boy was medium sized, with a sensitive face, blue eyes, curly brown hair, and slightly hollowed cheeks. All day, the mother had been waiting for this moment. She had spent three times as long as usual in puttering about the kitchen and cooking the same kind of a supper that she prepared every evening.

She blessed herself, bowed her head, and said grace, both father and son waiting in boredom while she performed this ritual. She always did the serving, and she served her son first, giving him a large cut of the thick steak she had fried, and then, filling his plate with potatoes and other vegetables. The father looked on silent and dour, watching her pass the plate to her son.

"Now you can serve the poor relation," he said as she started to serve him.

His remark passed unheeded, but Patrick frowned. They began eating.

"Well now that you're a man, with your schooling finished, and your fine college degree signed, sealed, and paid for, you can start paying back your old man the money he's spent making you so smart and highly educated. Maybe you'll start repaying your father and mother for what they've done for you and for the fine education they've given you," the father said, speaking slowly and with undue casualness as he ate.

Patrick did not reply. This was the old man's regular line.

"Joseph, why in the name of God would you be talking to your son like that, and this his birthday. You know that now the boy is working, he'll be giving us back everything we've given him, and with interest," Mrs. McMurtrie said.

"Of course he will," the father said with a note of irony in his voice. "I was just thinking out loud," he added.

They ate on in silence. It seemed as though the mother would cry, but no tears came. Patrick was uncomfortable. He wanted to be over with the meal, and to be out of the house and with Sarah. The strained atmosphere at the dinner table was not unusual to him. It was a replica of what happened nearly every night. The old man hated him. There was no love between his father and mother. For years now he had known his father as a dour and bitter man, hating everything about his home, always making sarcastic remarks, constantly starting family squabbles. And for years now also, he had known his mother as a sad and spiritless woman, fanatically religious, always seeming to suffer from the sharp gibes of her husband, sometimes fighting back, sometimes bearing herself with a painfully martyred expression on her face as if she were just going into a lion's den to die for her faith. He looked on her. That same expression. His mother embarrassed him. She loved him with such possessiveness.

Patrick's father always looked for something in the son's conduct which could be used against the mother. Patrick often looked upon himself as a kind of family no man's land. He remembered how ever since he was a boy this had gone on, with fighting and the old man's drinking. But in those days he had been innocent and afraid of his father. Even so, he had quietly detested him. Now, he did not detest his father. He was, at times, even sorry for the old man. Often, he was contemptuous of him. And his mother, she embarrassed him. She was so damned religious, and demanded that he be the same. Every Sunday, he had to go to Mass with her. For years now, he had been fulfilling his religious duties, even to the reception of Holy Communion, only to please his mother. His hypocrisy often disgusted him. But he could not bring himself to tell his mother that he was an atheist. She was such a sad woman. She had so little in life to which she could cling. And then, it would give the old man a trump card to play against her. The father always said that he had no education, and that the son's education had served to make him into a heathen and a snob, who soon wouldn't act as if he even knew his old parents.

Suddenly, while they were eating, Mrs. McMurtrie began to cry. Her husband sarcastically asked why she was crying. She answered that it was because she was so happy.

"Joseph, remember when Patrick was a little gossoon, and you would be so often taking him to the park, and there he would be chasing the squirrels. Patrick, my son, you always loved to chase the squirrels, and you couldn't say squirrel. You would always call them, 'quirrels.' You'd come home with your father and tell me of the great time you had, chasing the 'quirrels'," she said.

"Yes mother," Patrick said, striving not to show that he was bored.

"Ah woman, will you forget that talk. That's all happened years ago, and what's the good in remembering it all of the time. Tell me, do I ever hear anything out of you but when he was a little gossoon?"

"And son," she went on, ignoring her husband. "You were the good little fellow. On Sundays often, I would dress you up in your Sunday clothes, and take you to Mass with me, and sometimes, I'd be taking you to see your Aunt Ellen, Lord have mercy on her soul. Yes, 'tis proud of you I'd be then. And now you're a fine young man, and it's prouder I am of you. And Lord have mercy on me, but how you would cry for ice cream when you were at your Aunt Ellen's. I wish she could be here with us now to see the fine young man you have become. But the Lord took her."

"Yes, and whenever you cried for ice cream, you'd get it too," the father said.

"Why Joseph!" she exclaimed, shocked.

"You always spoiled him by giving him everything he asked for. Is it any wonder he reads the books I see around here?" the father said.

"There's nothing wrong with the books I read," Patrick said.

"No, there's nothing wrong with Darwin, and men coming from monkeys and all that high and mighty nonsense. No, nothing wrong with heathen books," the father said.

"You don't know anything about the books I bring home and read," Patrick said.

"See, Mary! Did you hear what he said to me! Many's the time, woman, that I warned you you were spoiling him. Here's the fruit of your willfulness. Here we save all our life to educate him, and how does he repay us? He calls his father ignorant. So we're ignorant now?" the father said, and suddenly he turned from the mother and faced Patrick. "Well my lad, it's not ignorant I'd be if I spent the money educating myself that I spent on you and your miseducation. Coming home now that you're a college graduate and acting like a snob!" He turned back and with a melodramatic gesture of the right arm, he said, "Woman, I warned you!"

"Oh quit putting on a show and acting as if I were still a two-year-old," Patrick said.

"Son, you must not be saying such things to your father. If he provokes you or not, he's your father," the mother said.

"Hell, I didn't ask him to be," Patrick said, disgusted.

"Patrick son!" the mother exclaimed in that injured martyr-like tone of voice that she so frequently used.

"Mary McMurtrie, before he dies, he'll disown his old father," Joseph McMurtrie said solemnly, shaking his finger as he spoke.

"Well from the way you go on, you'd think you're a section boss here at home, and I'm one of the hunkies working for you," Patrick said.

Patrick hadn't meant to answer his father's provocation. The answer had come against his will and his determination as it so often did.

"See Mary McMurtrie! It's your doin'! See, he's twenty-one now and been to college, and right away, he knows it all. Pretty soon, he'll be too good to deign to live in the same flat with us. He'll be leaving us ignorant old greenhorns. He'll be leaving us to go and marry that whore he runs around with," the father said, speaking with a bitterness that seemed to rise out of the depths of his being.

"Listen! Cut that out! You hear me!" Patrick said, blanching with anger.

"Well then show a little respect for your father," McMurtrie said, changing his tone of voice when he perceived the reaction he had produced in his son.

"People should do something in this world to earn respect," Patrick shot back at his father.

Patrick warned himself to exert more self-control. He understood more than his father did. He shouldn't let his old man get him so sore. With understanding, things should take on a different light. He knew that his father was jealous of him, bitter, unhappy, and that the old man had never loved his mother. Understanding these things, sensing causes underlying his father's conduct, he should take his father's words in stride. But damn it, it was too thick. The old hypocritical fathead calling Sarah a whore!

The father had been eyeing his son closely, and observed a change as if Patrick were softening while these reflections hastily passed through his mind.

"I'm boss in this house, and I want a little respect shown me! She's a whore anyway. What other kind of a girl could she be, sleeping with you?" the father said.

The old man couldn't stand anybody else having any enjoyment or happiness in life, Patrick told himself, now determined to maintain his self-control.

"Saint Joseph pray for me," the mother exclaimed woefully as a response to what her husband had just said.

"Watch what you're saying," Patrick said to his father.

"As long as this is my house, don't ever bring that woman of yours into it," the father said.

"Mother of God, protect my son from evil companions," the mother said.

"How do you know she'd want to come here?" Patrick said.

"Why should she? Why in the name of God should she be wanting to come into a decent household?" the father said.

"What the hell decency is there in this house?" Patrick asked, disgust rising above his efforts at self-control.

Shaking, the father rose and pointed an accusing finger at Patrick.

"Out of my house, you young cur!" the father said.

"My son is not going to be put out of this house. Not while I breathe the breath of life," the mother said.

Mrs. McMurtrie clasped her hands and silently prayed while tears rolled down her cheeks.

"Goddamn you!" Patrick said, flinging out each syllable.

"I hope that God will never give you or that whore of yours a decent day as long as you live!" McMurtrie said.

Patrick walked out of the room.

II

Patrick sat in his bedroom with his door closed so that he could not hear his father and mother fighting. It was a small room, with books scattered around it, and holy pictures on the walls. Right over the bed, there was a framed picture of the bleeding Sacred Heart. No, he didn't want to hear them talking and scrapping. It was often a puzzle to him that his old man never got bored with the sound of his own voice uttering the same complaints against his mother that he had been uttering for years and years in their squabbling. He never seemed able to probe down to what seemed to him the real reason for his father's hatred and jealousy. What had happened in the old man's life to cause this? He knew that the old man had never been happy with his mother. And he could understand that. Who would want her for a wife? Who would want to sleep with her? As far back as he could remember, she had always been the same. The same religious fanaticism. The same air of sadness and tiredness. She could give any man the creeps. She had always made both him and his father feel that their home was populated with death. Always images of the same suffering Christ on the Cross plastered all around the house! He looked around the room at the holy picture. Christ was suffering over his dresser. All of the pictures were cheap and banal. Assuming that there was a God, these pictures were a disservice to Him and to His supposedly True Faith. They made Him out as no more of a character than his own father and mother, or than some ignorant Irish priest. He couldn't get at the bottom of his old man. Perhaps, the old man hadn't wanted to marry her? Perhaps the old man hadn't wanted a kid? He didn't know. The old man was jealous of him now because he was young, had gotten a little education, and might have a different kind of a life.

How many times hadn't his old man come rolling home drunk? But always, his father had turned on respectability like a fountain to use in arguments with him. Yes, his father was a damned old hypocrite. Both his father and his mother were failures in life. They were mismated and they had botched their lives. Neither of them had ever seemed to be happy, except when his mother was smothering him with affection or praying, or when his old man was drunk with his cronies in a saloon or speakeasy. They were trying in their own way to drag him down to their own level. And he wouldn't be dragged down. He wouldn't! They were failures at living. They were going to make the same thing out of him if he let them. His mother wanted him to settle down into a successful nonentity. Well he wouldn't. He didn't have much of a job, but he would do something, make something out of his life. He didn't know what, but he would. Because he was out of college, he wasn't going to give up studying and trying to think. He was his mother's excuse for living. Somehow, he hated to hurt her. He didn't care about hurting his father. But she seemed so tragic a figure. Did she ever smile? Did she ever enjoy herself? Just looking at her suggested to him something of the cause of his father's bitterness.

He did things that he hated himself for doing, just because of his mother. Once a month, or once every two months, just to satisfy her, he said that he had gone to confession, and then, when she went to Mass with him, he received Holy Communion. Sacrilege! It caused no fear, no terror in his soul. His non-existent soul, he added with a smile. He asked himself were there many others in America doing the same thing as he was doing? Were there others with mothers and fathers such as his, and were they compromising themselves and their dignity in their own eyes by pretending to be Catholics, receiving the Sacraments of the Church sacrilegiously in order to preserve a little domestic peace and to nurture the illusions of older people!

Just now, his old man had gotten him damned sore when he had slandered Sarah. He loved Sarah, and he would live with her all his life. He wanted to marry her now, but she always counselled him to wait because neither of them had much money, and because of his home situation. What the hell business did the old man have saying what he'd said about her? Sarah was unlike any one he had ever known. And the old bastard calling her a *whore*! It was only self-control that had saved his father from getting something that he hadn't in the least bargained for. And what was going to happen when he did marry? He could see his father and mother alone in this house, eating themselves away with unhappiness and mutual hatred while they lived on waiting only to die. There they would be, each getting older, the old man becoming more and more bitter, the old lady growing more and more sad. She would throw anything she could in the way of his marrying Sarah. She would fight with all means to keep her son to herself. And it was clearly a case of who should be the one that was to be sacrificed. He or his mother? He and Sarah, rather, or else his mother? Why was it this way? Why did life have to be this way? Why did parents have to cling to their children like drowning persons clinging and clutching a lifeline for dear life itself. All damned fool banal questions he was asking himself, and yet they were real, and they cut through the very fibers of his life at this very moment. It was all more than he could make out. He stood up and told himself that he was twenty-one, and that technically, he had reached manhood's estate. He had to be a man. He had to walk over his mother's unhappiness and misery, or else, he couldn't be a man.

To thine own self be true . . .

He quoted the line with seriousness and determination. He wouldn't be just a dutiful son and a nonentity in an office all his life. He vowed that he wouldn't.

He dropped back on his bed, and reflected that what was the worst feature of this whole situation was that there was no solution to it. No matter how he thought it out, no matter how much he understood of the motives of his father and mother, and of his own motives for that matter, where did his understanding lead him to? It could not reduce one bit the pain and the agony and sorrow of it. He could not give up Sarah without suffering intensely. If he did that, he would have no heart to go on, to go on and fight to make something decent out of his life, to go on and rise above the ranks of mediocrity. With her, he might work, go to night school, study law, and make a career for himself. That was a plan he had been thinking about. And if he did not give up Sarah, what about his mother? It was painful to think of his mother and father in this house alone, waiting to die after he had left them. And Hell, what was it now to live here? And where was it getting any of the three of them? *What* was it getting them? Look at the scene at suppertime tonight. And there they were going at one another now in the dining room.

He sat on the bed, glum. He heard his father slam the front door. The old man would come home drunk to raise hell tonight, he told himself.

III

Patrick was ready to leave when his mother entered the room. She clutched him fiercely.

"You're all that I have. My son! My son! My baby boy that I nursed. My baby!"

Held in an embrace by his mother, Patrick felt almost physically ill.

She kissed his forehead.

"I have to go, Mother. I got to meet a fellow and I'm late and keeping him waiting on a street corner," he said.

Jealousy flashed in her eyes.

"Is it a lad you're meeting?"

"Why, of course Mother," he said, thinking to himself that she probably was sure that he was going to see Sarah.

"Patrick, you wouldn't lie to your mother?"

"You know I wouldn't, Mother. Why should I?"

And while he said this, he thought to himself that she forced him to lie to her; she had forced him to lie to her for years and years now. And she didn't know it, didn't know that it was impossible to tell her the truth about almost everything that he really felt or believed.

Wiping away a tear, she stood before him like a personification of desolation. That goddamn look of hers! Always that way! Always having to look at her standing there so silent, so injured and so sorrowful. He could understand a great deal about his father, just by seeing her now, standing there before him.

Suddenly, she drew a pair of rosary beads from her pocket. They were expensive, with a solid gold crucifix. She held them before him with great pride.

He waited for her to say something.

"For my son on his twenty-first birthday, from his mother," she said, and her smile was a miserable effort.

"Gee, thanks Mother! But you shouldn't have done that for me. They're expensive," he said.

"I had them blessed," she said.

She was so damned unfair and foolish, he reflected. And the pity of her was that she didn't even know. And giving him rosary beads! His mother was a fool.

"Son, never lose your religion. God is good. Never lose your faith in him," she said in a strained voice.

Again she wiped a tear away. Patrick was moved to pity his mother. But he was unable to express his emotion to her. And he dared not. If he did, then, that only served to make the tie between her and himself the more intolerable. And so often, the ties which held flesh and blood together were so artificial. This realization made him hate all society, because it was society that kept firm these artificial ties. And just look at the hopelessness it had made in his home.

He put his straw hat on, and waited, anxious to get out, acutely uncomfortable here with his mother.

"Son, tell me the truth! Are you going to see that girl?"

"Why mother, I told you I was going to see a fellow, and go to a movie with him."

"Son, she might be a nice girl, but she's not for you. I'm your mother and I know it," she said.

Patrick did not answer her.

"Patrick, isn't there a nice Catholic girl you grew up with that you could take out now and again?" she said.

"Mother, I'm late. And I'm going to be busy because I'm going to night school and study law in the fall. I won't be able to bother about girls," he said, feeling that he should blurt right out and tell her, force the issue into a showdown; but he was unable to force himself to do just that.

"Patrick, you do bother about that girl. I know you do. I can tell it. I'm your mother, and no one knows you better than your mother. I have been seeing how different you are since you've known that girl. I tell you this for your own good."

He asked himself why didn't he just tell her to mind her damned business?

"Son, you won't be having your mother with you always. You should stay in with me some nights. And that's little I'm asking of you," she said.

"Mother, I got to go," he said.

Whether she did it purposefully or not, he wasn't sure, but she always succeeded in making him feel so damned guilty. And guilty of what? Just of trying to be himself and live his own life.

"I'll be home early," he said, unable to bear that look of hers.

She kissed him passionately, and he left. At the door, he turned and said goodbye to her with what sympathy he could force into his voice.

"Goodbye," she said, again with all that sadness in her voice, saying it as if she were bidding him farewell for the final time in this world.

From the window, she watched him disappear down the street. She sat alone, rocking in the darkened parlor, tears filling her eyes.

IV

Walking to the streetcar, Patrick thought gloomily that things would go on without any change just as long as they three lived together. If his mother died, what then? It would be better if she died first. If his father went first, he'd be left with her around his neck, depending on him, using every sentimentality offered to her by society to keep herself like a chain holding him at her level. Unless he wanted to continue going through such suppers and scenes as that of tonight's, he had only one path to choose – to leave. And he couldn't do that while his mother lived. He knew that he couldn't. If she would only die. Death would be best for her. He thought of Sarah. Suddenly, he was fearful to the point of dread. He and Sarah would get married, and one day they would be old, and one of them would die and leave the other behind. But that was years away. And they wouldn't grow old together like his mother and father had. They would build a free and beautiful life together. They would!

On the streetcar, he accidentally put his hand into his coat pocket, and felt the rosary beads that his mother had given him. He drew his hand out as if he had touched something disgusting. The beads brought him back to thoughts of his mother just when he had happily dismissed her from his mind. He thought of the meaning of her religion to her. It was all that she had. Her faith in him gave her nothing but misery, and earned from him nothing but annoyance and contempt and a kind of sympathy that would be insulting to any dignified human being. He hated her religion. Yet it did her good, saved her from utter misery and loneliness. He didn't care, he hated it! People had to learn to be brave and free, to face what life flung at them, and not weakly to ask the consolation of religion. But there she was. She came from a different world than he, and a different country, and she was a lone, forlorn woman in the present world. Yes, death would be gentle to her, a smooth, rippling, sleepy approach into darkness. And it would produce an irony that she would never experience. There was no waking after death, and she would die, and she would not wake up in any Heaven. She would die, and there would be no more of her, and all her dreary life would have been in vain. He wanted to revolt against it all. Life was a lousy business. You had to stand up to the whole lousy business, he told himself with feeling and passion. Goddamn it, he would!

But he was going to Sarah. And when he and Sarah were married and they had children, they would raise them intelligently, intelligently and free from all that he had been raised in. He vowed that he would. He had no God to whom he could vow. He vowed it to himself. Sarah! She was so lovely. And once with her, now, he would tell her all that happened, tell her all that he had been thinking.

The car stopped and he got off. He was going to Sarah now, and all of his home life would drop from his mind for a little while, and he would find joy and love with her. He walked briskly, a young man on his way to see his girl.

A Goat for Azazel (A.D. 1688)

BY KATHERINE ANNE PORTER

Martha Goodwin, fourteen-year-old, elder daughter of a pious brick mason named John Goodwin, was behaving very strangely. She had been behaving with conspicuous strangeness since she was eleven years old and it had long been suspected that she was in the grip of a diabolical possession. Cotton Mather early noted her symptoms and marked their progress. The Goodwins lived in Charlestown, and during a Sabbath visit to his father-in-law, John Phillips, Mather heard an encouraging bit of gossip.

Not only Martha, but all four of Goodwin's children had fallen, almost overnight, into a state of mind very puzzling and sinister. Little Mercy, seven years old, was in a continual tantrum. She yelled and her body grew rigid while she was being dressed; she refused to do the useful household task suitable to her age; and she would not, without a fearful struggle, allow herself to be put to bed at the customary hour. Naturally the Devil found an easy abiding-place in the bodies of children, conceived as they were, poisoned to the bone with original sin, but a sound beating would usually dislodge him. He sat firmly in this child against all such persuasions. The slightest rebuke from her parents affected her like a lightning shock. She fell prone, turned blue in the face, her eyes rolled upward and her teeth clenched in a paroxysm of lockjaw. The elder son, sixteen years old, shouted that he was a wolf, retired into corners and howled bestially. The third child, John, suffered with shooting pains, and showed signs of epilepsy. He would sprawl on the floor and scream that he could not get up again because his head was nailed to the floor.

Martha was a pretty, inventive, restless girl. She suffered all the afflictions of the others, with a few added symptoms acutely her own.

One afflicted child had been troublesome enough, but four of them succeeded in terrorizing their parents completely. They called on their pastor and several other ministers to come and help them rout the invisible hosts that had chosen their humble household as a battlefield.

The last minister to be invited was Cotton Mather. With his genius for instant action, Cotton Mather was the first man there. The prayer-meeting was called for an afternoon. He arrived alone, early in the morning, held his prayer service by himself, recognized at a glance all the signs of true demoniacal posssion in the children, and advised their father to look about for the witch.

At this the children howled in dead earnest, and their sufferings were redoubled. By the time the other ministers arrived, among them Mr. John Hale of Beverly and Mr. Samuel Moyes of Salem, the children had been struck stone-deaf and could not hear the prayers. When the reverend gentlemen produced their Bibles, the devil-possessed were provoked to roll on the floor and kick at them.

The uproar continued for days, amid daily festivals of prayer and the fascinated attentions of the neighbors. The sufferings of the children rivaled those of the children of Sweden, Mather's favorite witch ground. Pins were discovered sticking lightly under their skins. They vomited pins and nails and other unnatural substances. They wore themselves out with acrobatic feats, bending backwards until their heads touched their heels, while their arms and legs appeared to be wrenched from the sockets by invisible hands.

At nightfall, recovered somewhat, they would eat hearty suppers and settle down for a good sleep. Cotton Mather suggested a three-day fast, and they weakened noticeably under it. Being fed again, their torments were renewed with sinister complications.

Martha named the witch. Some time before, she had quarrelled with the laundress, a girl of her own age, accusing her of stealing some linens. The girl was the daughter of Bridget Glover, an Irish woman who supported her family, with the help of her older children, by washing clothes for the neighbors. She was considered a little crazy, because she was excitable, and when she was excited she spoke Gaelic. But she had a free command of vituperation in English and her loose way of talking offended a great many people. She was a Catholic, really worse than a Quaker, and she had been called a witch more than once.

Bridget Glover joined in the quarrel and defended her child. She went over to the Goodwin house and shouted angrily and made incoherent threats. It was a foolish row over the back fence, but through skillful handling by Cotton Mather it became the most sensational episode in Boston for the next six months. The exact words spoken by Bridget Glover will never be known. Indeed, the facts of the case cannot now be learned, for it was recorded by Cotton Mather, who was interpreting by a formula, and the event followed the perfect classical pattern. Each member of the Goodwin family gave a different version of her speeches, but all agreed that she had spoken repeatedly of the Devil and had cursed them in the manner of a witch. Cotton Mather conferred with his friend Mr. Hale, who agreed with him that this was matter for the authorities. Bridget Glover was formally accused of witchcraft, and brought before the magistrates for examination.

When they began to question her, so the story runs, she stammered a moment, lapsed into Gaelic, and never again spoke a word of English. It was necesary to conduct her trial through an interpreter. There is little doubt that she was full of fairy lore, a firm believer in ancient signs and wonders. This was not strange, nor even criminal. Good Congregationalists had to be reminded from the pulpit, now and again, that they must not turn the sieve and shears, wear amulets, and recite charms when they dug for healing herbs. The records are so confused in Bridget's case that there is no way of knowing what arts she practised. The Irish bravado overcame her when confronted with her enemies, and she boasted that indeed she was a witch, and a good one. She had done all they charged her with and more; she hinted she could tell great things if she pleased.

The interpreters said so, at least. They also interrupted, on their own responsibility, to add that she appeared to be dominated in turn by a black magic superior to her own and was restrained from telling tales by being forced to talk in a language which the demons believed no one else in Boston could understand. The crack-brained logic of the demons left their servant defenseless, and the trial went on smoothly.

Point by point the evidence corresponded with the best traditions. Rag figures stuffed with goat's wool were found in her house and produced in court. She admitted she had made them, and said her way of tormenting her victims was to wet her finger in her mouth and stroke these dolls. The Goodwin children were brought in, fell to roaring at the sight of her, and when she touched one of the dolls they flew obligingly into fits.

Cotton Mather sat at the examination and took his endless notes. It was better than he hoped for.

The witch was invited to name her counsel. "Have you no one to stand by you?" asked a magistrate.

"I have,' she said, and looked pertly into the air. "No, he's gone!"

She explained, the faithful interpreters said, that she meant her Prince. This seemed so curious they doubted if she was sane. Half a dozen physicians came to talk with her. They inquired first about the state of her soul. "You ask me a very solemn question, I cannot tell what to say to it." They desired her to repeat the Pater Noster. She stumbled in some of the passages and excused her bad Latin by saying she could not pronounce those words if they gave her all the world. The doctors, too, had read the best authorities on witchcraft. They decided that she was sane, and a witch.

Cotton Mather, in his own account of this episode, told how he posted himself with the interpreters outside her cell, where they heard her quarrelling with her spectral demon, saying she had confessed to revenge herself for his falseness to her. Mather harried the fantastical creature, visiting her almost every day as she sat chained in her cell. In rambling wild talk she let her fancy go, according to the interpreters: and told of meetings with her Prince in company with other worshippers of his, though she would not name them; and confessed that she knew her Prince to be the Devil. Mather told her that her Prince had cheated her badly. "If that be so, I am sorry," said Bridget. She refused to answer some of his questions, explaining that her spirits forbade her to speak. As a Catholic she so feared and hated his heretic prayers that she implored him not to pray for her until her spirits gave her leave to listen.

She was found guilty and sentenced to be hanged. Mather could not rest on this. He went around and collected all the neighborhood gossip about her. Festering grievances and old hatreds were reopened; a Mrs. Hughes remembered that her small son had waked one night crying that a woman was in the room, she had reached under the bedclothes and tried to tear out his bowels. She said that Bridget, when accused of this, had confessed it was herself in spectre. This Mrs. Hughes, under Mather's questioning, enjoyed great refreshment of memory. A friend of hers had died six years before, declaring with her last breath that Bridget Glover had murdered her in spectre. Further – and this is the perfect Mather touch – the dying woman had warned Mrs. Hughes to remember this, for in six years there would be great occasion to mention it.

The six years were now finished. After sitting in prison for some months, Bridget Glover was taken out and hanged. On the scaffold she spoke out clearly and strongly in Irish. The interpreter came down off the ladder and translated the speech to Mather, waiting below. She said that the children would not be relieved by her death, for there were others besides herself had a hand in their sufferings.

This was truth with unconscious irony. The ones who had a hand in it published this statement at once, and the Goodwin children fell into fresh complexities of torment.

Cotton Mather sat in the Goodwin house and urged the wretched little animals onward. They had begun with a fine holiday of rebellion, and now found themselves caught in a horrible device that really frightened them. They were no longer allowed to invent their own tortures, but suffered assault from without. Invisible hands smacked them rudely, and large bruises appeared on their bodies to prove it. On being assured that the spectres had done it, they said they could see the shadows moving about the room. Demoralized with terror, they would point them out, and Cotton Mather would aim a blow at this place. Strangely enough, the child who pointed, though his back was turned, would receive a stout thwack also. Howling, he would speak the names that occurred, or had been suggested, to him, and Cotton Mather wrote them down, with the comment that all the persons named had been since suspected of witchcraft. Invariably, he would observe within a few days that a suspected woman would be wearing an unaccountable bruise on the very part of her body where he had struck at her spectre a few days previously. He does not explain how he went about making these discoveries. He failed in gathering enough evidence to justify the arrest of any one of them.

The solemn farce went on. The children were now quite bewildered, but they still had presence of mind enough to remember the main issue. During all the months that Bridget Glover sat chained waiting for her death, they concerned themselves with putting off the bedtime hour, getting out of their chores, and escaping family prayer. The neighbors crowded in as to a deathbed. This was better than a deathbed or a hanging, for it had the tang of novelty and supernatural danger. The children barked, purred, growled, leaped like wild animals, and attempted to fly like birds, or like witches. The watchers restrained them from harming themselves. When they pulled their neck-cloths so tightly they almost choked, someone was always on hand to relieve them. They almost fell in the fire, and they almost drowned themselves, but someone nearby hauled them out in the nick of time. If anyone dared to touch a Bible, those religion-surfeited infants almost died. They tore their clothes and broke glasses and spilled their cups, and mewed with delight; and to save their lives they could not do the simplest task without making a frightful mess of it. No one dared to punish them – were they not innocent victims of the Devil?

Mather continued to tell them the spectres had done everything, and did not fail verbally to point the way to grace. "Child, pray to the Lord Jesus Christ," he admonished them in turn. Immediately their teeth clenched over their tongues and they stared at him. "Child, look to Him," he advised, and their eyes were pulled instantly so far into their heads he professed a fear that they would never emerge again.

This grew monotonous, and Mather chose the interesting member of the family for closer observation. He took Martha to live in his house. She was gifted, pretty, and full of wit, and the others were merely noisy and stubborn and tiresome.

Away from the stuffy, disordered cottage, Martha behaved herself very nicely at first. The big fine Mather house with its handsome furniture, silver, books, servants, impressed her. Good food, a soft bed, and the gentleness of Abigail, Mather's young wife, were very disarming. Everything was pleasant except the persistent praying and the constant watching of all her movements.

She grew restless in a few days. In a voice of distress she announced to Cotton Mather that They had found her out, and at once she had a fit of choking and her throat swelled until she was threatened with strangulation. Mather held her and stroked her throat until the fit passed. Whenever the fits returned, he could always cure her with this stroking, a remedy in common use by the lower order of witches.

For several months the Mather household lived in tumult. Martha was the center of attraction, and she repaid the attentions given her. A dozen times a day Mather forced her to her knees to pray with him. She clapped her hands over her ears and declared They were raising such a clamor she could not hear a word. At times she walked with a heavy limp, and she explained that They had clamped Bridget Glover's chain on her leg. Mather would strike at the invisible chain and it would fall away. In his headlong battle with the Devil, he used with precision the methods of witchcraft described by those professional witchfinders Perkins, Gaule, Bernard; and Martha responded properly. She surmised hidden silver in the well, and it was found there. She spoke in strange languages, and "her belly would on a sudden be puft up strangely," one of the marks of diabolical possession as quoted by Increase Mather in his useful table; now, I believe, noted as one of the common symptoms of intestinal worms; and she did all these things with high dramatic effect.

She was forever getting into states where Cotton Mather must hurry to her rescue, and at times his powers of exorcism were tried severely. After a while, her mood would change into a charming gaiety. For days she would talk, "never wickedly," wrote Mather with affectionate admiration, "but always wittily and beyond herself." He loved wit and gaiety, and he dared not confess this taste to the society he lived in; but he could not deny himself the perverse joy he took in Martha's youth and spirits. She was so entertaining in these moods he could not reprove her. His role of religious guardian and exorcist forbade him to play a foil to her, and her spirits flashed themselves away in empty air, unsatisfied. Relapsing into her dark mood, she would say, "I want to steal, or be drunk – then I would get well."

Martha was the first, and the most imaginative, of all the girls who were to follow her in a blind destructive rebellion against the perversion of life through religion, in the theocratic state. Revolt was working in all directions; it was fermenting in politics, in the church, in labor, in the economic system; after two generations the whole body of society was heaving with premonitions of change. The children merely followed their sure instincts, but they were not understood, and Cotton Mather at twenty-eight years was in a position of power he was in no way fitted to assume. He used any weapon that came his way, but his personal desires blinded his judgment, and so he chose badly. He was bound to make of this absurd episode an issue of first importance in the history of his career, and he succeeded. He had proved his power as a witch-finder in the case of Bridget Glover, and he believed that a cure of Martha would establish finally the supernatural authority he craved: to be marked and set apart as the intimate of God, the most potent enemy of the Devil in New England, and in the world. First he must convince the Governor and the magistrates and the ministers of Boston that he could truly cast out devils. The rest would follow.

Martha's personality was a disturbing element, not to his greater plan but in his secret self. Neither of them realized fully the nature of the tension between them, and they played a gruesome game of blindman's buff. She tormented and tantalized him endlessly, and he held her and prayed with her while she struggled in her recurrent frenzies. At times these scenes were mere romps between them; at other moments they touched the edge of horror: he stared fascinated as she flung herself down before him writhing, crying for him to save her from her demons. He listened to her blasphemies as long as he dared, then stroked and soothed her into calm. She would work herself into a dangerous state and kick and strike at him; but always the blow that began in violence ended in a light pat of the finger tips or a soft nudge of the toe.

Day and night were the same to Martha. She would rise out of her sleep crying that her devil-horse was waiting for her. Mounting a chair, she would gallop about the room. Once, seated on air in the posture of a woman on horseback, she galloped up a flight of stairs, and Mather admired this feat so much he almost forgot its devilish inspiration. In this mood her boisterious humor grew very broad in the best seventeenth-century manner. If her stomach made sounds of disturbed digestion, she would exclaim, "Something is going away from me!", clasp her head in her palm and complain of faintness. Mather, listening solemnly for some statement from the demon inhabiting her, would declare indeed he had heard the squeaking of a mouse. If he tried to persuade her to speak the Holy Name, she would answer flippantly, "Oh, you know what it is! It is G and O and D!"

All profitable and edifying literature threw her into confusion. Books in favor of the Quakers calmed her, but she could not endure a word against them. She enjoyed popish books, and went blind at the sight of the Assembly catechism. She hugged the accursed Book of Common Prayer to her bosom, calling it her Bible. Mather noted with mystification and some chagrin that his own books worked like a poison in her. He gave her his story of bewitched Ann Cole, of Hartford, who was unutterably pious, even in her fits. Ann Cole's pieties gave Martha the worst convulsions of all.

It began to look as if the battle were lost, for Mather was so enchanted with her vitality and imagination he was losing control over her. Her tenderness then took an odd turn. She decided to flatter him outrageously. Flying as if pursued by an army of devils she burst in at his study door, paused with a sigh of relief, and told him she had come there for sanctuary. The devils could not enter there, the place was holy and God forbade it to them. She sat the whole afternoon by his side, demurely reading the Bible. At dark she went to the door and set her foot experimentally over the threshold. Her ghostly steed was waiting for her, her devils seized her, and she was off on her wild career seated on air.

Mather had waited long for some demonstration that his study was in fact a holy of holies. He wished for definitive proof. He pursued her, and dragged her again over the magic doorsill. She resisted furiously, fell, scuffled with her feet, and threw her weight upon him so that he was almost forced to carry her outright. After incredible toil the goal was gained and the delightful miracle repeated itself. They were both out of breath, but she recovered first, stood up beaming, and said, "Now I am well!"

This was plainly a marvel very creditable to them both. Mather called in several ministers and repeated the scene successfully half a dozen times before witnesses who infallibly would spread the story in its proper light. It then occurred to him, or was suggested, that further demonstrations of this kind were dangerous, as savoring slightly of witchcraft in themselves. Besides, it was no longer necessary. Martha for no apparent reason became perfectly subdued.

It was now early fall. Abigail was expecting her third child, and the constant excitement had wearied her. She lived in deep retirement, and no comment of hers is recorded concerning this episode. Martha was to stay on for a while to insure her recovery. She spent her afternoons reading pious books in Mather's study, and the household quieted down.

During this inexplicable period of calm, Mather began preparing his pamphlet on Martha's case, together with a sermon entitled "The Nature and Reality of

Witchcraft." Martha grew very annoyed at this, and her manner towards him underwent a mysterious change. Previously she had treated him with some respect, even in her rages; she had made love to him in her primitive way. Now she was bold and impudent; with her cutting young-girl wit she slashed at her patron and protector. He was startled and displeased at the new kind of demon that had got into Martha. Possibly she had not believed he was taking it all so seriously. When she discovered how completely she had befooled him, she was a changed girl.

In all his life no one had dared to interrupt Cotton Mather at his holy labors. Martha knocked loudly at his door whenever she pleased, and invented scandalous pretexts to annoy him. "There is someone below would be glad to see you!" she shouted one day. Mather went down, found no one, and scolded her for telling falsehoods. She retorted, "Mrs. Mather is always glad to see you!"

He understood nothing about women, and he never learned anything about them; this outburst of jealousy confounded him. A dozen times a day she was at his door, and would have him out on one excuse or another. The attention that had been given her was not going to be diverted to a sermon about her if she could help it. She threw heavy books and other objects at him, being careful not to hit him. She would follow him upstairs and down, heckling and ridiculing him about his foolish sermon, vowing she would revenge herself on him for writing it.

She rummaged through his papers, a desperate impertinence, and got hold of his precious document on witchcraft. She had read it while he was writing it, at least a hundred times, says Mather. Now she could not get one word of it straight, but made a parody of it as she went, with such aptness and humor Mather laughed in spite of himself. At once she grew very earnest, and in a bitter voice she prophesied that he "should quickly come to disgrace by that history."

She told him every day as clearly as she could in symbolic acts and words that she was making him ridiculous, but his obsessional self-concentration kept him blinded. He went on exhibiting her, and she rose to her audiences like the gifted actress she was.

A number of young ministers came to witness her performances. Mather talked to them in Latin; if he told her to look to God, he said, her eyes would be fairly put out. The clever girl clenched her eyelids. This was impressive, and they began trying her demon with languages. He knew Greek and Hebrew also. The Indian dialects floored the demon, and the gentlemen conversed in these. Then they all knelt and prayed affectionately for Martha, while she sprawled gracelessly on the floor, with her belly swelled strangely, and made croaking noises. She whistled, sang, shouted, and covered her ears to shut out the painful sound of prayer. Rising to her knees, she tried to strike Mather, could not, and begged the others to strike him for her: "He has wounded me in the *head*!" she wept. "Lord, have mercy on a daughter vexed with a Devil," prayed Mather. Martha sank her voice into her throat, as if a demon of grisly humor spoke within her: "There's two or three of us."

This was almost the end. Martha's energies were about exhausted, her inventiveness would go no further. In the evening of this day, she grew merry for a while, and later went quietly to bed. In the night she began weeping terribly, and when Mather went to quiet her she told him she repented of all she had said and done. She was beginning to realize her situation and to be ashamed.

At Christmas, she relapsed and gave a lively imitation of a drunken person, babbling and reeling and spewing. Mather was pained, insisted that she had had nothing to drink, and ended by admiring her talent for impersonation. She recovered shortly, wept again, and made one of her enigmatic remarks: "They will disgrace me when they can do nothing more." Mather thought she spoke of her demons.

Martha was growing up. She knew well that her day was over. A sudden sickness came upon her. She pulled and tossed and moaned and sweated in some profound disturbance, crying out that she was afraid to die alone, someone must die with her. Even in this state, she paraphrased a psalm so brilliantly that Mather was amazed again, for the last time. She resigned herself to death, prophecied Indian wars and a great tragedy upon the country, and recovered.

Her brothers and small sister, without Martha to inflame them, had been reduced to their usual behavior. Mather sent her home.

Here Martha's personal history ceases, but not the consequences of this fateful period of her life. She became, Mather recorded merely, very docile, very silent; and remained a submissive Christian girl. He made a legend of her, and the drama of Martha Goodwin and Bridget Glover took hold of the popular imagination and was recalled again and again during the Salem Witchcraft, four years later.

Mather preached his sermon on the nature and reality of witchcraft, and afterward published it, an initiate statement of the inner organization of the witch cult in New England, and elsewhere, its rules, ceremonies, feasts, and dark purposes. He was gradually persuading himself that the putting to death of witches was a blood-sacrifice tending to placate the Devil. His mind was a little confused between the role played by the ancient Hebrew scapegoat and an obscure doctrine of the early Christians that Christ shed his blood not as an offering to God the Father for the remission of sins but as an act of propitiation to the Devil on behalf of mankind. A passage from the witchcraft section of his *Magnalia Christi Americana* is poetically applicable to Bridget Glover's part in the Goodwin episode: "When two goats were offered unto the Lord (and only unto the Lord) we read that one of them was to fall by lot to Azazel . . . it is no other than the name of the Devil himself."

The Man in the Brooks Brothers Shirt

BY MARY MCCARTHY

The new man who came into the club car was coatless. He was dressed in gray trousers and a green shirt of expensive material that had the monogram "W.B." embroidered in darker green on the sleeve. His tie matched the green of the monogram, and his face, which emerged rather sharply from this tasteful symphony in cool colors, was blush pink. The greater part of his head appeared to be pink, also, though actually toward the back there was a good deal of closely cropped pale gray hair that harmonized with his trousers. He looked, she decided, like a middle-aged baby, like a young pig, like something in a seed catalogue. In any case, he was plainly Out of the Question, and the hope that had sprung up, as for some reason it always did, with the sound of a new step soft on the flowered Pullman carpet, died a new death. Already the trip was half over. They were now several hours out of Omaha; nearly all the Chicago passengers had put in an appearance; and still there was no one, no one at all. She must not mind, she told herself; the trip West was of no importance; yet she felt a curious, shamefaced disappointment, as if she had given a party and no guests had come.

She turned again to the lady on her left, her *vis-à-vis* at breakfast, a person with dangling earrings, a cigarette-holder, and a lorgnette, who was somebody in the New Deal and carried about with her a typewritten report of the hearings of some committee which she was anxious to discuss. The man in the green shirt crowded himself into a loveseat directly opposite, next to a young man with glasses and loud socks who was reading Negley Farson's "Way of a Transgressor." Sustaining her end of a well-bred, well-informed, liberal conversation, she had an air of perfect absorption and earnestness, yet she became aware, without ever turning her head, that the man across the way had decided to pick her up. Full of contempt for the man, for his coatlessness, for his color-scheme, for his susceptibility, for his presumption, she nevertheless allowed her voice to rise a little in response to him. The man countered by turning to his neighbor and saying something excessively audible about Negley Farson. The four voices, answering each other, began to give an antiphonal effect. Negley Farson was a fine fellow, she heard him pronounce; he could vouch for it, he knew him *personally*. The bait was crude, she reflected. She would have preferred the artificial fly to the angleworm, but still. . . . After all, he might have done worse; judged by eternal standards, Farson might not be much, but in the cultural atmosphere of the Pullman car, Farson was a titan. Moreover, if one judged the man by his intention, one could not fail to be touched. He was doing his best to *please* her. He had guessed from her conversation that she was an intellectual, and was placing the name of Farson as a humble offering at her feet. And the simple vulgarity of the offering somehow enhanced its value; it was like one of those homemade cakes with Paris-green icing that she used to receive on her birthday from her colored maid.

Her own neighbor must finally have noticed a certain displacement of attention, for she got up announcing that she was going in to lunch, and her tone was stiff with reproof and disappointment so that she seemed, for a moment, this rococo suffragette, like a nun who discovers that her favorite novice lacks the vocation. As she tugged open the door to go out, a blast of hot Nebraska air rushed into the club car, where the air-cooling system had already broken down.

The girl in the seat had an impulse to follow her. It would surely be cooler in the diner, where there was not so much glass. If she stayed and let the man pick her up, it would be a question of eating lunch together, and there would be a little quarrel about the check, and if she let him win she would have him on her hands all the way to Sacramento. And he was certain to be tiresome. That monogram in Gothic script spelled out the self-made man. She could foresee the political pronouncements, the pictures of the wife and children, the hand squeezed under the table. Nothing worse than that, fortunately, for the conductors on these trains were always very strict. Still, the whole thing would be so vulgar; one would expose oneself so to the derision of the other passengers. It was true, she was always wanting something exciting and romantic to happen; but it was not really romantic to be the-girl-who-sits-in-the-club-car-and-picks-up-men. She closed her eyes with a slight shudder: some predatory view of herself had been disclosed for an instant. She heard her aunt's voice saying, "I don't know why you make yourself so cheap," and "It doesn't pay to let men think you're easy." Then she was able to open her eyes again, and smile a little, patronizingly, for of course it hadn't worked out that way. The object of her trip was, precisely, to tell her aunt in Portland that she was going to be married again.

She settled down in her seat to wait and began to read an advance copy of a new novel. When the man would ask her what-that-book-is-you're-so-interested-in (she had heard the question before), she would be able to reply in a tone so simple and friendly that it could not give offense, "Why, you probably haven't heard of it. It's not out yet." (Yet, she thought, she had not brought the book along for purposes of ostentation: it had been given her by a publisher's assistant who saw her off at the train, and now she had nothing else to read. So, really, she could not be accused of insincerity. Unless it could be that her whole way of life had been assumed for purposes of ostentation, and the book, which looked accidental, was actually part of that larger and truly deliberate scheme. If it had not been this book, it would have been something else, which would have served equally well to impress a pink middle-aged stranger.)

The approach, when it came, was more unorthodox than she had expected. The man got up from his seat and said, "Can I talk to you?" Her retort, "What have you got to say?" rang off-key in her own ears. It was as if Broadway had answered Indiana. For a moment the man appeared to be taken aback, but then he laughed. "Why, I don't know; nothing special. We can talk about that book, I guess."

She liked him, and with her right hand made a gesture that meant, "All right, go on." The man examined the cover. "I haven't heard about this. It must be new."

"Yes." Her reply had more simplicity in it than she would have thought she could achieve. "It isn't out yet. This is an advance copy."

"I've read something else by this fellow. He's good."

"You have?" cried the girl in a sharp, suspicious voice. It was incredible that this well-barbered citizen should not only be familiar with but have a taste for the work of an obscure revolutionary novelist. On the other hand, it was incredible that he should be lying. The artless and offhand manner in which he pronounced the novelist's name indicated no desire to shine, indicated in fact that he placed no value on that name, that it was to him a name like Hervey Allen or Arthur Brisbane or

Westbrook Pegler or any other. Two alternatives presented themselves: either the man belonged to that extraordinary class of readers who have perfect literary digestions, who can devour anything printed, retaining what suits them, eliminating what does not, and liking all impartially, because, since they take what they want from each, they are always actually reading the same book (she had had a cousin who was like that about the theater, and she remembered how her aunt used to complain, saying "It's no use asking Cousin Florence whether the show at the stock company is any good this week; Cousin Florence has never seen a bad play") – either that, or else the man had got the name confused and was really thinking of some popular writer all the time.

Still, the assertion, shaky as it was, had given him status with her. It was as if he had spoken a password, and with a greater sense of assurance and propriety, she went on listening to his talk. His voice was rather rich and dark; the accent was middle-Western, but underneath the nasalities there was something soft and furry that came from the South. He lived in Cleveland, he told her, but his business kept him on the go a good deal; he spent nearly half his time in New York.

"You do?" she exclaimed, her spirits rising. "What *is* your business?" Her original view of him had already begun to dissolve, and it now seemed to her that the instant he had entered the club car she had sensed that he was no ordinary provincial entrepreneur.

"I'm a traveling salesman," he replied genially.

In a moment she recognized that this was a joke, but not before he had caught her look of absolute dismay and panic. He leaned toward her and laughed. "If it sounds any better to you, he said, "I'm in the steel business."

"It doesn't," she replied, recovering herself, making her words prim with political disapproval. But he *knew*; she had given herself away; he had trapped her features in an expression of utter snobbery.

"You're a pink, I suppose," he said, as if he had noticed nothing. "It'd sound better to you if I said I was a burglar."

"Yes," she acknowledged, with a comic air of frankness, and they both laughed. Much later, he gave her a business card that said he was an executive in Little Steel, but he persisted in describing himself as a traveling salesman, and she saw at last that it was an accident that the joke had turned on her: the joke was a wry, humble, clownish one that he habitually turned on himself.

When he asked if she would join him in a drink before lunch, she accepted readily. "Let's go into the diner, though. It may be cooler."

"I've got a bottle of whiskey in my compartment. I *know* it's cool there."

Her face stiffened. A compartment was something she had not counted on. But she did not know (she never had known) how to refuse. She felt bitterly angry with the man for having exposed her – so early – to this supreme test of femininity, a test she was bound to fail, since she would either go into the compartment, not wanting to (and he would know this and feel contempt for her malleability), or she would stay out of the compartment, wanting to have gone in (and he would know this, too, and feel contempt for her timidity).

The man looked at her face.

"Don't worry," he said in a kind, almost fatherly voice. "It'll be perfectly proper. I promise to leave the door open." He took her arm and gave it a slight, reassuring squeeze, and she laughed out loud, delighted with him for having, as she thought, once again understood and spared her.

In the compartment, which was off the club car, it *was* cooler. The highballs, gold in the glasses, tasted, as her own never did, the way they looked in the White Rock advertisements. There was something about the efficiency with which his luggage, in brown calf, was disposed in that small space, about the white coat of the black waiter who kept coming in with fresh ice and soda, about the chicken sandwiches they finally ordered for lunch, that gave her that sense of ritualistic "rightness" that the Best People are supposed to bask in. The open door contributed to this sense: it was exactly as if they were drinking in a show window, for nobody went by who did not peer in, and she felt that she could discern envy, admiration, and censure in the quick looks that were shot at her. The man sat at ease, unconscious of these attentions, but she kept her back straight, her shoulders high with decorum, and let her bare arms rise and fall now and then in short parabolas of gesture.

But if for the people outside she was playing the great lady, for the man across the table she was the Bohemian Girl. It was plain that she was a revelation to him, that he had never under the sun seen anyone like her. And he was quizzing her about her way of life with the intense, unashamed, wondering curiosity of a provincial seeing for the first time the sights of a great but slightly decadent city. Answering his questions she was able to see herself through his eyes (brown eyes, which were his only good feature, but which somehow matched his voice and thus enhanced the effect, already striking, of his having been put together by a good tailor). What she got from his view of her was a feeling of uniqueness and identity, a feeling she had once had when, at twenty, she had come to New York and had her first article accepted by a liberal weekly, but which had slowly been rubbed away by four years of being on the inside of the world that had looked magic from Portland, Oregon. Gradually, now, she was becoming very happy, for she knew for sure in this compartment that she was beautiful and gay and clever, and worldly and innocent, serious and frivolous, capricious and trustworthy, witty and sad, bad and really good, all mixed up together, all at the same time. She could feel the power running in her, like a medium on a particularly good night.

As these multiple personalities bloomed on the single stalk of her ego, a great glow of charity, like the flush of life, suffused her. This man, too, must be admitted into the mystery; this stranger must be made to open and disclose himself like a Japanese water flower. With a messianic earnestness she began to ask him questions, and though at first his answers displayed a sort of mulish shyness ("I'm just a traveling salesman," "I'm a suburban businessman," "I'm an economic royalist"), she knew that sooner or later he would tell her the truth, the rock-bottom truth, and was patient with him. It was not the first time she had "drawn a man out" – the phrase puckered her mouth, for it had never seemed like that to her. Certain evenings spent in bars with men she had known for half an hour came back to her; she remembered the beautiful frankness with which the cards on each side were laid on the table till love became a wonderful slow game of double solitaire and nothing that happened afterwards counted for anything beside those first few hours of self-revelation. Now as she put question after question she felt once more like a happy burglar twirling the dial of a well-constructed safe, listening for the locks to click and reveal the combination. When she asked him what the monogram on his shirt stood for, unexpectedly the door flew open.

He told her his name, and went on irrelevantly, "I get these shirts at Brooks Brothers. They'll put the monogram on if you order the shirts custom-made. I always order a dozen at a time. I get everything at Brooks Brothers except ties and shoes. Leonie thinks it's stodgy of me."

Leonie was his wife. They had a daughter, little Angela, and they lived in a fourteen-room house in the Gates Mills section of Cleveland. He also had a son by another marriage, little Frank, and Frank and Leonie got on wonderfully, he was glad to say, but then nobody could deny that Leonie had a wonderful disposition. Leonie was a home girl, quite different from Eleanor, who had been his first wife and was now a decorator in New York. Leonie loved her house and children. Of course, she was interested in culture too, particularly the theater, and there were always a lot of young men from the Cleveland Playhouse hanging around her; but then she was a Bryn Mawr girl, and you had to expect a woman to have different interests from a man.

Leonie was a Book of the Month Club member and she also subscribed to the two liberal weeklies. "She'll certainly be excited," the man said, grinning with pleasure, "when she hears I met somebody from the *Liberal* on this trip. But she'll never be able to understand why you wasted your time talking to poor old Bill."

The girl smiled at him.

"I *like* to talk to you," she said, suppressing the fact that nothing on earth would have induced her to talk to Leonie.

"I read an article in those magazines once in a while," he continued dreamily. "Once in a while they have something good, but on the whole they're too wishy-washy for me. Now that I've had this visit with you, though, I'll read your magazine every week, trying to guess which of those things in the front you wrote."

"I'm *never* wishy-washy," said the girl, laughing. "But is your wife radical?"

"Good Lord, no! She calls herself a liberal, but actually I'm more of a radical than Leonie is."

"How do you mean?"

"Well, you take the election. I'm going to vote for Landon because it's expected of me, and my vote won't put him in."

"But you're really for Roosevelt?"

"No," said the man, a little impatiently. "I don't like Roosevelt either. I don't like a man that's always hedging his bets. Roosevelt's an old woman. Look at the way he's handling these CIO strikes. He doesn't have the guts to stick up for Lewis, and he doesn't have the sense to stay out of the whole business." He leaned across the table and added, almost in a whisper, "You know who I'd like to vote for?"

The girl shook her head.

"Norman Thomas!"

"But you're a steel man!" said the girl.

The man nodded.

"Nobody knows how I feel, not even Leonie." He paused to think. "I was in the last war," he said finally, "and I had a grand time. I was in the cavalry and there weren't any horses. I was the youngest American major in the World War, and after the armistice we were stationed in Cologne, and we got hold of a Renault and every weekend we'd drive all night so we could have a day on the Riviera." He chuckled to himself. "But the way I look at it, there's a new war coming and it isn't going to be like that. God Almighty, we didn't hate the Germans!"

"And now?"

"You wait," he said. "Last time it was supposed to be what you people call an ideological war – for democracy and all that. But it wasn't. That was just advertising.

You liberals have all of a sudden found out that it was Mr. Morgan's war. You think that's terrible. But let me tell you that Mr. Morgan's war was a hell of a lot nicer to fight than this new one will be. Because this one will be ideological, and it'll be too damned serious. You'll wish that you had the international bankers and munitions men to stop the fight when things get too rough. I'd like to see this country stay out of it. That's why I'm for Thomas."

"You're a very interesting man," said the girl, tears coming to her eyes, perhaps because of the whiskey. "I've never known anyone like you. You're not the kind of businessman I write editorials against."

"You people are crazy, though," he said genially. "You're never going to get anywhere in America with that proletariat stuff. Every working man wants to live the way I do. He doesn't want me to live the way he does. You people go at it from the wrong end. I remember a Socialist organizer came down fifteen years ago into Southern Illinois. I was in the coal business then, working for my first wife's father. This Socialist was a nice fellow. . . ."

His voice was dreamy again, but there was an undercurrent of excitement in it. It was as if he were reviving some buried love affair, or, rather, some wispy young *tendresse* that had never come to anything. The Socialist organizer had been a distant connection of his first wife's; the two men had met and had some talks; later the Socialist had been run out of town; the man had stood aloof, neither helping nor hindering.

"I wonder what's become of him," he said finally. "In jail somewhere, I guess."

"Oh no," said the girl. "You don't understand modern life. He's a big bureaucrat in the CIO. Just like a businessman, only not so well paid."

The man looked puzzled and vaguely sad. "He had a lot of nerve," he murmured, then added quickly, in a loud, bumptious tone, "But you're all nuts!"

The girl bit her lips. The man's vulgarity was undeniable. For some time now she had been attempting (for her own sake) to whitewash him, but the crude raw material would shine through in spite of her. It had been possible for her to remain so long in the compartment only on the basis of one of two assumptions, both of them literary, (a) that the man was a frustrated Socialist, (b) that he was a frustrated man of sensibility, a kind of Sherwood Anderson character. But the man's own personality kept popping up, perversely, like a Jack-in-the-box, to confound these theories. The most one could say was that the man was frustrated. She had hoped to "give him back to himself," but these fits of self-assertion on his part discouraged her by making her feel that there was nothing very good to give. She had, moreover, a suspicion that his lapses were deliberate, even malicious, that the man knew what she was about and why she was about it, and had made up his mind to thwart her. She felt a Take-me-as-I-am, and I'll-drag-you-down-to-my-level challenge behind his last words. It was like the resistance of the patient to the psychoanalyst, of the worker to the Marxist: she was offering to release him from the chains of habit, and he was standing up and clanking those chains comfortably and impudently in her face. On the other hand, she *knew*, just as the analyst knows, just as the Marxist knows, that somewhere in his character there was the need of release and the humility that would accept aid – and there was, furthermore, a kindness and a general cooperativeness which would make him pretend to be a little better than he was, if that would help her to think better of herself.

For the thing was, the man and the little adventure of being with him had a kind of human appeal that she kept giving in to against her judgment. *She liked him.*

Why, it was impossible to say. The attraction was not sexual, for, as the whiskey went down in the bottle, his face took on a more and more porcine look that became so distasteful to her that she could hardly meet his gaze, but continued to talk to him with a large, remote stare, as if he were an audience of several hundred people. Whenever she did happen to catch his eye, to really look at him, she was as disconcerted as an actor who sees a human expression answering him from beyond the footlights. It was not his air of having money, either, that drew her to him, though that, she thought humorously, helped, but it hindered too. It was partly the homespun quality (the use of the word, "visit," for example, as a verb meaning "talk" took her straight back to her childhood and to her father, carpet-slippered, in a brown leather chair), and partly of course his plain delight in her, which had in it more shrewdness than she had thought at first, for, though her character was new and inexplicable to him, in a gross sense he was clearly a connoisseur of women. But beyond all this, she had glimpsed in him a vein of sympathy and understanding that made him available to any human being, just as he was, apparently, available as a reader to any novelist – and this might proceed, not, as she had assumed out in the club car, from stupidity, but from a restless and perennially hopeful curiosity.

Actually, she decided, it was the combination of provincialism and adventurousness that did the trick. This man *was* the frontier, though the American frontier had closed, she knew, forever, somewhere out in Oregon in her father's day. Her father, when that door had shut, had remained on the inside. In his youth, as she had learned to her surprise, from some yellowed newspaper clippings her aunt had forgotten in an old bureau drawer, he had been some kind of wildcat radical, full of workmen's compensation laws and state ownership of utilities; but he had long ago hardened into a corporation lawyer, Eastern style. She remembered how once she had challenged him with those clippings, thinking to shame him with the betrayal of ideals and how calmly he had retorted, "Things were different then." "But you fought the *railroads*," she had insisted. "And now you're their lawyer." "You had to fight the railroads in those days," he had answered innocently, and her aunt had put in, with her ineffable plebeian sententiousness, "Your father always stands for what is right." But she saw now that her father had honestly perceived no contradiction between the two sets of attitudes, which was the real proof that it was not he, so much as the times, that had changed.

Yet this man she was sitting with had somehow survived, like a lonely dinosaur, from that former day. It was not even a true survival, for if he was, as he said, forty-one, that would make him thirty years younger than her father, and he would be barely able to recall the Golden Age of American imperialism, to which, nevertheless, he plainly belonged. Looking at him, she thought of other young empires and recalled the Roman busts in the Metropolitan, marble faces of businessmen, shockingly rugged and modern and recognizable after the smooth tranquillity of the Greeks. Those early businessmen had been omnivorous, too, great readers, eaters, travelers, collectors, and, at the beginning, provincial also, small-town men newly admitted into world-citizenship, faintly uneasy but feeling their oats.

In the course of this analysis she had glided all the way from aversion to tenderness. She saw the man now as a man without a country, and felt a desire to reinstate him. But where? The best she could do was communicate to him a sense of his own isolation and grandeur. She could ensconce him in the dignity of sadness.

Meanwhile, the man had grown almost boisterously merry. It was late afternoon; the lunch things had long ago been taken away; and the bottle was nearly empty.

Outside the flat yellow farmland went by, comfortably dotted with haystacks; the drought and the cow-bones strewn over the Dust Bowl seemed remote as a Surrealist painting. Other passengers still paused to look in at the open door on their way to the club car, but the girl was no longer fully aware of them: they existed, as it were, only to give the perspective, to deepen that warm third dimension that had been established within the compartment. The man was lit up with memories of the war, droll stories of horse-play and drinking parties, a hero who was drowned while swimming in a French river, trips to Paris, Notre Dame, and target-practice in the Alps. It had been, she could see, an extension of college days, a sort of lower-middle-class Grand Tour, a wonderful male rough-house that had left a man such as this with a permanent homesickness for fraternity and a loneliness that no stag party could quite ease.

"I suppose I'm boring you," said the man, still smiling to himself, "but – it's a funny thing to say – I haven't had such a good time since the war. So that you remind me of it, and I can't stop talking, I don't know why."

"*I* know," she said, full of gentle omniscience. (This was her best side, and she knew it. But did that spoil it, keep it from being good?)

"It's because you've made a new friend, and you probably haven't made one for twenty years, not since the war. Nobody does, after they've grown-up."

"Maybe so," said the man. "Getting married, no matter how many times you do it, isn't the same thing. If you even *think* you'd like to marry a girl, you have to start lying to her. It's a law of nature, I guess. You have to protect yourself. I don't mean about cheating – that's small potatoes. . . ."

A meditative look absorbed his face. "Jesus Christ," he said, "I don't even *know* Leonie any more, and vice versa, but that's the way it ought to be. A man doesn't want his wife to understand him. That's not her job. Her job is to have a nice house and nice kids and give good parties he can have his friends to. If Leonie understood me, she wouldn't be able to do that. Probably we'd both go to pot."

Tears came to her eyes again. The man's life and her own life seemed unutterably tragic.

"I was in love with my husband," she said. "We understood each other. He never had a thought he didn't tell me."

"But you got a divorce," said the man. "Somebody must have misunderstood somebody else *somewhere* along the line."

"Well," she admitted, "maybe he *didn't* understand *me* so well. He was awfully surprised. . . ." She giggled like a soubrette. The giggle was quite out of character at the moment, but she had not been able to resist it. Besides (she was sure) it was these quick darts and turns, these flashing inconsistencies that gave her the peculiar, sweet-sour, highly volatile charm that was her *specialité de la maison*.

"Surprised when you picked up with somebody else?" asked the man. She nodded.

"What happened to that?"

"After I got divorced, I didn't want to marry him any more."

"So now you're on your own?"

The question seemed almost idle, but she replied in a distinct, emphatic voice, as if he were deaf and she had an important message for him.

"No," she said. "I'm going to be married in the fall."

"Are you in love with this one?"

"Oh, yes," she said. "He's charming. And he and I are much more alike than Jim and I were. He's a little bit of a bum and I am too. And he's selfish, which is a good thing for me. Jim was so *good*. And so vulnerable. The back of his neck was just like a little boy's. I always remember the back of his neck."

She spoke earnestly, but she saw that the man did not understand. Nobody had ever understood – and she herself did not quite know – why this image retained such power over her, why all her feelings of guilt and shame had clustered around the picture of a boyish neck (the face had not been boyish, but prematurely lined) bared like an early martyr's for the sword. "How could I have done it?" she whispered to herself again, as she still did nearly every day, and once again she was suffused with horror.

"He was too good for me," she said at last. "I felt like his mother. Nobody would ever have known it, but he needed to be protected."

That was it. That was what was so awful. Nobody would ever have known. But she had crawled into his secret life and nestled there, like the worm in the rose. How warm and succulent it had been! And when she had devoured it all, she had gone away. "Oh God," she muttered under her breath. It was no excuse that she had loved him. The worm indubitably loves the rose.

Hurriedly, to distract herself, she began to talk about her love affairs. First names with thumbnail descriptions rolled out till her whole life sounded to her like a drugstore novel. And she found herself over-anxious to explain to him why in each case the thing had not borne fruit, how natural it was that she should have broken with John, how reasonable that she should never have forgiven Ernest. It was as if she had been a prosecuting attorney drawing up a brief against each of her lovers, and, not liking the position, she was relieved when the man interrupted her.

"Seems to me," he said, "you're still in love with that husband of yours."

"Do you think so really?" she asked, leaning forward. "Why?"

Perhaps at last she had found him, the one she kept looking for, the one who could tell her what she was really like. For this she had gone to palmists and graphologists, hoping not for a dark man or a boat trip, but for some quick blaze of gypsy insight that would show her her own lineaments. If she once knew, she had no doubt that she could behave perfectly; it was merely a question of finding out. How, she thought, can you act upon your feelings if you don't know what they are? As a little girl whispering to a young priest in the confessional she had sometimes felt sure. The Church could classify it all for you. If you talked or laughed in church, told lies, had impure thoughts or conversations, you were bad; if you obeyed your parents or guardians, went to confession and communion regularly, said prayers for the dead, you were good. Protestants, like her father, were neutral; they lived in a gray world beyond good and evil. But when as a homely high-school girl, she had rejected the Church's filing system, together with her aunt's illiterate morality, she had given away her sense of herself. For a while she had believed that it was a matter of waiting until you grew older and your character was formed; then you would be able to recognize it as easily as a photograph. But she was now twenty-four, and had heard other people say she had a strong personality; she herself however was still in the dark. This hearty stranger in the green shirt – perhaps he could really tell whether she was in love with her husband. It was like the puzzle about the men with marks on their foreheads: A couldn't know whether his own forehead was marked, but B and C knew, of course, and he could, if he were bright, deduce it from their behavior.

"Well," replied the man, "of all the fellows you've talked about, Jim's the only one I get a picture of. Except your father – but that's different; he's the kind of a man I know about."

The answer disappointed her. It was too plain and folksy to cover the facts. It was true that she had loved her husband *personally*, for himself, and this had never happened to her with any one else. Nobody else's idiosyncrasies had ever warmed her; nobody else had she ever watched asleep. Yet that kind of love had, unfortunately, rendered her impotent to love him in the ordinary way, had, in fact, made it necessary for her to be unfaithful to him, and so, in the course of time, to leave him altogether. Or could it not be put in another way? Could she not say that all that conjugal tenderness had been a brightly packaged substitute for the Real Thing, for the long carnal swoon she had never quite been able to execute in the marriage bed? She had noticed that in those households where domesticity burns brightest and the Little Attentions rain most prodigally, the husband is seldom admitted to his real conjugal rights.

But it was impossible to explain this to the man. Already the conversation had dropped once or twice into ribaldry, but she was determined to preserve the decorum of the occasion. It was dark outside now and the waiter was back again, serving little brook trout on plates that had the Union Pacific's crest on them. Yet even as she warned herself how impossible it was, she heard her voice rushing on in a torrent of explicitness.

(This had all happened so many times before, ever since, as a schoolgirl, she had exchanged dirty jokes with the college boys from Eugene and seen them stop the car and lunge at her across the gearshift. While all the time, she commiserated with herself, she had merely been trying to be a good fellow, to show that she was sophisticated and grown-up, and not to let them suspect (oh, never!) that her father did not allow her to go out with boys and that she was a neophyte, a helpless fledgling, with no small talk and no coquetry at all. It had not been *fair* (she could still italicize it, bitterly) for them to tackle her like a football dummy; she remembered the struggles back and forth on the slippery leather seats of sports roadsters, the physical awkwardness of it all being somehow the crowning indignity; she remembered also the rides home afterwards, and how the boy's face would always be sullen and closed – he was thinking that he had been cheated, made a fool of, and resolving never to ask her again, so that she would finally become notorious for being taken out only once. How indecent and anti-human it had been, like the tussle between the drowning man and the lifeguard! And of course she had invited it, just as she was inviting it now, but what she was really asking all along was not that the male should assault her, but that he should believe her a woman. This freedom of speech of hers was a kind of masquerade of sexuality, like the rubber breasts that homosexuals put on for drags, but, like the dummy breasts, its brazenness betrayed it: it was a poor copy and a hostile travesty all at once. But the men, she thought, did not look into it so deeply; they could only respond by leaping at her – which, after all, she supposed, was their readiest method of showing her that her impersonation had been convincing. Yet that response, when it came, never failed to disconcert and frighten her: I had not counted on this, she could always whisper to herself, with a certain sad bewilderment. For it was all wrong, it was unnatural: art is to be admired, not acted on, and the public does not belong on the stage, nor the actors in the audience.)

But once more the man across the table spared her. His face was a little heavy with drink, but she could see no lechery in it, and he listened to her as calmly as a priest. The sense of the nightmare lifted; free will was restored to her.

"You know what my favorite quotation is?" she asked suddenly. She must be getting drunk, she knew, or she would not have said this, and a certain cool part of her personality protested. I must not quote poetry, she thought, I must stop it; God help us, if I'm not careful, we'll be singing Yale songs next. But her voice had broken away from her; she could only follow it, satirically, from a great distance. "It's from Chaucer," she went on, when she saw that she had his attention. "Criseyde says it, 'I am myne owne woman, welle at aise.'"

The man had some difficulty in understanding the Middle English, but when at last he had got it straight, he looked at her with bald admiration.

"Golly," he said, "you are, at that!"

The train woke her the next morning as it jerked into Cheyenne. It was still dark. The Pullman shade was drawn, and she imagined at first that she was in her own lower berth. She knew that she had been drunk the night before, but reflected with satisfaction that Nothing Had Happened. It would have been terrible if . . . She moved slightly and touched the man's body.

She did not scream, but only jerked away in a single spasmodic movement of rejection. This can't be, she thought angrily, it can't be. She shut her eyes tight. When I open them again, she said, he will be gone. I can't face it, she thought, holding herself rigid; the best thing to do is to go back to sleep. For a few minutes she actually dozed and dreamed she was back in Lower Seven with the sheets feeling extraordinarily crisp and clean and the curtains hanging protectively about her. But in the dream her pillow shook under her as the porter poked it to call her for breakfast, and she woke again and knew that the man was still beside her and had moved in his sleep. The train was pulling out of the station. If it had not been so early, outside on the platform there would have been tall men in cowboy hats. Maybe, she thought, I passed out and he put me to bed. But the body next to her was naked, and horror rippled over her again as she realized by the coarseness of the sheets touching her that she was naked too. Oh my God, she said, get me out of this and I will do anything you want.

Waves of shame began to run through her, like savage internal blushes, as fragments of the night before presented themselves for inspection. They had sung songs, all right, she remembered, and there had been some question of disturbing the other passengers, and so the door had been shut. After that the man had come around to her side of the table and kissed her rather greedily. She had fought him off for a long time, but at length her will had softened. She had felt tired and kind, and thought, why not? Then there had been something peculiar about the lovemaking itself – but she could not recall what it was. She had tried to keep aloof from it, to be present in body but not in spirit. Somehow that had not worked out and she had been dragged in and humiliated. There was some comfort in this vagueness, but recollection quickly stabbed her again. There were (oh, holy Virgin!) four-letter words that she had been forced to repeat, and, at the climax, a rain of blows on her buttocks that must surely (dear God!) have left bruises. She must be careful not to let her aunt see her without any clothes on, she told herself, and remembered how once she had visualized sins as black marks on the white soul. This sin, at least, no one would see. But all at once she became aware of the significance of the sheets. The bed had been made up. And that meant that the Pullman porter. . . . She closed her eyes, exhausted, unable to finish the thought. The Negley Farson man, the New Deal lady, the waiter, the porter seemed to press in on her, a crowd of jeering material witnesses. If only nobody could know. . . .

But perhaps it was not too late. She had a sudden vision of herself in a black dress, her face scrubbed and powdered, her hair neatly combed, sitting standoffishly in her seat, watching Wyoming and Nevada go by and reading her publisher's copy of a new avant-garde novel. It *could* be done. If she could get back before the first call for breakfast, she might be able to carry it off. There would be the porter, of course, but he would not dare gossip to passengers. Softly, she climbed out of the berth and began to look for her clothes. In the darkness, she discovered her slip and dress neatly hung by the wash basin – the man must have put them there, and it was fortunate, at least, that he was such a shipshape character, for the dress would not be rumpled. On the floor she collected her stockings and a pair of white crêpe de Chine pants, many times mended, with a button off and a little brass pin in its place. Feeling herself blush for the pin, she sat down on the floor and pulled her stockings on. One garter was missing. She put on the rest of her clothes, and then began to look for the garter, but though she groped her way over every inch of the compartment, she could not find it. She sank to the floor again with one stocking hanging loosely down, buried her head in her arms and cried. She saw herself locked in an intolerable but ludicrous dilemma: it was impossible to face the rest of the train with one stocking hanging down; but it was also impossible to wait for the man to wake up and enlist him in retrieving the garter; it was impossible to send the porter for it later in the morning, and more impossible to call for it in person. But as the comic nature of the problem grew plain to her, her head cleared. With a final sob she stripped off her stockings and stuffed them into her purse. She stepped barefooted into her shoes, and was fumbling in her purse for a comb when the man turned over and groaned.

He remembers, she thought in terror, as she saw his arm reach out dimly white and plump in the darkness. She stood very still, waiting. Perhaps he would go back to sleep. But there was a click, and the reading light above the berth went on. The man looked at her in bewilderment. She realized that she had forgotten to buckle her belt.

"Dearest," he said, "what in the world are you doing?"

"I'm dressed," she said. "I've got to get out before they wake up. Good-bye."

She bent over with the intention of kissing him on the forehead. Politeness required something, but this was the most she could bring herself to do. The man seized her arms and pulled her down, sitting up himself beside her. He looked very fat and the short hair on his chest was gray.

"You can't go," he said, quite simply and naturally, but as if he had been thinking about it all night long. "I love you. I'm crazy about you. This is the most wonderful thing that's ever happened to me. You come to San Francisco with me and we'll go to Monterey, and I'll fix it up with Leonie to get a divorce."

She stared at him incredulously, but there was no doubt of it: he was serious. His body was trembling. Her heart sank as she saw that there was no longer any question of her leaving; common decency forbade it. Yet she was more frightened than flattered by his declaration of love. It was as if some terrible natural force were loose in the compartment. His seriousness, moreover, was a rebuke; her own squeamishness and sick distaste, which a moment before had seemed virtuous in her, now appeared heartless, even frivolous, in the face of his emotion.

"But I'm engaged," she said, rather thinly.

"You're not in love with him," he said. "You couldn't have done what you did last night if you were." As the memory of lovemaking returned to him, his voice grew embarrassingly hoarse.

"I was tight," she said flatly in a low voice.

"A girl like you doesn't let a man have her just because she's drunk."

She bowed her head. There was no possible answer she could give. "I must go," she repeated. In a way she knew that she would have to stay, and knew, too, that it was only a matter of hours, but, just as a convict whose sentence is nearly up will try a jail break and get shot down by the guards, so the girl, with Sacramento not far ahead, could not restrain herself from begging, like a claustrophobic, for immediate release. She saw that the man was getting hurt and angry, but still she held herself stiffly in his embrace and would not look at him. He turned her head round with his hand. "Kiss me," he said, but she pulled away.

"I have to throw up."

He pointed to the toilet seat, which was covered with green upholstery. (She had forgotten that Pullman compartments had this indecent feature.) She raised the cover and vomited, while the man sat on the bed and watched her. This was the nadir, she thought bitterly; surely nothing worse than this could ever happen to her. She wiped the tears from her eyes and leaned against the wall. The man made a gesture toward her.

"Don't touch me," she said, "or I'll be sick again. It would be better if I went back to my berth."

"Poor little girl," he said tenderly. "You feel bad, don't you?"

He got out of the berth and took a fresh bottle of whiskey from a suitcase.

"I'll have to save the Bourbon for the conductor," he said in a matter-of-fact, friendly voice. "He'll be around later on, looking for his cut."

For the first time that morning the girl laughed. The man poured out two small drinks and handed her one of them. "Take it like medicine," he advised.

She sat down on the berth and crossed her legs. The man put on a dressing gown and pulled up a chair opposite her. They raised their glasses. The smell of the whiskey gagged her and she knew that it was out of the question, physically, for her to get drunk a second time. Yet she felt her spirits lift a little. There was an air of professional rowdyism about their drinking neat whiskey early in the morning in a dishevelled compartment that took her fancy.

"What about the porter?"

"Oh," said the man genially. "I've squared him. I gave him ten last night and I'll give him another ten when I get off. He thinks you're wonderful. He said to me, 'Mr. Breen, you sure done better than most.'"

"Oh!" said the girl, covering her face with her hands. "Oh! Oh!" For a moment she felt that she could not bear it, but as she heard the man laugh she made her own discomfiture comic and gave an extra groan or two that were purely theatrical. She raised her head and looked at him shamefaced, and then giggled. This vulgarity was more comforting to her than any assurances of love. If the seduction (or whatever it was) could be reduced to its lowest common denominator, could be seen in farcical terms, she could accept and even, wryly, enjoy it. The world of farce was a sort of moral underworld, a cheerful, well-lit hell where a Fall was only a pratfall after all.

Moreover, this talk had about it the atmosphere of the locker room or the stag-line, an atmosphere more bracing, more astringent than the air of Bohemia. The ten-dollar tips, the Bourbon for the conductor indicated competence and connoisseur-ship, which, while not of the highest order, did extend from food and drink and haberdashery all the way up to women. That was what had been missing in the men she had known in New York – the shrewd buyer's eye, the swift, brutal appraisal. That was what you found in the country clubs and beach clubs and yacht clubs – but you never found it in the café of the Brevoort. The men she had known during these last four years had been, when you faced it, too easily pleased: her success had been gratifying but hollow. It was not difficult, after all, to be the prettiest girl at a party for the sharecroppers. At bottom, she was contemptuous of the men who had believed her perfect, for she knew that in a bathing suit at Southampton she would never have passed muster, and though she had never submitted herself to this cruel test, it lived in her mind as a threat to her. A copy of *Vogue* picked up at the beauty parlor, a lunch at a restaurant that was beyond her means, would suffice to remind her of her peril. And if she had felt safe with the different men who had been in love with her it was because – she saw it now – in one way or another they were all of them lame ducks. The handsome ones, like her fiancé, were good-for-nothing, the reliable ones, like her husband, were peculiar-looking, the well-to-do ones were short and wore lifts in their shoes or fat with glasses, the clever ones were alcoholic or slightly homosexual, the serious ones were Jews or foreigners or else wore beards or black shirts or were desperately poor and had no table manners. Somehow each of them was handicapped for American life and therefore humble in love. And was she too disqualified, did she really belong to this fraternity of cripples, or was she not a sound and normal woman who had been spending her life in self-imposed exile, a princess among the trolls?

She did not know. She would have found out soon enough had she stayed on in Portland, but she had not risked it. She had gone away East to college and never come back until now. And very early in her college life she had got engaged to a painter, so that nothing that happened in the way of cutting in at the dances at Yale and Princeton really "counted." She had put herself out of the running and was patently not trying. Her engagement had been a form of insurance, but the trouble was that it not only insured her against failure but also against success. Should she have been more courageous? She could not tell, even now. Perhaps she *was* a princess because her father was a real gentleman who lunched at his club and traveled by drawing room or compartment; but on the other hand, there was her aunt. She could not find out for herself; it would take a prince to tell her. This man now – surely he came from that heavenly world, that divine position at the center of things where choice is unlimited. And he had chosen *her*.

But that was all wrong. She had only to look at him to see that she had cheated again, had tried to get into the game with a deck of phony cards. For this man also was out of the running. He was too old. Sound as he was in every other respect, time had made a lame duck of him. If she had met him ten years before, would he have chosen her then?

He took the glass from her hands and put his arms around her. "My God," he said, "if this had only happened ten years ago!"

She held herself stony in his embrace, and felt indeed like a rock being lapped by some importunate wave. There was a touch of dignity in the simile, she thought, but what takes place in the end? – Erosion. At that the image suddenly turned and presented another facet to her: dear Jesus, she told herself, frightened, I'm really as hard as nails. Then all at once she was hugging the man with an air of warmth that was not quite spurious and not quite sincere (for the distaste could not quite be smothered but only ignored); she pressed her ten fingers into his back and for the first time kissed him carefully on the mouth.

The glow of self-sacrifice illuminated her. This, she thought decidedly, is going to be the only real act of charity I have ever performed in my life; it will be the only time I have ever given anything when it honestly hurt me to do so. That her asceticism should have to be expressed in terms of sensuality deepened, in a curious way, its value, for the sacrifice was both paradoxical and positive; this was no simple abstention like a meatless Friday or a chaste Sunday: it was the mortification of the flesh achieved through the performance of the act of pleasure.

Quickly she helped him take off the black dress, and stretched herself out on the berth like a slab of white lamb on an altar. While she waited with some impatience for the man to exhaust himself, for the indignity to be over, she contemplated with a burning nostalgia the image of herself, fully dressed, with the novel, in her Pullman seat, and knew, with the firmest conviction, that for once she was really and truly good, not hard or heartless at all.

"You need a bath," said the man abruptly, raising himself on one elbow and looking sharply down at her as she lay relaxed on the rumpled sheet. The curtain was halfway up, and outside the Great Salt Lake surrounded them. They had been going over it for hours, that immense, gray-brown blighting Dead Sea, which looked, not like an actual lake, but like a mirage seen in the desert. She had watched it for a long time, while the man beside her murmured of his happiness and his plans for their future; they had slept a little and when they opened their eyes again, it was still there, an interminable reminder of sterility, polygamy, and waste.

"Get up," he went on, "and I'll ring for the porter to fix it for you."

He spoke harshly: this was the drill sergeant, the voice of authority. She sprang to attention, her lips quivering. Her nakedness, her long, loose hair, which a moment before had seemed voluptuous to her, now all at once became bold and disorderly, like an unbuttoned tunic at an army inspection. This was the first wound he had dealt her, but how deep the sword went in, back to the teachers who could smoke cigarettes and gossip with you in the late afternoon and then rebuke you in the morning class, back to the relations who would talk with you as an equal and then tell your aunt you were too young for silk stockings, back through all the betrayers, the friendly enemies, the Janus-faced overseers, back to the mother who could love you and then die.

"I don't want a bath," she asserted stubbornly. "I'm perfectly clean." But she knew, of course, that she had not bathed since she left New York, and, if she had been allowed to go her own way, would not have bathed until she reached Portland – who would think of paying a dollar for a bath on the train? In the ladies' room, where soot and spilt powder made a film over the dressing-tables and the hair-receivers stared up, archaic as cuspidors, one sponged oneself hastily under one's wrapper, and, looking at one's neighbors jockeying for position at the mirror, with their dirty kimonos, their elaborate make-up kits, and their uncombed permanents, one felt that one had been fastidious enough, and hurried away, out of the sweet, musty, unused smell of middle-aged women dressing. "I'm perfectly clean," she repeated. The man merely pressed the bell, and when the porter announced that the bath was ready, shoved her out into the corridor in his Brooks Brothers dressing gown with a cake of English toilet soap in her hands.

In the ladies' lounge, the colored maid had drawn the bath and stood just behind the half-drawn curtain, waiting to hand her soap and towels. And though, ordinarily, the girl had no particular physical modesty, at this moment it seemed to her insupportable that anyone should watch her bathe. There was something terrible and familiar about the scene – herself in the tub, washing, and a woman standing tall above her – something terrible and familiar indeed about the whole episode of being forced to cleanse herself. Slowly she remembered. The maid was, of course, her aunt, standing over her tub on Saturday nights to see that she washed every bit of herself, standing over her at the medicine cabinet to see that she took the castor oil, standing over her bed in the mornings to see if the sheets were wet. Not since she had been grown-up, had she felt this peculiar weakness and shame. It seemed to her that she did not have the courage to send the maid away, that the maid was somehow the man's representative, his spy, whom it would be impious to resist. Tears of futile, self-pitying rage came into her eyes, and she told herself that she would stay in the bath all day, rather than go back to the compartment. But the bell rang in the dressing-room, and the maid rustled the curtain, saying, "Do you want anything more? I'll leave the towels here," and the door swung behind her, leaving the girl alone.

She lay in the bath a long time, gathering her forces. In the tepid water, she felt for the first time a genuine Socialist ardor. For the first time in her life, she truly hated luxury, hated Brooks Brothers and Bergdorf Goodman and Chanel and furs and good food. All the pretty things she had seen in shops and coveted appeared to her suddenly gross, super-fatted, fleshly, even, strangely, unclean. By a queer reversal, the very safety pin in her underwear, which she had blushed for earlier in the morning came to look to her now as a kind of symbol of moral fastidiousness, just as the sores of a mendicant saint can, if thought of in the right way, testify to his spiritual health. A proud, bitter smile formed on her lips, as she saw herself as a citadel of socialist virginity, that could be taken and taken again, but never truly subdued. The man's whole assault on her now seemed to have had a political character; it was an incidental atrocity in the long class war. She smiled again, thinking that she had come out of it untouched, while he had been reduced to a jelly.

All morning in the compartment he had been in a state of wild and happy excitement, full of projects for reform and renewal. He was not sure what ought to happen next; he only knew that everything must be different. In one breath, he would have the two of them playing golf together at Del Monte; in the next, he would imagine that he had given her up and was starting in again with Leonie on a new basis. Then he would see himself throwing everything overboard and going to live in sin in a villa in a little French town. But at that moment a wonderful technical innovation for the manufacture of steel would occur to him, and he would be anxious to get back to the office to put it through. He talked of giving his fortune to a pacifist organization in Washington, and five minutes later made up his mind to send little Frank, who showed signs of being a problem child, to a damn good military school. Perhaps he would enlarge his Gates Mills house; perhaps he would sell it and move to New York. He would take her to the theater and the best restaurants; they would go to museums and ride on bus-tops. He would become a CIO organizer, or else he would give her a job in the personnel department of the steel company, and she could live in Cleveland with him and Leonie. But no, he would not do that, he would marry her, as he had said in the first place, or, if she would not marry him, he would keep her in an apartment in New York. Whatever happened she must not get off the train. He had come to regard her as a sort of rabbit's foot that he must keep by him at any price.

Naturally, she told herself, the idea was absurd. Yet suddenly her heart seemed to contract and the mood of indulgent pity ebbed away from her. She shivered and pulled herself out of the tub. His obstinacy on this point frightened her. If he should bar her way when the time came . . . ? If there should he a struggle . . . ? If she should have to pull the communication cord . . . ? She told herself that such things do not happen, that during the course of the day she would surely be able to convince him that she must go. (She had noticed that the invocation of her father inevitably moved him. "We mustn't do anything to upset your father," he would say. "He must be a very fine man." And tears would actually come to his eyes. She would play that, she thought, for all it was worth.) Yet her uneasiness did not abate. It was as if, carelessly, inadvertently, almost, she had pulled a switch that had set a whole strange factory going, and now, too late, she discovered that she did not know how to turn it off. She could have run away, but some sense of guilt, of social responsibility, of primitive awe, kept her glued to the spot, watching and listening, waiting to be ground to bits. Once, in a beauty parlor, she had been put under a defective dryer that remained on high no matter where she turned the regulator; her neck seemed to be burning up, and she could, at any time, have freed herself by simply getting out of the chair; yet she had stayed there the full half hour, until the operator came to release her. "I think," she had said then, lightly, "there is something wrong with the machine." And when the operator had examined it, all the women had gathered round, clucking, "How did you ever stand it?" She had merely shrugged her shoulders. It had seemed, at the time, better to suffer than to "make a fuss." Perhaps it was something like this that had held her to the man today, the fear of a scene and a kind of morbid competitiveness that would not allow the man to outdistance her in feeling. Yet suddenly she knew that it did not matter what her motives were: she could not, *could not*, get off the train until the man was reconciled to her doing so, until this absurd, ugly love story should somehow be concluded.

If only she could convert him to something, if she could say, "Give up your business, go to Paris, become a Catholic, join the CIO, join the army, join the Socialist Party, go off to the war in Spain." For a moment the notion engaged her. It would be wonderful, she thought, to be able to relate afterwards that she had sent a middle-aged businessman to die for the Republicans at the Alcazar. But almost at once she recognized that this was too much to hope for. The man back in the compartment was not equal to it; he was equal to a divorce, to a change of residence, at most to a change of business, but not to a change of heart. She sighed slightly, facing the truth about him. His gray flannel dressing gown lay on a chair beside her. Very slowly, she wrapped herself in it; the touch of the material made gooseflesh rise. Something about this garment – the color, perhaps, or the unsuitable size – reminded her of the bathing suits one rents at a public swimming pool. She gritted her teeth and pulled open the door. She did not pause to look about but plunged down the corridor with lowered head; though she passed no one, it seemed to her that she was running the gauntlet. The compartment, with its naked man and disordered bed, beckoned her on now, like a home.

When she opened the door, she found the man dressed, the compartment made up, and a white cloth spread on the collapsible table between the seats. In a few minutes the waiter of the night before was back with orange juice in cracked ice and corned beef hash and fish cakes. It was as if the scenery, which had been struck the night before, had been set up again for the matinee. The difference was that the door remained shut. Nevertheless, though there were no onlookers, atmospheric conditions in the compartment had changed; the relationship of the pair took on a certain sociable formality. The little breakfast passed off like a ceremonial feast. All primi-tive peoples, she thought, had known that a cataclysmic experience, whether joyful or sad, had in the end to be liquidated in an orderly meal. The banquets in Homer came to her mind, the refreshments the Irish put out at a wake, the sweetmeats the Arabs nibble after love, the fairy stories that end And-the-king-ordered-a-great-dinner-to-be-served-to-all-his-people. Upheavals of private feeling, like the one she had just been through, were as incalculable and anti-social as death. With a graceful inclination of her head, she accepted a second fish cake from the waiter, and felt herself restored to the human race.

There was to be no more lovemaking, she saw, and from the moment she felt sure of this, she began to be a little bit in love. The long day passed as if in slow motion, in desultory, lingering, tender talk. Dreamy confidences were murmured, and trailed off, casual and unemphatic, like the dialogue in a play by Chekhov. The great desert lake out the window disappeared and was replaced by the sage brush country, which seemed to her a pleasant, melancholy symbol of the contemporary waste land. The man's life lay before her; it was almost as if she could reach out and touch it, poke it, explore it, shine it up, and give it back to him. The people in it grew distinct to her, though they swam in a poetic ambience. She could see his first wife, an executive in her forties, good-looking, well-turned-out, the kind of woman that eats at Longchamps or the Algonquin; and then Leonie, finer-drawn, younger, with a certain Marie Laurencin look that pale, pretty, neutral-colored rich women get; then herself, still younger, still more highly organized – and all the time the man, a ludicrous and touching Ponce de Leon, growing helplessly older and coarser in inverse relation to the women he needed and wanted.

And she could see the Brussels carpet in a Philadelphia whorehouse, where he had first had a woman, the judge's face at the divorce hearing, the squash court at the club, the aquamarine bathtubs in his house, the barbecue pit, the fraternity brothers, the Audubon prints in his study, the vacuum bottle on the night table. Somehow it had become essential to them both that she should know *everything*. They might have been collaborators, drawing up a dossier for a new "Babbitt." This is what I am, he was saying: the wallpaper in the larger guest room is a blue and white Colonial design; I go to bed at ten and Leonie sits up and reads; I like kippers for breakfast; we have Heppelwhite chairs in the sitting room; the doctor is worried about my kidneys, and I feel lonely when I first wake up.

There were the details, the realistic "touches," and then there was the great skeleton of the story itself. In 1917 he was a chemistry major, just out of the state university, with a job for the next year teaching at a high school, and plans, after that, for a master's degree, and perhaps a job in the department at Cornell, where he had an uncle in the Agricultural School. The father had been a small businessman in a Pennsylvania coal town, the grandfather a farmer, the mother a little lady from Tennessee. But then there came the Officers' Training Camp, and the brilliant war record, and the right connections, so that the high-school job was never taken, and instead he was playing handball at the Athletic Club in the evenings, and working as a metallurgist for the steel company during the day. Soon he was moved into pro-duction, but somehow he was too amiable and easy-going for this, and after his first marriage, he went into the coal business. When he came back to the steel company, it was as a purchasing agent, and here his shrewdness and *bonhomie* were better employed. He became Chief Purchasing Agent and Fourth Vice-President; it was doubtful whether he would ever go further.

For ten years, he confided, he had been visited now and then by a queer sense of having missed the boat, but it was all vague with him: he had no idea of when the boat had sailed or what kind of boat it was or where it went to. Would he have done better to take the teaching job? It hardly seemed so. Plainly, he was no scientist – the steel company had seen this at once – and, had he taken that other road, at best he would have finished as the principal of a high school or the head of the chemistry department in a small-time state university. No, she thought, he was not a scientist manqué, but simply a nice man, and it was a pity that society had offered him no nicer way of being nice than the job of buying materials for a company in Little Steel. The job, she saw, was one of the least compromising jobs he could have held and still made money; by regarding his business life as a nexus of personal friend-ships he had tried to hold himself aloof from the banks and the blast furnaces. He was full of fraternal feelings, loyalties, even, toward the tin salesmen and iron mag-nates and copper executives and their wives who wined him and dined him and took him to the latest musical shows over and over again. ("Don't mistake me," he said, "most of those fellows and their women are mighty fine people"). Still – there was always the contract, waiting to be signed the next morning, lying implacably on the desk.

Here he was, affable, a good mixer, self-evidently a sound guy, and yet these qualities were somehow impeached by the commercial use that was made of them, so that he found himself, as he grew older, hunting, more and more anxiously, for new and non-commercial contexts in which to assert his gregariousness. He refused the conventional social life of Cleveland. At the country club dances, he was gener-ally to be found in the bar, shooting dice with the bartender; he played a little stud poker, but no bridge. In New York, he would stay at the Biltmore or the Murray Hill, buy his clothes at Brooks Brothers, and eat – when Leonie was not with him – at Cavanagh's, Luchow's or the Lafayette. But the greater part of his time he spent on trains, talking to his fellow-passengers, getting their life stories. ("Golly," he interjected, "if I were a writer like you!") This was one of his greatest pleasures, he said, and he would never go by plane if he could help it. In the three and a half days that it took a train to cross the continent, you could meet somebody who was a little bit different, and have a good, long visit with them. Sometimes, also, he would stop over and look up old friends, but lately that had been disappointing – so many of them were old or on the wagon, suffering from ulcers or cirrhosis of the liver.

He spread his hands suddenly. There it was, he indicated; he was sharing it all with her, like a basket lunch. And, as she accepted it, nodding from time to time in pleasure and recognition, supplementing it occasionally from her own store, she knew that the actual sharing of his life was no longer so much in question. During this afternoon of confidences, he had undergone a catharsis. He was at rest now, and happy, and she was free. He would never be alone again, she thought; in fact, it was as if he had never been alone at all, for by a tremendous act of perception, she had thrust herself back into his past, and was settled there forever, like the dear compan-ion, the twin, we pray for as children, while our parents, listening, laugh. She had brought it off, and now she was almost reluctant to leave him. A pang of joy went through her as she examined her own sorrow and found it to be real. All day she believed she had been acting a tragic part in something called One Perfect Night, but slowly, without her being aware of it, the counterfeit had passed into the true. She did not understand exactly how it had happened. Perhaps it was because she had come so very, very close – *tout comprendre, c'est tout aimer* – and perhaps it was because she was good at the task he had assigned her: at the sight of his life, waiting to be understood, she had rolled up her sleeves with all the vigor of a first-class cook confronting a brand-new kitchen.

"I love you," she said suddenly. "I didn't before, but now I do."

The man glanced sharply at her.

"Then you won't get off the train . . . ?"

"Oh, yes," she said, for now at last she could be truthful with him. "I'll certainly get off. One reason I love you, I suppose, is because I am getting off."

His dark eyes met hers in perfect comprehension.

"And one reason I'm going to let you do it," he said, "is because you love me."

She lowered her eyes, astonished, once more, at his shrewdness.

"Hell," he said, "it's a funny thing, but I'm so happy now that I don't care whether I ever see you again. I probably won't feel that way after you're gone. Right now I think I can live on this one day for the rest of my life."

"I hope you can," she said, her voice trembling with sincerity. "My dear, dear Mr. Breen, I hope you can." Then they both began to laugh wildly because she could not call him by his first name.

Still, he had not quite relinquished the idea of marrying her, and, once, very late in the afternoon, he struck out at her with unexpected, clumsy ferocity.

"You need a man to take care of you," he exclaimed. "I hate to see you go back to that life you've been living in New York. Your father ought to make you stay home in Portland. In a few years, you'll be one of those bohemian horrors with oily hair and long earrings. It makes me sick to think about it."

She pressed her lips together, and was amazed to find how hurt she was. It was unthinkable that he should speak of her way of life with such contempt; it was as if he had made a point of telling her that her gayest, wickedest, most extravagant hat was ugly and out-of-fashion.

"But you fell in love with me because I *am* bohemian," she said, forcing herself to smile, to take a suave and reasonable tone.

"No," he said, in a truculently sentimental voice. "It's because underneath all that you're just a sweet girl."

She shook her head impatiently. It was not true, of course, but it was hopeless to argue with him about it. Clearly, he took some cruel satisfaction in telling her that she was different from what she was. That implied that he had not fallen in love with her at all, but with some other person: the whole extraordinary little idyll had been based on a misunderstanding. Poor Marianna, she thought, poor pickings, to be loved under cover of darkness in Isabella's name! She did not speak for a long time.

Night fell again, and the little dinner that was presently served lacked the glamour of the earlier meals. The Union Pacific's menu had been winnowed out; they were reduced to steak and Great Big Baked Potatoes. She wished that they were out in the diner, in full view, eating some unusual dish and drinking a bottle of white wine. Even here in the compartment, she had hoped that he would offer her wine; the waiter suggested it, but the man shook his head without consulting her; his excesses in drink and love were beginning to tell on him; he looked tired and sick.

But by ten o'clock, when they were well out of Reno, she had warmed to him again. He had been begging her to let him send her a present; the notion displeased her at first; she felt a certain arrogant condescension in it; she refused to permit it, refused, even, to give him her address. Then he looked at her suddenly, with all the old humility and square self-knowledge in his brown eyes.

"Look," he said, "you'll be doing me a kindness. You see, that's the only thing a man like me can do for a woman is buy her things and love her a hell of a lot at night. I'm different from your literary boyfriends and your artistic boyfriends. I can't write you a poem or paint your picture. The only way I can show that I love you is to spend money on you.

"Money's your medium," she said, smiling, happy in this further insight he had given her, happy in her own gift of concise expression.

He nodded and she gave her consent. It must, however, be a very *small* present, and it must not, on any account, be jewelry, she said, not knowing precisely why she imposed this latter condition.

As they moved into the last hour of the trip, the occasion took on an elegiac solemnity. They talked very little; the man held both of her hands tightly. Toward the end, he broke the silence to say, "I want you to know that this has been the happiest day of my life." As she heard these words, a drowsy, sensuous contentment invaded her; it was as if she had been waiting for them all along; this was the climax, the spiritual orgasm. And it was just as she had known from the very first: in the end, he had not let her down. She had not been wrong in him after all.

They stood on the platform as the train came into Sacramento. Her luggage was piled up around them; one suitcase had a missing handle and was tied up with a rope. The man made a noise of disapproval.

"Your father," he said, "is going to feel terrible when he sees *that*." The girl laughed; the train slowed down; the man kissed her passionately several times, ignoring the porter who waited beside them with a large, Hollywood-darky smile on his face.

"If I were ten years younger," the man said, in a curious, measured tone, as if he were taking an oath, "I'd never let you get off this train." It sounded, she thought, like an apology to God.

In the station the air was hot and thick. She sat down to wait, and immediately she was damp and grubby; her stockings were wrinkled; her black suede shoes had somehow got dusty, and, she noticed for the first time, one of the heels was run over. Her trip home seemed peculiarly pointless, for she had known for the last eight hours that she was never going to marry the young man back in New York.

On the return trip, her train stopped in Cleveland early in the morning. In a new fall suit she sat in the club car, waiting. Mr. Breen hurried into the car. He was wearing a dark-blue business suit and had two packages in his hand. One of them was plainly a florist's box. She took it from him and opened it, disclosing two of the largest and most garish purple orchids she had ever seen. He helped her pin them on her shoulder and did not appear to notice how oddly they harmonized with her burnt sienna jacket. The other box contained a bottle of whiskey; *in memoriam*, he said.

They had the club car to themselves, and for the fifteen minutes the train waited in the station he looked at her and talked. It seemed to her that he had been talking ever since she left him, talking volubly, desperately, incoherently, over the long-distance telephone, via air mail, by Western Union and Postal Telegraph. She had received from him several pieces of glamour-girl underwear and a topaz brooch, and had been disappointed and a little humiliated by the taste displayed. She was glad now that the train stopped at such an outlandish hour, for she felt that he cut a ridiculous figure, with his gifts in his hand, like a superannuated stage-door johnny.

She herself had little to say, and sat passive, letting the torrent of talk and endearment splash over her. Sooner or later, she knew, the law of diminishing returns would begin to operate, and she would cease to reap these overwhelming profits from the small investment of herself she had made. At the moment, he was begging her to marry him, describing a business conference he was about to attend, and asking her approval of a vacation trip he was planning to take with his wife. Of these three elements in his conversation, the first was predominant, but she sensed that already she was changing for him, becoming less of a mistress and more of a confidante. It was significant that he was not (as she had feared) hoping to ride all the way to New York with her: the business conference, he explained, prevented that.

It never failed, she thought, to be a tiny blow to guess that a man is losing interest in you, and she was tempted, as on such occasions she always had been, to make some gesture that would quicken it again. If she let him think she would sleep with him, he would stay on the train, and let the conference go by the board. He had weighed the conference, obviously, against a platonic interlude, and made the sensible decision. But she stifled her vanity, and said to herself that she was glad that he was showing some signs of self-respect; in the queer, business-English letters he had written her, and on the phone for an hour at a time at her father's house, he had been too shockingly abject.

She let him get off the train, still talking happily, pressed his hand warmly but did not kiss him.

It was three weeks before he came to see her in her New York apartment, and then, she could tell, he was convalescent. He had become more critical of her and more self-assured. Her one-and-a-half rooms in Greenwich Village gave him claustrophobia, he declared, and when she pointed out to him that the apartment was charming, he stated flatly that it was not the kind of place he liked, nor the kind of place she ought to be living in. He was more the businessman and less the suitor, and though he continued to ask her to marry him, she felt that the request was somewhat formal; it was only when he tried to make love to her that his real, hopeless, humble ardor showed itself once more. She fought him off though she had an inclination to yield, if only to reestablish her ascendancy over him. They went to the theater two nights, and danced, and drank champagne, and the third morning he phoned her from his hotel that he had a stomach attack and would have to go home to Cleveland with a doctor.

More than a month went by before she saw him again. This time he refused to come to her apartment, but insisted that she meet him at his suite in the Ambassador. They passed a moderate evening: the man contented himself with dining at Longchamps. He bought her a large Brie cheese at the Voisin down the street, and told her an anti-New-Deal joke. Just below the surface of his genial manner, there was an hostility that hurt her. She found that she was extending herself to please him. All her gestures grew over-feminine and demonstrative; the lift of her eyebrows was a shade too arch: like a *passée belle*, she was overplaying herself. I must let go, she told herself; the train is pulling out; if I hang on, I'll be dragged along at its wheels. She made him take her home early.

A little later she received a duck he had shot in Virginia. She did not know how to cook it and it stayed in her icebox so long that the neighbors complained of the smell.

When she got a letter from him that had been dictated to his stenographer, she knew that his splurge was over. After that, she saw him once – for cocktails. He ordered double martinis and got a little drunk. Then his friendliness revived briefly, and he begged her with tears in his eyes to "forget all this Red nonsense and remember that you're just your father's little girl at heart." Walking home alone, trying to decide whether to eat in a tea room or cook herself a chop, she felt flat and sad, but in the end she was glad that she had never told him of her broken engagement.

When her father died, the man must have read the account in the papers, for she got a telegram that read: SINCEREST CONDOLENCES YOU HAVE LOST THE BEST FRIEND YOU WILL EVER HAVE. She did not file it away with the other messages, but tore it up carefully and threw it in the wastebasket. It would have been dreadful if anyone had seen it.

Josephine, the Songstress or, The Mice Nation

BY FRANZ KAFKA

Our singer is called Josephine. Those who have not heard her sing do not know the power of song. There is no one who is not carried away by her singing; and this is all the more remarkable as our race on the whole is not fond of music. The calm of peace is the best music for us; our lives are hard, and even when we try to dismiss the cares of the day we cannot lift ourselves to a thing so remote from our ordinary lives as music. But we do not complain about this very much, we never go to that extreme; we consider our greatest asset to be a certain practical shrewdness, which we find very necessary indeed, and this shrewdness enables us to smile and so console ourselves for everything, even for missing the joy of music – that is, if we were to desire it, which never happens. Josephine is the only exception; she loves music and also knows how to interpret it; she is the only one, and when she goes, music will disappear from our lives, who knows for how long?

I have often reflected as to just what really is the situation in music. We are completely unmusical, so how does it happen that we can understand Josephine's singing, or at least think we do, for Josephine denies that we understand her. The simplest answer would be that the beauty of her singing is so great that even the dullest sense cannot resist it. But this would not be a satisfactory answer. If this were actually so, we would have had a feeling of the unusual from the very first and always afterwards, a feeling that what we heard in this voice was something that we had never heard before, something we altogether lacked the capacity to hear, and which Josephine alone, and no one else, made us able to hear. But in my opinion, it is exactly this that is not so. I do not feel this, nor have I noticed anything of the sort in others. To our intimates we openly admit that Josephine's singing manifests nothing remarkable as singing in itself.

Is it really singing then? We do have traditions of song, in spite of our unmusical nature; there was singing in the old days of our people; sagas tell about it, and songs have even been preserved, which, to tell the truth, no one can sing any more. So we have some notion of what singing is like, and Josephine's art does not actually agree with that notion. Is it really singing then? Maybe it is just squeaking? And at any rate we all know what squeaking is; it is the artistic skill peculiar to our people, or rather no skill at all, but a characteristic manifestation of our life. We all squeak, but no one actually thinks of passing it off as art; we squeak without paying any attention to it, without even noticing it, and in fact many of us are not at all aware that squeaking is one of our characteristic traits. If it is true, therefore, that Josephine does not sing, but just squeaks, and – as it seems to me at least – hardly exceeds the ordinary limits of squeaking, then there still remains to be explained the enigma of her great success, and it is all the more an enigma.

For what she produces is not just simply squeaking. If one stood some distance from her and listened – or better yet, if one were to try it like this – have Josephine sing with other voices, and let the listener set himself the problem of distinguishing hers; without a doubt he would make out nothing more than an ordinary squeaking, a bit striking at the most for its delicacy or weakness. And yet if you stood right in front of her, it would prove to be something more than just squeaking. It is necessary to see as well as hear her in order to understand her art. Even if it is only our everyday squeaking, the fact that a person should stand up so solemnly to do nothing out of the ordinary, is something unusual in itself. There is no art, certainly, to cracking a nut, and no one would think of collecting an audience together just to entertain it by cracking nuts. All the same, if somebody did do this and succeeded in his intention, it would no longer be just a question of nut-cracking. Or if it were only a question of cracking nuts, it would become evident then that we had neglected this art because we possessed such easy mastery of it, and that this nut-cracker was showing us its true nature for the first time, and it would even enhance the effect if he were somewhat less proficient in nut-cracking than the rest of us.

Maybe it is the same way with Josephine's singing; we admire in her that which we do not admire at all in ourselves, and in this last she agrees with us fully. I was once present when – as of course, often happens – someone called her attention to the general popular squeaking. I have never seen such a haughty, insolent smile as the one that appeared on her face; to all outward appearances Josephine is refinement itself, strikingly refined even among a people such as ours, which is rich in feminine personalities of this sort, yet at that moment she actually seemed vulgar. But with her great sensitivity, she herself must have realized this immediately, for she managed to get herself under control. This in any event is her way of repudiating every connection between her art and squeaking. For those of the opposite opinion she has nothing but contempt, and most likely, unconfessed hatred. This is no ordinary vanity, for the opposition, to which I myself half belong, certainly admires her no less than does the crowd, but Josephine wants not only to be admired, but to be admired in exactly the way she decides. Admiration alone is of no importance to her. And when you sit in front of her you begin to understand this; opposition can only be maintained at a distance: sitting in front of her, you realize that what she squeaks is not ordinary squeaking.

Since squeaking is one of our more thoughtless habits, it might be supposed that squeaking can be heard in Josephine's audience; we enjoy her art, and when we enjoy ourselves, we squeak; but her audience does not squeak, it is still as a mouse. We are as silent as though participating in that peace for which we all yearn, and of which at the very least we are deprived by our own squeaking. Is it her singing itself that enraptures us, or is it rather the solemn stillness surrounding that weak little voice? Once it happened that while Josephine was singing, some insane little thing in the audience began to squeak too in all innocence. Now it was altogether the same kind of squeaking that we heard from Josephine: a squeaking, still hesitant for all its practice, came from out there in front, and from back in the audience there came a self-oblivious childish little squeaking. It would have been impossible to point out the difference, yet we immediately hissed and whistled the disturber down, which was quite unnecessary, as even without that she would have stolen away in fear and shame, while Josephine swelled her triumphal squeak and spreading her arms wide and lifting her head as high as she could, grew quite beside herself.

She is always like that. Every petty thing, every accident, every hindrance, a creak in the floor, someone grinding his teeth, any trouble with the lighting – all these she considers as designed to add to the effect of her singing. It is her opinion, to be sure, that she sings to deaf ears. There is no lack of enthusiasm and applause, but as for what she calls real understanding, she learned long ago to give up any hope of that. This being the case, she finds interruptions very useful. Any external thing that opposes itself to the purity of her singing and that can be overcome in an easy struggle – or even without a struggle, but simply by force of contrast – any such thing can contribute to the awakening of the crowd, and help to teach it, not, of course, understanding, but at least veneration and respect.

If petty issues serve her so well, how much more do the large ones. Our lives are very troubled, every day there come alarms, anxieties, hopes, fears, and a person could not possibly bear all this without the support of his fellows at every moment of the day and night. Yet even so, it often becomes just too difficult; at times as many as a thousand shoulders will tremble under a burden actually intended for only one. Then Josephine thinks that her moment has come. She will be standing there already, the delicate creature, with her diaphragm vibrating in an alarming way. It is as though she were concentrating all her strength in her singing, as though she were deprived of everything in herself, of every force, of almost every capacity for life not contributing directly to her singing, as though she were stripped and made ready for sacrifice, confided only to the protection of beneficent spirits; it is as though while so utterly rapt in her singing, a cold breath might kill her in passing. But just at the sight of this, we, her so-called enemies, would say to one another, "How can she even squeak if she has to strain herself so terribly, not to sing – we won't even mention singing – but simply to wring somehow a common, ordinary squeak from herself?" So it seems to us, but, as I have said, this is but a fleeting impression – an unavoidable one, it is true, but quick to pass. For we too are soon immersed in the emotion of the crowd, which is listening with bated breath, warm in the contact of body against body.

And most often, in order to collect around her a crowd of these people – who are almost always in motion, darting here and there on missions which are often not very clear – all Josephine would have to do is assume an attitude with her head thrown back, mouth half open, and eyes turned upward, signifying that she was about to sing. She can do this wherever she pleases, it does not have to be a place that can be seen from a distance, any obscure corner chosen on the moment's whim will do just as well. The news that she is going to sing will spread immediately, and processions are soon on the way. But frequently there will be obstacles, for Josephine likes to sing especially in times of disturbance when multifarious cares and troubles will have driven us upon many different paths, and try as we may, we cannot gather together as quickly as Josephine would like; and she may have to stand there in that solemn attitude of hers for quite a while without enough listeners present. Then she flies into such a rage, then she stamps her feet, swears in a very unlady-like way, and even goes as far as to bite. But even this sort of behavior does no harm to her prestige in our eyes; instead of trying to keep her exaggerated demands somewhat in check, we exert ourselves to satisfy them: messengers will be sent out to bring more listeners, this being kept secret from her; then people will be seen stationed on all the paths round about to wave to the oncomers to hurry; and this will all go on until barely enough of us have at last been collected together.

What makes the people go to so much trouble about Josephine? Such a question is no easier to answer than the one about her singing, with which it is connected. The first question might even be cancelled and identified completely with the second one, if it were possible to maintain that the people have surrendered themselves to

Josephine unconditionally because of her singing. This, however, is not the case. Our people hardly know what unconditional surrender means; people such as these, who love slyness more than anything else, inoffensive slyness, of course, and child- ish whispering, and idle yet innocent gossip that does nothing more than exercise the tongue – under no circumstances can such people surrender themselves uncondi- tionally. Josephine no doubt senses this, and it is against this that she struggles with every effort of her weak voice.

But general opinions of this kind should by no means be overestimated, for the people do surrender themselves to Josephine, only not unconditionally. It is not easy, for instance, to laugh at Josephine. You might admit to yourself that there is much food for laughter in Josephine – and in an abstract sense we are always close to laughter; in spite of all the sorrows of our life, a kind of mild laughter is habitual to us – but we do not laugh at Josephine. At times I have the impression that the people conceive of their relationship to Josephine as one by which this frail, pitiable and somehow remarkable creature – remarkable, in her opinion, for her singing – has been entrusted to their care. The reason for this is clear to no one, but it seems to be an established fact. And no one laughs at that which has been entrusted to one; to laugh at that would be to fail in one's duty. The utmost malice that the most mali- cious among us can show towards Josephine is to say now and then, "Laughter fails us when we look at Josephine."

And so the people take care of Josephine the way a father would who has adopted a child that stretches out its little hand to him – whether in pleading or command, one could not tell. Our nation might be thought unequal to such paternal obligations, but actually, it discharges them, in this case at least, in exemplary fash- ion; no single individual is capable of doing what the nation as a whole can in this respect. The difference between the powers of that nation and the powers of the individual is so enormous in fact, that it suffices for the nation but to draw its pro- tégé into the warmth of its nearness in order to protect it. No one, to tell the truth, dares mention such things to Josephine. "I don't give a squeak for your protection," she would say. And we would think, "Yes indeed, that is just what you do, really." And besides, it does not disprove anything when Josephine rebels; it is rather the way of a child and the gratitude of a child, and it is the way of a father not to pay any attention to it.

But other things are involved which are more difficult to explain on the basis of this relationship between the people and Josephine. Josephine, you see, has the opposite opinion, and thinks that it is she who protects the nation. Her singing rescues us, supposedly, from dangerous political and economic situations – no less than that – and if it does not drive misfortune away, it at least gives us the strength to bear it. She does not put it in this way exactly, nor in any other way – she says little in general, she is silent among all the chatterers – but it flashes from her eyes, it can be read from her closed mouth – among us only a few can keep their mouths closed, and she is one of them. At bad news – and many a day it is one piece of bad news after another, some false, some half-true – she gets up immediately, although she usually drags herself wearily along the ground, and she stretches her neck to try to get a general view of her flock, like a shepherd before a storm. Of course, children make similar claims in their wild, ungovernable way, but Josephine's are not as unjustified as theirs. Certainly, she does not save us, nor does she infuse us with any new strength; it is easy to pose as the savior of such a nation, which, accustomed as it is to suffering, unsparing of itself, quick to decision, and familiar with death, seems timid only because of the foolhardy atmosphere in which it lives constantly, and being, besides, as prolific as it is daring – it is easy, I say, to pass oneself off after the event as the savior of such a people, a people that somehow always manages to save itself, even if at such a cost that the student of history – as a rule we neglect the study of history completely – blenches with horror. And yet it is true that precisely in emergencies we listen to Josephine's voice better than otherwise. The menaces hanging over our heads make us quieter, humbler and more compliant with Josephine's dictatorial ways; we gather together eagerly, press close to one another eagerly, especially as it is for an occasion having nothing to do with the agonizing main question; it is as if we were drinking a last hurried cup of peace together before the battle – and hurry would be necessary, which Josephine forgets all too often. It would not be a song-recital so much as a gathering together of the nation, and what is more, a gathering where all would be silent save for that little squeaking out front; the hour would be far too grave to spend in chatter.

Of course, such a state of affairs would not satisfy Josephine at all. In spite of the nervous uneasiness which fills Josephine because her position has never been quite clarified, she is so blinded by her self-importance that she fails to notice many things, and without too much trouble can be induced to overlook even a great deal more; a crowd of flatterers is continually busy towards this end, which is really in the general interest. But to sing as a side-show, unnoticed, off in a corner at a gathering of the nation – certainly she would never sacrifice her singing for that, in spite of the fact that this would be no small thing in itself.

But she does not even have to do that, for her art is not unnoticed. Although we are really preoccupied with quite different things, and silence reigns by no means simply for the sake of the singing, and many of us do not even look up, but bury our faces in the fur of our neighbors, making it seem as though Josephine were exerting herself before us in vain, yet it cannot be denied that something of her squeaking reaches us irresistibly. This squeaking, lifted up at a time when silence is enjoined upon all others, is almost like a message from the nation to each of its individuals; in the midst of a crisis Josephine's thin squeaking is like the miserable existence of our people amidst the tumult of a hostile world. It does us good to think that Josephine, this nonentity as a voice, this nonentity as a performer, can still assert herself and find a way to reach us. At such moments, certainly, we could not endure a really artistic singer, even if one were to be found among us; we would refuse unanimously to put up with such nonsense. May Josephine be shielded from the realization that our listening to her is evidence against her singing. But she probably suspects this anyhow, otherwise why would she deny so passionately that we do listen to her? Yet she always manages to sing or squeak this supicion out of her mind.

But even without this, there would still be one sure consolation for her, the fact that to a certain extent we actually do listen to her, in the same way, probably, that one would listen to an artistic singer; and she achieves effects for us for which an artistic singer would strive in vain, and which are granted only to her insufficient powers. It is most likely that this has something to do on the whole with our way of life.

Our people have no youth, just barely a tiny moment of childhood. It is true that demands are regularly raised that children be granted a special liberty, a special indulgence, the right to a little freedom from care, to a little silly romping, to a little play; we are called on to recognize this right and help make it an actuality; demands like these are raised and almost everybody approves of them, nothing is more worthy of approval, but there is also nothing which the facts of our life can less permit. The demands are approved, attempts are made to carry them out, but soon everything returns to the old state of affairs. Our life is such that a child has to take care of itself as soon as it can run about a little and recognize the world around it; the areas in which for economic reasons we must live dispersed are too great, our foes are too many, the dangers prepared for us everywhere too incalculable – we cannot remove children from the struggle for existence; if we did it would only mean their untimely ends. But to these sad reasons there should be added a more encouraging one, the fertility of our race. One generation – and each is numerous – presses close upon the others, children do not have time enough to be children. If other nations bring up their children carefully, if they establish schools for their little ones, if their children, these nations' future, stream out of their schools daily, for some time at least it is the same children that appear there day in and day out. We have no schools, and at the very shortest intervals of time there pour forth from our people immense swarms of children, merrily spluttering and chirping until they can squeak, rolling or tumbled along by the pressure of the others until they can run, clumsily carrying everthing along by their mass until they can see: our children! And not the way it is in the schools of those others, not the same children, not at all, but always and ever again new ones, without end or interruption; hardly does a child come forth but it is no longer a child, and new child faces, indistinguishable in their numbers and hurry, rosy with their joy, are already pressing behind it. As pretty as all this may be and as much as others may justly envy us for it, it must be admitted that we cannot exactly give our children a real childhood. And this has its consequences. A certain undying, ineradicable childishness pervades our people; in direct contradiction to the best in us, our unerring sense of the practical, we will often act like complete fools, and just the way children act foolishly: senselessly, extravagantly, on a big scale, frivolously, and all this often for the sake only of a little fun. And although, as is only natural, the joy we get out of it can no longer have the full force of the joy of children, at least some part of that is certainly present. And Josephine has profited at all times by this childish streak in our people.

But our people are not only childish, they are also to some extent prematurely old; childhood and old age are different with us than with others. We have no youth, we become adult immediately, and then we stay adult too long; a certain weariness and hopelessness leave a broad imprint upon the generally sturdy and optimistic character of our people. It is likely that our lack of musical sense has some connection with this. We are too old for music; its inspiration and its soaring flights do not go with our inertia, we wearily wave it away; we confine ourselves to squeaking; a little squeaking now and then is the thing for us. Who knows, perhaps there are musically talented persons among us; but if there are, they are inevitably suppressed by the character of their fellow citizens before they can unfold. Josephine, on the other hand, can sing or squeak, or whatever she calls it, to her heart's content and not bother us; it agrees with us, and we can put up with it very well. If there is any music in it, it has been reduced to an infinitesimal minimum; a certain tradition of music is preserved, but without letting it trouble us in the slightest.

However, Josephine has even more to give to a people of this humor. At her concerts, especially in times of crisis, only those who are quite young take any interest in the singer as such; they alone marvel at the way she curls her lips, expels the air from between her delicate front teeth, faints away in admiration of her own sounds, and then takes this collapse as a pretext for urging herself on to new achievements that become more and more incomprehensible. But it is plain to see that most of the crowd has withdrawn into itself. Here in their short respites from battle the people sit and dream; it is as though each individual were relaxing his limbs, as though the restless one were able to lay himself down for once and stretch out at his pleasure in the great warm bed of the people. And now and then Josephine's squeaks sound through these dreams – she calls it sparkling, we call it jerky; but anyhow it is appropriate here as nowhere else, finding its expectant moment in a way music hardly ever does. Something of our poor short childhood is in it, something of our lost and unrecoverable joy, but also something of our busy present-day life, something of its small, inconceivable and yet persistent and inextinguishable cheerfulness. And all this is expressed, really, without any grand gestures, but softly, whisperingly, familiarly, often a little huskily. Naturally, it is squeaking. What else could it be? Squeaking is the language of our people. But many squeak all their lives, and do not know it, while here squeaking is liberated from the bonds of daily life, and for a short while we too are liberated by it. We positively do not want to miss these concerts.

But it is still a long way from this to Josephine's contention that at these moments she infuses us with new energy, etc., etc. A long way, that is, for ordinary people, but not for Josephine's flatterers. "How can it be otherwise?" they will ask with really shameless impudence. "How else can you explain so great an attendance, especially in the face of immediate danger, an attendance so great that it has often interfered with proper and timely measures of defense against that danger?" Now this last is true, unfortunately, but it does not redound to Josephine's credit, particularly when one adds that whenever these gatherings were suddenly broken up by the enemy so that many of us had to lose our lives then and there, Josephine, who was responsible for all this, having perhaps actually attracted the enemy by her squeaking, would always be occupying the safest spot, and protected by her claque, very quietly and hurriedly, would be the first to disappear. Although everybody really knows about this, the next time that Josephine rises to sing at any place and time she pleases they will again hurry over. You might conclude from this that Josephine is almost above the law, that she can do whatever she wants to, even when it endangers the community, yet be forgiven everything. If this were so, Josephine's demands would be completely understandable. This freedom granted to her, this extraordinary gift, which really controverts the law and has never been given to anyone else, might be considered indeed a confession of that which Josephine claims, that the people do not understand her, that they marvel helplessly at her art, feel unworthy of her, and try by what is no less than an act of desperation to make good the suffering they cause her, and that in the same way that her art is beyond their comprehension, her person and its wishes are beyond their authority. Now this in any event is altogether untrue; perhaps the people yield to Josephine too quickly in details, but they surrender themselves unconditionally neither to her nor to anyone else.

For a long time now, perhaps since the very beginning of her artistic career, Josephine has fought to be released from all work in recognition of her singing; she is to be freed from care as to her daily bread and from all else connected with the struggle for existence, and this is to be shifted – probably – to the people as a whole. Someone easily carried away – there are such – might conclude this demand to be intrinsically justified simply by its exceptional nature and by the very state of mind capable of conceiving such a demand. Our people, however, have drawn other conclusions and have quietly rejected it. Nor have they troubled themselves very much to refute the arguments in its support. Josephine has pointed out, for example, that her voice might suffer from the exertions of labor, that as a matter of fact, the exertions of labor are slight compared to those of singing; besides, they deprive her of any chance of getting enough rest after singing and of strengthening herself for the next concert, she has to exhaust herself completely in the process, and that even so, it is impossible for her under these circumstances ever to attain the peak of her performance. The people listen to her and go on as before. These people, so easily moved, sometimes cannot be moved at all. Sometimes their refusal is so stern that Josephine herself is taken aback; she appears to give in, does her work properly and sings as well as she can; but this only lasts for a while, then she returns to the struggle with new energy – of which, for this purpose, she seems to have an inexhaustible supply.

Now it is of course obvious that Josephine is not fighting really for her literal demands. She is sensible, she is not afraid of work, since, indeed, the fear of work is alien to us on the whole; even if her demands were to be granted she would live no differently than before, her work would not interfere with her singing at all, and her singing itself, no doubt, would not get any better. So what she is really fighting for is but a public and unambiguous recognition of her art that will outlive time, and tower far above anything known till now. While almost everything else seems attainable to her, this stubbornly eludes her. Perhaps she ought to have directed her attack in a different quarter from the very beginning, perhaps she herself has recognized her mistake by now, but it is too late to retreat, retreat would mean being unfaithful to herself; therefore she has to stand or fall by this demand.

If she really had the enemies she claims to have, she might be able to watch the struggle amusedly, without lifting a finger herself. But she has no enemies, and even if some of us have objections to her now and then, this struggle amuses no one; if only because the nation shows a cold, judicial attitude here such as is rarely seen among us. And even if some one approved of this attitude in this particular case, he would be deprived of all joy by the very thought that the nation might act similarly towards him at some other time. Like the demand itself, the refusal as such does not really matter; what matters is that the nation can show such a solid front towards one of its own members, all the more solid in so far as it otherwise humbly takes a paternal, and more than paternal, interest in this same member.

If a single person had represented the nation as a whole here, one might think that as long as this person had been indulging Josephine, he had had a lasting and ardent desire to put a stop finally to his indulgence, that he had been indulgent to superhuman lengths in the firm conviction that indulgence would reach its true limits, nevertheless; if he had indulged her more than necessary, it was only in order to speed the matter up, only in order to spoil Josephine and incite her to more and more demands, until she had actually made this last one; and then indeed he had decided – abruptly, because it had been long prepared – on the final, conclusive refusal. Now this was most certainly not the case; the people do not have to play such tricks; besides, their esteem for Josephine is sincere and well-proven, and Josephine's demand was without a doubt so extreme that any simple child could have predicted its outcome. Yet it is possible that such conjectures play a part in Josephine's version of the affair and add more bitterness to the pain of having been refused.

But even if she does entertain such conjectures, they do not frighten her off. Lately the struggle has become even sharper; whereas before she only waged it with words, she has now begun to use other means – more effective ones, in her opinion, but in ours more fraught with danger to herself.

Some of us think that the reason Josephine is becoming so urgent is that she feels herself growing older, her voice getting weaker, and therefore it seems high time to her to begin her final struggle for recognition. I do not believe this is so. If it were, Josephine would not be Josephine. There is no such thing for her as growing old and losing her voice. When she wants something she is not influenced in her purpose by external things, but by an inner logic. She reaches for the highest laurels, not because they seem for a moment to hang a little lower, but because they actually are the highest; if it were in her power, she would hang them even higher.

But in any event this contempt for external obstacles does not hinder her from using the most dishonorable methods. Her rights are beyond all question for her, so what difference does it make how she attains them – especially since in this world, as it seems to her, the honorable methods are precisely the ones that always fail. It is just for this reason, perhaps, that she has shifted the struggle for her rights from the field of singing to one not very dear to her. Her claque has circulated remarks of hers to the effect that she feels quite capable of singing so that it would be a real pleasure to all classes of the people, including the remotest sections of her opposition, a real pleasure in the sense meant by Josephine, not in the sense in which the people have always claimed to have got pleasure from her singing. But, she added, since she could not adulterate the sublime and flatter the vulgar, things would have to remain as they were. It is different, however, with her struggle to be released from work; of course this also involves her singing, but she does not carry on the fight here directly by means of the precious weapon of song; any means she employs are good enough here.

So the rumor was spread, for example, that unless her demand was granted, Josephine would shorten her coloratura passages. I had never heard of these coloratura passages, nor have I ever noticed anything of the sort in her singing. Nevertheless, Josephine was going to shorten her coloratura passages: not eliminate them entirely for the time being, but just shorten them. It is said that she carried out this threat, but I at all events was never struck by any differences from her previous performances. The people as a whole went on listening as before, nor was there any change in their treatment of Josephine's demand. However, it is undeniable that there is often something as truly graceful about Josephine's thinking as there is about her figure. For example, after this last performance, she announced – as if her original decision had been too harsh or abrupt for the people – that at her next performance she would restore the coloratura passages in their entirety. But after the next concert she again changed her mind; she was definitely all through now with her full-length coloratura passages, and they would not be restored again until her demand had received a favorable answer. The people listened to all these announcements, decisions and changes of decision distractedly, the way an adult absorbed in his own thoughts listens distractedly to the chattering of a child, full of kindly feelings in principle, but out of reach.

But Josephine will not give up. For instance, she claimed recently to have hurt her foot at work, which made it difficult for her to stand as she sang; since she could only sing while standing, she would now have to shorten her songs. But no one believed that she had really been hurt, in spite of the way she limped and had herself supported by her followers. Granted even the special sensitivity of her little body, we are nevertheless a people of workers, and Josephine belongs to this people, and if we were all to limp every time we scraped off some skin, the whole population would never stop limping. It made no difference that she had herself led around like a cripple and showed herself much more often than usual in this pitiful condition, the people went on listening to her singing as gratefully and delightedly as ever, and no great fuss was made about the shortened performances.

As she could not go on limping forever, she invented something new; she pretended to be tired or in bad humor or to feel faint. And then, in addition to a concert, we had a play. We would see Josephine surrounded by her followers, who would be begging and pleading with her to sing. It would seem that she wanted to sing very much, but was unable to. Then they would comfort and coax her and carry her almost bodily to the place fixed upon in advance, where she was to sing. She would give in finally with unimaginable tears, but as she would get ready to sing with what was ostensibly a supreme effort, feebly, her arms not outstretched as usual, but hanging limply at her sides so that you got the impression that they were perhaps a little too short – just as she was about to sing, it would suddenly come to nothing again; first there would be a sudden, helpless jerk of her head, and then she would collapse before our eyes. But after that, to be sure, she would quickly pick herself up and begin singing – not much differently, I think, than before. Perhaps if you had an ear for the finest nuances, you might have detected a note of agitation that was slightly out of the ordinary, but which only heightened the effect. And at the end she would be even less tired than before; she would leave with a firm step – if her tripping little walk can be called that – refusing all assistance from her claque, and measuring the crowd, which would respectfully make way for her, with a cold glance. This is the way things were until a short while ago, but the latest development, however, is her disappearance just at a moment when she was expected to sing. Not only have her followers looked for her; many others have volunteered in the search; but it has been of no avail. Josephine has disappeared, she does not want to sing, she does not even want to be asked to; this time she has abandoned us altogether.

It is strange how falsely she can reason, clever as she is; so falsely that you would think she did not reason at all, but was simply driven along by her fate, which in this world can only be a sad one. She has given up singing of her own accord, destroyed of her own accord the power she had gained over our feelings. How could she ever have gained this power, knowing our feelings so little? She hides herself and does not sing, but the people – a mass resting upon itself, which, despite appearances to the contrary, can only give, essentially, and can never receive gifts, not even from Josephine – the people continue, without apparent disappointment, calmly and majestically on their way.

For Josephine herself, the way must lead downwards. The time will soon come when her last squeak will sound and forever die. She is a small episode in the eternal history of our people, and the people will survive the loss. This will by no means be easy; how will it ever again be possible to hold our gatherings in complete silence? For were they not silent, really, even with Josephine? Was her actual squeaking noticeably louder and more vivid than our memory of it will be? Rather, did not the people in their wisdom esteem Josephine's singing so highly just because it was imperishable in this way?

For this reason, perhaps, we shall not be deprived of so very much; but Josephine, delivered from the earthly cares, which in her opinion are prepared for the elect, will lose herself joyfully among the unnumbered multitudes of the heroes of our nation, and, since we keep no history, will soon be forgotten in an intenser deliverance, like all her brothers.

Translated from the German by Clement Greenberg

Of This Time, of That Place

BY LIONEL TRILLING

It was a fine September day. By noon it would be summer again but now it was true autumn with a touch of chill in the air. As Joseph Howe stood on the porch of the house in which he lodged, ready to leave for his first class of the year, he thought with pleasure of the long indoor days that were coming. It was a moment when he could feel glad of his profession.

On the lawn the peach tree was still in fruit and young Hilda Aiken was taking a picture of it. She held the camera tight against her chest. She wanted the sun behind her but she did not want her own long morning shadow in the foreground. She raised the camera but that did not help, and she lowered it but that made things worse. She twisted her body to the left, then to the right. In the end she had to step out of the direct line of the sun. At last she snapped the shutter and wound the film with intense care.

Howe, watching her from the porch, waited for her to finish and called good morning. She turned, startled, and almost sullenly lowered her glance. In the year Howe had lived at the Aikens', Hilda had accepted him as one of her family, but since his absence of the summer she had grown shy. Then suddenly she lifted her head and smiled at him, and the humorous smile confirmed his pleasure in the day. She picked up her bookbag and set off for school.

The handsome houses on the streets to the college were not yet fully awake but they looked very friendly. Howe went by the Bradby house where he would be a guest this evening at the first dinner party of the year. When he had gone the length of the picket fence, the whitest in town, he turned back. Along the path there was a fine row of asters and he went through the gate and picked one for his buttonhole. The Bradbys would be pleased if they happened to see him invading their lawn and the knowledge of this made him even more comfortable.

He reached the campus as the hour was striking. The students were hurrying to their classes. He himself was in no hurry. He stopped at his dim cubicle of an office and lit a cigarette. The prospect of facing his class had suddenly presented itself to him and his hands were cold, the lawful seizure of power he was about to make seemed momentous. Waiting did not help. He put out his cigarette, picked up a pad of theme paper and went to his classroom.

As he entered, the rattle of voices ceased and the twenty-odd freshmen settled themselves and looked at him appraisingly. Their faces seemed gross, his heart sank at their massed impassivity, but he spoke briskly.

"My name is Howe," he said and turned and wrote it on the blackboard. The carelessness of the scrawl confirmed his authority. He went on, "My office is 412 Slemp Hall and my office hours are Monday, Wednesday and Friday from eleven thirty to twelve thirty."

He wrote, "M., W., F., 11:30-12:30." He said, "I'll be very glad to see any of you at that time. Or if you can't come then, you can arrange with me for some other time." He turned again to the blackboard and spoke over his shoulder. "The text for the course is Jarman's *Modern Plays*, revised edition. The Co-op has it in stock." He wrote the name, underlined "revised edition" and waited for it to be taken down in the new notebooks.

When the bent heads were raised again he began his speech of prospectus. "It is hard to explain –" he said, and paused as they composed themselves. "It is hard to explain what a course like this is intended to do. We are going to try to learn something about modern literature and something about prose composition."

As he spoke, his hands warmed and he was able to look directly at the class. Last year on the first day the faces had seemed just as cloddish, but as the term wore on they became gradually alive and quite likable. It did not seem possible that the same thing could happen again.

"I shall not lecture in this course," he continued. "Our work will be carried on by discussion and we will try to learn by an exchange of opinion. But you will soon recognize that my opinion is worth more than anyone else's here."

He remained grave as he said it, but two boys understood and laughed. The rest took permission from them and laughed too. All Howe's private ironies protested the vulgarity of the joke but the laughter made him feel benign and powerful.

When the little speech was finished, Howe picked up the pad of paper he had brought. He announced that they would write an extemporaneous theme. Its subject was traditional, "Who I am and why I came to Dwight College." By now the class was more at ease and it gave a ritualistic groan of protest. Then there was a stir as fountain pens were brought out and the writing arms of the chairs were cleared and the paper was passed about. At last all the heads bent to work and the room became still.

Howe sat idly at his desk. The sun shone through the tall clumsy windows. The cool of the morning was already passing. There was a scent of autumn and of varnish, and the stillness of the room was deep and oddly touching. Now and then a student's head was raised and scratched in the old elaborate students' pantomime that calls the teacher to witness honest intellectual effort.

Suddenly a tall boy stood within the frame of the open door. "Is this," he said, and thrust a large nose into a college catalogue, "is this the meeting place of English 1A? The section instructed by Dr. Joseph Howe?"

He stood on the very sill of the door, as if refusing to enter until he was perfectly sure of all his rights. The class looked up from work, found him absurd and gave a low mocking cheer.

The teacher and the new student, with equal pointedness, ignored the disturbance. Howe nodded to the boy, who pushed his head forward and then jerked it back in a wide elaborate arc to clear his brow of a heavy lock of hair. He advanced into the room and halted before Howe, almost at attention. In a loud clear voice he announced, "I am Tertan, Ferdinand R., reporting at the direction of Head of Department Vincent."

The heraldic formality of this statement brought forth another cheer. Howe looked at the class with a sternness he could not really feel, for there was indeed something ridiculous about this boy. Under his displeased regard the rows of heads dropped to work again. Then he touched Tertan's elbow, led him up to the desk and stood so as to shield their conversation from the class.

"We are writing an extemporaneous theme," he said. "The subject is, 'Who I am and why I came to Dwight College.' "

He stripped a few sheets from the pad and offered them to the boy. Tertan hesitated and then took the paper but he held it only tentatively. As if with the effort of making something clear, he gulped, and a slow smile fixed itself on his face. It was at once knowing and shy.

"Professor," he said, "to be perfectly fair to my classmates" – he made a large gesture over the room – "and to you" – he inclined his head to Howe – "this would not be for me an extemporaneous subject."

Howe tried to understand. "You mean you've already thought about it – you've heard we always give the same subject? That doesn't matter."

Again the boy ducked his head and gulped. It was the gesture of one who wishes to make a difficult explanation with perfect candor. "Sir," he said, and made the distinction with great care, "the topic I did not expect but I have given much ratiocination to the subject."

Howe smiled and said, "I don't think that's an unfair advantage. Just go ahead and write."

Tertan narrowed his eyes and glanced sidewise at Howe. His strange mouth smiled. Then in quizzical acceptance, he ducked his head, threw back the heavy dank lock, dropped into a seat with a great loose noise and began to write rapidly.

The room fell silent again and Howe resumed his idleness. When the bell rang, the students who had groaned when the task had been set now groaned again because they had not finished. Howe took up the papers and held the class while he made the first assignment. When he dismissed it, Tertan bore down on him, his slack mouth held ready for speech.

"Some professors," he said, "are pedants. They are Dryasdusts. However, some professors are free souls and creative spirits. Kant, Hegel and Nietzsche were all professors." With this pronouncement he paused. "It is my opinion," he continued, "that you occupy the second category."

Howe looked at the boy in surprise and said with good-natured irony, "With Kant, Hegel, and Nietzsche?"

Not only Tertan's hand and head but his whole awkward body waved away the stupidity. "It is the kind and not the quantity of the kind," he said sternly.

Rebuked, Howe said as simply and seriously as he could, "It would be nice to think so." He added, "Of course I am not a professor."

This was clearly a disappointment but Tertan met it. "In the French sense," he said with composure. "Generically, a teacher."

Suddenly he bowed. It was such a bow, Howe fancied, as a stage-director might teach an actor playing a medieval student who takes leave of Abelard – stiff, solemn, with elbows close to the body and feet together. Then, quite as suddenly, he turned and left.

A queer fish, and as soon as Howe reached his office he sifted through the batch of themes and drew out Tertan's. The boy had filled many sheets with his unformed headlong scrawl. "Who am I?" he had begun. "Here, in a mundane, not to say commercialized academe, is asked the question which from time long immemorably out of mind has accreted doubts and thoughts in the psyche of man to pester him as a nuisance. Whether in St. Augustine (or Austin as sometimes called) or Miss Bashkirtsieff or Frederic Amiel or Empedocles, or in less lights of the intellect than these, this posed question has been ineluctable."

Howe took out his pencil. He circled "academe" and wrote "vocab." in the margin. He underlined "time long immemorably out of mind" and wrote "Diction!" But this seemed inadequate for what was wrong. He put down his pencil and read ahead to discover the principle of error in the theme. "Today as ever, in spite of gloomy prophets of the dismal science (economics) the question is uninvalidated. Out of the starry depths of heaven hurtles this spear of query demanding to be caught on the shield of the mind ere it pierces the skull and the limbs be unstrung."

Baffled but quite caught, Howe read on. "Materialism, by which is meant the philosophic concept and not the moral idea, provides no aegis against the question which lies beyond the tangible (metaphysics). Existence without alloy is the question presented. Environment and heredity relegated aside, the rags and old clothes of practical life discarded, the name and the instrumentality of livelihood do not, as the prophets of the dismal science insist on in this connection, give solution to the interrogation which not from the professor merely but veritably from the cosmos is given. I think, therefore I am (cogito etc.) but who am I? Tertan I am, but what is Tertan? Of this time, of that place, of some parentage, what does it matter?"

Existence without alloy: the phrase established itself. Howe put aside Tertan's paper and at random picked up another. "I am Arthur J. Casebeer, Jr.," he read. "My father is Arthur J. Casebeer and my grandfather was Arthur J. Casebeer before him. My mother is Nina Wimble Casebeer. Both of them are college graduates and my father is in insurance. I was born in St. Louis eighteen years ago and we still make our residence there."

Arthur J. Casebeer, who knew who he was, was less interesting than Tertan, but more coherent. Howe picked up Tertan's paper again. It was clear that none of the routine marginal comments, no "sent. str." or "punct." or "vocab." could cope with this torrential rhetoric. He read ahead, contenting himself with underscoring the errors against the time when he should have the necessary "conference" with Tertan.

It was a busy and official day of cards and sheets, arrangements and small decisions and it gave Howe pleasure. Even when it was time to attend the first of the weekly Convocations he felt the charm of the beginning of things when intention is still innocent and uncorrupted by effort. He sat among the young instructors on the platform and joined in their humorous complaints at having to assist at the ceremony but actually he got a clear satisfaction from the ritual of prayer and prosy speech and even from wearing his academic gown. And when the Convocation was over the pleasure continued as he crossed the campus, exchanging greetings with men he had not seen since the spring. They were people who did not yet, and perhaps never would, mean much to him, but in a year they had grown amiably to be part of his life. They were his fellow townsmen.

The day had cooled again at sunset and there was a bright chill in the September twilight. Howe carried his voluminous gown over his arm, he swung his doctoral hood by its purple neckpiece and on his head he wore his mortarboard with its heavy gold tassel bobbing just over his eye. These were the weighty and absurd symbols of his new profession and they pleased him. At twenty-six Joseph Howe had discovered that he was neither so well off nor so bohemian as he had once thought. A small income, adequate when supplemented by a sizable cash legacy, was genteel poverty when the cash was all spent. And the literary life – the room at the Lafayette or the small apartment without a lease, the long summers on the Cape, the long afternoons and the social evenings – began to weary him. His writing filled his mornings and should perhaps have filled his life, yet it did not. To the amusement of his friends and with a certain sense that he was betraying his own freedom, he had used the last of his legacy for a year at Harvard. The small but respectable reputation of his two volumes of verse had proved useful – he continued at Harvard on a fellowship and when he emerged as Dr. Howe he received an excellent appointment, with prospects, at Dwight.

He had his moments of fear when all that had ever been said of the dangers of the academic life had occurred to him. But after a year in which he had tested every possibility of corruption and seduction he was ready to rest easy. His third volume of verse, most of it written in his first year of teaching, was not only ampler but, he thought, better than its predecessors.

There was a clear hour before the Bradby dinner party and Howe looked forward to it. But he was not to enjoy it, for lying with his mail on the hall table was a copy of this quarter's issue of *Life and Letters*, to which his landlord subscribed. Its severe cover announced that its editor, Frederic Woolley, had this month contributed an essay called "Two Poets," and Howe, picking it up, curious to see who the two poets might be, felt his own name start out at him with cabalistic power – Joseph Howe. As he continued to turn the pages his hand trembled.

Standing in the dark hall, holding the neat little magazine, Howe knew that his literary contempt for Frederic Woolley meant nothing, for he suddenly understood how he respected Woolley in the way of the world. He knew this by the trembling of his hand. And of the little world as well as the great, for although the literary groups of New York might dismiss Woolley, his name carried high authority in the academic world. At Dwight it was even a revered name, for it had been here at the college that Frederic Woolley had made the distinguished scholarly career from which he had gone on to literary journalism. In middle life he had been induced to take the editorship of *Life and Letters*, a literary monthly not widely read but heavily endowed and in its pages he had carried on the defense of what he sometimes called the older values. He was not without wit, he had great knowledge and considerable taste and even in the full movement of the "new" literature he had won a certain respect for his refusal to accept it. In France, even in England, he would have been connected with a more robust tradition of conservatism, but America gave him an audience not much better than genteel. It was known in the college that to the subsidy of *Life and Letters* the Bradbys contributed a great part.

As Howe read, he saw that he was involved in nothing less than an event. When the Fifth Series of *Studies in Order and Value* came to be collected, this latest of Frederic Woolley's essays would not be merely another step in the old direction. Clearly and unmistakably, it was a turning point. All his literary life Woolley had been concerned with the relation of literature to mortality, religion, and the private and delicate pieties and he had been unalterably opposed to all that he had called "inhuman humanitarianism." But here, suddenly, dramatically late, he had made an about-face, turning to the public life and to the humanitarian politics he had so long despised. This was the kind of incident the histories of literature make much of. Frederick Woolley was opening for himself a new career and winning a kind of new youth. He contrasted the two poets, Thomas Wormser who was admirable, Joseph Howe who was almost dangerous. He spoke of the "precious subjectivism" of Howe's verse. "In times like ours," he wrote, "with millions facing penury and want, one feels that the qualities of the *tour d'ivoire* are well-nigh inhuman, nearly insulting. The *tour d'ivoire* becomes the *tour d'ivresse* and it is not self-intoxicated poets that our people need." The essay said more:

> The problem is one of meaning. I am not ignorant that the creed of the
> esoteric poets declares that a poem does not and should not *mean* any-

thing, that it *is* something. But poetry is what the poet makes it, and if he is a true poet he makes what his society needs. And what is needed now is the tradition in which Mr. Wormser writes, the true tradition of poetry. The Howes do no harm, but they do no good when positive good is demanded of all responsible men. Or do the Howes indeed do no harm? Perhaps Plato would have said they do, that in some ways theirs is the Phrygian music that turns men's minds from the struggle. Certainly it is true that Thomas Wormser writes in the lucid Dorian mode which sends men into battle with evil.

It was easy to understand why Woolley had chosen to praise Thomas Wormser. The long, lilting lines of *Corn Under Willows* hymned, as Woolley put it, the struggle for wheat in the Iowa fields and expressed the real lives of real people. But why out of the dozen more notable examples he had chosen Howe's little volume as the example of "precious subjectivism" was hard to guess. In a way it was funny, this multiplication of himself into "the Howes." And yet this becoming the multiform political symbol by whose creation Frederic Woolley gave the sign of a sudden new life, this use of him as a sacrifice whose blood was necessary for the rites of rejuvenation, made him feel oddly unclean.

Nor could Howe get rid of a certain practical resentment. As a poet he had a special and respectable place in the college life. But it might be another thing to be marked as the poet of a wilful and selfish obscurity.

As he walked to the Bradbys', Howe was a little tense and defensive. It seemed to him that all the world knew of the "attack" and agreed with it. And indeed the Bradbys had read the essay but Professor Bradby, a kind and pretentious man, said, "I see my old friend knocked you about a bit, my boy," and his wife Eugenia looked at Howe with her childlike blue eyes and said, "I shall scold Frederic for the untrue things he wrote about you. You aren't the least obscure." They beamed at him. In their genial snobbery they seemed to feel that he had distinguished himself. He was the leader of Howeism. He enjoyed the dinner party as much as he had thought he would.

And in the following days, as he was more preoccupied with his duties, the incident was forgotten. His classes had ceased to be mere groups. Student after student detached himself from the mass and required or claimed a place in Howe's awareness. Of them all it was Tertan who first and most violently signalled his separate existence. A week after classes had begun Howe saw his silhouette on the frosted glass of his office door. It was motionless for a long time, perhaps stopped by the problem of whether or not to knock before entering. Howe called, "Come in!" and Tertan entered with his shambling stride.

He stood beside the desk, silent and at attention. When Howe asked him to sit down, he responded with a gesture of head and hand as if to say that such amenities were beside the point. Nevertheless he did take the chair. He put his ragged crammed briefcase between his legs. His face, which Howe now observed fully for the first time, was confusing, for it was made up of florid curves, the nose arched in the bone and voluted in the nostril, the mouth loose and soft and rather moist. Yet the face was so thin and narrow as to seem the very type of asceticism. Lashes of unusual length veiled the eyes and, indeed, it seemed as if there were a veil over the whole countenance. Before the words actually came, the face screwed itself into an attitude of preparation for them.

"You can confer with me now?" Tertan said.

"Yes, I'd be glad to. There are several things in your two themes I want to talk to you about." Howe reached for the packet of themes on his desk and sought for Tertan's. But the boy was waving them away.

"These are done perforce," he said. "Under the pressure of your requirement. They are not significant, mere duties." Again his great hand flapped vaguely to dismiss his themes. He leaned forward and gazed at his teacher.

"You are," he said, "a man of letters? You are a poet?" It was more declaration than question.

"I should like to think so," Howe said.

At first Tertan accepted the answer with a show of appreciation, as though the understatement made a secret between himself and Howe. Then he chose to misunderstand. With his shrewd and disconcerting control of expression, he presented to Howe a puzzled grimace. "What does that mean?" he said.

Howe retracted the irony. "Yes. I am a poet." It sounded strange to say.

"That," Tertan said, "is a wonder." He corrected himself with his ducking head. "I mean that is wonderful."

Suddenly he dived at the miserable briefcase between his legs, put it on his knees and began to fumble with the catch, all intent on the difficulty it presented. Howe noted that his suit was worn thin, his shirt almost unclean. He became aware, even, of a vague and musty odor of garments worn too long in unaired rooms. Tertan conquered the lock and began to concentrate upon a search into the interior. At last he held in his hand what he was after, a torn and crumpled copy of *Life and Letters*.

"I learned it from here," he said, holding it out.

Howe looked at him sharply, his hackles a little up. But the boy's face was not only perfectly innocent, it even shone with a conscious admiration. Apparently nothing of the import of the essay had touched him except the wonderful fact that his teacher was a "man of letters." Yet this seemed too stupid and Howe, to test it, said, "The man who wrote that doesn't think it's wonderful."

Tertan made a moist hissing sound as he cleared his mouth of saliva. His head, oddly loose on his neck, wove a pattern of contempt in the air. "A critic," he said, "who admits *prima facie* that he does not understand." Then he said grandly, "It is the inevitable fate."

It was absurd, yet Howe was not only aware of the absurdity but of a tension suddenly and wonderfully relaxed. Now that the "attack" was on the table between himself and this strange boy and subject to the boy's funny and absolutely certain contempt, the hidden force of his feeling was revealed to him in the very moment that it vanished. All unsuspected, there had been a film over the world, a transparent but discoloring haze of danger. But he had no time to stop over the brightened aspect of things. Tertan was going on. "I also am a man of letters. Putative."

"You have written a good deal?" Howe meant to be no more than polite and he was surprised at the tenderness he heard in his words.

Solemnly the boy nodded, threw back the dank lock and sucked in a deep anticipatory breath. "First, a work of homiletics, which is a defense of the principles of religious optimism against the pessimism of Schopenhauer and the humanism of Nietzsche."

"Humanism? Why do you call it humanism?"

"It is my nomenclature for making a deity of man," Tertan replied negligently. "Then three fictional works, novels. And numerous essays in science, combating materialism. Is it your duty to read these if I bring them to you?"

Howe answered simply, "No, it isn't exactly my duty but I shall be happy to read them."

Tertan stood up and remained silent. He rested his bag on the chair. With a certain compunction – for it did not seem entirely proper that, of two men of letters, one should have the right to blue-pencil the other, to grade him or to question the quality of his "sentence structure" – Howe reached for Tertan's papers. But before he could take them up, the boy suddenly made his bow-to-Abelard, the stiff inclination of the body with the hands seeming to emerge from the scholar's gown. Then he was gone.

But after his departure something was still left of him. The timbre of his curious sentences, the downright finality of so quaint a phrase as "It is the inevitable fate" still rang in the air. Howe gave the warmth of his feeling to the new visitor who stood at the door announcing himself with a genteel clearing of the throat.

"Dr. Howe, I believe?" the student said. A large hand advanced into the room and grasped Howe's hand. "Blackburn, sir, Theodore Blackburn, vice-president of the Student Council. A great pleasure, sir."

Out of a pair of ruddy cheeks a pair of small eyes twinkled good-naturedly. The large face, the large body were not so much fat as beefy and suggested something "typical," monk, politician, or innkeeper.

Blackburn took the seat beside Howe's desk. "I may have seemed to introduce myself in my public capacity, sir," he said. "But it is really as an individual that I came to see you. That is to say, as one of your students to be."

He spoke with an "English" intonation and he went on, "I was once an English major, sir."

For a moment Howe was startled, for the roast-beef look of the boy and the manner of his speech gave a second's credibility to one sense of his statement. Then the collegiate meaning of the phrase asserted itself, but some perversity made Howe say what was not really in good taste even with so forward a student, "Indeed? what regiment?"

Blackburn stared and then gave a little pouf-pouf of laughter. He waved the misapprehension away. "*Very* good, sir. It certainly is an ambiguous term." He chuckled in appreciation of Howe's joke, then cleared his throat to put it aside. "I look forward to taking your course in the romantic poets, sir," he said earnestly. "To me the romantic poets are the very crown of English literature."

Howe made a dry sound, and the boy, catching some meaning in it, said, "Little as I know them, of course. But even Shakespeare who is so dear to us of the Anglo-Saxon tradition is in a sense but the preparation for Shelley, Keats and Byron. And Wadsworth."

Almost sorry for him, Howe dropped his eyes. With some embarrassment, for the boy was not actually his student, he said softly, "Wordsworth."

"Sir?"

"Wordsworth, not Wadsworth. You said Wadsworth."

"Did I, sir?" Gravely he shook his head to rebuke himself for the error. "Wordsworth, of course – slip of the tongue." Then, quite in command again, he went on. "I have a favor to ask of you, Dr. Howe. You see, I began my college course as an English major," – he smiled – "as I said."

"Yes?"

"But after my first year I shifted. I shifted to the social sciences. Sociology and government – I find them stimulating and very *real*." He paused, out of respect for reality. "But now I find that perhaps I have neglected the other side."

"The other side?" Howe said.

"Imagination, fancy, culture. A well-rounded man." He trailed off as if there were perfect understanding between them. "And so, sir, I have decided to end my senior year with your course in the romantic poets."

His voice was filled with an indulgence which Howe ignored as he said flatly and gravely, "But that course isn't given until the spring term."

"Yes, sir, and that is where the favor comes in. Would you let me take your romantic prose course? I can't take it for credit, sir, my program is full, but just for background it seems to me that I ought to take it. I do hope," he concluded in a manly way, "that you will consent."

"Well, it's no great favor, Mr. Blackburn. You can come if you wish, though there's not much point in it if you don't do the reading."

The bell rang for the hour and Howe got up.

"May I begin with this class, sir?" Blackburn's smile was candid and boyish.

Howe nodded carelessly and together, silently, they walked to the classroom down the hall. When they reached the door Howe stood back to let his student enter, but Blackburn moved adroitly behind him and grasped him by the arm to urge him over the threshold. They entered together with Blackburn's hand firmly on Howe's biceps, the student inducting the teacher into his own room. Howe felt a surge of temper rise in him and almost violently he disengaged his arm and walked to the desk, while Blackburn found a seat in the front row and smiled at him.

II

The question was, At whose door must the tragedy be laid?

All night the snow had fallen heavily and only now was abating in sparse little flurries. The windows were valanced high with white. It was very quiet, something of the quiet of the world had reached the class and Howe found that everyone was glad to talk or listen. In the room there was a comfortable sense of pleasure in being human.

Casebeer believed that the blame for the tragedy rested with heredity. Picking up the book he read, "The sins of the fathers are visited on their children." This opinion was received with general favor. Nevertheless Johnson ventured to say that the fault was all Pastor Manders' because the Pastor had made Mrs. Alving go back to her husband and was always hiding the truth. To this Hibbard objected with logic enough, "Well then, it was really all her husband's fault. He *did* all the bad things." De Witt, his face bright with an impatient idea, said that the fault was all society's. "By society I don't mean upper-crust society," he said. He looked around a little defiantly, taking in any members of the class who might be members of upper-crust society. "Not in that sense. I mean the social unit."

Howe nodded and said, "Yes, of course."

"If the society of the time had progressed far enough in science," De Witt went on, "then there would be no problem for Mr. Ibsen to write about. Captain Alving plays around a little, gives way to perfectly natural biological urges, and he gets a social disease, a venereal disease. If the disease is cured, no problem. Invent salvarsan and the disease is cured. The problem of heredity disappears and li'l Oswald just doesn't get paresis. No paresis, no problem – no problem, no play." This was carrying the ark into battle and the class looked at De Witt with respectful curiosity. It was his usual way and on the whole they were sympathetic with his struggle to prove to Howe that science was better than literature. Still, there was something in his reckless manner that alienated them a little.

"Or take birth control, for instance," De Witt went on. "If Mrs. Alving had some knowledge of contraception, she wouldn't have had to have li'l Oswald at all. No li'l Oswald, no play."

The class was suddenly quieter. In the back row Stettenhover swung his great football shoulders in a righteous sulking gesture, first to the right, then to the left. He puckered his mouth ostentatiously. Intellect was always ending up by talking dirty.

Tertan's hand went up and Howe said, "Mr. Tertan." The boy shambled to his feet and began his long characteristic gulp. Howe made a motion with his fingers, as small as possible, and Tertan ducked his head and smiled in apology. He sat down. The class laughed. With more than half the term gone, Tertan had not been able to remember that one did not rise to speak. He seemed unable to carry on the life of the intellect without this mark of respect for it. To Howe the boy's habit of rising seemed to accord with the formal shabbiness of his dress. He never wore the casual sweaters and jackets of his classmates. Into the free and comfortable air of the college classroom he brought the stuffy sordid strictness of some crowded metropolitan high school.

"Speaking from one sense," Tertan began slowly, "there is no blame ascribable. From the sense of determinism, who can say where the blame lies? The preordained is the preordained and it cannot be said without rebellion against the universe, a palpable absurdity."

In the back row Stettenhover slumped suddenly in his seat, his heels held out before him, making a loud dry disgusted sound. His body sank until his neck rested on the back of his chair. He folded his hands across his belly and looked significantly out of the window, exasperated not only with Tertan but with Howe, with the class, with the whole system designed to encourage this kind of thing. There was a certain insolence in the movement and Howe flushed. As Tertan continued to speak, Howe stalked casually toward the window and placed himself in the line of Stettenhover's vision. He stared at the great fellow, who pretended not to see him. There was so much power in the big body, so much contempt in the Greek-athlete face under the crisp Greek-athlete curls, that Howe felt almost physical fear. But at last Stettenhover admitted him to focus and under his disapproving gaze sat up with slow indifference. His eyebrows raised high in resignation, he began to examine his hands. Howe relaxed and turned his attention back to Tertan.

"Flux of existence," Tertan was saying, "produces all things, so that judgment wavers. Beyond the phenomena, what? But phenomena are adumbrated and to them we are limited."

Howe saw it for a moment as perhaps it existed in the boy's mind – the world of shadows which are cast by a great light upon a hidden reality as in the old myth of the cave. But the little brush with Stettenhover had tired him and he said irritably, "But come to the point, Mr. Tertan."

He said it so sharply that some of the class looked at him curiously. For three months he had gently carried Tertan through his verbosities, to the vaguely respectful surprise of the other students, who seemed to conceive that there existed between this strange classmate and their teacher some special understanding from which they were content to be excluded. Tertan looked at him mildly and at once came brilliantly to the point. "This is the summation of the play," he said and took up his book and read, "'Your poor father never found any outlet for the over-mastering joy of life that was in him. And I brought no holiday into his home, either. Everything seemed to turn upon duty and I am afraid I made your poor father's home unbearable to him, Oswald.' Spoken by Mrs. Alving."

Yes, that was surely the "summation" of the play and Tertan had hit it, as he hit, deviously and eventually, the literary point of almost everything. But now, as always, he was wrapping it away from sight. "For most mortals," he said, "there are only joys of biological urgings, gross and crass, such as the sensuous Captain Alving. For certain few there are the transmutations beyond these to a contemplation of the utter whole."

Oh, the boy was mad. And suddenly the word, used in hyperbole, intended almost for the expression of exasperated admiration, became literal. Now that the word was used, it became simply apparent to Howe that Tertan was mad.

It was a monstrous word and stood like a bestial thing in the room. Yet it so completely comprehended everything that had puzzled Howe, it so arranged and explained what for three months had been perplexing him that almost at once its horror became domesticated. With this word Howe was able to understand why he had never been able to communicate to Tertan the value of a single criticism or correction of his wild, verbose themes. Their conferences had been frequent and long but had done nothing to reduce to order the splendid confusion of the boy's ideas. Yet, impossible though its expression was, Tertan's incandescent mind could always strike for a moment into some dark corner of thought.

And now it was suddenly apparent that it was not a faulty rhetoric that Howe had to contend with. With his new knowledge he looked at Tertan's face and wondered how he could have so long deceived himself. Tertan was still talking and the class had lapsed into a kind of patient unconsciousness, a coma of respect for words which, for all that most of them knew, might be profound. Almost with a suffusion of shame, Howe believed that in some dim way the class had long ago had some intimation of Tertan's madness. He reached out as decisively as he could to seize the thread of Tertan's discourse before it should be entangled further.

"Mr. Tertan says that the blame must be put upon whoever kills the joy of living in another. We have been assuming that Captain Alving was a wholly bad man, but what if we assume that he became bad only because Mrs. Alving, when they were first married, acted toward him in the prudish way she says she did?"

It was a ticklish idea to advance to freshmen and perhaps not profitable. Not all of them were following.

"That would put the blame on Mrs. Alving herself, whom most of you admire. And she herself seems to think so." He glanced at his watch. The hour was nearly over. "What do you think, Mr. De Witt?"

De Witt rose to the idea, he wanted to know if society couldn't be blamed for educating Mrs. Alving's temperament in the wrong way. Casebeer was puzzled, Stettenhover continued to look at his hands until the bell rang.

Tertan, his brows louring in thought, was making as always for a private word. Howe gathered his books and papers to leave quickly. At this moment of his discovery and with the knowledge still raw, he could not engage himself with Tertan. Tertan sucked in his breath to prepare for speech and Howe made ready for the pain and confusion. But at that moment Casebeer detached himself from the group with which he had been conferring and which he seemed to represent. His constituency remained at a tactful distance. The mission involved the time of an assigned essay. Casebeer's presentation of the plea – it was based on the freshmen's heavy duties at the fraternities during Carnival Week – cut across Tertan's preparations for speech. "And so some of us fellows thought," Casebeer concluded with heavy solemnity, "that we could do a better job, give our minds to it more, if we had more time."

Tertan regarded Casebeer with mingled curiosity and revulsion. Howe not only said that he would postpone the assignment but went on to talk about the carnival and even drew the waiting constituency into the conversation. He was conscious of Tertan's stern and astonished stare, then of his sudden departure.

Now that the fact was clear, Howe knew that he must act on it. His course was simple enough. He must lay the case before the Dean. Yet he hesitated. His feeling for Tertan must now, certainly, be in some way invalidated. Yet could he, because of a word, hurry to assign to official and reasonable solicitude what had been, until this moment, so various and warm? He could at least delay and, by moving slowly, lend a poor grace to the necessary, ugly act of making his report.

It was with some notion of keeping the matter in his own hands that he went to the Dean's office to look up Tertan's records. In the outer office the Dean's secretary greeted him brightly and at his request brought him the manila folder with the small identifying photograph pasted in the corner. She laughed "He was looking for the birdie in the wrong place," she said.

Howe leaned over her shoulder to look at the picture. It was as bad as all the Dean's-office photographs were, but it differed from all that Howe had ever seen. Tertan, instead of looking into the camera, as no doubt he had been bidden, had, at the moment of exposure, turned his eyes upward. His mouth, as though conscious of the trick played on the photographer, had the shy superior look that Howe knew.

The secretary was fascinated by the picture. "What a funny boy," she said. "He looks like Tartuffe!"

And so he did, with the absurd piety of the eyes and the conscious slyness of the mouth and the whole face bloated by the bad lens.

"Is he *like* that?" the secretary said.

"Like Tartuffe? No."

From the photograph there was little enough comfort to be had. The records themselves gave no clue to madness, though they suggested sadness enough. Howe read of a father, Stanislaus Tertan, born in Budapest and trained in engineering in Berlin, once employed by the Hercules Chemical Corporation – this was one of the factories that dominated the sound end of the town – but now without employment. He read of a mother Erminie (Youngfellow) Tertan, born in Manchester, educated at a Normal School at Leeds, now housewife by profession. The family lived on Greenbriar Street which Howe knew as a row of once elegant homes near what was now the factory district. The old mansions had long ago been divided into small and primitive apartments. Of Ferdinand himself there was little to learn. He lived with his parents, had attended a Detroit high school and had transferred to the local school in his last year. His rating for intelligence, as expressed in numbers, was high, his scholastic record was remarkable, he held a college scholarship for his tutition.

Howe laid the folder on the secretary's desk. "Did you find what you wanted to know?" she asked.

The phrases from Tertan's momentous first theme came back to him. "Tertan I am, but what is Tertan? Of this time, of that place, of some parentage, what does it matter?"

"No, I didn't find it," he said.

Now that he had consulted the sad half-meaningless record he knew all the more firmly that he must not give the matter out of his own hands. He must not release Tertan to authority. Not that he anticipated from the Dean anything but the greatest kindness for Tertan. The Dean would have the experience and skill which he himself couhd not have. One way or another the Dean could answer the question, "What is Tertan?" Yet this was precisely what he feared. He alone could keep alive – not forever but for a somehow important time – the question, "What is Tertan?" He alone could keep it still a question. Some sure instinct told him that he must not surrender the question to a clean official desk in a clear official light to be dealt with, settled and closed.

He heard himself saying, "Is the Dean busy at the moment? I'd like to see him."

His request came thus unbidden, even forbidden, and it was one of the surprising and startling incidents of his life. Later, when he reviewed the events, so disconnected in themselves or so merely odd, of the story that unfolded for him that year, it was over this moment, on its face the least notable, that he paused longest. It was frequently to be with fear and never without a certainty of its meaning in his own knowledge of himself that he would recall this simple, routine request and the feeling of shame and freedom it gave him as he sent everything down the official chute. In the end, of course, no matter what he did to "protect" Tertan, he would have had to make the same request and lay the matter on the Dean's clean desk. But it would always be a landmark of his life that, at the very moment when he was rejecting the official way, he had been, without will or intention, so gladly drawn to it.

After the storm's last delicate flurry, the sun had come out. Reflected by the new snow, it filled the office with a golden light which was almost musical in the way it made all the commonplace objects of efficiency shine with a sudden sad and noble significance. And the light, now that he noticed it, made the utterance of his perverse and unwanted request even more momentous.

The secretary consulted the engagement pad. "He'll be free any minute. Don't you want to wait in the parlor?"

She threw open the door of the large and pleasant room in which the Dean held his Committee meetings and in which his visitors waited. It was designed with a homely elegance on the masculine side of the eighteenth century manner. There was a small coal-fire in the grate and the handsome mahogany table was strewn with books and magazines. The large windows gave on the snowy lawn and there was such a fine width of window that the white casements and walls seemed at this moment but a continuation of the snow, the snow but an extension of casement and walls. The outdoors seemed taken in and made safe, the indoors seemed luxuriously freshened and expanded.

Howe sat down by the fire and lighted a cigarette. The room had its intended effect upon him. He felt comfortable and relaxed, yet nicely organized, some young diplomatic agent of the eighteenth century, the newly fledged Swift carrying out Sir William Temple's business. The rawness of Tertan's case quite vanished. He crossed his legs and reached for a magazine.

It was that famous issue of *Life and Letters* that his idle hand had found and his blood raced as he sifted through it and the shape of his own name, Joseph Howe, sprang out at him, still cabalistic in its power. He tossed the magazine back on the table as the door of the Dean's office opened and the Dean ushered out Theodore Blackburn.

"Ah, Joseph!" the Dean said.

Blackburn said, "Good morning, Doctor." Howe winced at the title and caught the flicker of amusement over the Dean's face. The Dean stood with his hand high on the doorjamb and Blackburn, still in the doorway, remained standing almost under his long arm.

Howe nodded briefly to Blackburn, snubbing his eager deference. "Can you give me a few minutes?" he said to the Dean.

"All the time you want. Come in." Before the two men could enter the office, Blackburn claimed their attention with a long full "Er." As they turned to him, Blackburn said, "Can *you* give *me* a few minutes, Dr. Howe?" His eyes sparkled at the little audacity he had committed, the slightly impudent play with hierarchy. Of the three of them Blackburn kept himself the lowest, but he reminded Howe of his subaltern relation to the Dean.

"I mean, of course," Blackburn went on easily, "when you've finished with the Dean."

"I'll be in my office shortly," Howe said, turned his back on the ready "Thank you, sir," and followed the Dean into the inner room.

"Energetic boy," said the Dean. "A bit beyond himself but very energetic. Sit down."

The Dean lighted a cigarette, leaned back in his chair, sat easy and silent for a moment, giving Howe no signal to go ahead with business. He was a young Dean, not much beyond forty, a tall handsome man with sad, ambitious eyes. He had been a Rhodes scholar. His friends looked for great things from him and it was generally said that he had notions of education which he was not yet ready to try to put into practice.

His relaxed silence was meant as a compliment to Howe. He smiled and said, "What's the business, Joseph?"

"Do you know Tertan – Ferdinand Tertan, a freshman?"

The Dean's cigarette was in his mouth and his hands were chasped behind his head. He did not seem to search his memory for the name. He said, "What about him?"

Clearly the Dean knew something and he was waiting for Howe to tell him more. Howe moved only tentatively. Now that he was doing what he had resolved not to do, he felt more guilty at having been so long deceived by Tertan and more need to be hoyal to his error.

"He's a strange fellow," he ventured. He said stubbornly, "In a strange way he's very brilliant." He concluded, "But very strange."

The springs of the Dean's swivel chair creaked as he came out of his sprawl and leaned forward to Howe. "Do you mean he's so strange that it's something you could give a name to?"

Howe looked at him stupidly. "What do you mean?" he said.

"What's his trouble?" the Dean said more neutrally.

"He's very brilliant, in a way. I looked him up and he has a top intelligence rating. But somehow, and it's hard to explain just how, what he says is always on the edge of sense and doesn't quite make it."

The Dean looked at him and Howe flushed up. The Dean had surely read Woolley on the subject of "the Howes" and the *tour d'ivresse*. Was that quick glance ironical?

The Dean picked up some papers from his desk and Howe could see that they were in Tertan's impatient scrawl. Perhaps the little gleam in the Dean's glance had come only from putting facts together.

"He sent me this yesterday," the Dean said. "After an interview I had with him. I haven't been able to do more than glance at it. When you said what you did, I realized there was something wrong."

Twisting his mouth, the Dean looked over the letter. "You seem to be involved," he said without looking up. "By the way, what did you give him at mid-term?"

Flushing, setting his shoulders, Howe said firmly, "I gave him A-minus."

The Dean chuckled. "Might be a good idea if some of our nicer boys went crazy – just a little." He said, "Well," to conclude the matter and handed the papers to Howe. "See if this is the same thing you've been finding. Then we can go into the matter again."

Before the fire in the parlor, in the chair that Howe had been occupying, sat Blackburn. He sprang to his feet as Howe entered.

"I said my office, Mr. Blackburn." Howe's voice was sharp. Then he was almost sorry for the rebuke, so clearly and naively did Blackburn seem to relish his stay in the parlor, close to authority.

"I'm in a bit of a hurry, sir," he said, "and I did want to be sure to speak to you, sir."

He was really absurd, yet fifteen years from now he would have grown up to himself, to the assurance and mature beefiness. In banks, in consular offices, in brokerage firms, on the bench, more seriously affable, a little sterner, he would make use of his ability to be administered by his job. It was almost reassuring. Now he was exercising his too-great skill on Howe. "I owe you an apology, sir," he said.

Howe knew that he did but he showed surprise.

"I mean, Doctor, after your having been so kind about letting me attend your class, I stopped coming." he smiled in deprecation. "Extra-curricular activities take up so much of my time. I'm afraid I undertook more than I could perform."

Howe had noticed the absence and had been a little irritated by it after Blackburn's elaborate plea. It was an absence that might be interpreted as a comment on the teacher. But there was only one way for him to answer. "You've no need to apologize," he said. "It's wholly your affair."

Blackburn beamed. "I'm so glad you feel that way about it, sir. I was worried you might think I had stayed away because I was influenced by –" He stopped and lowered his eyes.

Astonished, Howe said, "Influenced by what?"

"Well, by –" Blackburn hesitated and for answer pointed to the table on which lay the copy of *Life and Letters*. Without looking at it, he knew where to direct his hand. "By the unfavorable publicity, sir." He hurried on. "And that brings me to another point, sir. I am vice-president of Quill and Scroll, sir, the student literary society, and I wonder if you would address us. You could read your own poetry, sir, and defend your own point of view. It would be very interesting."

It was truly amazing. Howe looked long and cruelly into Blackburn's face, trying to catch the secret of the mind that could have conceived this way of manipulating him, this way so daring and inept – but not entirely inept – with its malice so without malignity. The face did not yield its secret. Howe smiled broadly and said, "Of course I don't think you were influenced by the unfavorable publicity."

"I'm still going to take – regularly, for credit – your romantic poets course next term," Blackburn said.

"Don't worry, my dear fellow, don't worry about it."

Howe started to leave and Blackburn stopped him with, "But about Quill, sir?"

"Suppose we wait until next term? I'll be less busy then."

And Blackburn said, "Very good, sir, and thank you."

In his office the little encounter seemed less funny to Howe, was even in some indeterminate way disturbing. He made an effort to put it from his mind by turning to what was sure to disturb him more, the Tertan letter read in the new interpretation. He found what he had always found, the same florid leaps beyond fact and meaning, the same headlong certainty. But as his eye passed over the familiar scrawl it caught his own name and for the second time that hour he felt the race of his blood.

"The Paraclete," Tertan had written to the Dean, "from a Greek word meaning to stand in place of, but going beyond the primitive idea to mean traditionally the helper, the one who comforts and assists, cannot without fundamental loss be jettisoned. Even if taken no longer in the supernatural sense, the concept remains deeply in the human consciousness inevitably. Humanitarianism is no reply, for not every man stands in the place of every other man for this other's comrade comfort. But certain are chosen out of the human race to be the consoler of some other. Of these, for example, is Joseph Barker Howe, Ph.D. Of intellects not the first yet of true intellect and lambent instructions, given to that which is intuitive and irrational, not to what is logical in the strict word, what is judged by him is of the heart and not the head. Here is one chosen, in that he chooses himself to stand in the place of another for comfort and consolation. To him more than another I give my gratitude, with all respect to our Dean who reads this, a noble man, but merely dedicated, not consecrated. But not in the aspect of the Paraclete only is Dr. Joseph Barker Howe established, for he must be the Paraclete to another aspect of himself, that which is driven and persecuted by the lack of understanding in the world at large, so that he in himself embodies the full history of man's tribulations and, overflowing upon others, notably the present writer, is the ultimate end."

This was love. There was no escape from it. Try as Howe might to remember that Tertan was mad and all his emotions invalidated, he could not destroy the effect upon him of his student's stern, affectionate regard. He had betrayed not only a power of mind but a power of love. And however firmly he held before his attention the fact of Tertan's madness, he could do nothing to banish the physical sensation of gratitude he felt. He had never thought of himself as "driven and persecuted" and he did not now. But still he could not make meaningless his sensation of gratitude. The pitiable Tertan sternly pitied him, and comfort came from Tertan's never-to-be-comforted mind.

III

In an academic community, even an efficient one, official matters move slowly. The term drew to a close with no action in the case of Tertan, and Joseph Howe had to confront a curious problem. How should he grade his strange student, Tertan?

Tertan's final examination had been no different from all his other writing, and what did one "give" such a student? De Witt must have his A, that was clear.

Johnson would get a B. With Casebeer it was a question of a B-minus or a C-plus, and Stettenhover, who had been crammed by the team tutor to fill half a blue book with his thin feminine scrawl, would have his C-minus which he would accept with mingled indifference and resentment. But with Tertan it was not so easy.

The boy was still in the college process and his name could not be omitted from the grade sheet. Yet what should a mind under suspicion of madness be graded? Until the medical verdict was given, it was for Howe to continue as Tertan's teacher and to keep his judgment pedagogical. Impossible to give him an F: he had not failed. B was for Johnson's stolid mediocrity. He could not be put on the edge of passing with Stettenhover, for he exactly did not pass. In energy and richness of intellect he was perhaps even De Witt's superior, and Howe toyed grimly with the notion of giving him an A, but that would lower the value of the A De Witt had won with his beautiful and clear, if still arrogant, mind. There was a notation which the Registrar recognized – Inc. for Incomplete and in the horrible comedy of the situation, Howe considered that. But really only a mark of M for Mad would serve.

In his perplexity, Howe sought the Dean, but the Dean was out of town. In the end, he decided to maintain the A-minus he had given Tertan at midterm. After all, there had been no falling away from that quality. He entered it on the grade sheet with something like bravado.

Academic time moves quickly. A college year is not really a year, lacking as it does three months. And it is endlessly divided into units which, at their beginning, appear larger than they are – terms, half-terms, months, weeks. And the ultimate unit, the hour, is not really an hour, lacking as it does ten minutes. And so the new term advanced rapidly and one day the fields about the town were all brown, cleared of even the few thin patches of snow which had lingered so long.

Howe, as he lectured on the romantic poets, became conscious of Blackburn emanating wrath. Blackburn did it well, did it with enormous dignity. He did not stir in his seat, he kept his eyes fixed on Howe in perfect attention, but he abstained from using his notebook, there was no mistaking what he proposed to himself as an attitude. His elbow on the writing-wing of the chair, his chin on the curled fingers of his hand, he was the embodiment of intellectual indignation. He was thinking his own thoughts, would give no public offence, yet would claim his due, was not to be intimidated. Howe knew that he would present himself at the end of the hour.

Blackburn entered the office without invitation. He did not smile, there was no cajolery about him. Without invitation he sat down beside Howe's desk. He did not speak until he had taken the blue book from his pocket. He said, "what does this mean, sir?"

It was a sound and conservative student tactic. Said in the usual way it meant, "How could you have so misunderstood me?" or "What does this mean for my future in the course?" But there were none of the humbler tones in Blackburn's way of saying it.

Howe made the established reply, "I think that's for you to tell me."

Blackburn continued icy. "I'm sure I can't, sir."

There was a silence between them. Both dropped their eyes to the blue book on the desk. On its cover Howe had penciled: "F. This is very poor work."

Howe picked up the blue book. There was always the possibility of injustice. The teacher may be bored by the mass of papers and not wholly attentive. A phrase, even the student's handwriting, may irritate him unreasonably. "Well," said Howe, "let's go through it."

He opened the first page. "Now here: you write, 'In "The Ancient Mariner,"
Coleridge lives in and transports us to a honey-sweet world where all is rich and
strange, a world of charm to which we can escape from the humdrum existence of
our daily lives, the world of romance. Here, in this warm and honey-sweet land of
charming dreams we can relax and enjoy ourselves.'"

Howe lowered the paper and waited with a neutral look for Blackburn to speak.
Blackburn returned the look boldly, did not speak, sat stolid and lofty. At last Howe
said, speaking gently, "Did you mean that, or were you just at a loss for something
to say?"

"You imply that I was just 'bluffing'?" The quotation marks hung palpable in the
air about the word.

"I'd like to know. I'd prefer believing that you were bluffing to believing that
you really thought this."

Blackburn's eyebrows went up. From the height of a great and firm-based idea
he looked at his teacher. He clasped the crags for a moment and then pounced,
craftily, suavely. "Do you mean, Dr. Howe, that there aren't two opinions possible?"

It was superbly done in its air of putting all of Howe's intellectual life into the
balance. Howe remained patient and simple. "Yes, many opinions are possible, but
not this one. Whatever anyone believes of 'the Ancient Mariner,' no one can in
reason believe that it represents a – a honey-sweet world in which we can relax."

"But that is what I *feel*, sir."

This was well done too. Howe said, "Look, Mr. Blackburn. Do you really relax
with hunger and thirst, the heat and the sea-serpents, the dead men with staring
eyes, Life in Death and the skeletons? Come now, Mr. Blackburn."

Blackburn made no answer and Howe pressed forward. "Now you say of
Wordsworth, 'Of peasant stock himself, he turned from the effete life of the salons
and found in the peasant the hope of a flaming revolution which would sweep away
all the old ideas. This is the subject of his best poems.'"

Beaming at his teacher with youthful eagerness, Blackburn said, "Yes, sir, a rebel,
a bringer of light to suffering mankind. I see him as a kind of Prothemeus."

"A kind of what?"

"Prothemeneus, sir."

"Think, Mr. Blackburn. We were talking about him only today and I mentioned
his name a dozen times. You don't mean Prothemeus. You mean –" Howe waited
but there was no response.

"You mean Prometheus."

Blackburn gave no assent and Howe took the reins. "You've done a bad job here,
Mr. Blackburn, about as bad as could be done." He saw Blackburn stiffen and his
genial face harden again. "It shows either a lack of preparation or a complete lack of
understanding." He saw Blackburn's face begin to go to pieces and he stopped.

"Oh, sir," Blackburn burst out, "I've never had a mark like this before, never
anything below a B, never. A thing like this has never happened to me before."

It must be true, it was a statement too easily verified. Could it be that other
instructors accepted such flaunting nonsense? Howe wanted to end the interview.
"I'll set it down to lack of preparation," he said. "I know you're busy. That's not an
excuse but it's an explanation. Now suppose you really prepare and then take
another quiz in two weeks. We'll forget this one and count the other."

Blackburn squirmed with pleasure and gratitude. "Thank you, sir. You're really
very kind, very kind."

Howe rose to conclude the visit. "All right then – in two weeks."

It was that day that the Dean imparted to Howe the conclusion of the case of Tertan. It was simple and a little anticlimactic. A physician had been called in, and had said the word, given the name.

"A classic case, he called it," the Dean said. "Not a doubt in the world," he said. His eyes were full of miserable pity and he clutched at a word. "A classic case, a classic case." To his aid and to Howe's there came the Parthenon and the form of the Greek drama, the Aristotelian logic, Racine and the Well-Tempered Clavichord, the blueness of the Aegean and its clear sky. Classic – that is to say, without a doubt, perfect in its way, a veritable model, and, as the Dean had been told, sure to take a perfectly predictable and inevitable course to a foreknown conclusion.

It was not only pity that stood in the Dean's eyes. For a moment there was fear too. "Terrible," he said, "it is simply terrible."

Then he went on briskly. "Naturally we've told the boy nothing. And naturally we won't. His tuition's paid by his scholarship and we'll continue him on the rolls until the end of the year. That will be kindest. After that the matter will be out of our control. We'll see, of course, that he gets into the proper hands. I'm told there will be no change, he'll go on like this, be as good as this, for four to six months. And so we'll just go along as usual."

So Tertan continued to sit in Section 5 of English 1A, to his classmates still a figure of curiously dignified fun, symbol to most of them of the respectable but absurd intellectual life. But to his teacher he was now very different. He had not changed – he was still the greyhound casting for the scent of ideas and Howe could see that he was still the same Tertan, but he could not feel it. What he felt as he looked at the boy sitting in his accustomed place was the hard blank of a fact. The fact itself was formidable and depressing. But what Howe was chiefly aware of was that he had permitted the metamorphosis of Tertan from person to fact.

As much as possible he avoided seeing Tertan's upraised hand and eager eye. But the fact did not know of its mere factuality, it continued its existence as if it were Tertan, hand up and eye questioning, and one day it appeared in Howe's office with a document.

"Even the spirit who lives egregiously, above the herd, must have its relations with the fellowman," Tertan declared. He laid the document on Howe's desk. It was headed "Quill and Scroll Society of Dwight College. Application for Membership."

"In most ways these are crass minds," Tertan said, touching the paper. "Yet as a whole, bound together in their common love of letters, they transcend their intellectual lacks since it is not a paradox that the whole is greater than the sum of its parts."

"When are the elections?" Howe asked.

"They take place tomorrow."

"I certainly hope you will be successful."

"Thank you. Would you wish to implement that hope?" A rather dirty finger pointed to the bottom of the sheet. "A faculty recommender is necessary," Tertan said stiffly, and waited.

"And you wish me to recommend you?"

"It would be an honor."

"You may use my name."

Tertan's finger pointed again. "It must be a written sponsorship, signed by the sponsor." There was a large blank space on the form under the heading, "Opinion of Faculty Sponsor."

This was almost another thing and Howe hesitated. Yet there was nothing else to do and he took out his fountain pen. He wrote, "Mr. Ferdinand Tertan is marked by his intense devotion to letters and by his exceptional love of all things of the mind." To this he signed his name which looked bold and assertive on the white page. It disturbed him, the strange affirming power of a name. With a business-like air, Tertan whipped up the paper, folded it with decision and put it into his pocket. He bowed and took his departure, leaving Howe with the sense of having done something oddly momentous.

And so much now seemed odd and momentous to Howe that should not have seemed so. It was odd and momentous, he felt, when he sat with Blackburn's second quiz before him and wrote in an excessively firm hand the grade of C-minus. The paper was a clear, an indisputable failure. He was carefully and consciously committing a cowardice. Blackburn had told the truth when he had pleaded his past record. Howe had consulted it in the Dean's office. It showed no grade lower than a B-minus. A canvass of some of Blackburn's previous instructors had brought vague attestations to the adequate powers of a student imperfectly remembered and sometimes surprise that his abilities could be questioned at all.

As he wrote the grade, Howe told himself that his cowardice sprang from an unwillingness to have more dealings with a student he disliked. He knew it was simpler than that. He knew he feared Blackburn: that was the absurd truth. And cowardice did not solve the matter after all. Blackburn, flushed with a first success, attacked at once. The minimal passing grade had not assuaged his feelings and he sat at Howe's desk and again the blue book lay between them. Blackburn said nothing. With an enormous impudence, he was waiting for Howe to speak and explain himself.

At last Howe said sharply and rudely, "Well?" His throat was tense and the blood was hammering in his head. His mouth was tight with anger at himself for his disturbance.

Blackburn's glance was almost baleful. "This is impossible, sir."

"But there it is," Howe answered.

"Sir?" Blackburn had not caught the meaning but his tone was still haughty.

Impatiently Howe said, "There it is, plain as day. Are you here to complain again?"

"Indeed I am, sir." There was surprise in Blackburn's voice that Howe should ask the question.

"I shouldn't complain if I were you. You did a thoroughly bad job on your first quiz. This one is a little, only a very little, better." This was not true. If anything, it was worse.

"That might be a matter of opinion, sir."

"It is a matter of opinion. Of my opinion."

"Another opinion might be different, sir."

"You really believe that?" Howe said.

"Yes." The omission of the "sir" was monumental.

"Whose, for example?"

"The Dean's, for example." Then the fleshy jaw came forward a little. "Or a certain literary critic's, for example."

It was colossal and almost too much for Blackburn himself to handle. The solidity of his face almost crumpled under it. But he withstood his own audacity and went on. "And the Dean's opinion might be guided by the knowledge that the person who gave me this mark is the man whom a famous critic, the most eminent judge of literature in this country, called a drunken man. The Dean might think twice about whether such a man is fit to teach Dwight students."

Howe said in quiet admonition, "Blackburn, you're mad," meaning no more than to check the boy's extravagance.

But Blackburn paid no heed. He had another shot in the locker. "And the Dean might be guided by the information, of which I have evidence, documentary evidence," – he slapped his breastpocket twice – "that this same person personally recommended to the college literary society, the oldest in the country, that he personally recommended a student who is crazy, who threw the meeting into an uproar, a psychiatric case. The Dean might take that into account."

Howe was never to learn the details of that "uproar." He had always to content himself with the dim but passionate picture which at that moment sprang into his mind, of Tertan standing on some abstract height and madly denouncing the multitude of Quill and Scroll who howled him down.

He sat quiet a moment and looked at Blackburn. The ferocity had entirely gone from the student's face. He sat regarding his teacher almost benevolently. He had played a good card and now, scarcely at all unfriendly, he was waiting to see the effect. Howe took up the blue book and negligently sifted through it. He read a page, closed the book, struck out the C-minus and wrote an F.

"Now you may take the paper to the Dean," he said. "You may tell him that after reconsidering it, I lowered the grade."

The gasp was audible. "Oh sir!" Blackburn cried. "Please!" His face was agonized. "It means my graduation, my livelihood, my future. Don't do this to me."

"It's done already."

Blackburn stood up. "I spoke rashly, sir, hastily. I had no intention, no real intention, of seeing the Dean. It rests with you – entirely, entirely. I *hope* you will restore the first mark."

"Take the matter to the Dean or not, just as you choose. The grade is what you deserve and it stands."

Blackburn's head dropped. "And will I be failed at midterm, sir?"

"Of course."

From deep out of Blackburn's great chest rose a cry of anguish. "Oh sir, if you want me to go down on my knees to you, I will, I will."

Howe looked at him in amazement.

"I will, I will. On my knees, sir. This mustn't, mustn't happen."

He spoke so literally, meaning so very truly that his knees and exactly his knees were involved and seeming to think that he was offering something of tangible value to his teacher, that Howe, whose head had become icy clear in the nonsensical drama, thought, "The boy is mad," and began to speculate fantastically whether something in himself attracted or developed aberration. He could see himself standing absurdly before the Dean and saying, "I've found another. This time it's the Vice-president of the Council, the manager of the debating team and secretary of Quill and Scroll."

One more such discovery, he thought, and he himself would be discovered! And there, suddenly, Blackburn was on his knees with a thump, his huge thighs straining his trousers, his hand outstretched in a great gesture of supplication.

With a cry, Howe shoved back his swivel chair and it rolled away on its casters half across the little room. Blackburn knelt for a moment to nothing at all, then got to his feet.

Howe rose abruptly. He said, "Blackburn, you will stop acting like an idiot. Dust your knees off, take your paper and get out. You've behaved like a fool and a malicious person. You have half a term to do a decent job. Keep your silly mouth shut and try to do it. Now get out."

Blackburn's head was low. He raised it and there was a pious light in his eyes. "Will you shake hands, sir?" he said. He thrust out his hand.

"I will not," Howe said.

Head and hand sank together. Blackburn picked up his blue book and walked to the door. He turned and said, "Thank you, sir." His back, as he departed, was heavy with tragedy and stateliness.

IV

After years of bad luck with the weather, the College had a perfect day for commencement. It was wonderfully bright, the air so transparent, the wind so brisk that no one could resist talking about it.

As Howe set out for the campus he heard Hilda calling from the back yard. She called, "Professor, professor," and came running to him.

Howe said, "What's this 'professor' business?"

"Mother told me," Hilda said. "You've been promoted. And I want to take your picture."

"Next year," said Howe. "I won't be a professor until next year. And you know better than to call anybody 'professor.'"

"It was just in fun," Hilda said. She seemed disappointed.

"But you can take my picture if you want. I won't look much different next year." Still, it was frightening. It might mean that he was to stay in this town all his life.

Hilda brightened. "Can I take it in this?" she said, and touched the gown he carried over his arm.

Howe laughed. "Yes, you can take it in this."

"I'll get my things and meet you in front of Otis," Hilda said. "I have the background all picked out."

On the campus the commencement crowd was already large. It stood about in eager, nervous little family groups. As he crossed, Howe was greeted by a student, capped and gowned, glad of the chance to make an event for his parents by introducing one of his teachers. It was while Howe stood there chatting that he saw Tertan.

He had never seen anyone quite so alone, as though a circle had been woven about him to separate him from the gay crowd on the campus. Not that Tertan was not gay, he was the gayest of all. Three weeks had passed since Howe had last seen him, the weeks of examination, the lazy week before commencement, and this was now a different Tertan. On his head he wore a panama hat, broadbrimmed and fine, of the shape associated with South American planters. He wore a suit of raw silk, luxurious but yellowed with age and much too tight, and he sported a whangee cane. He walked sedately, the hat tilted at a devastating angle, the stick coming up and down in time to his measured tread. He had, Howe guessed, outfitted himself to greet the day in the clothes of that ruined father whose existence was on record in the Dean's office. Gravely and arrogantly he surveyed the scene in it, his whole bearing seemed to say, but not of it. With his haughty step, with his flashing eye, Tertan was coming nearer. Howe did not wish to be seen. He shifted his position slightly. When he looked again, Tertan was not in sight.

The chapel clock struck the quarter hour. Howe detached himself from his chat and hurried to Otis Hall at the far end of the campus. Hilda had not yet come. He went up into the high portico and, using the glass of the door for a mirror, put on his gown, adjusted the hood on his shoulders and set the mortarboard on his head. When he came down the steps Hilda had arrived.

Nothing could have told him more forcibly that a year had passed than the development of Hilda's photographic possessions from the box camera of the previous fall. By a strap about her neck was hung a leather case, so thick and strong, so carefully stitched and so molded to its contents that it could only hold a costly camera. The appearance was deceptive, Howe knew, for he had been present at the Aikens' pre-Christmas conference about its purchase. It was only a fairly good domestic camera. Still, it looked very impressive. Hilda carried another leather case from which she drew a collapsible tripod. Decisively she extended each of its gleaming legs and set it up on the path. She removed the camera from its case and fixed it to the tripod. In its compact efficiency the camera almost had a life of its own, but Hilda treated it with easy familiarity, looked into its eye, glanced casually at its gauges. Then from a pocket she took still another leather case and drew from it a small instrument through which she looked first at Howe, who began to feel inanimate and lost, and then at the sky. She made some adjustment on the instrument, then some adjustment on the camera. She swept the scene with her eye, found a spot and pointed the camera in its direction. She walked to the spot, stood on it and beckoned to Howe. With each new leather case, with each new instrument and with each new adjustment she had grown in ease and now she said, "Joe, will you stand here?"

Obediently Howe stood where he was bidden. She had yet another instrument. She took out a tape measure on a mechanical spool. Kneeling down before Howe, she put the little metal ring of of the tape under the tip of his shoe. At her request, Howe pressed it with his toe. When she had measured her distance, she nodded to Howe who released the tape. At a touch, it sprang back into the spool. "You have to be careful if you're going to get what you want," Hilda said. "I don't believe in all this snap-snap-snapping," she remarked loftily. Howe nodded in agrement, although he was beginning to think Hilda's care excessive.

Now at last the moment had come. Hilda squinted into the camera, moved the tripod slightly. She stood to the side, holding the plunger of the shutter-cable. "Ready," she said. "Will you relax, Joseph, please?" Howe realized that he was standing frozen. Hilda stood poised and precise as a setter, one hand holding the little cable, the other extended with curled dainty fingers like a dancer's, as if expressing to her subject the precarious delicacy of the moment. She pressed the plunger and there was the click. At once she stirred to action, got behind the camera, turned a new exposure. "Thank you," she said. "Would you stand under that tree and let me do a character study with light and shade?"

The childish absurdity of the remark restored Howe's ease. He went to the little tree. The pattern the leaves made on his gown was what Hilda was after. He had just taken a satisfactory position when he heard in the unmistakable voice, "Ah, Doctor! Having your picture taken?"

Howe gave up the pose and turned to Blackburn who stood on the walk, his hands behind his back, a little too large for his bachelor's gown. Annoyed that Blackburn should see him posing for a character study in light and shade, Howe said irritably, "Yes, having my picture taken."

Blackburn beamed at Hilda. "And the little photographer," he said. Hilda fixed her eyes on the ground and stood closer to her brilliant and aggressive camera. Blackburn, teetering on his heels, his hands behind his back, wholly prelatical and benignly patient, was not abashed at the silence. At last Howe said, "If you'll excuse us, Mr. Blackburn, we'll go on with the picture."

"Go right ahead, sir. I'm running along." But he only came closer. "Dr. Howe," he said fervently, "I want to tell you how glad I am that I was able to satisfy your standards at last."

Howe was surprised at the hard insulting brightness of his own voice and even Hilda looked up curiously as he said, "Nothing you have ever done has satisfied me and nothing you could ever do would satisfy me, Blackburn."

With a glance at Hilda, Blackburn made a gesture as if to hush Howe – as though all his former bold malice had taken for granted a kind of understanding between himself and his teacher, a secret which must not be betrayed to a third person. "I only meant, sir," he said, "that I was able to pass your course after all."

Howe said, "You didn't pass my course. I passed you out of my course. I passed you without even reading your paper. I wanted to be sure the college would be rid of you. And when all the grades were in and I did read your paper, I saw I was right not to have read it first."

Blackburn presented a stricken face. "It was very bad, sir?"

But Howe had turned away. The paper had been fantastic. The paper had been, if he wished to see it so, mad. It was at this moment that the Dean came up behind Howe and caught his arm. "Hello, Joseph," he said. "We'd better be getting along, it's almost late."

He was not a familiar man, but when he saw Blackburn, who approached to greet him, he took Blackburn's arm too. "Hello, Theodore," he said. Leaning forward on Howe's arm and on Blackburn's, he said, "Hello, Hilda dear." Hilda replied quietly, "Hello, Uncle George."

Still clinging to their arms, still linking Howe and Blackburn, the Dean said, "Another year gone, Joe, and we've turned out another crop. After you've been here a few years, you'll find it reasonably upsetting – you wonder how there can be so many graduating classes while you stay the same. But of course you don't stay the same." Then he said, "Well," sharply, to dismiss the thought. He pulled Blackburn's arm and swung him around to Howe. "Have you heard about Teddy Blackburn?" he asked. "He has a job already, before graduation, the first man of his class to be placed." Expectant of congratulations, Blackburn beamed at Howe. Howe remained silent.

"Isn't that good?" the Dean said. Still Howe did not answer and the Dean, puzzled and put out, turned to Hilda. "That's a very fine-looking camera, Hilda." She touched it with affectionate pride.

"Instruments of precision," said a voice. Instruments of precision. Of the three with joined arms, Howe was the nearest to Tertan, whose gaze took in all the scene except the smile and the nod which Howe gave him. The boy leaned on his cane. The broadbrimmed hat, canting jauntily over his eye, confused the image of his face that Howe had established, suppressed the rigid lines of the ascetic and brought out the baroque curves. It made an effect of perverse majesty.

"Instruments of precision," said Tertan for the last time, addressing no one, making a casual comment to the universe. And it occurred to Howe that Tertan might not be referring to Hilda's equipment. The sense of the thrice-woven circle of the boy's loneliness smote him fiercely. Tertan stood in majestic jauntiness, superior to all the scene, but his isolation made Howe ache with a pity of which Tertan was more the cause than the object, so general and indiscriminate was it.

Whether in his sorrow he made some unintended movement toward Tertan which the Dean checked or whether the suddenly tightened grip on his arm was the Dean's own sorrow and fear, he did not know. Tertan watched them in the incurious way people watch a photograph being taken and suddenly the thought that, to the boy, it must seem that the three were posing for a picture together made Howe detach himself almost rudely from the Dean's grasp.

"I promised Hilda another picture," he announced – needlessly, for Tertan was no longer there, he had vanished in the last sudden flux of visitors who, now that the band had struck up, were rushing nervously to find seats.

"You'd better hurry," the Dean said. "I'll go along, it's getting late for me." He departed and Blackburn walked stately by his side.

Howe again took his position under the little tree which cast its shadow over his face and gown. "Just hurry, Hilda, won't you?" he said. Hilda held the cable at arm's length, her other arm crooked and her fingers crisped. She rose on her toes and said "Ready," and pressed the release. "Thank you," she said gravely and began to dismantle her camera as he hurried off to join the procession.

The Hand That Fed Me

BY ISAAC ROSENFELD

D*ec. 21*

Dear Ellen,

It was very sweet of you to send me a Christmas card. It was really a wonderful gesture, and so simple! When you prepared your Christmas list you included me – and that's all there was to it.

You know, in that one day of ours I never did manage to find out who your friends were (not that I wasn't eager to!). But I imagine your list went something like this: aunts, uncles, cousins; girlfriends; boyfriends. It amuses me to think that I must have been included in the latter group, in the company, let us say, of John, Bob, Steve, Chick, etc. I am quite willing to share the honor with them, even though the names of my colleagues must be entirely imaginary and even though you probably put my own name last on the list. But perhaps you had me in mind all along, knowing what a gesture that would be! Naturally, you must have assumed I'm not in the army. I'm not quarreling with you, but there's something a little glib in that assumption. Why, so far as you are concerned, should I *not* be in the army? Do you follow me? Is it simply a habit of thinking so that whenever – rarely ! – you do come to me, you immediately say, "Joe? Oh, he's still around." I can see no other way, unless, God save my mind, you've taken to obtaining information from my friends, whom you have sworn to secrecy. But how should you know who my friends are, since I never found out yours?

Of course, I may have mentioned Otto to you – he was very much on my mind that day. Would you believe it, while we were walking down Hoyne Avenue and I was, permit me, impressing you with all I had, I kept wondering what Otto would do in similar circumstances, and I was gloating, sure that he would never have been able to give such a fine account of himself! Furthermore, I still gloat over it although – for all the fine impression I made – you never answered my letters and even once, when I called on you (for perhaps the tenth time) you actually hid from me. I know all about it. Your brother came to the door and he seemed to have half a mind to admit me; but behind him I could hear a commotion of shushing and whispering, and I'm sure it was you, ducking into the pantry and telling them to say you were out and on no account to let me in.

Of course, what makes all this slightly ridiculous, is the fact that it happened three years ago. But why did you wait three years before sending me a card? What was wrong with the Christmas of the very same year, or the one of the year following? Ah, I know how your mind works. On Christmas, 1939, you *suppressed* all thought of me. In 1940 you allowed yourself to think, but only to the following extent: "If I send him a Christmas card now, he'll think I've been *unable* to forget him. So we'll wait another year or two. By that time it'll be quite clear, when he gets my card, not that I've been unable to forget him, but that I have so good a memory that I can even recall the name and address of a man whom I saw only once, three years ago." Am I right?

But it's a trivial thing and why attach so much importance to it? I suppose you would have me believe that. You would have me believe that your card was only a way of acknowledging a pleasant day that you had hitherto failed to acknowledge. Something brought it to your mind – say, an onion you had eaten recently. And so the card, yes?

Not on your life, Ellen, not for one moment will I believe it. For if it were only a trivial matter, would you have waited three years? You would have sent me a card at once, or even phoned me on the following day, as you'd promised. Trivialities are the things women rush into, feeling they're important. The important things, however, are what they mull over, plot, deliberate, all to no end. It took you three years, Ellen, to convince yourself that a single afternoon you had spent with me was trivial!

So there you are.

But one more thing. On your card you have written, "From Ellen. Do you remember me?" A pretty little disingenuous note! I assure you, your card was sent in the deepest conviction that I had not once ceased to think of you. I'm sure of it. If you thought I'd forgotten you, you wouldn't have dared send a card. What, a man should receive a card from a certain Ellen and wonder who she is? Any time you'd leave yourself open! Or, on the other hand, was it a rather coy way of insinuating that you'd all but forgotten me? You see, if you are willing to admit that I may have forgotten you, isn't that another way of suggesting that you barely, barely manage to remember me?

Nonsense! I know perfectly well that you've never forgotten me. – But who are you, Shakespeare, that the smallest scrap of your writing should be covered with commentaries? Enough of that.

Do you remember me? Indeed!

Joseph Feigenbaum

Dec. 22

Dear Ellen,

It just occurred to me that while I wrote you at some length, yesterday, I forgot the obvious subject of our correspondence – Xmas. So I'm writing you again to wish you a merry Xmas.

Yours,

J. F.

P.S. Of course, I could just as well send a Xmas card.

Dec. 23

Dear Ellen,

Since I wrote to you twice, I might just as well have said something worth saying. After all, even if we have "forgotten" each other, we still have our three years to look back on – years, may I add, all the more interesting because we did not, in any way, spend them together.

Please understand my motive. If it seems sentimental to you, then you're a fool, and I've no fear of offending you when I say so. And besides what can you do about it? Can you threaten to break off our friendship? Can you threaten to stop writing? As if you would ever write! You see, Ellen, by avoiding me you've put yourself completely in my power. But that's hardly worth pointing out.

Our whole meeting comes back to me. I remember that summer, no work, no friends, no conversation, the realization I was meant for WPA. What a wonderful summer of self-discovery! Believe me, chaos is the mother of knowledge. It's a distinguished family: indolence, poverty, frustration, *seediness* – these are the blood relations of that little monster, Mr. Knowthyself. I shall never again be afraid of turning myself inside out, like an empty pocket – what treasures of lint and fuzz! Do you follow me, Ellen? I mean to say, it is sometimes a good thing to shake yourself out, and go around unhappy – you lose most of your delusions. A happy man takes a great risk – of believing that he is what he seems to be.

Well, I was forced to go on WPA; forced outwardly, that is, for inwardly I went as a free man. I knew what to expect. My friends ("my generation" as it became fashionable to call them) were all on one cultural project or another. I would go on the Writers' Project and fill out a time sheet as well as any one else. All such matters, which are done with only half a will, are called ways of keeping body and soul together; actually, they are ways of keeping them apart. That is, you do what you do, and you don't have to worry about undergoing any changes. WPA was a great social invention, it was refrigeration on a mass scale. It took us as we were, and froze us as we were; it preserved us, it kept us from decaying. But what's all this? I merely wanted to say a few things it was impossible to say when we walked out of the relief station together, and I find that I am overdramatizing myself.

I hadn't thought there would be such a long line at the C.R.A. office, so many Negroes, Poles, old men. Not a single applicant for the Writers' Project among them. It is so much better to be an unemployed writer than an unemployed any-thing-else that I felt especially sorry for them. An unemployed plumber, for example – a man who is starving because there are no toilet bowls for him to fix. There is something so pathetic in that! A writer, at least, is always writing. Whatever hap-pens, he records it. It begins to rain – he says to himself: it is raining. He walks down the stairs – he says to himself: I am walking down the stairs. He is always writing in his head, and it does him good. But what good does it do a man to go around fixing toilet bowls in his head? Pig misery! So there I was, looking at the men around me and recording them, putting down their coughs, their leanness, the dirt, the stubble on their faces, and meanwhile thinking: here am I, a writer, this is me, etc., etc.

Ellen, you look at yourself only in mirrors. Relying on a piece of glass the way you do, you probably have little notion of the actual figure you cut. That day, when you were not smearing on lipstick while looking into a compact-mirror, you were sucking the point of a pencil, and rolling it between your lips. That you, who refuse to write to me, should have come into my life at the point of a pencil!

Now I might almost begin to flatter you – to dwell on the image of a girl, a little above average in height, more than ordinary in appearance, a girl, though I suspect the word, quite beautiful, standing there in the basement among all the coughing old men, surrounded by steampipes, benches, notices plastered on the wooden walls: *Bekanntmachung, Avviso*. And all the while this girl rolls the point of a pencil in her mouth. Do you know, after you had caught my eye, you stuck your tongue out at me. First the pencil, and then the tongue. Ellen, Ellen!

It would have meant very little. It would only have been a study in violent contrast, squalor and flirtation, sex and the relief office – and, as a matter of fact, I was not sure at the beginning that it meant anything more. But immediately the element of personal worth entered. Almost at once I talked to you, you will recall, as though you were more than a pretty girl with a pencil stuck in your mouth. It was you who did the flirting, made the advances. Do I wear make-up? Do I carry a purse full of compacts, powderboxes, lipsticks? Understand, I accuse you of nothing. I am glad you behaved as you did. Perhaps because I am not thin and old and coughing, you saw to it that I should notice you. But it was I who saw to all the rest.

I want you to observe that you were ahead of me in the line. When your preliminary interview was over and your preliminary papers were filled out, you could have gone home. I expected you, at any moment, while you were idling around the basement, I expected you to break away, perhaps with a slight nod in my direction, and go home. But I knew you would not. I said nothing, you will remember, I even pretended not to notice you. But how carefully I watched you, and how pleased I was! There you were, waiting for me, and it was all voluntary on your part, and even somewhat embarrassing. The pretexts you invented! First you sat down on one of the benches and stretched and yawned as though you were tired. Then you removed your shoes and rubbed your feet – such pretty feet, if I may say, and just barely dirty! By that time I thought I might dare acknowledge that I knew you were waiting for me. I smiled. I motioned to you. But you would not admit it. You wouldn't look at me. You curled up on the bench where you sat and pretended to go to sleep – a wonder no one saw you and put you out. I knew you were waiting for me, that you had already acknowledged me even more deeply than I had acknowledged you – since at the outset I was only responding to a flirtation, but what were you responding to? I don't flirt. You were therefore responding to me! It made me so happy, somewhat dizzy, it was even slightly alarming. I sang a song, I joked with the man who stood ahead of me in line, a short and chubby Negro whom I liked immensely. I offered him cigarettes. When he took only one, I slipped some more into his hip pocket, so carefully, I might have been stealing his wallet. He was now my friend. Having become your friend, I was everybody's friend. I even smiled at the relief worker who interviewed me, a bitter hag who resented my happiness and detained me with unnecessary questions, as though to extract my secret. And when I was through with her and came out, startled to find you absent from the bench, only to see you standing at the door, so clearly, so obviously waiting!

That whole afternoon, Ellen, the walk to your house, your friendliness, your kindness in asking me up and inviting me to have lunch with you! Even now I can hardly believe that I should ever have received such gifts of kindness. Such absolute friendship, comradeship, trust, good will, and with it all the constant promise of intimacy: one moment you are at my shoulder, the next, you take my arm, or my hand, or you pretend a mosquito has landed and you slap my cheek. And what a lunch! Rye bread and borscht, served by your father, and with such good nature, even after he had learned my name and drawn certain unavoidable inferences. Borscht, furthermore, with bits of green onion floating in it. I was so happy to learn you were Russian! I consider myself a Russian, you understand. As a Jew, I am also a German, an Italian, a Frenchman, a Pole, I am all Europe – but a Russian, foremost.

I am sure that all this did not come to naught because I am a Jew. To begin with, you are the kind of gentile who knows how to say "goy" – a word I distinctly heard you use. There is only one nation on the earth – the nation of those who call the rest of the world "goyim." We Jews use it in contempt, because of our fears, but it is capable of elevation into a word of pride and brotherhood. No, that is not the reason why we "broke up." There are only two possibilities, one very flattering to me, the other, degrading.

To take the base one first, I observed, when I entered your house and when I was eating lunch, that you avoided all reference to WPA. Your presented me to your father, and later to your brother, as an old friend from school whom you bumped into downtown while looking for a job. You would not admit that you had applied for WPA, and you would not have them know that I, too, had done so. What a false and wicked pride, and – since you evidently know something about such matters – what utter disloyalty to your class! Your father, a carpenter as I recall, was obviously unemployed. He had that look about him. And your brother, who was building a model airplane in the middle of the day, evidently had nothing better to do. So what was there to be ashamed of? And what if your mother, as I gather from her absence, was the only one working in the family? What of it? Must you be ashamed? But perhaps you were even more ashamed of me than of yourself. Perhaps the very fact that you met me in a relief station was enough to queer me. Then why flirt with me and bring me to your home?

But apart from all that, what a fool you were not to go through with your WPA application. I scoured all the rolls, inquired at all the projects where you might conceivably have been taken on, but no one had heard of you. Ah, what you missed! Myself, I went on to the Writers' Project and compiled a 100,000 word report on pigeon racing in Chicago, including a life-size biography of Josiah Breen, the pigeon fancier. And what did you do? Pickle works, belt-buckle factory, typist, stenographer, secretary? You are a traitor to your class, Ellen, to your better instincts and your better capacities, and you allowed what we call "the most crucial experience of our generation" to slip by you. But this is a digression.

As I say, you may have been ashamed to know me, or to continue seeing me because I was going on WPA. Or perhaps, even because I had caught you in the act, applying for the national dispensation. This, of course, is only a possibility; and I may be wrong. Assuming that I am, and that you had your own and better reasons, there remains another possibility, which I am very eager to entertain. It does me good.

This is mystery. It involves a whole world, of which you are the hub. At the center, beside you, let me place a young man, of respectable, and somewhat better family than your own, a man whom we shall call Willard. Am I warm? When we met, you had already known Willard for a period of two years. He, a serious fellow, perhaps a student of law, or already a lawyer, could not help but have serious intentions. He doesn't laugh very often, your Willard; and when you do, opening your mouth wide, it disconcerts him. Furthermore, when you suck pencils in his presence, or show him your tongue, he is more than a little embarrassed. But what can you do about it? You were to marry him. You were then, I should judge, twenty-four, the age when one begins observing that a woman is not growing any younger. Besides, you are *used* to him, miserable habit. He is good to you, he's solid, he looks down on WPA, he smokes cigars. What then? How else are you to act when this wistful, melancholy, timid, cynical and so appealing young writer comes along and speaks to you as a man has never spoken before, and dwells on you, and intimates, and sighs and stares? It is, after all, shocking to discover that one's fiancé is not the ultimate man on earth, and that another, a man you met in a basement, who has never kissed you or walked you through the park, is capable of preempting the emotions you have already consigned and wrapped and, furthermore, of providing you with new ones. *Nyet, krasavitsa moya?*

Ellen, if this be true, then your reticence is a tribute! Thank you for ignoring me, thank you for your silence. For it means you realized, in those few hours, that going with me would make irrecoverable your whole past life and its commitments. After all, women have been known to keep several men on a string. Thank you for not binding me. For it means you feared the string, and where it might lead you. And what if the string should break? The fear that a string might break is the fear of love!

But look at all these pages I have written, and where will I find an envelope large enough? Ellen, unintentionally, merely out of a desire to say a few things I had not said before, I have invoked more of the past than I had intended. It has brought me back to that helpless, pitiful state of mind – I despise it – where a man lives on promises. I have drugged myself into believing what I believed three years ago your promise to call me, to write to me, to see me again. Now I know you will write, if only a few words, and I know you will answer me at once.

Always yours,

Joe

Dec. 29

Dear Ellen,

Christmas passed, and nearly six days have gone by. I tell myself that you have been very busy over the holidays, that you haven't found time to write. But I knew full well that if you were going to write, you would already have done so. Why do you deny me this? Is it my pride or your presumption? Have I touched too sensitive, too deep a point? Or could it be that I have merely bored you?

I tell myself I have bored her. But how can that be when I still believe in the love she seemed to have offered me? Is it possible? If the world were made up of such haphazard, ill fitting emotions, no pattern at all would exist – it just wouldn't hang together.

Excuse me if I have used the word love in vain. But the more I have thought of you, the more I have grown to believe that I have a right to use it. It is almost as though I have written these letters to make myself believe that you love me. God knows what I have written! God knows why I go on!

I suppose every man sometimes has the urge to pour himself out, release all the stops and let go. My sense of caution should tell me that few men have the right to confess; only murderers and hardened criminals, never men who are merely unhappy. Those who have really committed crimes, those who have an actual guilt lying over them – they have something to say. But the rest of us – perhaps we become liars when we open our mouths, liars or pathetic wishers, and half of what we say may be false, and the other half merely the result of a vain striving for a sense of personal history.

Then why do I go on? Why do I persist in writing to you in the face of what must surely amount to a personal humiliation? I'll tell you why – and may the telling damn you! A man feels humiliated only when he is cast down from one position to a lower one. Some men never learn their lesson. No sooner humiliated, they attempt to injure someone else in return. These are the unpleasant characters, the personalities charged with an explosive that any touch may set off. Your Willard may be of such a type – not because he is mean; he may even be sweet in his own way – but only insofar as he lacks subtlety. But our other type of man is a different sort entirely. When he is humiliated he does not bound back with a rage that destroys his perception. Instead, he learns. He sees most clearly what concerns him most closely; and he accepts it and makes it a part of himself. When he has been utterly humiliated, he observes that he has touched bottom; having reached bottom, he knows there's no lower he can fall. There's a comfort, a perpetual cushion in certain kinds of misery – you rest on it, just as a contented man rests at the top of his career. Top or bottom, either way – but no struggling in the middle!

Does this succeed in explaining myself to you? Most likely not. I feel you must learn something about the way in which I live, in order to understand why, after three years have passed, I shower you with letters, to which I expect no answer.

I live in what I consider to be a state of exile. Among the friends I have at present is a certain Zampechini, an Italian refugee, and a certain Lutzek, a German refugee. I have told them, "Boys, we are in exile together. Not from our separate countries – but from history." But why proceed in this fashion, at this level, way over your head? It is enough to state briefly the following conditions:

1. I am alone.
2. The last six women I approached unconditionally turned me down.
3. There is a war on and I am out of it on all fronts; neither losing nor profiting by it, and not even employed.
4. I live in a rooming house, on the allowance my father very grudgingly gives me.
5. Ever since WPA folded up,

but never mind the rest.

I was going to tell you more. I wanted, first, to tell you everything; then, a little; now, nothing. Ah, what's the difference? I cannot bear to tell you what I have suffered, because I am proud of it, and it would only bore you. Enough. Let this be a last effort at explanation in a letter full of abortive efforts. As a man who, quite confidently, has touched bottom, both in what he has suffered and in personal esteem, I feel nothing I do can injure me. Your rebuffs are *not, definitely not* a further humiliation. I understand myself too well. I am of the brotherhood of paupers who endure everything at their own expense. And so, if I go out of my way and out of my time to reach after a promised happiness of three years back, this, too, a deliberate delusion, is also at my own expense. And perhaps even the greatest irony is my knowing that while you refuse to answer my letters, you also fail to understand them.

But, no fear. I shall plague you no longer.

Feigenbaum

Dec. 31

Dear Ellen,

Contrary to the word I had given, I called on you yesterday. I am writing today to identify myself, to make it perfectly clear that it was I, and no one else, who called.

He said you were out. Who, I do not know. Perhaps it was "your Willard." I believed him, made no further inquiries. I left no message and no name. In a fit of humiliation I withheld my name. I am writing today to repudiate that humiliation. It was not of the bottom variety; it was of the rising sort that struggles midway between its origins and its hopes. It was not true to nature. My humiliation admits no hopes.

Now that there can be no doubt in your mind as to the identity of your caller, I may go on to the next point. By calling on you I satisfied a partial longing. Naturally, complete satisfaction would have come only with my seeing you. But as it is I saw your house, the door which opened, the stairs that led up, the door that closed in my face. Willard does not count. I am indifferent to him. My point is that with yesterday's closing of the door I accepted as closed our whole relationship. I shall no longer plague you with letters, no longer make any attempt to see you. And this is the truth. You may rely on it, not because I have promised you – my promises are evidently as little to be trusted as yours. But it is so because I have at last accepted it, and have willed it to be so. I find that this decision, against which I have been fighting ever since your Xmas card came, has, surprisingly, liberated me.

For what I have to say actually has nothing to do with humiliation. Very simply, Ellen, I love you. It is so easy to say, and one can say it as well as another. Why did I have to torture myself?

I love you. And why do I love you? Because you came to me. Because, in the basement of the relief station you noticed me before I noticed you, and because your flirting was not in response to an act of mine, but an overture, an opening entirely of your own. For this, all my gratitude. Because, at a moment when you did not yet exist for me, I already existed for you. Isn't this reason enough?

No, it needs further explaining. I feel that the more I love you, the less you understand me. You must know that a man like myself, so deeply displeased, dissatisfied with himself as I am, can only be saved by an act of graciousness. A blessing, external and gratuitous must come to him. For he will destroy whatever is internal, whatever comes out of himself. The lower he falls, the more he will demand and the louder he will clamor for salvation. An absolute beggar demands the entire world.

This is why I love you. But if I love you because you flirted with me, I am, at the same time, inclined to disapprove of your flirtatiousness. I could understand flirtatiousness in a nun. But in a woman like yourself, Ellen! A nun, let us assume, is repressed. But you! Not repression but *bonheur*, bliss at every pore. Now that I no longer need withhold anything, now that I am free, I may tell you what I felt when I first saw you. Believe me, and here enters another irony, my first sight of you was intuitive proof that I would have you! That is what is called spontaneous love. Love pre-exists in the heart, and when it finds its object it leaps out and enters it and does its business, establishing a conviction, while the timid soul still tells itself it has no more than an "interest." But I do not delude myself. I saw and at once believed, and I knew what I saw and what I believed, and so strong was my conviction that even the three years that passed and the frustrations of the last week have not deprived me of it. Yes, I was sure. Furthermore, I still am. For it will not go away. I still see you as I saw you then, excited, plump, in a tight black dress, your arms bare, your hair loose, your feet in sandal-shoes. I have torn that dress from you a thousand times, but I have done it reverently, in my mind observing that same delicacy, that attention to detail I would observe in fact. Thus I have seen you naked, and I do not revile myself with the thought that what is only imaginary for me must be actual for one or many a man. It is my possession. The nakedness with which I have endowed you is solid and unique, both in the actuality it has for me, and in its expression, which is entirely its own and not compounded of other women. Nor is the look of your body a wish fulfilment, for I do not assemble you out of separate female perfections – that art of daydreaming! No, for your breasts, as I imagine them, are even too large for my preference and your thighs could do with a little less hair. I have, furthermore, distilled a set of odors to go with your hair and your armpits, and these, again, are distinctive; and I have supplied your skin with textures, and have given you appropriate sounds – laughter for love play, a sharp intaking of the breath for passion, and a wildness of hissing and moaning devoid of all language. This is that solemn nakedness to which we bring not only our passion, but our capacity for a sensual revenge. But it is not brutal; it is tender. And above all it is persistent in the face of a thousand complications I can never make out.

And then the pencil in your mouth, the tongue stuck at me, and the conversation and your waiting for me and the walk and the invitation to your house, the lunch, and your promise and the happiness almost, almost reached, and the conviction established beyond overthrowing! Was it from this that I was to expect denial?

We lean toward the imperfect – it was too good to be true. But this is no explanation. It will satisfy only a shallow, a skeptical intelligence. The perfect must be true! What else is perfection, and why do we demand it? But however I explain it, I still do not understand. I refuse to believe my own reasons.

What then? I love you enough to think evil of you. I am angry enough to know that what I saw and believed, you, too, saw – but did not believe. You acknowledged a conviction without sharing it. And nothing human can be colder!

Look how similarities endanger us. You, with the pencil in your mouth, knew me well enough, from your own traits, to destroy me. I am of the same erotic type as you. I, too, must be fed. My whole life can be explained by hunger. You knew you would have to offer, give, yield. If only you had not known! If only your perception had been clouded with that animal stupidity for which we are, occasionally, so grateful in women! Or, if only I had known better! I should have known that a woman will make a concession on one point only when she has prepared some reservation on another. As it was, you managed to concede everything, yet withheld everything. The evil in your flirtatiousness was that it went beyond flirtation; it offered love, real love, in order to snatch it away. It was the old game played to its fullest, criminal in its intelligence, the *absolute* cheat.

Well, it's over and done with. Of course, in outdoing me you also had to deny yourself. But a woman will count her self-denial at a small cost when the game is so large and she masters it. But it's over, it's over. Yet it persists. Certain patterns are dangerous. We form them once and follow them always. And if a man will attach, as I have done, a whole morality to a single incident, he will always be at the mercy of "incidents." The insight he will gain will give him no peace. He will be forced to employ it everywhere, with all the subtle damage it can do him. And at a time like the present when there is no place for unhappy men, no understanding they can count on, no mood they can share, what good will their insight do them?

But, Ellen, I release you. I go back to my own cares, reluctantly, I admit, but with a certain confidence. My place in the world – see how quickly one can spring from his place in bed to his place in the world! Can a woman do as much? – My place in the world is assured, no matter how difficult it be, for I am my own assurance. I am that man – and there are many like me – whose place is entirely contained in his own being. So long as I exist, that is my place, my function. I do not justify myself. I merely point this out: I have so little, so little pride, so little belief, so little outward appetite, I am so pared down to my own core, that I cannot help believing I am an essential man. And besides, WPA will come back, have no fear. Do you think I wrote my report on pigeon racing for nothing? It stands there in the files, waiting, ready to be taken up again. Some day, when the war is over, and the machines have been removed from the old buildings, after the dust has settled and the activity has died down, the steel vaults will be unlocked and the steel files will be brought out, and the pigeons will flutter again. Once again the world will take account of us – we bare, pared, essential men. The earth will once again acknowledge loneliness, as real as her own mountains. What else can be done? We may be a generation – we may, as well, be an eternity. But perhaps a new wrinkle in disasters? Perhaps the night and the wolves and the waves we howled about back in the thirties – when there was still a little twilight – will really come down to blot out, swallow, and wash us away? What will be will be.

One only looks to his own accountable and natural future. But here, I shan't write much longer. The New Year is coming. Ellen, Ellen, at last I am free. One moment you were my great bitterness, and now I am in the clear, rid of you. My life will find another bitterness, perhaps of a higher fresher quality, perhaps even a bitterness in some successful thing. What does it matter? I am cushioned at the bottom and only look forward to what I may expect. For after all, what is humiliation? It does not endure forever. And when it has led us underground to our last comfort, look, it has served its purpose and it is gone. Who knows when new heights may not appear? A man has only so much in common with his experience. The rest he derives from God knows where.

I believe some men are capable of rising out of their own lives. They stand on the same ground as their brothers, but they are, somehow, transcendental, while their brothers are underground. Their only secret is a tremendous willingness – they do not struggle with themselves!

Ellen, all I mean to say is this: I still believe in human happiness, and in my own to boot. If I cannot make my claim on you, I will make it on life, demand that existence satisfy the longings it arouses. It must, it must! For that is happiness: the conviction that something is necessary.

But how dare I speak of happiness? Ater all, I was once convinced that you were necessary. And what is necessity without fulfilment? Is it possible? I shall say it is. Be gentle to the unfulfilled, be good to it. We are accustomed to sing the joys of the happy, the fulfilled men. Let us also sing the joys of the desolate, the empty men. Theirs is the necessity without fulfillment, but it is possible that even to them – who knows? – some joy may come.

I forgive you and release you, Ellen. You are beautiful – go. But God, if you only knew, if you only knew how willing I am – always – to take the risk of my happiness!

A Happy New Year!
Love,

Joseph

Cass Mastern's Wedding Ring

BY ROBERT PENN WARREN

Long ago Jack Burden was a graduate student, working for his Ph.D. in American History, in the state university of his native State. This Jack Burden (of whom the present Jack Burden, *Me*, is a legal, biological, and perhaps even metaphysical continuator) lived in a slatternly apartment with two other graduate students, one industrious, stupid, unlucky, and alcoholic, and the other idle, intelligent, lucky, and alcoholic. At least they were alcoholic for a period after the first of the month, when they received the miserable check paid them by the university for their miserable work as assistant teachers. The industry and ill luck of one canceled out against the idleness and luck of the other and they both amounted to the same thing, and they drank what they could get when they could get it. They drank because they didn't really have the slightest interest in what they were doing now and didn't have the slightest hope for the future. They could not even bear the thought of pushing on to finish their degrees, for that would mean leaving the university (leaving the first-of-the-month drunks, the yammer about "work" and "ideas" in smoke-blind rooms, the girls who staggered slightly and giggled indiscreetly on the dark stairs leading to the apartment) to go to some normal school on a sun-baked crossroads or a junior college long on Jesus and short on funds, to go to face the stark reality of drudgery and dry rot and prying eyes and the slow withering of the green wisp of dream which had, like some window plant in an invalid's room, grown out of a bottle. Only the bottle hadn't had water in it. It had had something which looked like water, smelled like kerosene, and tasted like carbolic acid: one-run corn whiskey.

Jack Burden lived with them, in the slatternly apartment among the unwashed dishes in the sink and on the table, the odor of stale tobacco smoke, the dirty shirts and underwear piled in corners. He even took a relish in the squalor, in the privilege of letting a last crust of buttered toast fall to the floor to lie undisturbed until the random heel should grind it into the mud-colored carpet, in the spectacle of the fat roach moving across the cracked linoleum of the bathroom floor while he steamed in the tub. Once he had brought his mother to the apartment for tea, and she had sat on the edge of the overstuffed chair, holding a cracked cup and talking with a brittle and calculated charm out of a face which was obviously being held in shape by a profound exercise of will. She saw a roach venture out from the kitchen door. She saw one of Jack Burden's friends crush an ant on the inner lip of the sugar bowl and flick the carcass from his finger. The nail of the finger itself was not very clean. But she kept right on delivering the charm, out of the rigid face. He had to say that for her.

But afterwards, as they walked down the street, she had said: "Why do you live like that?"

"It's what I'm built for, I reckon," Jack Burden said.

"With those people," she said.

"They're all right," he said, and wondered if they were, and wondered if he was. His mother didn't say anything for a minute, making a sharp, bright clicking sound on the pavement with her heels as she walked along, holding her small shoulders trimly back, carrying her famished-cheeked, blue-eyed, absolutely innocent face slightly lifted to the pulsing sunset world of April like a very expensive present the world ought to be glad to even have a look at. And back then, fifteen years ago, it was still something to look at, too. Sometimes Jack Burden (who was *Me* or what *Me* was fifteen years ago) would be proud to go into a place with her, and have people stare the way they would, and just for a minute he would be happy. But there is a lot more to everything than just walking into a hotel lobby or restaurant.

Walking along beside him she said meditatively: "That dark-haired one – if he got cleaned up – he wouldn't be bad looking."

"That's what a lot of other women think," Jack Burden said, and suddenly felt a nauseated hatred of the dark-haired one, the one who had killed the ant on the sugar bowl, who had the dirty nails. But he had to go on, something made him go on: "Yes, and a lot of them don't even care about cleaning him up. They'll take him like he is. He's the great lover of the apartment. He put the sag in the springs of that divan we got."

"Don't be vulgar," she said, because she definitely did not like what is known as vulgarity in conversation.

"It's the truth," he said.

She didn't answer, and her heels did the bright clicking. Then she said, "If he'd throw those awful clothes away – and get something decent."

"Yeah," Jack Burden said, "on his seventy-five dollars a month."

She looked at him now, down at his clothes. "Yours are pretty awful, too," she said.

"Are they?" Jack Burden demanded.

"I'll send you money for some decent clothes," she said.

A few days later the check came and a note telling him to get a "couple of decent suits and accessories." The check was for two hundred and fifty dollars. He did not even buy a necktie. But he and the two other men in the apartment had a wonderful blowout, which lasted for five days, and as a result of which the industrious and unlucky one lost his job and the idle and lucky one got too sociable and, despite his luck, contracted what is quaintly known as a social disease. But nothing happened to Jack Burden, for nothing ever happened to Jack Burden, who was invulnerable. Perhaps that was the curse of Jack Burden: he was invulnerable.

So, as I have said, Jack Burden lived in the slatternly apartment with the two other graduate students, for even after being fired the unlucky, industrious one still lived in the apartment. He simply stopped paying anything but he stayed. He borrowed money for cigarettes. He sullenly ate the food the others brought in and cooked. He lay around during the day, for there was no reason to be industrious any more, ever again. Once at night, Jack Burden woke up and thought he heard the sound of sobs from the living room, where the unlucky, industrious one slept on a wall-bed. Then one day the unlucky, industrious one was not there. They never did know where he had gone, and they never heard from him again.

But before that they lived in the apartment, in an atmosphere of brotherhood and mutual understanding. They had this in common: they were all hiding. The difference was in what they were hiding from. The two others were hiding from the future, from the day when they would get degrees and leave the university. Jack Burden, however, was hiding from the present. The other two took refuge in the present. Jack Burden took refuge in the past. The other two sat in the living room and argued and drank or played cards or read, but Jack Burden was sitting, as like as not, back in his bedroom before a little pine table, with the notes and papers and books before him, scarcely hearing the voices. He might come out and take a drink or take a hand of cards or argue or do any of the other things they did, but what was real was back in that bedroom on the pine table.

What was back in the bedroom on the pine table?

A large packet of letters, eight tattered, black-bound account books tied together with faded red tape, a photograph, 5 x 8 inches, mounted on cardboard and stained in its lower half by water, and a plain gold ring, man-sized, with some engraving in it, on a loop of string. The past. Or that part of the past which had gone by the name of Cass Mastern.

Cass Mastern was one of Jack Burden's father's two maternal uncles, a brother of his mother, Lavinia Mastern, a great-uncle to Jack Burden. The other great-uncle was named Gilbert Mastern, who died in 1914, at the age of ninety-four or five, rich, a builder of railroads, a sitter on boards of directors, and left the packet of letters, the black account books, and the photograph, and a great deal of money to a grandson (and not a penny to Jack Burden). Some ten years later the heir of Gilbert Mastern, recollecting that his cousin Jack Burden, with whom he had no personal acquaintance, was a student of history, or something of the sort, sent him the packet of letters, the account books, and the photograph, asking if he, Jack Burden, thought that the enclosures were of any "financial interest" since he, the heir, had heard that libraries sometimes would pay a "fair sum for old papers and antebellum relics and keepsakes." Jack Burden replied that, since Cass Mastern had been of no historical importance as an individual, it was doubtful that any library would pay more than a few dollars, if anything, for the material, and asked for instructions as to the disposition of the parcel. The heir replied that under the circumstances Jack Burden might keep the things for "sentimental reasons."

So Jack Burden made the acquaintance of Cass Mastern, his great-uncle, who had died in 1864 at a military hospital in Atlanta, who had been only a heard but forgotten name to him, and who was the pair of dark, wide-set, deep eyes which burned out of the photograph, through the dinginess and dust and across more than fifty years. The eyes, which were Cass Mastern, stared out of a long, bony face, but a young face with full lips above a rather thin, curly black beard. The lips did not seem to belong to that bony face and the burning eyes.

The young man in the picture, standing visible from the thighs up, wore a loose-fitting, shapeless jacket, too large in the collar, short in the sleeves, to show strong wrists and bony hands clasped at the waist. The thick dark hair, combed sweepingly back from the high brow, came down long and square-cut, after the fashion of time, place, and class, almost to brush the collar of the coarse, hand-me-down-looking jacket, which was the jacket of an infantryman in the Confederate Army.

But everything in the picture, in contrast with the dark, burning eyes, seemed accidental. That jacket, however, was not accidental. It was worn as the result of calculation and anguish, in pride and self-humiliation, in the conviction that it would be worn in death. But death was not to be that quick and easy. It was to come slow and hard, in a stinking hospital in Atlanta. The last letter in the packet was not in Cass Mastern's hand. Lying in the hospital with his rotting wound, he dictated his farewell letter to his brother, Gilbert Mastern. The letter, and the last of the account books in which Cass Mastern's journal was kept, were eventually sent back home to

Mississippi, and Cass Mastern was buried somewhere in Atlanta, nobody had ever known where.

It was, in a sense, proper that Cass Mastern – in the gray jacket, sweat-stiffened, and prickly like a hair shirt, which it was for him at the same time that it was the insignia of a begrudged glory – should have gone back to Georgia to rot slowly to death. For he had been born in Georgia, he and Gilbert Mastern and Lavinia Mastern, Jack Burden's grandmother, in the red hills up toward Tennessee. "I was born," the first page of the first volume of the journal said, "in a log cabin in north Georgia, in circumstances of poverty, and if in later years I have lain soft and have supped from silver, may the Lord not let die in my heart the knowledge of frost and of coarse diet. For all men come naked into the world, and in prosperity 'man is prone to evil as the sparks fly upward.'" The lines were written when Cass was a student at Transylvania College, up in Kentucky, after what he called his "darkness and trouble" had given place to the peace of God. For the journal began with an account of the "darkness and trouble" – which was a perfectly real trouble, with a dead man and a live woman and long nailscratches down Cass Mastern's bony face. "I write this down," he said in the journal, "with what truthfulness a sinner may attain unto that if ever pride is in me, of flesh or spirit, I can peruse these pages and know with shame what evil has been in me, and may be in me, for who knows what breeze may blow upon the charred log and fan up flame again?"

The impulse to write the journal sprang from the "darkness and trouble," but Cass Mastern apparently had a systematic mind, and so he went back to the beginning, to the log cabin in the red hills of Georgia. It was the older brother, Gilbert, some fifteen years older than Cass, who lifted the family from the log cabin. Gilbert, who had run away from home when a boy and gone West to Mississippi, was well on the way to being "a cotton-snob" by the time he was twenty-seven or eight, that is, by 1850. The penniless and no doubt hungry boy walking barefoot onto the black soil of Mississippi was to become, ten or twelve years later, the master sitting the spirited roan stallion (its name was Powhatan – that from the journal) in front of the white verandah. How did Gilbert make his first dollar? Did he cut the throat of a traveler in the cane-brake? Did he black boots at an inn? It is not recorded. But he made his fortune, and sat on the white verandah and voted Whig. After the war when the white verandah was a pile of ashes and the fortune was gone, it was not surprising that Gilbert, who had made one fortune with his bare hands, out of the very air, could now, with all his experience and cunning and hardness (the hardness harder now for the four years of riding and short rations and disappointment), snatch another one, much greater than the first. If in later years he ever remembered his brother Cass and took out the last letter, the one dictated in the hospital in Atlanta, he must have mused over it with a tolerant irony. For it said: "Remember me, but without grief. If one of us is lucky, it is I. I shall have rest and I hope in the mercy of the Everlasting and in His blessed election. But you, my dear brother, are condemned to eat bread in bitterness and build on the place where the charred embers and ashes are and to make bricks without straw and to suffer in the ruin and guilt of our dear land and in the common guilt of man. In the next bed to me there is a young man from Ohio. He is dying. His moans and curses and prayers are not different from any others to be heard in this tabernacle of pain. He marched hither in his guilt as I in mine. And in the guilt of his land. May a common Salvation lift us both from the dust. And dear brother, I pray God to give you strength for what is to come." Gilbert must have smiled, looking back, for he had eaten little bread in bitterness. He had had his own kind of strength. By 1870 he was again well off. By 1875 he was rich. By 1880 he had a fortune, was living in New York, was a name, a thick, burly man, slow of movement, with a head like a block of bare granite. He had lived out of one world into another. Perhaps he was even more at home in the new than in the old. Or perhaps the Gilbert Masterns are always at home in any world. As the Cass Masterns are never at home in any world.

But to return: Jack Burden came into possession of the papers from the grandson of Gilbert Mastern. When the time came for him to select a subject for his dissertation for his Ph.D., his professor suggested that he edit the journal and letters of Cass Mastern, and write a biographical essay, a social study based on those and other materials. So Jack Burden began his first journey into the past.

It seemed easy at first. It was easy to reconstruct the life of the log cabin in the red hills. There were the first letters back from Gilbert, after he had begun his rise (Jack Burden managed to get possession of the other Gilbert Mastern papers of the period before the Civil War). There was the known pattern of that life, gradually altered toward comfort as Gilbert's affluence was felt at that distance. Then, in one season, the mother and father died, and Gilbert returned to burst, no doubt, upon Cass and Lavinia as an unbelievable vision, a splendid impostor in black broadcloth, varnished boots, white linen, heavy gold ring. He put Lavinia in a school in Atlanta, bought her trunks of dresses, and kissed her good-bye. ("Could you not have taken me with you, dear Brother Gilbert? I would have been ever so dutiful and affectionate a sister," so she wrote to him, in the copy-book hand, in brown ink, in a language not her own, a language of schoolroom propriety. "May I not come to you now? Is there no little task which I –" But Gilbert had other plans. When the time came for her to appear in his house she would be ready.) But he took Cass with him, a hobbledehoy now wearing black and mounted on a blooded mare.

At the end of three years Cass was not a hobbledehoy. He had spent three years of monastic rigor at *Valhalla*, Gilbert's house, under the tuition of a Mr. Lawson and of Gilbert himself. From Gilbert he learned the routine of plantation management. From Mr. Lawson, a tubercular and vague young man from Princeton, New Jersey, he learned some geometry, some Latin, and a great deal of Presbyterian theology. He liked the books, and once Gilbert (so the journal said) stood in the doorway and watched him bent over the table and then said, "At least you may be good for *that*."

But he was good for more than that. When Gilbert gave him a small plantation, he managed it for two years with such astuteness (and such luck, for both season and market conspired in his behalf) that at the end of the time he could repay Gilbert a substantial part of the purchase price. Then he went, or was sent, to Transylvania. It was Gilbert's idea. He came into the house on Cass's plantation one night to find Cass at his books. He walked across the room to the table where the books lay, by which Cass now stood. Gilbert stretched out his arm and tapped the open book with his riding crop. "You might make something out of that," he said. The journal reported that, but it did not report what book it was that Gilbert's riding crop tapped. It is not important what book it was. Or perhaps it is important, for something in our mind, in our imagination, wants to know the fact. We see the red, square, strong hand ("My brother is strong-made and florid") protruding from the white cuff, grasping the crop which in that grasp looks fragile like a twig. We see the flick of the little leather loop on the open page, a flick brisk, not quite contemptuous, but we cannot make out the page.

In any case, it probably was not a book on theology, for it seems doubtful that

Gilbert, in such a case, would have used the phrase "make something out of that." It might have been a page of the Latin poets, however, for Gilbert would have discovered that, in small doses, they went well with politics or the law. So Transylvania College it was to be, suggested, it developed, by Gilbert's neighbor and friend, Mr. Davis, Mr. Jefferson Davis, who had once been a student there. Mr. Davis had studied Greek.

At Transylvania, in Lexington, Cass discovered pleasure. "I discovered that there is an education for vice as well as for virtue, and I learned what was to be learned from the gaming table, the bottle, and the racecourse, and from the illicit sweetness of the flesh." He had come out of the poverty of the cabin and the monastic regime of *Valhalla* and the responsibilities of his own little plantation; and he was tall and strong and, to judge from the photograph, well favored, with the burning dark eyes. It was no wonder that he "discovered pleasure" – or that pleasure discovered him. For, though the journal does not say so, in the events leading up to the "darkness and trouble," Cass seems to have been, in the beginning at least, the pursued rather than the pursuer.

The pursuer is referred to in the journal as "She" and "Her." But I learned the name. "She" was Annabelle Trice, Mrs. Duncan Trice, and Mr. Duncan Trice was a prosperous young banker of Lexington, Kentucky, who was an intimate of Cass Mastern and apparently one of those who led him into the paths of pleasure. I learned the name by going back to the files of the Lexington newspapers for the middle 1850s to locate the story of a death. It was the death of Mr. Duncan Trice. In the newspaper it was reported as an accident. Duncan Trice had shot himself by accident, the newspaper said, while cleaning a pair of pistols. One of the pistols, already cleaned, lay on the couch where he had been sitting, in his library, at the time of the accident. The other, the lethal instrument, had fallen to the floor. I had known, from the journal, the nature of the case, and when I had located the special circumstances, I had learned the identity of "She." Mr. Trice, the newspaper said, was survived by his widow, née Annabelle Puckett, of Washington, D. C.

Shortly after Cass had come to Lexington, Annabelle Trice met him. Duncan Trice brought him home, for he had received a letter from Mr. Davis, recommending the brother of his good friend and neighbor, Mr. Gilbert Mastern. (Duncan Trice had come to Lexington from Southern Kentucky, where his own father had been a friend of Samuel Davis, the father of Jefferson, when Samuel lived at *Fairview* and bred racers.) So Duncan Trice brought the tall boy home, who was no longer a hobbledehoy, and set him on a sofa and thrust a glass into his hand and called in his pretty, husky-voiced wife, of whom he was so proud, to greet the stranger. "When she first entered the room, in which the shades of approaching twilight were gathering though the hour for the candles to be lit had scarcely come, I thought that her eyes were black, and the effect was most striking, her hair being of such a fairness. I noticed, too, how softly she trod and with a gliding motion which, though she was perhaps of a little less than moderate stature, gave an impression, of regal dignity –

> *et avertens rosea cervice refulsit*
> *ambrosiaeque comae divinum vertice odorem*
> *spiravere, pedes vestis defluxit ad imos,*
> *et vera incessu patuit dea.*

So the Mantuan said, when Venus appeared and the true goddess was revealed by her gait. She came into the room and was the true goddess as revealed in her movement, and was, but for Divine Grace (if such be granted to a parcel of corruption such as I), my true damnation. She gave me her hand and spoke with a tingling huskiness which made me think of rubbing my hand upon a soft deep-piled cloth, like velvet, or upon a fur. It would not have been called a musical voice such as is generally admired. I know that, but I can only set down what effect it worked upon my own organs of hearing."

Was she beautiful? Well, Cass set down a very conscientious description of every feature and proportion, a kind of tortured inventory, as though in the midst of the "darkness and trouble," at the very moment of his agony and repudiation he had to take one last backward look even at the risk of being turned into the pillar of salt. "Her face was not large though a little given to fullness. Her mouth was strong but the lips were red and moist and seemed to be slightly parted or about to part themselves. The chin was short and firmly molded. Her skin was of a great whiteness, it seemed then before the candles were lit, but afterwards I was to see that it had a bloom of color upon it. Her hair, which was in a remarkable abundance and of great fairness was drawn back from her face and worn in large coils low down to the neck. Her waist was very small and her breasts, which seemed naturally high and round and full, were the higher for the corseting. Her dress, of a dark blue silk, I remember, was cut low to the very downward curve of the shoulders, and in the front showed how the breasts were lifted like twin orbs."

Cass described her that way. He admitted that her face was not beautiful. "Though agreeable in its proportions," he added. But the hair was beautiful, and "of an astonishing softness, upon your hand softer and finer than your thought of silk." So even in that moment, in the midst of the "darkness and trouble," the recollection intruded into the journal of how that abundant, fair hair had slipped across his fingers. "But," he added, "her beauty was her eyes."

He had remarked how, when she first came in, into the shadowy room, her eyes had seemed black. But he had been mistaken, he was to discover, and that discovery was the first step toward his undoing. After the greeting ("she greeted me with great simplicity and courtesy and bade me again take my seat"), she remarked on how dark the room was and how the autumn always came to take one unawares. Then she touched a bellpull and a Negro boy entered. "She commanded him to bring light and to mend the fire, which was sunk to ash, or near so. He came back presently with a seven-branched candle stick which he put upon the table back of the couch on which I sat. He struck a lucifer but she said 'Let me light the candles.' I remember it as if yesterday. I was sitting on the couch. I had turned my head idly to watch her light the candles. The little table was between us. She leaned over the candles and applied the lucifer to the wicks, one after another. She was leaning over, and I saw how the corset lifted her breasts together, but because she was leaning the eyelids shaded her eyes from my sight. Then she raised her head a little and looked straight at me over the new candle flames, and I saw all once that her eyes were not black. They were blue, but a blue so deep that I can only compare it to the color of the night sky in autumn when the weather is clear and there is no moon and the stars have just well come out. And I had not known how large they were. I remember saying that to myself with perfect clearness, 'I had not know how large they were,' several times, slowly, like a man marveling. Then I knew that I was blushing and I felt my tongue dry like ashes in my mouth and I was in the manly state.

"I can see perfectly clearly the expression on her face even now, but I cannot interpret it. Sometimes I have thought of it as having a smiling hidden in it, but I cannot be sure. (I am only sure of this: that man is never safe and damnation is ever at hand, O God and my Redeemer!) I sat there, one hand clenched upon my knee and the other holding an empty glass, and I felt that I could not breathe. Then she said to her husband, who stood in the room behind me, 'Duncan, do you see that Mr. Mastern is in need of refreshment?' "

The year passed. Cass, who was a good deal younger than Duncan Trice, and as a matter of fact several years younger than Annabelle Trice, became a close companion of Duncan Trice and learned much from him, for Duncan Trice was rich, fashionable, clever, and high-spirited ("much given to laughter and full-blooded"). Duncan Trice led Cass to the bottle, the gaming table and the racecourse, but not to "the illicit sweetness of the flesh." Duncan Trice was passionately and single-mindedly devoted to his wife. ("When she came into a room, his eyes would fix upon her without shame, and I have seen her avert her face and blush for the boldness of his glance when company was present. But I think that it was done by him unawares, his partiality for her was so great.") No, the other young men, members of the Trice circle, led Cass first to the "illicit sweetness." But despite the new interests and gratifications, Cass could work at his books. There was even time for that, for he had great strength and endurance.

So the year passed. He had been much in the Trice house, but no word beyond the "words of merriment and civility" had passed between him and Annabelle Trice. In June, there was a dancing party at the house of some friend of Duncan Trice. Duncan Trice, his wife, and Cass happened to stroll at some moment into the garden and to sit in a little arbor, which was covered with a jasmine vine. Duncan Trice returned to the house to get punch for the three of them, leaving Annabelle and Cass seated side by side in the arbor. Cass commented on the sweetness of the scent of jasmine. All at once, she burst out ("her voice low-pitched and with its huskiness, but in a vehemence which astonished me"), "Yes, yes, it is too sweet. It is suffocating. I shall suffocate." And she laid her right hand, with the fingers spread, across the bare swell of her bosom above the pressure of the corset.

"Thinking her taken by some sudden illness," Cass recorded in the journal, "I asked if she were faint. She said no, in a very low, husky voice. Nevertheless I rose, with the expressed intention of getting a glass of water for her. Suddenly she said, quite harshly and to my amazement, because of her excellent courtesy, 'sit down, sit down, I don't want water!' So somewhat distressed in mind that unwittingly I might have offended, I sat down. I looked across the garden where in the light of the moon several couples promenaded down the paths between the low hedges. I could hear the sound of her breathing beside me. It was disturbed and irregular. All at once she said, 'How old are you, Mr. Mastern?' I said twenty-two. Then she said, 'I am twenty-nine.' I stammered something, in my surprise. She laughed as though at my confusion, and said 'Yes, I am seven years older than you, Mr. Mastern. Does that surprise you, Mr. Mastern?' I replied in the affirmative. Then she said, 'seven years is a long time. Seven years ago you were a child, Mr. Mastern.' Then she laughed, with a sudden sharpness, but quickly stopped herself to add, 'But I wasn't a child. Not seven years ago, Mr. Mastern.' I did not answer her, for there was no thought clear in my head. I sat there in confusion, but in the middle of my confusion I was trying to see what she would have looked like as a child. I could call up no image. Then her husband returned from the house."

A few days later Cass went back to Mississippi to devote some months to his plantation, and, under the guidance of Gilbert, to go once to Jackson, the capital, and once to Vicksburg. It was a busy summer. Now Cass could see clearly what Gilbert intended: to make him rich and to put him into politics. It was a flattering and glittering prospect, and one not beyond reasonable expectation for a young man whose brother was Gilbert Mastern. ("My brother is a man of great taciturnity and strong mind, and when he speaks, though he practices no graces and ingratiations, all men, especially those of the sober sort who have responsibility and power, weigh his words with respect.") So the summer passed, under the strong hand and cold eye of Gilbert. But toward the end of the season, when already Cass was beginning to give thought to his return to Transylvania, an envelope came addressed to him from Lexington, in an unfamiliar script. When Cass unfolded the single sheet of paper a small pressed blossom, or what he discovered to be such, slipped out. For a moment he could not think what it was, or why it was in his hand. Then he put it to his nostrils. The odor, now faint and dusty, was the odor of Jasmine.

The sheet of paper had been folded twice, to make four equal sections. In one section, in a clean, strong, not large script, he read:

"Oh, Cass!" That was all.

It was enough.

One drizzly autumn afternoon, just after his return to Lexington, Cass called at the Trice house to pay his respects. Duncan Trice was not there, having sent word that he had been urgently detained in the town and would be home for a late dinner. Of that afternoon, Cass wrote: "I found myself in the room alone with her. There were shadows, as there had been that afternoon, almost a year before, when I first saw her in that room, and when I had thought that her eyes were black. She greeted me civilly, and I replied and stepped back after having shaken her hand. Then I realized that she was looking at me fixedly, as I at her. Suddenly, her lips parted slightly and gave a short exhalation, like a sigh or suppressed moan. As of one accord, we moved toward each other and embraced. No words were passed between us as we stood there. We stood there for a long time, or so it seemed. I held her body close to me in a strong embrace, but we did not exchange a kiss, which upon recollection has since seemed strange. But was it strange? Was it strange that some remnant of shame should forbid us to look each other in the face? I felt and heard my heart racing within my bosom. With a loose feeling as though it were unmoored and were leaping at random in a great cavity within me, but at the same time I scarcely accepted the fact of my situation. I was somehow possessed by incredulity, even as to my identity, as I stood there and my nostrils were filled with the fragrance of her hair. It was not to be believed that I was Cass Mastern, who stood thus in the house of a friend and benefactor. There was no remorse or horror at the turpitude of the act, but only the incredulity which I have referred to. (One feels incredulity at observing the breaking of a habit, but horror at the violation of a principle. Therefore what virtue and honor I had known in the past had been an accident of habit and not the fruit of will. Or can virtue be the fruit of human will? The thought is pride.)

"As I have said, we stood there for a long time in a strong embrace, but with her face lowered against my chest, and my own eyes staring across the room and out a window into the deepening obscurity of the evening. When she finally raised her face, I saw that she had been silently weeping. Why was she weeping? I have asked myself that question. Was it because even on the verge of committing an irremediable wrong she could weep at the consequence of an act which she felt powerless to avoid? Was it because the man who held her was much younger than she and his embrace gave her the reproach of youth and seven years? Was it because he had come seven years too late and could not come in innocence? It does not matter what the cause. If it was the first, then the tears can only prove that sentiment is no substitute for obligation, if the second, then they only prove that pity of the self is no substitute for wisdom. But she shed the tears and finally lifted her face to mine with those tears bright in her large eyes, and even now, though those tears were my ruin, I cannot wish them unshed, for they testify to the warmth of her heart and prove that whatever her sin (and mine) she did not step to it with a gay foot and with the eyes hard with lust and fleshly cupidity.

"The tears were my ruin, for when she lifted her face to me some streak of tenderness was mixed into my feelings, and my heart seemed to flood itself into my bosom to fill that great cavity wherein it had been leaping. She said, 'Cass' – the first time she had ever addressed me by my Christian name. 'Yes,' I replied. 'Kiss me,' she said very simply, 'you can do it now.' So I kissed her. And thereupon in the blindness of our mortal blood and in the appetite of our hearts we performed the act. There in that very room with the servants walking with soft feet somewhere in the house and with the door to the room open and with her husband expected, and not yet in the room the darkness of evening. But we were secure in our very recklessness, as though the lustful heart could give forth a cloud of darkness in which we were shrouded, even as Venus once shrouded Aeneas in a cloud so that he passed unspied among men to approach the city of Dido. In such cases as ours the very recklessness gives security as the strength of the desire seems to give the sanction of justice and righteousness.

"Though she had wept and had seemed to perform the act in a sadness and desperation, immediately afterward she spoke cheerfully to me. She stood in the middle of the room pressing her hair into place, and I stumblingly ventured some remark about our future, a remark very vague for my being was still confused, but she responded, 'Oh, let us not think about it now,' as though I had broached a subject of no consequence. She promptly summoned a servant and asked for lights. They were brought and thereupon I inspected her face to find it fresh and unmarked. When her husband came, she greeted him familiarly and affectionately, and as I witnessed it my own heart was wrenched, but not, I must confess, with compunction. Rather with a violent jealousy. When he spoke to me, so great was my disturbance that I was sure that my face could but betray it."

So began the second phase of the story of Cass Mastern. All that year, as before, he was often in the house of Duncan Trice, and as before he was often with him in field sports, gambling, drinking, and race-going. He learned, he says, to "wear his brow unwrinkled," to accept the condition of things. As for Annabelle Trice, he says that sometimes looking back, he could scarcely persuade himself that "she had shed tears." She was, he says, "of a warm nature, reckless and passionate of disposition, hating all mention of the future (she would never let me mention times to come), agile, resourceful, and cheerful in devising to gratify our appetites, but with a womanly tenderness such as any man might prize at a sanctified hearthside." She must indeed have been agile and resourceful, for to carry on such a liaison undetected in that age and place must have been a problem. There was a kind of summer house at the foot of the Trice garden, which one could enter unobserved from an alley. Some of their meetings occurred there. A half-sister of Annabelle Trice, who lived in

Lexington, apparently assisted the lovers or winked at their relationship, but, it seems, only after some pressure by Annabelle, for Cass hints at "a stormy scene." So some of the meetings were there. But now and then Duncan Trice had to be out of town on business, and on those occasions Cass would be admitted, late at night, to the house, even during a period when Annabelle's mother and father were staying there; so he actually lay in the very bed belonging to Duncan Trice.

There were, however, other meetings, unplanned and unpredictable moments snatched when they found themselves left alone together. "Scarce a corner, cranny, or protected nook or angle of my friend's trusting house did we not at one time or another defile, and that even in the full and shameless light of day," Cass wrote in the journal, and when Jack Burden, the student of history, went to Lexington and went to see the old Trice home he remembered the sentence. The town had grown up around the house, and the gardens, except for a patch of lawn, were gone. But the house was well maintained (some people named Miller lived there and by and large respected the place) and Jack Burden was permitted to inspect the premises. He wandered about the room where the first meeting had taken place and she had raised her eyes to Cass Mastern above the newly lighted candles and where, a year later, she had uttered the sigh, or suppressed moan, and stepped to his arms; and out into the hall, which was finely proportioned and with a graceful stair; and into a small, shadowy library; and to a kind of back hall, which was a well "protected nook or angle" and had, as a matter of fact, furniture adequate to the occasion. Jack Burden stood in the main hall, which was cool and dim, with dully glittering floors, and in the silence of the house, recalled that period, some seventy years before, of the covert glances, the guarded whispers, the abrupt rustling of silk in the silence (the costume of the period certainly had not been designed to encourage casual vice), the sharp breath, the reckless sighs. Well, all of that had been a hell of a long time before, and Annabelle Trice and Cass Mastern were long since deader than mackerel, and Mrs. Miller, who came down to give Jack Burden a cup of tea (she was flattered by the "historical" interest in her house, though she didn't guess the exact nature of the case), certainly was not "agile" and didn't look "resourceful" and probably had used up all her energy in the Ladies Altar Guild of Saint Luke's Episcopal Church and in the D.A.R.

The period of the intrigue, the second phase of the story of Cass Mastern, lasted all of one academic year, part of the summer (for Cass was compelled to go back to Mississippi for his plantation affairs and to attend the wedding of his sister Lavinia, who married a well-connected young man named Willis Burden), and well through the next winter, when Cass was back in Lexington. Then, on March 19, 1854, Duncan died, in his library (which was a "protected nook or angle" of his house), with a lead slug nearly the size of a man's thumb in his chest. It was quite obviously an accident.

The widow sat in church, upright and immobile. When she once raised her veil to touch at her eyes with a handkerchief, Cass Mastern saw that the cheek was "pale as marble but for a single flushed spot, like the flush of fever." But even when the veil was lowered he detected the fixed, bright eyes glittering "within that artificial shadow."

Cass Mastern, with five other young men of Lexington, cronies and boon companions of the dead man, carried the coffin. "The coffin which I carried seemed to have no weight, although my friend had been of large frame and had inclined to stoutness. As we proceeded with it, I marveled at the fact of its lightness, and once the fancy flitted into my mind that he was not in the coffin at all, that it was empty, and that all the affair was a masquerade or mock show carried to ludicrous and blasphemous length, for no purpose, as in a dream. Or to deceive me, the fancy came. I was the object of the deception, and all the other people were in league and conspiracy against me. But when that thought came, I suddenly felt a sense of great cunning and a wild exhilaration. I had been too sharp to be caught so. I had penetrated the deception. I had the impulse to hurl the coffin to the ground and see its emptiness burst open and to laugh in triumph. But I did not, and I saw the coffin sink beneath the level of the earth on which we stood and receive the first clods.

"As soon as the sound of the first clods striking the coffin came to me, I felt a great relief, and then a most overmastering desire. I looked toward her. She was kneeling at the foot of the grave, with what thoughts I could not know. Her head was inclined slightly and the veil was over her face. The bright sun poured over her black-clad figure. I could not take my eyes from the sight. The posture seemed to accentuate the charms of her person and to suggest to my inflamed senses the suppleness of her members. Even the funereal tint of her costume seemed to add to the provocation. The sunshine was hot upon my neck and could be felt through the stuff of my coat upon my shoulders. It was preternaturally bright so that I was blinded by it and my eyes were blinded and my senses swam. But all the while I could hear, as from a great distance, the scraping of the spades upon the piled earth and the muffled sound of earth falling into the excavation."

That evening Cass went to the summer house in the garden. It was not by appointment, simply on impulse. He waited there a long time, but she finally appeared, dressed in black "which was scarce darker than the night." He did not speak, or make any sign as she approached, "gliding like a shadow among shadows," but remained standing where he had been, in the deepest obscurity of the summer house. Even when she entered, he did not betray his presence. "I cannot be certain that any premeditation was in my silence. It was prompted by an overpowering impulse which gripped me and sealed my throat and froze my limbs. Before that moment, and afterwards, I knew that it is dishonorable to spy upon another, but at the moment no such considerations presented themselves. I had to keep my eyes fixed upon her as she stood there thinking herself alone in the darkness of the structure. I had the fancy that since she thought herself alone I might penetrate into her being, that I might learn what change, what effect, had been wrought by the death of her husband. The passion which had seized me to the very extent of paroxysm that afternoon at the very brink of my friend's grave was gone. I was perfectly cold now. But I had to know, to try to know. It was as though I might know myself by knowing her. (It is the human defect – to try to know oneself by the self of another. One can only know oneself in God and in His great eye.)

"She entered the summer house and sank upon one of the benches, not more than a few feet from my own location. For a long time I stood there, peering at her. She sat perfectly upright and rigid. At last I whispered her name, as low as might be. If she heard it, she gave no sign. So I repeated her name, in the same fashion, and again. Upon the third utterance, she whispered, 'yes,' but she did not change her posture or turn her head. Then I spoke more loudly, again uttering her name, and instantly, with a motion of wild alarm she rose, with a strangled cry, and her hands lifted toward her face. She reeled, and it seemed that she would collapse to the floor, but she gained control of herself and stood there staring at me. Stammeringly, I made my apology, saying that I had not wanted to startle her, that I had understood her to answer yes to my whisper before I spoke, and I asked her, 'Did you not answer to my whisper?'

She replied that she had.

'Then why were you distressed when I spoke again?' I asked her.

'Because, I did not know that you were here,' she said.

'But,' I said, 'you say that you had just heard my whisper and had answered to it, and now you say that you did not know I was here.'

'I did not know that you were here,' she repeated, in a low voice, and the import of what she was saying dawned upon me.

'Listen,' I said, 'when you heard the whisper – did you recognize it was my voice?'

She stared at me, not answering.

'Answer me,' I demanded, for I had to know.

She continued to stare, and finally replied hesitantly, 'I do not know.'

'You thought it was –' I began, but before I could utter the words she had flung herself upon me, clasping me in desperation like a person frantic with drowning, and ejaculated: 'No, no, it does not matter what I thought, you are here, you are here!' And she drew my face down and pressed her lips against mine to stop my words. Her lips were cold, but they hung upon mine.

I too was perfectly cold, as of a mortal chill. And the coldness was the final horror of the act which we performed, as though two dolls should parody the shame and filth of man to make it doubly shameful.

After, she said to me, 'Had I not found you here tonight, it could never have been between us again.'

'Why?' I demanded.

'It was a sign,' she said.

'A sign?' I asked.

'A sign that we cannot escape, that we –' and she interrupted herself, to resume, whispering fiercely in the dark, 'I do not want to escape – it is a sign – whatever I have done is done.' She grew quiet for a moment, then she said, 'Give me your hand.'

I gave her my right hand. She grasped it, dropped it, and said, 'the other, the other hand.'

I held it out, across my own body, for I was sitting on her left. She seized it with her own left hand, bringing her hand upward from below to press my hand flat against her bosom. Then, fumblingly, she slipped a ring upon my finger, the finger next to the smallest.

'What is that?' I asked.

'A ring,' she answered, paused, and added, 'It is his ring.'

Then I recalled that he, my friend, had always worn a wedding ring, and I felt the metal cold upon my flesh. 'Did you take it off of his finger?' I asked, and the thought shook me.

'No,' she said.

'No?' I questioned.

'No,' she said, 'he took it off. It was the only time he ever took it off.'

I sat beside her, waiting for what, I did not know, while she held my hand pressed against her bosom. I could feel it rise and fall. I could say nothing.

Then she said, 'do you want to know how – how he took it off?'

'Yes,' I said in the dark, and waiting for her to speak, I moved my tongue out upon my dry lips.

'Listen,' she commanded me in an imperious whisper, 'that evening after – after it happened – after the house was quiet again, I sat in my room, in the little chair by the dressing table, where I always sit for Phebe to let down my hair. I had sat there out of habit, I suppose, for I was numb all over. I watched Phebe preparing the bed for the night.' (Phebe was her waiting maid, a comely yellow wench somewhat given to the fits and sulls.) 'I saw Phebe remove the bolster and then look down at a spot where the bolster had lain, on my side of the bed. She picked something up and came toward me. She stared at me – and her eyes, they are yellow, you look into them and you can't see what is in them – she stared at me – a long time – and then she held out her hand, clenched shut and she watched me – and then – slow, so slow – she opened up the fingers – and there lay the ring on the palm of her hand – and I knew it was his ring but all I thought was, it is gold and it is lying in a gold hand. For Phebe's hand was gold – I had never noticed how her hand is the color of pure gold. Then I looked up and she was still staring at me, and her eyes were gold, too, and bright and hard like gold. And I knew that she knew.'

'Knew?' I echoed, like a question, for I knew, too, now. My friend had learned the truth – from the coldness of his wife, from the gossip of servants – and had drawn the gold ring from his finger and carried it to the bed where he had lain with her and had put it beneath her pillow and had gone down and shot himself but under such circumstances that no one save his wife would ever guess it to be more than an accident. But he had made one fault of calculation. The yellow wench had found the ring.

'She knows,' she whispered, pressing my hand hard against her bosom, which heaved and palpitated with a new wildness. 'She knows – and she looks at me – she will always look at me.' Then suddenly her voice dropped, and a wailing intonation came into it: 'She will tell. All of them will know. All of them in the house will look at me and know – when they hand me the dish – when they come into the room – and their feet don't make any noise!' She rose abruptly, dropping my hand. I remained seated, and she stood there beside me, her back toward me, the whiteness of her face and hands no longer visible, and to my sight the blackness of her costume faded into the shadow, even in such proximity. Suddenly, in a voice which I did not recognize for its hardness, she said in the darkness above me, 'I will not abide it, I will not abide it!' Then she turned, and with a swooping motion leaned to kiss me upon the mouth. Then she was gone from my side and I heard her feet running up the gravel of the path. I sat there in the darkness for a time longer, turning the ring upon my finger."

After that meeting in the summer house, Cass did not see Annabelle Trice for some days. He learned that she had gone to Louisville, where, he recalled, she had close friends. She had, as was natural, taken Phebe with her. Then he heard that she had returned, and that night, late, went to the summer house in the garden. She was there, sitting in the dark. She greeted him. She seemed, he wrote later, peculiarly cut off, remote, and vague in manner, like a somnambulist or a person drugged. He asked about her trip to Louisville, and she replied briefly that she had been down the river to Paducah. He remarked that he had not known that she had friends in Paducah, and she said that she had none there. Then, all at once, she turned on him, the vagueness changing to violence, and burst out, "You are prying – you are prying into my affair – and I will not tolerate it." Cass stammered out some excuse before she cut in to say, "But if you must know, I'll tell you. I took her there."

For a moment Cass was genuinely confused, "Her?" he questioned. "Phebe," she replied, "I took her to Paducah, and she's gone."

"Gone – gone where?"

"Down the river," she answered, repeated, "down the river," and laughed abruptly, and added, "and she won't look at me any more like that."

"You sold her?"

"Yes, I sold her. In Paducah, to a man who was making up a coffle of Negroes for New Orleans. And nobody knows me in Paducah, nobody knew I was there, nobody knows I sold her, for I shall say she ran away into Illinois. But I sold her. For thirteen hundred dollars."

"You got a good price," Cass said, "even for a yellow girl as sprightly as Phebe." And, as he reports in the journal, he laughed with some "bitterness and rudeness," though he does not say why.

"Yes," she replied, "I got a good price. I made him pay every penny she was worth. And then do you know what I did with the money, do you?"

"When I came off the boat at Louisville, there was an old man, a nigger, sitting on the landing stage, and he was blind and picking on a guitar and singing 'Old Dan Tucker.' I took the money out of my bag and walked to him and laid it in his old hat."

"If you were going to give the money away – if you felt the money was defiled – why didn't you free her?" Cass asked.

"She'd stay right here, she wouldn't go away, she would stay right here and look at me. Oh, no, she wouldn't go away, for she's the wife of a man the Motley's have, their coachman. Oh, she'd stay right here and look at me and tell, tell what she knows, and I'll not abide it!"

Then Cass said "If you had spoken to me I would have bought the man from Mr. Motley and set him free, too."

"He wouldn't have sold," she said, "the Motleys won't sell a servant."

"Even to be freed?" Cass continued, and she cut in, "I tell you I won't have you interfering with my affairs, do you understand that?" And she rose from his side and stood in the middle of the summer house, and, he reports, he saw the glimmer of her face in the shadow and heard her agitated breathing. "I thought you were fond of her," Cass said.

"I was," she said, "until – until she looked at me like that."

"You know why you got that price for her?" Cass asked, and without waiting for an answer, went on: "Because she's yellow and comely and well-made. Oh, the drovers wouldn't take her down chained in a coffle. They wouldn't wear her down. They'll take her down the river soft. And you know why?"

"Yes, I know why," she said, "and what is it to you? Are you so charmed by her?"

"That is unfair," Cass said.

"Oh, I see, Mr. Mastern," she said, "oh, I see, you are concerned for the honor of a black coachman. It is very delicate sentiment, Mr. Mastern. Why –" and she came to stand above him as he still sat on the bench, "why did you not show some such delicate concern for the honor of your friend? Who is now dead."

According to the journal, there was, at this moment, "a tempest of feeling" in his breast. He wrote: "Thus I heard put into words for the first time the accusation which has ever, in all climes, been that most calculated to make wince a man of proper nurture or natural rectitude. What the hardened man can bear to hear from the still small voice within, may yet be when spoken by any external tongue an accusation dire enough to drain his very cheeks of blood. But it was not only that accusation in itself, for in very truth I had supped full of that horror and made it my long familiar. It was not merely the betrayal of my friend. It was not merely the death of my friend, at whose breast I had leveled the weapon. I could have managed somehow to live with those facts. But I suddenly felt that the world outside of me was shifting and the substance of things, and that the process had only begun of a general disintegration of which I was the center. At that moment of perturbation, when the cold sweat broke on my brow, I did not frame any sentence distinctly to my mind. But I have looked back and wrestled to know the truth. It was not the fact that a slave woman was being sold away from the house where she had had protection and kindness and away from the arms of her husband into debauchery. I knew that such things had happened in fact, and I was no child, for after my arrival in Lexington and my acquaintance with the looser sort of companions, the sportsmen and the followers of the races, I had myself enjoyed such diversions. It was not only the fact that the woman for whom I had sacrificed my friend's life and my honor could, in her new suffering, turn on me with a cold rage and the language of insult so that I did not recognize her. It was, instead, the fact that all of these things – the death of my friend, the betrayal of Phebe, the suffering and rage and great change of the woman I had loved – all had come from my single act of sin and perfidy, as the boughs from the bole and the leaves from the bough. Or to figure the matter differently, it was as though the vibration set up in the whole fabric of the world by my act had spread infinitely and with ever increasing power and no man could know the end. I did not put it into words in such fashion, but I stood there shaken by a tempest of feeling."

When Cass had somewhat controlled his agitation, he said, "To whom did you sell the girl?"

"What's it to you?" she answered.

"To whom did you sell the girl?" he repeated.

"I'll not tell you," she said.

"I will find out," he said. "I will go to Paducah and find out."

She grasped him by the arm, driving her fingers deep into the flesh, "like talons," and demanded, "Why – why are you going?"

"To find her," he said. "To find her and buy her and set her free." He had not premeditated this. He heard the words, he wrote in the journal, and knew that that was his intention. "To find her and buy her and set her free," he said, and felt the grasp on his arm released and then in the dark suddenly felt the rake of her nails down his cheek, and heard her voice in a kind of "wild sibilance" saying, "If you do – if you do – oh, I'll not abide it – I will not!"

She flung herself from his side and to the bench. He heard her gasp and sob, "a hard dry sob like a man's." He did not move. Then he heard her voice, "If you do – if you do – she looked at me that way, and I'll not abide it – if you do –" Then after a pause, very quietly: "If you do, I shall never see you again."

He made no reply. He stood there for some minutes, he did not know how long, then he left the summer house, where she still sat, and walked down the alley.

The next morning he left for Paducah. He learned the name of the trader, but he also learned that the trader had sold Phebe (a yellow wench who answered to Phebe's description) to a "private party" who happened to be in Paducah at the time but who had gone on down river. His name was unknown in Paducah. The trader had presumably sold Phebe so that he would be free to accompany his coffle when it had been made up. He had now headed, it was said, into south Kentucky, with a few bucks and wenches, to pick up more. As Cass had predicted, he had not wanted to wear Phebe down by taking her in the coffle. So getting a good figure of profit in Paducah, he had sold her there. Cass went south as far as Bowling Green, but lost track of his man there. So, rather hopelessly, he wrote a letter to the trader, in care of the market at New Orleans, asking for the name of the purchaser and any information about him. Then he swung back north to Lexington.

At Lexington he went down to West Short Street, to the Lewis G. Robards barracoon, which Mr. Robards had converted from the Old Lexington Theater a few years earlier. He had a notion that Mr. Robards, the leading trader of the section, might be able, through his down-river connections, to locate Phebe, if enough of a commission was in sight. At the barracoon there was no one in the office except a boy, who said that Mr. Robards was down river but that Mr. Simms was "holding things down" and was over at the "house" at an "inspection." So Cass went next door to the house. (When Jack Burden was in Lexington investigating the life of Cass Mastern, he saw the "house" still standing, a two-storey brick building of the traditional residential type, roof running lengthwise, door in center of front, window on each side, chimney at each end, lean-to in back. Robards had kept his "choice stock" there and not in the coops, to wait for "inspection.")

Cass found the main door unlocked at the house, entered the hall, saw no one, but heard laughter from above. He mounted the stairs and discovered, at the end of the hall, a small group of men gathered at an open door. He recognized a couple of them, young hangers-on he had seen about town and at the track. He approached and asked if Mr. Simms was about. "Inside," one of the men said, "showing." Over the heads, Cass could see into the room. First he saw a short, strongly made man, a varnished looking man, with black hair, black neck-cloth, large bright black eyes, and black coat, with a crop in his hand. Cass knew immediately that he was a French "speculator," who was buying "fancies" for Louisiana. The Frenchman was staring at something beyond Cass's range of vision. Cass moved farther and could see within.

There he saw the man whom he took to be Mr. Simms, a nondescript fellow in a plug hat, and beyond him the figure of a woman. She was a very young woman, some twenty years old perhaps, rather slender, with skin slightly darker than ivory, probably an octoroon, and hair crisp rather than kinky, and deep dark liquid eyes, slightly bloodshot, which stared at a spot above and beyond the Frenchman. She did not wear the ordinary plaid osnaburg and kerchief of the female slave up for sale, but a white, loosely cut dress, with elbow-length sleeves, and skirts to the floor and no kerchief, only a band to her hair. Beyond her, in the neatly furnished room ("quite genteel," the journal called it, while noting the barred windows), Cass saw a rocking chair and little table, and on the table a sewing basket with a piece of fancy needle-work lying there with the needle stuck in it, "as though some respectable young lady or householder had dropped it casually aside upon rising to greet a guest." Cass recorded that somehow he found himself staring at the needlework.

"Yeah," Mr. Simms was saying, "Yeah." And grasped the girl by the shoulder to swing her slowly around for a complete view. Then he seized one of her wrists and lifted the arm to shoulder level and worked it back and forth a couple of times to show the supple articulation, saying, "yeah." That done, he drew the arm forward, holding it toward the Frenchman, the hand hanging limply from the wrist which he held. (The hand was, according to the journal, "well molded, and the fingers tapered.") "Yeah," Mr. Simms said, "look at that-air hand. Ain't no lady got a littler, teensier hand. And round and soft, yeah?"

"Ain't she got nuthen else round and soft?" one of the men at the door called, and the others laughed.

"Yeah," Mr. Simms said, and leaned to take the hem of her dress, which with a delicate flirting motion he lifted higher than her waist, while he reached out with his other hand to wad the cloth and draw it into a kind of "awkward girdle" about her waist. Still holding the wad of cloth he walked around her, forcing her to turn (she turned "without resistance and as though in a trance") with his motion until her small buttocks were toward the door. "Round and soft, boys," Mr. Simms said, and gave her a good whack on the near buttock to make the flesh tremble. "Ever git yore hand on anything rounder ner softer, boys?" he demanded. "Hit's a cushion, I declare. And shake like sweet jelly."

"God-a-mighty and got on stockings," one of the men said.

While the other men laughed, the Frenchman stepped to the side of the girl, reached out to lay the tip of his riding crop at the little depression just above the beginning of the swell of the buttocks. He held the tip delicately there for a moment, then flattened the crop across the back and moved it down slowly, evenly across each buttock, to trace the fullness of the curve. "Turn her," he said in his foreign voice.

Mr. Simms obediently carried the wad around, and the body followed in the half revolution. One of the men at the door whistled. The Frenchman laid his crop across the woman's belly as though he were a "carpenter measuring something or as to demonstrate its flatness," and moved it down as before, tracing the structure, until he came to rest across the thighs, below the triangle. Then he let his hand fail to his side, with the crop. "Open your mouth," he said to the girl.

She did so, and he peered earnestly at her teeth. Then he leaned and whiffed her breath. "It is a good breath," he admitted, as though grudgingly.

"Yeah," Mr. Simms said, "yeah, you ain't a-finden no better breath."

"Have you any others?" the Frenchman demanded. "On hand?"

"We got 'em," Mr. Simms said.

"Let me see," the Frenchman said, and moved toward the door with, apparently, the "insolent expectation" that the group there would dissolve before him. He went out into the hall, Mr. Simms following. While Mr. Simms locked the door, Cass said to him, "I wish to speak to you, if you are Mr. Simms."

"Huh?" Mr. Simms said ("grunted" according to the journal), but looking at Cass became suddenly civil for he could know from dress and bearing that Cass was not one of the casual hangers-on. So Mr. Simms admitted the Frenchman to the next room to inspect its occupant, and returned to Cass. Cass remarked in the journal that trouble might have been avoided if he had been more careful to speak in private, but he wrote that at the time the matter was so much upon his mind that the men who stood about were as shadows to him.

He explained his wish to Mr. Simms, described Phebe as well as possible, gave the name of the trader in Paducah, and offered a liberal commission. Mr. Simms seemed dubious, promised to do what he could, and then said, "But nine outa ten you won't git her, Mister. And we got sumthen here better. You done seen Delphy, and she's nigh white as airy woman, and a sight more juicy, and that gal you talk about is nuthen but yaller. Now Delphy –"

"But the young gemmun got a hankeren fer yaller," one of the hangers-on said, and laughed, and the others laughed too.

Cass struck him across the mouth. "I struck him with the side of my fist," Cass wrote, "to bring blood. I struck him without thought, and I recollect the surprise which visited me when I saw the blood on his chin and saw him draw a bowie from his shirt-front. I attempted to avoid his first blow, but received it upon my left shoulder. Before he could withdraw, I had grasped his wrist in my right hand, forced it down so that I could also use my left hand, which still had some strength left at that moment, and with a turning motion of my body I broke his arm across my right hip, and then knocked him to the floor. I recovered the bowie from the floor, and with it faced the man who seemed to be the friend of the man who was now prostrate. He had a knife in his hand, but he seemed disinclined to pursue the discussion."

Cass declined the assistance of Mr. Simms, pressed a handkerchief over his wound, walked out of the building and toward his lodgings, and collapsed on West Short Street. He was carried home. The next day he was better. He learned that Mrs. Trice had left the city, presumably for Washington. A couple of days later his wound infected, and for some time he lay in delirium between life and death. His recovery was slow, presumably retarded by what he termed in the journal his "will toward darkness." But his constitution was stronger than his will, and he recovered, to know himself as the "chief of sinners and a plague-spot on the body of the human world." He would have committed suicide except for the fear of damnation for that act, for though "hopeless of Grace I yet clung to the hope of Grace." But sometimes the very fact of damnation because of suicide seemed to be the very reason for suicide: he had brought his friend to suicide and the friend, by that act, was eternally damned; therefore he, Cass Mastern, should, in justice, insure his own damnation by the same act. "But the Lord preserved me from self-slaughter for ends which are His and beyond my knowledge."

Mrs. Trice did not come back to Lexington.

He returned to Mississippi. For two years he operated his plantation, read the Bible, prayed, and, strangely enough, prospered greatly, almost as though against his will. In the end he repaid Gilbert his debt, and set free his slaves. He had some notion of operating the plantation with the same force on a wage basis. "You fool," Gilbert said to him, "be a private fool if you must, but in God's name don't be a public one. Do you think you can work them, them being free? One day work, one day loaf. Do you think you can have a passell of free niggers next door to a plantation with slaves? If you did have to set them free, you don't have to spend the rest of your natural life nursing them. Get them out of this country, and take up law or medicine. Or preach the Gospel and at least make a living out of all this praying." Cass tried for more than a year to operate the plantation with his free negroes, but was compelled to confess that the project was a failure. "Get them out of the country," Gilbert said to him. "And why don't you go with them. Why don't you go North?"

"I belong here," Cass replied.

"Well, why don't you preach abolition right here?" Gilbert demanded. "Do something, do anything, but stop making a fool of yourself trying to raise cotton with free niggers."

"Perhaps I shall preach abolition," Cass said, "someday. Even here. But not now.

I am not worthy to instruct others. Not now. But meanwhile there is my example. If it is good, it is not lost. Nothing is ever lost."

"Except your mind," Gilbert said, and flung heavily from room.

There was a sense of trouble in the air. Only Gilbert's great wealth and prestige and scarcely concealed humorous contempt for Cass saved Cass from ostracism, or worse. ("His contempt for me is a shield," Cass wrote. "He treats me like a wayward and silly child who may learn better and who does not have to be taken seriously. Therefore my neighbors do not take me seriously.") But trouble did come. One of Cass's negroes had a broad-wife on a plantation near by. After she had had some minor trouble with the overseer, the husband stole her from the plantation and ran away. Toward the Tennessee border the pair were taken. The man, resisting officers, was shot; the woman was brought back. "See," Gilbert said, "all you have managed to do is get one nigger killed and one nigger whipped. I offer my congratulations." So Cass put his free negroes on a boat bound up river, and never heard of them again.

"I saw the boat head out into the channel, and watched wheels churn against the strong current, and my spirit was troubled. I knew that the negroes were passing from one misery to another, and that the hopes they now carried would be blighted. They had kissed my hands and wept for joy, but I could take no part in their rejoicing I had not flattered myself that I had done anything for them. What I had done I had done for myself, to relieve my spirit of a burden, burden of their misery and their eyes upon me. The wife of my dead friend had found the eyes of the girl Phebe upon her and had gone wild and had ceased to be herself and had sold the girl into misery. I had found their eyes upon me and had freed them into misery, lest I should do worse. For many cannot bear their eyes upon them, and enter into evil and cruel ways in their desperation. There was in Lexington a decade and more before my stay in that city, a wealthy lawyer named Fielding L. Turner, who had married a lady of position from Boston. This lady, Caroline Turner, who had never had blacks around her and who had been nurtured in sentiments oppossed to the institution of human servitude, quickly became notorious for her abominable cruelties performed in her fits of passion. All persons of the community reprehended her floggings, which she perform with her own hands, uttering meanwhile little cries in her throat, according to report. Once while she was engaged in flogging a servant in an apartment on the second floor of her palatial home, a small negro boy entered the room and began to whimper. She seized him and bodily hurled him through the window of the apartment so that he fell upon a stone below and broke his back to become a cripple for his days. To protect her from the process of law and the wrath of the community, Judge Turner committed her to a lunatic asylum. But later the physicians said her to be of sound mind and released her. Her husband in his will left her no slaves, for to do so would, the will said, be to doom them to misery in life and a speedy death. But she procured slaves, among them a yellow coachman named Richard, mild of manner, sensible, and of plausible disposition. One day she had him chained and proceeded to flog him. But he tore himself from the chains that held him to the wall and seized the woman by the throat and strangled her. Later he was captured and hanged for murder, though many wished that his escape had been contrived. This story was told me in Lexington. One lady said to me: 'Mrs. Turner did not understand negroes.' And another: 'Mrs. Turner did it because she was from Boston where the abolitionists are.' But I did not understand. Then, much later, I began to understand. I understood that Mrs. Turner flogged her negroes for the same reason that the wife of my friend sold Phebe down the river: she could not bear their eyes upon her. I understand, for I can no longer bear their eyes upon me. Perhaps only a man like my brother Gilbert can in the midst of evil retain enough of innocence and strength to bear their eyes upon him and to do a little justice in the terms of the great injustice."

So Cass, who had a plantation with no one to work it, went to Jackson, the capital of the state, and applied himself to the law. Before he left, Gilbert came to him and offered to take over the plantation and work it with a force of his people from his own great place on a share basis. Apparently he was still trying to make Cass rich. But Cass declined, and Gilbert said: "You object to my working it with slaves, is that it? Well, let me tell you, if you sell it, it will be worked with slaves. It is black land and will be watered with black sweat. Does it make any difference then, which black sweat falls on it?" And Cass replied that he was not going to sell the plantation. Then Gilbert, in an apopletic rage, bellowed: "My God, man, it is land, don't you understand, it is land, and land cries out for man's hand!" But Cass did not sell. He installed a caretaker in the house, and rented a little land to a neighbor for pasture.

He went to Jackson, sat late with his books, and watched trouble gathering over the land. For it was the autumn of 1858 when he went to Jackson. On January 8, 1861, Mississippi passed the Ordinance of Secession. Gilbert had opposed secession, writing to Cass: "The fools, there is not a factory for arms in the state. Fools not to have prepared themselves if they have foreseen the trouble. Fools, if they have not foreseen it, to act thus in the face of facts. Fools not to temporize now and, if they must, prepare themselves to strike a blow. I have told responsible men to prepare. All fools." To which Cass replied: "I pray much for peace." But later, he wrote: "I have talked with Mr. French, who is, as you know, the Chief of Ordnance, and he says that they have only old muskets for troops, and those but flintlocks. The agents have scraped the state for shotguns, at the behest of Governor Pettus. Shotguns, Mr. French said, and curled his lips. And what shotguns, he added, and then told me of a weapon contributed to the cause, an old musket barrel strapped with metal to a piece of cypress rail crooked at one end. An old slave gave this treasure to the cause, and does one laugh or weep?" (One can guess what Gilbert would have done, reading the letter.) After Jefferson Davis had come back to Mississippi, having resigned from the Senate, and had accepted the command of the troops of Mississippi with the rank of Major-General, Cass called upon him, at the request of Gilbert. He wrote to Gilbert: "The General says that they have given him 10,000 men, but not a stand of modern rifles. But the General also said, they have given me a very fine coat with fourteen brass buttons in front and a black velvet collar. Perhaps we can use the buttons in our shotguns, he said, and smiled."

Cass saw Mr. Davis once more, for he was with Gilbert on the steamboat *Natchez* which carried the new President of the Confederacy on the first stage of his journey from his plantation, Brierfield, to Montgomery. "We were on old Mr. Tom Leather's boat," Cass wrote in the journal, "which had been supposed to pick up the President at a landing a few miles below Brierfield. But Mr. Davis was delayed in leaving his house and was rowed out to us. I leaned on the rail and saw the little black skiff proceeding toward us over the red water. A man waved from the skiff to us. The captain of the *Natchez* observed the signal, and gave a great blast of his boat's whistle which made our ears tingle and shivered out over the expanse of waters. Our boat stopped and the skiff approached. Mr. Davis was received on board. As the steamboat moved on, Mr. Davis looked back and lifted his hand in salute to the negro servant (Isaiah Montgomery whom I had known at Brierfield) who stood in the skiff, which rocked in the wash of the steamboat, and waved his farewell. Later, as we proceeded upriver toward the bluffs of Vicksburg, he approached my brother, with whom I was standing on the deck. We had previously greeted him. My brother again, and more intimately, congratulated Mr. Davis, who replied that he could take no pleasure in the honor. 'I have,' he said, 'always looked upon the Union with a superstitious reverence and have freely risked my life for its dear flag on more than one battlefield, and you, gentlemen, can conceive the sentiment now in me that the object of my attachment for many years has been withdrawn from me.' And he continued, 'I have in the present moment only the melancholy pleasure of an easy conscience.' Then he smiled, as he did rarely. Thereupon he took his leave of us and retired within. I had observed how worn to emaciation was his face by illness and care, and how thin the skin lay over the bone. I remarked to my brother that Mr. Davis did not look well. He replied, 'a sick man, it is a fine how-de-do to have a sick man for a president.' I responded that there might be no war, that Mr. Davis hoped for peace. But my brother said, 'make no mistake, the Yankees will fight and they will fight well and Mr. Davis is a fool to hope for peace.' I replied, 'all good men hope for peace.' At this my brother uttered an indistinguishable exclamation and said, 'what we want now that they've got into this is not a good man but a man who can win, and I am not interested in the luxury of Mr. Davis' conscience.' Then my brother and I continued our promenade in silence, and I reflected that Mr. Davis was a good man. But the world is full of good men, I reflect as I write these lines, and yet the world drives hard into darkness and the blindness of blood, even as now late at night I sit in this hotel room in Vicksburg, and I am moved to ask the meaning of our virtue. May God hear our prayer!"

Gilbert received a commission as colonel in a cavalry regiment. Cass enlisted as a private in the Second Mississippi Rifles. "You could be a captain," Gilbert said, "or a major. You've got brains enough for that. And," he added, "damned few of them have." Cass replied that he preferred to be a private soldier, "marching with other men." But he could not tell his brother why, or tell his brother that, though he would march with other men and would carry a weapon in his hand, he would never take the life of an enemy. "I must march with these men who march," he wrote in the journal, "for they are my people and I must partake with them of all bitterness, and that more fully. But I cannot take the life of another man. How can I who have taken the life of my friend, take the life of an enemy, for I have used up my right to blood?" So Cass marched away to war, carrying the musket which was, for him, but a meaningless burden, and wearing on a string, against the flesh of his chest, beneath the fabric of the gray jacket, the ring which had once been Duncan Trice's wedding ring and which Annabelle Trice, that night in the summer house, slipped onto his finger as his hand lay on her bosom.

Cass marched to Shiloh, between the fresh fields, for it was early April, and then into the woods that screened the river. (Dogwood and redbud would have been out then.) He marched into the woods, heard the lead whistle by his head, saw the dead men on the ground, and the next day came out of the woods and moved in the sullen withdrawal toward Corinth. He had been sure that he would not surivive the battle. But he had survived, and moved down the crowded road "as in a dream." And he wrote: "And I felt that henceforward I should live in that dream." The dream took him into Tennessee again – Chickamauga, Knoxville, Chattanooga, and the nameless skirmishes, and the bullet for which he waited did not find him. He became known as a man of extreme courage. At Chickamauga, when his company wavered in the enemy fire and seemed about to break in its attack, he moved steadily up the slope and could not understand his own inviolability. And the men regrouped, and followed. "It seemed strange to me," he wrote, "that I who in God's will sought death and could not find it, should in my seeking lead men to it who did not seek." When Colonel Hickman congratulated him, he could "find no words" for answer.

But if he had put on the gray jacket in anguish of spirit and in hope of expiation, he came to wear it in pride, for it was a jacket like those worn by the men with whom he marched. "I have seen men do brave things," he wrote, "and they ask for nothing." More and more into the journals crept the comments of the professional soldier between the prayers and the scruples – criticism of command (of Bragg after Chickamauga), satisfaction and an impersonal pride in manoeuvre or gunnery ("the practice of Marlowe's battery excellent"), and finally the admiration for the feints and delays executed by Johnston's virtuosity on the approaches to Atlanta, at Buzzard's Roost, Snake Creek Gap, New Hope Church, Kenesaw Mountain ("there is always a kind of glory, however stained or obscured, in whatever man's hand does well, and General Johnston does well").

Then, outside Atlanta, the bullet found him. He lay in the hospital and rotted slowly to death. But even before the infection set in, when the wound in the leg seemed scarcely serious, he knew would die. "I shall die," he wrote in the journal, "and shall be spared the end and the last bitterness of war. I have lived to do no man good, and have seen others suffer for my sin. I do not question the Justice of God, that others have suffered for my sin, for it may be that only by the suffering of the innocent does God affirm that men are brothers, and brothers in His Holy Name. And in this room with me now, men suffer for sins not theirs, as for their own. It is a comfort to know that I suffer only for my own." He knew not only that he was to die, but that the war was over. "It is over. It is all over but the dying, which will go on. Though the boil has come to a head and has burst, yet must the pus flow. Men shall yet come together and die in the common guilt of man and in the guilt that sent them hither from far places and distant firesides. But God in His Mercy has spared me the end. Blessed be His Name."

There was no more in the journal. There was only the letter to Gilbert, written in the strange hand, dictated by Cass after he had grown too weak to write. "Remember me, but without grief. If one of us is lucky, it is I . . ."

Atlanta fell. In the last confusion, the grave of Cass Mastern was not marked. Someone at the hospital, a certain Albert Calloway, kept Cass's papers and the ring which he had carried on the cord around his neck, and much later, after the war in fact, sent them to Gilbert Mastern with a courteous note. Gilbert preserved the journal, the letters from Cass, the picture of Cass, and the ring on its cord, and after Gilbert's death, the heir finally sent the packet to Jack Burden, the student of history and the grand-nephew of Cass and Gilbert Mastern. So they came to rest on the little pine table in Jack Burden's bedroom in the slatternly apartment which he occupied with the two older graduate students, the unlucky, industrious, and alcoholic one, and the lucky, idle, and alcoholic one.

Jack Burden lived with the Mastern papers for a year and a half. He wanted to know all of the facts of the world in which Cass and Gilbert Mastern had lived, and he did know many of the facts. And he felt that he knew Gilbert Mastern. Gilbert Mastern had kept no journal, but he felt that he knew him, the man with the head like the block of bare granite, who had lived through one world into another and had been at home in both. But the day came when Jack Burden sat down at the pine table and realized that he did not know Cass Mastern. He did not have to know Cass Mastern to get the degree; he only had to know the facts about Cass Mastern's world. But without knowing Cass Mastern, he could not put down the facts about Cass Mastern's world. Not that Jack Burden said that to himself. He simply sat there at the pine table, night after night, staring at the papers before him, twisting the ring on its cord, staring at the photograph, and writing nothing. Then he would get up to get a drink of water, and would stand in the dark kitchen, holding an old jelly glass in his hand, waiting for the water to run cold from the tap.

The Prison

BY ANDRÉ MALRAUX

The library at Altenburg was impressive. A central column pushed the Roman arches high up into the shadows where bookshelves disappeared, for the room was lit only by electric lamps set at eye level. The night entered through a vast stained glass window. Here and there were a few gothic sculptures, photographs of Tolstoy and Nietzsche, a glass showcase containing letters from the latter to Uncle Walter, a portrait of Montaigne, the death masks of Pascal and Beethoven (those members of the family, my father thought). In a large alcove, his uncle was waiting for him behind a desk that looked like a kitchen table, deliberately isolated – set on a wooden stand a step high, which permitted him to dominate his interlocutor: from just such ostentatious penury did Philip II in his cell look down disdainfully on the nave of the Escurial.

When the train had stopped my father had seen him on the platform: though he didn't know him, he knew his crutches. Standing very straight, with two retainers beside him, his uncle watched his approach with a curious immobility in which he cloaked his infirmity; a very high collar and a little black tie were visible under the light Byronic cape that reached below his knees; gold-rimmed glasses rested on the broken nose of Michelangelo – Michelangelo at the end of a long academic career. . . . A formal welcome in the best manner had been immediately followed by:

"We rise at eight."

To my father's astonishment they had set off on foot. The retainers followed; the solemn outlines of the spruce trees under the sky where a dark lint of clouds was formed by the evil summer wind, the horses' steps and the muffled creaking of the carriage behind were in tone with the silent advance of the rubber-tipped crutches. Some four hundred yards ahead of them the priory, toward which all the dark lines of the valley converged, had finally appeared, its beauty massive and austere. Walter Berger, leaning on his left crutch, had extended his right arm:

"There it is." And modestly: "A barn. Just a barn."

What would the chateau be! my father thought.

"It's a barn. . . ." Walter had repeated, scorning any reply. And they had finally gotten into the carriage.

Walter looked at the barely illuminated portraits and the rows of books in the shadows, as though expecting this cloister of the mind to lift my father to a state of grace. The light struck his face from below, accentuating its quality of unfinished sculpture. He had taken off his glasses and the low light that threw its contours into relief created an illusion of his dead brother's face. This was the man that my grandfather, after a rupture of fifteen years, had wanted as his executor – and it was to send them to him that he had bought the journals that spoke of my father's activity in Turkey.

"I loved Dietrich," Walter said as though bestowing an honor, but not without emotion.

There was in his voice, as in his regard, something absent – as if he had been afraid of committing himself by what he said, or as if his remark had not quite distracted him from some meditation. However, he inquired:

"He had poison ready, I was told, in case the veronal should not . . . be effective!"

"There was a little vial of strychnine on the bedside table. But the revolver was under the bolster too, uncocked."

Standing every week for so many years, at the same hour, at the same place outside the church. . . .

Walter nearly began a sentence, stopped, finally decided:

"Would you be able to illuminate me – I say only: illuminate me – as to the reasons that might have . . . impelled Dietrich to this . . . accident?"

"No. I should even say: on the contrary. Two days before his death we dined together; we happened by chance to talk about Napoleon. He asked me, rather ironically: 'If you could choose a life, whose would you choose?' 'And you?' He thought about it quite a while and all of a sudden said, gravely: 'Well you know, really, *no matter what happens*, if I could live over another life I wouldn't want to be anyone but Dietrich Berger.'"

"I wouldn't want to be anyone but Dietrich Berger," Walter repeated softly. "It is possible for man to care deeply – fanatically – about his own self, even when he is already separated from life. . . ."

From outside, through the rainy evening, came the idiot cries of the chickens. Walter reached his hand toward my father, questioningly:

"And you have no reason to think that during the day that followed, some . . . happening. . . ."

"The suicide was in the 'no matter what happens.'"

"Just the same, you didn't suspect anything? (I say only: suspect. . . .)"

He said: suspect; that was all, simply suspect; nothing more than suspect.

"I was convinced that people who talk about suicide never kill themselves."

The man, my father thought bitterly, to whom my few moments of success or happiness gave more joy or pride than to any other in the world.

Walter murmured in a tone of recollection, the immobility of his mouth accentuated by the low light:

"Still one does recognize death, when it has struck often before. . . ."

"I had never seen a man die to whom I was attached."

"But those Balkan peoples . . . violent, agitated. . . ."

"I have come from Central Asia. The life of the Moslems is a stroke of chance in the universal destiny: they never commit suicide. It's true I have seen many of them die, in Tripolitania. But the ones I saw die were not my friends."

Outside, the drops crackled on the flat leaves of the spindle-trees, as on paper; at regular intervals a heavier drop falling from some gutter, resounded.

"When I was a child," Walter said in a low voice, "I was very much afraid of death. Every year that has brought me closer to it has brought me closer to indifference in regard to it. . . . It was Joubert, I think who said, 'The evening of life brings with it its lamp.'"

My father didn't reply. He was sure that Walter was lying; he could feel anguish breaking through.

"Why," said Walter, "did Dietrich wish to be buried as a Catholic? It's strange – I say only: strange – and hardly reconcilable with suicide. He knew that the Church grants religious burial to suicides only in so far as it admits their . . . irresponsibility."

He seemed jealous of the resoluteness with which his brother had died – and at the same time, proud.

"Irresponsibility was not his strong point. But after all, he rejected the Church, not the Sacraments."

My father hesitated, then went on:

"I believe what happened must have been very painful. You know that the will was sealed. The sentence: 'My formal wish is to be buried as a Catholic,' was written on a separate page and was found on the bedside table where the strychnine was; but the first version had been : '*My formal wish is not to be buried as a Catholic.*' He crossed out the negative later, drawing a large number of lines through it. Probably he hadn't the strength any longer to tear the paper up and write it over again."

"Fear?" Walter suggested.

"Or the end of revolt: humility."

"And besides, what does one ever know? In essentials, man is what he conceals. . . ."

Walter shrugged his shoulders and brought his aged hands together, as children do to make a mud pie:

"A pitiful little heap of secrets. . . ."

"A man is what he does!" my father replied almost brutally. Temperamentally, he was exasperated by what he called, as though speaking of pickpocketing, the psychology-of-secrets. Assuming that my grandfather's suicide had had a "cause," that cause, whether the most banal or the saddest of secrets, was less significant than the strychnine and the revolver – than the resolution by which he had *chosen* death, a death that resembled his life.

"In the realm of secrets," he went on in a more moderate tone, "men are a little too easily equal."

"Yes, you are what is called, I believe, a man of action. . . ."

"It is not action that has made me understand that in essentials, as you put it, man is higher than his secrets."

From the funeral room he saw again the bed, mussed by the men from the hospital who had just taken the body away, and timidly straightened out by Jeanne, with the hollow in it like that of a sleeper; the electricity was still on, as though no one – not even himself – had dared to drive away death by pulling back the curtains. In the half-open closet he saw a little birthday spruce, with all its tiny candles. . . . There was an ashtray on the night table: in it were three cigarette butts: my grandfather had smoked either before he took the veronal, or before he fell asleep. On the edge of the ashtray, an ant was running. It had gone on following its course in a straight line, climbed up on the revolver lying there. Except for a distant automobile horn, and the clop-clop of a carriage in the street, my father heard only the indifferent noise of the little traveling-clock, still going. Mechanical and living like that scratching, all over the earth there stretched the order of the communities of insects, below man's mysterious freedom. Death was there, in the troubling light given off by electric bulbs when one has become aware of daylight beyond the curtains, and the imperceptible trace that people leave who dispose of corpses; from the side of the living came the continual noise of the horn, the sound of the horse's steps receding, the morning calls of birds, human voices – stifled, alien. At that hour, near Kaboul, near Samarkand, the donkey caravans were slowly proceeding, hoofs and stamping lost in Moslem tedium.

The human adventure, the earth. And all that, like his father's finished life, could have been other. . . . He felt himself little by little invaded by an unknown feeling, as he had been on the nocturnal heights of Asia by the presence of the sacred, while around him the padded wings of the little sand-owls beat silently. . . . It was again, but far deeper, the agonizing freedom of that evening in Marseilles, when he watched the shadows sliding in a tenuous odor of cigarettes and absinthe – when Europe was so foreign to him, and he watched it, as freed from time he might have watched an hour from a distant past slide by, with all its unaccustomed retinue. So now he felt all of life itself become unaccustomed thereby he found himself suddenly released – mysteriously foreign to the earth and surprised by it, as he had been after his home-coming by that street where the men of his race slide by in the green hour. . . .

He had finally pulled the curtains. Beyond the classic scrollwork of the great iron door the leaves were the bright green of early summer; a little farther began the darker foliage, down to the almost black lines of the spruce. He became conscious of imagining that all that vegetation was violent.

Like a single human fate, the whole of life was an adventure. He looked at the infinite multiplicity of that banal landscape, listened to the long whisper of Reichbach's awakening, as in his childhood he had looked beyond the constellations at the smaller and smaller stars, until he could see no farther. And from the mere presence of the people passing there, hurrying in the morning sun, alike and differ-ent as leaves, there seemed to issue a secret that did not come only from the death that was still in ambush behind his back, a secret that was far less of death than of life – a secret that would not have been less poignant if man had been immortal.

"I have known that . . . feeling," said Walter. "And it seems to me sometimes that I will find it again, when I am old. . . ."

My father gazed at this man of seventy-five who said: when I am old. . . . Walter fixed his eyes on him, lifted his hand:

"They tell me that you recently dedicated one of your courses to my friend Friedrich Nietzsche, when you were among those . . . Turks? I was in Turin – I hap-pened to be in Turin . . . when I learned that he had just gone crazy there. I hadn't seen him: I had just arrived. Overbeck, who had been informed of it, tumbled, so to speak, from Basel to my lodgings: he had to take the poor man away immediately and hadn't even enough money for the tickets. As usual! You . . . know Nietzsche's face" (Walter indicated the portrait behind him); "but the photographs don't convey his expression: he had a feminine sweetness, in spite of his . . . ogre's moustache. That expression was gone."

His head was still motionless, his voice still withdrawn – as if he were speaking, not to my father but to the books and the illustrious photographs in the shadows, as if no listener would have been quite worthy of understanding him; or rather (my father's impression developed as he listened to him) as if the associates who would have understood what he was going to say were all of another epoch, as if no one, today, would take the trouble to understand, and he were talking only out of cour-tesy, lassitude and a sense of duty. There was in his whole attitude the same haughty modesty that was expressed by his little elevated desk.

"When Overbeck, in his distress had cried 'Friedrich!' the poor man had embraced him and immediately afterwards asked him in a distracted voice: 'Have you ever heard of Friedrich Nietzsche?' Overbeck reached out his hand clumsily. 'I? no, I'm a stupid man. . . .' "

Walter's hand, still raised, imitated Overbeck's. My father loved Nietzsche more than any other writer. Not for his preaching, but for the incomparable generosity of intelligence that he found in him. He listened, uneasy, fascinated.

"Then Friedrich had talked about the honors that were being planned for him. All right . . . we took him away. Luckily we had run into a friend of Overbeck's, a . . . dentist, who was used to handling cases of insanity. . . . I didn't have much money available, so we had to take third class tickets. What could we do! It was a long trip, in those days, from Turin to Basel. The train was almost filled up with poor people, Italian laborers. We knew from Friedrich's fellow-lodgers that he was subject to violent attacks. Finally, we found three seats. I stood in the corridor. Overbeck sat on Friedrich's left; Miescher, the dentist, on his right; next to them was a peasant woman. She looked like Overbeck, the same grandmotherly face. . . . In her basket there was a chicken that kept sticking its head out incessantly; the woman shoved it back in. It was enough to drive you into a fury – I say: a fury! What must it have been for a . . . sick man! I was expecting some terrible incident.

"The train entered the Saint Gothard tunnel, which had just been finished. It took thirty-five minutes then to go through it – thirty-five minutes – and there was no light in the cars, at least in third class. The rocking in the dark, the smell of soot, the feeling that the trip would never end. . . . In spite of the clanking of the train, I could hear the chicken's beak pecking at the basket, and I was waiting. How could we deal with a crisis in that darkness?"

Except for his hardly moving lips, his whole face was still motionless in the theatrical light; but beneath his voice, punctuated by the drops falling from the tiles, there rumbled all the revenge that goes with certain kinds of compassion.

"And suddenly – you . . . are aware that a number of Friedrich's writings were still unpublished – a voice began to rise in the dark, above the clatter of the cars. Friedrich was singing – with perfect articulation, he who stammered in conversation – he was singing a poem we had never heard before; and it was his last poem, *Venice*.

"I do not like Friedrich's music. It is mediocre. But that song was . . . well, really: sublime.

"He had finished well before we left the tunnel. When we came out of the dark everything was the same as before. As before. . . . The same wretched carriage. The same peasant woman, the chicken, the laborers, the dentist. And we, and he, besotted. The mystery you have been talking about, I never felt it so strongly. All that was so . . . fortuitous. . . . And Friedrich much more troubling than a corpse. It was life – I say simply: life. . . . A very . . . curious event had occurred: the song was as strong as life. I had just made a discovery. An important one. In the prison that Pascal speaks of, men have managed to draw from within themselves an answer that permeates, so to speak, with immortality those who are worthy of it. And in that railroad carriage. . . ."

For the first time he made a rather flowing gesture, not with his hand, but with his fist, as though wiping off a blackboard.

"And in that railroad carriage, you see, and sometimes since – I say only: sometimes – the millennia of stars in the sky have seemed to me as much eclipsed by man, as our individual destinies are eclipsed by the stars in the sky. . . ."

He had stopped looking at my father, who was the more troubled by his sudden and apparently absent eloquence, because it took the same form as his own. Even as a child he had never seen Walter; and those ellipses, those abrupt and instinctive images had always been alien to Dietrich Berger. But already Walter had resumed the strange tone of disdain that seemed to be directed, beyond my father, to some invisible interlocutor:

"People passionately in love – I believe that is the expression? – oppose love to death. I never experienced it myself. But I know that certain works withstand the dizziness that comes from the contemplation of our dead, of the stars in the sky, of history. . . . There are a few of them here. No, not those gothic ones; you . . . know the head of the young man from the museum of the Acropolis? The first piece of sculpture to represent a human face, simply a human face; freed from monsters . . . from death . . . from the gods. That day, man was also drawn forth by man from clay. . . . That photograph, there, behind you. I have had the experience of studying it after looking a long time into a microscope. . . . The mystery of matter doesn't touch it."

The low, vast grating of the rain grew more and more delicate on the leaves, like the sound of burned paper disintegrating, came from outside; the big drop was still forming, and resounding as it fell into a puddle, regularly. Walter's voice became more withdrawn than ever:

"The great mystery is not that we should be thrown by chance between the profusion of matter and that of the stars; it is that in this prison we should extract from ourselves images strong enough to negate our nothingness. . . ."

Through the dormer-window, the mushroom-like smell of the trees dripping in the still tepid night came in along with the grating of the woodland silence, mingling with the dusty smell of bindings in the library sunk in darkness. In my father's mind, Nietzsche's song over the metallic din of the wheels, mixed with the image of the old man of Reichbach awaiting death behind the drawn curtains of his room, with the funeral repast, the caricature that corpses impose on those who approach them, the metallic beat of the handles of the coffin being carried away on men's shoulders.

. . . The privilege that Walter was speaking of, how much more power it had against the stars in the sky than against pain! – though even then it would perhaps have triumphed over a dead man's face, if the face were not a face that one loved. . . . For Walter, man was only the "pitiful little heap of secrets" made to nourish those works that as far as the far depths of the shadows surrounded his immobile face; for my father, all the stars in the sky were imprisoned in the feeling that caused a being already inhabited by the wish for death, at the end of a not brilliant and often painful life, to say: "If I could choose another life, I would choose my own. . . ."

Walter tapped his fingers nervously on the book on which his hands were resting. My father recalled the face where the only marks of suicide were a poignant serenity, the disappearance of wrinkles, the agonizing youth of death. . . . And he observed before him the almost similar face, with its strong planes of shadow, the glassy eyes motionless, and on the table, in full light, Walter's trembling hands, the same as his own though larger, the woodcutter's hands of Bergers of Reichbach, veins and hair grey.

Translated from the French by Eleanor Clark

The Interior Castle

BY JEAN STAFFORD

Pansy Vanneman, injured in an automobile accident, often woke up before dawn when the night noises of the hospital still came, in hushed hurry, through her half-open door. By day, when the nurses talked audibly with the interns, laughed without inhibition, and took no pains to soften their footsteps on the resounding composition floors, the routine of the hospital seemed as bland and commonplace as that of a bank or a factory. But in the dark hours, the whispering and the quickly stilled clatter of glasses and basins, the moans of patients whose morphine was wearing off, the soft squeak of a stretcher as it rolled past on its way from the emergency ward – these suggested agony and death. Thus, on the first morning, Pansy had faltered to consciousness long before daylight and had found herself in a ward from every bed of which, it seemed to her, came the bewildered protest of someone about to die. A caged light burned on the floor beside the bed next to hers. Her neighbor was dying and a priest was administering Extreme Unction. He was stout and elderly and he suffered from asthma so that the struggle of his breathing, so close to her, was the basic pattern and all the other sounds were superimposed upon it. Two middle-aged men in overcoats knelt on the floor beside the high bed. In a foreign tongue, the half-gone woman babbled against the hissing and sighing of the Latin prayers. She played with her rosary as if it were a toy: she tried, and failed, to put it into her mouth.

Pansy felt horror, but she felt no pity. An hour or so later, when the white ceiling lights were turned on and everything – faces, counterpanes, and the hands that groped upon them – was transformed into a uniform gray sordor, the woman was wheeled away in her bed to die somewhere else, in privacy. Pansy did not quite take this in, although she stared for a long time at the new, empty bed that had replaced the other.

The next morning, when she again woke up before the light, this time in a private room, she recalled the woman with such sorrow that she might have been a friend. Simultaneously, she mourned the driver of the taxicab in which she had been injured, for he had died at about noon the day before. She had been told this as she lay on a stretcher in the corridor, waiting to be taken to the x-ray room; an intern passing by, had paused and smiled down at her and had said, "Your cab-driver is dead. You were lucky."

Six weeks after the accident, she woke one morning just as daylight was showing on the windows as a murky smear. It was a minute or two before she realized why she was so reluctant to be awake, why her uneasiness amounted almost to alarm. Then she remembered that her nose was to be operated on today. She lay straight and motionless under the seersucker counterpane. Her blood-red eyes in her darned face stared through the window and saw a frozen river and leafless elm trees and a grizzled esplanade where dogs danced on the ends of leashes, their bundled-up owners stumbling after them, half blind with sleepiness and cold. Warm as the hospital room was, it did not prevent Pansy from knowing, as keenly as though she were one of the walkers, how very cold it was outside. Each twig of a nearby tree was stark. Cold red brick buildings nudged the low-lying sky which was pale and inert like a punctured sac.

In six weeks, the scene had varied little: there was promise in the skies neither of sun nor of snow; no red sunsets marked these days. The trees could neither die nor leaf out again. Pansy could not remember another season in her life so constant, when the very minutes themselves were suffused with the winter pallor as they dropped from the moon-faced clock in the corridor. Likewise, her room accomplished no alterations from day to day. On the glass-topped bureau stood two potted plants telegraphed by faraway well-wishers. They did not fade, and if a leaf turned brown and fell, it soon was replaced; so did the blossoms renew themselves. The roots, like the skies and like the bare trees, seemed zealously determined to maintain a status quo. The bedside table, covered every day with a clean white towel, though the one removed was always immaculate, was furnished sparsely with a water glass, a bent drinking tube, a sweating pitcher, and a stack of paper handkerchiefs. There were a few letters in the drawer, a hairbrush, a pencil, and some postal cards on which, from time to time, she wrote brief messages to relatives and friends: "Dr. Nash says that my reflexes are shipshape (*sic*) and Dr. Rivers says the frontal fracture has all but healed and that the occipital is coming along nicely. Dr. Nicholas, the nose doctor, promises to operate as soon as Dr. Rivers gives him the go-ahead sign (*sic*)."

The bed itself was never rumpled. Once fretful and now convalescent, Miss Vanneman might have been expected to toss or to turn the pillows or to unmoor the counterpane; but hour after hour and day after day she lay at full length and would not even suffer the nurses to raise the head-piece of the adjustable bed. So perfect and stubborn was her body's immobility that it was as if the room and the landscape, mortified by the ice, were extensions of herself. Her resolute quiescence and her disinclination to talk, the one seeming somehow to proceed from the other, resembled, so the nurses said, a final coma. And they observed, in pitying indignation, that she might as *well* be dead for all the interest she took in life. Amongst themselves they scolded her for what they thought a moral weakness: an automobile accident, no matter how serious, was not reason enough for anyone to give up the will to live or to be happy. She had not to come down bluntly to the facts – had the decency to be grateful that it was the driver of the cab and not she who had died. (And how dreadfully the man had died!) She was twenty-five years old and she came from a distant city. These were really the only facts known about her. Evidently she had not been here long, for she had no visitors, a lack which was at first sadly moving to the nurses but which became to them a source of unreasonable annoyance: had anyone the right to live so one-dimensionally? It was impossible to laugh at her, for she said nothing absurd; her demands could not be complained of because they did not exist; she could not be hated for a sharp tongue nor for a supercilious one; she could not be admired for bravery or for wit or for interest in her fellow creatures. She was believed to be a frightful snob.

Pansy, for her part, took a secret and mischievous pleasure in the bewilderment of her attendants and the more they courted her with offers of magazines, crossword puzzles, amd a radio which she could rent from the hospital, the farther she retired from them into herself and into the world which she had created in her long hours here and which no one could ever penetrate nor imagine. Sometimes she did not even answer the nurses' questions; as they rubbed her back with alcohol and steadily discoursed, she was as remote from them as if she were miles away. She did not think that she lived on a higher plane than that of the nurses and the doctors but that she lived on a different one and that at this particular time – this time of exploration and habituation – she had no extra strength to spend on making herself known to them. All she had been before and all the memories she might have brought out to disturb the monotony of, say, the morning bath, and all that the past meant to the future when she would leave the hospital, were of no present consequence to her. Not even in her thoughts did she employ more than a minimum of memory. And when she did remember, it was in flat pictures, rigorously independent of one another: she saw her thin, poetic mother who grew thinner and more poetic in her canvas deck-chair at Saranac reading *Lalla Rookh*. She saw herself in an inappropriate pink hat drinking iced tea in a garden so oppressive with the smell of phlox that the tea itself tasted of it. She recalled an afternoon in autumn in Vermont when she had heard three dogs' voices in the north woods and she could tell, by the characteristic minor key struck three times at intervals, like bells from several churches, that they had treed something: the eastern sky was pink and the trees on the horizon looked like some eccentric vascular system meticulously drawn on colored paper.

What Pansy thought of all the time was her own brain. Not only the brain as the seat of consciousness, but the physical organ itself which she envisaged, romantically, now as a jewel, now as a flower, now as a light in a glass, now as an envelope of rosy vellum containing other envelopes, one within the other, diminishing infinitely. It was always pink and always fragile, always deeply interior and invaluable. She believed that she had reached the innermost chamber of knowledge and that perhaps her knowledge was the same as the saint's achievement of pure love. It was only convention, she thought, that made one say "sacred heart" and not "sacred brain."

Often, but never articulately, the color pink troubled her and the picture of herself in the wrong hat hung steadfastly before her mind's eye. None of the other girls had worn hats and since autumn had come early that year, they were dressed in green and rusty brown and dark yellow. Poor Pansy wore a white eyelet frock with a lacing of black ribbon around the square neck. When she came through the arch, overhung with bittersweet, and saw that they had not yet heard her, she almost turned back, but Mr. Oliver was there and she was in love with him. She was in love with him though he was ten years older than she and had never shown any interest in her beyond asking her once, quite fatuously but in an intimate voice, if the yodeling of the little boy who peddled clams did not make her wish to visit Switzerland. Actually, there was more to this question than met the eye, for some days later Pansy learned that Mr. Oliver, who was immensely rich, kept an apartment in Geneva. In the garden that day, he spoke to her only once. He said, "My dear, you look exactly like something out of Katherine Mansfield," and immediately turned and within her hearing asked Beatrice Sherburne to dine with him that night at the Country Club. Afterward, Pansy went down to the sea and threw the beautiful hat onto the full tide and saw it vanish in the wake of a trawler. Thereafter, when she heard the clam boy coming down the road, she locked the door and when the knocking had stopped and her mother called down from her chaise longue, "Who was it, dearie?" she replied, "A salesman."

It was only the fact that the hat had been pink that worried her. The rest of the memory was trivial, for she knew that she could never again love anything as ecstatically as she loved the spirit of Pansy Vanneman, enclosed within her head.

But her study was not without distraction, and she fought two adversaries: pain and Dr. Nicholas. Against Dr. Nicholas, she defended herself valorously and in fear; but pain, the pain, that is, that was independent of his instruments, she sometimes forced upon herself adventurously like a child scaring himself in a graveyard.

Dr. Nicholas greatly admired her crushed and splintered nose which he daily probed and peered at, exclaiming that he had never seen anything like it. His shapely hands ached for their knives; he was impatient with the skull-fracture man's cautious delay. He spoke of "our" nose and said "we" would be a new person when we could breathe again. His own nose, the trademark of his profession, was magnificent. Not even his own brilliant surgery could have improved upon it nor could a first-rate sculptor have duplicated its direct downward line which permitted only the least curvature inward toward the end; nor the delicately rounded lateral declivities; nor the thin-walled, perfectly matched nostrils. Miss Vanneman did not doubt his humaneness nor his talent – he was a celebrated man – but she questioned whether he had imagination. Immediately beyond the prongs of his speculum lay her treasure whose price he no more than the nurses could not estimate. She believed he could not destroy it, but she feared that he might maim it: might leave a scratch on one of the brilliant facets of the jewel, bruise a petal of the flower, smudge the glass where the light burned, blot the envelopes, and that then she would die or would go mad. While she did not question that in either eventuality her brain would after a time redeem its original impeccability, she did not quite yet wish to enter upon either kind of eternity, for she was not certain that she could carry with her her knowledge as well as its receptacle.

Blunderer that he was, Dr. Nicholas was an honorable enemy, not like the demon, pain, which skulked in a thousand guises within her head, and which often she recklessly willed to attack her and then drove back in terror. After the rout, sweat streamed from her face and soaked the neck of the coarse hospital shirt. To be sure, it came usually of its own accord, running like a wild fire through all the convolutions to fill with flame the small sockets and ravines and then, at last, to withdraw, leaving behind a throbbing and an echo. On these occasions, she was as helpless as a tree in a wind. But at the other times when, by closing her eyes and rolling up the eyeballs in such a way that she fancied she looked directly on the place where her brain was, the pain woke sluggishly and came toward her at a snail's pace. Then, bit by bit, it gained speed. Sometimes it faltered back, subsided altogether, and then it rushed like a tidal wave driven by a hurricane, lashing and roaring until she lifted her hands from the counterpane, crushed her broken teeth into her swollen lip, stared in panic at the soothing walls with her ruby eyes, stretched out her legs until she felt their bones must snap. Each cove, each narrow inlet, every living bay was flooded and the frail brain, a little hat-shaped boat, was washed from its mooring and set adrift. The skull was as vast as the world and the brain was as small as a seashell.

Then came calm weather and the safe journey home. She kept vigil for a while, though, and did not close her eyes, but gazing pacifically at the trees, conceived of the pain as the guardian of her treasure who would not let her see it; that was why she was handled so savagely whenever she turned her eyes inward. Once this watch was interrupted: by chance she looked into the corridor and saw a shaggy mop slink past the door, followed by a senile porter. A pair of ancient eyes, as rheumy as an old dog's, stared uncritically in at her and the toothless mouth formed a brutish word. She was so surprised that she immediately closed her eyes to shut out the shape of the word and the pain dug up the unmapped regions of her head with mattocks, ludicrously huge. It was the familiar pain, but this time, even as she endured it, she observed with detachment that its effect upon her was less than that of its contents, the by-products, for example, of temporal confusion and the bizarre misapplication of the style of one sensation to another. At the moment, for example, although her brain reiterated to her that it was being assailed, she was stroking her right wrist with her left hand as though to assuage the ache, long since dispelled, of the sprain in the joint. Some minutes after she had opened her eyes and left off soothing her wrist, she lay rigid experiencing the sequel to the pain, an ideal terror. For, as before on several occasions, she was overwhelmed with the knowledge that the pain had been consummated in the vessel of her mind and for the moment the vessel was unbeautiful: she thought, quailing, of those plastic folds as palpable as the fingers of locked hands containing in their very cells, their fissures, their repulsive hemispheres, the mind, the Soul, the inscrutable intelligence.

The porter, then, like the pink hat and like her mother and the hounds' voices, loitered with her.

II

Dr. Nicholas came at nine o'clock to prepare her for the operation. With him came an entourage of white-frocked acolytes, and one of them wheeled in a wagon on which lay knives and scissors and pincers, cans of swabs and gauze. In the midst of these was a bowl of liquid whose rich purple color made it seem strange like the brew of an alchemist.

"All set?" he asked her, smiling. "A little nervous, what? I don't blame you. I've often said I'd rather lose an arm than have a submucous resection." Pansy thought for a moment he was going to touch his nose. His approach to her was roundabout. He moved through the yellow light shed by the globe in the ceiling which gave his forehead a liquid gloss; he paused by the bureau and touched a blossom of the cyclamen; he looked out the window and said, to no one and to all, "I couldn't start my car this morning. Came in a cab." Then he came forward. As he came, he removed a speculum from the pocket of his short-sleeved coat and like a cat, inquiring of the nature of a surface with its paws, he put out his hand toward her and drew it back, gently murmuring, "You must not be afraid, my dear. There is no danger, you know. Do you think for a minute I would operate if there were?"

Dr. Nicholas, young, brilliant, and handsome was an aristocrat, a husband, a father, a clubman, a Christian, a kind counselor, and a trustee of his school alumni association. Like many of the medical profession, even those whose speciality was centered on the organ of the basest sense, he interested himself in the psychology of his patients: in several instances, for example, he had found that severe attacks of sinusitis were coincident with emotional crises. Miss Vanneman more than ordinarily captured his fancy since her skull had been fractured and her behavior throughout had been so extraordinary that he felt he was observing at firsthand some of the results of shock, that incommensurable element, which frequently were too subtle to see. There was, for example, the matter of her complete passivity during a lumbar puncture, reports of which were written down in her history and were enlarged upon for him by Dr. Rivers' intern who had been in charge. Except for a tremor in her throat and a deepening of pallor, there were no signs at all that she was aware of what was happening to her. She made no sound, did not close her eyes nor clench her fists. She had had several punctures; her only reaction had been to the very first one, the morning after she had been brought in. When the intern explained to her that he was going to drain off cerebrospinal fluid which was pressing against her brain, she exclaimed, "My God!" but it was not an exclamation of fear. The young man had been unable to name what it was he had heard in her voice; he could only say that it had not been fear as he had observed it in other patients.

He wondered about her. There was no way of guessing whether she had always had a nature of so tolerant and undemanding a complexion. It gave him a melancholy pleasure to think that before her accident she had been high-spirited and loquacious; he was moved to think that perhaps she had been a beauty and that when she had first seen her face in the looking glass she had lost all joy in herself. It was very difficult to tell what the face had been, for it was so bruised and swollen, so hacked up and lopsided. The black stitches the length of the nose, across the saddle, across the cheekbone, showed that there would be unsightly scars. He had ventured once to give her the name of a plastic surgeon but she had only replied with a vague, refusing smile. He had hoisted a manly shoulder and said, "You're the doctor."

Much as he pondered, coming to no conclusions, about what went on inside that pitiable skull, he was, of course, far more interested in the nose, deranged so badly that it would require his topmost skill to restore its functions to it. He would be obliged not only to make a submucous resection, a simple run-of-the-mill operation, but to remove the vomer, always a delicate task but further complicated in this case by the proximity of the bone to the frontal fracture line which conceivably was not entirely closed. If it were not and he operated too soon and if a cold germ then found its way into the opening, his patient would be carried off by meningitis in the twinkling of an eye. He wondered if she knew in what potential danger she lay; he desired to assure her that he had brought his craft to its nearest perfection and that she had nothing to fear of him, but feeling that she was perhaps both ignorant and unimaginative and that such consolation would create a fear rather than dispel one, he held his tongue and came nearer to the bed.

Watching him, Pansy could already feel the prongs of his pliers opening her nostrils for the insertion of his fine probers. The pain he caused her with his instruments was of a different kind from that she felt unaided: it was a naked, clean, and vivid pain which made her faint and ill and made her wish to die. Once she had fainted as he ruthlessly explored and after she was brought around, he continued until he had finished his investigation. The memory of this outrage had afterward several times made her cry.

This morning she looked at him and listened to him with hatred. Fixing her eyes upon the middle of his high, protuberant brow, she imagined the clutter behind it and she despised its obtuse imperfection, the reason's oblique comprehension of itself. In his bland unawareness, this nobody, this nose-bigot, was about to play with fire and she wished him ill.

He said, "I can't blame you. No, I expect you're not looking forward to our little party. But I expect you'll be glad to be able to breathe again."

He stationed his lieutenants. The intern stood opposite him on the left side of the bed. The surgical nurse wheeled the wagon within easy reach of his hands and stood beside it. Another nurse stood at the foot of the bed. A third drew the shades at the windows and attached the blinding light which shone down on the patient hotly, and then she left the room, softly closing the door. Pansy stared at the silver ribbon tied in a great bow round the green crepe paper of one of the flower pots. It made her realize for the first time that one of the days she had lain here had been Christmas, but she had no time to consider this strange and thrilling fact, for Dr. Nicholas was genially explaining his anaesthetic. He would soak packs of gauze in the purple fluid, a cocaine solution, and he would place them then in her nostrils, leaving them there for an hour. He warned her that the packing would be disagreeable (he did not say "painful") but that it would be well worth a few minutes of discomfort not to be in the least sick after the operation. He asked her if she were ready and when she nodded her head, he adjusted the mirror on his forehead and began.

At the first touch of his speculum, Pansy's fingers mechanically bent to the palms of her hands and she stiffened. He said, "A pack, Miss Kennedy," and Pansy closed her eyes. There was a rush of plunging pain as he drove the sodden gobbet of gauze high up into her nose and something bitter burned in her throat so that she retched. The doctor paused a moment and the surgical nurse wiped her mouth. He returned to her with another pack, pushing it with his bodkin doggedly until it lodged against the first. Stop! Stop! cried all her nerves, wailing along the surface of her skin. The coats that covered them were torn off and they shuddered like naked people screaming, Stop! Stop! But Dr. Nicholas did not hear. Time and again he came back with a fresh pack and did not pause at all until one nostril was finished. She opened her eyes and saw him wipe the sweat off his forehead and saw the dark intern bending over her, fascinated. Miss Kennedy bathed her temples in ice water and Dr. Nicholas said, "There. It won't be much longer. I'll tell them to send you some coffee, though I'm afraid you won't be able to taste it. Ever drink coffee with chicory in it? I have no use for it."

She snatched at his irrelevancy and, though she had never tasted chicory, she said severely, "I love it."

Dr. Nicholas chuckled. "De gustibus. Ready? A pack, Miss Kennedy."

The second nostril was harder to pack since the other side was now distended and the passage was anyhow much narrower, as narrow, he had once remarked, as that in the nose of an infant. In such pain as passed all language and even the farthest fetched analogies, she turned her eyes inward thinking that under the obscuring cloak of the surgeon's pain, she could see her brain without the knowledge of its keeper. But Dr. Nicholas and his aides would give her no peace. They surrounded her with their murmuring and their foot-shuffling and the rustling of their starched uniforms, and her eyelids continually flew back in embarrassment and mistrust. She was claimed entirely by this present, meaningless pain and suddenly and sharply, she forgot what she had meant to do. She was aware of nothing but her ascent to the summit of something; what it was she did not know, whether it was a tower or a peak or Jacob's ladder. Now she was an abstract word, now she was a theorem of geometry, now she was a kite flying, a top spinning, a prism flashing, a kaleidoscope turning.

But none of the others in the room could see inside and when the surgeon was finished, the nurse at the foot of the bed said, "Now you must take a look in the mirror. It's simply too comical." And they all laughed intimately like old, fast friends. She smiled politely and looked at her reflection: over the gruesomely fattened snout, her scarlet eyes stared in fixed reproach upon the upturned lips, grey with bruises. But even in its smile of betrayal, the mouth itself was puzzled: it reminded her that something had been left behind, but she could not recall what it was. She was hollowed out and was as dry as a white bone.

III

They strapped her ankles to the operating table and put leather nooses round her wrists. Over her head was a mirror with a thousand facets in which she saw a thousand travesties of her face. At her right side was the table, shrouded in white, where lay the glittering blades of the many knives, thrusting out fitful rays of light. All the cloth was frosty; everything was white or silver and as cold as snow. Dr. Nicholas, a tall snowman with silver eyes and silver fingernails, came into the room soundlessly for he walked on layers and layers of snow which deadened his footsteps; behind him came the intern, a smaller snowman, less impressively proportioned. At the foot of the table, a snow figure put her frozen hands upon Pansy's helpless feet. The doctor plucked the packs from the cold, numb nose. His laugh was like a cry on a bitter, still night: "I will show you now," he called across the expanse of snow, "that you can feel nothing." The pincers bit at nothing, snapped at the air and cracked a nerveless icicle. Pansy called back and heard her own voice echo: "I feel nothing."

Here the walls were gray, not tan. Suddenly the face of the nurse at the foot of the table broke apart and Pansy first thought it was in grief. But it was a smile and she said, "Did you enjoy your coffee?" Down the gray corridors of the maze, the words rippled, ran like mice, birds, broken beads: Did you enjoy your coffee? your coffee? your coffee? Similarly once in another room that also had gray walls, the same voice had said, "Shall I give her some whiskey?" She was overcome with gratitude that this young woman (how pretty she was with her white hair and her white face and her china-blue eyes!) had been with her that first night and was with her now.

In the great stillness of the winter, the operation began. The knives carved snow. Pansy was happy. She had been given a hypodermic just before they came to fetch her and she would have gone to sleep had she not enjoyed so much this trickery of Dr. Nicholas whom now she tenderly loved.

There was a clock in the operating room and from time to time she looked at it. An hour passed. The snowman's face was melting; drops of water hung from his fine nose, but his silver eyes were as bright as ever. Her love was returned, she knew: he loved her nose exactly as she loved his knives. She looked at her face in the domed mirror and saw how the blood had streaked her lily-white cheeks and had stained her shroud. She returned to the private song: Did you enjoy your coffee? your coffee?

At the half-hour, a murmur, sanguine and slumbrous, came to her and only when she had repeated the words twice did they engrave their meaning upon her. Dr. Nicholas said, "Stand back now, nurse. I'm at this girl's brain and I don't want my elbow jogged." Instantly Pansy was alive. Her strapped ankles arched angrily; her wrists strained against their bracelets. She jerked her head and she felt the pain flare; she had made the knife slip.

"Be still!" cried the surgeon. "Be quiet, please!"

He had made her remember what it was she had lost when he had rammed his gauze into her nose: she bustled like a housewife to shut the door. She thought, I must hurry before the robbers come. It would be like the time Mother left the cellar door open and the robber came and took, of all things, the terrarium.

Dr. Nicholas was whispering to her. He said, in the voice of a lover, "If you can stand it five minutes more, I can perform the second operation now and you won't have to go through this again. What do you say?"

She did not reply. It took her several seconds to remember why it was her mother had set such store by the terrarium and then it came to her that the bishop's widow had brought her an herb from Palestine to put in it.

The intern said, "You don't want to have your nose packed again, do you?"

The surgical nurse said, "She's a good patient, isn't she, sir?"

"Never had a better," replied Dr. Nicholas. "But don't call me 'sir.' You must be a Canadian to call me 'sir.'"

The nurse at the foot of the bed said, "I'll order some more coffee for you.

"How about it, Miss Vanneman?" said the doctor. "Shall I go ahead?"

She debated. Once she had finally fled the hospital and fled Dr. Nicholas, nothing could compel her to come back. Still, she knew that the time would come when she could no longer live in seclusion, she must go into the world again and must be equipped to live in it; she banally acknowledged that she must he able to breathe. And finally, though the world to which she would return remained unreal, she gave the surgeon her permission.

He had now to penetrate regions that were not anaesthetized and this he told her frankly, but he said that there was no danger at all. He apologized for the slip of the tongue he had made: in point of fact, he had not been near her brain, it was only a figure of speech. He began. The knives ground and carved and curried and scoured the wounds they made; the scissors clipped hard gristle and the scalpels chipped off bone. It was as if a tangle of tiny nerves were being cut dexterously, one by one; the pain writhed spirally and came to her who was a pink bird and sat on the top of a cone. The pain was a pyramid made of a diamond; it was an intense light; it was the hottest fire, the coldest chill, the highest peak, the fastest force, the furthest reach, the newest time. It possessed nothing of her but its one infinitesimal scene: beyond the screen as thin as gossamer, the brain trembled for its life, hearing the knives hunting like wolves outside, sniffing and snapping. Mercy! Mercy! cried the scalped nerves.

At last, miraculously, she turned her eyes inward tranquilly. Dr. Nicholas had said, "The worst is over. I am going to work on the floor of your nose," and at his signal she closed her eyes and this time and this time alone, she saw her brain lying in a shell-pink satin case. It was a pink pearl, no bigger than a needle's eye, but it was so beautiful and so pure that its smallness made no difference. Anyhow, as she watched, it grew. It grew larger and larger until it was an enormous bubble that contained the surgeon and the whole room within its rosy luster. In a long ago summer, she had often been absorbed by the spectacle of flocks of yellow birds that visited a cedar tree and she remembered that everything that summer had been some shade of yellow. One year of childhood, her mother had frequently taken her to have tea with an aged schoolmistress upon whose mantelpiece there was a herd of ivory elephants; that had been the white year. There was a green spring when early in April she had seen a grass snake on a boulder, but the very summer that followed was violet, for vetch took her mother's garden. She saw a swatch of blue tulle lying in a raffia basket on the front porch of Uncle Marion's brown house. Never before had the world been pink, whatever else it had been. Or had it been, one other time? She could not be sure and she did not care. Of one thing she was certain: never had the world enclosed her before and never had the quiet been so smooth.

For only a moment the busybodies left her to her ecstasy and then, impatient and gossiping, they forced their way inside, slashed at her resisting trance with questions and congratulations, with statements of fact and jokes. "Later," she said to them dumbly. "Later on, perhaps. I am busy now." But their voices would not go away. They touched her, too, washing her face with cloths so cold they stung, stroking her wrists with firm, antiseptic fingers. The surgeon, squeezing her arm with avuncular pride, said, "Good girl," as if she were a bright dog that had retrieved a bone. Her silent mind abused him: "You are a thief," it said, "you are a heartless vagabond and you should be put to death." But he was leaving, adjusting his coat with an air of vainglory, and the intern, abject with admiration, followed him from the operating room smiling like a silly boy.

Shortly after they took her back to her room, the weather changed, not for the better. Momentarily the sun emerged from its concealing murk, but in a few minutes the snow came with a wind that promised a blizzard. There was great pain, but since it could not serve her, she rejected it and she lay as if in a hammock in a pause of bitterness. She closed her eyes, shutting herself up within her treasureless head.

Two Prostitutes

BY ALBERTO MORAVIA

Toward the beginning of the summer Giacomo found himself entirely alone. He thought that he had many friends and knew a number of women, but no sooner had a few acquaintances gone off on their holidays than he was left high and dry. Actually, like everyone else, he moved in a limited circle of persons, and now it occurred to him that when he was an old man such leave-takings would be final and his solitude complete.

He fell into the habit of getting up very late and staying in his boarding house room until it was time for lunch, smoking or reading distractedly in bed. After lunch he went out for a cup of coffee, bought a newspaper and took it back to his room. Sometimes, when he was especially tired, he liked to let the paper fall from his hand and go off to sleep. In mid-afternoon he got up, washed, dressed and went out.

He went to a café in the most fashionable street, where they served small individual bottles of German beer of which Giacomo was very fond. As he slowly sipped the cold beer he observed the sidewalk and the people seated at the outdoor tables around him. All the idlers of the city, the prettiest girls and the best-dressed young men, met at this point of the street and among these tables. Many of them stood directly in front of the café windows, pretending to chatter, but actually striking a pose for the benefit of anyone who might be looking and, in their turn, watching out of the corner of one eye what was going on about them. Women went in lively fashion, with cigarettes in their hands, from one table to another, laughing and talking in a loud manner, and the waiters with their trays were barely able to fray a path among the crowd. There was a lot of joking, calling out from person to person and gossipy talk that made for a certain atmosphere of self-sufficiency, as if those present were gathered not on the open street but in an exclusive drawing room. Indeed if a shabby man, or a solitary and friendless one like Giacomo ventured in, he seemed like an uninvited and unwelcome guest. It was a strictly private affair between those who were sitting at the tables and those who were walking up and down in front of them. Above this scene the full-grown foliage of large plane trees threw a flickering pattern of light and shade over tables, glasses, faces and clothes. It was hot, but not stuffy, and the sky was cloudless and burning. As twilight came the people scattered, each one going to his own house, and the waiter cleared the tables and drew the curtains together.

After he had finished his first bottle of beer Giacomo usually ordered another. By this time it was sunset, and he got up and walked slowly home. In the evening he came back to the café and witnessed a repetition of the scenes of the afternoon: the same parading display and the same social atmosphere, but by lamplight and on a smaller scale. On this broad, airy street, winding up a hill with palaces and gardens on either side, the evenings were particularly agreeable. The wind blew gently under the plane trees and voices rang out cheerily in the soft, tired air while women's faces took on a mysterious look among the shadows. Less people passed by than in the daytime and it was possible to observe them more closely. Giacomo ordered an ice in a tall glass and ate it slowly and conscientiously, as if he were being paid to do exactly what he was doing: to eat an ice and watch the people go by.

He felt empty and calm, and at times he could even persuade himself that he was master of his lonely and abandoned situation. But he was prey to a latent anxiety, which at the most unexpected moments gripped his heart. Sometimes he realized that his gluttonous enjoyment of beer and ices betrayed the fact that he could expect nothing more out of life than these simple pleasures. Or again a casual look, word or gesture on the part of some of the other habitués of the café suddenly revealed to him how much fuller and richer their lives were than his. He had a dim feeling of pain and resolved that before the end of the summer he would take some step toward regaining his own freedom. For in his moments of anxiety he felt that he was no longer free, even if he appeared to be so, but that he was impotently enslaved to a solitude which was not of his own seeking.

One night on his way home from the usual hour at the café he was attracted by the dim light from the cellar window of a nightclub farther along the street. He remembered having heard that in winter this was a gathering place for women in search of amorous adventure, and he was curious to see whether now in midsummer he could find there a companion for the night. He went down a few steps, pushed open a glass door and found himself in the bar. The shaded lamps left it half dark inside and the summer heat mingled disagreeably with the lingering smell of stale tobacco. In front of the shelves lined with bottles along the wall, the barman's face was positively black with heat, as if something like an apoplectic stroke had drawn all the blood into his head. But he moved about normally enough in his shiny white jacket, with his hands gliding over the zinc bar, the steam coffee-maker, the water taps, the bottles of olives and all the other accessories of his trade. For the moment Giacomo could think of nothing better to do than to perch on a stool and ask for a liqueur.

He had hardly settled down and begun to perspire under the low ceiling than he realized that what he was looking for was not in the bar but in the back room, which he could now see was composed of a series of booths, each one containing a couple of tables and upholstered benches, the latter fitted into recesses under the windows or in the walls. At this moment the booths were all empty except for two women who were sitting on a bench under the window of one of them.

For a short while, although he scrutinized them keenly, he could not make out exactly what sort they were. They were stylishly but unostentatiously dressed, blondes both of them, with one appearing seven or eight years younger than the other and wearing her hair loose over her shoulders. She had a healthy complexion with no make-up on it, large blue-green eyes, a pointed nose and full red lips. She wore no hat and a sport jacket lay over the bench beside her, leaving her in a short-sleeved blouse. The older woman's hair was carefully waved and she wore a tiny hat tilted precariously over one side of her forehead. She too had light-colored eyes, but they were close together and deep-set under fleshy lids, which gave her a vicious and hypocritical air. Her eyes, as well as her cheeks and exceedingly narrow curved lips, were heavily made up. She was more stylish than her companion, and at first sight perhaps more beautiful, but in an elaborate and banal urban manner. At second glance Giacomo decidedly preferred the younger, if for no other reason simply because there was something less conventional about her.

The two women sat there motionless, without saying a word, while Giacomo looked the one with the hat straight in the face and at the other from a side view.

What suddenly convinced him that they were prostitutes was the excessive and inappropriate air of dignity assumed by the older of the two, and her almost ugly, dark hands, with purplish red polish on the nails, which were laid on the table. The younger woman had polish on her nails too, but her hands were pale and slender.

"Here's your drink, sir," the barman said all of a sudden, putting down a glass. Under ordinary circumstances Giacomo would not have had the courage to question him about the two women, but in the present atmosphere of unreality he had acquired a bold front which successfully masked his essential awkwardness and timidity.

"Who are those two?" he asked abruptly.

The barman was running a damp rag over the bar, and without raising his head or stopping his work he answered: "I don't know, sir. They were here the other evening, but before that I'd never seen them."

However, his tone of voice clearly indicated that they were women of the sort for which Giacomo was looking.

"Please take my glass over to that table," said Giacomo, and getting down from his stool he went to sit at the table beside that of the two women.

He was still in the same relative position, that is looking at the younger one from the side and with the other directly across from him. The latter, who could not help seeing him, lowered her gaze, while her companion, who could have ignored his presence, shot him a bold glance out of the corner of her greenish eye, which had a vaguely hilarious expression. It seemed to Giacomo as if the woman with the hat on saw this glance and disapproved of it. But perhaps, he thought, he was mistaken.

The barman brought over his glass, put it down on the table and went back to the bar, leaving the three of them alone in the booth. The younger woman spoke up in a clear voice:

"It's plain now that that friend of yours isn't coming. An ill-mannered fellow I call him."

"Sh!" said the older woman with annoyance.

"Why shouldn't I talk now?" asked the younger. "I repeat that if he doesn't come he's ill-mannered."

"Very well," said the older, sitting as stiffly as if she were afraid her hat would slip down over her nose, "but why shout about it?"

"Who's shouting?"

"You are."

"All right. I shan't argue. . . ." But she had spoken gaily and without anger, perhaps, Giovanni thought, merely in order to catch his attention. "Give me a cigarette, will you?" she added.

Giacomo had laid his cigarette-case beside his glass on the table and he was quick to lean over and hold it out. The girl was no less quick to accept, then she took the case in her hand and offered it to her friend, who appeared to hesitate between the desire for a smoke and resentment of the other's behavior.

"It's not really proper to take a cigarette upon so short an acquaintance," she observed regretfully. But she took one and looked at the name of the brand before putting it in her mouth. Then, with the motion of a fine lady allowing a perfect gentleman to give her a light, she leaned over the table toward Giacomo's lighter. The other had already lit up and was blowing smoke out through her nostrils.

"Hot, isn't it?" observed Giacomo, turning instinctively toward the older of the two women, who he felt was still hostile to him.

This conventional remark seemed to please her, as if it were a mark of unde-served respect.

"Frightful," she said in a cool and worldly tone of voice, drawing in small mouthfuls of smoke and blowing them out again without inhaling while she stared at the tip of her cigarette. "I don't remember when there was ever anything like it."

"I'm perspiring all over," said the younger woman with a laugh, raising her arm to show the dampness of her blouse underneath it.

As she did so her breasts quite perceptibly inflated the silk, revealing the weight of them rather than the shape. "It's impossible to breathe in this hole," she added.

The older woman appeared to disapprove of this exhibition and gave a chiding look at her companion. Then she said, turning to Giacomo: "This is really a place to come to in the winter, isn't it? In summer, one's better off at an outdoor café."

Apparently she was set on carrying on a drawing room conversation, in spite of the fact that she had allowed him to sit near them and regardless of her companion's bold behavior.

"Yes," he replied. "Outdoor cafés are best, especially those in a pleasant park."

"That's where we always go," she said quickly.

"What do you mean, 'always'?" interrupted the other.

"All the time," and she flicked the ash off the end of her cigarette, bending her head slightly to one side. "This evening is an exception. . . . We are waiting for a friend . . ."

The younger woman began to laugh: "A fine sort of friend, when we don't even know his name . . ."

"What's that?" said the older one defensively, but without moving. "His name is . . . Meluschi."

The young woman laughed again.

"That's the name of our landlord! What's the connection?"

"My sister has a great way of joking," said the older one to Giacomo.

"I'm not joking at all," rejoined the other. "He's no friend of yours, much less of mine. In fact we more or less picked him up on the street." There was something almost sensually cruel about her outspokenness. Her eyes shone maliciously and her nostrils quivered.

"In the first place we were in a café," the older woman said, turning to Giacomo as if he alone could understand her. "He came over very politely and asked if he could talk to us, just the way you did tonight." And she added, in the direction of her sister: "If you go on like that, who knows what this gentleman will think of us?"

But her companion went right on laughing, shifting about in her chair with her face flushed from mirth.

"He's thought it already, never fear . . . or else he'd never have come over here with a face like that on him. Isn't that so, Mr.? . . . What is your name, anyhow? Yesterday we didn't ask, and you see what's happened . . ."

"My name is Giacomo," said the young man, half amused and half put out by the girl's words. Then he added with an effort:

"Yes, I did come over with such a thought in mind, but I may have been mis-taken. . . ."

"Oh no, you were not mistaken at all!" And she gave a hearty laugh.

"And what's your name?"

"My name's Rina," the older woman interposed, "and my sister's is Lori."

Her sister laughed again.

"Your name isn't Rina at all; it's Teresa. And mine is not Lori but Giovanna."

"I like Rina and Lori better, because they're short. That's enough now, Lori. . . ."

"Can't anyone laugh?"

"It's all right to laugh, but you're loud and vulgar."

"I'm nothing of the sort," said Lori, but she grew serious, as if her sister's last remark had struck home.

"What's your last name?" Giacomo asked.

"Panigatti," said Rina, modestly lowering her eyes.

"There's a town in Sicily called Canicatti," said Giacomo, enjoying her discomfiture.

"No, it's Panigatti, and we are not Sicilians. . . ."

"Where do you come from?"

"We come from Verona," she answered, but her younger sister winked and interposed: "We really come from Meolo, but she doesn't like the sound of that because it reminds her of a cat's meowing."

"Will you have something to drink?" Giacomo asked.

"Yes, champagne, champagne!" said the younger sister with mock enthusiasm.

"I suggest we go to some other place. What do you say?" And the older woman picked her gloves up from the table and began to slip them on.

"What about your friend Meluschi?" asked Giacomo.

"It looks to me as if he really weren't coming," said Rina. But her sister shouted impetuously: "He certainly won't turn up again; he must have been just a loafer. . . ."

All three of them got up and went toward the door. Giacomo went over to the bar and asked how much he owed.

"Are you paying for all three drinks?" asked the barman.

"Yes, and a package of Egyptian cigarettes."

"Two thousand liras in all," the barman said. The amount was small.

Giacomo took the cigarettes and handed over the money. From behind the bar the barman bowed and said good night.

They came out on the wide sidewalk under the heavy foliage of the plane trees. Outside the area where they cast their shadows a full moon lit up the asphalted street and the flower beds on the outer edge of the sidewalk. The colors of the flowers, red, blue, green and yellow, seemed strange and unreal in the moonlight.

"Where shall we go?" Giacomo asked.

"Somewhere where we can drink," answered the younger woman. "I've gone long enough without a drop. I'm as dry as. . . ."

"How about the Splendid Bar?" said the older one, stepping out on the sidewalk and deliberately making her gestures show up in the moonlight.

"It's stifling down there," protested her sister.

"I say we go to the Ancus Martius Grotto," proposed Giacomo.

This was a place not very far away, a nightclub in a cellar that was decorated to look like an ancient ruin, with fake classical vases and inscriptions all around. Hidden behind columns and carved out of the soft tufa stone there were a number of small rooms, dark corners and recesses where it was possible to talk at ease. The older woman did not appear very pleased; perhaps it was not fashionable enough to suit her. But the younger one enthusiastically took Giacomo's arm.

"Yes, let's go to the Grotto. Who was Ancus Martius anyhow?"

"One of the kings of ancient Rome."

They walked slowly along the deserted sidewalk until they came to the entrance of the Grotto, a red brick stair leading to the cellar. Two enormous amphorae, one on either side of the door, gave a clue to the whole style. At the bottom of the stair there was a broken and blackened stone with an inscription in dog-Latin. As they passed this and started down a second flight of stairs they were greeted by the smell of mingled smoke, wine and mold, together with a hollow, far-away noise of voices and music from the large and winding rooms below. From the landing they could see rows of tables under the low vaults, with people sitting around them over carafes of wine. Arches, columns, pilasters all contributed to the imitation of a primitive underground basilica.

"Wonderful!" said Lori, clapping her hands. "It's really old, isn't it? . . . It looks like . . . what do they call those places where the ancient Christians used to meet?"

"The catacombs," Giacomo suggested.

"Yes . . . the catacombs . . . and to think you've never brought me here before!" This last remark was addressed to her sister.

"I've never really liked it," said the latter.

The people sitting at the tables watched them go by without showing the least curiosity. For the most part they were unpretentious young men and their girls; occasionally a large group drank and joked noisily, making the vaults echo. Far away, on a bandstand at the other end of the grotto, three or four violin and cello players could be seen moving their arms up and down.

"Let's go through here," said Giacomo.

They made their way among the tables of the main room and through a narrow hall lined with red bricks to a smaller room decorated in Pompeian style. The purposely unfinished frescoes on the walls portrayed cupids, satyrs and naked women against a dark red background and gave the impression of having been scientifically restored. Over them customers had pencilled their names and various jokes and exclamations. A wrought-iron lamp hung from the ceiling and most of the room was occupied by a large table with a few stools around it. Giacomo sat down at the head of the table with the older sister to the right and the younger to the left of him.

"What will you have to drink?" he asked.

"Anything at all, as long as it's good," said Lori.

Her sister said she would like a liqueur, but it seemed that there was none to be had.

"We have red and white Chianti, and Orvieto on tap, and bottled wines," said the waiter.

"What sweet wines have you?"

"Marsala, Passito, Aleatico. . . ."

"Bring us some Aleatico."

"So you come from Meolo," said Giacomo, picking up the conversation.

"Yes," answered the younger sister. "But I live in Milan and my sister lives here. Every now and then we exchange visits: she comes to stay with me or I go to stay with her."

"I don't care for Milan," said Rina. "The winters are too cold. I've been ill and need sunshine."

"What was the matter with you?" Giacomo asked.

"I'm delicate," she explained, touching her chest with one hand. Her chest was, indeed, almost hollow, as Giacomo had already noticed. But her deep-set eyes under the fleshy lids had a vicious expression that aroused his curiosity.

"That's not it," Lori put in. "The truth is she's in love with someone who lives here."

"What does he do?" asked Giacomo.

"He's in business," said the older sister with the same modesty with which she had declared that her last name was Panigatti.

"He's a cheese salesman," said the younger, holding two fingers up to her nose as if to indicate that he smelled of his trade.

Then the waiter brought the wine. Giacomo uncorked the bottle and poured it into the thick green glasses.

"It's good," Lori said, looking at Giacomo. "Very sweet."

"Aleatico," her sister confirmed.

Giacomo drank his first glassful in a single swallow and poured himself another. The two women had emptied their glasses too, and Giacomo filled them and ordered another bottle.

"Where is your friend just now?" he asked Rina prudently.

"He's on the road."

"Oh, there's no danger of his putting in a sudden appearance," said her sister with a laugh. "He always wires or calls up. He's a very good fellow."

"Lori, don't talk about him like that. You don't even know him."

"He's not so very wonderful," Lori said unexpectedly. "You're quite right to deceive him. I don't blame you."

The older woman said nothing. Giacomo decided that she was the one to be his conquest, or that he should at least make some advance. Inconspicuously he put his hand on her knee under the table. She looked at him hypocritically and said: "Where are you from?"

"From Ancona," Giacomo answered.

His hand roughly pushed aside her dress and travelled from the knee up her thigh. Above very tight garters her bare skin seemed to be bursting. She had on all sorts of fancy underwear, silks, laces, tiny buttons and an elaborate system of suspenders.

"That's a beautiful city," she said, without moving or pushing Giacomo's hand away.

Her dress was riding way up to one side, leaving one leg bare. "Do you think I can't see you?" shouted her sister, with, however, no jealousy in her voice. "But as far as I'm concerned, go right ahead."

Giacomo withdrew his hand, but a moment later he was sorry and put it back, for she had seemed to ask nothing better. For the sake of being fair he put his other arm around the younger sister's waist. She laughed and looked at him sideways out of her big, malicious eyes, holding her glass in her hand. Giacomo bent over and brushed her neck with his lips.

The older sister pushed Giacomo's hand away and pulled down her dress. She seemed to do this not out of anger but because some people were passing by the entrance to the small room.

"What do you do in Milan?" Giacomo asked.

"What do I do?" she repeated with a laugh.

"She's a model," supplied her sister.

"I used to be," said the younger woman deliberately. "Now I do just what you do here."

"Why do you say such a thing?" asked the other irritably. "You're trying to pass yourself off for something different from what you are."

"What do you know about that!" said Lori slowly with mock astonishment. She was slightly drunk and the color and expression of her eyes wavered from one moment to the next. "And what is it that you do, if I may ask?"

"I don't do anything," said Rina, shrugging her shoulders contemptuously. "I'm a lady of leisure . . ."

"What do you know about that! Then I do the same thing. I'm a lady of leisure too. . . ."

Rina looked daggers at her sister, but did not reply. Then she said warningly to Giacomo: "If you encourage her to go on drinking like that, there's no telling what she'll say."

Lori turned suddenly bitter.

"I haven't had too much to drink, I'll have you know! And then Giacomo here is different. He doesn't put on airs the way you do. . . ."

"Come, come," said Giacomo conciliatingly, patting the girl's knee. She paid no attention, and he ventured to move his hand up her legs. She held them close together, and go as far as he would he found no trace of slip, stockings or underpinnings of any kind. From her smooth, cool thighs, very different from her sister's, he reached all the way to her stomach, which perhaps because of the way she was sitting down and leaning over fell into a fold and gave the impression of being round and well fed. She was quite naked under her dress, but with no ulterior motive, simply because it was uncomfortable to feel clinging underwear in the hot weather. Meanwhile, heedless of his hand, she went on shouting at her sister:

"I make no bones about it. I don't pretend to live with one man alone and then bring a stranger home with me every evening."

The older woman stared at her unblinkingly, with her tiny hat tilted over her narrow eyes.

"I make no bones about it, I say," repeated the other less vehemently, as if she regretted her previous violence. "And you, be still there!" she added, turning her anger on Giacomo.

"I told you not to encourage her drinking," said the sister.

By now Giacomo felt drunk himself and the girl's unashamed nakedness excited him. Drunkenness and excitement combined to make him grow suddenly impatient.

"What would you say if we two got out of here and left her?" he whispered to Lori, taking advantage of a moment when Rina was fitting a cigarette into a long holder.

But to his surprise the girl showed a most unexpected loyalty to her sister.

"Ask her," she said. "When I'm staying with her she decides everything."

Somewhat astonished, Giacomo turned to the older woman; lowering his voice, not so much because he was afraid that the other would hear him as because he was ashamed of what he was saying.

"I wonder if we mightn't move along. . . . I was thinking I might go somewhere else, perhaps with just one of you."

"No, not with just one of us," Rina rejoined promptly. "It's either both of us or nothing."

"Why so?"

"Because that's the way we do it."

"What shall I do with two women?" Giacomo wondered. The idea of their being sisters intrigued him. "And how much is it for you both?"

"Twenty thousand liras. Ten thousand each."

Giacomo could not help thinking that this was quite a lot, but Rina's tone of voice was such as to rule out any possibility of bargaining.

"Very well," he said. "But where shall we go?"

"To your place," she answered.

"I haven't a place of my own," said Giacomo. "I live in a boarding house."

"Then I don't know."

"Can't we go to where you live?"

"I must preserve the sanctity of my home," she said with mellifluous pride.

"You take people there all the time!" her sister said languidly, her bitterness tempered by the effects of the wine.

"Which one of you am I to believe?" Giacomo asked. Then, realizing that he had made a faux pas, he added: "Well, just this once anyhow. . . ." And he took Rina's hand.

Rina smiled and shook her head. "I can't take you home. It's impossible."

"How so?"

"It's just impossible, that's all."

Giacomo saw that he had to take another tack. "Then let's go to a hotel," he said.

"Out of the question! They always ask to see your papers. . . ."

"What was the name of that hotel where we went a few days ago with that . . . ?" put in the younger sister with a strange hesitation in her voice ". . . Hotel Corona, wasn't it?"

"Very well, then," said Giacomo with annoyance. "When the time comes we'll just go our separate ways."

A silence followed. Rina puffed in a mysterious and worldly manner at her cigarette, looking at Giacomo benevolently out of her deep-set, fleshy eyes.

"How much do you suppose it would have cost you to take all three of us to a hotel?" she asked.

"I don't know . . . Two thousand liras, I suppose."

"More than that, because you'd have had to take one double and one single room. At least three thousand, I make it."

"What are you driving at?"

"If you promise not to make any noise, then give us the extra three thousand liras you'd have spent at the hotel – and we'll go to my house. . . ."

The younger sister could not help laughing at the perplexity on Giacomo's face.

"A good business woman, isn't she?" she observed, putting her head down between her arms on the table and closing her eyes.

"All right," said Giacomo. "Let's go immediately."

"Let's go."

All three got up and the older sister, who seemed to be in a hurry, went ahead of the other two down the long, arched, brick-lined hall. Giacomo took the younger one into his arms. She pushed him away with mockingly exaggerated gestures, as if to imply that her sister might notice, then all of a sudden she let him kiss her. They drew quickly apart.

"It's good to have a kiss every now and then," she whispered with a smile.

"Yes, it is," he answered.

They retraced their steps among the tables in the various rooms. The low vaulted ceilings echoed voices, clinking glasses and the indistinct hum of the music all mingled together, and the air seemed heavier and more smoke-laden than when they had come in. Giacomo began to think that he too had had too much to drink. Outside it was almost warmer than underground. The air hung motionless under the plane trees and the street lamps lit up their mass of dense, inert leaves.

"We must find a taxi," said the older sister, as if she were coming away from a fashionable private party.

They walked down to the nearby square, but there was no taxi in sight.

"Where is this home of yours, anyhow?" Giacomo asked gaily. He was walking between them, arm in arm, and letting them lead him along.

"Remember the sanctity of the home!" said the younger sister with a giggle.

The older one named a street some distance off, in the outskirts of the city.

"We'll have to take a bus," said Giacomo, "and make connections with a tram at the end of the line."

There was really nothing else they could do. Fortunately the bus came soon and they got in. Giacomo paid the three fares and they sat down, the older one occupying a seat to herself and the other two sharing one behind her.

"You'd have found a hotel more convenient," the younger sister said in a loud voice as the bus started. "You'll have a long walk coming home. But the hotels here are so fussy. I know one in Milan where they ask no questions and don't even require a deposit on the room. . . ."

Some of the people in the half-empty bus turned around to look at Giacomo and his companion, but the hour was late and they were apparently too tired to smile. The bus hurtled recklessly through the narrow streets of the central part of the city with beetling palaces on either side. The older woman turned around and said to Giacomo emphatically:

"How long do you plan to stay? Your wife must miss you. She doesn't see much of you, does she, with all these long trips?"

"Wife? Do you know his wife? . . . Are you really married?"

"Yes, married to you," Giacomo said, laughing and taking her hand. But she pulled it away and whispered with mock severity:

"Watch out. . . . My sister's looking."

"Hurrah for the sanctity of the home!" Giacomo said.

"Yes, three cheers for the sanctity of the home!"

More of the passengers looked at them with curiosity in their eyes.

"Can't you keep quiet for a minute?" asked the older sister, turning around.

"I'll talk when I choose," replied the younger.

After this reply the older one drew herself up and definitely turned her back on them. Apparently she had decided in desperation to try to give the impression that she had nothing to do with them at all. She opened her bag and began to powder her nose. In the mirror of the compact Giacomo could see the hardness and ill humor of her eyes under the fleshy lids.

The bus made its last stop in a dark square. Through the black, pointed leaves of the palm trees in a public garden they could see the round, yellow headlight of a tram.

"That's ours," said the older woman, quickening her pace.

The tram was almost full, but they managed to seat themselves in the same arrangement as before. At the second stop a man about fifty years old with a conical head and greying hair got in. He was dressed in a black suit, a white shirt and a black tie and had a prominent red-tipped nose in the middle of his wooden face. He sat down beside Rina and raised his hat somewhat as if it were the cover of a pot.

"When are you going back to Milan?" Giacomo asked his companion.

"Not for some time," the girl said. "I want to have some fun. My sister's always taking me to the best places, but the people we run into there have a way of never turning up again, like the one with whom we had an appointment this evening. I'd rather go to a businessmen's restaurant. . . . They tell me that the . . ." – and here she named a fashionable establishment – ". . . is just the place to go."

Her sister stirred on her seat but did not turn around.

"Yes," Giacomo assented. "They have good food there."

"I want to have fun, I say," the girl went on. "What's the name of that place where they have a vaudeville show and between acts you can dance on the floor?"

"The Eden?" Giacomo suggested.

"I went there some time ago with a man from the south . . . he was very generous with his money. . . . What would you say if we were to go together one of these evenings?"

"Why not?"

"I'm crazy about places like that."

Giacomo did not reply, and she went on:

"Will you look me up if you come to Milan?"

"Where do you live?"

"I'll give you the exact address," she said, looking at him with a sort of drunken satisfaction. "You can come whenever you like. I don't believe in the sanctity of the home."

The man in black turned around and scrutinized them carefully. Rina's neck and shoulders were held so stiffly that not even the rocking motion of the tram could shake them.

"That wine of yours really went to my head," the girl said after a pause. "It was good stuff, though. . . ."

The tram came to a stop. Rina got up and without speaking went toward the door. The man in black passed in front of her while she waited there and again took off his hat. She nodded graciously, as if she were grateful to him for this mark of respect after the sort of talk she had heard from her sister.

"Where are you going?" called out Lori, getting up in her turn. "Is it our stop?"

The sister said nothing, but got out, with Giacomo and Lori following her. The tram went on and they were left in the midst of a very large, flat, asphalt-paved space, surrounded on three sides by tall apartment-houses with very few lighted windows. Straight ahead of them two rows of lamps ran along either side of a paved road apparently leading into an uncultivated area where there were no houses in sight.

"Are we there?" asked the girl, looking around her. "I never seem to recognize it."

The older sister waited until the man in black had walked away. Then she said angrily:

"Yes, we're there. But I don't want you to stay with me ever again."

"Why not? What's the matter?"

"I've told you often enough," said her sister, her anger mounting as she spoke. "You might have the decency in the part of town where I live and the tram I take every day not to carry on that way. You talked nonsense all the way out here, and in such a loud voice. . . ."

"What did I say?"

"Everyone on the tram knows me . . . What are they going to think? Did you see that gentleman sitting next to me? He's Mr. Picchio, a lawyer, who lives in my house, on the same floor. He'll say my sister is a little slut who brings men home with her. . . ."

"But what does it matter?"

"It matters a lot. I don't want people to talk about me behind my back."

"Look here," said the younger sister, planting herself in the middle of the open space with her hands on her hips. "Look here, what's the use of all this fuss? What your neighbors will say is no more than the truth. Go along with you!" And she came back to Giacomo's side.

"Very well," said the other, "but this is the last time I'm inviting you for a visit."

They walked a little way in silence. Then Rina went up to the entrance of one of the large apartment houses.

"For heaven's sake be quiet," she whispered to Giacomo as she turned the key in the lock.

They came into a lobby with a black marble ledge running all the way around the floor. A star-shaped hanging glass lamp cast myriads of sparkling facets on the walls. Thence they passed into a room enclosing the stairs. Rina walked around the cage of the self-running elevator and went to a door at the end of a hall.

"Quietly," she said again, as they went in.

After they had shut the door behind them she lit a lamp enclosed in a square white glass box. The apartment seemed to be furnished in extremely modern style. Everywhere there were cubical or box-shaped pieces of furniture, chromium lamps, glass tables and tubular chairs. Rina led Giacomo down a narrow corridor to a closed door.

"We might as well go straight into the bedroom," she said.

The room was a small one and most of it was taken up by a low, wide double bed. The design on the bedcover was composed of squares fitted one inside another, in various shades of all different colors, from pale blue to violet, red and brown, and the same material was used in the upholstery of the chairs. A wardrobe made up of a series of sections joined together, with a revolving mirror in the middle, took up most of one wall. There were globe-shaped lamps on low tables. Everything was spotlessly clean, and in spite of the bright colors of the bedcover the atmosphere of the room was somewhat dull and sad, like that of an up-to-date, modest hotel. Rina carefully took off her hat and put it in the wardrobe. Then she went into a corner and pulled her dress off over her head, leaving herself clad in a perforated black slip. She had hardly any breasts, Giacomo thought to himself, but her body was pleasing enough, with the wide hips and plump legs. Not knowing quite what to do and finding her within his reach he put his arms around her waist and pulled her to him. She allowed him to kiss her but displayed no feeling.

"I'll fix the bed," she said, "and you can undress in the bathroom over there if you like. . . ."

She bent over the bed to pull off the bedcover and lifted up her silk-stockinged leg, showing again how the garter was too tight above the knee. Then she turned down the sheet, which was clean and still creased from ironing. Plainly her statement about the sanctity of the home had some real meaning. Giacomo wondered whether he should get undressed, but he was ashamed to lie down naked and alone in the big double bed. She was sitting on the edge of the bed now, with her back to him, pulling off her stockings. The younger sister had disappeared and through the half-open door he could hear her stirring about in the bathroom. Giacomo observed that it was very hot and asked Rina if she could open the window.

"After we've put out the light," she answered. "Otherwise someone might look in and see."

Just then Lori came out of the bathroom and went over to stand in front of the mirror in the wardrobe. Giacomo saw her look at herself with curiously concentrated attention, then, as if her mind were on something else, slowly unbutton her blouse from top to bottom. When it was unbuttoned she hesitated for a moment, then equally slowly took it off, revealing herself naked underneath. She had rather large breasts, which seemed to be dragged down by their weight, but the tips of them were pointed upward and from the stiff way they shook with every movement it was clear that their shape was a natural one and not the effect of age or weariness. She walked by Giacomo, hung her blouse over the back of a chair and went over to a gramophone placed on a stool in one corner of the room.

"Let's have some music," she said.

As she leaned over to wind the gramophone she looked up through her loose hair at Giacomo with a happy expression on her face. Her breasts hardly moved at all, and Giacomo was surprised because the effort of turning the handle made the rest of her body shake all over. As a popular tune started up she came over to him and held out her arms.

"Let's dance," she said.

They wheeled around, but when the music grew louder Rina called out from a chair at the dressing-table:

"Turn that thing off!"

Instead of obeying her Giacomo led his partner out into the corridor. His timidity was gone; now that he was launched upon the adventure there was nothing to do but carry it to a logical conclusion. Soon both Rina and Lori would be fully undressed and all three of them would lie down on the wide double bed.

The idea was so very agreeable that it actually checked his impatience to perform. He wished somehow to handle Lori alone because he was half ashamed to do so before her sister. But just as he was gradually trying to change a dance step into a closer embrace the music came to a sudden stop.

"It's that fool of a Rina," the girl said, freeing herself abruptly from his arms and rushing into the bedroom, where Giacomo discontentedly followed her.

"Why did you turn off the gramophone? We were dancing," she said to her sister, who was just lowering its cover.

"I told you before I didn't want any noise," Rina answered. "Didn't you make enough racket in the tram? You put me to shame before Mr. Picchio and I don't know whether I'll ever be able to look him in the face again."

They stood facing each other, one naked, the other in her slip. "What do I care about Mr. Picchio?" her sister shouted. "Perhaps he's caught on to the fact that you go out after men. But what of it?"

"I care, though. And then it's not true. You're the one that goes man-hunting in Milan."

"And what do you do, in the name of heaven?"

"Never mind what I do . . . Just remember that as long as you're in my house you have to behave. . . . This evening you've put me to shame. . . . There are things you can do on your own hook, but please don't do them here. . . ."

"The sanctity of the home, eh?" The girl gave a forced laugh, then her face turned red with anger. "I don't give a rap for this filthy home of yours. I'd just as soon go away this minute."

"Go on away; you'll be doing me a favor," said her sister in a less secure and almost intimidated tone of voice.

"I'm going, never fear," said the girl furiously, taking her blouse off the chair and beginning to button it up in a hurry.

"Go on then," said Rina, but she was plainly suffering from the other's decision.

"I'm going, and you'll never see me again." With her face still red she pulled out from behind the wardrobe a canvas suitcase trimmed in leather. Then she opened a drawer and began to pack her belongings helter-skelter.

"Come now," said Giacomo, going over to her. "Come, come."

"Let me alone," she said, pushing him away.

"As far as I'm concerned, go on," said her sister, who was standing near the gramophone with a disconcerted expression.

"I'm going away from your filthy house, never fear."

"Go, then," said her sister sorrowfully. "Go as quickly as you can."

This time Lori did not answer. She leaned the suitcase against her thigh, raised her knee and closed it. Then passing angrily between Giacomo and her sister she took a crumpled hat off a rack and went out of the room.

"Lori!" Rina called, as if her feelings had got the better of her.

There was no answer and a moment later the apartment was shaken by the angry slamming of the front door. Rina sat down on the edge of the bed and put her head between her hands.

The whole thing had taken place so swiftly that Giacomo had not yet recovered from his earlier presumption that he was successfully launched upon the adventure and had only to let himself be carried along to a happy ending. He was still puffed up with self-assurance and yet the affair had already gone up in smoke. He felt stabbing pangs of annoyance, disappointment and futility. Looking at the woman who sat in her black slip on the edge of the bed she had vainly prepared a short time before, he saw that she was in tears.

"To think of all I did for her!" she said in a quivering voice. "When she was a small child and I was sixteen years old I worked to support her. What would she have become without me? I gave her summer holidays, bought her clothes and everything. . . . When she was older I found her a job as a model. . . For years I deprived myself in order to send her money. . . And now, see how she has treated me!"

She shook her head and looked up at him from beneath her fleshy eyelids, and now there was nothing vicious in her eyes.

"Come, come!" said Giacomo, forcing himself to sit down beside her and taking her hand in his. "She'll come back."

"No, I know her. She'll not come back so soon, in fact she'll never come back at all." And she drew a handkerchief out from under the pillow and blew her nose.

Giacomo wondered whether he should suggest that the two of them go ahead as if nothing had happened. Even in her tearful and dishevelled state Rina would probably have consented, but she would have made a most unsuitably melancholy partner in lovemaking.

"I think I may as well go home," he said, getting up.

"I'm not urging you to stay," she said, following his example. "I feel so very badly. . . . You saw how she treated me. . . . The wicked, ungrateful girl!"

So saying she went into the corridor. At the door Giacomo took her into his arms and gave her a kiss. She returned it with something like gratitude.

"I'm sorry," she said.

"It doesn't matter," Giacomo answered.

When he got outside he looked hopefully around for the angry Lori. But he could see only great black pools of asphalt, rows of street lamps and dark apartment houses. "One more day is gone," he reflected spitefully. And he started off in the direction of the lamps.

Translated from the Italian by Frances Frenaye

The Jail
(Nor Even Yet Quite Relinquish –)

BY WILLIAM FAULKNER

So, although in a sense the jail was both older and less old than the courthouse, in actuality, in time, in observation and memory, it was older even than the town itself. Because there was no town until there was a courthouse, and no courthouse until (like some unsentient unweaned creature torn violently from the dug of its dam) the floorless lean-to rabbit-hutch housing the iron chest was reft from the log flank of the jail and transmogrified into a by-neo-Greek-out-of-Georgian-England edifice set in the center of what in time would be the town Square (as a result of which, the town itself had moved one block south – or rather, no town then and yet, the court-house itself the catalyst: a mere dusty widening of the trace, trail, pathway in a forest of oak and ash and hickory and sycamore and flowering catalpa and dogwood and judas tree and persimmon and wild plum, with on one side old Alec Holston's tavern and coaching-yard, and a little farther along, Ratcliffe's trading post-store and the blacksmith's, and diagonal to all of them, *en face* and solitary beyond the dust, the log jail; moved – the town – complete and intact, one block southward, so that now, a century and a quarter later, the coaching-yard and Ratcliffe's store were gone and old Alec's tavern and the blacksmith's were a hotel and a garage, on a main thoroughfare true enough but still a business side-street, and the jail across from them, though transformed also now into two storeys of Georgian brick by the hand ((or anyway pocketbooks) of Sartoris and Sutpen and Louis Grenier, faced not even on a side-street but on an alley);

And so, being older than all, it had seen all: the mutation and the change: and, in that sense, had recorded them (indeed, as Gavin Stevens, the town lawyer and the county amateur Cincinnatus, was wont to say, if you would peruse in unbroken – ay, overlapping – continuity the history of a community, look not in the church registers and the courthouse records, but beneath the successive layers of calsomine and creosote and whitewash on the walls of the jail, since only in that forcible carceration does man find the idleness in which to compose, in the gross and simple terms of his gross and simple lusts and yearnings, the gross and simple recapitula-tions of his gross and simple heart); invisible and impacted, not only beneath the annual inside creosote-and-whitewash of bullpen and cell, but on the blind outside walls too, first the simple mud-chinked log ones and then the symmetric brick, not only the scrawled illiterate and repetitive unimaginative doggerel and the perspec-tiveless almost prehistoric sexual picture-writing, but the images, the panorama not only of the town of its days and years until a century and better had been accom-plished, filled not only with its mutation and change from a halting-place: to a community: to a settlement: to a village: to a town, but with the shapes and motions, the gestures of passion and hope and travail and endurance, of the men and women and children in their successive overlapping generations long after the subjects which had reflected the images were vanished and replaced and again replaced, as when you stand say alone in a dim and empty room and believe, hypnotized beneath the vast weight of man's incredible and enduring *Was*, that perhaps by turning your head aside you will see from the corner of your eye the turn of a moving limb – a gleam of crinoline, a laced wrist, perhaps even a Cavalier plume – who knows? provided there is will enough, perhaps even the face itself three hundred years after it was dust – the eyes, two jellied tears filled with arrogance and pride and satiety and knowledge of anguish and foreknowledge of death, saying no to death across twelve generations, asking still the old same unanswerable question three centuries after that which reflected them had learned that the answer didn't matter, or – better still – had forgotten the asking of it – in the shadowy fathomless dreamlike depths of an old mirror which has looked at too much too long;

But not in shadow, not this one, this mirror, these logs: squatting in the full glare of the stump-pocked clearing during those first summers, solitary on its side of the dusty widening marked with an occasional wheel but mostly by the prints of horses and men: Pettigrew's private pony express until he and it were replaced by a monthly stagecoach from Memphis, the race horse which Jason Compson traded to Ikkemotubbe, old Mohataha's son and the last ruling Chickasaw chief in that section, for a square of land so large that, as the first formal survey revealed, the new courthouse would have been only another of Compson's outbuildings had not the town Corporation bought enough of it (at Compson's price) to forefend themselves being trespassers, and the saddle-mare which bore Doctor Habersham's worn black bag (and which drew the buggy after Doctor Habersham got too old and stiff to mount the saddle), and the mules which drew the wagon in which, seated in a rocking chair beneath a French parasol held by a Negro slave girl, old Mohataha would come to town on Saturdays (and came that last time to set her capital X on the paper which ratified the dispossession of her people forever, coming in the wagon that time too, barefoot as always but in the purple silk dress which her son, Ikkemotubbe, had brought her back from France, and a hat crowned with the royal-colored plume of a queen, beneath the slave-held parasol still and with another female slave child squatting on her other side holding the crusted slippers which she had never been able to get her feet into, and in the back of the wagon the petty rest of the unmarked Empire flotsam her son had brought to her which was small enough to be moved; driving for the last time out of the woods into the dusty widening before Ratcliffe's store where the Federal land agent and his marshal waited for her with the paper, and stopped the mules and sat for a little time, the young men of her bodyguard squatting quietly about the halted wagon after the eight-mile walk, while from the gallery of the store and of Holston's tavern the settlement – the Ratcliffes and Compsons and Peabodys and Pettigrews ((not Grenier and Holston and Habersham, because Louis Grenier declined to come in to see it, and for the same reason old Alec Holston sat alone on that hot afternoon before the smoldering log in the fireplace of his taproom, and Doctor Habersham was dead and his son had already departed for the West with his bride, who was Mohataha's granddaughter, and his father-in-law, Mohataha's son, Ikkemotubbe)) – looked on, watched: the inscrutable ageless wrinkled face, the fat shapeless body dressed in the cast-off garments of a French queen, which on her looked like the Sunday costume of the madame of a rich Natchez or New Orleans brothel, sitting in a battered wagon inside a squatting ring of her household troops, her young men dressed in their Sunday clothes for traveling too: then she said, 'Where is this Indian territory?' And they told her: West. 'Turn the mules west,' she said, and someone did so, and she took the pen from the agent and made her X on the paper and handed the pen back and the wagon moved, the young men rising too, and she vanished across that summer afternoon to that terrific and infinitesimal creak and creep of ungreased wheels, herself immobile beneath the rigid parasol, grotesque and regal, bizarre and moribund, like obsolescence's self riding off the stage its own obsolete catafalque, looking not once back, not once back toward home);

But most of all, the prints of men – the fitted shoes which Doctor Habersham and Louis Grenier had brought from the Atlantic seaboard, the cavalry boots in which Alec Holston had ridden behind Francis Marion, and – more myriad almost than leaves, outnumbering all the others lumped together – the moccasins, the deerhide sandals of the forest, worn not by the Indians but by white men, the pioneers, the long hunters, as though they had not only vanquished the wilderness but had even stepped into the very footgear of them they dispossessed (and mete and fitting so, since it was by means of his feet and legs that the white man conquered America; the closed and split U's of his horses and cattle overlay his own prints always, merely consolidating his victory) – (the jail) watched them all, red men and white and black – the pioneers, the hunters, the forest men with rifles, who made the same light rapid soundless toed-in almost heelless prints as the red men they dispossessed and who in fact dispossessed the red men for that reason: not because of the grooved barrel but because they could enter the red man's milieu and make the same footprints that he made; the husbandman printing deep the hard heels of his brogans because of the weight he bore on his shoulders: axe and saw and plow-stock, who dispossessed the forest man for the obverse reason: because with his saw and axe he simply removed, obliterated, the milieu in which alone the forest man could exist; then the land specu-lators and the traders in slaves and whiskey who followed the husbandmen, and the politicians who followed the land speculators, printing deeper and deeper the dust of that dusty widening, until at last there was no mark of Chickasaw left in it any more; watching (the jail) them all, from the first innocent days when Doctor Habersham and his son and Alex Holston and Louis Grenier were first guests and then friends of Ikkemotubbe's Chickasaw clan; then an Indian agent and a land-office and a trading post, and suddenly Ikkemotubbe and his Chickasaws were themselves the guests without being friends of the Federal Government; then Ratcliffe, and the trading post was no longer simply an Indian trading post, though Indians were still welcome, of course (since, after all, they owned the land or anyway were on it first and claimed it), then Compson with his race horse and presently Compson began to own the Indian accounts for tobacco and calico and jean pants and cooking-pots on Ratcliffe's books (in time he would own Ratcliffe's books too) and one day Ikkemotubbe owned the race horse and Compson owned the land itself, some of which the city fathers would have to buy from him at his price in order to establish a town; and Pettigrew with his tri-weekly mail, and then a monthly stage and the new faces coming in faster than old Alex Holston, arthritic and irascible, hunkered like an old surly bear over his smol-dering hearth even in the heat of summer (he alone now of that original three, since old Grenier no longer came in to the settlement, and old Doctor Habersham was dead, and the old doctor's son, in the opinion of the settlement, had already turned Indian and renegade even at the age of twelve or fourteen) any longer made any effort, wanted, to associate names with; and now indeed the last moccasin print vanished from that dusty widening, the last toed-in heelless light soft quick long-striding print pointing West for an instant, then trodden from the sight and memory of man by a heavy leather heel engaged not in the traffic of endurance and hardihood and survival, but in money-taking with it (the print) not only the moccasins but the deer-hide leggins and jerkin too, because Ikkemotubbe's Chickasaws now wore eastern factory-made jeans and shoes sold them on credit out of Ratcliffe's and Compson's general store, walking in to the settlement on the white man's Saturday, carrying the alien shoes rolled neatly in the alien pants under their arms, to stop at the bridge over Compson's creek long enough to bathe their legs and feet before donning the pants and shoes, then coming on to squat all day on the store gallery eating cheese and crackers and peppermint candy (bought on credit too out of Compson's and Ratcliffe's showcase) and now not only they but Habersham and Holston and Grenier too were there on sufferance, anachronistic and alien, not really an annoyance yet but simply a discomfort;

Then they were gone; the jail watched that: the halted ungreased unpainted wagon, the span of underfed mules attached to it by fragments of eastern harness supplemented by raw deer-hide thongs, the nine young men – the wild men, tameless and proud, who even in their own generation's memory had been free and, in that of their fathers, the heirs of kings – squatting about it, waiting, quiet and composed, not even dressed in the ancient forest-softened deerskins of their freedom but in the formal regalia of the white man's inexplicable ritualistic sabbaticals: broadcloth trousers and white shirts with boiled-starch bosoms (because they were traveling now; they would be visible to outworld, to strangers: – and carrying the New England-made shoes under their arms too since the distance would be long and walking was better barefoot), the shirts collarless and cravatless true enough and with the tails worn outside, but still board-rigid, gleaming, pristine, and in the rocking chair in the wagon, beneath the slave-borne parasol, the fat shapeless old matriarch in the regal sweat-stained purple silk and the plumed hat, barefoot too of course but, being a queen, with another slave to carry her slippers, putting her cross to the paper and then driving on, vanishing slowly and terrifically to the slow and terrific creak and squeak of the ungreased wagon – apparently and apparently only, since in reality it was as though, instead of putting an inked cross at the foot of a sheet of paper, she had lighted the train of a mine set beneath a dam, a dyke, a barrier already straining, bulging, bellying, not only towering over the land but leaning, looming, imminent with collapse, so that it only required the single light touch of the pen in that brown illiterate hand, and the wagon did not vanish slowly and terrifically from the scene to the terrific sound of its ungreased wheels, but was swept, hurled, flung not only out of Yoknapatawpha County and Mississippi but the United States too, immobile and intact – the wagon, the mules, the rigid shapeless old Indian woman and the nine heads which surrounded her – like a float or a piece of stage property dragged rapidly into the wings across the very backdrop and amid the very bustle of the property-men setting up for the next scene and act before the curtain had even had time to fall;

There was no time; the next act and scene itself clearing its own stage without waiting for property-men; or rather, not even bothering to clear the stage but commencing the new act and scene right in the midst of the phantoms, the fading wraiths of that old time which had been exhausted, used up, to be no more and never return: as though the mere and simple orderly ordinary succession of days was not big enough, comprised not scope enough, and so weeks and months and years had to be considered and compounded into one burst, one surge, one soundless roar filled with one word: town: city: with a name: Jefferson; men's mouths and their incredulous faces (faces to which old Alex Holston had long since ceased trying to give names or, for that matter, even to recognize) were filled with it; that was only yesterday, and by tomorrow the vast bright rush and roar had swept the very town one block south, leaving in the tideless backwater of an alley on a side-street the old jail which, like the old mirror, had already looked at too much too long, or like the patriarch who, whether or not he decreed the conversion of the mud-chinked cabin into a mansion, had at least foreseen it, is now not only content but even prefers the old chair on the back gallery, free of the rustle of blueprints and the uproar of bickering architects in the already dismantled living room;

It (the old jail) didn't care, tideless in that backwash, insulated by that city block of space from the turmoil of the town's birthing, the mud-chinked log walls even carcerant of the flotsam of an older time already on its rapid way out too: an occasional runaway slave or drunken Indian or shoddy would-be heir of the old tradition of Mason or Hare or Harpe (biding its time until, the courthouse finished, the jail too would be translated into brick, but, unlike the courthouse, merely a veneer of brick, the old mud-chinked logs of the ground floor still intact behind the patterned and symmetric sheathe); no longer even watching now, merely cognizant, remembering: only yesterday was a wilderness ordinary, a store, a smithy, and already today was not a town, a city, but the town and city: named; not a courthouse but *the* courthouse, rising surging like the fixed blast of a rocket, not even finished yet but already looming, beacon focus and lodestar, already taller than anything else, out of the rapid and fading wilderness – not the wilderness receding from the rich and arable fields as tide recedes, but rather the fields themselves, rich and inexhaustible to the plow, rising sunward and airward out of swamp and morass, themselves thrusting back and down brake and thicket, bayou and bottom and forest, along with the copeless denizens – the wild men and animals – which once haunted them, waiting, dreaming, imagining, no other – lodestar and pole, drawing the people – the men and women and children, the maidens, the marriageable girls and the young men, flowing, pouring in with their tools and goods and cattle and slaves and gold money, behind ox- or mule-teams, by steamboat up Ikkemotubbe's old river from the Mississippi; only yesterday Pettigrew's pony express had been displaced by a stagecoach, yet already there was talk of a railroad less than a hundred miles to the north, to run all the way from Memphis to the Atlantic Ocean;

Going fast now: only seven years, and not only was the courthouse finished, but the jail too: not a new jail of course but the old one veneered over with brick, into two storeys, with white trim and iron-barred windows: only its face lifted, because behind the veneer were still the old ineradicable bones, the old ineradicable remembering: the old logs immured intact and lightless between the tiered symmetric bricks and the whitewashed plaster, immune now even to having to look, see, watch that new time which in a few years more would not even remember that the old logs were there behind the brick or had ever been, an age from which the drunken Indian had vanished, leaving only the highwayman, who had wagered his liberty on his luck, and the runaway nigger who, having no freedom to stake, had wagered merely his milieu; that rapid, that fast: Sutpen's untameable Paris architect long since departed, vanished (one hoped) back to wherever it was he had made that aborted midnight try to regain and had been overtaken and caught in the swamp, not (as the town knew now) by Sutpen and Sutpen's wild West Indian headman and Sutpen's bear bounds, nor even by Sutpen's destiny nor even by his (the architect's) own, but by that of the town: the long invincible arm of Progress itself reaching into that midnight swamp to pluck him out of that bayed circle of dogs and naked Negroes and pine torches, and stamped the town with him like a rubber signature and then released him, not flung him away like a squeezed-out tube of paint, but rather (inattentive too) merely opening its fingers, its hand; stamping his (the architect's) imprint not on just the courthouse and the jail, but on the whole town, the flow and trickle of his bricks never even faltering, his molds and kilns building the two churches and then that Female Academy a certificate from which, to a young woman of North Mississippi or West Tennessee, would presently have the same mystic significance as an invitation dated from Windsor castle and signed by Queen Victoria would for a young female from Long Island or Philadelphia;

That fast now: tomorrow, and the railroad did run unbroken from Memphis to Carolina, the light-wheeled bulb-stacked wood-burning engines shrieking among the swamps and cane-brakes where bear and panther still lurked, and through the open woods where browsing deer still drifted in pale bands like unwinded smoke: because they – the wild animals, the beasts – remained, they coped, they would endure; a day, and they would flee, lumber, scuttle across the clearings already overtaken and relinquished by the hawk-shaped shadows of mail planes; they would endure, only the wild men were gone; indeed, tomorrow, and there would be grown men in Jefferson who could not even remember a drunken Indian in the jail; another tomorrow – so quick, so rapid, so fast – and not even a highwayman any more of the old true sanguinary girt and tradition of Hare and Mason and the mad Harpes; even Murrell, their thrice-compounded heir and apotheosis, who had taken his heritage of simple rapacity and bloodlust and converted it into a bloody dream of outlaw-empire, was gone, finished, as obsolete as Alexander, checkmated and stripped not even by man but by Progress, by a pierceless front of middle-class morality, which refused him even the dignity of execution as a felon, but instead merely branded him on the hand like an Elizabethan pickpocket – until all that remained of the old days for the jail to incarcerate was the runaway slave, for his little hour more, his little minute yet while the time, the land, the nation, the American earth, whirled faster and faster toward the plunging precipice of its destiny;

That fast, that rapid: a commodity in the land now which until now had dealt first in Indians: then in acres and sections and boundaries: – an economy: Cotton: a king: omnipotent and omnipresent: a destiny of which (obvious now) the plow and the axe had been merely the tools; not plow and axe which had effaced the wilderness, but Cotton: petty globules of Motion weightless and myriad even in the hand of a child, incapable even of wadding a rifle, let alone of charging it, yet potent enough to sever the very taproots of oak and hickory and gum, leaving the acre-shading tops to wither and vanish in one single season beneath that fierce minted glare; not the rifle nor the plow which drove at last the bear and deer and panther into the last jungle fastuesses of the river bottoms, but Cotton; not the soaring cupola of the courthouse drawing people into the country, but that same white tide sweeping them in: that tender skim covering the winter's brown earth, burgeoning through spring and summer into September's white surf crashing against the flanks of gin and warehouse and ringing like bells on the marble counters of the banks: altering not just the face of the land, but the complexion of the town too, creating its own parasitic aristocracy not only behind the columned porticoes of the plantation houses, but in the counting-rooms of merchants and bankers and the sanctums of lawyers, and not only these last, but finally nadir complete: the county offices too: of sheriff and tax-collector and bailiff and turnkey and clerk: doing overnight to the old jail what Sutpen's architect with all his brick and iron smithwork, had not been able to accomplish – the old jail which had been unavoidable, a necessity, like a public comfort-station, and which, like the public comfort-station, was not ignored but simply by mutual concord, not seen, not looked at, not named by its purpose and aim, yet which to the older people of the town, in spite of Sutpen's architect's face-lifting, was still the old jail – now translated into an integer, a moveable pawn on the county's political board like the sheriff's star or the clerk's bond or the bailiff's wand of office; converted indeed now, elevated (an apotheosis) ten feet above the level of the town, so that the old buried log walls now contained the living-quarters for the turnkey's family and the kitchen from which his wife catered, at so much a meal, to the city's and the county's prisoners – perquisite not for work or capability for work, but for political fidelity and the numerality of votable kin by blood or marriage – a jailor or turnkey, himself someone's cousin and with enough other cousins and inlaws of his own to have assured the election of sheriff or chancery- or circuit-clerk – a failed farmer who was not at all the victim of his time but, on the contrary, was its master, since his inherited and inescapable incapacity to support his family by his own efforts had matched him with an era and a land where government was founded on the working premise of being primarily an asylum for ineptitude and indigence, for the private business failures among your or your wife's kin whom otherwise you yourself would have to support – so much his destiny's master that, in a land and time where a man's survival depended not only on his ability to drive a straight furrow and to fell a tree without maiming or destroying himself, that fate had supplied to him one child: a frail anemic girl with narrow workless hands lacking even the strength to milk a cow, and then capped its own vanquishment and eternal subjugation by the paradox of giving him for his patronymic the designation of the vocation at which he was to fail: Farmer; this was the incumbent, the turnkey, the jailor; the old tough logs which had known Ikke-motubbe's drunken Chickasaws and brawling teamsters and trappers and flatboat-men (and – for that one short summer night – the four highwaymen, one of whom might have been the murderer, Wiley Harpe), were now the bower framing a win-dow in which mused hour after hour and day and month and year, the frail blonde girl not only incapable of (or at least excused from) helping her mother cook, but even of drying the dishes after her mother (or father perhaps) washed them – mus-ing, not even waiting for anyone or anything, as far as the town knew, not even pensive, as far as the town knew: just musing amid her blonde hair in the window facing the country town street, day after day and month after month and – as the town remembered it – year after year for what must have been three or four of them, inscribing at some moment the fragile and indelible signature of her meditation in one of the panes of it (the window): her frail and workless name, scratched by a diamond ring in her frail and workless hand, and the date: *Cecilia Farmer April 16th 1861*;

At which moment the destiny of the land, the nation, the South, the State, the County, was already whirling into the plunge of its precipice, not that the State and the South knew it, because the first seconds of fall always seem like soar: a weight-less deliberation preliminary to a rush not downward but upward, the falling body reversed during the second by transubstantiation into the upward rush of earth; a soar, an apex, the South's own apotheosis of its destiny and its pride, Mississippi and Yoknapatawpha County not last in this, Mississippi among the first of the eleven to ratify secession, the regiment of infantry which John Sartoris raised and organized with Jefferson for its headquarters, going to Virginia numbered Two in the roster of Mississippi regiments, the jail watching that too but just by cognizance from a block away: that noon, the regiment not even a regiment yet but merely a voluntary asso-ciation of untried men who knew they were ignorant and hoped they were brave, the four sides of the Square lined with their fathers or grandfathers and their moth-ers and wives and sisters and sweethearts, the only uniform present yet that one in which Sartoris stood with his virgin sabre and his pristine colonel's braid on the courthouse balcony, bareheaded too while the Baptist minister prayed and the Richmond mustering officer swore the regiment in; and then (the regiment) gone; and now not only the jail but the town too hung without motion in a tideless back-wash: the plunging body advanced far enough now into space as to have lost all sense of motion, weightless and immobile upon the light pressure of invisible air, gone now all diminishment of the precipice's lip, all increment of the vast increase-less earth: a town of old men and women and children and an occasional wounded soldier (John Sartoris himself, deposed from his colonelcy by a regimental election after Second Manassas, came home and oversaw the making and harvesting of a crop on his plantation before he got bored and gathered up a small gang of irregular cavalry and carried it up into Tennessee to join Forrest), static in *quo*, rumored, murmured of war only as from a great and incredible dreamy distance, like far summer thunder; until the spring of '64, the once-vast fixed impalpable increaseless and threatless earth now one omnivorous roar of rock (a roar so vast and so spew-ing, flinging ahead of itself, like the spray above the maelstrom, the preliminary anesthetic of shock so that the agony of bone and flesh will not even be felt, as to contain and sweep along with it the beginning, the first ephemeral phase, of this story, permitting it to boil for an instant to the surface like a chip or a twig – a matchstick or a bubble, say, too weightless to give resistance for destruction to func-tion against: in this case, a bubble, a minute globule which was its own impunity, since what it – the bubble – contained, having no part in rationality and being con-temptuous of fact, was immune even to the rationality of rock) – a sudden battle centering around Colonel Sartoris's plantation house four miles to the north, the line of a creek held long enough for the main Confederate body to pass through Jefferson to a stronger line on the river heights south of the town, a rear-guard action of cavalry in the streets of the town itself (and this was the story, the begin-ning of it; all of it too, the town might have been justified in thinking, presuming they had had time to see, notice, remark and then remember, even that little) – the rattle and burst of pistols, the hooves, the dust, the rush and scurry of a handful of horsemen led by a lieutenant, up the street past the jail, and the two of them – the frail and useless girl musing in the blonde mist of her hair beside the windowpane where three or four (or whatever it was) years ago she had inscribed with her grand-mother's diamond ring her paradoxical and significantless name (and where, so it seemed to the town, she had been standing ever since), and the soldier, gaunt and tattered, battle-grimed and fleeing and undefeated, looking at one another for that moment across the fury and pell mell of battle;

Then gone; that night the town was occupied by Federal troops; two nights later, it was on fire (the Square, the stores and shops and the professional offices), gutted (the courthouse too), the blackened jagged topless jumbles of brick wall enclosing like a ruined jaw the blackened shell of the courthouse between its two rows of topless columns, which (the columns) were only blackened and stained, being tougher than fire: but not the jail, it escaped, untouched, insulated by its windless backwater from fire; and now the town was as though insulated by fire or perhaps cauterized by fire from fury and turmoil, the long roar of the rushing omnivorous rock fading on to the east with the fading uproar of the battle: and so in effect it was a whole year in advance of Appomattox (only the undefeated undefeatable women, vulnerable only to death, resisted, endured, irreconcilable); already, before there was a name for them (already their prototype before they even existed as a species), there were carpetbaggers in Jefferson – a Missourian named Redmond, a cotton- and quartermaster-supplies speculator, who had followed the Northern army to Memphis in '61 and (nobody knew exactly how or why) had been with (or at least on the fringe of) the military household of the brigadier commanding the force which occupied Jefferson, himself – Redmond – going no farther, stopping, staying, none knew the why for that either, why he elected Jefferson, chose that alien fire-gutted site (himself one, or at least the associate, of them who had set the match) to be his future home; and a German private, a blacksmith, a deserter from a Pennsylvania regiment, who appeared in the summer of '64, riding a mule, with (so the tale told later, when his family of daughters had become matriarchs and grand-mothers of the town's new aristocracy) for saddle-blanket sheaf on sheaf of virgin and uncut United States banknotes, so Jefferson and Yoknapatawpha County had mounted Golgotha and passed beyond Appomattox a full year in advance, with returned soldiers in the town, not only the wounded from the battle of Jefferson, but whole men: not only the furloughed from Forrest in Alabama and Johnston in Georgia and Lee in Virginia, but the stragglers, the unmaimed flotsam and refuse of that single battle now drawing its final constricting loop from the Atlantic Ocean at Old Point Comfort, to Richmond: to Chattanooga: to Atlanta: to the Atlantic Ocean again at Charleston, who were not deserters but who could not rejoin any still-intact Confederate unit for the reason that there were enemy armies between (so that in the almost faded twilight of that land, the knell of Appomattox made no sound; when in the spring and early summer of '65 the formally and officially paroled and disbanded soldiers began to trickle back into the county, there was anticlimax; they returned to a land which not only had passed through Appomattox over a year ago, it had that year in which to assimilate it, that whole year in which not only to ingest surrender but (begging the metaphor, the figure) to convert, metabolize it, and then defecate it as fertilizer for the four-years' fallow land they were already in train to rehabilitate a year before the Virginia knell rang the formal change, the men of '65 returning to find themselves alien in the very land they had been bred and born in and had fought for four years to defend, to find a working and already solvent economy based on the premise that it could get along without them: (and now the rest of this story, since it occurs, happens, here: not yet June in '65; this one had indeed wasted no time getting back: a stranger, alone; the town did not even know it had ever seen him before, because the other time was a year ago and had lasted only while he galloped through it firing a pistol backward at a Yankee army, and he had been riding a horse – a fine though a little too small and too deli-cate blooded mare – where now he rode a big mule, which for that reason – its size –

was a better mule than the horse was a horse, but it was still a mule, and of course the town could not know that he had swapped the mare for the mule on the same day that he traded his lieutenant's sabre – he still had the pistol – for the stocking full of seed corn he had seen growing in a Pennsylvania field and had not let even the mule have one mouthful of it during the long journey across the ruined land between the Atlantic seaboard and the Jefferson jail, riding up to the jail at last, still gaunt and tattered and dirty and still undefeated and not fleeing now but instead making or at least planning a single-handed assault against what any rational man would have considered insurmountable odds ((but then, that bubble had ever been immune to the ephemerae of facts)); perhaps, probably – without doubt: apparently she had been standing leaning musing in it for three or four years in 1864; nothing had happened since, not in a land which had even anticipated Appomattox, capable of shaking a meditation that rooted, that durable, that veteran – the girl watched him get down and tie the mule to the fence, and perhaps while he walked from the fence to the door he even looked for a moment at her, though possibly, perhaps even probably, not, since she was not his immediate object now, he was not really concerned with her at the moment, because he had so little time, he had none, really: still to reach Alabama and the small hill farm which had been his father's and would now be his, if – no, when – he could get there, and it had not been ruined by four years of war and neglect, and even if the land was still plantable, even if he could start planting the stocking of corn tomorrow, he would be weeks and even months late; during that walk to the door and as he lifted his hand to knock on it, he must have thought with a kind of weary and indomitable outrage of how, already months late, he must still waste a day or maybe even two or three of them before he could load the girl onto the mule behind him and head at last for Alabama – this, at a time when of all things he would require patience and a clear head, trying for them ((courtesy too, which would he demanded now)), patient and urgent and polite, undefeated, trying to explain, in terms which they could understand or at least accept, his simple need and the urgency of it, to the mother and father whom he had never seen before and whom he never intended, or anyway anticipated, to see again, not that he had anything for or against them either: he simply intended to be too busy for the rest of his life, once they could get on the mule and start for home; not seeing the girl then, during the interview, not even asking to see her for a moment when the interview was over, because he had to get the license now and then find the preacher: so that the first word he ever spoke to her was a promise delivered through a stranger; it was probably not until they were on the mule – the frail useless hands whose only strength seemed to be that sufficient to fold the wedding license into the bosom of her dress and then cling to the belt around his waist – that he looked at her again or ((both of them)) had time to learn one another's middle name);

That was the story, the incident, ephemeral of an afternoon in late May, unrecorded by the town and the county because they had little time too: (the county and the town) had anticipated Appomattox and kept that lead, so that in effect Appomattox itself never overhauled them; it was the long pull of course, but they had – as they would realize later – that priceless, that unmatchable year; on New Year's Day, 1865, while the rest of the South sat staring at the northeastern horizon beyond which Richmond lay, like a family staring at the closed door to a sick-room, Yoknapatawpha County was already nine months gone in reconstruction; by New Year's '66, the gutted walls (the rain of two winters had washed them clean of the smoke and soot) of the Square had been temporarily roofed and were stores and shops and offices again, and they had begun to restore the courthouse: not temporary, this, but restored, exactly as it had been, between the two columned porticoes, one north and one south, which had been tougher than dynamite and fire, because it was the symbol: the County and the City: and they knew how, who had done it before; Colonel Sartoris was home now, and General Compson, the first Jason's son, and though a tragedy had happened to Sutpen and his pride – a failure not of his pride nor even of his own bones and flesh, but of the lesser bones and flesh which he had believed capable of supporting the edifice of his dream – they still had the old plans of his architect and even the architect's molds, and even more: money, (strangely, curiously) Redmond, the town's domesticated carpetbagger, symbol of a blind rapacity almost like a biological instinct, destined to cover the South like a migration of locusts; in the case of this man, arriving a full year before its time and now devoting no small portion of the fruit of his rapacity to restoring the very building the destruction of which had rung up the curtain for his appearance on the stage, had been the formal visa on his passport to pillage; and by New Year's of '76, this same Redmond with his money and Colonel Sartoris and General Compson had built a railroad from Jefferson north into Tennessee to connect with one from Memphis to the Atlantic Ocean; nor content there either, north and south: another ten years (Sartoris and Redmond and Compson quarreled, and Sartoris and Redmond bought – probably with Redmond's money – Compson's interest in the railroad, and the next year Sartoris and Redmond had quarreled and the year after that, because of simple physical fear, Redmond killed Sartoris from ambush on the Jefferson Square and fled, and at last even Sartoris's supporters – he had no friends: only enemies and frantic admirers – began to understand the result of that regimental election in the fall of '62) and the railroad was a part of that system covering the whole South and East like the veins in an oak leaf and itself mutually adjunctive to the other intricate systems covering the rest of the United States, so that you could get on a train in Jefferson now and, by changing and waiting a few times, go anywhere in North America;

No more into the United States, but into the *rest* of the United States, because the long pull was over now; only the aging unvanquished women were unreconciled (irreconcilable, reversed and irrevocably reverted against the whole moving unanimity of panorama until, old unordered vacant pilings above a tide's flood, they themselves had an illusion of motion, facing irreconcilably backward toward the old lost battles, the old aborted cause, the old four ruined years whose very physical scars ten and twenty and twenty-five changes of season had annealed back into the earth; twenty-five and then thirty-five years; not only a century and an age, but a way of thinking died; the town itself wrote the epilogue and epitaph: 1900, on Confederate Decoration Day, Mrs. Virginia Depre, Colonel Sartoris's sister, twitched a lanyard and the spring-restive bunting collapsed and flowed, leaving the marble effigy – the stone infantry-man on his stone pedestal on the exact spot where forty years ago the Richmond officer and the local Baptist minister had mustered in the Colonel's regiment, and the old men in the gray and braided coats (all officers now, none less in rank than captain) tottered into the sunlight and fired shotguns at the bland sky and raised their cracked quavering voices in the shrill hackle-lifting yelling which Lee and Jackson and Longstreet and the two Johnstons (and Grant and Sherman and Hooker and Pope and McClellan and Burnside too for the matter of that) had listened to amid the smoke and the din; epilogue and epitaph, because apparently neither the U.D.C. ladies who instigated and bought the monument, nor the architect who designed it nor the masons who erected it, had noticed that the marble eyes under the shading marble palm stared not toward the north and the enemy, but toward the south, toward (if anything) his own rear – looking perhaps, the wits said (could say now, with the old war thirty-five years past and you could even joke about it – except the women, the ladies, the unsurrendered, the irreconcilable, who even after another thirty-five years would still get up and stalk out of picture houses showing *Gone With the Wind*), for reinforcements; or perhaps not a combat soldier at all, but a provost marshal's man looking for deserters, or perhaps himself for a safe place to run to: because that old war was dead; the sons of those tottering old men in gray had already died in blue coats in Cuba, the macabre mementos and testimonials and shrines of the new war already usurping the earth before the blasts of blank shotgun shells and the weightless collapsing of bunting had unveiled the final ones to the old;

Not only a new century and a new way of thinking, but of acting and behaving too: now you could go to bed in a train in Jefferson and wake up tomorrow morning in New Orleans or Chicago; there were electric lights and running water in almost every house in town except the cabins of Negroes; and now the town bought and brought from a great distance a kind of gray crushed ballast-stone called macadam, and paved the entire street between the depot and the hotel, so that no more would the train-meeting hacks filled with drummers and lawyers and court-witnesses need to lurch and heave and strain through the winter mud-holes; every morning a wagon came to your very door with artificial ice and put it in your icebox on the back gallery for you, the children in rotational neighborhood gangs following it (the wagon), eating the fragments of ice which the Negro driver chipped off for them; and that summer a specially-built sprinkling-cart began to make the round of the streets each day; a new time, a new age: there were screens in windows now; people (white people) could actually sleep in summer night air, finding it harmless, uninimical: as though there had waked suddenly in man (or anyway in his women-folks) a belief in his inalienable civil right to be free of dust and bugs;

Moving faster and faster: from the speed of two horses on either side of a polished tongue, to that of thirty then fifty then a hundred under a tin bonnet no bigger than a washtub: which from almost the first explosion, would have to be controlled by police; already in a back yard on the edge of town, an ex-blacksmith's-apprentice, a grease-covered man with the eyes of a visionary monk, was building a gasoline buggy, casting and boring his own cylinders and rods and cams, inventing his own coils and plugs and valves as he found he needed them, which would run, and did: crept popping and stinking out of the alley at the exact moment when the banker Bayard Sartoris, the Colonel's son, passed in his carriage: as a result of which, there is on the books of Jefferson today a law prohibiting the operation of any mechanically-propelled vehicle on the streets of the corporate town: who (the same banker Sartoris) died in one (such was progress, that fast, that rapid) lost from control on an icy road by his (the banker's) grandson, who had just returned from (such was progress) two years of service as a combat airman on the Western Front and now the camouflage paint is weathering slowly from a French point-seventy-five field piece squatting on one flank of the base of the Confederate monument, but even before it faded there was neon in the town and A.A.A. and C.C.C. in the county, and WPA ("and XYZ and etc.," as "Uncle Pete" Gombault, a lean clean tobacco-chewing old man, incumbent of a political sinecure under the designation of United States marshal – an office held back in reconstruction times, when the State of Mississippi was a United States military district, by a Negro man who was still living in 1925 – firemaker, sweeper, janitor and furnace-attendant to five or six lawyers and doctors and one of the banks – and still known as "Mulberry" from the avocation which he had followed before and during and after his incumbency as marshal: peddling illicit whiskey in pint and half-pint bottles from a cache beneath the roots of a big mulberry tree behind the drugstore of his pre-1865 owner – put it) in both; WPA and XYZ marking the town and the county as war itself had not : gone now were the last of the forest trees which had followed the shape of the Square, shading the unbroken second-storey balcony onto which the lawyers' and doctors' offices had opened, which shaded in its turn the fronts of the stores and the walkway beneath; and now was gone even the balcony itself with its wrought-iron balustrade on which in the long summer afternoons the lawyers would prop their feet to talk; and the continuous iron chain looping from wooden post to post along the circumference of the courthouse yard, for the farmers to hitch their teams to; and the public watering trough where they could water them, because gone was the last wagon to stand on the Square during the spring and summer and fall Saturdays and trading-days, and not only the Square but the streets leading into it were paved now, with fixed signs of interdiction and admonition applicable only to something capable of moving faster than thirty miles an hour; and now the last forest tree was gone from the courthouse yard too, replaced by formal synthetic shrubs contrived and schooled in Wisconsin greenhouses, and in the courthouse (the city hall too) a courthouse and city hall gang, in miniature of course (but that was not its fault but the fault of the city's and the country's size and population and wealth) but based on the pattern of Chicago and Kansas City and Boston and Philadelphia (and which, except for its minuscularity, neither Philadelphia nor Boston nor Kansas City nor Chicago need have blushed at) which every three or four years would try again to raze the old courthouse in order to build a new one, not that they did not like the old one nor wanted the new, but because the new one would bring into the town and county that much more increment of unearned federal money;

And now the paint is preparing to weather from an anti-tank howitzer squatting on rubber tires on the opposite flank of the Confederate monument; and gone now from the fronts of the stores are the old brick made of native clay in Sutpen's architect's old molds, replaced now by sheets of glass taller than a man and longer than a wagon and team, pressed intact in Pittsburgh factories and framing interiors bathed now in one shadowless corpse-glare of fluorescent light; and, now and at last, the last of silence too: the county's hollow inverted air one resonant boom and ululance of radio: and thus no more Yoknapatawpha's air nor even Mason and Dixon's air, but America's: the patter of comedians, the baritone screams of female vocalists, the babbling pressure to buy and buy and still buy arriving more instantaneous than light, two thousand miles from New York and Los Angeles; one air, one nation: the shadowless fluorescent corpse-glare bathing the sons and daughters of men and women, Negro and white both, who were born to and who passed all their lives in denim overalls and calico, haggling by cash or the installment-plan for garments copied last week out of *Harper's Bazaar* or *Esquire* in East Side sweat-shops:

because an entire generation of farmers has vanished, not just from Yoknapatawpha's but from Mason and Dixon's earth: the self-consumer: the machine which displaced the man because the exodus of the man left no one to drive the mule, now that the machine was threatening to extinguish the mule; time was when the mule stood in droves at daylight in the plantation mule-lots across the plantation road from the serried identical ranks of two-room shotgun shacks in which lived in droves with his family the Negro tenant- or share- or furnish-hand who bridled him (the mule) in the lot at sunup and followed him through the plumb-straight monotony of identical furrows and back to the lot at sundown, with (the man) one eye on where the mule was going and the other eye on his (the mule's) heels; both gone now, the one, to the last of the forty- and fifty- and sixty-acre hill farms inaccessible from unmarked dirt roads, the other to New York and Detroit and Chicago and Los Angeles ghettos, or nine out of ten of him that is, the tenth one mounting from the handles of a plow to the springless bucket seat of a tractor, dispossessing and displacing the other nine just as the tractor had dispossessed and displaced the other eighteen mules to whom that nine would have been complement; then Warsaw and Dunkerque displaced that tenth in his turn, and now the planter's not-yet-drafted son drove the tractor: and then Pearl Harbor and Tobruk and Utah Beach displaced that son, leaving the planter himself on the seat of the tractor, for a little while that is or so he thought, forgetting that victory or defeat both are bought at the same exorbitant price of change and alteration; one nation, one world: young men who had never been farther from Yoknapatawpha County than Memphis or New Orleans (and that not often), now talked glibly of street intersections in Asiatic and European capitals, returning no more to inherit the long monotonous endless unendable furrows of Mississippi cotton fields, living now (with now a wife and next year a wife and child and the year after that a wife and children) in automobile trailers or G.I. barracks on the outskirts of liberal arts colleges, and the father and now grandfather himself still driving the tractor across the gradually diminishing fields between the long looping skeins of electric lines bringing electric power from the Appalachian mountains, and the subterrene steel veins bringing the natural gas from the Western plains, to the little lost lonely farmhouses glittering and gleaming with automatic stoves and washing machines and television antennae;

One nation: no longer anywhere, not even in Yoknapatawpha County, one last irreconcilable fastness of stronghold from which to enter the United States, because at last even the last old sapless indomitable unvanquished widow or maiden aunt had died and the old deathless Lost Cause had become a faded (though still select) social club or caste, or form of behavior when you remembered to observe it on the occasions when young men from Brooklyn, exchange students at Mississippi or Arkansas or Texas Universities, vended tiny Confederate battle flags among the thronged Saturday afternoon ramps of football stadia; one world: the tank gun: captured from a regiment of Germans in an African desert by a regiment of Japanese in American uniforms, whose mothers and fathers at the time were in a California detention camp for enemy aliens, and carried (the gun) seven thousand miles back to be set halfway between, as a sort of secondary flying buttress to a memento of Shiloh and The Wilderness; one universe, one cosmos: contained in one America: one towering frantic edifice poised like a card-house over the abyss of the mortgaged generations; one boom, one peace: one swirling rocket-roar filling the glittering zenith as with golden feathers, until the vast hollow sphere of his air, the vast and terrible burden beneath which he tries to stand erect and lift his battered and indomitable head – the very substance in which he lives and, lacking which, he would vanish in a matter of seconds – is murmurous with his fears and terrors and disclaimers and repudiations and his aspirations and dreams and his baseless hopes, bouncing back at him in radar waves from the constellations;

And still – the old jail endured, sitting in its rumorless cul-de-sac, its almost seasonless backwater in the middle of that rush and roar of civic progress and social alteration and change like a collarless (and reasonably clean: merely dingy: with a day's stubble and no garters to his socks) old man sitting in his suspenders and stocking feet, on the back kitchen steps inside a walled courtyard; actually not isolated by location so much as insulated by obsolescence: on the way out of course (to disappear from the surface of the earth along with the rest of the town on the day when all America, after cutting down all the trees and leveling the hills and mountains with bulldozers, would have to move underground to make room for, get out of the way of, the motor cars) but like the track-walker in the tunnel, the thunder of the express mounting behind him, who finds himself opposite a niche or crack exactly his size in the wall's living and impregnable rock, and steps into it, inviolable and secure while destruction roars past and on and away, grooved ineluctably to the spidery rails of its destiny and destination; not even – the jail – worth selling to the United States for some matching allocation out of the federal treasury; not even (so fast, so far, was Progress) any more a real pawn, let alone knight or rook, on the County's political board, not even plum in true worth of the word: simply a modest sinecure for the husband of someone's cousin, who had failed not as a father but merely as a fourth-rate farmer or day-laborer;

It survived, endured; it had its inevictable place in the town and the county; it was even still adding modestly not just to its but to the town's and the county's history too: somewhere behind that dingy brick facade, between the old durable hand-molded brick and the cracked creosote-impregnated plaster of the inside walls (though few in the town or county any longer knew that they were there) were the old notched and mortised logs which (this, the town and county did remember; it was part of its legend) had held someone who might have been Wiley Harpe; during that summer of 1864, the federal brigadier who had fired the Square and the courthouse had used the jail as his provost-marshal's guard-house; and even children in high school remembered how the jail had been host to the Governor of the State while he discharged a thirty-day sentence for contempt of court for refusing to testify in a paternity suit brought against one of his lieutenants: but isolate, even its legend and record and history, indisputable in authenticity yet a little oblique, elliptic or perhaps just ellipsoid, washed thinly over with a faint quiet cast of apocraphy: because there were new people in the town now, strangers, outlanders, living in new minute glass-walled houses set as neat and orderly and antiseptic as cribs in a nursery ward, in new subdivisions named Fairfield or Longwood or Halcyon Acres which had once been the lawn or backyard or kitchen garden of the old residences (the old obsolete columned houses still standing among them like old horses surged suddenly out of slumber in the middle of a flock of sheep), who had never seen the jail; that is, they had looked at it in passing, they knew where it was, when their kin or friends or acquaintances from the East or North or California visited them or passed through Jefferson on the way to New Orleans or Florida, they could even repeat some of its legend or history to them: but they had had no contact with it; it was not a part of their lives; they had the automatic stoves and furnaces and milk deliveries and lawns the size of installment-plan rugs; they had never had to go to the jail on the morning after June tenth or July Fourth or Thanksgiving or Christmas or New Year's (or for that matter, on almost any Monday morning) to pay the fine of houseman or gardener or handyman so that he could hurry on home (still wearing his hangover or his barely-stanched razor-slashes) and milk the cow or clean the furnace or mow the lawn;

So only the old citizens knew the jail any more, not old people but old citizens: men and women old not in years but in the constancy of the town, or against that constancy, concordant (not coeval of course, the town's date was a century and a quarter ago now, but in accord against that continuation) with that thin durable continuity born a hundred and twenty-five years ago out of a handful of bandits captured by a drunken militia squad, and a bitter ironical incorruptible wilderness mail-rider, and a monster wrought-iron padlock – that steadfast and durable and unhurryable continuity against or across which the vain and glittering ephemerae of progress and alteration washed in substanceless repetitive evanescent scarless waves, like the wash and glare of the neon sign on what was still known as the Holston House diagonally opposite, which would fade with each dawn from the old brick walls of the jail and leave no trace; only the old citizens still knew it: the intractable and obsolescent of the town who still insisted on wood-burning ranges and cows and vegetable gardens and handymen who had to be taken out of hock on the mornings after Saturday nights and holidays; or the ones who actually spent the Saturday- and holiday-nights inside the barred doors and windows of the cells or bullpen for drunkenness or fighting or gambling – the servants, housemen and gardeners and handymen, who would be extracted the next morning by their white folks, and the others (what the town knew as the New Negro, independent of that commodity) who would sleep there every night beneath the thin ruby checker-barred wash and fade of the hotel sign, while they worked their fines out on the street; and the County, since its cattle-thieves and moon-shiners went to trial from there, and its murderers – by electricity now (so fast, that fast, was Progress) – to eternity from there; in fact it was still, not a factor perhaps, but at least an integer, a cipher, in the county's political establishment; at least still used by the Board of Supervisors, if not as a lever, at least as something like Punch's stuffed club, not intended to break bones, not aimed to leave any permanent scars;

So only the old knew it, the irreconcilable Jeffersonians and Yokenapatawphians who had (and without doubt firmly intended to continue to have) actual personal dealings with it on the blue Monday mornings after holidays, or during the semi-yearly terms of Circuit or Federal Court: – until suddenly you, a stranger, an out-lander say from the East or the North or the Far West, passing through the little town by simple accident, or perhaps relation or acquaintance or friend of one of the outland families which had moved into one of the pristine and recent subdivisions, yourself turning out of your way to fumble among road signs and filling stations out of frank curiosity, to try to learn, comprehend, understand what had brought your cousin or friend or acquaintance to elect to live here – not specifically here, of course, not specifically Jefferson, but such as here, such as Jefferson – suddenly you would realize that something curious was happening or had happened here – that instead of dying off as they should as time passed, it was as though the old irreconcilables were actually increasing in number; as though with each interment of one, two more shared that vacancy: where in 1900, only thirty-five years afterward, there could not have been more than two or three capable of it, either by knowledge or memory of leisure, or even simple willingness and inclination, now, in 1951, eighty-six years afterward, they could be counted in dozens (and in 1965 a hundred years afterward, in hundreds because – by now you had already begun to understand why your kin or friend or acquaintance had elected to come to such as this with his family and call it his life – by then the children of that second outland invasion following a war, would also have become not just Mississippians but Jeffersonians and Yoknapatawphians: by which time – who knows? – not merely the pane, but the whole window, perhaps the entire wall, may have been removed and embalmed intact into a museum by an historical, or anyway a cultural, club of ladies – why, by that time, they may not even know, or even need to know; only that the window-pane bearing the girl's name and the date is that old, which is enough; has lasted that long: one small rectangle of wavy, crudely-pressed, almost opaque glass, bearing a few faint scratches apparently no more durable than the thin dried slime left by the passage of a snail, yet which has endured a hundred years) who are capable and willing too to quit whatever they happen to be doing – sitting on the last of the wooden benches beneath the last of the locust and chinaberry trees among the potted conifers of the new age dotting the courthouse yard, or in the chairs along the shady sidewalk before the Holston House, where a breeze always blows – to lead you across the street and into the jail (with courteous neighborly apologies to the jailer's wife sitting or turning on the stove the peas and grits and side-meat – purchased in bargain-lot quantities by shrewd and indefatigable peditation from store to store – which she will serve to the prisoners for dinner or supper at so much a head plate – payable to the County, which is no mean factor in the sinecure of her husband's incumbency) into the kitchen and so to the cloudy pane bearing the faint scratches which, after a moment, you will descry to be a name and a date;

Not at first, of course, but after a moment, a second, because at first you would be a little puzzled, a little impatient because of your illness-at-ease from having been dragged without warning or preparation into the private kitchen of a strange woman cooking a meal; you would think merely *What? So what?* annoyed and even a little outraged, until suddenly, even while you were thinking it, something has already happened; the faint frail illegible meaningless even inferenceless scratching on the ancient poor-quality glass you stare at, has moved, under your eyes, even while you stared at it, coalesced, seeming actually to have entered into another sense than vision: a scent, a whisper, filling that hot cramped strange room already fierce with the sound and reek of frying pork-fat: the two of them in conjunction – the old milky obsolete glass, and the scratches on it: that tender ownerless obsolete girl's name and the old dead date in April almost a century ago – speaking, murmuring, back from, out of, across from, a time as old as lavender, older than album or stereopticon, as old as daguerreotype itself;

And being a stranger and a guest would have been enough, since, a stranger and a guest, you would have shown the simple courtesy and politeness of asking the questions naturally expected of you by the host or anyway volunteer guide, who had dropped whatever he was doing (even if that had been no more than sitting with others of his like on a bench in a courthouse yard or on the sidewalk before a hotel) in order to bring you here; not to mention your own perfectly natural desire for, not revenge perhaps, but at least compensation, restitution, vindication, for the shock and annoyance of having been brought here without warning or preparation, into the private quarters of a strange woman engaged in something as intimate as cooking a meal; but by now you had not only already begun to understand why your kin or friend or acquaintance had elected, not Jefferson but such as Jefferson, for his life, but you had heard that voice, that whisper, murmur, frailer than the scent of lavender, yet (for that second anyway) louder than all the seethe and fury of frying fat; so you ask the questions, not only which are expected of you, but whose answers you yourself must have if you are to get back into your car and fumble with any attention and concentration among the road signs and filling stations, to get on to wherever it is you had started when you stopped by chance or accident in Jefferson for an hour or a day or a night, and the host – guide – answers them, to the best of his ability out of the town's composite heritage of remembering that long back, told, repeated, inherited to him by his father; or rather, his mother: from her mother: or better still, to him when he himself was a child, direct from his great-aunt: the spinsters, maiden and childless out of a time when there were too many women because too many of the young men were maimed or dead: the indomitable and undefeated, maiden progenitresses of spinster and childless descendants still capable of rising up and stalking out in the middle of *Gone With the Wind*;

And again one sense assumes the office of two or three: not only hearing, listening, and seeing too, but you are even standing on the same spot, the same boards she did that day she wrote her name into the window and on the other one three years later watching and hearing through and beyond that faint fragile defacement the sudden rush and thunder: the dust: the crackle and splatter of pistols: then the face, gaunt, battle-dirty, stubbled-over; urgent of course, but merely harried, harassed; not defeated, turned for a fleeing instant across the turmoil and the fury, then gone: and still the girl in the window (the guide – host – has never said one or the other; without doubt in the town's remembering after a hundred years it has changed that many times from blonde to dark and back to blonde again; which doesn't matter, since in your own remembering that tender mist and vail will be forever blonde) not even waiting: musing; a year, and still not even waiting: meditant, not even unimpatient; just patienceless, in the sense that blindness and zenith are colorless; until at last the mule, not out of the long northeastern panorama of defeat and dust and fading smoke, but drawn out of it by that impregnable, that invincible, that incredible, that terrifying passivity, coming at that one fatigueless unflagging jog all the way from Virginia – the mule which was a better mule in 1865 than the blood mare had been a horse in -'2 and -'3 and -'4, for the reason that this was now 1865, and the man, still gaunt and undefeated: merely harried and urgent and short of time to get on to Alabama and see the condition of his farm – or (for that matter) if he still had a farm, and now the girl, the fragile and workless girl not only incapable of milking a cow but of whom it was never even demanded, required, suggested, that she substitute for her father in drying the dishes, mounting pillon on a mule behind a paroled cavalry subaltern out of a surrendered army who had swapped his charger for a mule and the sabre of his rank and his defeatless pride for a stocking full of seed corn, whom she had not known or even spoken to long enough to have learned his middle name or his preference in food, or told him hers, and no time for that even now: riding, hurrying toward a country she had never seen, to begin a life which was not even simple frontier, engaged only with wilderness and shoeless savages and the tender hand of God, but one which had been rendered into a desert (assuming that it was still there at all to be returned to) by the iron and fire of civilization;

Which was all your host (guide) could tell you, since that was all he knew, inherited, inheritable from the town: which was enough, more than enough in fact, since all you needed was the face framed in its blonde and delicate vail behind the scratched glass; yourself, the stranger, the outlander from New England or the prairies or the Pacific Coast, no longer come by the chance or accident of kin or friend or acquaintance or roadmap, but drawn too from ninety years away by that incredible and terrifying passivity, watching in your turn through and beyond that old milk dim disfigured glass that shape, that delicate frail and useless bone and flesh departing pillon on a mule without one backward look to the reclaiming of an abandoned and doubtless even ravaged (perhaps even usurped) Alabama hill farm – being lifted onto the mule (the first time he touched her probably, except to put the ring on: not to prove nor even to feel, touch, if there actually was a girl under the calico and the shawls; there was no time for that yet; but simply to get her up there so they could start), to ride a hundred miles to become the farmless mother of farmers (she would bear a dozen, all boys, herself no older, still fragile, still workless among the churns and stoves and brooms and stacks of wood which even a woman could split into kindlings; unchanged), bequeathing to them in their matronymic the heritage of that invincible inviolable ineptitude;

Then suddenly, you realize that that was nowhere near enough, not for that face – bridehood, motherhood, grandmotherhood, then widowhood and at last the grave – the long peaceful connubial progress toward matriarchy in a rocking chair nobody else was allowed to sit in, then a headstone in a country churchyard not for that passivity, that stasis, that invincible captaincy of soul which didn't even need to wait but simply to be, breathe tranquilly, and take food – infinite not only in capacity but in scope too: that face, one maiden muse which had drawn a man out of the running pell mell of a cavalry battle, a whole year around the long iron perimeter of duty and oath, from Yoknapatawpha County, Mississippi, across Tennessee into Virginia and up to the fringe of Pennsylvania before it curved back into its closing fade along the headwaters of the Appomattox river and at last removed from him its iron hand: where, a safe distance at last into the rainy woods from the picket lines and the furled flags and the stacked muskets, a handful of men leading spent horses, the still-warm pistols still loose and quick for the hand in the unstrapped scabbards, gathered in the failing twilight – privates and captains, sergeants and corporals and subalterns – talking a little of one last desperate cast southward where (by last report) Johnston was still intact, knowing that they would not, that they were done not only with vain resistance but with indomitability too; already departed this morning in fact for Texas, the West, New Mexico; a new land even if not yet (spent too – like the horses – from the long harassment and anguish of remaining indomitable and undefeated) a new hope, putting behind them for good and all the lost of both: the young dead bride – drawing him (that face) even back from this too, from no longer having to remain undefeated too: who swapped the charger for the mule and the sabre for the stocking of seed corn: back across the whole ruined land and the whole disastrous year by that virgin inevictable passivity more inescapable than lodestar;

Not that face; that was nowhere near enough; no symbol there of connubial matriarchy, but fatal instead with all insatiate and deathless sterility; spouseless, barren, and undescended; not even demanding more than that: simply requiring it, requiring all – Lilith's lost and insatiable face drawing the substance – the will and hope and dream and imagination – of all men (you too: yourself and the host too) into that one bright fragile net and snare; not even to be caught, over-flung, by one single unerring cast of it, but drawn to watch in patient and thronging turn the very weaving of the strangling golden strands – drawing the two of you from almost a hundred years away in your turn – yourself the stranger, the outlander with a B.A. or (perhaps even) M.A. from Harvard or Northwestern or Stanford, passing through Jefferson by chance or accident on the way to somewhere else, and the host who in three generations has never been out of Yoknapatawpha further than a few prolonged Saturday nights in Memphis or New Orleans, who has heard of Jenny Lind, not because he has heard of Mark Twain and Mark Twain spoke well of her, but for the same reason that Mark Twain spoke well of her; not that she sang songs, but that she sang them in the old West in the old days, and the man sanctioned by public affirmation to wear a pistol openly in his belt is an inevictable part of the Missouri and the Yokenapatawpha dream too, but never of Duse or Bernhardt or Maximilian of Mexico, let alone whether the Emperor of Mexico even ever had a wife or not (saying – the host – : 'You mean, she was one of them? maybe even that emperor's wife?' and you 'Why not? Wasn't she a Jefferson girl?') – to stand, in this hot strange little room furious with frying fat, among the roster and chronicle, the deathless murmur of the sublime and deathless names and the deathless faces, the faces omnivorous and insatiable and forever incontent: demon-nun and angel-witch, empress, siren, Erinys: Mistinguett too, invincible possessed of a half-century more of years than the mere three score or so she bragged and boasted, for you to choose among, which one she was – not *might* have been, nor even *could* have been, but *was*: so vast, so limitless in capacity is man's imagination to disperse and burn away the rubble-dross of fact and probability, leaving only truth and dream – then gone, you are outside again, in the hot noon sun: late; you have already wasted too much time: to unfumble among the road signs and filling stations to get back onto a highway you know, back into the United States; not that it matters, since you know again now that there is no time: no space: no distance: a fragile and workless scratching almost depthless in a sheet of old barely transparent glass, and (all you had to do was look at it a while; all you have to do now is remember it) there is the clear undistanced voice as though out of the delicate antenna-skeins of radio, further than empress's throne, than splendid insatiation, even than matriarch's peaceful rocking chair, across the vast instantaneous intervention, from the long long time ago: *'Listen, stranger; this was myself: this was I.'*

Gimpel the Fool

BY ISAAC BASHEVIS SINGER

I am Gimpel the fool. I don't think myself a fool. On the contrary. But that's what folks call me. They gave me the name while I was still in school. I had seven names in all: imbecile, donkey, flax-head, dope, glump, ninny and fool. The last name stuck. What did my foolishness consist of? I was easy to take in. They said, "Gimpel, you know the rabbi's wife has been brought to childbed?" So I skipped school. Well, it turned out to be a lie. How was I supposed to know? She hadn't had a big belly. But I never looked at her belly. Was that really so foolish? The gang laughed and hee-hawed, stomped and danced and chanted a good-night prayer. And instead of the raisins they give when a woman's lying in, they stuffed my hand full of goat turds. I was no weakling. If I slapped someone he'd see all the way to Cracow. But I'm really not a slugger by nature. I think to myself, "Let it pass." So they take advantage of me.

I was coming home from school and heard a dog barking. I'm not afraid of dogs, but of course I never want to start up with them. One of them may be mad, and if he bites there's not a Tartar in the world who can help you. So I made tracks. Then I looked around and saw the whole market place wild with laughter. It was no dog at all but Wolf-Leib the thief. How was I supposed to know it was he? It sounded like a howling bitch.

When the pranksters and leg-pullers found that I was easy to fool, every one of them tried his luck with me. "Gimpel, the Czar is coming to Frampol; Gimpel, the moon fell down in Turbeen; Gimpel, little Hodl Furpiece found a treasure behind the bathhouse." And I like a golem believed everyone. In the first place, everything is possible, as it is written in the Wisdom of the Fathers, I've forgotten just how. Second, I had to believe when the whole town came down on me! If I ever dared to say, "Ah, you're kidding!" there was trouble. People got angry. "What do you mean! You want to call everyone a liar?" What was I to do? I believed them, and I hope at least that did them some good.

I was an orphan. My grandfather who brought me up was already bent toward the grave. So they turned me over to a baker, and what a time they gave me there! Every woman or girl who came to bake a pan of cookies or dry a batch of noodles had to fool me at least once. "Gimpel, there's a fair in heaven; Gimpel, the rabbi gave birth to a calf in the seventh month. A cow flew over the roof and laid brass eggs." A student from the Yeshivah came once to buy a roll, and he said: "You Gimpel, while you stand here scraping with your baker's shovel the Messiah has come. The dead have arisen." "What do you mean?" I said. "I heard no one blow the ram's horn!" He said, "Are you deaf?" And all began to cry: "We heard it, we heard!" Then in came Reitze the candle-dipper and called out in her hoarse voice, "Gimpel, your father and mother have stood up from the grave. They're looking for you." To tell the truth, I knew very well that nothing of the sort had happened, but all the same while folks were talking, I threw on my wool vest and went out. Maybe something had happened. What did I stand to lose by looking? Well, what a cat-music of jeers went up. And then I took a vow to believe nothing more. But that was no go either. They confused me so that I didn't know the big end from the small.

I went to the rabbi to get some advice. He said: "It is written, better to be a fool all your days than for one hour to be evil. You are not a fool. They are the fools. For he who causes his neighbor to feel shame loses paradise himself." Nevertheless, the rabbi's daughter took me in. As I left the rabbinical court she said, "Have you kissed the wall yet?" I said, "No, what for?" She answered, "It's a law, you've got to do it after every visit." Well, there didn't seem to be any harm in it. And she burst out laughing. It was a fine trick. She put one over on me, all right.

I wanted to go off to another town, but then everyone got busy matchmaking and they were after me so they nearly tore my coattails off. They talked at me and talked until I got water on the ear. She was no chaste maiden, but they told me she was virgin pure. She had a limp, and they said it was deliberate, from coyness. She had a bastard, and they told me the child was her little brother. I cried, "You're wasting your time. I'll never marry that whore." But they said indignantly, "What a way to talk! Aren't you ashamed of yourself? We can take you to the rabbi and have you fined for giving her a bad name." I saw then that I wouldn't escape them so easily and I thought, "They're set on making me their butt. But when you're married the husband's the master, and if that's all right with her it's agreeable to me, too. Besides, you can't pass through life unscathed, nor expect to."

I went to her clay house, which was built on the sand, and the whole gang, hollering and chorusing, came after me. They acted like bear-baiters. When we came to the well they stopped, all the same. They were afraid to start anything with Elka. Her mouth would open as if it were on a hinge, she had a fierce tongue. I entered the house. Lines were strung from wall to wall and clothes were drying. Barefoot she stood by the tub doing a wash. She was dressed in a worn hand-me-down gown of plush. She had her hair put up in braids and pinned across her head. It took my breath away, almost, the reek of it all.

Evidently she knew who I was. She took a look at me and said: "– Look who's here. He's come, the drip. Grab a seat."

I told her all; I denied nothing. "Tell me the truth," I said, "are you really a virgin, and is that mischievous Yechiel actually your little brother? Don't be deceitful with me, for I'm an orphan."

"I'm an orphan myself," she answered, "and whoever tries to twist you up, may the end of his nose take a twist. But don't let them think they can take advantage of me. I want a dowry of fifty guilders, and let them take up a collection besides. Otherwise, they can kiss my you-know-what." She was very plainspoken. I said: "It's the bride and not the groom who gives a dowry." Then she said: "Don't bargain with me. Either a flat yes or a flat no – go back where you came from." I thought that no bread would ever be baked from *this* dough. But ours is not a poor town. They consented to everything and proceeded with the wedding. It so happened that there was a dysentery epidemic at the time. The ceremony was held at the cemetery gates, near the little corpse-washing hut. The fellows got drunk. While the marriage contract was being drawn up, I heard the most pious high magistrate ask, "Is the bride a widow or a divorced woman?" And the sexton's wife answered for her, for she was supposed to instruct her, "Both a widow and divorced." It was a black moment for me. But what was I to do, run away from under the marriage-canopy?

There was singing and dancing. An old granny danced opposite me hugging a woven white *chalah*. The master of revels made a "God 'a mercy" in memory of the bride's parents. The schoolboys threw burrs, as on *Tisha B'av* fast-day. There were a lot of gifts after the sermon: a noodle board, a kneading trough, a bucket, brooms, ladles, household articles galore. Then I took a look and saw two strapping young men carrying a crib. "What do we need this cradle for?" I asked. So they said, "Don't rack your brains about it. It's okay, it'll come in handy." I realized I was going to be rooked. Take it another way, though, what did I stand to lose?

I reflected: "I'll see what comes of it. A whole town can't go altogether crazy."

At night I came where my wife lay, but she wouldn't let me in. "Say, look here, is this what they married us for?" I said. And she said, "My monthlies have come on me." "But yesterday they took you to the ritual bath, and that's afterwards, isn't it supposed to be?" "Today isn't yesterday," said she, "and yesterday's not today. You can beat it, if you don't like it." In short, I waited.

Not four months after she was brought to childbed. The towns-folk hid their laughter with their knuckles. But what could I do? She suffered intolerable pains and clawed at the walls. "Gimpel," she cried, "I'm going. Forgive me!" The house filled with women. They were boiling pans of water. The screams rose to the welkin. The thing to do was to go to the synagogue to repeat psalms and that was what I did.

The townsfolk liked that, all right. I stood in a corner saying psalms and prayers and they shook their heads at me. "Pray, pray!" they told me. "Prayer never made any woman pregnant." One of the congregation put a straw to my mouth and said, "Hay for the cows." There was something to that, too, by God!

She gave birth to a boy. Friday at the synagogue the sexton stood up before the Ark, pounded on the reading-table and announced, "The wealthy Red Gimpel invites the congregation to a feast in honor of the birth of a son." The whole House of Worship rang with laughter. My face was flaming. But there was nothing I could do. Ater all, I *was* the one responsible for the circumcision honors and rituals.

Half the town came running. You couldn't wedge another soul in. Women brought peppered chick-peas, and there was a keg of beer from the tavern. I ate and drank as much as anyone and they all congratulated me. Then there was a circumcision and I named the boy after my father, may he rest in peace. When all were gone and I was left with my wife alone, she thrust her head through the bed-curtain and called me to her. "Gimpel," said she, "why are you silent? Has your ship gone and sunk?" "What shall I say," I answered. "A fine thing you've done to me. If my mother had known of it she'd have died a second time." She said: "Are you crazy, or what?" "How can you make such a fool," I said, "of one who should be the lord and master?" "What's the matter with you?" she said. "What have you taken it into your head to imagine?" I saw that I must speak bluntly and openly. "Do you think this is the way to use an orphan?" I said. "You have borne a bastard." She answered, "Drive this foolishness out of your head. The child is yours." "How can he be mine?" I argued. "He was born seventeen weeks after the wedding." She told me then that he was premature. I said, "Isn't he a little too premature?" She said she had had a grandmother who carried just as short a time and she resembled this grandmother of hers as one drop of water does another. She swore to it with such oaths that you would have believed a peasant at the fair if he had used them. To tell the plain truth, I didn't believe her; but when I talked it over next day with the schoolmaster he told me that the very same thing had happened to Adam and Eve. Two they went up to bed, and four they descended.

"There isn't a woman in the world who is not the granddaughter of Eve," he said.

That was how it was, they argued me dumb. But then, who really knows how such things are?

I began to forget my sorrow. I loved the child madly, and he loved me too. As soon as he saw me he'd wave his little hands and want me to pick him up and when he was colicky I was the only one who could quiet him. I bought him a little bone teething ring, and a little gilded cap. He was forever catching the evil eye from someone and then I had to run to get one of those abracadabras for him that would get him out of it. I worked like an ox. You know how expenses go up when there's an infant in the house. I don't want to lie about it, I didn't dislike Elka either, for that matter. She swore at me and cursed, and I couldn't get enough of her. What strength she had! One of her looks could rob you of the power of speech. And her orations! Pitch and sulphur, that's what they were full of, and yet somehow also full of charm. I adored her every word. She gave me bloody wounds, though.

In the evening I brought her a white loaf besides the dark one, and also poppy-seed rolls which I baked myself. I thieved because of her and swiped everything I could lay hands on, macaroons, raisins, almonds, cakes. I hope I may be forgiven for stealing from the Saturday pots the women left to warm in the baker's oven. I would take out scraps of meat, a chunk of pudding, a chicken leg or head, a piece of tripe, whatever I could nip quickly. Elka ate and became fat and handsome.

I had to sleep away from home all during the week, at the bakery. On Friday nights when I got home, she always made an excuse of some sort. Either she had heartburn, or a stitch in the side, or hiccups or headaches. You know what women's excuses are. I had a bitter time of it. It was rough. To add to it, this little brother of hers, the bastard, was growing bigger. He'd put lumps on me, and when I wanted to hit back, she'd open her mouth and curse so powefully that I saw a green haze floating before my eyes. Ten times a day she threatened to divorce me. Another man in my place would have taken French leave and disappeared. But I'm the type that bears it and says nothing. What's one to do? Shoulders are from God, and burdens too.

One night there was a calamity in the bakery; the oven burst and we almost had a fire. There was nothing to do but go home, so I went home. Let me, I thought, also taste the joy of sleeping in bed in mid-week. I didn't want to wake the sleeping mite, and tip-toed into the house. Coming in it seemed to me that I heard not the snoring of one but as it were a double snore, one a thin enough snore and the other like the snoring of a slaughtered ox. Oh, I didn't like that; I didn't like it at all. I went up to the bed, and things suddenly turned black. Next to Elka there lay a man's form. Another in my place would have made an uproar, and enough noise to rouse the whole town, but the thought occurred to me that I might wake the child. A little thing like that, why frighten a little swallow like that, I thought. All right, then, I went back to the bakery and stretched out on a sack of flour, and till morning I never shut an eye. I shivered as if I had had malaria. "Enough of being a donkey," I said to myself. "Gimpel isn't going to be a sucker all his life. There's a limit even to the foolishness of a fool like Gimpel."

In the morning I went to the rabbi to get a divorce, and it made a great commotion in the town. They sent the beadle for Elka right away. She came, carrying the child. And what do you think she did? She denied it, denied everything, bone and stone! "He's out of his head," she said. "I know nothing of dreams or divinations." They yelled at her, warned her, hammered on the table, but she stuck to her guns: it was false accusation, she said.

The butchers and the horse-traders took her part. One of the lads from the slaughter-house came by and said to me, "We've got our eye on you, you're a marked man." Meanwhile, the child started to bear down and soiled itself. In the rabbinical court there was an ark of the covenant, and they couldn't allow that, so they sent Elka away.

I said to the rabbi, "What shall I do?"

"You must divorce her at once," said he.

"And what if she refuses?" I asked.

He said, "You must serve the divorce, that's all you'll have to do."

I said, "Well, all right, Rabbi. Let me think about it."

"There's nothing to think about," said he. "You mustn't remain under the same roof with her."

"And if I want to see the child?" I asked.

"Let her go, the harlot," said he, "and her brood of bastards with her."

The verdict he gave was that I mustn't even cross her threshold. Never again, as long as I should live.

During the day it didn't bother me so much. I thought, "It was bound to happen, the abscess had to burst." But at night when I stretched out upon the sacks, I felt it all very bitterly. A longing took me for her and for the child. I wanted to be angry, but that's my misfortune exactly, I don't have it in me to be really angry. "In the first place," this was how my thoughts went, "there's bound to be a slip sometimes. You can't live without errors. Probably that lad who was with her led her on and gave her presents and what not, and women are often long on hair and short on sense, and so he got round her. And then since she denies it so, maybe I was only seeing things? Hallucinations do happen. You see a figure, or a mannikin or something, but when you come up closer it's nothing, there's not a thing there. And if that's so, I'm doing her an injustice." And when I got so far in my thoughts, I started to weep. I sobbed so that I wet the flour where I lay. In the morning I went to the rabbi and told him that I had made a mistake. The rabbi wrote on with his quill, and he said that if that were so he would have to reconsider the whole case. Until he had finished, I wasn't to go near my wife, but I might send her bread and money by messenger.

Nine months passed before all the rabbis could come to an agreement. Letters went back and forth. I hadn't realized that there could be so much erudition about a matter like this.

Meantime Elka gave birth to still another child, a girl this time. On the Sabbath I went to the synagogue and invoked a blessing on her. They called me up to the Torah, and I named the child for my mother-in-law, may she rest in peace. The louts and loud-mouths of the town that came into the bakery gave me a going over. All Frampol refreshed its spirits because of my trouble and grief. However, I resolved that I would always believe what I was told. What's the good of *not* believing? Today it's your wife you don't believe; tomorrow it's God himself you won't take stock in.

By an apprentice who was her neighbor I sent her daily a corn or a wheat loaf or a piece of pastry, rolls or bagel or, when I got the chance, a slab of pudding, a slice of honeycake, or wedding strudel. Whatever came my way. The apprentice was a good-hearted lad, and more than once he added something on his own. He had formerly annoyed me a lot, plucking my nose and digging me in the ribs, but when he started to be a visitor to my house he became kind and tolerant. "Hey, you, Gimpel," he said to me, "you have a very decent little wife, and two fine kids. You don't deserve them."

"But the things people say about her," I said.

"Well, they have long tongues," be said, "and nothing to do with them but babble. You can ignore it as you can ignore the cold of last winter."

One day the rabbi sent for me and said, "Are you certain, Gimpel, that you were wrong about your wife?"

I said, "I'm certain."

"Why, but look here! You yourself saw it."

"It must have been a shadow," I said.

"The shadow of what?"

"Just of one of the beams, I think."

"You can go home, then. You owe thanks to the Yanover Rabbi. He found an obscure reference in Maimonides that favored you."

I seized the rabbi's hand and kissed it.

I wanted to run home immediately. It's no small thing to be separated for so long a time from wife and child. Then I reflected, "I'd better go back to work now, and go home in the evening." I said nothing to anyone, notwithstanding that as far as my heart was concerned it was like one of the holy days. The women teased and twitted me as they did every day, but my thought was, "Go on, with your loose talk. The truth is out, like the oil upon the water. Maimonides says it's right, and therefore it is right!"

At night, when I had covered the dough to let it rise, I took my share of bread and a little sack of flour, and started homeward. The moon was full and the stars were glistening something to terrify the soul. I hurried onward, and before me darted a long shadow. It was winter, and a fresh snow had fallen. I had a mind to sing, but it was growing late and I didn't want to wake the householders. Then I felt like whistling, but remembered that you don't whistle at night because it brings the demons out. So I was silent and walked as fast as I could.

Dogs in the Christian yards barked at me when I passed, but I thought, "Bark your teeth out! What are you but mere dogs? Whereas I am a man, the husband of a fine wife, the father of promising children."

I approached the house and my heart started to pound as though it were the heart of a criminal. I felt no fear, but my heart went thump! thump! . . . Well, no drawing back. I quietly lifted the latch and went in. Elka was asleep. I looked at the infant's cradle. The shutter was closed but the moon forced its way through the cracks. I saw the newborn child's face there and loved it as soon as I saw it. Immediately. Each tiniest bone. Then I came nearer to the bed. And what did I see but the apprentice lying there beside Elka. The moon went out all at once. It was utterly black, and I trembled both hand and foot. My teeth chattered. The bread fell from my hands and my wife waked and said, "Who is that, ah?"

I muttered, "It's me . . ."

"Gimpel?" she asked. "How do you come here? I thought it was forbidden."

"The rabbi said," I answered, and shook as with a fever.

"Listen to me, Gimpel," she said, "go out to the shed and see if the goat's all right. It seems she's been sick." I have forgotten to say that we had a goat. When I heard she was unwell I went into the yard. The nannygoat was a good little creature.

I had a nearly human feeling for her.

With hesitant steps, I went up to the shed and opened the door. The goat stood there on her four feet. I felt her everywhere, drew her by the horns, examined her udders and found nothing wrong. She had probably eaten too much bark. "Good night, little goat," I said. "Keep well." And the little beast answered with a "Maa" as though to thank me for the good will.

I went back. The apprentice had vanished.

"Where," I asked, "is the lad?"

"What lad?" my wife answered.

"What do you mean?" I said. "The apprentice. You were sleeping with him."

"The things I have dreamed this night and the night before," she said, "may they come true and lay you low, body and soul. An evil spirit has taken root in you and dazzles your sight." She screamed out, "You hateful creature! You moon-calf! You spook! You uncouth mane! Get out, or I'll scream all Frampol out of bed."

Before I could move, her little brother sprang out from behind the oven and struck me a blow on the back of the head. I thought he had broken my neck. I felt that something about me was deeply wrong, and I said, "Don't make a scandal. All that's needed now is that people should accuse me of raising spooks and *Dybbuks*." For that was what she had meant. "No one will touch bread of my baking."

In short, I somehow calmed her.

"Well," she said, "that's enough. Lie down, and be shattered by wheels."

Next morning I called the apprentice aside. "Listen here, brother!" I said. And so on and so forth. "What do you say?" He stared at me as though I had dropped from the roof or something.

"I swear!" he said. "You'd better go to a herb-doctor or some healer. I'm afraid you have a screw loose, but I'll bush it up for you." And that's how the thing stood.

To make a long story short, I lived twenty years with my wife. She bore me six children, four daughters and two sons. All kinds of things happened, but I neither saw nor heard. I believed, and that's all. The rabbi recently said to me, "Belief in itself is beneficial. It is written that a saint lives by his faith."

Suddenly my wife took sick. It began with a trifle, a little growth upon the breast. But she evidently was not destined to live long; she had no years. I spent a fortune on her. I have forgotten to say that by this time I had a bakery of my own, and was considered in Frampol to be something of a rich man. Daily the healer came, and every witch-doctor in the neighborhood was brought. They decided to use leeches, and after that to try cupping. They even called a doctor from Lublin, but it was too late. Before she died she called me to her bed and said, "Forgive me, Gimpel."

I said, "What is there to forgive? You have been a good and faithful wife."

"Woe, Gimpel," she said, "it was ugly how I deceived you all these years. I want to go clean to my Maker, and so I have to tell you that the children are not yours."

If I had been clouted on the head with a piece of wood, it couldn't have bewildered me more.

"Whose are they? —" I asked.

"I don't know," she said, "there were a lot. . . . But they're not yours." And as she spoke, she tossed her head to the side, her eyes turned glassy and it was all up with Elka. On her whitened lips there remained a smile.

I imagined that, dead as she was, she was saying, "I deceived Gimpel. That was the essence of my brief life."

One night, when the period of mourning was done, once as I lay dreaming on the flour sacks, there came the Spirit of Evil himself and said to me, "Gimpel, why do you sleep?"

I said, "What should I be doing? Eating *kreplach*?"

"The whole world deceives you," he said, "and you ought to deceive the world in your turn."

"How can I deceive all the world?" I asked him.

He answered, "You might accumulate a bucket of urine every day, and at night pour it into the dough. Let the sages of Frampol eat filth."

"What about Judgment in the world to come?" I said.

"There is no world to come," he said. "They've sold you a bill of goods and talked you into believing you carried a cat in your belly. What nonsense!"

"Well then," I said, "and is there a God?"

He answered, "There is no God, either."

"What," I said, "*is* there, then?"

"A thick mire."

He stood before my eyes, this spokesman, with a goatish beard and horns, long-toothed and with a tail.

Hearing such words, I wanted to snatch him by the tail but I tumbled from the flour sacks and nearly broke a rib. Then it happened that I had to answer the call of nature, and passing I saw the risen dough which seemed to say to me, "Do it!" In brief, I let myself be persuaded.

At dawn the apprentice came. We kneaded the bread, scattered kummel on it and set it to bake. Then the apprentice went away and I was left sitting in the little trench by the oven, on a pile of rags. "Well, Gimpel," I thought, "you've revenged yourself on them for all the shame they've put on you." Outside the frost glittered, but it was warm beside the oven. The flames heated my face. I bent my head and fell into a doze.

I saw in a dream, at once, Elka in her shrouds. She called to me, "What have you done, Gimpel?"

I said to her, "It's all your fault," and started to cry.

"You fool!" she said. "You fool! Because I was false is everything false too? I never deceived anyone but myself. I'm paying for it all, Gimpel. They spare you nothing here."

I looked at her face. It was black. I was startled and waked, and remained sitting dumb. I sensed that everything hung in the balance. A false step now and I'd lose eternal life. But God gave me His help. I seized the long shovel and took out the loaves, carried them into the yard and started to dig a hole in the frozen earth. My apprentice came back as I was doing it. "What are you doing, boss?" he said, and grew pale as a corpse.

"I know what I'm doing," I said, and I buried it all under his very eyes.

Then I went home, took my hoard from its hiding place, and divided it among the children.

"I saw your mother tonight," I said. "She's growing very dark, poor thing."

They were so astounded, they couldn't speak a word.

"Be well," I said, "and forget that such a one as Gimpel ever existed." I put on my short coat, a pair of boots, took the bag which held my prayer shawl in one hand, my stick in the other and kissed the *mezzuzah*. When people saw me in the street they were greatly surprised.

"Where are you going?" they said.

I answered, "Into the world." And so I departed from Frampol.

I wandered over the land, and good people did not neglect me. After many years I became old and white, I heard a great deal, many lies and falsehoods, but the longer I lived the more I understood that there were really no lies. Whatever doesn't really happen is dreamed at night. It happens to one if it doesn't happen to another, tomorrow if not today, or a century hence if not next year. What difference can it make? Often I heard tales of which I said, "Now this is a thing that cannot happen." But before a year had elapsed, I heard that it actually had come to pass somewhere. Even sheer inventions have their truth.

Going from place to place, eating at strange tables, it often happens that I spin yarns – improbable things that could never have happened about devils, magicians, windmills and the like. The children run after me, "Granddaddy, tell us a story." Sometimes they ask for particular stories and I try to please them. A fat young boy once said to me, "Grandfather, it's the same story you told us before." The little rogue, he was right.

So it is with dreams, too. It is many years since I left Frampol, but as soon as I shut my eyes I am there again. And whom do you think I see? Elka. She is standing by the washtub, as at our first encounter, but her face is shining and her eyes are as radiant as the eyes of a saint, and she speaks outlandish words to me, exotic things. When I wake, I have forgotten it all. But while the dream lasts I am comforted. She answers all my queries, and what comes out is that all is right. I weep and implore her, "Let me be with you." And she consoles me and tells me to be patient. The time is nearer than it is far. Sometimes she strokes and kisses me, and weeps upon my face. When I awaken I feel her lips and taste the salt of her tears.

No doubt the world is entirely an imaginary world, but it is only once removed from the true world. At the door of the hovel where I lie, there stands the plank on which the dead are taken away. The gravedigger-Jew has his spade ready. The grave waits and the worms are hungry, the shrouds are prepared, I carry them in my beggar's sack. Another *schnorrer* is waiting to inherit my handful of straw. When the time comes, I will go joyfully. Whatever may be there, it will be real, without complication, without ridicule, without deception. God be praised: there even Gimpel cannot be deceived.

Translated from the Yiddish by Saul Bellow

The Magic Barrel

BY BERNARD MALAMUD

Not long ago there lived in uptown New York, in a small, most meager room, though crowded with books, Leo Finkle, a rabbinical student in the Yeshivah University. Finkle, after six years of study, was to be ordained in June and had been advised by an acquaintance that he might find it easier to win himself a congregation if he were married. Since he had no present prospects of marriage, after two tormented days of turning it over in his mind, he called in Pinye Salzman, a marriage broker, whose two-line advertisement he had read in the *Forward*.

The matchmaker appeared one night out of the dark fourth-floor hallway of the graystone rooming house, grasping a black, strapped portfolio that had been worn thin with use. Salzman, who had been long in the business, was of slight but dignified build, wearing an old hat and an overcoat too short and tight for him. He smelled frankly of fish, which he loved to eat, and although he was missing a few teeth, his presence was not displeasing, because of an amiable manner curiously contrasted by mournful eyes. His voice, his lips, his wisp of beard, his bony fingers were animated, but give him a moment of repose and his mild blue eyes soon revealed a depth of sadness, a characteristic that put Leo a little at ease although the situation, for him, was inherently tense.

He at once informed Salzman why he had asked him to come, explaining that his home was in Cleveland, and that but for his parents, who had married comparatively late in life, he was alone in the world. He had for six years devoted himself entirely to his studies, as a result of which, quite understandably, he had found himself without time for a social life and the company of young women. Therefore he thought it the better part of trial and error – of embarrassing fumbling – to call in an experienced person to advise him in these matters. He remarked in passing that the function of the marriage broker was ancient and honorable, highly approved in the Jewish community, because it made practical the necessary without hindering joy. Moreover, his own parents had been brought together by a matchmaker. They had made, if not a financially profitable marriage – since neither had possessed any worldly goods to speak of – at least a successful one in the sense of their everlasting devotion to one another. Salzman listened in embarrassed surprise, sensing a sort of apology. Later, however, he experienced a glow of pride in his work, an emotion that had left him years ago, and he heartily approved of Finkle.

The two men went to their business. Leo had led Salzman to the only clear place in the room, a table near a window that overlooked the lamp-lit city. He seated himself at the matchmaker's side but facing him, attempting by an act of will to suppress the unpleasant tickle in his throat. Salzman eagerly unstrapped his portfolio and removed a loose rubber band from a thin packet of much-handled cards. As he flipped through them, a gesture and sound that physically hurt Leo, the student pretended not to see and gazed steadfastly out the window. Although it was still February, winter was on its last legs, signs of which he had for the first time in years begun to notice. He now observed the round white moon, moving high in the sky through a cloud-menagerie, and watched with half-open mouth as it penetrated a huge hen, and dropped out of her like an egg laying itself. Salzman, though pretending through eyeglasses he had just slipped on, to be engaged in scanning the writing on the cards, stole occasional glances at the young man's distinguished face, noting with pleasure the long, severe scholar's nose, brown eyes heavy with learning, sensitive yet ascetic lips, and a certain almost hollow quality of the dark cheeks. He gazed around at shelves upon shelves of books and let out a soft but happy sigh.

When Leo's eyes fell upon the cards, he counted six spread out in Salzman's hand.

"So few?" he said in disappointment.

"You wouldn't believe me how much cards I got in my office," Salzman replied. "The drawers are already filled to the top, so I keep them now in a barrel, but is every girl good for a new rabbi?"

Leo blushed at this, regretting all he had revealed of himself in a curriculum vitae he had sent to Salzman. He had thought it best to acquaint him with his strict standards and specifications, but in having done so now felt he had told the marriage broker more than was absolutely necessary.

He hesitantly inquired, "Do you keep photographs of your clients on file?"

"First comes family, amount of dowry, also what kind promises," Salzman replied, unbuttoning his tight coat and settling himself in the chair. "After comes pictures, rabbi."

"Call me Mr. Finkle. I'm not a rabbi yet."

Salzman said he would, but instead called him doctor, which he changed to rabbi when Leo was not listening too attentively.

Salzman adjusted his horn-rimmed spectacles, gently cleared his throat and read in an eager voice the contents of the top card:

"Sophie P. Twenty-four years. Widow for one year. No children. Educated high school and two years college. Father promises eight thousand dollars. Has wonderful wholesale business. Also real estate. On the mother's side comes teachers, also one actor. Well known on Second Avenue."

Leo gazed up in surprise, "Did you say a widow?"

"A widow don't mean spoiled, rabbi. She lived with her husband maybe four months. He was a sick boy, she made a mistake to marry him."

"Marrying a widow has never entered my mind."

"This is because you have no experience. A widow, specially if she is young and healthy like this girl, is a wonderful person to marry. She will be thankful to you the rest of her life. Believe me, if I was looking now for a bride, I would marry a widow."

Leo reflected, then shook his head.

Salzman hunched his shoulders in an almost imperceptible gesture of disappointment. He placed the card down on the wooden table and began to read another:

"Lily H. High school teacher. Regular. Not a substitute. Has savings and new Dodge car. Lived in Paris one year. Father is successful dentist thirty-five years. Interested in professional man. Well Americanized family. Wonderful opportunity.

"I know her personally," said Salzman. "I wish you could see this girl. She is a doll. Also very intelligent. All day you could talk to her about books and theyater and what not. She also knows current events."

"I don't believe you mentioned her age?"

"Her age?" Salzman said, raising his brows in surprise. "Her age is thirty-two years."

Leo said after a while, "I'm afraid that seems a little too old."

Salzman let out a laugh. "So how old are you, rabbi?"

"Twenty-seven."

"So what is the difference, tell me, between twenty-seven and thirty-two? My own wife is seven years older than me; So what did I suffer? – Nothing. If Rothschild's daughter wants to marry you, would you say on account her age, no?"

"Yes," Leo said dryly.

Salzman shook off the no in the yes. "Five years don't mean a thing. I give you my word that when you will live with her for one week you will forget her age. What does it mean five years – that she lived more and knows more than somebody who is younger? On this girl, God bless her, years are not wasted. Each one that it comes makes better the bargain."

"What subject does she teach in high school?"

"Languages. If you heard the way she reads French, you will think it is music. I am in the business twenty-five years, and I recommend her with my whole heart. Believe me, I know what I'm talking, rabbi."

"What's on the next card?" Leo said abruptly.

Salzman reluctantly turned up the third card:

"Ruth K. Nineteen years. Honor student. Father offers thirteen thousand dollars cash to the right bridegroom. He is a medical doctor. Stomach specialist with marvelous practice. Brother-in-law owns own garment business. Particular people."

Salzman looked up as if he had read his trump card.

"Did you say nineteen?" Leo asked with interest.

"On the dot."

"Is she attractive?" He blushed. "Pretty?"

Salzman kissed his fingertips. "A little doll: On this I give you my word. Let me call the father tonight and you will see what means pretty."

But Leo was troubled. "You're sure she's that young?"

"This I am positive. The father will show you the birth certificate."

"Are you positive there isn't something wrong with her?" Leo insisted.

"Who says there is wrong?"

"I don't understand why an American girl her age should go to a marriage broker."

A smile spread over Salzman's face.

"So for the same reason you went, she comes."

Leo flushed. "I am pressed for time."

Salzman, realizing he had been tactless, quickly explained. "The father came, not her. He wants she should have the best, so he looks around himself. When we will locate the right boy he will introduce him and encourage. This makes a better marriage than if a young girl without experience takes for herself. I don't have to tell you this."

"But don't you think this young girl believes in love?" Leo spoke uneasily.

Salzman was about to guffaw but caught himself and said soberly, "Love comes with the right person, not before."

Leo parted dry lips but did not speak. Noticing that Salzman had snatched a quick glance at the next card, he cleverly asked, "How is her health?"

"Perfect," Salzman said, breathing with difficulty. "Of course, she is a little lame on her right foot from an auto accident that it happened to her when she was twelve years, but nobody notices on account she is so brilliant and also beautiful."

Leo got up heavily and went to the window. He felt curiously bitter and upbraided himself for having called in the marriage broker. Finally, he shook his head.

"Why not?" Salzman persisted, the pitch of his voice rising.

"Because I hate stomach specialists."

"So what do you care what is his business? After you marry her, do you need him? Who says he must come every Friday night to your house?"

Ashamed of the way the talk was going, Leo dismissed Salzman, who went home with melancholy eyes.

Though he had felt only relief at the marriage broker's departure, Leo was in low spirits the next day. He explained it as arising from Salzman's failure to produce a suitable bride for him. He did not care for his type of clientele. But when Leo found himself hesitating over whether to seek out another matchmaker, one more polished than Pinye, he wondered if it could be – his protestations to the contrary, and although he honored his father and mother – that he did not, in essence, care for the matchmaking institution? This thought he quickly put out of mind yet found himself still upset. All day he ran around in a fog – missed an important appointment, forgot to give out his laundry, walked out of a Broadway cafeteria without paying and had to run back with the ticket in his hand; had even not recognized his landlady in the street when she passed with a friend and courteously called out, "A good evening to you, Doctor Finkle." By nightfall, however, he had regained sufficient calm to sink his nose into a book and there found peace from his thoughts.

Almost at once there came a knock on the door. Before Leo could say enter, Salzman, commercial cupid, was standing in the room. His face was gray and meager, his expression hungry, and he looked as if he would expire on his feet. Yet the marriage broker managed, by some trick of the muscles, to display a broad smile.

"So good evening. I am invited?"

Leo nodded, disturbed to see him again, yet unwilling to ask him to leave.

Beaming still, Salzman laid his portfolio on the table. "Rabbi, I got for you tonight good news."

"I've asked you not to call me rabbi. I'm still a student."

"Your worries are finished. I have for you a first-class bride."

"Leave me in peace concerning this subject." Leo pretended lack of interest.

"The world will dance at your wedding."

"Please, Mr. Salzman, no more."

"But first must come back my strength," Salzman said weakly. He fumbled with the portfolio straps and took out of the leather case an oily paper bag, from which he extracted a hard seeded roll and a small smoked white fish. With one motion of his hand he stripped the fish out of its skin and began ravenously to chew. "All day in a rush," he muttered.

Leo watched him eat.

"A sliced tomato you have maybe?" Salzman hesitantly inquired.

"No."

The marriage broker shut his eyes and ate. When he had finished he carefully cleaned up the crumbs and rolled up the remains of the fish in the paper bag. His spectacled eyes roamed the room until he discovered, amid some piles of books, a one-burner gas stove. Lifting his hat he humbly asked, "A glass tea you got, rabbi?"

Conscience-stricken, Leo rose and brewed the tea. He served it with a chunk of lemon and two cubes of lump sugar, delighting Salzman.

After he had drunk his tea, Salzman's strength and good spirits were restored.

"So tell me, rabbi," he said amiably, "you considered any more the three clients I mentioned yesterday?"

"There was no need to consider."

"Why not?"

"None of them suits me."

"What, then, suits you?"

Leo let it pass because he could give only a confused answer.

Without waiting for a reply, Salzman asked, "You remember this girl I talked to you – the high school teacher?" "Age thirty-two?"

But, surprisingly, Salzman's face lit in a smile. "Age twenty-nine."

Leo shot him a look. "Reduced from thirty-two?"

"A mistake," Salzman avowed. "I talked today with the dentist. He took me to his safety deposit box and showed me the birth certificate. She was twenty-nine years last August. They made her a party in the mountains where she went for her vacation. When her father spoke to me the first time I forgot to write the age and I told you thirty-two, but now I remember this was a different client, a widow."

"The same one you told me about? I thought she was twenty-four?"

"A different. Am I responsible that the world is filled with widows?"

"No, but I'm not interested in them, nor for that matter, in schoolteachers."

Salzman passionately pulled his clasped hands to his breast. Looking at the ceiling he exclaimed, "Jewish children, what can I say to somebody that he is not interested in high school teachers? So what then you are interested?"

Leo flushed but controlled himself.

"In who else you will be interested," Salzman went on, "if you not interested in this fine girl that she speaks four languages and has personally in the bank ten thousand dollars? Also her father guarantees further twelve thousand. Also she has a new car, wonderful clothes, talks on all subjects, and she will give you a first-class home and children. How near do we come in our life to paradise?"

"If she's so wonderful, why wasn't she married ten years ago?"

"Why?" said Salaman with a heavy laugh. "– Why? Because she is *partikler*. This is why. She wants only the *best*."

Leo was silent, amused at how he had trapped himself. But Salzman had aroused his interest in Lily H., and he began seriously to consider calling on her. When the marriage broker observed how intently Leo's mind was at work on the facts he had supplied, he felt positive they would soon come to an agreement.

Late Saturday afternoon, conscious of Salzman, Leo Finkle walked with Lily Hirschorn along Riverside Drive. He walked briskly and erectly, wearing with distinction the black fedora he had that morning taken with trepidation out of the dusty hatbox on his closet shelf, and the heavy black Saturday coat he had thoroughly whisked clean. Leo also owned a walking stick, a present from a distant relative, but had decided not to use it. Lily, petite and not unpretty, had on something signifying the approach of spring. She was *au courant*, animatedly, with all subjects, and he weighed her words and found her surprisingly sound – score another for Salzman, whom he uneasily sensed to be somewhere around, hiding perhaps high in a tree along the street, flashing the lady signals; or perhaps a cloven-hoofed Pan, piping nuptial ditties as he danced his invisible way before them, strewing wild buds on the walk and purple summer grapes in their path, symbolizing fruit of a union, of which there was yet none.

Lily startled Leo by remarking, "I was thinking of Mr. Salzman, a curious figure, wouldn't you say?"

Not certain what to answer, he nodded.

She bravely went on, blushing, "I for one am grateful for his introducing us. Aren't you?"

He courteously replied, "I am."

"I mean," she said with a little laugh – and it was all in good taste, or at least gave the effect of being not in bad – "do you mind that we came together so?"

He was not afraid of her honesty, recognizing that she meant to set the relationship aright, and understanding that it took a certain amount of experience in life, and courage, to want to do it quite that way. One had to have some sort of past to make that kind of beginning.

He said that he did not mind. Salzman's function was traditional and honorable – valuable for what it might achieve, which, he pointed out, was frequently nothing.

Lily agreed with a sigh. They walked on for a while and she said after a long silence, again with a nervous laugh, "Would you mind if I asked you something a little bit personal? Frankly, I find the subject fascinating." Although Leo shrugged, she went on half embarrassedly, "How was it that you came to your calling? I mean, was it a sudden passionate inspiration?"

Leo, after a time, slowly replied, "I was always interested in the Law."

"You saw revealed in it the presence of the Highest?"

He nodded and changed the subject. "I understand you spent a little time in Paris, Miss Hirschorn?"

"Oh, did Mr. Salzman tell you, Rabbi Finkle?" Leo winced but she went on, "It was ages and ages ago and almost forgotten. I remember I had to return for my sister's wedding."

But Lily would not be put off. "When," she asked in a trembly voice, "did you become enamored of God?"

He stared at her. Then it came to him that she was talking not about Leo Finkle, but a total stranger, some mystical figure, perhaps even passionate prophet that Salzman had conjured up for her – no relation to the living or dead. Leo trembled with rage and weakness. The trickster had obviously sold her a bill of goods, just as he had him, who'd expected to become acquainted with a young lady of twenty-nine, only to behold, the moment he laid eyes upon her strained and anxious face, a woman past thirty-five and aging very rapidly. Only his self-control, he thought, had kept him this long in her presence.

"I am not," he said gravely, "a talented religious person," and in seeking words to go on, found himself possessed by fear and shame. "I think," he said in a strained manner, "that I came to God not because I loved Him, but because I did not."

This confession he spoke harshly because its unexpectedness shook him.

Lily wilted. Leo saw a profusion of loaves of bread sailing like ducks high over his head, not unlike the loaves by which he had counted himself to sleep last night. Mercifully, then, it snowed, which he would not put past Salzman's machinations.

He was infuriated with the marriage broker and swore he would throw him out of the room the moment he reappeared. But Salzman did not come that night, and when Leo's anger had subsided, an unaccountable despair grew in its place. At first he thought this was caused by his disappointment in Lily, but before long it became evident that he had involved himself with Salzman without a true knowledge of his own intent. He gradually realized – with an emptiness that seized him with six hands – that he had called in the broker to find him a bride because he was incapable of doing it himself. This terrifying insight he had derived as a result of his meeting and conversation with Lily Hirschorn. Her probing questions had somehow irritated him into revealing – to himself more than her – the true nature of his relationship with God, and from that it had come upon him, with shocking force, that apart from his parents, he had never loved anyone. Or perhaps it went the other way, that he did not love God so well as he might, because he had not loved man. It seemed to Leo that his whole life stood starkly revealed and he saw himself, for the first time, as he truly was – unloved and loveless. This bitter but somehow not fully unexpected revelation brought him to a point of panic controlled only by extraordinary effort. He covered his face with his hands and wept.

The week that followed was the worst of his life. He did not eat, and lost weight. His beard darkened and grew ragged. He stopped attending lectures and seminars and almost never opened a book. He seriously considered leaving the Yeshivah, although he was deeply troubled at the thought of the loss of all his years of study – saw them like pages from a book strewn over the city – and at the devastating effect of this decision upon his parents. But he had lived without knowledge of himself, and never in the Five Books and all the Commentaries – mea culpa – had the truth been revealed to him. He did not know where to turn, and in all this desolating loneliness there was no *to whom*, although he often thought of Lily but not once could bring himself to go downstairs and make the call. He became touchy and irritable, especially with his landlady, who asked him all manner of questions; on the other hand, sensing his own disagreeableness, he waylaid her on the stairs and apologized abjectly, until mortified, she ran from him. Out of this, however, he drew the consolation that he was yet a Jew and that a Jew suffered. But gradually, as the long and terrible week drew to a close, he regained his composure and some idea of purpose in life: to go on as planned. Although he was imperfect, the ideal was not. As for his quest of a bride, the thought of continuing afflicted him with anxiety and heartburn, yet perhaps with this new knowledge of himself he would be more successful than in the past. Perhaps love would now come to him and a bride to that love. And for this sanctified seeking who needed a Salzman?

The marriage broker, a skeleton with haunted eyes, returned that very night. He looked, withal, the picture of frustrated expectancy – as if he had steadfastly waited the week at Miss Lily Hirschorn's side for a telephone call that never came.

Casually coughing, Salzman came immediately to the point:

"So how did you like her?"

Leo's anger rose and he could not refrain from chidivng the matchmaker: "Why did you lie to me, Salzman?"

Salzman's pale face went dead white, as if the world had snowed on him.

"Did you not state that she was twenty-nine?" Leo insisted.

"I give you my word –"

"She was thirty-five. *At least* thirty-five."

"Of this I would not be too sure. Her father told me –"

"Never mind. The worst of it was that you lied to her."

"How did I lie to her, tell me?"

"You told her things about me that weren't true. You made me out to be more, consequently less than I am. She had in mind a totally different person, a sort of semi-mystical Wonder Rabbi."

"All I said, you was a religious man.

"I can imagine."

Salzman sighed. "This is my weakness that I have," he confessed. "My wife says to me I shouldn't be a salesman, but when I have two fine people that they would be wonderful to be married, I am so happy that I talk too much." He smiled wanly. "This is why Salzman is a poor man."

Leo's anger went. "Well, Salzman, I'm afraid that's all."

The marriage broker fastened hungry eyes on him.

"You don't want any more a bride?"

"I do," said Leo, "but I have decided to seek her in a different way. I am no longer interested in an arranged marriage. To be frank, I now admit the necessity of premarital love. That is, I want to be in love with the one I marry."

"Love?" said Salzman, astounded. After a moment he said, "For us, our love is our life, not for the ladies. In the ghetto they –"

"I know, I know," said Leo. "I've thought of it often. Love, I have said to myself, should be a byproduct of living and worship rather than its own end. Yet for myself I find it necessary to establish the level of my need and to fulfill it."

Salzman shrugged but answered, "Listen, rabbi, if you want love, this I can find for you also. I have such beautiful clients that you will love them the minute your eyes will see them."

Leo smiled unhappily. "I'm afraid you don't understand."

But Salzman hastily unstrapped his portfolio and withdrew a manila packet from it.

"Pictures," he said, quickly laying the envelope on the table.

Leo called after him to take the pictures away, but as if on the wings of the wind, Salzman had disappeared.

March came. Leo had returned to his regular routine. Although he felt not quite himself yet – lacked energy – he was making plans for a more active social life. Of course it would cost something, but he was an expert in cutting corners; and when there were no corners left he could make circles rounder. All the while Salzman's pictures had lain on the table, gathering dust. Occasionally as Leo sat studying, or enjoying a cup of tea, his eyes fell on the manila envelope, but he never opened it.

The days went by and no social life to speak of developed with a member of the opposite sex – it was difficult, given the circumstances of his situation. One morning Leo toiled up the stairs to his room and stared out the window at the city. Although the day was bright his view of it was dark. For some time he watched the people in the street below hurrying along and then turned with a heavy heart to his little room. On the table was the packet. With a sudden relentless gesture he tore it open. For a half-hour he stood there, in a state of excitement, examining the photographs of the ladies Salzman had included. Finally, with a deep sigh he put them down. There were six, of varying degrees of attractiveness, but look at them long enough and they all became Lily Hirschorn: all past their prime, all starved behind bright smiles, not a true personality in the lot. Life, despite their anguished struggles and frantic yoohooings, had passed them by; they were photographs in a briefcase that stank of fish. After a while, however, as Leo attempted to return the pictures into the envelope, he found another in it, a small snapshot of the type taken by a machine for a quarter. He gazed at it a moment and let out a cry.

Her face deeply moved him. Why, he could at first not say. It gave him the impression of youth – all spring flowers, yet age – a sense of having been used to the bone, wasted; this all came from the eyes, which were hauntingly familiar, yet absolutely strange. He had a strong impression that he had met her before, but try as he might he could not place her, although he could almost recall her name, as if he had read it written in her own handwrting. No, this couldn't be; he would have remembered her. It was not, he affirmed, that she had an extraordinary beauty – no, although her face was attractive enough; it was that *something* about her moved him. Feature for feature, even some of the ladies of the photographs could do better; but she leaped forth to the heart – had lived, or wanted to – more than just wanted, perhaps regretted it – had somehow deeply suffered: it could he seen in the depths of those reluctant eyes, and from the way the light enclosed and shone from her, and within her, opening whole realms of possibility: this was her own. Her he desired. His head ached and eyes narrowed with the intensity of his gazing, then, as if a black fog had blown up in the mind, he experienced fear of her and was aware that he had received an impression, somehow, of filth. He shuddered, saying softly, it is thus with us all. Leo brewed some tea in a small pot and sat sipping it, without sugar, to calm himself. But before he had finished drinking, again with excitement he examined the face and found it good: good for him. Only such a one could truly understand Leo Finkle and help him to seek whatever he was seeking. How she had come to be among the discards in Salzman's barrel he could never guess, but he knew he must urgently go find her.

Leo rushed downstairs, grabbed up the Bronx telephone book, and searched for Salzman's home address. He was not listed, nor was his office. Neither was he in the Manhattan book. But Leo remembered having written down the address on a slip of paper after he had read Salzman's advertisement in the "personals" column of the *Forward*. He ran up to his room and tore through his papers, without luck. It was exasperating. Just when he needed the matchmaker he was nowhere to be found. Fortunately Leo remembered to look in his wallet. There on a card he found his name written and a Bronx address. No phone number was listed, which, Leo now recalled, was the reason he had originally communicated with Salzman by letter. He got on his coat, put a hat on over his skull cap and hurried to the subway station. All the way to the far end of the Bronx he sat on the edge of his seat. He was more than once tempted to take out the picture and see if the girl's face was as he remembered it, but he refrained, allowing the snapshot to remain in his inside coat pocket, content to have her so close. When the train pulled into the station he was waiting at the door and bolted out. He quickly located the street Salzman had advertised.

The building he sought was less than a block from the subway, but it was not an office building, nor even a loft, nor a store in which one could rent office space. It was an old and grimy tenement. Leo found Salaman's name in pencil on a soiled tag under the bell and climbed three dark flights to his apartment. When he knocked, the door was opened by a thin, asthmatic, gray-haired woman, in felt slippers.

"Yes?" she said, expecting nothing. She listened without listening. He could have sworn he had seen her somewhere before but knew it was illusion.

"Salzman – does he live here? Pinye Salzman," he said, "the matchmaker?"

She stared at him a long time. "Of course." He felt embarrassed. "Is he in?"

"No." Her mouth was open, but she offered nothing more.

"This is urgent. Can you tell me where his office is?"

"In the air." She pointed upward.

"You mean he has no office?" Leo said.

"In his socks."

He peered into the apartment. It was sunless and dingy, one large room divided by a half-open curtain, beyond which he could see a sagging metal bed. The nearer side of the room was crowded with rickety chairs, old bureaus, a three-legged table, racks of cooking utensils, and all the apparatus of a kitchen. But there was no sign of Salzman or his magic barrel, probably also a figment of his imagination. An odor of frying fish made Leo weak to the knees.

"Where is he?" he insisted. "I've got to see your husband."

At length she answered, "So who knows where he is? Every time he thinks a new thought he runs to a different place. Go home, he will find you."

"Tell him Leo Finkle."

She gave no sign that she had heard.

He went downstairs, deeply depressed.

But Salzman, breathless, stood waiting at his door.

Leo was overjoyed and astounded. "How did you get here before me?"

"I rushed."

"Come inside."

They entered. Leo fixed tea and a sardine sandwich for Salzman.

As they were drinking he reached behind him for the packet of pictures and handed them to the marriage broker.

Salzman put down his glass and said expectantly, "You found maybe somebody you like?"

"Not among these."

The marriage broker turned sad eyes away.

"Here's the one I like." Leo held forth the snapshot.

Salzman slipped on his glasses and took the picture into his trembling hand. He turned ghastly and let out a miserable groan.

"What's the matter?" cried Leo.

"Excuse me. Was an accident this picture. She is not for you."

Salzman frantically shoved the manila packet into his portfolio. He thrust the snapshot into his pocket and fled down the stairs.

Leo, after momentary paralysis, gave chase and cornered the marriage broker in the vestibule. The landlady made hysterical outcries but neither of them listened.

"Give me back the picture, Salzman."

"No." The pain in his eyes was terrible.

"Tell me who she is then."

"This I can't tell you. Excuse me."

He made to depart, but Leo, forgetting himself, seized the matchmaker by his tight coat and shook him frenziedly.

"Please," sighed Salzman. "*Please.*"

Leo ashamedly let him go. "Tell me who she is," he begged. "It's very important for me to know."

"She is not for you. She is a wild one – wild, without shame. This is not a bride for a rabbi."

"What do you mean wild?"

"Like an animal. Like a dog. For her to be poor was a sin. This is why she is dead now."

"In God's name, what do you mean?"

"Her I can't introduce to you," Salzman cried.

"Why are you so excited?"

"Why he asks," Salzman said, bursting into tears. "This is my baby, my Stella, she should burn in hell."

Leo hurried up to bed and hid under the covers. Under the covers he thought his whole life through. Although he soon fell asleep he could not sleep her out of his mind. He woke, beating his breast. Though he prayed to be rid of her, his prayers went unanswered. Through days of torment he struggled endlessly not to love her; fearing success, he escaped it. He then concluded to convert her to goodness, himself to God. The idea alternately nauseated and exalted him.

He perhaps did not know that he had come to a final decision until he encountered Salzman in a Broadway cafeteria. He was sitting alone at a rear table, sucking the bony remains of a fish. The marriage broker appeared haggard, and transparent to the point of vanishing.

Salzman looked up at first without recognizing him. Leo had grown a pointed beard and his eyes were weighted with wisdom.

"Salzman," he said, "love has at last come to my heart."

"Who can love from a picture?" mocked the marriage broker.

"It is not impossible."

"If you can love her, then you can love anybody. Let me show you some new clients that they just sent me their photographs. One is a little doll."

"Just her I want," Leo murmured.

"Don't be a fool, doctor. Don't bother with her."

"Put me in touch with her, Salzman," Leo said humbly. "Perhaps I can do her a service."

Salzman had stopped chewing, and Leo understood with emotion that it was now arranged.

Leaving the cafeteria, he was, however, afflicted by a tormenting suspicion that Salzman had planned it all to happen this way.

Leo was informed by letter that she would meet him on a certain corner, and she was there one spring night, waiting under a street lamp. He appeared, carrying a small bouquet of violets and rosebuds, Stella stood by the lamp post, smoking. She wore white with red shoes, which fitted his expectations, although in a troubled moment he had imagined the dress red, and only the shoes white. She waited uneasily and shyly. From afar he saw that her eyes – clearly her father's – were filled with desperate innocence. He pictured, in hers, his own redemption. Violins and lit candles revolved in the sky. Leo ran forward with the flowers outthrust.

Around the corner, Salzman, leaning against a wall, chanted prayers for the dead.

Seize the Day

BY SAUL BELLOW

When it came to concealing his troubles, Tommy Wilhelm was not less capable than the next fellow. So at least he thought, and there was a certain amount of evidence to back him up. He had once been an actor – no, not quite, an extra – and he knew what acting should be. Also, he was smoking a cigar, and when a man is smoking a cigar, wearing a hat, he has an advantage; it is harder to find out how he feels. He came from the twenty-third floor down to the lobby on the mezzanine to collect his mail before breakfast and he believed – he hoped – that he looked passably well: doing all right. It was a matter of sheer hope because there was not much that he could add to his present effort. On the fourteenth floor he looked for his father to enter the elevator; they often met at this hour on the way to breakfast. If he worried about his appearance it was mainly for his old father's sake. But there was no stop on the fourteenth, and the elevator sank and sank. Then the smooth door opened and the great, dark red, uneven carpet that covered the lobby billowed toward Wilhelm's feet. In the foreground, the lobby was dark, sleepy. French drapes like sails kept out the sun, but three high narrow windows were open, and in the blue air Wilhelm saw a pigeon about to light on the great chain that supported the marquee of the movie house directly underneath the lobby. For one moment he heard the wings beating strongly.

Most of the guests at the Hotel Gloriana were people past the age of retirement. Along Broadway in the Seventies, Eighties and Nineties, a great part of New York's vast population of old men and women lives. Unless the weather is too cold or wet they fill the benches about the tiny railed parks and along the subway gratings from Verdi Square to Columbia University, they crowd the shops and cafeterias, the dime stores, the tearooms, the bakeries, the beauty parlors, the reading rooms and club rooms. Among these old people at the Gloriana Wilhelm felt out of place. He was comparatively young, in his middle forties, large and blond, with big shoulders; his back was heavy and strong, if already a little stooped or thickened, too.

After breakfast the old guests sat down on the green leather armchairs and sofas in the lobby and began to gossip and look into the papers; they had nothing to do but wait out the day. But Wilhelm was used to an active life and liked to go out energetically in the morning. And for several months, because he had no position, he had kept up his morale by rising early; he was shaved and in the lobby by eight o'clock. He bought the paper and some cigars and drank a Coca-Cola or two before he went in to breakfast with his father. After breakfast: out, out, out to attend to business. The getting out had in itself become the chief business. But he had realized that he could not keep this up much longer, and today he was afraid. He was aware that his routine was about to break up and he sensed that a huge trouble long presaged but till now formless was due. Before evening he'd know.

Nevertheless he followed his daily course, and crossed the lobby.

Rubin, the man at the newsstand, had poor eyes. They may not have been actually weak but they were poor in expression, with lacy lids that furled down at the corners. He dressed well. It didn't seem necessary, he was behind the counter most of the time, but he dressed very well. He had on a rich brown suit; the cuffs embarrassed the hairs on his small hands. He wore a Countess Mara painted necktie. As Wilhelm approached Rubin did not see him; he was looking out dreamily at the Hotel Ansonia, which was visible from his corner several blocks away. The Ansonia, the neighborhood's great landmark, was built by Stanford White. It looks like a baroque palace from Prague or Munich enlarged a hundred times, with towers, domes, huge swells and bubbles of metal gone green from exposure, iron fretwork and festoons. Black television antennae are densely planted on its round summits. Under the changes of weather it may look like marble or like sea water, black as slate in the fog, white as tufa in sunlight. This morning it looked like the image of itself reflected in deep water, white and cumulous above, with cavernous distortions underneath. Together, the two men gazed at it.

Then Rubin said, "Your dad is in to breakfast already, the old gentleman."

"Oh, yes? Ahead of me, today?"

"That's a real knocked-out shirt you got on," said Rubin. "Where's it from, Saks?"

"No, it's a Jack Fagman – Chicago."

Even when his spirits were low, Wilhelm could still wrinkle his forehead in a pleasing way. Some of the slow, silent movements of his face were very attractive. He went back a step as if to stand away from himself and get a better look at his shirt. His glance was comic, a comment upon his untidiness. He liked to wear good clothes, but once he had put it on each article appeared to go its own way. Wilhelm, laughing, panted a little; his teeth were small, his cheeks when he laughed and puffed grew round, and he looked much younger than his years. In the old days when he was a college freshman and wore a raccoon coat and a beanie on his large blond head his father used to say that, big as he was, he could charm a bird out of a tree. Wilhelm had great charm still.

"I like this dove-gray color," he said in his sociable, good-natured way. "It isn't washable. You have to send it to the cleaner. It never smells as good as washed. But it's a nice shirt. It cost sixteen, eighteen bucks."

This shirt had not been bought by Wilhelm; it was a present from his boss – his former boss, with whom he had had a falling out. But there was no reason why he should tell Rubin the history of it. Although perhaps Rubin knew. Rubin was the kind of man who knew, and knew and knew. Wilhelm also knew many things about Rubin, for that matter – about Rubin's wife and Rubin's business, Rubin's health. None of these could be mentioned, and the great weight of the unspoken left them little to talk about.

"Well, y'lookin' pretty sharp today," Rubin said.

And Wilhelm said gladly, "Am I? Do you really think so?" He could not believe it. He saw his reflection in the glass cupboard full of cigar boxes, among the grand seals and paper damask and the gold-embossed portraits of famous men, Garcia, Edward the Seventh, Cyrus the Great. You had to allow for the darkness and deformations of the glass but he thought he didn't look too good. A wide wrinkle like a comprehensive bracket sign was written upon his forehead, the point between his brows, and there were patches of brown on his dark blond skin. He began to be half amused at the shadow of his own marveling, troubled, desirous eyes, and his nostrils and his lips. Fair-haired hippopotamus! that was how he looked to himself. He saw a big round face, a red mouth, stump teeth. And the hat, too; and the cigar, too. I should have done hard labor all my life, he reflected. Hard honest labor that tires you out and makes you sleep. I'd have worked off my energy and felt better. Instead, I had to distinguish myself . . . yet.

He had put forth plenty of effort, but that was not the same as working hard, was it? And if as a young man he had got off to a bad start it was due to this very same face. Early in the 1930s, because of his striking looks, he had been very briefly considered star material, and he had gone to Hollywood. There for seven years, stubbornly, he tried to become a screen artist. Long before that time his ambition or delusion had ended but through pride and perhaps also through laziness he had remained in California. At last he turned to other things, but those seven years of persistence and defeat had unfitted him somehow for trades and businesses, and then it was too late to go into one of the professions. He had been slow to mature, and he had lost ground, and so he hadn't been able to get rid of his energy and he was convinced that this energy itself had done him the greatest harm.

"I didn't see you at the gin game last night," said Rubin.

"I had to miss it. How did it go?"

For the last few weeks Wilhelm had played gin almost nightly, but yesterday he had felt that he couldn't afford to lose any more. He had never won. Not once. And while the losses were small they weren't gains, were they? They were losses. He was tired of losing, and tired also of the company, and so he had gone by himself to the movies.

"Oh," said Rubin, "it was okay. Carl made a chump of himself yelling at the guys. This time Dr. Tamkin didn't let him get away with it. He told him the psychological reason why."

"What was the reason?"

Rubin said, "I can't quote him. Who could? You know the way Tamkin talks. Don't ask me. Do you want the *Trib*? Aren't you going to look at the closing quotations?"

"It won't help much to look. I know what they were yesterday at three," said Wilhelm. "But I suppose I better had get the paper." It seemed necessary for him to lift one shoulder in order to put his hand into his jacket pocket. There, among little packets of pills and crushed cigarette butts and strings of cellophane, the red tapes of packages which he sometimes used as dental floss, he recalled that he had dropped some pennies.

"That doesn't sound so good," said Rubin. He meant to be conversationally playful, but his voice had no tone and his eyes, slack and lid-blinded, turned elsewhere. He didn't want to hear. It was all the same to him. Maybe he already knew, being the sort of man who knew and knew.

No, it wasn't good. Wilhelm held three orders of lard in the commodities market. He and Dr. Tamkin had bought this lard together four days ago at 12.96 and the price at once began to fall and was still falling. In the mail this morning there was sure to be a call for additional margin payment. One came every day.

The psychologist, Dr. Tamkin, had got him into this. Tamkin lived at the Gloriana and attended the card game. He had explained to Wilhelm that you could speculate in commodities at one of the uptown branches of a good Wall Street house without making the full deposit of margin legally required. It was up to the branch manager. If he knew you – and all the branch managers knew Tamkin – he would allow you to make short-term purchases. You needed only to open a small account.

"The whole secret of this type of speculation," Tamkin had told him, "is in the alertness. You have to act fast – buy it and sell it; sell it and buy in again. But quick! Get to the window and have them wire Chicago at just the right second. Strike and strike again! Then get out the same day. In no time at all you turn over fifteen, twenty thousand dollars' worth of soybeans, coffee, corn, hides, wheat, cotton." Obviously, the doctor understood the market well. Otherwise he could not make it sound so simple. "People lose because they are greedy and can't get out when it starts to go up. They gamble, but I do it scientifically. This is not guesswork. You must take a few points and get out. Why, ye gods!" said Dr. Tamkin with his bulging eyes, his bald head and his drooping lip. "Have you stopped to think how much dough people are making in the market?"

Wilhelm with a quick change from gloomy attention to the panting laugh which entirely changed his face had said, "Ho, have I ever! What do you think? Who doesn't know it's way beyond 1928-29 and still on the rise? Who hasn't read the Fulbright investigation? There's money everywhere. Everyone is shoveling it in. Money is . . . is. . . ."

"And can you rest – can you sit still while this is going on?" said Dr. Tamkin. "I confess to you I can't. I think about people, just because they have a few bucks to invest, making fortunes. They have no sense, they have no talent, they just have the extra dough and it makes them more dough. I get so worked up and tormented and restless, so restless! I haven't even been able to practice my profession. With all this money around you don't want to be a fool, while everyone else is making. I know guys who make five, ten thousand a week just by fooling around. I know a guy at the Hotel Pierre. There's nothing to him, but he has a whole case of Mumm's champagne at lunch. I know another guy on Central Park South . . . but what's the use of talking. They make millions. They have smart lawyers who get them out of taxes by a thousand schemes."

"Whereas I got taken," said Wilhelm. "My wife refused to sign a joint return. One fairly good year and I got into the thirty-two per cent bracket and was stripped bare. What of all my bad years?"

"It's a businessmen's government," said Dr. Tamkin. "You can be sure that these men making five thousand a week. . . ."

"I don't need that sort of money," Wilhelm had said. "But oh! if I could only work out a little steady income from this. Not much. I don't ask much. But how badly I need! . . . I'd be so grateful if you'd show me how to work it."

"Sure I will. I do it regularly. I'll bring you my receipts if you like. And do you want to know something? I approve of your attitude very much. You want to avoid catching the money fever. This type of activity is filled with hostile feeling and lust. You should see what it does to some of these fellows. They go on the market with murder in their hearts."

"What's that I once heard a guy say?" Wilhelm remarked. "A man is only as good as what he loves."

"That's it – just it," Tamkin said. "You don't have to go about it their way. There's also a calm and rational, a psychological approach."

Wilhelm's father, old Dr. Adler, lived in an entirely different world from his son, but he had warned him once against Dr. Tamkin. Rather casually – he was a very bland old man – he said, "Wilky, perhaps you listen too much to this Tamkin. He's interesting to talk to. I don't doubt it. I think he's pretty common but he's a persuasive man. However, I don't know how reliable he may be."

It made Wilhelm profoundly bitter that his father should speak to him with such detachment about his welfare. Dr. Adler liked to appear affable. Affable! His own son, his one and only son, could not speak his mind or ease his heart to him. I wouldn't turn to Tamkin, he thought, if I could turn to him. At least Tamkin sympathizes with me and tries to give me a hand, whereas Dad doesn't want to be disturbed.

Old Dr. Adler had retired from practice; he had a considerable fortune and could easily have helped his son. Recently, Wilhelm had told him, "Father – it so happens that I'm in a bad way now. I hate to have to say it. You realize that I'd rather have good news to bring you. But it's true. And since it's true, Dad – what else am I supposed to say? It's true."

Another father might have appreciated how difficult this confession was – so much bad luck, weariness, weakness and failure. Wilhelm had tried to copy the old man's tone when he made it and sounded gentlemanly, low-voiced, tasteful. He didn't allow his voice to tremble; he made no stupid gesture. But the doctor had no answer. He only nodded. You might have told him that Seattle was near Puget Sound, or that the Giants and Dodgers were playing a night game, so little was he moved from his expression of healthy, handsome, good-humored old age. He behaved toward his son as he had formerly done toward his patients, and it was a great grief to Wilhelm; it was almost too much to bear. Couldn't he see – couldn't he feel? Had he lost his family sense?

Greatly hurt, Wilhelm struggled however to be fair. Old people are bound to change, he said. They have hard things to think about. They must prepare for where they are going. They can't live by the old schedule any longer and all their perspectives change, and other people grow alike, kin or acquaintances. Dad is no longer the same person, Wilhelm reflected. He was thirty-two when I was born, and now he's going on eighty. Furthermore, it's time I stopped feeling like a kid toward him, a small son.

The handsome old doctor stood well above the other old people in the hotel. He was idolized by everyone. This was what people said: "That's old Professor Adler who used to teach internal medicine. He was a diagnostician, one of the best in New York, and had a tremendous practice. Isn't he a wonderful-looking old guy? It's a pleasure to see such a fine old scientist, clean and immaculate. He stands straight and understands every single thing you say. He still has all his buttons. You can discuss any subject with him." The clerks, the elevator operators, the telephone girls and waitresses and chambermaids, the management flattered and pampered him. That was what he wanted. He had always been a vain man. To see how his father loved himself sometimes made Wilhelm madly indignant.

He folded over the *Tribune* with its heavy, black, crashing sensational print and read without recognizing any of the words, for his mind was still on his father's vanity. He had created his own praise. People were primed and did not know it. And what did he need praise for? In a hotel where everyone was busy and contacts were so short he could be in people's thoughts only for a moment. He could never matter much to them. Wilhelm let out a long, hard breath and raised the brows of his round and somewhat circular eyes. He stared beyond the thick borders of the paper.

. . . love that well
Which thou must leave ere long.

Involuntary memory brought him these lines. At first he thought they referred to his father, but then he understood that they were for himself, rather. *He* should love that well. *This thou perceivest . . . which makes thy love more strong.* Under Dr. Tamkin's influence Wilhelm had recently begun to remember the poems he used to read. Dr. Tamkin knew, or said he knew, the great English poets and once in a while he mentioned a poem of his own. It was a long time since anyone had spoken to Wilhelm about this sort of thing. He didn't like to think about his college days, but if there was one course that now made sense it was Literature I. The textbook was Lieder and Lovett's *British Poetry and Prose*, a black heavy book with thin pages. "Did I read that?" he asked himself. Yes, he had read it and there was one accomplishment at least he could recall with pleasure. He had read *Yet once more, O ye laurels*. How pure this was to say! It was beautiful. *Sunk though he be beneath the watery floor* . . . Such things had always swayed him, and now the power of such words was far, far greater.

Wilhelm respected the truth but he could lie, and one of the things he lied often about was his education. He said he was an alumnus of Penn State; in fact he had left school before his sophomore year was finished. His sister Catherine had a B.S. degree. Wilhelm's late mother was a graduate of Bryn Mawr. He was the only member of the family who had no education. This was another sore point. His father was ashamed of him.

But he had heard the old man bragging to another old man, saying, "My son is a sales executive. He didn't have the patience to finish school. But he does all right for himself. His income is up in the five figures, somewhere."

"What . . . thirty, forty thousand?" said his stooped old friend.

"Well, he needs at least that much for his style of life. Yes, he needs that."

Despite his troubles, Wilhelm almost laughed. Why, that boasting old hypocrite. He knew the sales executive was no more. For many weeks there had been no executive, no sales, no income. But how we love looking fine in the eyes of the world – how beautiful are the old when they are doing a snow-job! It's Dad, thought Wilhelm, who is the salesman. He's selling me. *He* should have gone on the road.

But what of the truth? Ah, the truth was that there were problems, and of these problems his father wanted no part. His father was ashamed of him. The truth, Wilhelm thought, was very awkward. He pressed his lips together, and his tongue went soft; it pained him far at the back, in the cords and throat, and a knot of ill formed in his chest. Dad never was a pal to me when I was young, he reflected. He was at the office or the hospital, or lecturing. He expected me to look out for myself and never gave me much thought. Now he looks down on me. And maybe in some respects he's right.

No wonder Wilhelm delayed the moment when he would have to go into the dining room. He had moved to the end of Rubin's counter. He had opened the *Tribune*; the fresh pages drooped from his hands; the cigar was smoked out and the hat did not defend him. He was wrong to suppose that he was more capable than the next fellow when it came to concealing his troubles. They were clearly written out upon his face. He wasn't even aware of it.

There was the matter of the different names which, in the hotel, came up frequently. "Are you Dr. Adler's son?" "Yes, but my name is Tommy Wilhelm." And the doctor would say, "My son and I use different monickers. I uphold tradition. He's for the new." The Tommy was Wilhelm's own invention. He adopted it when he went to Hollywood, and dropped the Adler. Hollywood was his own idea, too. He used to pretend that it had all been the doing of a certain talent scout named Maurice Venice. But the scout never made him a definite offer of a studio connection. He had approached Wilhelm, but the results of the screen test had not been good. After the test Wilhelm took the initiative and pressed Maurice Venice until he got him to say, "Well, I suppose you might make it out there." And on the strength of this, Wilhelm had left college and had gone to California.

Someone had said, and Wilhelm agreed with the saying, that in Los Angeles all the loose objects in the country were collected, as if America had been tilted and everything that wasn't tightly screwed down had slid into Southern California. He himself had been one of these loose objects. Sometimes he told people, "I was too mature for college. I was a big boy, you see. 'Well,' I thought, 'when do you start to become a man?'" After he had driven a painted flivver and had worn a yellow slicker with slogans on it, and played illegal poker, and gone out on coke dates, he had *had* college. He wanted to try something new and quarreled with his parents about his career. And then a letter came from Maurice Venice.

The story of the scout was long and intricate and there were several versions of it. The truth about it was never told. Wilhelm had lied first boastfully and then out of charity to himself. But his memory was good, he could still separate what he had invented from the actual happenings, and this morning he found it necessary as he stood by Rubin's showcase with his *Tribune* to recall the crazy course of the true events. 'I didn't seem even to realize that there was a Depression. How could I have been such a jerk as not to prepare for anything and just go on luck and inspiration.' With round gray eyes expanded and his large shapely lips closed in severity toward himself he forced open all that had been hidden. 'Dad I couldn't affect one way or another. Mama was the one who tried to stop me, and we carried on and yelled and pleaded. The more I lied the louder I raised my voice, and charged-like a hippopotamus. Poor Mother! How I disappointed her.' Rubin heard Wilhelm give a broken sigh as he stood with the forgotten *Tribune* crushed under his arm.

When Wilhelm was aware that Rubin watched him loitering and idle, apparently not knowing what to do with himself this morning, he turned to the Coca-Cola machine. He swallowed hard at the coke bottle and coughed over it, but he ignored his coughing for he was still thinking, his eyes upcast and his lips cosed behind his hand. By a peculiar twist of habit he wore his coat collar turned up always, as though there were a wind. It never lay flat. But on his broad back, stooped with its own weight, its strength warped almost into deformity, the collar of his sports coat appeared anyway to be no wider than a ribbon.

He was listening to the sound of his own voice as he explained, twenty-five years ago in the living room on West End Avenue, "But Mother, if I don't pan out as an actor I can still go back to school."

But she was afraid he was going to destroy himself. She said. "Wilky, Dad could make it easy for you if you wanted to go into medicine." To remember this stifled him.

"I can't stand hospitals. Besides, I might make a mistake and hurt someone or even kill a patient. I couldn't stand that. Besides, I haven't got that sort of brains."

Then his mother had made the mistake of mentioning her nephew Artie, Wilhelm's cousin who was an honor student at Columbia in math and languages. That dark little gloomy Artie with his disgusting narrow face, and his moles and selfish sniffing ways and his unclean table manners, the boring habit he had of conjugating verbs when you went for a walk with him. "Romanian is an easy language. You just add a -*tl* to everything." He was now a professor, this same Artie with whom he had played near the Soldiers and Sailors monument on Riverside Drive.

Not that to be a professor was itself so great. How could anyone bear to know so many languages? And Artie also had to remain Artie, which was a bad deal. But perhaps success had changed him. Now that he had a place in the world perhaps he was better. Did he love his languages, and live for them, or was his cousin Artie also, in his heart, cynical? So many people nowadays were. No one seemed satisfied, and Wilhelm was horrified by the cynicism of successful people. Cynicism was bread and meat to everyone. And irony. Perhaps it couldn't be helped. It was probably even necessary. Wilhelm however feared it intensely. Whenever at the end of the day he was unusually fatigued he attributed it to cynicism. Too much of the world's business done. Too much falsity. He had various words to express the effect this had on him. Chicken! Unclean! Congestion! he exclaimed in his heart. Rat race! Phoney! Murder! Play-the-Game! Buggers!

At first the letter from the talent scout was nothing but a flattering sort of joke. Wilhelm's picture in the college paper when he was running for class treasurer was seen by Maurice Venice who wrote to him about a screen test. Wilhelm at once took the train to New York. He found the scout to be huge and oxlike, so stout that his arms seemed caught from beneath in a grip of flesh and fat; it looked as though it must be positively painful. He had little hair. Yet he enjoyed a healthy complexion. His breath was noisy and his voice rather difficult and husky because of the fat in his throat. He had on a double-breasted suit of the type then known as the pill-box; it was chalk-striped, pink on blue, the trousers hugged his ankles.

They met and shook hands and sat down. Together these two big men dwarfed the tiny Broadway office and made the furnishings look like toys. Wilhelm had the color of a Golden Grimes apple when he was well, and then his thick blond hair was vigorous and his wide shoulders were unwarped; he was leaner in the jaws, his eyes fresher and wider; his legs were still awkward but he was impressively handsome. And he was now about to make his first great mistake. Like, he sometimes thought, I was going to pick up a weapon and strike myself a blow with it.

Looming over his desk in the small office darkened by over-built midtown – sheer walls, gray spaces, dry lagoons of tar and pebbles – Maurice Venice proceeded to establish his credentials. He said, "My letter was on the regular stationery, but maybe you want to check on me?"

"Who *me*," said Wilhelm. "Why?"

"There's guys who think I'm in a racket and make a charge for the test. I don't ask a cent. I'm no agent. There ain't no commission."

"I never even thought of it," said Wilhelm. Was there perhaps something fishy about this Maurice Venice? He protested too much.

In his husky, fat-weakened voice he finally challenged Wilhelm. "If you're not sure, you can call the distributor and find out who am I, Maurice Venice."

Wilhelm wondered at him. "Why shouldn't I be sure. Of course I am."

"Because I can see the way you size me up, and because this is a dinky office. Like you don't believe me. Go ahead. Call. I won't care if you're cautious. I mean it. There's quite a few people who doubt me at first. They can't really believe that fame and fortune are going to hit 'em."

"But I can tell you I do believe you," Wilhelm had said, and bent inward to accommodate the pressure of his warm, panting laugh. It was purely nervous. His neck was ruddy and neatly shaved about the ears – he was fresh from the barber-shop; his face anxiously glowed with his desire to please and to make a fine impression. It was all wasted on Venice, who was just as concerned about the impression *he* was making.

"If you're surprised, I'll just show you what I mean," Venice had said. "It was about fifteen months ago right in this identical same office when I saw a beautiful thing in the paper. It wasn't even a photo but a drawing, a brassiere ad, but I knew right away that this was star material. I called up the paper to ask who the girl was, they gave me the name of the advertising agency; I phoned the agency and they gave me the name of the artist; I got hold of the artist and he gave me the number of the model agency. Finally, finally, I got her number and phoned her and said, 'this is Maurice Venice, scout for Kaskaskia Films.' So right away she says, 'Yah, so's your old lady.' Well, when I saw I wasn't getting nowhere with her I said to her, 'Well, Miss. I don't blame you. You're a very beautiful thing and must have a dozen admirers after you all the time, boyfriends who like to call and pull your leg and give a tease. But as I happen to be a very busy fellow and don't have the time to horse around or argue, I tell you what to do. Here's my number, and here's the number of the Kaskaskia Distributors Inc. Ask them who am I, Maurice Venice. The scout.' She did it. A little while later she phoned me back, all apologies and excuses, but I didn't want to embarrass her and get off on the wrong foot with an artist. I know better than to do that. So I told her it was a natural precaution, never mind. I wanted to run a screen test right away. Because I seldom am wrong about talent. If I see it, it's there. Get that, please. And do you know who that little girl is today?"

"No," Wilhelm said eagerly. "Who is she?"

Venice said impressively, "Nita Christenberry."

Wilhelm sat utterly blank. This was failure. He didn't know the name, and Venice was waiting for his response and would be angry.

And in fact Venice had been offended. He said, "What's the matter with you! Don't you read a magazine? She's a starlet."

"I'm sorry," Wilhelm answered. "I'm at school and don't have time to keep up. If I don't know her, it doesn't mean a thing. She made a big hit, I'll bet."

"You can say that again. Here's a photo of her." He handed Wilhelm some pictures. She was a bathing beauty – short, the usual breasts, hips and smooth thighs. Yes, quite good, as Wilhelm recalled. She stood on high heels and wore a Spanish comb and mantilla. In her hand was a fan.

He had said, "She looks awfully peppy."

"Isn't she a divine girl? And what personality! Not just another broad in the show business, believe me." He had a surprise for Wilhelm. "I have found happiness with her," he said.

"You have?" said Wilhelm, slow to understand.

"Yes, boy, we're engaged."

Wilhelm saw another photograph, taken on the beach. Venice was dressed in a terry-cloth beach outfit and he and the girl, cheek to cheek, were looking into the camera. Below, in white ink, was written *Love at Malibu Colony*.

"I'm sure you'll be very happy. I wish you. . ."

"I *know*," said Venice firmly. "I'm going to be happy. When I saw that drawing, the breath of fate breathed on me. I felt it over my entire body."

"Say, it strikes a bell suddenly," Wilhelm had said. "Aren't you related to Martial Venice the producer?"

Venice was either a nephew of the producer or the son of a first cousin. Decidedly he had not made good. It was easy enough for Wilhelm to see this now. The office was so poor, and Venice bragged so nervously, and identified himself so scrupulously – the poor guy. He was the obscure failure of an aggressive and power-ful clan. As such he had the greatest sympathy from Wilhelm.

Venice had said, "Now I suppose you want to know where you come in. I seen your school paper, by accident. You take quite a remarkable picture."

"It can't be so much," said Wilhelm, more panting than laughing.

"You don't want to tell me my business," Venice said, "Leave it to me. I studied up on this."

"I never imagined . . . Well, what kind of roles do you think I'd fit?"

"All this time that we've been talking, I've been watching. Don't think I haven't. You remind me of someone. Let's see who it can be . . . one of the great old-timers. Is it Milton Sills? No, that's not the one. Conway Tearle, Jack Mulhall? George Bancroft? No, his face was ruggeder. One thing I can tell you, though, a George Raft type you're not – those tough, smooth, black little characters."

"No, I wouldn't seem to be."

"No, you're not that flyweight type, with the fists, from a nightclub, and the glamorous sideburns, doing the Tango or the Bolero. Not Edward G. Robinson, either . . . I'm thinking aloud. Or the Cagney fly-in-your-face role, a cabbie, with that mouth and those punches."

"I realize that."

"Not suave like William Powell, or a lyric juvenile like Buddy Rogers. I suppose you don't play the sax? No. But . . ."

"But what?"

"I have you placed as the type that loses the girl to the George Raft type or the William Powell type. You are steady, faithful, you get stood up. The older women would know better. The mothers are on your side. With what they know, if it was up to them, they'd take you in a minute. You're very sympathetic, even the young girls feel that. You'd make a good provider. But they go more for the other types. It's as clear as anything."

This was not how Wilhelm saw himself. And as he surveyed the old ground he recognized now that he had been not only confused but hurt. Why, he thought, he cast me even then for a loser.

Wilhelm had said, with half a mind to be defiant, "Is that your opinion?"

It never occurred to Venice that a man might object to stardom in such a role. "Here is your chance," he said. "Now you're just in college. What are you study-ing?" He snapped his fingers. "Stuff." Wilhelm himself felt this way about it. "You may plug along fifty years before you get anywheres. This way, in one jump, the world knows who you are. You become a name like Roosevelt, Swanson. From east to west, out to China, into South America. This is no bunk. You become a lover to the whole world. The world wants it, needs it. One fellow smiles, a billion people smile. One fellow cries, the other billion sob with him. Listen, bud," Venice pulled himself together to make an effort. On his imagination there was some great weight which he could not discharge. He wanted Wilhelm, too, to feel it. He twisted his large, clean, well-meaning rather foolish features as though he were their unwilling captive, and said in his choked, fat-obstructed voice, "Listen, everywhere there are people trying hard, miserable, in trouble, downcast, tired, trying and trying. They need a break, right? A breakthrough, a help, luck or sympathy."

"That certainly is the truth," said Wilhelm. He had seized the feeling and he waited for Venice to go on. But Venice had no more to say; he had concluded. He gave Wilhelm several pages of blue hectographed script, stapled together, and told him to prepare for the screen test. "Study your lines in front of a mirror," he said. "Let yourself go. The part should take ahold of you. Don't be afraid to make faces and be emotional. Shoot the works. Because when you start to act, you're no more an ordinary person, and those things don't apply to you. You don't behave the same way as the average."

And so Wilhelm had never returned to Penn State. His roommate sent his things to New York for him, and the school authorities had to write to Dr. Adler to find out what had happened.

Still, for three months, Wilhelm delayed his trip to California. He wanted to start out with the blessings of his family, but they were never given. He quarreled with his parents and his sister. And then, when he was best aware of the risks and knew a hundred reasons against going and had made himself sick with fear, he left home. This was typical of Wilhelm. After much thought and hesitation and debate he invariably took the course he had rejected innumerable times. Ten such decisions made up the history of his life. He had decided that it would be a bad mistake to go to Hollywood, and then he went. He had made up his mind not to marry his wife, but ran off and got married. He had resolved not to invest money with Tamkin, and then had given him a check.

But Wilhelm had been eager for life to start. College was merely another delay. Venice had approached him and said that the world had named Wilhelm to shine before it. He was to be freed from the anxious and narrow life of the average. Moreover, Venice had claimed that he never made a mistake. His instinct for talent was infallible, he said.

But when Venice saw the results of the screen test he did a quick about-face. In those days Wilhelm had had a speech difficulty. It was not a true stammer, it was a thickness of speech which the sound track exaggerated. The film showed that he had many peculiarities, otherwise unnoticeable. When he shrugged, his hands drew up within his sleeves. The vault of his chest was huge, but he really didn't look strong under the lights. Though he called himself a hippopotamus, his walk was bearlike, quick and rather soft, toes turned inward, as though his shoes were an impediment. About one thing, Venice had been right. Wilhelm was photogenic, and his wavy blond hair (now graying) came out well, but after the test he refused to encourage him. He tried to get rid of him. He couldn't afford to take a chance on him, he had made too many mistakes already and lived in fear of his powerful relatives.

Wilhelm had told his parents, "Venice says I owe it to myself to go." How ashamed he was now of this lie! He had begged Venice not to give him up. He had said, "Can't you help me out? It would kill me to go back to school now."

Then when he reached the coast he learned that a recommendation from Maurice Venice was the kiss of death. Venice was in more need of help and charity than he, Wilhelm, had ever been. A few years later when Wilhelm was down on his luck and working as an orderly in a Los Angeles hospital, he saw Venice's picture in the papers. He was under indictment for pandering. Closely following the trial Wilhelm found out that Venice had indeed been employed by Kaskaskia Films but that he had evidently made use of the connection to organize a ring of call girls. Then what did he want with me? Wilhelm had cried to himself. He was unwilling to believe anything very bad about Venice. Perhaps he was foolish and unlucky, a fall-guy, a dupe, a sucker. But you didn't give a man fifteen years in prison for that. Wilhelm often thought that he might write him a letter to say how sorry he was. He remembered the breath of fate and Venice's certainty that he would be happy. Nita

Christenberry was sentenced to three years. Wilhelm recognized her although she had changed her name.

By that time too Wilhelm had taken a new name. In California he became Tommy Wilhelm. Dr. Adler would not accept the change. Today, he still called his son Wilky, as he had done for more than forty years. Well, now, Wilhelm was thinking, the paper crowded in disarray under his arm, there's really very little that a man can change at will. He can't change his lungs, or nerves, or constitution or temperament. They're not under his control. When he's young and strong and impulsive and dissatisfied with the way things are he wants to rearrange them to assert his freedom. He can't overthrow the government or be differently born; he only has a little scope and maybe a foreboding, too, that essentially you can't make changes. Nevertheless, he makes a gesture and becomes Tommy Wilhelm. Wilhelm had always had a great longing to be Tommy. He had never, however, succeeded in feeling like Tommy, and in his soul had always remained Wilky. When he was drunk he reproached himself horribly as Wilky, and said to himself that it was a good thing perhaps that he had not become a success as Tommy, since that would not have been a genuine success. Wilhelm would have feared that not he but Tommy had brought it off, cheating Wilky of his birthright. Yes, it had been an absurd thing to do, but it was his imperfect judgment at the age of twenty which should be blamed. He had cast off his father's name, and with it his father's opinion of him. It was, he knew it was, his bid for liberty, Adler being in his mind the title of the species, Tommy the freedom of the person. But Wilky was his inescapable self.

In middle age you no longer thought such thoughts. Then it came over you that from one grandfather you had inherited such and such a head of hair which looked like honey when it whitens or sugars in the jar; from another, broad thick shoulders; an oddity of speech from one uncle, and small teeth from another, and the gray eyes with darkness diffused even into the whites, and a wide-lipped mouth like a statue from Peru. Wandering races have such looks, the bones of one tribe, the skin of another. From his mother he had gotten sensitive feelings, a soft heart, brooding, hypochondria, a tendency to be confused under pressure.

The changed name was a mistake, and he would admit it as freely as you liked. But this mistake couldn't be undone now, so why must his father continually remind him how he had sinned? It was too late. You would have to return to the pathetic day when the sin was committed. And where was that day? Past and dead. Whose humiliating memories were these? His and not his father's. What had he to think back on that he could call good? Very, very little. You had to forgive. First, to forgive yourself, and then general forgiveness. Didn't he suffer from his mistakes far more than his father could?

"Oh, God," Wilhelm prayed. "Let me out of my trouble. Let me out of my thoughts, and let me do something better with myself. For all the time I have wasted I am very sorry. Let me out of this clutch and get into a different life. For I am all balled up. Have mercy."

II

The mail.

The clerk who gave it to him did not care what sort of appearance he made this morning. He only glanced at him from under his brows, upward, as the letters changed hands. Why should the hotel people waste courtesies on him? They had his number. The clerk knew that he was handing him, along with the letters, a bill for his rent. Wilhelm assumed a look that removed him from all such things. But it was bad. To pay the bill he would have to withdraw money from his brokerage account, and the account was being watched because of the drop in lard. According to the *Tribune's* figures lard was still twenty points below last year's level. There were government price supports. Wilhelm didn't know how these worked but he understood that the farmer was protected and that the SEC kept an eye on the market and therefore he believed that lard would be sent up again and he wasn't greatly worried as yet. But in the meantime, his father might have offered to pick up his hotel tab. Why didn't he? What a selfish old man he was! He saw his son's hardships; he could so easily help him. How little it would mean to him, and how much to Wilhelm! Where was the old man's heart? Maybe, thought Wilhelm, I was sentimental in the past and exaggerated his kindliness – warm family life. It may never have been there.

Not long ago his father had said to him in his usual affable, pleasant way, "Well, Wilky, here we are under the same roof again, after all these years."

Wilhelm was glad for an instant. At last they would talk over old times. But he was also on guard against insinuations. Wasn't his father saying, "Why are you here in a hotel with me and not at home in Brooklyn with your wife and two boys? You're neither a widower nor a bachelor. You have brought me all your confusions. What do you expect me to do with them?"

So Wilhelm studied the remark for a bit, then said, "The roof is twenty-six stories up. But how many years has it been?"

"That's what I was asking you."

"Gosh, Dad, I'm not sure. Wasn't it the year Mother died? What year was that?"

He asked this question with an innocent frown on his Golden Grimes, dark blond face. *What year was it!* As though he didn't know the year, the month, the day, the very hour of his mother's death.

"Wasn't it 1931?" said Dr. Adler.

"Oh, was it?" said Wilhelm. And to hide the sadness and the overwhelming irony of the question he gave a nervous wag of the head and felt the ends of his collar rapidly and gave his panting laugh. But it came out of his mouth dryly.

"Do you know?" his father said. "You must realize, an old fellow's memory becomes unreliable. It was in winter, that I'm sure of. 1932?"

Yes, it was age. Don't make an issue of it, Wilhelm advised himself. If you were to ask the old doctor in what year he interned, he'd tell you correctly. All the same, don't make an issue. Don't quarrel with your own father. Have pity on an old man's failings.

"I believe the year was closer to 1934, Dad," he said.

But Dr. Adler was thinking, Why the devil can't he stand still when we're talking. He's either hoisting his pants up and down by the pockets or jittering with his feet. A regular mountain of tics, he's getting to be. Wilhelm had a habit of moving his feet back and forth as though, hurrying into a house, he had to clean his shoes first on the door mat.

Then Wilhelm had said, "Yes, that was the beginning of the end, wasn't it, Father?"

Wilhelm often astonished Dr. Adler. Beginning of the end? What could he mean – what was he fishing for? Whose end? The end of family life? The old man was puzzled but he would not give Wilhelm an opening to introduce his complaints. He had learned that it was better not to take up Wilhelm's strange challenges. So he merely agreed pleasantly, for he was a master of social behavior, and said, "It was an awful misfortune for us all."

He thought, What business has he to complain to *me* of his mother's death?

Face to face they had stood, each declaring himself silently after his own way. – It was – it was not, the beginning of the end – *some* end.

Unaware of anything odd in his doing it, for he did it all the time, Wilhelm had pinched out the coal of his cigarette and dropped the butt in his pocket, where there were many more. And as he gazed at his father, the little finger of his right hand began to twitch and tremble; of that he was unconscious, too.

And yet Wilhelm believed that when he put his mind to it he could have perfect and even distinguished manners, outdoing his father. Despite the slight thickness in his speech – it amounted almost to a stammer when he started the same phrase over several times in his effort to eliminate the thick sound – he could be fluent. Other-wise, he would never have made a good salesman. He claimed also that he was a good listener. When he listened, he made a tight mouth and rolled his eyes thought-fully. He would soon tire and begin to utter short, loud, impatient breaths, and he would say, "Oh yes . . . yes . . . yes. I couldn't agree more." When he was forced to differ he would declare, "Well, I'm not sure. I don't really see it that way. I'm of two minds about it." He would never willingly hurt any man's feelings.

But in conversation with his father he was apt to lose control of himself. After any talk with Dr. Adler, Wilhelm generally felt dissatisfied, and his dissatisfaction reached its greatest intensity when they discussed family matters. Ostensibly he had been trying to help the old man to remember a date, but in reality he meant to tell him, "You were set free when Ma died. You wanted to forget her. You'd like to get rid of Catherine, too. Me, too. You're not kidding anyone." – Wilhelm striving to put this across, and the old man not having it. In the end he was left struggling, while his father seemed unmoved.

And then once more Wilhelm had said to himself, 'But man! You're not a kid. Even then you weren't a kid!' He looked down over the front of his big, indecently big, spoiled body. He was beginning to lose his shape, his gut was fat, and he looked like a hippopotamus. His younger son called him "a hummuspotamus" – that was little Paul. And here he was still struggling with his old dad, filled with ancient grievances. Instead of saying, "Good-bye, youth! Oh, good-bye those marvelous, foolish wasted days. What a big clunk I was – I *am*."

Wilhelm was still paying heavily for his mistakes. His wife Margaret would not give him a divorce, and he had to support her and the two children. She would regularly agree to divorce him, and then think things over again and set new and more difficult conditions. No court would have awarded her the amounts he paid. One of today's letters, as he had expected, was from her. For the first time, he had sent her a post-dated check and she protested. She also enclosed bills for the boys' educational insurance policies, due next week. Wilhelm's mother-in-law had taken out these policies in Beverly Hills, and since her death two years ago he had to pay the premiums. Why couldn't she have minded her own business! They were his kids, and he took care of them and always would. He had planned to set up a trust fund. But that was on his former expectations. Now he had to rethink the future, because of the money problem. Meanwhile, here were the bills to be paid. When he saw the two sums punched out so neatly on the cards he cursed the company and its IBM equipment. His heart and his head were congested with anger. Everyone was supposed to have money. It was nothing to the company. It ran pictures of funerals in the magazines and frightened the suckers, and then punched out little holes, and the customers would lie awake to think out ways to raise the dough. They'd be ashamed not to have it. They couldn't let a great company down, either, and they got the scratch. In the old days they would put a man in prison for debt, but there were subtler things now.

They made it a shame not to have money and put everybody to work. Well, and what else had Margaret sent him? He tore the envelope open with his thumb swearing that he would send any other bills back to her. There was, luckily, nothing more. He put the hole-punched cards in his pocket. Didn't Margaret know that he was nearly at the end of his rope? Of course. Her instinct told her that this was her opportunity and she was giving him the works.

He went into the dining room, which was under Austro-Hungarian management at the Hotel Gloriana. It was run like a European establishment. The pastries were excellent, especially the strudel. He often had apple strudel and coffee in the afternoon.

As soon as he entered he saw his father's small head in the sunny bay at the farther end, and heard his neat voice. It was with an odd sort of perilous expression that Wilhelm crossed the dining room.

Dr. Adler liked to sit in a corner that looked across Broadway down to the Hudson and New Jersey. On the other side of the street was a supermodern cafeteria with gold and purple mosaic columns. On the second floor a private-eye school, a dental laboratory, a reducing parlor, a veteran's club and a Hebrew school shared the space. The old man was sprinkling sugar on his strawberries. Small hoops of brilliance were cast by the water glasses on the white tablecloth, despite a faint murkiness in the sunshine. It was early summer. and the long window was turned inward; a moth was on the pane; the putty was broken and the white enamel on the frames was streaming with wrinkles.

"Ha, Wilky," said the old man to his tardy son. "You haven't met our neighbor Mr. Perls, have you? From the fifteenth floor."

"How d'do," Wilhelm said. He did not welcome this stranger; he began at once to find fault with him. Mr. Perls carried a heavy cane with a crutch tip. Dyed hair, a skinny forehead – these were not reasons for bias. Nor was it Mr. Perls's fault that Dr. Adler was using him, not wishing to have breakfast with his son alone. But a gruffer voice within Wilhelm spoke, asking, Who is this damn, frazzle faced herring with his dyed hair and his fish teeth and this drippy mustache? Another one of Dad's German friends. Where does he collect all these guys? What is the stuff on his teeth? I never saw such pointed crowns. Are they stainless steel, or a kind of silver? How can a human face get into this condition. Uch! Staring with his widely spaced gray eyes, Wilhelm sat, his broad back stooped under the sports jacket. He clasped his hands on the table with an implication of suppliance. Then he began to relent a little toward Mr. Perls, beginning at the teeth. Each of those crowns represented a tooth ground to the quick, and estimating a man's grief with his teeth as two percent of the total, and adding to that his flight from Germany and the probable origin of his wincing wrinkles, not to be confused with the wrinkles of his smile, it came to a sizable load.

"Mr. Perls was a hosiery wholesaler," said Dr. Adler.

"Is this the son you told me was in the selling line?" said Mr. Perls.

Dr. Adler replied, "I have only this one son. One daughter. She was a medical technician before she got married – anesthetist. At one time she had an important position in Mount Sinai."

He couldn't mention his children without boasting. In Wilhelm's opinion, there was little to boast of. Catherine, like Wilhelm, was big and fair-haired. She had married a court reporter who had a pretty hard time of it. She had taken a professional name, too – Philippa. At forty she was still ambitious to become a painter. Wilhelm didn't venture to criticize her work. It didn't do much to him, he said, but then he was no critic. Anyway, he and his sister were generally on the outs and he didn't often see her paintings. She worked very hard, but there were fifty thousand people in New York with paints and brushes, each practically a law unto himself. It was the Tower of Babel in paint. *He* didn't want to go far into this. Things were chaotic all over.

Dr. Adler thought that Wilhelm looked particularly untidy this morning – unrested, too, his eyes red-rimmed from excessive smoking. He was breathing through his mouth and he was evidently much distracted and rolled his red-shot eyes barbarously. As usual, his coat collar was turned up as though he had had to go out in the rain. When he went to business he pulled himself together a little; otherwise he let himself go and looked like hell.

"What's the matter, Wilky, didn't you sleep last night?"

"Not very much."

"You take too many pills of every kind – first stimulants and then depressants, anodynes followed by analeptics, until the poor organism doesn't know what's happened. Then the Luminal won't put people to sleep, and the Pervitin or Benzedrine won't wake them. God knows! These things get to be as serious as poisons, and yet everyone puts all their faith in them."

"No, Dad, it's not the pills. It's that I'm not used to New York anymore. For a native, that's very peculiar, isn't it? It was never so noisy at night as now, and every little thing is a strain. Like the alternate parking. You have to run out at eight to move your car. And where can you put it? If you forget for a minute they tow you away. Then some fool puts advertising leaflets under your windshield wiper and you have heart failure a block away because you think you've got a ticket. When you do get stung with a ticket, you can't argue. You haven't got a chance in court and the city needs the revenue."

"But in your line you have to have a car, eh?" said Mr. Pens.

"Lord knows why any lunatic would want one in the city who didn't need it for his livelihood."

Wilhelm's old Pontiac was parked in the street. Formerly, when on an expense account, he had always put it up in a garage. Now he was afraid to move the car from Riverside Drive lest he lose his space, and he used it only on Saturdays when the Dodgers were playing in Ebbets Field and he took his boys to the game. Last Saturday when the Dodgers were out of town he had gone out to visit his mother's grave.

Dr. Adler had refused to go along. He couldn't bear his son's driving. Forgetfully, Wilhelm traveled for miles in second gear; he was seldom in the right lane and he neither gave signals nor watched for lights. The upholstery of his Pontiac was filthy with grease and ashes. One cigarette burned in the ashtray, another in his hand, a third on the floor with maps and other waste paper and Coca-Cola bottles. He dreamed at the wheel or argued and gestured and therefore the old doctor would not ride with him.

Then Wilhelm had come back from the cemetery angry because the stone bench between his mother's and his grandmother's graves had been overturned and broken by vandals. "Those damn teenage hoodlums get worse and worse," he said. "Why they must have used a sledge hammer to break the seat smack in half like that. If I could catch one of them!" He wanted the doctor to pay for a new seat, but he was cool to the idea. He said he was going to have himself cremated.

Mr. Perls said, "I don't blame you if you get no sleep up where you are." His voice was tuned somewhat sharp, as though he were slightly deaf. "Don't you have Parigi the singing teacher there? God, they have some queer elements in this hotel. On which floor is that Estonian woman with all her cats and dogs? They should have made her leave long ago."

"They've moved her down to twelve," said Dr. Adler.

Wilhelm ordered a large Coca-Cola with his breakfast. Working in secret at the small envelopes in his pocket he found two pills by touch. Much fingering had worn and weakened the paper. Under cover of a napkin he swallowed a Phenaphen sedative and a Unicap, but the doctor was sharp-eyed and said, "Wilky, what are you taking now.

"It's just my vitamin pills." He put his cigar butt in an ashtray on the table behind him for his father did not like the odor. Then he drank his Coca-Cola.

"That's what you drink for breakfast, and not orange juice?" said Mr. Perls. He seemed to sense that he would not lose Dr. Adler's favor by taking this questionable tone with his son.

"The caffeine stimulates brain activity," said the old doctor. "It does all kinds of things to the respiratory center."

"It's just a habit of the road, that's all," Wilhelm said. "If you drive around long enough it turns your brains, your stomach and everything else."

His father explained, "Wilky used to be with the Rojax Corporation. He was their northeastern sales representative for a good many years but recently ended the connection."

"Yes," said Wilhelm, "I was with them from the end of the war. He sipped the Coca-Cola and chewed the ice, glancing at one and the other with his attitude of large, shaky, patient dignity. The waitress set two boiled eggs before him.

"What kind of line does this Rojax company manufacture?" said Mr. Perls.

"Kiddies' furniture. Little chairs, rockers, tables, jungle-gyms, slides, swings, seesaws."

Wilhelm let his father do the explaining. Large and stiff-backed, he tried to sit patiently, but his feet were abnormally restless. All right! His father had to impress Mr. Perls? He would go along once more, and play his part. Fine! He would play along and help his father maintain his style. Style was the main consideration.

"I was with the Rojax Corporation for almost ten years," he said. "We parted ways because they wanted me to share my territory. They took a son-in-law into the business – a new fellow. It was his idea."

To himself, Wilhelm said, Now God alone can tell why I have to lay my whole life bare to this blasted herring here. I'm sure nobody else does it. Other people keep their business to themselves. Not me.

He continued, "But the rationalization was that it was too big a territory for one man. I had a monopoly. That wasn't so. The real reason was that they had gotten to the place where they would have to make me an officer of the corporation. Vice-presidency. I was in line for it, but instead this son-in-law got in, and . . .

Dr. Adler thought Wilhelm was discussing his grievances much too openly and said, "My son's income was up in the five figures."

As soon as money was mentioned, Mr. Perls's voice grew eagerly sharper. "Yes? What, the thirty-two per cent bracket? Higher even, I guess?" He asked for a hint, and he named the figures not idly but with a sort of hugging relish. Uch! How they love money, thought Wilhelm. They adore money! Holy money! Beautiful money! It was getting so that people were feeble-minded about everything except money. While, if you didn't have it, you were a dummy, a dummy! You had to excuse yourself from the face of the earth. Chicken! that's what it was. The world's business. If only he could find a way out of it.

Such thinking brought on the usual congestion. It would grow into a fit of passion if he permitted it. Therefore he stopped talking and began to eat.

Before he struck the egg with his spoon, he dried the moisture with his napkin. Then he battered it (in his father's opinion) more than was necessary. A faint grime was left by his fingers on the white of the egg after he had picked away the shell. Dr. Adler saw it with silent repugnance. What a Wilky he had given to the world! Why, he didn't even wash his hands in the morning. He used an electric razor so that he didn't have to touch water. The doctor couldn't bear Wilky's dirty habits. Only once – and never again, he swore – had he visited his room. Wilhelm, in pajamas and stockings, had sat on his bed drinking gin from a coffee mug and rooting for the Dodgers on television. "That's two and two on you, Duke. Come on – hit it, now." He came down on the bed – bam! The bed looked kicked to pieces. Then he drank the gin as though it were tea, and urged his team on with his fist. The smell of dirty clothes was outrageous. By the bedside lay a quart bottle, and foolish magazines and mystery stories for the hours of insomnia. Wilhelm lived in worse filth than a savage. When the doctor spoke to him about this he answered, "Well, I have no wife to look after my things." And who – *who!* – had done the leaving? Not Margaret. The doctor was certain that she wanted him back.

Wilhelm drank his coffee with a trembling hand. In his full face his abused, bloodshot gray eyes moved back and forth. Jerkily he set his cup back and put half the length of a cigarette into his mouth; he seemed to hold it with his teeth, like a cigar.

"I can't let them get away with it," he said. "It's also a question of morale."

His father corrected him. "Don't you mean a moral question, Wilky?"

"I mean that, too. I have to do something to protect myself. I was promised executive standing." Correction before a stranger mortified him, and his dark blond face changed color, more pale, and then more dark. He went on talking to Perls but his eyes spied on his father. "I was the one who opened the territory for them. I could go back for one of their competitors and take away their customers. My customers. Morale enters into it because they've tried to take away my confidence."

"Would you offer a different line to the same people?" Mr. Perls wondered.

"Why not? I know what's wrong with the Rojax product."

"Nonsense," said his father. "Just nonsense and kid's talk, Wilky. You're only looking for trouble and embarrassment that way. What would you gain by such a silly feud? You have to think about making a living and meeting your obligations."

Hot and bitter, Wilhelm said with pride, while his feet moved angrily under the table, "I don't have to be told about my obligations. I've been meeting them for years. In more than twenty years I've never had a penny of help from anybody. I preferred to dig a ditch on the WPA but never asked anyone to meet my obligations for me."

"Wilky has had all kinds of experiences," said Dr. Adler.

The old doctor's face had a wholesome reddish and almost translucent color, like a ripe apricot. The wrinkles beside his ears were deep because his skin conformed so tightly to the bones. With all his might, he was a healthy and fine small old man. He wore a white vest of a light check pattern. His hearing aid doodad was in the pocket. An unusual shirt of red and black stripes covered his chest. He bought his clothes in a college shop, farther uptown. Wilhelm thought he had no business to get himself up like a jockey, out of respect for his profession.

"Well," said Mr. Perls. "I can understand how you feel. You want to fight it out. By a certain time of life, to have to start all over again can't be a pleasure, though a good man can always do it. But anyway you want to keep on with a business you know already, and not have to meet a whole lot of new contacts."

Wilhelm again thought, Why does it have to be me and my life that's discussed, and not him and his life? He would never allow it. But I am an idiot. I have no reserve. To me it can be done. I talk. I must ask for it. Everybody wants to have intimate conversations, but the smart fellows don't give out, only the fools. The smart fellows talk intimately about the fools, and examine them all over and give them advice. Why do I allow it? The hint about his age had hurt him. No, you can't admit it's as good as ever, he conceded. Things do give out.

"In the meanwhile," Dr. Adler said, "Wilky is taking it easy and considering various propositions. Isn't that so?"

"More or less," said Wilhelm. He suffered his father to increase Mr. Perls's respect for him. The WPA ditch had brought the family into contempt. He was a little tired. The spirit, the peculiar burden of his existence lay upon him like an accretion, a load, a hump. In any moment of quiet, when sheer fatigue prevented him from struggling, he was apt to feel this mysterious weight, this growth or collection of nameless things which it was the business of his life to carry about. That must be what a man was for. This large, odd, excited, fleshy, blond, abrupt personality named Wilhelm, or Tommy, was here, present, in the present – Dr. Tamkin had been putting into his mind many suggestions about the present moment, and here and now – this Wilky, or Tommy Wilhelm, forty-four years old, father of two sons, at present living in the Hotel Gloriana, was assigned to be the carrier of a load which was his own self, his characteristic self. There was no figure or estimate for the value of this load. But it is probably exaggerated by the subject, T. W. Who is a visionary sort of animal. Who has to believe that he can know why he exists. Though he has never seriously tried to find out why.

Mr. Perls said, "If he wants time to think things over and have a rest, why doesn't he run down to Florida for a while? Off season it's cheap and quiet. Fairyland. The mangoes are just coming in. I got two acres down there. You'd think you were in India."

Mr. Perls utterly astonished Wilhelm when he spoke of Fairyland with a foreign accent. Mangoes – India? What did he mean, India?

"Once upon a time," said Wilhelm, "I did some public relations work for a big hotel down in Cuba. If I could get them a notice in Leonard Lyons or one of the other columns it might be good for another holiday there, gratis. I haven't had a vacation for a long time, and I could stand a rest after going so hard. You know that's true, Father." He meant that his father knew how deep the crisis was becoming, how badly he was strapped for money, and that he could not rest but would be crushed if he stumbled, and that his obligations would destroy him. He couldn't falter. He thought, 'the money! When I had it, I flowed money. They bled it away from me. I hemorrhaged money. But now it's almost all gone, and where am I supposed to turn for more?'

He said, "As a matter of fact, Father, I am tired as hell."

But Mr. Perls began to smile, and said, "I understand from Dr. Tamkin that you're going into some kind of investment with him, partners."

"You know, he's a very ingenious fellow," said Dr. Adler. " I really enjoy hearing him go on. I wonder if he really is a medical doctor."

"Isn't he?" said Perls. "Everybody thinks he is. He talks about his patients. Doesn't he write prescriptions?"

"I don't really know what he does," said Dr. Adler. "He's a cunning man."

"He's a psychologist, I understand," said Wilhelm.

"I don't know what sort of psychologist or psychiatrist he may be," said his father. "He's a little vague. It's growing into a major industry, and a very expensive one. Fellows have to hold down very big jobs in order to pay those fees. Anyway, this Tamkin is clever. He never said he practiced here, but I believe he was a doctor in California. They don't seem to have much legislation out there to cover these things, and I hear a thousand dollars will get you a degree from a Los Angeles correspondence school. He gives the impression of knowing something about chemistry, and things like hypnotism. I wouldn't trust him, though."

"And why wouldn't you?" Wilhelm demanded.

"Because he's probably a liar. Do you believe he invented all the things he claims?"

Mr. Perls was grinning.

"He was written up in *Fortune*," said Wilhelm. "Yes, in *Fortune* magazine. He showed me the article. I've seen his clippings."

"That doesn't make him legitimate," said Dr. Adler. "It might have been another Tamkin. Make no mistake, he's an operator. Perhaps even crazy."

"Crazy, you say?"

Mr. Perls put in, "He could be both sane and crazy. In these days nobody can tell for sure which is which."

"An electrical device for truck drivers to wear in their caps," said Dr. Adler, describing one of Tamkin's proposed inventions. "To wake them with a shock when they begin to he drowsy at the wheel. It's triggered by the change in blood pressure when they start to doze."

"It doesn't sound like such an impossible thing to me," said Wilhelm.

Mr. Perls said, "To me he described an underwater suit so a man could walk on the bed of the Hudson in case of an atomic attack. He said he could walk to Albany in it."

"Ha, ha, ha, ha, ha!" cried Dr. Adler in his old man's voice. "Tamkin's Folly. You could go on a camping trip under Niagara Falls."

"This is just his kind of fantasy," said Wilhelm. "It doesn't mean a thing. Inventors are supposed to be like that. I get funny ideas myself. Everybody wants to make something. Any American does."

But his father ignored this and said to Perls, "What other inventions did he describe?"

While the frazzle-faced Mr. Perls and his father in the unseemly, monkey-striped shirt were laughing, Wilhelm could not restrain himself and joined in with his own panting laugh. But he was in despair. They were laughing at the man to whom he had given a power-of-attorney over his last seven hundred dollars to speculate for him in the commodities market. They had bought all that lard. It had to rise today. By ten o'clock, or half-past ten, trading would be active, and he would see.

III

Between white tablecloths and glassware and glancing silverware, through over-full light, the long figure of Mr. Perls went away into the darkness of the lobby. He thrust with his cane, and dragged a large built-up shoe which Wilhelm had not included in his estimate of troubles. Dr. Adler wanted to talk about him. "There's a poor man, he said, "with a bone condition which is gradually breaking him up."

"One of those progressive diseases?" said Wilhelm.

"Very bad. I've learned," the doctor told him, "to keep my sympathy for the real ailments. This Perls is more to be pitied than any man I know."

Wilhelm understood he was being put on notice and did not express his opinion. He ate and ate. He did not hurry but kept putting food on his plate until he had gone through the muffins and his father's strawberries, and then some pieces of bacon that were left. He had several cups of coffee, and when he was finished he sat gigantically in a state of arrest and didn't seem to know what he should do next.

For a while, father and son were uncommonly still. Wilhelm's preparations to please Dr. Adler had failed completely, for the old man kept thinking, 'You'd never guess he had a clean upbringing. What a dirty devil this son of mine is. Why can't he try to sweeten his appearance a little. Why does he want to drag himself like this. And he makes himself look so idealistic!'

Wilhelm sat, mountainous. He was not really so slovenly as his father found him to be. In some aspects he even had a certain delicacy. His mouth though broad had a fine outline, and his brow and his gradually incurved nose, dignity, and in his blond hair there was white but there were also shades of gold and chestnut. When he was with the Rojax Corporation, Wilhelm had kept a small apartment in Roxbury, two rooms in a large house with a small porch and garden, and on mornings of leisure, in late spring weather like this, he used to sit expanded in a wicker chair with the sunlight pouring through the weave, and sunlight through the slug-eaten holes of the young hollyhocks and as deeply as the grass allowed into small flowers. This peace (he forgot that that time had its troubles, too), this peace was gone. It must not have belonged to him, really, for to be here in New York with his old father was more genuinely like his life. He was well aware that he didn't stand a chance of getting sympathy from his father, who said he kept it for real ailments. Moreover, he advised himself repeatedly not to discuss his vexatious problems with him, for his father, with some justice, wanted to be left in peace. Wilhelm also knew that when he began to talk about these things he made himself feel worse, he became congested with them and worked himself into a Dutch. Therefore he warned himself, 'Lay off, pal. It'll only be an aggravation.' From a deeper source, however, came other promptings. If he didn't keep his troubles before him, he risked losing them alto-gether and he knew by experience that this was worse. And furthermore, he could not succeed in excusing his father on the ground of old age. No. No he could not. I am his son, he thought. He is my father. He is as much father as I am son – old or not. Affirming this, though in complete silence, he sat, and sitting he kept his father at the table with him.

"Wilky," said the old man, "have you gone down to the baths here yet?"

"No, Dad, not yet."

"Well, you know the Gloriana has one of the finest pools in New York. Eighty feet, blue tile. It's a beauty."

Wilhelm had seen it. On the way to the gin game, you passed the stairway to the pool. He did not care for the odor of the wall-locked and chlorinated water.

"You ought to investigate the Russian and Turkish baths, and the sunlamps and massage. I don't hold with sunlamps. But the massage does a world of good, and there's nothing better than hydrotherapy, when you come right down to it. Simple water has a calming effect and would do you more good than all the barbiturates and alcohol in the world."

Wilhelm reflected that this advice was as far as his father's help and sympathy would extend.

"I thought," he said, "that the water cure was for lunatics."

The doctor received this as one of his son's jokes and said with a smile, "Well, it won't turn a sane man into a lunatic. It does a great deal for me. I couldn't live without my massages and steam."

"You're probably right. I ought to try it one of these days. Yesterday, late in the afternoon, my head was about to bust and just had to have a little air, so I walked around the reservoir, and I sat down for a while in a playground. It rests me to watch the kids play potsy and skip-rope."

The doctor said with approval, "Well, now, that's more like the idea."

"It's the end of the lilacs," said Wilhelm. "When they burn it's the beginning of summer. At least, in the city. Around the time of year when the candy stores take down the windows and start to sell sodas on the sidewalk. But even though I was raised here, Dad, I can't take city life any more, and I miss the country. There's too much push here for me. It works me up too much. I take things too hard. I wonder why you never retired to a quieter place."

The doctor opened his small hand on the table in a gesture so old and so typical that Wilhelm felt it like an actual touch upon the foundations of his life. "I am a city boy myself, you must remember," Dr. Adler explained. "But if you find the city so hard on you, you ought to get out."

"I'll do that," said Wilhelm, "as soon as I can make the right connection. Meanwhile . . ."

His father interrupted, "Meanwhile I suggest you cut down on drugs."

"You exaggerate that, Dad. I don't really . . . I give myself a little boost against . . ." He almost pronounced the word "misery" but he kept his resolution not to complain.

The doctor, however, fell into the error of pushing his advice too hard. It was all he had to give his son and he gave it once more. "Water and exercise," he said.

He wants a young, smart, successful son, thought Wilhelm, and he said, "Oh, Father, it's nice of you to give me this medical advice, but steam isn't going to cure what ails me."

The doctor measurably drew back, warned by the sudden weak strain of Wilhelm's voice and all that the droop of his face, the swell of his belly against the restraint of his belt intimated.

"Some new business?" he asked unwillingly.

Wilhelm made a great preliminary summary which involved the whole of his body. He drew and held a long breath, and his color changed and his eyes swam. "New?" he said.

"You make too much of your problems," said the doctor. "They ought not to he turned into a career. Concentrate on real troubles – fatal sickness, accidents." The old man's whole manner said, 'Wilky, don't start this on me. I have a right at my age to be spared.'

Wilhelm himself prayed for restraint; he knew this weakness of his and fought it. He knew, also, his father's character. And he began mildly, "As far as the fatal part of it goes, everyone on this side of the grave is the same distance from death. No, I guess my trouble is not exactly new. I've got to pay premiums on two policies for the boys. Margaret sent them to me. She unloads everything on me. Her mother left her an income. She won't even file a joint tax return. I get stuck. Etcetera. But you've heard the whole story before."

"I certainly have," said the old man. "And I've told you to stop giving her so much money."

Wilhelm worked his lips in silence before he could speak. The congestion was growing. "Oh, but my kids, Father. My kids. I love them. I don't want them to lack anything."

The doctor said with a half-deaf benevolence, "Well, naturally. And she, I'll bet, is the beneficiary."

"Let her be. I'd sooner die myself before I collected a cent of such money."

"Ah yes," the old man sighed. He did not like the mention of death. "Did I tell you that your sister Catherine – Philippa, is after me again."

"What for?"

"She wants to rent a gallery for an exhibition."

Stiffly fair-minded, Wilhelm said, "Well, of course that's up to you, Father."

The round-headed old man with his fine feather-white, ferny hair said, "No, Wilky. There's not a thing on those canvases. I don't believe it; it's a case of the Emperor's clothes. I may be old enough for my second childhood, but at least the first is well behind me. I was glad enough to buy crayons for her when she was four. But now she's a woman of forty and too old to be encouraged in her delusions. She's no painter."

"I wouldn't go so far as to call her a born artist," said Wilhelm. "But you can't blame her for trying something worthwhile."

"Let her husband pamper her."

Wilhelm had done his best to be just to his sister, and he had sincerely meant to spare his father, but the old man's tight, benevolent deafness had its usual effect on him. He said, "When it comes to women and money, I'm completely in the dark. What makes Margaret act like this?"

"She's showing you that you can't make it without her," said the doctor. "She aims to bring you back by financial force."

"But if she ruins me, Dad, how can she expect me to come back? No, I have a sense of honor. What you don't see is that she's trying to put an end to me."

His father stared. To him this was absurd. And Wilhelm thought, Once a guy starts to slip, he figures he might as well be a clunk. A real big clunk. He even takes pride in it. But there's nothing to be proud of – hey, boy? Nothing. I don't blame Dad for his attitude.

"I don't understand that. But if you feel like this why don't you settle with her once and for all?"

"What do you mean, Dad?" said Wilhelm, surprised. "I thought I told you. Do you think I'm not willing to settle? Four years ago when we broke up, I gave her everything – goods, furniture, savings. I tried to show good will, but I didn't get anywhere. Why when I wanted Scissors, the dog, because the animal and I were so attached to each other – it was bad enough to leave the kids – she absolutely refused me. Not that she cared a damn about the animal. I don't think you've seen him. He's an Australian sheep dog. They usually have one blank or whitish eye which gives a misleading look, but they're the gentlest dogs, and have unusual delicacy about eating or talking. Let me at least have the companionship of this animal! Never!" Wilhelm was greatly moved. He wiped his face at all corners with his napkin. Dr. Adler felt that his son indulged himself too much in his emotions.

"Whenever she can hit me, she hits, and she seems to live for that alone. And she demands more and more, and still more. Two years ago she wanted to go back to college and get another degree. It increased my burden but I thought it would be wiser in the end if she got a better job through it. But still she takes as much from me as before. Next thing she'll want to be a Doctor of Philosophy. She says the women in her family live long, and I'll have to pay and pay for the rest of my life."

The doctor said impatiently, "Well these are details, not principles. Just details which you can leave out. The dog! You're mixing up all kinds of irrelevant things. Go to a good lawyer."

"But I've already told you, Dad. I got a lawyer, and she got one, too, and both of them talk and send me bills, and I eat my heart out. Oh Dad, Dad, what a hole I'm in!" said Wilhelm in utter misery. "The lawyers, see? draw up an agreement, and she says okay on Monday and wants more money on Tuesday. And it begins again."

"I always thought she was a strange kind of woman," said Dr. Adler. He felt that by disliking Margaret from the first and disapproving of the marriage he had done all that he could be expected to do.

"Strange, Father? I'll show you what she's like." Wilhelm took hold of his broad throat with brown-stained fingers and bitten nails and began to choke himself.

"What are you doing?" cried the old man.

"I'm showing you what she does to me."

"Stop that – stop it!" the old man said and tapped the table commandingly.

"Well, Dad, she hates me. I feel that she's strangling me. I can't catch my breath. She just has fixed herself on me to till me. She can do it at long distance. One of these days I'll be struck down by suffocation or apoplexy because of her. I just can't catch my breath."

"Take your hands off your throat, you foolish man," said his father. "Stop this bunk. Don't expect me to believe in all kinds of voodoo."

"If that's what you want to call it, all right." His face flamed and paled and swelled and his breath was laborious. "But I'm telling you that from the time I met her I've been a slave. The Emancipation Proclamation was only for colored people. A husband like me is a slave, with an iron collar. The churches go up to Albany and supervise the law. They won't have divorces. The court says, 'You want to be free. Then you have to work twice as hard – twice, at least! Work! you bum.' So then guys kill each other for the buck, and they may be free of a wife who hates them but they are sold to the company. The company knows a guy has got to have his salary, and takes full advantage of him. Don't talk to me about being free. A rich man may be free, on an income of a million net. A poor man may be free because nobody cares what he does. But a fellow in my position has to sweat it out until he drops dead."

His father replied to this, "Wilhelm, it's entirely your own fault. You don't have to allow it."

Stopped in his eloquence, Wilhelm could not speak for a while. Dumb and incompetent, he struggled for breath and frowned with effort into his father's face.

"I don't understand your problems," said the old man. "I never had any like them."

By now Wilhelm had lost his head beyond recovery and he waved his hands and said over and over, "Oh Dad, don't give me that stuff, don't give me that. Please don't give me that sort of thing."

"It's true," said his father. "I come from a different world. Your mother and I led an entirely different life."

"Oh, how can you compare Mother," Wilhelm said. "Mother was a help to you. Did she harm you ever?"

"There's no need to carry on like an opera, Wilky," said the doctor. "This is only your side of things."

"What? It's the truth," said Wilhelm.

The old man could not be persuaded and shook his round head and drew his vest down over the gilded shirt, and leaned back with a completeness of style that made this look, to anyone out of hearing, like an ordinary conversation between a middle-aged man and his respected father. Wilhelm towered and swayed, big and sloven, with his gray eyes red-shot and his honey-colored hair twisted in flaming shapes upwards. Injustice made him angry, made him beg. He wanted an understanding with his father. He tried to capitulate to him, and he said, "You can't compare Mother and Margaret, and neither can you and I be compared, because you, Dad, were a success. And a success – is a success. I never made a success."

The doctor's old face lost all of its composure and became hard and angry. His small breast rose sharply under the red and black shirt and he said, "Yes. Because of hard work. I was not self-indulgent, not lazy. My old man sold dry goods in Williamsburg. We were nothing, do you understand? I knew I couldn't afford to waste my chances."

"I wouldn't admit for one minute that I was lazy," said Wilhelm. "If anything, I tried too hard. I admit I made many mistakes. Like I thought I shouldn't do things you had done already. Study chemistry. You had done it already. It was in the family."

His father continued, "I didn't run around with fifty women, either. I was not a Hollywood star. I didn't have time to go to Cuba for a vacation. I stayed at home and took care of my family."

Oh, thought Wilhelm, his eyes turning upwards, why did I come here in the first place, to live near him. New York is like a gas. The colors are running. My head feels so tight, I don't know what I'm doing. He thinks I want to take away his money or that I envy him. He doesn't see what I want.

"Dad," Wilhelm said aloud, "you're being very unfair. It's true the movies was a false step. But I love my boys. I didn't abandon them. I left Margaret because I had to."

"Why did you have to?"

"Well –" said Wilhelm, struggling to condense his many reasons into a few plain words, "I had to – I had to."

With sudden and surprising bluntness his father said, "Did you have bed trouble with her? Then you should have stuck it out. Sooner or later everyone has it. Normal people stick it out. It passes. But you wouldn't, so now you must pay for your stupid romantic notions. Have I made my view clear?"

It was very clear. Wilhelm seemed to hear it repeated from various sides and inclined his head different ways, and listened and thought.

Finally he said, "I guess that's the medical standpoint. You may be right. I just couldn't live with Margaret. I wanted to stick it out, but I was getting very sick. She was one way and I was another. She wouldn't be like me, so I tried to be like her, and I couldn't do it."

"Are you sure she didn't tell *you* to go," the doctor said.

"I wish she had. I'd be in a better position now. No, it was me. I didn't want to leave, but I couldn't stay. Somebody had to take the initiative. I did. Now I'm the fall guy too."

Pushing aside in advance all the objections that his son would make, the doctor said, "Why did you lose your job with Rojax?"

"I didn't, I've told you."

"You're lying. You wouldn't have ended the connection. You need the money too badly. But you must have got into trouble." The small old man spoke with great strength. "Since you have to talk and can't let it alone, tell the truth. Was there a scandal – a woman?"

Wilhelm fiercely defended himself. "No, Dad, there wasn't any woman. I told you how it was."

"Maybe it was a man, then," the old man said wickedly.

Shocked, Wilhelm stared at him with burning pallor and dry lips. His skin looked a little yellow. "I don't think you know what you're talking about," he answered after a moment. "You shouldn't let your imagination run so free. Since you've been living here on Broadway you must think you understand life, up to date. You ought to know your own son a little better. Let's drop that, now."

"All right, Wilky, I'll withdraw that. But something must have happened in Roxbury nevertheless. You'll never go back. You're just talking wildly about representing a rival company. You won't. You've done something to spoil your reputation, I think. But you've got girlfriends who are expecting you back, isn't that so?"

"I take a lady out now and then while on the road," said Wilhelm. "I'm not a monk."

"No one special? Are you sure you haven't gotten into complications?"

He had tried to unburden himself and instead, Wilhelm thought, he had to undergo an inquisition to prove himself worthy of a sympathetic word. Because his father believed that he did all kinds of gross things.

"There is a woman in Roxbury that I went with. We fell in love and wanted to marry, but she got tired of waiting for my divorce. Margaret figured that. On top of which the girl was a Catholic and I had to go with her to the priest and make an explanation."

Neither did this last confession touch Dr. Adler's sympathies or sway his calm old head or affect the color of his complexion.

"No, no, no, no; all wrong," he said.

Again Wilhelm cautioned himself. Remember his age. He is no longer the same person. He can't bear trouble. I'm so choked up and congested anyway I can't see straight. Will I ever get out of the woods, and recover my balance? You're never the same afterwards. Trouble rusts out the system.

"You really *want* a divorce?" said the old man.

"For the price I pay I should be getting what I ask."

"In that case," Dr. Adler said, "it seems to me no normal person would stand for such treatment from a woman."

"Ah, Father, Father!" said Wilhelm. "It's always the same deal with you. Look how you lead me on. You always start out to help me with my problems, and be sympathetic and so forth. It gets my hopes up and I begin to be grateful. But before we're through I'm a hundred times more depressed than before. Why is that? You don't have sympathy. You want to shift all the blame on to me. Maybe you're wise to do it . . ." Wilhelm was beginning to lose himself. "All you seem to think about is your death. Well I'm sorry. But I'm going to die too. And I'm your son. It isn't my fault in the first place. There ought to be a right way to do this, and be fair to each other. But what I want to know is why do you start up with me if you're not going to help me? What do you want to know about my problems for, Father? So you can lay the whole responsibility on me – so that you won't have to help me? Do you want me to comfort you for having such a son?" Wilhelm had a great knot of wrong tied tight within his chest, and tears approached his eyes but he didn't let them out. He looked shabby enough as it was. His voice was thick and hazy, and he was stammering and could not bring his awful feelings forth.

"You have some purpose of your own," said the doctor, "in acting so unreasonable. What do you want from me? What do you expect?"

"What do I expect?" said Wilhelm. He felt as though he were unable to recover something. Like a ball in the surf, washed beyond reach, his self-control was going out. "I expect *help*!" The word escaped him in a loud, wild, frantic cry and startled the old man, and two or three breakfasters within hearing glanced their way. Wilhelm's hair, the color of whitened honey, rose dense and tall with the expansion of his face, and he said, "When I suffer . . . you aren't even sorry. That's because you have no affection for me, and you don't want any part of me."

"Why must I like the way you behave? No, I don't like it," said Dr. Adler.

"All right. You want me to change myself. But suppose I could do it – what would I become? What could I? Let's suppose that all my life I have had the wrong ideas about myself and wasn't what I thought I was. And wasn't even careful to take a few precautions, as most people do . . . like a woodchuck has a few exits to his tunnel. But what shall I do now? More than half my life is over. It's more than half. And now you tell me I'm not even normal."

The old man too had lost his calm. "You talk about being helped," he said. "When you thought you had to go into the service I sent a check to Margaret every month. As a family man you could have had an exemption. But no! The war couldn't be fought without you and you had to get yourself drafted and be an office boy in the Pacific theater. Any clerk could have done what you did. You had nothing better to do than become a G.I."

Wilhelm was going to reply, and half raised his bearish figure from the chair, his fingers spread and whitened by their grip on the table, but the old man would not let him begin. He said, "I see other elderly people here with children who aren't much good, and they keep backing them and holding them up at a great sacrifice. But I'm not going to make that mistake. It doesn't enter your mind that when I die – a year, two years from now – you'll still be here. I think of it."

He had intended to say that he had a right to be left in peace. Instead he gave Wilhelm the impression that he meant it was not fair for the better man of the two, and the more useful, the more admired, to leave the world first. Perhaps he meant that, too . . . a little; but he would not under normal circumstances come out with it so flatly.

"Father," said Wilhelm with an unusual openness of appeal, "don't you think I know how you feel? I have pity. I want you to live on and on. If you outlive me, that's perfectly okay by me . . ." As his father did not answer this avowal and turned away his glance, Wilhelm suddenly burst out, "No, but you hate me. And if I had money you wouldn't. By God, you have to admit it. The money makes the difference. Then we would be a fine father and son. If I was a credit to you so you could boast and brag about me all over the hotel. But I'm not the right type of son. I'm too old, I'm too old and too unlucky."

His father said, "I can't give you any money. There wouldn't be any end to it once I started. You and your sister would take every last buck from me. I'm still alive, not dead. I am still here. Life isn't over yet. I am as much alive as you or anyone. And I want nobody on my back. I give you the same advice, Wilky. Carry nobody on your back."

"Just keep your money," said Wilhelm miserably. "Keep it and enjoy it yourself. That's the ticket!"

IV

Ass! Idiot! Wild boar! Dumb mule! Slave! Lousy, wallowing hippopotamus! Wilhelm called himself as his bending legs carried him from the dining room. His pride! His inflamed feelings! His begging and feebleness! And trading insults with his old father . . . and spreading confusion over everything. Oh, how poor, contemptible and ridiculous he was! When he remembered how he had said, with great reproof, "Father, you might to know your own son," – why, how corny and abominable it was.

He could not get out of the sharply brilliant dining room fast enough. He was horribly worked up; his neck and shoulders, his entire chest ached as though they had been tightly tied with ropes. He smelled the salt odor of tears in his nose.

But at the same time, since there were depths in Wilhelm not unsuspected by himself, he received a suggestion from some remote element in his thoughts that the business of life, the real business – to carry the peculiar burden, to feel shame and impotence, to taste these quelled tears – the only important business, was being done. Maybe the making of mistakes expressed the very purpose of his life and the essence of his being here. Maybe he was supposed to make them and suffer from them on this earth. And though he had raised himself above Mr. Perls and his father because they adored money, still they were called to act energetically and this was better than to yell and cry, pray and beg, poke and blunder and go by fits and starts, and fall upon the thorns of life. And finally sink beneath that watery floor – would that be tough luck, or would it be good riddance?

But he raged once more against his father. Other people with money, while they're still alive, want to see it do some good. Granted he shouldn't support me. But have I asked him to do that? Have I ever asked for dough at all, either for Margaret or for the kids or for myself? It isn't the money, but only the assistance; not even assistance, but just the feeling. But he may be trying to teach me that a grown man should be cured of such feeling. Feeling got me in dutch at Rojax. I had the *feeling* that I belonged to the firm, and my *feelings* were hurt when they put Gerber in over me. Dad thinks I'm too simple. But I'm not so simple as he thinks. What about his feelings? He doesn't forget death for one single second, and that's what makes him like this. And not only is death on his mind but through the money he forces me to think about it too. It gives him power over me. He forces me that way, and then he's sore. If he was poor, I could care for him and show it. The way I could care, too, if I only had a chance. He'd see how much love and respect I had in me. It would make him a different man, too. He'd put his hands on me and give me his blessing.

Someone in a gray straw hat with a wide cocoa-colored band spoke to Wilhelm in the lobby. The light was dusky, splotched with red underfoot; green, the leather furniture; yellow, the indirect lighting.

"Hey, Tommy. Say, there."

"Excuse me," said Wilhelm, trying to reach a house phone. But this was Dr. Tamkin whom he was just about to call.

"You have a very obsessional look on your face," said Dr. Tamkin.

Wilhelm thought, Here he is. Here he is. If I could only figure *this* guy out.

"Oh," he said to Tamkin. "Have I got such a look? Well, whatever it is, you name it and I'm sure to have it."

The sight of Dr. Tamkin brought his quarrel with his father to a close. He found himself flowing into another channel.

"What are we doing?" he said. "What's going to happen to lard, today?"

"Don't worry yourself about that. All we have to do is hold on to it and it's sure to go up. But what's made you so hot under the collar, Wilhelm?"

"Oh, one of those family situations." This was the moment to take a new look at Tamkin, and he viewed him closely but gained nothing by the new effort. It was conceivable that Tamkin was everything that he claimed to be, and all the gossip false. But was he a scientific man, or not? If he was not, this might be a case for the district attorney's office to investigate. Was he a liar? That was a delicate question. Even a liar might be trustworthy in some ways. Could he trust Tamkin, could he? He feverishly, fruitlessly sought an answer.

But the time for this question was past, and he had to trust him now. After a long struggle to come to a decision, he had given him the money. Practical judgment was in abeyance. He had worn himself out, and the decision was no decision. How had this happened? But how had his Hollywood career begun? It was not because of Maurice Venice, who turned out to be a pimp. It was because Wilhelm himself was ripe for the mistake. His marriage, too, had been like that. Through such decisions somehow his life had taken form. And so, from the moment when he tasted the peculiar flavor of fatality in Dr. Tamkin, he could no longer keep back the money.

Five days ago, Tamkin had said, "Meet me tomorrow, and we'll go to the Market." Wilhelm therefore had had to go. At eleven o'clock they had walked to the brokerage office. On the way Tamkin broke the news to Wilhelm that though this was an equal partnership he couldn't put up his half of the money just yet; it was tied up for a week or so in one of his patents. Today he would be two hundred dollars short; next week, he'd make it up. But neither of them needed an income from the market, of course. This was only a sporting proposition anyhow, Tamkin said. Wilhelm had to answer, "Of course." It was too late to withdraw. What else could he do? Then came the formal part of the transaction, and it was frightening. The very shade of green of Tamkin's check looked wrong; it was a false, disheartening color. His handwriting was peculiar, even monstrous; the *e*'s were like *i*'s, the *t*'s and *i*'s the same and the *h*'s like wasps' bellies. He wrote like a fourth grader. Scientists, however, dealt mostly in symbols; they printed. This was Wilhelm's explanation.

Dr. Tamkin had given him his check for three hundred dollars. Wilhelm, in a blinded and convulsed aberration, pressed and pressed, to try to kill the trembling of his hand as he wrote out his check for a thousand. He set his lips tight, crouched with his huge back over the table, and wrote with crumbling, terrified fingers, knowing that if Tamkin's check bounced his own would not be honored either. His sole cleverness was to set the date ahead by one day to give the green check time to clear.

Next he had signed a power-of-attorney allowing Tamkin to speculate with his money, and this was an even more frightening document. Tamkin had never said a word about it, but here they were and it had to be done.

After delivering his signatures, the only precaution Wilhelm took was to come back to the manager of the brokerage office and ask him privately, "Uh, about Dr. Tamkin. We were in here a few minutes ago, remember?"

That day had been a weeping, smoky one and Wilhelm had gotten away from Tamkin on the pretext of having to run to the post office.

Tamkin had gone to lunch alone, and here was Wilhelm, back again, breathless, his hat dripping, needlessly asking the manager if he remembered.

"Yes, sir, I know," the manager had said. He was a cold, mild, lean German who dressed correctly and around his neck wore a pair of opera glasses with which he read the board. He was an extremely correct person except that he never shaved in the morning, not caring, probably, how he looked to the fumblers and the old people and the operators and the gamblers and the idlers of Broadway uptown. The Market closed at three-thirty. Maybe, Wilhelm guessed, he had a thick beard and took a lady out to dinner later and wanted to look fresh-shaven.

"Just a question," said Wilhelm. "A few minutes ago I signed a power-of-attorney so Dr. Tamkin could invest for me. You gave me the blanks."

"Yes, sir, I remember."

"Now this is what I want to know," Wilhelm had said. "I'm no lawyer and I only gave the paper a glance. Does this give Dr. Tamkin power-of-attorney over any other assets of mine – money, or property?"

The rain had dribbled from Wilhelm's deformed transparent raincoat; the buttons of his shirt, which always seemed tiny, were partly broken, in pearly quarters of the moon, and some of the dark, thick golden hairs that grew on his belly stood out. It was the manager's business to conceal his opinion of him; he was shrewd, gray, correct (although unshaven) and had little to say except on matters that came to his desk. He must have recognized in Wilhelm a man who reflected long and then made the decision he had rejected twenty separate times. Silvery, cool, level, long-profiled, experienced, indifferent, observant, with unshaven refinement, he scarcely looked at Wilhelm, who trembled with fearful awkwardness. The manager's face, low-colored, long-nostriled, acted as a unit of perception; his eyes merely did their reduced share. Here was a man, like Rubin, who knew and knew and knew. He, a foreigner, knew; Wilhelm, in the city of his birth, was ignorant.

The manager had said, "No, sir, it does not give him."

"Only over the funds I deposited with you?"

"Yes, that is right, sir."

"Thank you, that's what I wanted to find out," Wilhelm had said, grateful.

The answer comforted him. However, the question had no value. None at all. For Wilhelm had no other assets. He had given Tamkin his last money. There wasn't enough of it to cover his obligations anyway, and Wilhelm had reckoned that he might as well go bankrupt now as next month. "Either broke or rich," was how he had figured, and encouraged himself to try the gamble. Well, not rich; he did not expect that, but perhaps Tamkin might really show him how to earn what he needed in the market.

By now, however, he had forgotten his own reckoning and was aware only that he stood to lose his seven hundred dollars to the last cent.

Dr. Tamkin took the attitude that they were a pair of gentlemen experimenting with lard and grain futures. The money, a few hundred dollars, meant nothing much to either of them. He said to Wilhelm, "Watch. You'll get a big kick out of this and wonder why more people don't go into it. You think the Wall Street guys are so smart – geniuses? That's because most of us are psychologically afraid to think about the details. Tell me this. When you're on the road, and you don't understand what goes on under the hood of your car, you'll worry what'll happen if something goes wrong with the engine. Am I wrong?" No, he was right. "Well," said Dr. Tamkin with an expression of quiet triumph about his mouth, almost the suggestion of a jeer, "it's the same psychological principle, Wilhelm. They are rich because you don't understand what goes on. But it's no mystery, and by putting in a little money and applying certain principles of observation, you begin to grasp it. It can't be studied in the abstract. You have to take a specimen risk so that you feel the process, the money-flow, the whole complex. To know how it feels to be a seaweed you have to get in the water. In a very short time we'll take out a hundred per cent profit." Thus Wilhelm had to pretend at the outset that his interest in the market was theoretical.

"Well," said Tamkin when he met him now in the lobby, "what's the problem, what is this family situation? Tell me." He put himself forward as the keen mental scientist. Whenever this happened Wilhelm didn't know what to reply. No matter what he said or did it seemed that Dr. Tamkin saw through him.

"I had some words with my dad."

Dr. Tamkin saw nothing extraordinary in this. "It's the eternal same story," he said. "The elemental conflict of parent and child. It won't end, ever. Even with a fine old gentleman like your dad."

"I don't suppose it will. I've never been able to get anywhere with him. He objects to my feelings. He thinks they're sordid. I upset him and he gets mad at me. But maybe all old men are alike."

"Sons, too. Take it from one of them," said Dr. Tamkin. "All the same, you should be proud of such a fine old patriarch of a father. It should give you hope. The longer he lives, the longer your life-expectancy becomes."

Wilhelm answered, brooding, "I guess so. But I think I inherit more from my mother's side, and she died in her fifties."

"A problem arose between a young fellow I'm treating and his dad – I just had a consultation," said Dr. Tamkin, as he removed his dark gray hat.

"So early in the morning?" said Wilhelm with a glint of suspicion.

"Over the telephone, of course."

What a creature Tamkin was when he took off his hat! The indirect light showed the many intricacies of his bald skull, his gull's nose, his rather handsome eyebrows, his vain mustache, his deceiver's brown eyes. His figure was stocky, rigid, short in the neck, so that the large ball of the occiput touched his collar. His bones were peculiarly formed, as though twisted twice where the ordinary human bone was turned only once, and his shoulders rose in two pagoda-like points. At mid-body he was thick. He stood pigeon-toed, a sign perhaps that he was devious or had much to hide. The skin of his hands was aging, and his nails were moonless, concave, claw-like, and they appeared loose. His eyes were as brown as beaver fur and full of strange lines. The two large brown naked balls looked thoughtful – but were they? And honest – but this honest expression was not always of the same strength, nor was Wilhelm convinced that it was completely natural. He felt that Tamkin tried to make his eyes deliberately conspicuous, with studied art, and that he brought forth his hypnotic effect by exertion. Occasionally it failed or drooped, and when this happened the sense of his face passed downward to his heavy (possibly foolish?) red underlip.

Wilhelm wanted to talk about the lard-holdings, but Dr. Tamkin said, "This father and son case of mine would be instructive to you. It's a different psychological type completely than your dad. This man's father thinks that he isn't his son."

"Why not?"

"Because be has found out something about the mother carrying on with a friend of the family for twenty-five years."

"Well, what do you know!" said Wilhelm. His silent thought was, Pure bull. Nothing but bull!

"You must note how interesting the woman is, too. She has two husbands. Whose are the kids? The fellow detected her and she gave a signed confession that two of the four children were not the father's."

"It's amazing," said Wilhelm, but he said it in a rather distant way. He was always hearing such stories from Dr. Tamkin. If you were to believe Tamkin, most of the world was like this. Everybody in the hotel had a mental disorder, a secret history, a concealed disease. The wife of Rubin at the newsstand was supposed to be kept by Carl, the yelling, loud-mouthed gin-rummy player. The wife of Frank in the barbershop had disappeared with a G.I. while he was waiting for her to disembark at the French Lines pier. Everyone was like the faces on a playing card, upside down either way. Every public figure had a character neurosis. Maddest of all were the businessmen, the heartless, flaunting, boisterous business class who ruled this country with their hard manners and their bold lies and their absurd words that nobody could believe. They were crazier than anyone. They spread the plague. Wilhelm, thinking of the Rojax Corporation, was inclined to agree about the businessmen. And he supposed that Tamkin, for all his peculiarities, spoke a kind of truth and did a sort of good. It confirmed Wilhelm's suspicions to hear that there was a plague, and he said, "I couldn't agree with you more. They trade on anything, they steal everything, they're cynical right to the bones while holy as can be to the outside world."

"You have to realize," said Tamkin, speaking of his patient, or his client, "that the mother's confession isn't good. It's a confession of duress. I try to tell the young fellow he shouldn't worry about a phony confession. But what does it help him if I am rational with him?"

"No?" said Wilhelm, intensely nervous. "I think we ought to go over to the Market. It'll be opening pretty soon."

"Oh, come on," said Tamkin. "It isn't even nine o'clock, and there isn't much trading the first hour anyway. Things don't get hot in Chicago until half-past ten, and they're an hour behind us, don't forget. Anyway, I say lard will go up, and it will. Take my word. I've made a study of the guilt-aggression cycle which is behind it. I ought to know *something* about that. Straighten your collar."

"But meantime," said Wilhelm, "we have taken a licking this week. Are you sure your insight is at its best? Maybe when it isn't we should lay off and wait."

"Don't you realize," Dr. Tamkin told him, "you can't march in a straight line to the victory? You fluctuate toward it. From Euclid to Newton there was straight lines. The modern age analyzes the waves. On my own accounts, I took a licking in hides and coffee. But I have confidence. I'm sure I'll outguess them." He gave Wilhelm a narrow smile, friendly, calming, shrewd and wizard-like, patronizing, secret, potent. He saw his fears and smiled at them. "It's something," he remarked, "to see how the competition factor will manifest itself in different individuals."

"So? Let's go over."

"But I haven't had my breakfast yet."

"I've had mine."

"Come, have a cup of coffee."

"I wouldn't want to meet my dad." Looking through the glass doors Wilhelm saw that his father had left by the other exit. Wilhelm thought, 'He didn't want to run into me, either.' He said to Dr. Tamkin, "Okay, I'll sit with you, but let's hurry it up because I'd like to get to the Market while there's still a place to sit. Everybody and his uncle gets in ahead of you."

"I want to tell you about this boy and his dad. It's highly absorbing. The father was a nudist. Everybody went naked in the house. Maybe the woman found men *with* clothes attractive. Her husband didn't believe in cutting his hair, either. He practiced dentistry. In his office he wore riding pants and a pair of boots, and he wore a green eyeshade."

"Oh, come off it," said Wilhelm.

"This is a true case history."

Without warning, Wilhelm began to laugh. He himself had no premonition of his change of humor. His face became warm and pleasant, and he forgot his father, his anxieties; he panted bearlike, happily, through his teeth. "This sounds like a horse dentist. He wouldn't have to put on pants to treat a horse. Now what else are you going to tell me? Did the wife play the mandolin? Does the boy join the cavalry? Oh, Tamkin, you really are a killer-diller."

"Oh, you think I'm trying to amuse you," said Tamkin. "That's because you aren't familiar with my outlook. I deal in facts. Facts always are sensational. I'll say that a second time. Facts *always!* are sensational."

Wilhelm was reluctant to part with his good mood. The doctor had little sense of humor. He was looking at him earnestly.

"I'd bet you any amount of money," said Tamkin, "that the facts about you are sensational."

"Oh – ha, ha! You want them? You can sell them to a true confession magazine."

"People forget how sensational the things are that they do. They don't see it on themselves. It blends into the background of their daily life."

Wilhelm smiled. "Are you sure this boy tells you the truth?"

"Yes, because I've known the whole family for years."

"And you do psychological work with your own friends? I didn't know that was allowed."

"Well, I'm a radical in the profession. I have to do good wherever I can."

Wilhelm's face became ponderous again and pale. His whitened gold hair lay heavy on his head, and he clasped uneasy fingers on the table. Sensational, but oddly enough, dull, too. Now how do you figure that out? It blends with the background. Funny, but unfunny. True but false. Casual but laborious, Tamkin was. Wilhelm was most suspicious of him when he took his dryest tone.

"With me," said Dr. Tamkin, "I am at my most efficient when I don't need the fee. When I only love. Without financial reward. I remove myself from the social influence. Especially money. The spiritual compensation is what I look for. Bringing people into the here and now. The real universe. That's the present moment. The past is no good to us. The future is full of anxiety. Only the present is real – the here-and-now. Seize the day."

"Well," said Wilhelm, his earnestness returning, "I know you are a very unusual man. I like what you say about here-and-now. Are all the people who come to see you personal friends and patients, too? Like that tall handsome girl, the one who always wears those beautiful broomstick skirts and belts?"

"She was an epileptic, and a most bad and serious pathology, too. I'm curing her successfully. She hasn't had a seizure in six months, and she used to have one every week."

"And that young cameraman, the one who showed us those movies from the jungles of Brazil, isn't he related to her?"

"Her brother. He's under my care, too. He has some terrible tendencies, which are to be expected when you have an epileptic sibling. I came into their lives when they needed help desperately, and took hold of them. A certain man forty years older than she had her in his control and used to give her fits by suggestion whenever she tried to leave him. If you only knew one per cent of what goes on in the city of New York! You see, I understand what it is when the lonely person begins to feel like an animal. When the night comes and he feels like howling from his window like a wolf. I'm taking complete care of that young fellow and his sister. I have to steady him down or he'll go from Brazil to Australia the next day. The way I keep him in the here-and-now is by teaching him Greek."

This was a complete surprise! "What, do you know Greek?"

"A friend of mine taught me when I was in Cairo. I studied Aristotle with him to keep from being idle."

Wilhelm tried to take in these new claims and examine them. Howling from the window like a wolf when night comes – that was something really to think about. But the Greek! He realized that Tamkin was watching to see how he took it. More elements were continually being added. A few days ago Tamkin hinted that he had once been in the underworld, one of the Detroit Purple Gang. He was once head of a mental clinic in Toledo. He had worked with a Polish inventor on an unsinkable ship. He was a technical consultant in the field of television. In the life of a man of genius, all of these things might happen. But had they happened to Tamkin? Was he a genius?

He often said that he had attended some of the Egyptian royal family as a psychiatrist. "But everybody is alike, common or aristocrat," he told Wilhelm. "The aristocrat knows less about life."

An Egyptian princess whom he had treated in California, for horrible disorders he had described to Wilhelm, retained him to come back to the old country with her, and there he had had many of her friends and relatives under his care. They turned over a villa on the Nile to him. "For ethical reasons, I can't tell you many of the details about them," he said – but Wilhelm had already heard all these details, and strange and shocking they were, if true. *If* true – he could not be free from doubt. For instance, the general who had to wear ladies' silk stockings . . . and all the rest. Listening to the doctor when he was so strangely factual, he had to translate his words into his own language, and he could not translate fast enough or find terms of his own to fit what he heard.

"Those Egyptian big-shots invested in the market, too, for the heck of it. What did they need extra money for? By association, I almost became a millionaire myself, and if I had played it smart there's no telling what might have happened. I could have been the ambassador." The American – the Egyptian ambassador? "A friend of mine tipped me off on the cotton. I made a heavy purchase of it. I didn't have that kind of money, but everybody there knew me. It never entered their minds that a person of their social circle didn't have dough. The sale was made on the phone. Then, while the cotton shipment was at sea, the price tripled. When the stuff suddenly became so valuable, all hell broke loose on the world cotton market, they looked to see who was the owner of this big shipment. Me! They investigated my credit and found out I was a mere doctor, and they canceled. This was illegal. I sued them. But as I didn't have the money to fight them I sold the suit to a Wall Street lawyer for twenty thousand dollars. He fought it and was winning. They settled with him out of court for more than a million. But on the way back from Cairo, flying, there was a crash. All on board died. I have this guilt on my conscience, of being the murderer of that lawyer. Although he was a crook."

Wilhelm thought, 'I must be a real jerk to sit and listen to such impossible stories. I guess I am a sucker for people who talk about the deeper things of life, even the way he does.'

"We scientific men speak of irrational guilt, Wilhelm," said Dr. Tamkin, as if Wilhelm were a pupil in his class. "But in such a situation, because of the money, I wished him harm. I realize it. This isn't the time to describe all the details, but the money made me guilty. *M*oney and *M*urder both begin with *M*. *M*achinery. *M*ischief."

Wilhelm, his mind thinking for him at random, said, "What about *M*ercy? *M*ilk-of-human-kindness ?"

"One fact should be clear to you by now. Money-making is aggression. That's the whole thing. The functionalistic explanation is the only one. People come to the market to kill. They say, 'I'm going to make a killing.' It's not accidental. Only they haven't got the genuine courage to kill, and they erect a symbol of it. The money. They make a killing by a fantasy. Now, counting and numbering is always a sadistic activity. Like hitting. In the Bible, the Jews wouldn't allow you to count them. They knew it was sadistic."

"I don't understand what you mean," said Wilhelm. A strange uneasiness tore at him. The day was growing too warm and his head felt dim. "What makes them want to kill?"

"By and by, you'll get the drift," Dr. Tamkin assured him. His amazing eyes had some of the rich dryness of a brown fur. Innumerable crystalline hairs or spicules of light glittered dryly in their bold surfaces. "You can't understand without first spending years on the study of the ultimates of human and animal behavior, the deep chemical, organismic and spiritual secrets of life. I am a psychological poet."

"If you're this kind of poet," said Wilhelm, whose fingers in his pocket were feeling in the little envelopes for the Phenaphen capsules, "what are you doing in the market?"

"That's a good question. Maybe I am better at speculation because I don't care. Basically, I don't wish hard enough for money, and therefore I come with a cool head to it."

Wilhelm thought, Oh, sure! That's an answer, is it? I bet that if I took a strong attitude, he'd back down on everything. He'd grovel in front of me. – The way he looks at me on the sly, to see if I'm being taken in. He swallowed his Phenaphen pill with a long gulp of water. The rims of his eyes grew red as it went down. And then he felt calmer.

"Let me see if I can give you an answer that will satisfy you," said Dr. Tamkin. His flapjacks were set before him. He spread the butter on them, poured on brown maple syrup, quartered them and began to eat with hard, active muscular jaws which sometimes gave a creak at the hinges. He pressed the handle of his knife against his chest and said, "In here, the human bosom – mine, yours, everybody's – there isn't just one soul. There's a lot of souls. But there are two main ones, the real soul and a pretender soul. Now! Every man realizes that he has to love something or somebody. He feels that he must go outward. 'If thou canst not love, what art thou?' Are you with me?"

"Yes, doc, I think so," said Wilhelm listening – a little skeptically but nonetheless hard.

" 'What art thou?' Nothing. That's the answer, Nothing. In the heart of hearts – Nothing! So of course, you can't stand that and want to be Something, and you try. But instead of being this Something, the man puts it over on everybody instead. You can't be that strict to yourself. You love a *little*. Like, you have a dog" (Scissors!) "or give some money to a charity drive. Now that isn't love, is it? What is it? Egotism, pure and simple. It's a way to love the pretender soul. Vanity. Only vanity, is what it is. And social control. The interest of the pretender-soul is the same as the interest of the social life, the society mechanism. This is the main tragedy of human life. Oh, it is terrible! Terrible! You are not free. Your own betrayer is inside of you and sells you out. You have to obey him like a slave. He makes you work like a horse. And for what? For who?"

"Yes, for what?" The doctor's words caught Wilhelm's heart. "I couldn't agree more," he said. "When do we get free?"

"The purpose is to keep the whole thing going. The true soul is the one that pays the price. It suffers and gets sick, and it realizes that the pretender can't be loved. Because the pretender is a lie. The true soul loves the truth. And when the true soul feels like this, it wants to kill the pretender. The love has turned into hate. Then you become dangerous. A killer. You have to kill the deceiver."

"Does this happen to everybody?"

The doctor answered simply, "Yes, to everybody. Of course, for simplification purposes, I have spoken of the soul; it isn't the scientific term, but it helps you to understand it. Whenever the slayer slays, he wants to slay the soul in him which has gypped and deceived him. Who is his enemy? Him. And his lover? Also. Therefore, all suicide is murder, and all murder is suicide. It's the one and identical phenomenon. Biologically, the pretender soul takes away the energy of the true soul and makes it feeble, like a parasite. It happens unconsciously, unawaringly, in the depths of the organism. Ever take up parasitology?"

"No, it's my dad who's the doctor."

"You should read a book about it."

Wilhelm said, "But this means that the world is full of murderers. So it's not the world. It's a kind of hell."

"Sure," the doctor said. "At least a kind of purgatory. You walk on the bodies. They are all around. I can see them cry *de profundis* and wring their hands. I hear them, poor human things. I can't help hearing. And my eyes are open to it. This is the human tragedy-comedy."

Wilhelm tried to capture his vision. And again the doctor looked untrustworthy to him, and he doubted him. "Well," he said, "there are also kind, ordinary, helpful people. They're . . . out in the country. All over. What kind of morbid stuff do you read, anyway?" The doctor's room was full of books.

"I read the best literature, science and philosophy," Dr. Tamkin said proudly. Wilhelm had observed that in his room even the TV aerial was set upon a pile of volumes. "Korzybski, Aristotle, Freud, W. H. Sheldon, and all the great poets. You answer me like a layman. You haven't applied your mind strictly to this."

"Very interesting," said Wilhelm. He was aware that he hadn't applied his mind strictly to anything. "You don't have to think I'm a dummy, though. I have ideas, too." A glance at the clock told him that the market would soon open. They could spare a few minutes yet. There were still more things he wanted to hear from Tamkin. He realized that Tamkin spoke faultily, but then scientific men were not always strictly literate. It was the description of the two souls that had awed him. In Tommy he saw the pretender. And even Wilky might not be himself. Might the name of his true soul be the one by which his old grandfather had called him – Velvel? The name of a soul, however, must be only that – soul. What did it look like? Does my soul look like me? Is there a soul that looks like Dad? Like Tamkin? Where does the true soul gets its strength? Why does it have to love truth? Wilhelm was tormented, but tried to be oblivious to his torment. Secretly, he prayed the doctor would give him some useful advice and transform his life. "Yes, I understand you," he said. "It isn't lost on me."

"I never said you weren't intelligent, but only you just haven't made a study of it all. As a matter of fact you're a profound personality with very profound creative capacities but also disturbances. I've been concerned with you, and for some time I've been treating you."

"Without my knowing it? I haven't felt you doing anything. What do you mean? I don't think I like being treated without my knowledge. I'm of two minds . . . What's the matter, don't you think I'm normal?" And he really was divided in mind. That the doctor cared about him pleased him. This was what he craved, that someone should care about him, wish him well. Kindness, mercy, he wanted. But – and here he retracted his heavy shoulders in his peculiar way, drawing his hands up into his sleeves; his feet moved uneasily under the table – but he was worried, too, and even somewhat indignant. For what right had Tamkin to meddle without being asked? What kind of privileged life did this man lead? He took other people's money and speculated with it. Everybody came under his care. No one could have secrets from him.

The doctor looked at him with his deadly, brown, heavy impenetrable eyes, his naked shining head, his red hanging underlip, and said, "You have lots of guilt in you."

Wilhelm helplessly admitted, as he felt the heat rise to his wide face, "Yes, I think so too. But personally," he added, "I don't feel like a murderer. I always try to lay off. It's the others who get me. You know – make me feel oppressed. And if you don't mind, and it's all the same to you, I would rather know it when you start to treat me. And now, Tamkin, for Christ's sake, they're putting out the lunch menus already. Will you sign the check, and let's go!"

Tamkin did as he asked, and they rose. They were passing the bookkeeper's desk when he took out a substantial bundle of onion-skin papers and said, "These are receipts of the transactions. Duplicates. You'd better keep them as the account is in your name and you'll need them for income taxes. And here is a copy of a poem I wrote yesterday."

"I have to leave something at the desk for my father," Wilhelm said, and he put his hotel bill in an envelope with a note. *Dear Dad, Please carry me this month, Yours, W.* He watched the clerk, with his sullen pug's profile and stiff-necked look, push the envelope into his father's box.

"May I ask you really why you and your dad had words?" said Dr. Tamkin, who had hung back, waiting.

"It was about my future," said Wilhelm. He hurried down the stairs with swift steps, like a tower in motion, his hands in his trousers pockets. He was ashamed to discuss the matter. "He says there's a reason why I can't go back to my old territory, and there is. I told everybody I was going to he an officer of the corporation. And I was supposed to. It was promised. But then they welshed because of the son-in-law. I bragged and made myself look big."

"If you were humble enough, you could go back. But it doesn't make much difference. We'll make you a good living on the market."

They came into the sunshine of upper Broadway, not clear but throbbing through the dust and fumes, a false air of gas visible at eye-level as it spurted from the bursting buses. From old habit, Wilhelm turned up the collar of his jacket.

"Just a technical question," Wilhelm said. "What happens if your losses are bigger than your deposit?"

"Don't worry. They have ultra-modern electronic bookkeeping machinery, and it won't let you get in debt. It puts you out automatically. But I want you to read this poem. You haven't read it yet."

Light as a locust, a helicopter bringing mail from Newark Airport to La Guardia sprang over the city in a long leap.

The paper Wilhelm unfolded had ruled borders in red ink. He read:

MECHANISM VS FUNCTIONALISM
ISM VS HISM

If thee thyself couldst only see
Thy greatness that is and yet to be,
Thou would feel joy-beauty-what ecstasy
They are at thy feet, earth-moon-sea, the trinity.

Why forth then dost thou tarry
And partake thee only of the crust
And skim the earth's surface narry
When all creations art thy just?

Seek ye then that which art not there
In thine own glory let thyself rest.
Witness. Thy power is not bare.
Thou art King. Thou art at thy best.

Look then right before thee.
Open thine eyes and see.
At the foot of Mt. Serenity
Is thy cradle to eternity.

Utterly confused, Wilhelm said to himself explosively, What kind of mishmash, claptrap is this! What does he want from me? Damn him to hell, he might as well hit me on the head, and lay me out, kill me. What does he give me this for? What's the purpose? Is it a deliberate test? Does he want to mix me up? He's already got me mixed up completely. I was never good at riddles. Kiss those seven hundred bucks good-bye, and call it one more mistake in a long line of mistakes – Oh, Mama, what a line! He stood near the shining window of a fruit store, clutching Tamkin's paper, rather dazed, as though a charge of photographer's flash powder had gone up in his eyes. But he's waiting for my reaction. I have to say something to him about his poem. It really is no joke. What will I tell him? Who is this King? The poem is written to someone. But who? I can't even bring myself to talk. I feel too choked and strangled. With all the books he reads, how come the guy is so illiterate? And why do people just naturally assume that you'll know what they're talking about? No. I don't know, and nobody knows. The planets don't, the stars don't, infinite space doesn't. It doesn't square with Planck's Constant or anything else. So what's the good of it? Where's the need of it? What does he mean here by Mount Serenity? Could it be a figure of speech for Mount Everest? As he says people are all committing suicide, maybe those guys who climbed Everest were only trying to kill themselves, and if we want peace we should stay at the foot of the mountain. In the here-and-now. But it's also here-and-now on the slope, and on the top, where they climbed to seize the day. *Surface narry* is something he can't mean, I don't believe. I'm about to start foaming at the mouth. *Thy cradle . . . Who* is resting in his cradle – in his glory? My thoughts are at an end. I feel the wall. No more. So f**k it all! The money and everything. Take it away! When I have the money, they eat me alive, like those piranha fish in the movie about the Brazilian jungle. It was hideous when they ate up that Brahman bull in the river. He turned pale. Just like clay and in five minutes nothing was left except the skeleton still in one piece, floating away. When I haven't got it any more at least they'll let me alone. "Well, what do you think of this?" said Dr. Tamkin. He gave a special sort of wise smile, as though Wilhelm must now see what kind of man he was dealing with.

"Nice. Very nice. Have you been writing long?"

"I've been developing this line of thought for years and years. You follow it all the way?"

"I'm trying to figure out who this Thou is."

"Thou? Thou is you."

"Me! Why? This applies to me?"

"Why shouldn't it apply to you? You were in my mind when I composed it. Of course, the hero of the poem is sick humanity. If it would open its eyes it would be great."

"Yes, but how do I get into this?"

"The main idea of the poem is *con*struct or *de*struct. There is no ground in between. Mechanism is *de*struct. Money of course is *de*struct. When the last grave is dug, the gravedigger will have to he paid. If you could have confidence in nature you would not have to fear. It would keep you up. Creative is nature. Rapid. Lavish. Inspirational. It shapes leaves. It rolls the waters of the earth. Man is the chief of this. All creations are his just inheritance. You don't know what you've got within you. A person either creates or he destroys. There is no neutrality. . . ."

"I realized you were no beginner," said Wilhelm with great propriety. "I have only one criticism to make. I think why-forth is wrong. You should write *Wherefore then dost thou.*" And he reflected, So? I took a gamble. It'll have to be a miracle though to save me. My money will be gone, then it won't he able to destruct me. He can't just take and lose it, though. He's in it, too. I think he's in a bad way himself. He must be. I'm sure because, come to think of it, he sweated blood when he signed that check. But what have I let myself in for?

V

Patiently, in the window of the fruitstore, a man with a scoop spread crushed ice between his rows of vegetables. There were also Persian melons, lilacs, tulips with radiant black at the middle. The many street noises came back after a little while from the caves of the sky. Crossing the tide of Broadway traffic, Wilhelm was saying to himself, "The reason Tamkin lectures me is that somebody has lectured him, and the reason for the poem is that he wants to give me good advice. Everybody seems to know something. Even fellows like Tamkin. Many people know what to do, but how many can do it?"

He believed that he must, that he could and would recover the good things, the happy things, the easy tranquil things of life. He had made mistakes, but he could overlook these. He had been a fool, but that could be forgiven. The time wasted . . . must be relinquished. What else could one do about it? Things were too complex, but they might be reduced to simplicity again. Recovery was possible. First he had to get out of the city. No, first he had to pull out his money. . . .

From the carnival of the street – pushcarts, accordion and fiddle, shoeshine, begging, the dust going round like a woman on stilts – they entered the narrow crowded theater of the brokerage office. From front to back it was filled with the Broadway crowd. But how was lard doing this morning? From the rear of the hall Wilhelm tried to read the tiny figures. The German manager was looking through his binoculars.

Tamkin placed himself on Wilhelm's left and covered his conspicuous bald head. "The guy'll ask me about the margin," he muttered. They passed, however, unobserved.

"Look, the lard has held its place," he said.

Tamkin's eyes must be very sharp to read the figures over so many heads and at this distance – another respect in which he was unusual.

The room was always crowded. Everyone talked. Only at the front could you hear the flutter of the wheels within the hoard. Teletyped news items crossed the illuminated screen above.

"Lard. Now what about rye?" said Tamkin, rising on his toes. Here he was a different man, active and impatient. He parted people who stood in his way. His face turned resolute, and on either side of his mouth odd bulges formed under his mustache. Already he was pointing out to Wilhelm the appearance of a new pattern on the board.

"There's something up today," he said.

"Then why'd you take so long with breakfast?" said Wilhelm.

There were no reserved seats in the room, only customary ones. Tamkin always sat in the second row, on the commodities side of the aisle. Some of his acquaintances kept their hats on the chairs for him.

"Thanks. Thanks," said Tamkin, and he told Wilhelm, "I fixed it up yesterday."

"That was a smart thought," said Wilhelm. They sat down.

With folded hands, by the wall, sat an old Chinese businessman in a seersucker coat. Smooth and fat, he wore a white Vandyke. One day Wilhelm had seen him on Riverside Drive pushing two little girls along in a baby carriage – his grandchildren. Then there were two women in their fifties, supposed to be sisters, shrewd and able money-makers, according to Tamkin. They had never a word to say to Wilhelm. But they would chat with Tamkin. Tamkin talked to everyone.

Wilhelm sat between Mr. Rowland, who was elderly, and Mr. Rappaport, who was very old. Yesterday Rowland had told him that in the year 1908, when he was a junior at Harvard, his mother had given him twenty shares of steel for his birthday, and then he had started to read the financial news and had never practiced law but instead followed the market for the rest of his life. Now he speculated only in soybeans, of which he had made a specialty. By his conservative method, said Tamkin, he cleared two hundred a week. Small potatoes, but then he was a bachelor, retired, and didn't need money.

"Without dependents," said Tamkin. "He doesn't have the problems that you and I do."

Did Tamkin have dependents? He had everything that it was possible for a man to have – science, Greek, chemistry, poetry, and now dependents, too. That beautiful girl with epilepsy, perhaps. He often said that she was a pure, marvelous, spiritual child who had no knowledge of the world. He protected her, and, if he was not lying, adored her. And if you encouraged Tamkin by believing him, or even if you refrained from questioning him, his hints became more daring. Sometimes he said that he paid for her music lessons. Sometimes he seemed to have footed the bill for the brother's expedition to Brazil. And he spoke of paying for the support of the orphaned child of a dead sweetheart. These hints, made dully as asides, grew by repetition into sensational claims.

"For myself, I don't need much," said Tamkin. "But a man can't live for himself and I need the money for certain important things. What do you figure you have to have, to get by?"

"Not less than fifteen grand, after taxes. That's for my wife and the two boys."

"Isn't there anybody else?" said Tamkin with a shrewdness almost cruel. But his look grew more sympathetic as Wilhelm stumbled, not willing to recall another grief.

"Well . . . there was. But it wasn't a money matter."

"I should hope!" said Tamkin "If love is love, it's free. Fifteen grand, though, isn't too much for a man of your intelligence to ask out of life. Fools, hard-hearted criminals and murderers have millions to squander. They burn up the world – oil, coal, wood, metal, and soil and even the air and the sky. They consume, and they give back no benefit. A man like you, humble for life, who wants to feel and live, has trouble – not wanting," said Tamkin in his parenthetical fashion, "to exchange an ounce of soul for a pound of social power – he'll never make it without help in a world like this. But don't you worry. . . ."

Wilhelm grasped at this.

"Just you never mind. We'll go easily beyond your figure."

Dr. Tamkin gave Wilhelm comfort. He often asserted that he had made as much as a thousand a week in commodities. Wilhelm had examined the receipts, but until this moment it had never occurred to him that there must be debit-slips too; he had been shown only the credits.

"But fifteen grand is not an ambitious figure," Tamkin was telling him. "For that you don't have to wear yourself out on the road, dealing with narrow-minded people. A lot of them don't like Jews, either, I suppose?"

"I can't afford to notice. I'm lucky when I have my occupation. Tamkin, do you mean there's a hope for our money?"

"Oh, did I forget to mention what I did before closing yesterday? You see, I closed out one of the lard contracts and bought a hedge of December rye. The rye is up three points already and takes some of the sting out. But lard will go up, too."

"Where? God, yes, you're right!" said Wilhelm, eager, and got to his feet to look. New hope freshened his heart. "Why didn't you tell me before?"

And Tamkin, smiling like a benevolent magician, said, "You must learn to have trust. The slump in lard can't last. And just take a look at eggs. Didn't I predict they couldn't go any lower? They're rising and rising. If we had taken eggs we'd be far ahead."

"Then why didn't we take them?"

"We were just about to. I had a buying order in at .24, but the tide turned at .26¼ and we barely missed. Never mind. Lard will go back to last year's levels."

Maybe. But when? Wilhelm could not allow his hopes to grow strong. However, for a little while he could breathe more easily. Late morning trading was increasing. The shining numbers whirred on the board and sounded like a huge cage of artificial birds. Lard fluctuated between two points, but rye slowly climbed.

He closed his greatly earnest eyes and nodded his Buddha's head, too large to suffer such uncertainties. For several moments of peace he was removed to his small yard in Roxbury.

He breathed in the sugar of the pure morning.

He heard the long phrases of the birds.

No enemy wanted his life.

Wilhelm thought, I will get out of here. I don't belong in New York any more; and he sighed like a sleeper.

Tamkin said, "Excuse me," and left his seat. He could not sit still in the room but passed back and forth between the stocks and commodities sections. He knew dozens of people and was continually engaging in discussions. Was he giving advice, gathering information, or giving it, or practicing – whatever mysterious profession he practiced? Hypnotism? Perhaps he could put people in a trance while he talked to them. What a rare, peculiar bird he was, with those pointed shoulders, that bare head, his loose nails, almost claws, and those brown, soft, deadly, heavy eyes.

He spoke of things that mattered, and as very few people did this he could take you by surprise, excite you, move you. Maybe he wished to do good, maybe to give himself a lift to a higher level, maybe believe his own prophecies, maybe touch his own heart. Who could tell? He had picked up a lot of strange ideas; Wilhelm could only suspect, he could not say with certainty, that Tamkin hadn't made them his own.

Now Tamkin and he were equal partners, but Tamkin had put up only three hundred dollars. Suppose he did this not only once but five times; then an investment of fifteen hundred dollars gave him five thousand to speculate with. If he had power of attorney in every case, he could shift the money from one account to another. No, the German probably kept an eye on him. Nevertheless it was possible. Calculations like this made Wilhelm feel ill. Obviously Tamkin was a plunger. But how did he get by? He must be in his fifties. How did he support himself? Five years in Egypt; Hollywood before that. Michigan. Ohio. Chicago. A man of fifty has supported himself for at least thirty years. You could be sure that Tamkin had never worked in a factory or in an office. How did he make it? His taste in clothes was horrible, but he didn't buy cheap things. He wore corduroy or velvet shirts from Clyde's, painted neckties, striped socks. There was a slightly acid or pasty smell about his person; for a doctor, he didn't bathe much. Also, Dr. Tamkin had a good room at the Gloriana and had had it for about a year. But so was Wilhelm himself a guest, with an unpaid bill at present in his father's box. Did the beautiful girl with the skirts and belts pay him? Was he defrauding his so-called patients? So many questions impossible to answer could not be asked about an honest man. Nor perhaps about a sane man. Was Tamkin a lunatic then? That sick Mr. Perls at breakfast had said that there was no easy way to tell the sane from the mad, and he was right about that in any big city and especially in New York – the end of the world, with its complexity and machinery, bricks and tubes, wires and stones, holes and heights. And was everybody crazy here? What sort of people did you see? Every other man spoke a language entirely his own, which he had figured out by private thinking; he had his own ideas and peculiar ways. If you wanted to talk about a glass of water, you had to start back with God creating the heavens and earth; the Apple; Abraham, Moses and Jesus; Rome; the middle ages; gunpowder; the Revolution; back to Newton; up to Einstein; then War and Lenin and Hitler. After showing this and getting it all straight again you could proceed to talk about a glass of water. "I'm fainting, please get me a little water." You were lucky even then to make yourself understood. And this happened over and over and over with everyone you met. You had to translate and translate, explain and explain, back and forth, and it was the punishment of Hell itself not to understand or be understood, not to know the crazy from the sane, the wise from the fools, the young from the old or the sick from the well. The fathers were no fathers and the sons no sons. You had to talk with yourself in the daytime and reason with yourself at night. Who else was there to talk to in a city like New York?

A queer look came over Wilhelm's face with its eyes turned up and his silent mouth with its high upper lip. He went several degrees further when you are like this, dreaming that everybody is outcast, you realize that this must be one of the small matters. There is a larger body, and from this you cannot be separated. The glass of water fades out. You do not go from simple a and simple b to the great x and y, nor does it matter whether you agree about the glass but far beneath such items, what Tamkin would call the real soul says plain and understandable things to everyone. There sons and fathers are themselves, and a glass of water is only an ornament; it makes a hoop of brightness on the cloth; it is an angel's mouth. There truth for everybody may be found, and confusion is only . . . only temporary, thought Wilhelm.

The idea of this larger body had been planted in him a few days ago beneath Times Square, when he had gone downtown to pick up tickets for the baseball game on Saturday (a double-header at the Polo Grounds). He was going through an underground corridor, a place he had always hated and hated more than ever now. On the walls between the advertisements were words in chalk: *Sin No More*, and *Do Not Eat the Pig*, he had particularly noticed. And in the dark tunnel, in the haste, heat and darkness which disfigure and make freaks and fragments of nose and eyes and teeth, all of a sudden, unsought, a general love for all these imperfect and lurid-looking people burst out in Wilhelm's breast. He loved them. One and all, he passionately loved them. They were his brothers and his sisters. He was imperfect and disfigured himself, but what difference did that make if he was united with them by this blaze of love? And as he walked he began to say, "Oh my brothers – my brothers and my sisters," blessing them all as well as himself.

So what did it matter how many languages there were, or how hard it was to describe a glass of water? Or matter that a few minutes later he didn't feel like a brother toward the man who sold him the tickets?

On that very same afternoon he didn't hold so high an opinion of this same onrush of loving kindness. What did it come to? As they had the capacity and must use it once in a while, people were bound to have such involuntary feelings. It was only another one of those subway things. Like having a hard-on at random. But today, his day of reckoning, he consulted his memory again and thought, 'I must go back to that. That's the right clue and may do me the most good. Something very big. Truth-like.'

The old fellow on the right, Mr. Rappaport, was nearly blind and kept asking Wilhelm, "What's the new figure on November wheat? Give me July soybeans too." When you told him he didn't say thank you. He said okay, instead, or check, and turned away until he needed you again. He was very old, older even than Dr. Adler, and if you believed Tamkim he had once been the Rockefeller of the chicken business and had retired with a large fortune.

Wilhelm had a queer feeling about the chicken industry, that it was sinister. On the road, he frequently passed chicken farms. Those big, rambling, wooden buildings out in the neglected fields; they were like prisons. The lights burned all night in them to cheat the poor hens into laying. Then the slaughter. Pile all the coops of the slaughtered on end, and in one week they'd go higher than Mount Everest or Mount Serenity. The blood filling the Gulf of Mexico. The chicken shit, acid, burning the earth.

How old – old this Mr. Rappaport was! Purple stains were buried in the flesh of his nose and the cartilage of his ear was twisted like a cabbage heart. Beyond remedy by glasses, his eyes were smoky and faded.

"Read me that soybean figure now, boy," he said, and Wilhelm did. He thought perhaps the old man might give him a tip, or some useful advice or information about Tamkin. But no. He only wrote memoranda on a pad, and put the pad in his pocket. He let no one see what he had written. And Wilhelm thought this was the way a man who had grown rich by the murder of millions of animals, little chickens, would act. If there was a life to come he might have to answer for the killing of all those chickens. What if they all were waiting? But if there was a life to come, everybody would have to answer. But if there was a life to come, the chickens themselves would be all right.

Well! What stupid ideas he was having this morning. Phooey!

Finally old Rappaport did address a few remarks to Wilhelm. He asked him whether he had reserved his seat in the synagogue for Yom Kippur.

"No," said Wilhelm.

"Well, you better hurry up if you expect to say *Yiskor* for your parents. I never miss."

And Wilhelm thought, Yes, I suppose I should say a prayer for Mother once in a while. His mother had belonged to the Reform congregation. His father had no religion. At the cemetery Wilhelm had paid a man to say a prayer for her. He was among the tombs and he wanted to be tipped for the *El molai rachamin*. "Thou God of Mercy," he thought that meant. *B'gan Aden* – "in Paradise." Singing, they drew it out, *B'gan Ay-den*. The broken bench beside the grave made him wish to do something. Wilhelm often prayed in his own manner. He did not go to the synagogue but he would occasionally perform certain devotions, according to his feelings. Now he reflected, In Dad's eyes I am the wrong kind of Jew. He doesn't like the way I act. Only he is the right kind of Jew. Whatever you are, it always turns out to be the wrong kind.

Mr. Rappaport grumbled and whiffed at his long cigar, and the board, like a swarm of electrical bees, whirred.

"Since you were in the chicken business, I thought you'd speculate in eggs, Mr. Rappaport." Wilhelm, with his warm, panting laugh, sought to charm the old man.

"Oh. Yeah. Loyalty, hey?" said old Rappaport. "I should stick to them. I spent a lot of time amongst chickens. I got to be an expert chicken sexer. When the chick hatches you have to tell the boys from the girls. It's not easy. You need long, long experience. What do you think, it's a joke? A whole industry depends on it. Yes, now and then I buy a contract eggs. What have you got today?"

Wilhelm said anxiously, "Lard. Rye."

"Buy? Sell?"

"Bought."

"Uh," said the old man. Wilhelm could not determine what he meant by this. But of course you couldn't expect him to make himself any clearer. It was not in the code to give information to anyone. Sick with desire, Wilhelm waited for Mr. Rappaport to make an exception in his case. Just this once! Because it was critical. Silently, by a sort of telepathic concentration he begged the old man to speak the single word that would save him, give him the merest sign. "Oh, please – please help," he nearly said. If Rappaport would close one eye, or lay his head to one side, or raise his finger and point to a column in the paper or to a figure on his pad. A hint! A hint!

A long perfect ash formed on the end of the cigar, the white ghost of the leaf with all its veins and its fainter pungency. It was ignored, in its beauty, by the old man. For it was beautiful. Wilhelm he ignored as well.

Then Tamkin said to him, "Wilhelm, look at the jump our rye just took." December rye climbed three points as they tensely watched; the tumblers raced and the machine's lights buzzed.

"A point and a half more, and we can cover the lard losses," said Tamkin. He showed him his calculations on the margin of the *Times*.

"I think you should put in the selling order now. Let's get out with a small loss."

"Get out now? Nothing doing."

"Why not? Why should we wait?"

"Because," said Tamkin with a smiling, almost openly scoffing look, "you've got to keep your nerve when the market starts to go places. Now's when you can make something."

"I'd get out while the getting's good."

"No, you shouldn't lose your head like this. It's obvious to me what the mechanism is, back in the Chicago market. There's a short supply of December rye. Look, it's just gone up another quarter. We should ride it."

"I'm losing my taste for the gamble," said Wilhelm. "You can't feel safe when it goes up so fast. It's liable to come down just as quick."

Dryly, as though he were dealing with a child, Tamkin told him in a tone of tiring patience, "Now listen, Tommy. I have it diagnosed right. If you wish I should sell I can give the sell order. But this is the difference between healthiness and pathology. One is objective, doesn't change his mind every minute, enjoys the risk element. But that's not the neurotic character. The neurotic character . . ."

"Damn it, Tamkin!" said Wilhelm roughly. "Cut that out. I don't like it. Leave my character out of consideration. Don't pull any more of that stuff on me. I tell you I don't like it."

Tamkin therefore went no further; he backed down. "I meant," he said, softer, "that as a salesman you are basically an artist-type. The seller is in the visionary sphere of the business function. And then you're an actor, too."

"No matter what type I am –" An angry and yet weak sweetness rose into Wilhelm's throat. He coughed as though he had the flu. It was twenty years since he had appeared on the screen as an extra. He blew the bagpipes in a film called *Annie Laurie*. Annie had come to warn the young Laird; he would not believe her and called the bag-pipers to drown her out. He made fun of her while she wrung her hands. Wilhelm, in a kilt, barelegged, blew and blew and blew and not a sound came out. Of course all the music was recorded. He came down with the flu after that and still suffered sometimes from chest weakness.

"Something stuck in your throat?" said Tamkin. "I think maybe you are too disturbed to think clearly. You should try some of my 'here and now' mental exercises. It stops you from thinking so much about the future and the past and cuts down confusion."

"Yes, yes, yes, yes," said Wilhelm, his eyes fixed to December rye.

"Nature only knows one thing, and that's the present. Present, present, eternal present, like a big, huge, giant wave – colossal, bright and beautiful, full of life and death, climbing into the sky, standing in the seas. You must go along with the actual, the Here and Now, the glory . . ."

Chest weakness, Wilhelm's recollection went on. Margaret nursed him. They had two rooms of furniture which were afterwards foreclosed. She sat on the bed and read to him. He made her read for days, and she read stories, poetry, everything in the house. He felt dizzy, stifled when he tried to smoke. They had him wear a flannel vest.

> *Come then, Sorrow!*
> *Sweetest Sorrow!*
> *Like an own babe I nurse thee on my breast!*

Why did he remember that? Why?

"You have to pick out something that's in the actual, immediate present moment," said Tamkin. "And say to yourself – here and now, here and now, here and now. 'Where am I?' 'Here.' 'When is it?' 'Now.' Take an object or a person.

Anybody. 'Here and now I see a person. 'Here and now I see a man.' 'Here and now I see a man sitting on a chair.' Take me, for instance. Don't let your mind wander. 'Here and now I see a man in a brown suit. Here and now I see a corduroy shirt.' You have to narrow it down, one item at a time and not let your imagination shoot ahead. Be in the present. Grasp the now, the moment, the instant."

'Is he trying to hypnotize or con me?' Wilhelm wondered. 'To take my mind off selling? But even if I'm back at seven hundred bucks, then where am I?'

As if in prayer, his lids coming down with raised veins, frayed out, on his significant eyes, Tamkin said, "Here and now I see a button. Here and now I see the thread that sews the button. Here and now I see the green thread." Inch by inch he contemplated himself in order to show Wilhelm how calm it would make him. But Wilhelm was hearing Margaret's voice as she read, somewhat unwillingly,

Come then, Sorrow . . .

I thought to leave thee
And deceive thee,
But now of all the world I love thee best.

Then Mr. Rappaport's old hand pressed his thigh and he said, "What's my wheat? Those damn guys are blocking the way. I can't see."

VI

Rye was still ahead when they went out to lunch, and lard was holding its own.

They ate in the cafeteria with the gilded front. There was the same art inside as outside. The food looked sumptuous. Whole fishes were framed like pictures with carrots, and the salads were like terraced landscapes or like Mexican pyramids; slices of lemon and onion and radishes were like sun and moon and stars; the cream pies were about a foot thick and the cakes swollen as if sleepers had baked them in their dreams.

"What'll you have?" said Tamkin.

"Not much. I ate a big breakfast. I'll find a table. Bring me some yogurt and crackers and a cup of tea. I don't want to spend much time over lunch."

Tamkin said, "You've got to eat."

Finding an empty place at this hour was not easy. The old people idled and gossiped over their coffee. The elderly ladies were rouged and mascaraed and hennaed and used blue hair rinse and eye shadow and wore costume jewelry, and many of them were proud and stared at you with expressions that did not belong to their age. Were there no longer any respectable old ladies who knitted and cooked and looked after their grandchildren? Wilhelm's grandmother had dressed him in a sailor suit and danced him on her knee, blew on the porridge for him and said, "Admiral, you must eat." But what was the use of remembering this so late in the day?

He managed to find a table and Dr. Tamkin came along with a tray piled with plates and cups. He had Yankee pot roast, purple cabbage, potatoes, a big slice of watermelon and two cups of coffee. Wilhelm could not even swallow his yogurt. His chest pained him still.

At once Tamkin involved him in a lengthy discussion. Did he do it to stall Wilhelm and prevent him from selling out the rye – or to recover the ground lost when he had made Wilhelm angry by hints about the neurotic character? Or did he have no purpose except to talk?

"I think you worry a lot too much about what your wife and your father will say. Do they matter so much?"

Wilhelm replied, "A person can become tired of looking himself over and trying to fix himself up. You can spend the entire second half of your life recovering from the mistakes of the first half."

"I believe your dad told me he had some money to leave you.

"He probably does have something."

"A lot?"

"Who can tell," said Wilhelm guardedly.

"You ought to think over what you'll do with it."

"I may be too feeble to do anything by the time I get it. If I get anything."

"A thing like this you ought to plan out carefully. Invest it properly." He began to unfold schemes whereby you bought bonds, and used the bonds as security to buy something else and thereby earned twelve per cent safely on your money. Wilhelm failed to follow the details. Tamkin said, "If he made you a gift now, you wouldn't have to pay the inheritance taxes."

Bitterly, Wilhelm told him, "My father's death blots out all other considerations from his mind. He forces me to think about it, too. Then he hates me because he succeeds. When I get desperate – of course I think about money. But I don't want anything to happen to him. I certainly don't want him to die." Tamkin's brown eyes glittered shrewdly at him. "You don't believe it. Maybe it's not psychological. But on my word of honor. A joke is a joke, but I don't want to joke about stuff like this. When he dies, I'll be robbed, like. I'll have no more father."

"You love your old man?"

Wilhelm grasped at this. "Of course, of course I love him. My father. My mother. . . ." As he said this there was a great pull at the very center of his soul. When a fish strikes the line, you feel the live force in your hand. A mysterious being beneath the water, driven by hunger, has taken the hook and rushes away and fights, writhing. Wilhelm never identified what struck within him. It did not reveal itself. It got away.

And Tamkin, the confuser of the imagination, began to tell, or to fabricate, the strange history of *his* father. "He was a great singer," he said. "He left us five kids because he fell in love with an opera soprano. I never held it against him, but admired the way he followed the life-principle. I wanted to do the same. Because of unhappiness, at a certain age the brain starts to die back" (true, true! thought Wilhelm). "Twenty years later I was doing experiments in Eastman Kodak, Rochester, and I found the old fellow. He had five more children." (False, false!) "He wept; he was ashamed. I had nothing against him. I naturally felt strange."

"My dad is something of a stranger to me, too," said Wilhelm, and he began to muse. Where is the familiar person he used to be? Or I used to be? Catherine – she won't even talk to me any more, my own sister. It may not be so much my trouble that Papa turns his back on as my confusion. It's too much. The ruins of life, and on top of that confusion, chaos and old night. Is it an easier farewell for Dad if we don't part friends? He should maybe do it angrily – "Blast you with my curse!" And why, Wilhelm further asked, should he or anybody else pity me; or why should I be pitied sooner than another fellow? It is my childish mind that thinks people are ready to give it just because you need it.

Then Wilhelm began to think about his own two sons and to wonder how he appeared to them, and what they would think of him. Right now he had an advantage through baseball. When he went to fetch them, to go to Ebbets Field, though, he was not himself. He put on a front but he felt as if he had swallowed a fistful of sand. The strange, familiar house, horribly awkward; the dog, Scissors, rolled over on his back and barked and whined. Wilhelm acted as if there were nothing irregular, but a weary heaviness came over him. On the way to Flatbush he would think up anecdotes about old Pigtown and Charlie Ebbets for the boys and reminiscences of the old stars, but it was very heavy going. They did not know how much he cared for them. No. It hurt him greatly and he blamed Margaret for turning them against him. She wanted to ruin him, while she wore the mask of kindness. Up in Roxbury, he had to go and explain to the priest, who was not sympathetic. They don't care about individuals, their rules came first. Olive said she would marry him outside the Church when he was divorced. But Margaret would not let go. Olive's father was a pretty decent old guy, an osteopath, and he understood what it was all about. Finally he said, "See here, I have to advise Olive. She is asking me. I am mostly a freethinker myself, but the girl has to live in this town." And by now Wilhelm and Olive had had a great many troubles and she was beginning to dread his days in Roxbury, she said. He trembled at offending this small, pretty, dark girl whom he adored. When she would get up late on Sunday morning she would wake him almost in tears at being late for Mass. He would try to help her hitch her garters and smooth out her slip and dress and even put on her hat with shaky hands; then he would rush her to church and drive in second gear in his forgetful way trying to apologize and calm her. She got out a block from church to avoid gossip. Even so she loved him, and she would have married him if he had obtained the divorce. But Margaret must have sensed this. Margaret would tell him he did not really want a divorce; he was afraid of it. He cried, "Take everything I've got, Margaret. Let me go to Reno. Don't you want to marry again?" No. She went out with other men, but took his money. She lived to punish him.

Dr. Tamkin told Wilhelm, "Your dad is jealous of you."

Wilhelm smiled, "Of *me*? That's rich."

"Sure. People are always jealous of a man who leaves his wife."

"Oh," said Wilhelm scornfully. "When it comes to wives he wouldn't have to envy me."

"Yes, and your wife envies you, too. She thinks, 'He's free and goes with young women.' Is she getting old?"

"Not exactly old," said Wilhelm, whom the mention of his wife made sad. Twenty years ago, in a neat blue wool suit, in a soft hat made of the same cloth – he could plainly see her. He stooped his yellow head and looked under the hat at her clear, simple face, her living eyes moving, her straight small nose, her jaw beautifully, painfully clear in its form. It was a cool day, but he smelled the odor of pines in the sun, in the granite canyon. Just south of Santa Barbara, this was.

"She's forty-some years old," he said.

"I was married to a lush," said Tamkin. "A painful alcoholic. I couldn't take her out to dinner because she'd say she was going to the ladies' toilet and disappear into the bar. I'd ask the bartenders they shouldn't serve her. But I loved her deeply. She was the most spiritual woman of my entire experience."

"Where is she now?"

"Drowned," said Tamkin. "At Provincetown, Cape Cod. It must have been a suicide. She was that way – suicidal. I tried everything in my power to cure her. Because," said Tamkin, "my real calling is to be a healer. I get wounded. I suffer from it. I would like to escape from the sicknesses of others, but I can't. I am only on loan to myself, so to speak. I belong to humanity."

Liar! Wilhelm inwardly called him. Nasty lies. He invented a woman and killed her off and then called himself a healer, and made himself so earnest he looked like a bad-natured sheep. He's a puffed-up little bogus and humbug with smelly feet. A doctor! A doctor would wash himself. He believes he's making a terrific impression, and he practically invites you to take off your hat when he talks about himself; and he thinks he has imagination, but he hasn't. Neither is he smart.

Then what am I doing with him here, and why did I give him the seven hundred dollars? thought Wilhelm.

Oh, this was a day of reckoning. It was a day, he thought, on which, willing or not, he would take a good close look at the truth. He breathed hard and his misshapen hat came low upon his congested dark blond face. A rude look. Tamkin was a charlatan, and furthermore he was desperate. And furthermore – Wilhelm had always known this about him. But he appeared to have worked it out at the back of his mind that Tamkin for thirty or forty years had gotten through many a tight place, that he would get through this crisis too and bring him, Wilhelm, to safety also. And Wilhelm realized that he was on Tamkin's back. It made him feel that he had virtually left the ground and was riding upon the other man. He was in the air. It was for Tamkin to take the steps.

The doctor, if he was a doctor, did not look anxious. But then his face did not have much variety. Talking always about spontaneous emotion and open receptors and free impulses he had about as much expressiveness as a pin-cushion. When his hypnotic spell failed, his big underlip made him look weak-minded. Fear stared from his eyes, sometimes, so humble as to make you sorry for him. Once or twice Wilhelm had seen that look. Like a dog, he thought. Perhaps he didn't look it now, but he was very nervous, Wilhelm knew; but he could not afford to recognize this too openly. The doctor needed a little room, a little time. He should not be pressed now. So Tamkin went on, telling his tales.

Wilhelm said to himself, I am on his back – his back. I gambled seven hundred bucks, so I must take this ride. I have to go along with him. It's too late. I can't get off.

"You know," Tamkin said, "that blind old man Rappaport – he's pretty close to totally blind – is one of the most interesting personalities around here. If you could only get him to tell his true story. It's fascinating. This is what he told me: You often hear about bigamists with a secret life. But this old man never hid anything from anybody. He's a regular patriarch. Now, I'll tell you what he did. He had two whole families, separate and apart, one in Williamsburg and the other in the Bronx. The two wives knew about each other. The wife in the Bronx was younger; she's close to seventy now. When he got sore at one wife he went to live with the other one. Meanwhile he ran his chicken business in New Jersey. By one wife he had four kids, and by the other six. They're all grown, but they never have met their half brothers and sisters and don't want to. The whole bunch of them are listed in the telephone book."

"I can't believe it," said Wilhelm.

"He told me this himself. And do you know what else? While he had his eyesight, he used to read a lot, but the only books he would read were by Theodore

Roosevelt. He had a set in each of the places where he lived, and he brought his kids up on those books."

"Please," said Wilhelm, "don't feed me any more of this stuff, will you? Kindly do not. . . ."

"In telling you this," said Tamkin with one of his hypnotic subtleties, "I do have a motive. I want you to see how some people free themselves from morbid guilt feelings and follow their instincts. Innately, the female knows how to cripple by sickening a man with guilt. It is a very special destruct, and she sends her curse to make a fellow impotent. As if she says, 'Unless I allow it, you will never more be a man.' But men like my old dad or Mr. Rappaport answer, 'Woman, what are thou to me?' You can't do that yet. You're a halfway case. You want to follow your instinct, but you're too worried still. For instance, about your kids . . ."

"Now look here," said Wilhelm stamping his feet. "One thing! Don't bring up my boys. Just lay off."

"I was only going to say that they are better off than with conflicts in the home."

"I'm deprived of my children." Wilhelm bit his lip. It was too late to turn away. The anguish struck him. "I pay and pay. I never see them. They grow up without me. She makes them like herself. She'll bring them up to be my enemies. Please let's not talk about this."

But Tamkin said, "Why do you let her make you suffer so? It defeats the original object in leaving her. Don't play her game. Now, Wilhelm, I'm trying to do you some good. I want to tell you, don't marry suffering. Some people do. They get married to it, and sleep and eat together, just as husband and wife. If they go with joy they think it's adultery."

When Wilhelm heard this he had, in spite of himself, to admit that there was a great deal in Tamkin's words. Yes, thought Wilhelm, suffering is the only kind of life they are sure they can have, and if they quit suffering they're afraid they'll have nothing. He knows it. This time the faker knows what he's talking about.

Looking at Tamkin he believed he saw all this confessed from his usually barren face. Yes, yes, he too. One hundred falsehoods, but at last one truth. Howling like a wolf from the city window. No one can bear it any more. Everyone is so full of it that at last everybody must proclaim it. It! It!

Then suddenly Wilhelm rose and said, "That's enough of this. Tamkin, let's go back to the Market."

"I haven't finished my melon."

"Never mind that. You've had enough to eat. I want to go back." Dr. Tamkin slid the two checks across the table. "Who paid yesterday? It's your turn, I think."

It was not until they were leaving the cafeteria that Wilhelm remembered definitely that he had paid yesterday, too. But it wasn't worth arguing about.

Tamkin kept repeating as they walked down the street that there were many who were dedicated to suffering. But he told Wilhelm, "I'm optimistic in your case, and I have seen a world of maladjustment. There's hope for you. You don't really want to destroy yourself. You're trying hard to keep your feelings open, Wilhelm. I can see it. Seven percent of this country is committing suicide by alcohol. Another three, maybe, narcotics. Another sixty just fading away into dust by boredom. Twenty more who have sold their souls to the Devil. Then there's a small percentage of those who want to live. That's the only significant thing in the whole world of today. Those are the only two classes of people there are. Some want to live, but the great majority don't." This fantastic Tamkin began to surpass himself. "They don't. Or else, why these wars? I'll tell you more, he said. "The love of the dying amounts to one thing; they want you to die with them. It's because they love you. Make no mistake."

True, true! thought Wilhelm, profoundly moved by these revelations. How does he know these things? How can he be such a jerk, and even perhaps an operator, swindler, and understand so well what gives? I believe what he says. It simplifies much . . . everything. People are dropping like flies. I am trying to stay alive and work too hard at it. That's what's turning my brains. This working hard defeats its own end. Where should I start over? Let me go back a ways and try again.

Only a few hundred yards separated the cafeteria from the broker's, and within that short space Wilhelm turned again, in measurable degrees, from these wide considerations to the problems of the moment. The closer he approached to the Market, the more Wilhelm had to think about money.

They passed the newsreel theater where the ragged shoeshine kids called after them. The same old bearded man with his bandaged beggar face and his tiny ragged feet and the old press clipping on his fiddle case to prove he had once been a concert violinist, pointed his bow at Wilhelm saying, "You!" Wilhelm went by with worried eyes, bent on crossing Seventy-second Street. In full tumult the great afternoon current raced for Columbus Circle where the mouth of midtown stood open and the skyscrapers gave back the yellow fire of the sun.

As they approached the polished stone front of the new office building, Dr. Tamkin said, "Well, isn't that old Rappaport by the door? I think he should carry a white cane, but he will never admit there's a single thing the matter with his eyes."

Mr. Rappaport did not stand well; his knees were sunk, while his pelvis only half filled his trousers. His suspenders held them, gaping.

He stopped Wilhelm with an extended hand, having somehow recognized him. In his deep voice he commanded him, "Take me to the cigar store."

"You want me? . . . Tamkin!" Wilhelm whispered, "You take him."

Tamkin shook his head. "He wants you. Don't refuse the old gentleman." Significantly, he said in a lower voice, "This minute is another instance of the 'here-and-now.' You have to live in this very minute, and you don't want to. A man asks you for help. Don't think of the Market. It won't run away. Show your respect for the old boy. Go ahead, That may be more valuable."

"Take me," said the old chicken merchant again.

Greatly annoyed, Wilhelm wrinkled his face at Tamkin. He took the old man's big but light elbow at the bone. "Well let's step on it," he said. "Or wait – I want to have a look at the board first to see how we're doing."

But Tamkin had already started Mr. Rappaport forward. He was walking, and he scolded Wilhelm, saying "Don't leave me standing in the middle of the sidewalk. I'm afraid to get knocked over."

"Let's get a move on. Come," Wilhelm urged him as Tamkin went into the broker's.

The traffic seemed to come down Broadway out of the sky, where the hot spokes of the sun rolled from the south. Hot, stony odors rose from the subway grating in the street.

"These teenage hoodlums worry me. I'm a-scared of these Puerto Rican kids, and these young characters who take dope," said Mr. Rappaport. "They go around all hopped up."

"Hoodlums?" said Wilhelm. "I went to the cemetery and my mother's stone bench was split. I could have broken somebody's neck for what. Which store do you go to!"

"Across Broadway. That La Magnita sign next door to the Automat."

"What's the matter with this store here on this side?"

"They don't carry my brand, that's what's the matter."

Wilhelm cursed, but checked the words.

"What are you talking?"

"Those damn taxis," said Wilhelm. "They want to run everybody down."

They entered the cool, odorous shop. Mr. Rappaport put away his large cigars with great care in various pockets while Wilhelm muttered, "Come on, you old creeper. What a pokey old character! The whole world waits on him." Rappaport did not offer Wilhalm a cigar, but holding one up he asked, "What do you say at the size of these, huh? They're Churchill-type cigars."

He barely crawls along, thought Wilhelm. His pants are dropping off because he hasn't enough flesh for them to stick to. He's almost blind, and covered with spots, but this old man still makes money in the market. Is loaded with dough, probably. And I bet he doesn't give his children any. Some of them must be in their fifties. This is what keeps middle-aged men as children. He's master over the dough. Think – just think. Who controls everything? Old men of this type. Without needs. They don't need therefore they have. I need, therefore I don't have. That would be too easy.

"I'm older even than Churchill," said Rappaport.

Now he wanted to talk! But if you asked him a question in the Market, he couldn't be bothered to answer.

"I bet you are, said Wilhelm. "Come, let's get going.

"I was a fighter too, like Churchill," said the old man. When we licked Spain I went into the Navy. Yes I was a gob that time. What did I have to lose? Nothing. After the battle of San Juan Hill, Teddy Roosevelt kicked me off the beach."

"Come, watch the curb," said Wilhelm.

"I was curious and wanted to see what went on. I didn't have no business there, but I took a boat and rowed myself to the beach. Two of our guys was dead, layin' under the American flag to keep the flies off. So I says to the guy on duty, there, who was the sentry, 'Let's have a look at these guys. I want to see what went on here,' and he says, 'Naw,' but I talked him into it. So he took off the flag and there were these two tall guys, both gentlemen, lying in their boots. They was very tall. The two of them had long mustaches. They were high society boys. I think one of them was called Fish, from up the Hudson, a big-shot family. When I looked up, there was Teddy Roosevelt, with his hat off, and he was looking at these fellows, the only ones who got killed there. Then he says to me, 'What's the Navy want here? Have you got orders?' 'No, sir,' I says to him. 'Well, get the hell off the beach, then.'"

Old Rappaport was very proud of this memory. "Everything he said had such snap, such class. Man! I love that Teddy Roosevelt," he said, "I love him!"

Ah, what people are! He is almost not with us, and his life is nearly gone, but T. R. once yelled at him, so he loves him. I guess it is love, too, Wilhelm smiled. So maybe the rest of Tamkin's story was true, about the ten children and the wives and the telephone directory.

He said, "Come on, come on, Mr. Rappaport," and hurried the old man back by the large hollow elbow; he gripped it through the thin cotton cloth. Re-entering the brokerage office where under the lights the tumblers were speeding with the clack of drumsticks upon wooden blocks, more than ever resembling a Chinese theater, Wilhelm strained his eyes to see the board.

The lard figures were unfamiliar. That amount couldn't be lard! They must have put the figures in the wrong slot. He traced the line back to the margin. It was down to .19, and had dropped twenty points since noon. And what about the contract of rye? It had sunk back to its earlier position, and they had lost their chance to sell.

Old Mr. Rappaport said to Wilhelm, "Read me my wheat figure."

"Oh, leave me alone for a minute," he said, and positively hid his face from the old man behind one hand. He looked for Tamkin, Tamkin's bald head, or Tamkin with his gray straw and the cocoa-colored band. He couldn't see him. Where was he? The seats next to Rowland were taken by strangers. He thrust himself over the one on the aisle, Mr. Rappaport's former place, and pushed at the back of the chair ontil the new occupant, a red-headed man with a thin determined face, leaned forward to get out of his way but would not surrender the seat. "Where's Tamkin?" Wilhelm asked Rowland.

"Gee, I don't know. Is anything wrong?"

"You must have seen him. He came in a while back."

"No, but I didn't."

Wilhelm fumbled out a pencil from the top pocket of his coat and began to make calculations. His very fingers were numb, and in his agitation he was afraid he made mistakes with the decimal points and went over the subtraction and multiplication like a schoolboy at an exam. His heart, accustomed to many sorts of crisis, was now in a new panic. And, as he had dreaded, he was wiped out. It was unnecessary to ask the German manager. He could see for himself that the electronic bookkeeping device must have closed him out. The manager probably had known that Tamkin wasn't to be trusted, and on that first day he might have warned him. But you couldn't expect him to interfere.

"You get hit?" said Mr. Rowland.

And Wilhelm, quite coolly, said, "Oh, it could have been worse, I guess." He put the piece of paper into his pocket with its cigarette butts and packets of pills. The lie helped him out. Although, for a moment, he was afraid be would cry. But he hardened himself. The hardening effort made a violent, vertical pain go through his chest, like that caused by a pocket of air under the collar bones. To the old chicken millionaire who, by this time, had become acquainted with the drop in rye and lard, he also denied that anything serious had happened. "It's just one of those temporary slumps. Nothing to be scared about," he said, and remained in possession of himself. His need to cry, like someone in a crowd, pushed and jostled and abused him from behind, and Wilhelm did not dare turn. He said to himself, I will not cry in front of these people. I'll be damned if I'll break down in front of them like a kid, even though I never expect to see them again. No! No! And yet his unshed tears rose and rose and he looked like a man about to drown. But when they talked to him, he answered very distinctly. He tried to speak proudly.

". . . going away?" he heard Rowland ask. "What?"

"I thought you might be going away too. Tamkin said he was going to Maine this summer for his vacation."

"Oh, going away?"

Wilhelm broke off and went to look for Tamkin in the men's toilet. Across the corridor was the room where the machinery of the board was housed. It hummed and whirred like mechanical birds, and the tubes glittered in the dark. A couple of businessmen with cigarettes in their fingers were having a conversation in the lavatory. At the top of the closet door sat a gray straw hat with a cocoa-colored band. "Tamkin," said Wilhelm. He tried to identify the feet below the door. "Are you in there, Dr. Tamkin?" he said with stifled anger. "Answer me. It's Wilhelm."

The hat was taken down, the latch lifted, and a stranger came out who looked at him with annoyance.

"You waiting?" said one of the businessmen. He was warning Wilhelm that he was out of turn.

"Me? Not me," said Wilhelm. "I'm looking for a fellow."

Bitterly angry, he said to himself that Tamkin would pay him the two hundred dollars at least, his share of the original deposit. And before he takes the train to Maine, too. Before he spends a penny on vacation – that liar! We went into this as equal partners.

VII

I was the man beneath, Tamkin was on my back, and I thought I was on his. He made me carry him, too, besides Margaret. Like this they ride on me with hoofs and claws. Tear me to pieces, stamp on me and break my bones.

Once more the hoary old fiddler pointed his bow at Wilhelm as he hurried by. Wilhelm rejected his begging and denied the omen. He dodged heavily through traffic and with his quick small steps ran up the lower stairway of the Gloriana Hotel with its dark-tinted mirrors, kind to people's defects. From the lobby, he phoned Tainkin's room, and when no one answered he took the elevator up. A rouged woman in her fifties, with a mink stole, led three tiny dogs on a leash, high-strung creatures with prominent black eyes like dwarf deer and legs like twigs. This was the eccentric Estonian lady who had been moved with her pets to the twelfth floor.

She identified Wilhelm. "You are Dr. Adler's son," she said.

Formally, he nodded.

"I am a dear friend of your father."

He stood in the corner and would not meet her glance and she thought he was snubbing her and made a mental note to speak of it to the doctor.

The linen wagon stood at Tamkin's door, and the chambermaid's key with its big brass tongue was in the lock.

"Has Dr. Tamkin been here?" he asked her.

"No, I haven't seen him."

Wilhelm came in, however, to look around. He examined the photos on the desk trying to connect the faces with the strange people in Tamkin's stories. Big heavy volumes were stacked under the double-pronged TV aerial. *Science and Sanity*, he read, and there were several books on poetry. The *Wall Street Journal* hung in separate sheets from the bed-table under the weight of the silver water jug. A bathrobe with lightning streaks of red and white was laid across the foot of the bed with a pair of expensive batik pajamas. It was a box of a room, but from the windows you saw the river as far uptown as the Bridge, as far downtown as Hoboken. What lay between was deep, azure, dirty, complex, crystal, rusty, with the red bones of new apartments rising on the bluffs of New Jersey, and huge liners in their berths, the tugs with matted beards of cordage. Even the brackish river smell rose this high, like the smell of mop water. From every side he heard pianos, and the voices of men and women singing scales and opera, all mixed, and the sounds of pigeons on the ledges.

Again Wilhelm took the phone. "Can you locate Dr. Tamkin in the lobby for me?" he asked. And when the operator reported that she could not, Wilhelm gave the number of his father's room, but Dr. Adler was not in, either. "Well, please give me the masseur. I say the massage room. Don't you understand me? The men's health club. Yes, Max Schilper's – how am I supposed to know the name of it?"

There a strange voice said, "Toktor Adler?" It was the old Czech prizefighter with the deformed nose and ears who was attendant down there and gave out soap, sheets and sandals. He went away. A hollow endless silence followed. Wilhelm flicked the receiver with his nails, whistled into it, but could not summon either the attendant or the operator.

The maid saw him examining the bottles of pills on Tamkin's table and seemed suspicious of him. He was running low on Phenaphen pills and was looking for something else. But he swallowed one of his own tablets and went out and rang again for the elevator. He went down to the health club. Through the steamy windows, when he emerged, he saw the reflection of the swimming pool swirling green at the bottom of the lowest stairway. He went through the locker room curtains. Two men wrapped in towels were playing ping-pong. They were awkward and the ball bounded high. The Negro in the toilet was shining shoes. He did not know Dr. Adler by name and Wilhelm descended to the massage room. On the tables naked men were lying. It was not a brightly lighted place, and it was very hot, and under the white faint moons of the ceiling shone pale skins. Calendar pictures of pretty girls dressed in tiny fringes were pinned on the wall. On the first table, eyes deeply shut in heavy silent luxury, lay a man with a full square beard and short legs, stocky and black-haired. He might have been an orthodox Russian. Wrapped in a sheet, waiting, the man beside him was newly shaved and red from the steam bath. He had a big happy face and was dreaming. And after him was an athlete, strikingly muscled, powerful and young, with a strong white curve to his genital and a half angry smile on his mouth. Dr. Adler was on the fourth table, and Wilhelm stood over his father's pale, slight body. His ribs were narrow and small, his belly round, white, and high. It had its own being, like something separate. His thighs were weak, the muscles of his arms had fallen, his throat was creased.

The masseur in his undershirt bent and whispered in his ear, "It's your son," and Dr. Adler opened his eyes into Wilhelm's face. At once he saw the trouble in it, and by an instantaneous reflex he removed himself from the danger of contagion, and he said, serenely, "Well, have you taken my advice, Wilky?"

"Oh, Dad," said Wilhelm.

"– to take a swim and get a massage?"

"Did you get my note?" said Wilhelm.

"Yes, but I'm afraid you'll have to ask somebody else, because I can't. I had no idea you were so low on funds. How did you let it happen? Didn't you lay anything aside?"

"Oh, please, Dad," said Wilhelm, almost bringing his hands together in a clasp.

"I'm sorry," said the doctor. "I really am. But I have set up a rule. I've thought about it, I believe it is a good rule, and I don't want to change it. You haven't acted wisely. What's the matter?"

"Everything. Just everything. What isn't? I did have a little, but I haven't been very smart."

"You took some gamble? You lost it? Was it Tamkin? I told you, Wilky, not to build on that Tamkin. Did you? I suspect –"

"Yes, Dad, I'm afraid I trusted him."

Dr. Adler surrendered his arm to the masseur who was using winter-green oil. "Trusted! And got taken?"

"I'm afraid I kind of . . ." Wilhelm glanced at the masseur but he was absorbed in his work. He probably did not listen to conversations. "I did. I might as well say it. I should have listened to you."

"Well, I won't remind you how often I warned you. It must be very painful."

"Yes, Father, it is."

"I don't know how many times you have to be burned in order to learn something. The same mistake, over and over."

"I couldn't agree with you more," said Wilhelm with a face of despair. "You're so right, Father. It's the same mistake, and I get burned again and again. I can't seem to . . . I'm stupid, Dad, I just can't breathe. My chest is all up . . . I feel choked. I just simply can't catch my breath."

He stared at his father's nakedness. Gradually he became aware that Dr. Adler was making an effort to keep his temper. He was on the verge of an explosion. Wilhelm hung his face and said, "Nobody likes bad luck, eh Dad?"

"So! It's bad luck, now. A minute ago it was stupidity."

"It is stupidity – it's some of both. It's true that I can't learn. But I –"

"I don't want to listen to the details," said his father. "And I want you to understand that I'm too old to take on new burdens. I'm just too old to do it. And people who will just wait for help – must *wait* for help. They have got to stop waiting."

"It isn't all a question of money . . . there are other things a father can give to a son." He lifted up his gray eyes and his nostrils grew wide with a look of suffering appeal that stirred his father even more deeply against him.

He warningly said to him, "Look out, Wilky, you're tiring my patience very much."

"I try not to. But one word from you, just a word, would go a long way. I've never asked you for very much. But you are not a kind man, Father. You don't give the little bit I beg you for."

He recognized that his father was now furiously angry. Dr. Adler started to say something, and then raised himself and gathered the sheet over him as he did so. His mouth opened, wide, dark, twisted, and he said to Wilhelm, "You want to make yourself into my cross. But I am not going to pick up a cross. I'll see you dead, Wilky, by Christ, before I let you do that to me."

"Father, listen! Listen!"

"Go away from me now. It's torture for me to look at you, you slob!" cried Dr. Adler.

Wilhelm's blood rose up madly, in anger equal to his father's, but then it sank down and left him helplessly aching with misery. He said stiffly, and with a strange sort of formality, "Okay, Dad, that'll be enough. That's about all we should say." And he stalked out heavily by the door adjacent to the swimming pool and the steam room, and labored up two long flights from the basement. Once more he took the elevator to the lobby on the mezzanine.

He inquired at the desk for Dr. Tamkin.

The clerk said, "No, I haven't seen him. But I think there's something in the box for you."

"Me? Give it here," said Wilhelm and opened a telephone message from his wife. It read, "Please phone Mrs. Wilhelm on return. Urgent."

Whenever he received an urgent message from his wife he was always thrown into a great fear for the children. He ran to the phone booth, spilling out the change from his pockets onto the little curved steel shelf under the telephone, and dialed the Digby number.

"Yes?" said his wife. Scissors barked at the phone.

"Margaret?"

"Yes, hello." They never exchanged any other greeting. She instantly knew his voice.

"The boys all right?"

"They're out on their bicycles. Why shouldn't they be all right? Scissors, quiet!"

"Your message scared me," he said. "I wish you wouldn't make urgent so common."

"I had something to tell you."

Her familiar unbending voice awakened in him a kind of hungry longing, not for Margaret but for the peace he had once known.

"You sent me a post-dated check," she said. "I can't allow that. It's already five days past the first. You dated your check for the twelfth."

"Well, I have no money. I haven't got it. You can't send me to prison for that. I'll be lucky if I can raise it by the twelfth."

She answered, "You better get it, Tommy."

"Yes? What for?" he said. "Tell me. For the sake of what? To tell lies about me to everyone? You . . ."

She cut him off. "You know what for. I've got the boys to bring up."

Wilhelm in the narrow booth broke into a heavy sweat. He dropped his head and shrugged while with his fingers he arranged nickels, dimes and quarters in rows. "I'm doing my best," he said. "I've had some bad luck. As a matter of fact, it's been so bad that I don't know where I am. I couldn't tell you what day of the week this is. I can't think straight. I'd better not even try. This has been one of those days, Margaret. May I never live to go through another like it. I mean that with all my heart. So I'm not going to try to do any thinking today. Tomorrow I'm going to see some guys. One is a sales manager. The other is in television. But not to act," he hastily added. "On the business end."

"That's just some more of your talk, Tommy," she said. "You ought to patch things up with Rojax Corporation. They'd take you back. You've got to stop thinking like a youngster."

"What do you mean?"

"Well," she said, measured and unbending, remorselessly unbending. "You still think like a youngster. But you can't do that any more. Every other day you want to make a new start. But in eighteen years you'll be eligible for retirement. Nobody wants to hire a new man of your age."

"I know. But listen you don't have to sound so hard. I can't crawl back to them. And really you don't have to sound so hard. I haven't done you so much harm."

"Tommy, I have to chase you and ask you for money that you owe us, and I hate it."

She hated also to be told that her voice was hard.

"I'm making an effort to control myself," she told him.

He could picture her, her hair cut in graying bangs above her pretty, decisive face. She prided herself on being fair-minded. We could not bear, he thought, to know what we do. Even though blood is spilled. Even though the breath of life is taken from someone's nostrils. This is the way of the weak; quiet and fair. And then smash! smash!

"Rojax take me back? I'd have to crawl back. They don't need me. After so many years I should have got stock in the firm. How can I support the three of you, and live myself, on half my territory? And why should I even try when you won't lift a finger to help? I sent you back to school, didn't I? At that time you said . . ."

His voice was rising. She did not like that and intercepted him. "You misunderstood me," she said.

"You must realize you're killing me. You can't be as blind as all that. Thou shalt not kill! Don't you remember that?"

She said, "You're just raving now. When you calm down it'll be different. I have great confidence in your earning ability."

"Margaret, you don't grasp the situation. You'll have to get a job."

"Absolutely not. I'm not going to have two young children running loose."

"They're not babies," Wilhelm said. "Tommy is fourteen. Paulie is going to be ten."

"Look," Margaret said in her deliberate manner. "We can't continue this conversation if you're going to yell so, Tommy. They're at a dangerous age. There are teen-aged gangs. The parents working, or the families broken up."

Once again she was reminding him that it was he who had left her. She had the bringing up of the children as her burden, while he, must expect to pay the price of his freedom.

Freedom! he thought with consuming bitterness. Ashes in his mouth, not freedom. Give me my children. For they are mine, too.

Can you be the woman I lived with? he started to say. Have you forgotten that we slept so long together? Must you now deal with me like this, and have no mercy?

He would be better off with Margaret again, than he was today. This was what she wanted to make him feel, and she drove it home. "Are you in misery?" she was saying. "But you have deserved it." And he could not go back to her any more than he could beg Rojax to take him back. If it cost him his life, he could not. Margaret had ruined him with Olive. She hit him, and hit him, beat him, battered him, wanted to get the very life out of him. He could not, could not.

"Margaret, I want you please to reconsider about work. You have that degree now. Why did I pay your tuition?"

"Because it seemed practical. But it isn't. Growing boys need parental authority and a safe home."

He begged her, "Margaret, go easy on me. You ought to. I'm at the end of my rope and feel that I'm suffocating. You don't want to be responsible for a person's destruction. You've got to let up. I feel I'm about to burst." His face had swelled. He struck a blow upon the tin and wood and nails of the wall of the booth. "You've got to let me breathe. If I should keel over, what then? And it's something I can never understand about you. How you can treat someone like this whom you lived with so long. Who gave you the best of himself. Who tried. Who loved you." Merely to pronounce the word love made him tremble.

"Ah," she said with a sharp breath. "Now we're coming to it. How did you imagine it was going to be – big shot? Everything made smooth for you? I thought you were leading up to this."

She had not, perhaps, intended to reply as harshly as she did, but she brooded a great deal and now she could not forbear to punish him and make him feel pains like those she had to undergo.

He struck the wall again, this time with his knuckles, and he had scarcely enough air in his lungs to speak in a whisper, because his heart pushed upward with a frightful pressure. He got up and stamped his feet in the narrow enclosure, and bit his small teeth together and thought he was about to lose his reason.

"Haven't I always done my best?" he yelled, though his voice sounded weak and thin to his own ears. "Everything comes from me and nothing back again to me. There's no law that'll punish this, but you are committing a crime against me. Before God – and that's no joke. I mean that. Before God! . . . Sooner or later the boys will know it."

In a firm tone, levelly, Margaret said to him, "I won't stand to be howled at. When you can speak normally and have something sensible to say I'll listen, But not to this." She hung up.

Wilhelm tried to tear the apparatus from the wall. He ground his teeth and seized the black box with insane digging fingers and made a stifled cry, and pulled. Then he saw an elderly lady staring through the glass door, utterly appalled by him, and he ran from the booth leaving a large amount of change on the shelf. He hurried down the stairs and into the street.

On Broadway it was still bright afternoon and the gassy air was almost motionless under the leaden spokes of sunlight, and sawdust footprints lay about the doorways of butcher shops and fruit stores. And the great, great crowd, the inexhaustible current of millions of every race and kind pouring out, pressing round, of every age, of every genius, possessors of every human secret antique and future, in every face the refinement of one particular motive or essence – *I labor, I spend, I strive, I design, I love, I cling, I uphold, I give way, I envy, I long, I scorn, I die, I hide, I want.* Faster, much faster than any man could make the tally. The sidewalks were wider than a causeway, the street itself was immense, and it quaked and gleamed and it seemed to Wilhelm to throb at the last limit of endurance. And although the sunlight appeared like a broad tissue, its actual weight made him feel like a drunkard.

'I'll get a divorce if it's the last thing I do,' he swore. 'As for Dad . . . As for Dad . . . I'll have to sell the car for junk and pay the hotel. I'll have to go on my knees to Olive and say "Stand by me a while. Don't let her win. Olive!" ' And he thought, 'I'll try to start again with Olive. In fact, I must. Olive loves me. Olive –'

Beside a row of limousines near the curb he thought he saw Dr. Tamkin. Of course he had been mistaken before about the hat with the cocoa-colored band and didn't want to make the same mistake twice. But wasn't that Tamkin who was speaking so earnestly, with pointed shoulders, to someone under the canopy of the funeral parlor? For this was a huge funeral. He looked for his singular face under the dark, fashionable hat brim. There were two open cars filled with flowers, and a policeman tried to keep a path open to pedestrians. Right at the canopy-pole, now wasn't that that damned Tamkin talking away with a solemn face, gesticulating with an open hand?

"Tamkin!" shouted Wilhelm, pushing forward. But he was pushed to the side by a policeman clutching his nightstick at both ends, like a rolling pin. Wilhelm was even further from Tamkin now, and swore under his breath at the cop who continued to press him back, back, belly and ribs, saying, "Keep it moving there, please," his face red with impatient sweat, his brows like red fur. Wilhelm said to him haughtily, "You shouldn't push people like this."

The policeman, however, was not really to blame. He had been ordered to keep a way clear. Wilhelm was moved forward by the pressure of the crowd.

He cried, "Tamkin!"

But Tamkin was gone. Or rather, it was he himself who was carried from the street into the chapel. The pressure ended inside where it was dark and cool. The flow of fan-driven air dried his face, which he wiped hard with his handkerchief to stop the slight salt itch. He gave a sigh when he heard the organ notes that stirred and breathed from the pipes and he saw people in the pews. Men in formal clothes and black homburgs strode softly back and forth on the cork floor, up and down the center aisle. The white of the stained glass was like mother-of-pearl, the blue of the Star of David like velvet ribbon.

"Well," thought Wilhelm, "if that was Tamkin outside I might as well wait for him here where it's cool. Funny, he never mentioned he had a funeral to go to, today. But that's just like the guy."

But within a few minutes he had forgotten Tamkin. He stood along the wall with others and looked toward the coffin and the slow line that was moving past it, gazing at the face of the dead. Presently he too was in this line, and slowly, slowly, foot by foot, the beating of his heart anxious, thick, frightening, but somehow also rich, he neared the coffin and paused for his turn, and gazed down. He caught his breath when he looked at the corpse and his face swelled, his eyes shone, hugely with instant tears.

The dead man was grey-haired. He had two large waves of gray hair in front. But he was not old. His face was long, and he had a bony nose, slightly, delicately twisted. His brows were raised as though he had sunk into the final thought. Now at last he was with it, after the end of all distraction, and when his flesh was no longer flesh. And by this meditative look Wilhelm was so struck that he could not go away. In spite of the tinge of horror, and then the splash of heart-sickness that he felt, he could not go. He stepped out of line and remained beside the coffin; his eyes filled silently and through his still tears he studied the man as the line of visitors moved with veiled looks past the satin coffin toward the standing bank of lilies, lilacs, roses. With great stifling sorrow, almost admiration, Wilhelm nodded and nodded. On the surface, the dead man with his formal shirt and his tie and silk lapels and his powdered skin looked so proper; only a little beneath so – black, Wilhelm thought, so fallen in the eyes.

Standing a little apart, Wilhelm began to cry. He cried at first softly and from sentiment, but soon from deeper feeling. He sobbed loudly and his face grew distorted and hot, and the tears stung his skin. A man . . . another human creature, was what first went through his thoughts, but other and different things were torn from him. What'll I do? I'm stripped and kicked out . . . Oh Father, what do I ask of you? What'll I do about the kids – Tommy, Paul? My children. And Olive? My dear! Why, why, why – you must protect me against that devil who wants my life. Then take, take it. Take it from me.

Soon he was past words, past reason, coherence. He could not stop, because it was as if the source of all tears had suddenly sprung open within him, black, deep and hot, and they were pouring out and convulsed his body, bending his stubborn head, bowing his shoulders, twisting his face, crippling the very hands with which he held the handkerchief. His efforts to collect himself were useless. The great knot of ill and grief in his throat swelled upward and he gave in utterly and held his face and wept.

He, alone of all the people in the chapel was sobbing. No one knew who he was.

One woman said, "Is that perhaps the cousin from New Orleans they were expecting?"

"It must be somebody real close to carry on so."

"Oh my, oh my! To be mourned like that," said one man and looked at Wilhelm's heavy shaken shoulders, his clutched face, the whitened honey of his hair, with wide, glinting jealous eyes.

"The man's brother, maybe?"

"Oh, I doubt that very much," said another bystander. "They're not alike at all. Night and day."

The flowers and lights fused ecstatically in Wilhelm's blind wet eyes, the heavy sea-like music shuddered at his ears. It found him where he had hidden himself in the center of a crowd by the great and happy oblivion of tears. He heard it and sank deeper than sorrow, and by the way that can only be found through the midst of sorrow, through torn sobs and cries, he found the secret consummation of his heart's ultimate need.

The Renegade

BY ALBERT CAMUS

What a jumble! What a jumble! I must tidy up my mind. Since they cut out my tongue, another tongue, it seems, has been constantly wagging somewhere in my skull, something has been talking, or someone, that suddenly falls silent and then it all begins again – oh, I hear too many things I never utter, what a jumble, and if I open my mouth it's like pebbles rattling together. Order and method, the tongue says, and then goes on talking of other matters simultaneously – yes, I always longed for order. At least one thing is certain, I am waiting for the missionary who is to come and take my place. Here I am on the trail, an hour away from Taghâsa, hidden in a pile of rocks, sitting on my old rifle. Day is breaking over the desert, it's still very cold, soon it will be too hot, this country drives men mad and I've been here I don't know how many years. . . . No, just a little longer. The missionary is to come this morning, or this evening. I've heard he'll come with a guide, perhaps they'll have but one camel between them. I'll wait, I am waiting, it's only the cold making me shiver. Just be patient a little longer, lousy slave!

But I have been patient for so long. When I was home on that high plateau of the Massif Central, my coarse father, my boorish mother, the wine, the pork soup every day, the wine above all, sour and cold, and the long winter, the frigid wind, the snowdrifts, the revolting braken – oh, I wanted to get away, leave them all at once and begin to live at last, in the sunlight, with fresh water. I believed the priest, he spoke to me of the seminary, he tutored me daily, he had plenty of time in that Protestant region where he used to hug the walls as he crossed the village. He told me of the future and of the sun, Catholicism is the sun, he used to say, and he would get me to read, he beat Latin into my hard head ('The kid's bright but he's pig-headed') my head was so hard that, despite all my falls, it has never once bled in my life: 'Bull-headed,' my pig of a father used to say. At the seminary they were proud as punch, a recruit from the Protestant region was a victory, they greeted me like the sun at Austerlitz. The sun was pale and feeble, to be sure, because of the alcohol, they have drunk sour wine and the children's teeth are set on edge, *gra gra*, one really ought to kill one's father, but after all there's no danger that *he*'ll hurl himself into missionary work since he's now long dead, the tart wine eventually cut through his stomach, so there's nothing left but to kill the missionary.

I have something to settle with him and with his teachers, with my teachers who deceived me, with the whole of lousy Europe, everybody deceived me. Missionary work, that's all they could say, go out to the savages and tell them: 'Here is my Lord, just look at him, he never strikes or kills, he issues his orders in a low voice, he turns the other cheek, he's the greatest of masters, choose him, just see how much better he's made me, offend me and you will see.' Yes, I believed, *gra gra*, and I felt better, I had put on weight, I was almost handsome, I wanted to be offended. When we would walk out in tight black rows, in summer, under Grenoble's hot sun and would meet girls in cotton dresses, *I* didn't look away, I despised them, I waited for them to offend me and sometimes they would laugh. At such times I would think:

'Let them strike me and spit in my face,' but their laughter, to tell the truth, came to the same thing, bristling with teeth and quips that tore me to shreds, the offense and the suffering were sweet to me! My confessor couldn't understand when I used to heap accusations on myself: 'No, no, there's good in you!' Good! There was nothing but sour wine in me, and that was all for the best, how can a man become better if he's not bad, I had grasped that in everything they taught me. That's the only thing I did grasp, a single idea and, pig-headed bright boy, I carried it to its logical conclusion, I went out of my way for punishments, I groused at the normal, in short I too wanted to be an example in order to be noticed and so that after noticing me people would give credit to what had made me better, through me praise my Lord.

Fierce sun! It's rising, the desert is changing, it has lost its mountain-cyclamen color, O my mountain, and the snow, the soft enveloping snow, no, it's a rather grayish yellow, the ugly moment before the great resplendence. Nothing, still nothing from here to the horizon over yonder where the plateau disappears in a circle of still soft colors. Behind me, the trail climbs to the dune hiding Taghâsa whose iron name has been beating in my head for so many years. The first to mention it to me was the half-blind old priest who had retired to our monastery, but why do I say the first, he was the only one, and it wasn't the city of salt, the white walls under the blinding sun that struck me in his account but the cruelty of the savage inhabitants and the town closed to all outsiders, only one of those who had tried to get in, one alone, to his knowledge, had lived to relate what he had seen. They had whipped him and driven him out into the desert after having put salt on his wounds and in his mouth, he had met nomads who for once were compassionate, a stroke of luck, and since then I had been dreaming about his tale, about the fire of the salt and the sky, about the House of the Fetish and his slaves, could anything more barbarous, more exciting be imagined, yes, that was my mission and I had to go and reveal to them my Lord.

They all expatiated on the subject at the seminary to discourage me, pointing out the necessity of waiting, that it was not missionary country, that I wasn't ready yet, I had to prepare myself specially, know who I was, and even then I had to go through tests, then they would see! But go on waiting, ah, no ! – yes, if they insisted, for the special preparation and the try-out because they took place at Algiers and brought me closer, but for all the rest I shook my pighead and repeated the same thing, to get among the most barbarous and live as they did, to show them at home, and even in the House of the Fetish, through example, that my Lord's truth would prevail. They would offend me, of course, but I was not afraid of offenses, they were essential to the demonstration, and as a result of the way I endured them I'd get the upper hand of those savages like a strong sun. Strong, yes, that was the word I constantly had on the tip of my tongue, I dreamed of absolute power, the kind that makes people kneel down, that forces the adversary to capitulate, converts him in short, and the blinder, the crueler he is, the more he's sure of himself, mired in his own conviction, the more his consent establishes the royalty of whoever brought about his collapse. Converting good folk who had strayed somewhat was the shabby ideal of our priests, I despised them for daring so little when they could do so much, they lacked faith and I had it, I wanted to be acknowledged by the torturers themselves, to fling them on their knees and make them say:

'O Lord, here is thy victory,' to rule in short by the sheer force of words over an army of the wicked. Oh, I was sure of reasoning logically on that subject, never quite sure of myself otherwise, but once I get an idea I don't let go of it, that's my strong point, yes the strong point of the fellow they all pitied!

The sun has risen higher, my forehead is beginning to burn. Around me the stones are beginning to crack open with a dull sound, the only cool thing is the rifle's barrel, cool as the fields, as the evening rain long ago when the soup was simmering, they would wait for me, my father and mother who would occasionally smile at me, perhaps I loved them. But that's all in the past, a film of heat is beginning to rise from the trail, come on, missionary, I'm waiting for you, now I know how to answer the message, my new masters taught me, and I know they are right, you have to settle accounts with that question of love. When I fled the seminary in Algiers I had a different idea of the savages and only one detail of my imaginings was true, they are cruel. I had robbed the treasurer's office, cast off my habit, crossed the Atlas, the upper plateaus and the desert, the bus-driver of the Trans-Sahara line made fun of me: 'Don't go there,' he too, what had got into them all, and the gusts of sand for hundreds of wind-blown kilometers, progressing and backing in the face of the wind, then the mountains again made up of black peaks and ridges sharp as steel, and after them it took a guide to go out on the endless sea of brown pebbles, screaming with heat, burning with the fires of a thousand mirrors, to the spot on the confines of the white country and the land of the blacks, where stands the city of salt. And the money the guide stole from me, ever naive I had shown it to him, but he left me on the trail – just about here, it so happens – after having struck me: 'Dog, there's the way, the honor's all mine, go ahead, go on, they'll show you,' and they did show me, oh yes, they're like the sun that never stops, except at night, beating sharply and proudly, that is beating me hard at this moment, too hard, with a multitude of lances burst from the ground, oh shelter, yes shelter, under the big rock, before everything gets muddled.

The shade here is good. How can anyone live in the city of salt, in the hollow of that basin full of dazzling heat? On each of the sharp right-angle walls cut out with a pickax and coarsely planed, the gashes left by the pickax bristle with blinding scales, pale scattered sand yellows them somewhat except when the wind dusts the upright walls and terraces, then everything shines with dazzling whiteness under a sky likewise dusted even to its blue rind. I was going blind during those days when the stationary fire would crackle for hours on the surface of the white terraces that all seemed to meet as if, in the remote past, they had all together tackled a mountain of salt, flattened it first, and then had hollowed out streets, the insides of houses and windows directly in the mass, or as if – yes, this is more like it, they had cut out their white, burning hell with a powerful jet of boiling water just to show that they could live where no one ever could, thirty days' travel from any living thing, in this hollow in the middle of the desert where the heat of day prevents any contact among creatures, separates them by a portcullis of invisible flames and of searing crystals, where without transition the cold of night congeals them individually in their rock-salt shells, nocturnal dwellers in a dried-up ice-floe, black Eskimos suddenly shivering in their cubical igloos. Black because they wear long black garments and the salt that collects even under their nails, that they continue tasting bitterly and swallowing during the sleep of those polar nights, the salt they drink in the water from the only spring in the hollow of a dazzling groove, often spots their dark garments with something like the trail of snails after a rain.

Rain, O Lord, just one real rain, long and hard, rain from your heaven! Then at last the hideous city, gradually eaten away, would slowly and irresistibly cave in and, utterly melted in a slimy torrent, would carry off its savage inhabitants toward the sands. Just one rain, Lord! But what do I mean, what Lord, they are the lords and masters! They rule over their sterile homes, over their black slaves that they work to death in the mines and each slab of salt that is cut out is worth a man in the region to the south, they pass by, silent, wearing their mourning veils in the mineral whiteness of the streets, and at night, when the whole town looks like a milky phantom, they stoop down and enter the shade of their homes where the salt walls shine dimly. They sleep with a weightless sleep and, as soon as they wake, they give orders, they strike, they say they are a united people, that their god is the true god, and that one must obey. They are my masters, they are ignorant of pity and, like masters, they want to be alone, to progress alone, to rule alone, because they alone had the daring to build in the salt and the sands a cold torrid city. And I. . . .

What a jumble when the heat rises, I'm sweating, they never do, now the shade itself is heating up, I feel the sun on the stone above me, it's striking, striking like a hammer on all the stones and it's the music, the vast music of noon, air and stones vibrating over hundreds of kilometers, *gra*, I hear the silence as I did once before. Yes, it was the same silence, years ago, that greeted me when the guards led me to them, in the sunlight, in the center of the square, whence the concentric terraces rose gradually toward the lid of hard blue sky sitting on the edge of the basin. There I was, thrown on my knees in the hollow of that white shield, my eyes corroded by the swords of salt and fire issuing from all the walls, pale with fatigue, my ear bleeding from the blow given by my guide and they, tall and black, looked at me without saying a word. The day was at its mid-course. Under the blows of the iron sun, the sky resounded at length, a sheet of white-hot tin, it was the same silence and they stared at me, time passed, they kept on staring at me, and I couldn't face their stares, I panted more and more violently, eventually I wept, and suddenly they turned their backs on me in silence and all together went off in the same direction. On my knees, all I could see, in the red and black sandals, was their feet sparkling with salt as they raised the long black gowns, the tip rising somewhat, the heel striking the ground lightly, and when the square was empty I was dragged to the House of the Fetish.

Squatting as I am today in the shelter of the rock and the fire above my head pierces the rock's thickness, I spent several days within the dark of the House of the Fetish, somewhat higher than the others, surrounded by a wall of salt, but without windows, full of a sparkling night. Several days, and I was given a basin of brackish water and some grain that was thrown before me the way chickens are fed, I picked it up. By day the door remained closed and yet the darkness became less oppressive, as if the irresistible sun managed to flow through the masses of salt. No lamp, but by feeling my way along the walls I touched garlands of dried palms decorating the walls and, at the end, a small door, coarsely fitted, of which I could make out the bolt with my finger-tips. Several days, long after – I couldn't count the days or the hours, but my handful of grain had been thrown me some ten times and I had dug out a hole for my excrements that I covered up in vain, the stench of an animal-den hung on anyway – long after, yes, the door opened wide and they came in.

One of them came toward me where I was squatting in a corner. I felt the burning salt against my cheek, I smelt the dusty scent of the palms, I watched him approach. He stopped a yard away from me, he stared at me with his metallic eyes that shone without expression in his brown horse-face, then he raised his hand. Still impassive, he seized me by the lower lip which he twisted slowly until he tore my flesh and, without letting go, made me turn around and back up to the center of the room, he pulled on my lip to make me fall on my knees there, mad with pain and my mouth bleeding, then he turned away to join the others standing against the walls. They watched me moaning in the unbearable heat of the unbroken daylight that came in the wide-open door, and in that light suddenly appeared the Sorcerer with his raffia hair, his chest covered with a breastplate of pearls, his legs bare under a straw skirt, wearing a mask of reeds and wire with two square openings for the eyes. He was followed by musicians and women wearing heavy motley gowns that revealed nothing of their bodies. They danced in front of the door at the end, but a coarse scarcely rhythmical dance, they just barely moved, and finally the Sorcerer opened the little door behind me, the masters did not stir, they were watching me, I turned around and saw the Fetish, his double ax-head, his iron nose twisted like a snake.

I was carried before him, to the foot of the pedestal, I was made to drink a black, bitter, bitter water, and at once my head began to burn, I was laughing, that's the offense, I am offended. They undressed me, shaved my head and body, washed me in oil, beat my face with cords dipped in water and salt, and I laughed and turned my head away but, each time, two women would take me by the ears and offer my face to the Sorcerer's blows while I could see only his square eyes, I was still laughing, covered with blood. They stopped, no one spoke but me, the jumble was beginning in my head, then they lifted me up and forced me to raise my eyes toward the Fetish, I had ceased laughing. I knew that I was now consecrated to him to serve him, adore him, no, I was not laughing any more, fear and pain stifled me. And there, in that white house, between those walls that the sun was assiduously burning on the outside, my face taut, my memory exhausted, yes, I tried to pray to the Fetish, he was all there was and even his horrible face was less horrible than the rest of the world. Then it was that my ankles were tied with a cord that permitted just one step, they danced again, but this time in front of the Fetish, the masters went out one by one.

The door once closed behind them, the music again, and the Sorcerer lighted a bark-fire around which he pranced, his long silhouette broke on the angles of the white walls, fluttered on the flat surfaces, filled the room with dancing shadows. He traced a rectangle in a corner to which the women dragged me, I felt their dry and gentle hands, they set before me a bowl of water and a little pile of grain and pointed to the Fetish, I grasped that I was to keep my eyes fixed on him. Then the Sorcerer called them one after the other over to the fire, he beat some of them who moaned and who then went and prostrated themselves before the Fetish my god, while the Sorcerer kept on dancing and he made them all leave the room until only one was left, quite young, squatting near the musicians and not yet beaten. He held her by a shock of hair which he kept twisting around his wrist, she dropped backward with eyes popping until she finally fell on her back. Dropping her, the Sorcerer screamed, the musicians turned to the wall, while behind the square-eyed man the scream rose to an impossible pitch, and the woman rolled on the ground in a sort of fit and, at last on all fours, her head hidden in her locked arms, she too screamed, but with a hollow, muffled sound, and in this position, without ceasing to scream and to look at the Fetish, the Sorcerer took her nimbly and nastily, without the woman's face being visible, for it was covered with the heavy folds of her garment. And, wild as a result of the solitude, *I* screamed too, yes, howled with fright toward the Fetish until a kick hurled me against the wall, biting the salt as I am biting this rock today with my tongueless mouth, while waiting for the man I must kill.

Now the sun has gone a little beyond the middle of the sky. Through the breaks in the rock, I can see the hole it makes in the white-hot metal of the sky, a mouth voluble as mine, constantly vomiting rivers of flame over the colorless desert. On the trail in front of me, nothing, no cloud of dust on the horizon, behind me they must be looking for me, no, not yet, it's only in the late afternoon that they opened the door and I could go out a little, after having spent the day cleaning the house of the Fetish, set out fresh offerings, and in the evening the ceremony would begin, in which I was sometimes beaten, at others not, but always I served the Fetish, the Fetish whose image is engraved in iron in my memory and now in my hope also. Never had a god so possessed or enslaved me, my whole life day and night was devoted to him, and pain and the absence of pain, wasn't that joy, were due him and even, yes, desire, as a result of being present, almost every day, at that impersonal and nasty act which I heard without seeing it inasmuch as I now had to face the wall or else be beaten. But my face up against the salt, obsessed by the bestial shadows moving on the wall, I listened to the long scream, my throat was dry, a burning sexless desire squeezed my temples and my belly as in a vise. Thus the days followed one another, I barely distinguished them as if they had liquefied in the torrid heat and the treacherous reverberation from the walls of salt, time had become merely a vague lapping of waves in which there would burst out, at regular intervals, screams of pain or possession, a long ageless clay in which the Fetish ruled as this fierce sun does over my house of rocks, and now as I did then, I weep with unhappiness and longing, a wicked hope consumes me, I want to betray, I lick the barrel of my gun and its soul inside, its soul, only guns have souls – oh, yes! the day they cut out my tongue, I learned to adore the immortal soul of hatred!

What a jumble, what a rage, *gra gra*, drunk with heat and wrath, lying prostrate on my gun. Who's panting here? I can't endure this endless heat, this waiting, I must kill him. Not a bird, not a blade of grass, stone, an arid desire, their screams, this tongue within me talking, and, since they mutilated me, the long, flat, deserted suffering deprived even of the water of night, the night of which I would dream, when locked in with the god, in my den of salt. Night alone with its cool stars and dark fountains could save me, carry me off at last from the wicked gods of mankind, but even locked up I could not contemplate it. If the newcomer tarries more, I shall see it at least rise from the desert and sweep over the sky, a cold golden vine that will hang from the dark zenith and from which I can drink at length, moisten this black dried hole that no muscle of live flexible flesh revives now, forget at last that day when madness took away my tongue.

How hot it was, really hot, the salt was melting or so it seemed to me, the air was corroding my eyes, and the Sorcerer came in without his mask. Almost naked under grayish tatters, a new woman followed him and her face, covered with a tattoo reproducing the mask of the Fetish, expressed only an idol's ugly stupor. The only thing alive about her was her thin flat body that flopped at the foot of the god when the Sorcerer opened the door of the niche. Then he went out without looking at me, the heat rose, I didn't stir, the Fetish looked at me over that motionless body whose muscles stirred gently and the woman's idol-face didn't change when I approached. Only her eyes enlarged as she stared at me, my feet touched hers, the heat then began to shriek, and the idol, without a word, still staring at me with her dilated eyes, gradually slipped onto her back, slowly drew her legs up and raised them as she gently spread her knees. But, immediately afterward, *gra*, the Sorcerer was lying in wait for me, they all entered and tore me from the woman, beat me dreadfully on the sinful place, what sin, I'm laughing, where is it and where is virtue, they clapped me against a wall, a hand of steel gripped my jaws, another opened my mouth, pulled on my tongue until it bled, was it I screaming with that bestial scream, a cool cutting caress, yes cool at last, went over my tongue. When I came to, I was alone in the night, glued to the wall, covered with hardened blood, a gag of strange smelling dry grasses filled my mouth, it had stopped bleeding, but it was vacant and in that absence the only living thing was a tormenting pain. I wanted to rise, I fell back, happy, desperately happy to die at last, death too is cool and its shadow hides no god.

I did not die, a new feeling of hatred stood up one day, at the same time I did, walked toward the door of the niche, opened it, closed it behind me, I hated my people, the Fetish was there and, from the depths of the hole in which I was I did more than pray to him, I believed in him and denied all I had believed up to then. Hail! he was strength and power, he could be destroyed but not converted, he stared over my head with his empty, rusty eyes. Hail! He was the master, the only lord, whose indisputable attribute was malice, there are no good masters. For the first time, as a result of offenses, my whole body crying out a single pain, I surrendered to him and approved his maleficent order, I adored in him the evil principle of the world. A prisoner of his kingdom – the sterile city carved out of a mountain of salt, divorced from nature, deprived of those rare and fleeting flowerings of the desert, preserved from those strokes of chance or marks of affection such as an unexpected cloud or a brief violent downpour that are familiar even to the sun or the sands, the city of order in short, right angles, square rooms, rigid men – I freely became its tortured, hate-filled citizen, I repudiated the long history that had been taught me. I had been misled, solely the reign of malice was devoid of defects, I had been misled, truth is square, heavy, thick, it does not admit distinctions, good is an idle dream, an intention constantly postponed and pursued with exhausting effort, a limit never reached, its reign is impossible. Solely evil can reach its limits and reign absolutely, it must be served to establish its visible kingdom, then we shall see, but what does 'then' mean, solely evil is present, down with Europe, reason, honor, and the cross. Yes, I was to be converted to the religion of my masters, yes, indeed, I was a slave, but if I too become vicious I cease to be a slave, despite my shackled feet and my mute mouth. O, this heat is driving me crazy, the desert cries out everywhere under the unbearable light, and he, the Lord of kindness, whose very name revolts me, I disown him, for I know him now. He dreamed and wanted to lie, his tongue was cut out so that his word would no longer be able to deceive the world, he was pierced with nails even in his head, his poor head, like mine now, what a jumble, how weak I am, and the earth didn't tremble, I am sure, it was not a righteous man they had killed, I refuse to believe it, there are no righteous men but only evil masters who bring about the reign of relentless truth. Yes, the Fetish alone has power, he is the sole god of this world, hatred is his commandment, the source of all life, the cool water, cool like mint that chills the mouth and burns the stomach.

Then it was that I changed, they realized it, I would kiss their hands when I met them, I was on their side, never wearying of admiring them, I trusted them, I hoped they would mutilate my people as they had mutilated me. And when I learned that the missionary was to come, I knew what I was to do. That day like all the others, the same blinding daylight that had been going on so long! Late in the afternoon a guard was suddenly seen running along the edge of the basin, and, a few minutes later, I was dragged to the House of the Fetish and the door closed. One of them held me on the ground in the dark, under threat of his cross-shaped sword and the silence lasted for a long time until a strange sound filled the ordinarily peaceful town, voices that it took me some time to recognize because they were speaking my language, but as soon as they rang out the point of the sword was lowered toward my eyes, my guard stared at me in silence. Then two voices came closer and I can still hear them, one asking why that house was guarded and whether they should break in the door, Lieutenant, the other said: 'No' sharply, then added, after a moment, that an agreement had been reached, that the town accepted a garrison of twenty men on condition that they would camp outside the walls and respect the customs. The private laughed, 'They're knuckling under,' but the officer didn't know, for the first time in any case they were willing to receive someone to take care of the children and that would be the chaplain, later on they would see about the territory. The other said they would cut off the chaplain's you know what if the soldiers were not there. 'Oh, no!' the officer answered, 'In fact Father Beffort will come before the garrison; he'll be here in two days.' That was all I heard, motionless, lying under the sword, I was in pain, a wheel of needles and knives was whirling in me. They were crazy, they were crazy, they were allowing a hand to be laid on the city, on their invincible power, on the true god, and the fellow who was to come would not have his tongue cut out, he would show off his insolent goodness without paying for it, without enduring any offense. The reign of evil would be postponed, there would be doubt again, again time would be wasted dreaming of the impossible good, wearing oneself out in fruitless efforts instead of hastening the realization of the only possible kingdom and I looked at the sword threatening me, O sole power to rule over the world! O power, and the city gradually emptied of its sounds, the door finally opened, I remained alone, burned and bitter, with the Fetish, and I swore to him to save my new faith, my true masters, my despotic God, to betray well, whatever it might cost me.

Gra, the heat is abating a little, the stone has ceased to vibrate, I can go out of my hole, watch the desert gradually take on yellow and ochre tints that will soon be mauve. Last night I waited until they were asleep, I had blocked the lock on the door, I went out with the same step as usual, measured by the cord, I knew the streets, I knew where to get the old rifle, what gate wasn't guarded, and I reached here just as the night was beginning to fade around a handful of stars while the desert was getting a little darker. And now it seems days and days that I have been crouching in these rocks. Soon, soon, I hope he comes soon! In a moment they'll begin to look for me, they'll speed over the trails in all directions, they won't know that I left for them and to serve them better, my legs are weak, drunk with hunger and hate. O! over there, *gra*, at the end of the trail, two camels are growing bigger, ambling along, already multiplied by short shadows, they are running with that lively and dreamy gait they always have. Here they are, here at last!

Quick, the rifle, and I load it quickly. O Fetish, my god over yonder, may your power be preserved, may the offense be multiplied, may hate rule pitilessly over a world of the damned, may the wicked forever be masters, may the kingdom come, where in a single city of salt and iron black tyrants will enslave and possess without pity! And now, *gra gra*, fire on pity, fire on impotence and its charity, fire on all that postpones the coming of evil, fire twice, and there they are toppling over, falling, and the camels flee toward the horizon, where a geyser of black birds has just risen in the unchanged sky. I laugh, I laugh, the fellow is writhing in his detested habit, he is raising his head a little, he sees me – me his all-powerful shackled master, why does he smile at me, I'll crush that smile! How pleasant is the sound of a rifle-butt on the face of goodness, today, today at last, all is consummated and everywhere in the desert, even hours away from here, jackals sniff the non-existent wind, then set out in a patient trot toward the feast of carrion awaiting them. Victory! I raise my arms to a heaven moved to pity, a lavender shadow is just barely suggested on the opposite side, O nights of Europe, home, childhood, why must I weep in the moment of triumph?

He stirred, no the sound comes from somewhere else, and from the other direction here they come rushing like a flight of dark birds, my masters, who fail upon me, seize me, ah yes! strike, they fear their city sacked and howling, they fear the avenging soldiers I called forth, and this is only right, upon the sacred city. Defend yourselves now, strike! strike me first, you possess the truth! O my masters, they will then conquer the soldiers, they'll conquer the word and love, they'll spread over the deserts, cross the seas, fill the light of Europe with their black veils – strike the belly, yes, strike the eyes – sow their salt on the continent, all vegetation, all youth will die out, and dumb crowds with shackled feet will plod beside me in the world-wide desert under the cruel sun of the true faith, I'll not be alone. Ah! the pain, the pain they cause me, their rage is good and on this cross-shaped war-saddle where they are now quartering me, pity! I'm laughing, I love the blow that nails me down crucified.

How silent the desert is! Already night and I am alone, I'm thirsty. Still waiting, where is the city, those sounds in the distance, and the soldiers perhaps the victors, no, it can't be, even if the soldiers are victorious, they're not wicked enough, they won't be able to rule, they'll still say one must become better, and still millions of men between evil and good, torn, bewildered, O Fetish, why hast thou forsaken me? All is over, I'm thirsty, my body is burning, a darker night fills my eyes.

This long, this long dream, I'm awaking, no, I'm going to die, dawn is breaking, the first light, daylight for the living, and for me the inexorable sun, the flies. Who is speaking, no one, the sky is not opening up, no, no, God doesn't speak in the desert, yet whence comes that voice saying: 'If you consent to die for hate and power, who will forgive us?' Is it another tongue in me or still that other fellow refusing to die, at my feet, and repeating: 'Courage! courage! courage!'? Ah! supposing I were wrong again! Once fraternal men, sole recourse, O solitude, forsake me not! Here, here who are you, torn, with bleeding mouth, is it you, Sorcerer, the soldiers defeated you, the salt is burning over there, it's you my beloved master! Cast off that hate-ridden face, be good now, we were mistaken, we'll begin all over again, we'll rebuild the city of mercy, I want to go back home. Yes, help me, that's right, give me your hand. . . .

A handful of salt fills the mouth of the garrulous slave.

Translated from the French by Justin O'Brien

Any Day Now

BY James Baldwin

One evening Vivaldo came to visit them in their last apartment. They heard the whistles of tugboats all day and all night long. Vivaldo found Leona sitting on the bathroom floor, her hair in her eyes, her face swollen and dirty with weeping. Rufus had been beating her. He sat silently on the bed.

"Why?" cried Vivaldo.

"I don't know," Leona sobbed, "it can't be for nothing I did. He's always beating me, for nothing, for nothing!" She gasped for breath, opening her mouth like an infant and in that instant Vivaldo really hated Rufus and Rufus knew it. "He says I'm sleeping with other colored boys behind his back and it's not true, God knows it's not true!"

"Rufus knows it isn't true," Vivaldo said. He looked over at Rufus, who said nothing. He turned back to Leona. "Get up, Leona. Stand up. Wash your face."

He went into the bathroom and helped her to her feet and turned the water on. "Come on, Leona. Pull yourself together, like a good girl."

She tried to stop sobbing and splashed water on her face. Vivaldo patted her on the shoulder, astonished all over again to realize how frail she was. He walked into the bedroom.

Rufus looked up at him. "This is my house," he said, "and that's my girl. You ain't got nothing to do with this. Get your ass out of here."

"You could be killed for this," said Vivaldo. "All she has to do is yell. All *I* have to do is walk down to the corner and get a cop."

"You trying to scare me, motherf*****? Go *get* a cop."

"You must be out of your mind. They'd take one look at this situation and put you *under* the jailhouse." He walked to the bathroom door. "Come on, Leona. Get your coat. I'm taking you out of here."

"I'm not out of *my* mind," Rufus said, "but *you* are. Where you think you taking Leona?"

"I got no place to go," Leona muttered.

"Well, you can stay at my place until you find some place to go. I'm not leaving you here."

Rufus threw back his head and laughed. Vivaldo and Leona both turned to watch him. Rufus cried to the ceiling, "Motherf***** going to come to *my* house and walk out with *my* girl and he thinks this poor nigger's just going to sit and let him do it. Ain't this a bitch?"

He fell over on his side, still laughing.

Vivaldo shouted, "For Christ's sake, Rufus! *Rufus!*"

Rufus stopped laughing and sat straight up. "What? Who the hell do you think you're kidding? I know you only got one bed in your place!"

"Oh, Rufus," Leona wailed, "Vivaldo's only trying to help."

"You shut up," he said, instantly, and looked at her.

"Everybody ain't a animal," she muttered.

"You mean, like me?"

She said nothing. Vivaldo watched them both.

"You mean, like me, bitch? Or you mean like you?"

"If I'm a animal," she flared – and perhaps she was emboldened by the presence of Vivaldo – "I'd like you to tell me who made me one. Just tell me that!"

"Why, your husband did, you bitch. You told me yourself he had a thing on him like a horse. You told me yourself how he did you – he kept telling you how he had the biggest thing in Dixie, black *or* white. And you said you couldn't stand it. Ha-*ha*. *That's* one of the funniest things I *ever* heard," and he grimaced, making a dry, barking sound. "*Didn't* you tell me all that?"

"I guess," she said, wearily, after a silence, "I told you a lot of things I shouldn't have."

Rufus snorted. "I guess you did." He said – to Vivaldo, the room, the river – "it was her husband ruined this bitch. Your husband and all of them funky niggers screwed you in the Georgia bushes. That's why your husband threw you out. Why don't you tell the truth? I wouldn't have to beat you if you'd tell the truth." He grinned at Vivaldo. "Man, this chick can't *get* enough" – and he broke off, staring at Leona.

"Rufus," said Vivaldo, trying to he calm, "I don't know what you're putting down. I think you must be crazy. You got a great chick, who'd go all the way for you – and you know it – and you keep coming on with this Gone With The Wind crap. What's the matter with your head, baby?" He tried to smile; his lips threatened to split. "Baby, please don't do this. Please."

Rufus said nothing. He sat down on the bed, in the position in which he had been sitting when Vivaldo arrived.

"Come on, Leona," said Vivaldo at last and Rufus stood up, looking at them both with a little smile, with hatred.

"I'm just going to take her away for a few days, so you can both cool down. There's no point in going on like this."

"Sir Walter Scott – with a hard-on," Rufus sneered.

"Look," said Vivaldo, "If you don't trust me, man, I'll get a room at the Y. I'll come back here. Goddammit," he shouted, "I'm not trying to steal your girl. You know me better than that."

Rufus said, with an astonishing and a menacing humility, "I guess you don't think she's good enough for you."

"Oh, shit. You don't think she's good enough for *you*."

"No," said Leona, and both men turned to watch her, "ain't neither one of you got it right. Rufus don't think he's good enough for *me*."

She and Rufus stared at each other. A tugboat whistled, far away. Rufus smiled.

"You see? *You* bring it up all the time. *You* the one who brings it up. Now, how you expect me to make it with a bitch like you?"

"It's the way you was raised," she said, "and I guess you just can't help it."

Again, there was silence. Leona pressed her lips together and her eyes filled with tears. She seemed to wish to call the words back, to call time back, and begin everything over again. But she could not think of anything to say and the silence stretched. Rufus pursed his lips.

"Go on, you slut," he said, "go on and make it with your wop lover. He ain't going to be able to do you no good. Not now. You be back. You can't do without me now." And he lay face downward on the bed. "Me, I'll get me a good night's sleep for a change."

Vivaldo pushed Leona to the door, backing out of the room, watching Rufus. "I'll be back," he said.

"No, you won't," said Rufus. "I'll kill you if you do."

Leona looked at him quickly, bidding him to be silent, and Vivaldo closed the door behind him.

"Leona," he asked when they were in the streets, "how long has this been going on? Why do you take it?"

"Why," asked Leona, wearily, "do people take anything? Because they can't help it, I guess. Well, that's me. Before God, I don't know what to do." She began to cry again. The streets were very dark and empty. "I know he's sick and I keep hoping he'll get well and I can't make him see a doctor. He knows I'm not doing none of those things he says, he knows it!"

"But you can't go on like this, Leona. He can get both of you killed."

"He says it's me trying to get us killed." She tried to laugh. "He had a fight last week with some guy in the subway, some real ignorant, unhappy man just didn't like the idea of our being together, you know? and well, you know, he blamed that fight on me. He said I was encouraging the man. Why, Viv, I didn't even *see* the man until he opened his mouth. But, Rufus, he's all the time looking for it, he sees it where it ain't, he don't see nothing else no more. He says I ruined his life. Well, he sure ain't done mine much good."

She tried to dry her eyes. Vivaldo gave her his handkerchief and put one arm around her shoulders.

"You know, the world is hard enough and people is evil enough without all the time looking for it and stirring it up and making it worse. I keep telling him, I know a lot of people don't like what I'm doing. But I don't care, let them go their way, I'll go mine."

A policeman passed them, giving them a look. Vivaldo felt a chill go through Leona's body. Then a chill went through his own. He had never been afraid of policemen before; he had only despised them. But now he felt the impersonality of the uniform, the emptiness of the streets. He felt what the policeman might say and do if he had been Rufus, walking here with his arm around Leona.

He said, nevertheless, after a moment, "You ought to leave him. You ought to leave town."

"I tell you, Viv, I keep hoping – it'll all come all right somehow. He wasn't like this when I met him, he's not really like this at all. I *know* he's not. Something's got all twisted up in his mind and he can't help it."

They were standing under a street lamp. Her face was hideous, was unutterably beautiful with grief. Tears rolled down her thin cheeks and she made doomed, sporadic efforts to control the trembling of her little girl's mouth.

"I love him," she said, helplessly, "I love him, I can't help it. No matter what he does to me. He's just lost and he beats me because he can't find nothing else to hit."

He pulled her against him while she wept, a thin, tired, bewildered girl, and unwitting heiress of generations of bitterness. He could think of nothing to say. A light was slowly turning on inside him, and he saw dangers, mysteries, and chasms he had never seen before.

"Here comes a taxi," he said.

She straightened and tried to dry her eyes.

"I'll come with you," he said, "and come right back."

"No," she said, "just give me the keys. I'll be all right. You go on back to Rufus."

"Rufus said he'd kill me," he said, half smiling.

The taxi stopped beside them. He gave her his keys. She opened the door, keeping her face away from the driver.

"Rufus ain't going to kill nobody but himself," she said, "if he don't find a friend to help him." She paused half in, half out of the cab. "You the only friend he's got in the world, Vivaldo."

He gave her some money for the fare, looking at her with something, after all these months, explicit at last. They both loved Rufus. And they were both white. Now that it stared them so hideously in the face, each could see how desperately the other had been trying to avoid this confrontation.

"You'll *go* there now?" he asked. "You'll *go* to my place?"

"Yes. I'll go. You go back to Rufus. Maybe you can help him. He needs somebody to help him."

Vivaldo gave the driver his address on Bank Street and watched the taxi roll away. He turned and started back the way they had come.

The way seemed longer, now that he was alone, and darker. His awareness of the policeman, prowling somewhere in the darkness near him, made the silence ominous. He felt threatened. He felt totally estranged from the city in which he had been born; this city for which he sometimes felt a kind of stony affection because it was all he knew of home. Yet he had no home here – the hovel on Bank Street was not a home. He had always supposed that he would, one day, make a home here for himself. Now he began to wonder if anyone could ever put down roots in this rock; or, rather, he began to be aware of the shapes acquired by those who had. He began to wonder about his own shape.

He had often thought of his loneliness, for example, as a condition which testified to his superiority. But people who were not superior were, nevertheless, extremely lonely; and unable to break out of their solitude precisely because they had no equipment with which to enter it. His own loneliness, magnified so many million times, made the night air colder. He remembered to what excesses, into what traps and nightmares, his loneliness had driven him; and he wondered where such a violent emptiness might drive an entire city.

At the same time, as he came close to Rufus's house he was trying very hard not to think about Rufus.

He was in a section of warehouses; very few people lived down here. By day, trucks choked the streets, laborers stood on these ghostly platforms, moving great weights, and cursing. As he had once, for a long time, he had been one of them. He had been proud of his skill and his muscles and happy to be accepted as a man among men. Only it was they who saw something in him, which they could not accept, which made them uneasy. Every once in a while a man, lighting his cigarette, would look at him quizzically with a little smile. The smile masked an unwilling defensive hostility. They said he was a "bright kid," that he would "go places"; and they made it clear that they expected him to "go," to which places did not matter – he did not belong to them.

But at the bottom of his mind the question of Rufus nagged and stung. There had been a few colored boys in his high school but they had mainly stayed together, as far as he remembered. He had known boys who got a bang out of going out and beating up niggers. He was not the kind of person who beat up other people, especially not while travelling in a mob, any more than he was the kind of person who pulled wings off flies. But, as the suffering of the fly had never in the least engaged his imagination, neither had the fury of a nigger. It scarcely seemed possible – it scarcely, even, seemed fair – that colored boys who were beaten up in high school could grow up into colored men who wanted to beat up everyone in sight, including, or perhaps especially, people who had never, one way or another, given them a thought. He watched the light in Rufus's window, the only light on down here.

He climbed the stairs to Rufus's apartment and walked in without knocking. Rufus was standing near the door holding a knife.

"Is that for me or for you? Or were you planning to cut yourself a hunk of salami?"

He forced himself to stand where he was and to look directly at Rufus.

"I was thinking about putting it into you, motherf*****." But he had not moved. Vivaldo slowly let out his breath.

"Well, put it down. If I ever saw a poor bastard who needed his friends, you're it."

They watched each other for what seemed like a very long time and neither of them moved. They stared into each other's eyes, each, perhaps, searching for the friend each remembered. Vivaldo knew the face before him so well that he had ceased, in a way, to look at it and now his heart turned over to see what time had done to Rufus. He had not seen before the fine lines in the forehead, the deep, crooked line between the brows, the tension which soured the lips. He wondered what the eyes were seeing – they had not been seeing it years before. He had never associated Rufus with violence, for his walk was always deliberate and slow, his tone mocking and gentle: but now he remembered how Rufus played the drums.

He moved one short step closer, watching Rufus, watching the knife.

"Don't kill me, Rufus," he suddenly heard himself say. "I'm not trying to hurt you. I'm only trying to help."

The bathroom door was still open and the light still burned. The bald kitchen light burned mercilessly down on the two orange crates and the board which formed the kitchen table, and on the uncovered wash and bathtub. Dirty clothes lay flung in a corner. Beyond them, in the dim bedroom, two suitcases, Rufus's and Leona's, lay open in the middle of the floor. On the bed was a twisted grey sheet and a thin blanket.

Rufus stared at him. He seemed not to believe Vivaldo; he seemed to long to believe him. His face twisted, he dropped the knife, and fell against Vivaldo, throwing his arms around him, trembling.

Vivaldo led him into the bedroom and they sat down on the bed.

"Somebody's got to help me," said Rufus at last, "somebody's got to help me. This shit has got to stop."

"Can't you tell me about it? You're screwing up your life. And I don't know why."

Rufus sighed and fell back, his arms beneath his head, staring at the ceiling. "I don't know, either. I don't know up from down. I don't know what I'm doing no more."

The entire building was silent. The room in which they sat seemed very far away from the life breathing all around them, all over the island.

Vivaldo said, gently, "You know, what you're doing to Leona – that's not right. Even if she were doing what you say she's doing – it's not right. If all you can do is beat her, well, then, you ought to leave her."

Rufus seemed to smile. "I guess there *is* something the matter with my head."

Then he was silent again; he twisted his body on the bed. He looked over at Vivaldo.

"You put her in a cab?"

"Yes," Vivaldo said.

"She's gone to your place?"

"Yes."

"You going back there?"

"I thought maybe I'd stay here with you for a while – if you don't mind."

"What're you trying to do – be a warden or something?" He said it with a smile, but there was no smile in his voice.

"I just thought maybe you wanted company," said Vivaldo.

Rufus got off the bed and walked restlessly up and down the two rooms.

"I don't need no company. I done had enough company to last me the rest of my life." He walked to the window and stood there, his back to Vivaldo. "How I hate them – all those white sons of bitches out there. They're trying to kill me, you think I don't know? They got the world on a string, man, the miserable, white c***suckers, and they tying that string around my neck, they killing *me*." He turned into the room again; he did not look at Vivaldo. "Sometimes I lie here and I listen – just listen. They out there, scuffling, making that change, they think it's going to last forever. Sometimes I lie here and listen, listen for a bomb, man, to fall on this city and make all that noise stop. I listen to hear them moan, I want them to bleed and choke, I want to hear them *crying*, man, for somebody to come help them. They'll cry a long time before I come down there." He paused, his eyes glittering with tears and with hate. "It's going to happen one of these days, it's got to happen. I sure would like to see it." He walked back to the window. "Sometimes I listen to those boats on the river – I listen to those whistles – and I think wouldn't it be nice to get on a boat again and go someplace away from all these nowhere people where a man could be treated like a man." He wiped his eyes with the back of his hand, then suddenly brought his fist down on the windowsill. "I can't stand this place, I can't stand it! You got to fight with the landlord because the landlord's *white*! You got to fight with the elevator boy because the motherf*****'s *white*. Any bum on the Bowery can shit all over you because maybe he can't hear, can't see, can't walk, can't f*** – but he's white!"

"Rufus. Rufus. What about – ?" He wanted to say: What about me, Rufus? I'm white. He said, "Rufus, not everybody's like that."

"No? That's news to me."

"Leona loves you –"

"She loves the colored folks so much," said Rufus, "sometimes I just can't stand it. You know all that chick knows about me? The *only* thing she knows?" He put his hand on his sex, brutally, as though he would tear it out, and seemed pleased to see Vivaldo wince. He sat down on the bed again. "That's all."

"I think you're out of your mind," said Vivaldo. But fear drained his voice of conviction.

"But she's the only chick in the world for me," Rufus added after a moment, "ain't that a bitch?"

"You're destroying that girl. Is that what you want?"

"She's destroying me, too," said Rufus.

"Well, is *that* what you want?"

"What *do* two people want from each other," asked Rufus, "when they get together? Do *you* know?"

"Well, they don't want to drive each other crazy, man. I know that."

"You know more than I do," Rufus said, sardonically. "What do *you* want – when you get together with a girl?"

"What do I *want*?"

"Yeah, what do you want?"

"Well," said Vivaldo, fighting his panic, trying to smile, "I just want to get laid, man." But he stared at Rufus, feeling terrible things stir inside him.

"Yeah?" And Rufus looked at him curiously, as though he were thinking, *So that's the way white boys make it.* "Is that all?"

"Well" – he looked down – "I want the chick to love me. I want to make her love me. I want to be loved."

There was silence. Then Rufus asked, "Has it ever happened?"

"No," said Vivaldo, thinking of Catholic girls and whores, "I guess not."

"How do you *make* it happen?" Rufus whispered. "What do you *do*?" He looked over at Vivaldo. He half smiled. "What do *you* do?"

"What do you mean, what do I do?" He tried to smile; but he knew what Rufus meant.

"You just do it like you was told?" He tugged at Vivaldo's sleeve; his voice dropped. "That white chick – Jane – of yours – she ever give you a b*** j**?"

Oh, Rufus, he wanted to cry, *stop this crap!* and he felt tears well up behind his eyes. "I haven't had a chick that great," he said, briefly, thinking again of the dreadful Catholic girls with whom he had grown up, of his sister and his mother and father. He tried to force his mind back through the beds he had been in – his mind grew as black as a wall. "Except," he said, suddenly, "with whores," and felt, in the silence that then fell, that murder was sitting on the bed beside them. He stared at Rufus.

Rufus laughed. He lay back on the bed and laughed until tears began running from the corners of his eyes. It was the worst laugh Vivaldo had ever heard and he wanted to shake Rufus or slap him, anything to make him stop. But he did nothing; he lit a cigarette; the palms of his hands were wet. Rufus choked, sputtered, and sat up. He turned his agonized face to Vivaldo for an instant. Then: "Whores!" he shouted and began to laugh again.

"What's so funny?" Vivaldo asked quietly.

"If you don't see it, I can't tell you," Rufus said. He had stopped laughing, was very sober and still. "Everybody's on the A train – you take it uptown, I take it downtown – it's crazy." Then, again, he looked at Vivaldo with hatred. He said, "Me and Leona – she's the greatest lay I ever had. Ain't nothing we don't do."

"Crazy," said Vivaldo. He crushed out his cigarette on the floor. He was beginning to be angry. At the same time he wanted to laugh.

"But it ain't going to work," said Rufus. "It ain't going to work." They heard the whistles on the river; he walked to the window again. "I ought to get out of here. I better get out of here."

"Well, then, *go.* Don't hang around, waiting – just *go.*"

"I'm *going* to go," said Rufus. "I'm going to go. I just want to see Leona one more time," He stared at Vivaldo. "I just want to get laid – get b**** – loved, one more time."

"You know," said Vivaldo, "I'm not really interested in the details of your sex life."

Rufus smiled. "No? I thought all you white boys had a big thing about how us spooks was making out."

"Well," said Vivaldo, "I'm different."

"Yeah," said Rufus. "I can see that."

"I just want to be your friend," said Vivaldo. "That's all. But you don't want any friends, do you?"

"Yes, I do," said Rufus quickly. "Yes, I do." He paused; then, slowly, with difficulty, "Don't mind me. I know you're the only friend I've got left in the world, Vivaldo."

Then that's why you hate me, Vivaldo thought, feeling still and helpless and sad.

From the Black Notebook

BY DORIS LESSING

Breakfast was over, it was about ten in the morning, and we were glad to have something to fill our time until lunch. A short way past the hotel a track turned off the main road at right angles and wandered ruttily over the veld, following the line of an earlier African footpath. This track led to the Roman Catholic Mission about seven miles off in the wilderness. Sometimes the Mission car came in for supplies; sometimes farm laborers went by in groups to or from the Mission, which ran a large farm, but for the most part the track was empty. All that country was high-lying sandveld, undulating, broken sharply here and there by kopjes. When it rained the soil seemed to offer resistance, not welcome. The water danced and drummed in a fury of white drops to a height of two or three feet over the hard soil, but an hour after the storm, it was already dry again and the gullies and vleis were running high and noisy. It had rained the previous night so hard that the iron roof of the sleeping block had shaken and pounded over our heads, but now the sun was high, the sky unclouded, and we walked beside the tarmac over a fine crust of white sand which broke drily under our shoes to show the dark wet underneath.

There were five of us that morning, I don't remember where the others were. Perhaps it was a week-end when only five of us had come down to the hotel. Paul carried the rifle, looking every inch a sportsman and smiling at himself in this role. Jimmy was beside him, clumsy, fattish, pale, his intelligent eyes returning always to Paul, humble with desire, ironical with pain at his situation. I, Willi and Maryrose came along behind. Willi carried a book. Maryrose and I wore holiday clothes-colored dungarees and shirts.

As soon as we turned off the main road on to the sand track we had to walk slowly and carefully, because this morning after the heavy rain there was a festival of insects. Everything seemed to riot and crawl. Over the low grasses a million white butterflies with greenish white wings hovered and lurched. They were all white, but of different sizes. That morning a single species had hatched or sprung or crawled from their crysallises, and were celebrating their freedom. And on the grass itself, and all over the road were a certain species of brightly-colored grasshopper, in couples. There were millions of them too.

"And one grasshopper jumped on the other grasshopper's back," observed Paul's light but grave voice, just ahead. He stopped. Jimmy, beside him, obediently stopped too. We came to a standstill behind them both. "Strange," said Paul, "but I've never understood the inner or concrete meaning of that song before." It was grotesque, and we were all not so much embarrassed, as awed. We stood laughing, but our laughter was too loud. In every direction, all around us, were the insects, coupling. One insect, its legs firmly planted on the sand, stood still; while another, apparently identical, was clamped firmly on top of it, so that the one underneath could not move. Or an insect would be trying to climb on top of another, while the one under-neath remained still, apparently trying to aid the climber whose earnest or frantic heaves threatened to jerk both over sideways. Or a couple, badly-matched, would topple over, and the one that had been underneath would right itself and stand waiting while the other fought to resume its position, or another insect, apparently identical, ousted it. But the happy or well-mated insects stood all around us, one above the other, with their bright round idiotic black eyes staring. Jimmy went off into fits of laughter, and Paul thumped him on the back. "These extremely vulgar insects do not merit our attention," observed Paul. He was right. One of these insects, or half a dozen, or a hundred would have seemed attractive, with their bright paint-box colors, half-submerged in thin emerald grasses. But in thousands, crude green and crude red, with the black blank eyes staring – they were absurd, obscene, and above all, the very emblem of stupidity. "Much better to watch the butterflies," said Maryrose, doing so. They were extraordinarily beautiful. As far as we could see, the blue air was graced with white wings. And looking down into a distant vlei, the butterflies were a white glittering haze over green grass.

"But my dear Maryrose," said Paul, "you are doubtless imagining in that pretty way of yours that these butterflies are celebrating the joy of life, or simply amusing themselves, but such is not the case. They are merely pursuing vile sex, just like these ever-so-vulgar grasshoppers."

"How do you know?" enquired Maryrose, in her small voice, very earnest; and Paul laughed his full-throated laugh which he knew was so attractive, and fell back and came beside her, leaving Jimmy alone in front. Willi, who had been squiring Maryrose, gave way to Paul and came to me, but I had already moved forward to Jimmy, who was forlorn.

"It really *is* grotesque," said Paul, sounding genuinely put out. We looked where he was looking. Among the army of grasshoppers were two obtrusive couples. One was an enormous powerful-looking insect, like a piston with its great spring-like legs, and on its back a tiny ineffectual mate, unable to climb high enough up. And next to it, the position reversed: a tiny bright pathetic grasshopper was straddled by, dwarfed, almost crushed by an enormous powerful driving insect. "I shall try a small scientific experiment," announced Paul. He stepped carefully among the insects to the grasses at the side of the road, laid down his rifle, and pulled a stem of grass. He went down on one knee in the sand, brushing insects aside with an efficient and indifferent hand. Neatly he levered the heavy-bodied insect off the small one. But it instantly sprang back to where it was with a most surprisingly determined single leap. "We need two for this operation," announced Paul. Jimmy was at once tugging at a grass-stem, and took his place beside him, although his face was wrenched with loathing at having to bend down so close to the swarm. The two young men were now kneeling on the sandy road, operating their grass-stems. I and Willi and Maryrose stood and watched. Willi was frowning. "How frivolous," I remarked, ironical. Although, as usual, we were not on particularly good terms that morning, Willi allowed himself to smile at me and said with real amusement:

"All the same, it is interesting." And we smiled at each other, with affection and with pain because these moments were so seldom. And across the kneeling boys Maryrose watched us, with envy and pain. She was seeing a happy couple and feeling shut out. I could not bear it, and I went to Maryrose, abandoning Willi. Maryrose and I bent over the backs of Paul and Jimmy and watched.

"Now," said Paul. Again he lifted his monster off the small insect. But Jimmy was clumsy and failed, and before he could try again Paul's big insect was back in position. "Oh, you idiot," said Paul, irritated. It was an irritation he usually suppressed, because he knew Jimmy adored him. Jimmy dropped the grass-stem and laughed painfully; tried to cover up his hurt – but by now Paul had grasped the two stems, had levered the two covering insects, large and small, off the two others, large and small, and now they were two well-matched couples, two big insects together and two small ones.

"There," said Paul. "That's the scientific approach. How neat. How easy. How satisfactory."

There we all stood, the five of us, surveying the triumph of common sense. And we all began to laugh again, helplessly, even Willi; because of the utter absurdity of it. Meanwhile all around us thousands and thousands of painted grasshoppers were getting on with the work of propagating their kind without any assistance from us. And even our small triumph was soon over, because the large insect that had been on top of the other large insect fell off, and immediately the one which had been underneath mounted him or her.

"Obscene," said Paul gravely.

"There is no evidence," said Jimmy, trying to match his friend's light grave tone, but failing, since his voice was always breathless, or shrill, or too facetious: "There is no evidence that in what we refer to as nature things are any better-ordered than they are with us. What evidence have we that all these – miniature troglodytes are nicely sorted out male above female? Or even –" he added daringly, on his fatally wrong note "– male with female at all? For all we know, this is a riot of debauchery, males with males, females with females . . ." He petered out in a gasp of laughter. And looking at his heated, embarrassed, intelligent face, we all knew that he was wondering why it was that nothing he ever said, or could say, sounded easy, as when Paul said it. For if Paul had made that speech, as he might very well have done, we would all have been laughing. Instead of which we were uncomfortable, and were conscious that we were hemmed in by these ugly scrambling insects.

Suddenly Paul sprang over and trod deliberately, first on the monster couple, whose mating he had organized, and then on the small couple.

"Paul," said Maryrose, shaken, looking at the crushed mess of colored wings, eyes, white smear.

"A typical response of a sentimentalist," said Paul, deliberately parodying Willi – who smiled, acknowledging that he knew he was being mocked. But now Paul said seriously: "Dear Maryrose, by tonight, or to stretch a point, by tomorrow night, nearly all these things will be dead – just like your butterflies."

"Oh no," said Maryrose, looking at the dancing clouds of butterflies with anguish, but ignoring the grasshoppers. "But why?"

"Because there are too many of them. What would happen if they all lived? It would be an invasion. The Mashopi Hotel would vanish under a crawling mass of grasshoppers, it would be crushed to the earth, while inconceivably ominous swarms of butterflies danced a victory dance over the deaths of Mr. and Mrs. Boothby and their marriageable daughter."

Maryrose, offended and pale, looked away from Paul. We all knew she was thinking about her dead brother. At such moments she wore a look of total isolation, so that we all longed to put our arms around her.

Yet Paul continued, and now he began by parodying Stalin: "It is self-evident, it goes without saying – and in fact there is no need at all to say it, so why should I go to the trouble? – However, whether there is any need to say a thing or not is clearly besides the point. As is well known, I say, nature is prodigal. Before many hours are out, these insects will have killed each other by fighting, biting, deliberate homicide, suicide, or by clumsy copulation. Or they will have been eaten by birds which even at this moment are waiting for us to remove ourselves so that they can begin their feast. When we return to this delightful pleasure resort next weekend, or, if our political duties forbid, the weekend after, we shall take our well-regulated walks along this road and see perhaps one or two of these delightful red and green insects at their sport in the grass, and think, how pretty they are! And little will we reck of the million corpses that even then will be sinking into their last resting place all about us. I do not even mention the butterflies who, being incomparably more beautiful, though probably not more useful, we will actively, even assiduously miss – if we are not more occupied with our more usual decadent diversions."

We were wondering why he was deliberately twisting the knife in the wound of Maryrose's brother's death. She was smiling painfully. And Jimmy, tormented continuously by fear that he would crash and be killed, had the same small wry smile as Maryrose.

"The point I am trying to make, comrades . . ."

"We know what point you are trying to make," said Willi, roughly and angrily. Perhaps it was for moments like these that he was the "father figure" of the group, as Paul said he was. "Enough," said Willi. "Let's go and get the pigeons."

"It goes without saying, it is self-evident," said Paul, returning to Stalin's favorite opening phrases just so as to hold his own against Willi, "that mine host Boothby's pigeon pie will never get made if we go on in this irresponsible fashion."

We proceeded along the track, among the grasshoppers. About half a mile further on there was a small kopje, or tumbling heap of granite boulders; and beyond it, as if a line had been drawn, the grasshoppers ceased. They were simply not there, they did not exist, they were an extinct species. The butterflies, however, continued everywhere, like white petals dancing.

I think it must have been October or November. Not because of the insects – I'm too ignorant to date the time of the year from them, but because of the quality of the heat that day. It was a sucking, splendid, menacing heat. Late in a rainy season there would have been a champagne tang in the air, a warning of winter. But that day I remember the heat was striking our cheeks, our arms, our legs, even through our clothing. Yes, of course it must have been early in the season, the grass was short, tufts of clear sharp green in white sand. So that weekend was four or five months before the final one, which was just before Paul was killed. And the track we strolled along that morning was where Paul and I ran hand in hand that night months later through a fine seeping mist to fall together in the damp grass. Where? Perhaps near where we sat to shoot pigeons for the pie.

We left the small kopje behind, and now a big one rose ahead. The hollow between the two was the place Mrs. Boothby had said was visited by pigeons. We struck off the track to the foot of the big kopje, in silence. I remember us walking, silent, with the sun stinging our backs. I can *see* us, five small brightly-colored young people, walking in the grassy vlei through reeling white butterflies under a splendid blue sky.

At the foot of the kopje stood a clump of large trees under which we arranged ourselves. Another clump stood about twenty yards away. A pigeon cooed somewhere from the leaves in this second clump. It stopped at the disturbance we made, decided we were harmless and cooed on. It was a soft, somnolent drugging sound, hypnotic, like the sound of cicadas, which – now that we were listening – we realized were shrilling everywhere about us. The noise of cicadas is like having malaria and being full of quinine, an insane incessant shrilling noise that seems to come out the eardrums. Soon one doesn't hear it, as one ceases to hear the fevered shrilling of quinine in the blood.

"Only one pigeon," said Paul. "Mrs. Boothby has misled us."

He rested his rifle barrel on a rock, sighted the bird, tried without the support of the rock, and just when we thought he would shoot, laid the rifle aside.

We prepared for a lazy interval. The shade was thick, the grass soft and springy and the sun climbing towards midday position. The kopje behind us towered up into the sky, dominating, but not oppressive. The kopjes in this part of the country are deceptive. Often quite high, they scatter and diminish on approach, because they consist of groups or piles of rounded granite boulders; so that standing at the base of a kopje one might very well see clear through a crevice or small ravine to the vlei on the other side, with great, toppling glistening boulders soaring up like a giant's pile of pebbles. This kopje, as we knew, because we had explored it, was full of the earthworks and barricades built by the Mashona seventy, eighty years before as a defense against the raiding Matabele. It was also full of magnificent Bushmen paintings. At least, they had been magnificent until they had been defaced by guests from the hotel who had amused themselves throwing stones at them.

"Imagine," said Paul. "Here we are, a group of Mashona, beseiged. The Matabele approach, in all their horrid finery. We are outnumbered. Besides, we are not, so I am told? a warlike folk, only simple people dedicated to the arts of peace, and the Matabele always win. We know, we men, that we will die a painful death in a few moments. You lucky women, however, Anna and Maryrose, will merely be dragged off by new masters in the superior tribe of the altogether more warlike and virile Matabele."

"They would kill themselves first," said Jimmy. "'Wouldn't you, Anna? Wouldn't you, Maryrose?"

"Of course," said Maryrose, good-humored.

"Of course," I said.

The pigeon cooed on. It was visible, a small, shapely bird, dark against the sky. Paul took up the rifle, aimed and shot. The bird fell, turning over and over with loose wings, and hit earth with a thud we could hear from where we sat. "We need a dog," said Paul. He expected Jimmy to leap up and fetch it. Although we could see Jimmy struggling with himself, he in fact got up, walked across to the sister clump of trees, retrieved the now graceless corpse, flung it at Paul's feet, and sat down again. The small walk in the sun had flushed him, and caused great patches to appear on his shirt. He pulled it off. His torso, naked, was pale, fattish, almost childish. "That's better," he said, defiantly, knowing we were looking at him, and probably critically.

The trees were now silent. "One pigeon," said Paul. "A toothsome mouthful for our host."

From trees far away came the sound of pigeons cooing, a murmuring gentle sound. "Patience," said Paul. He rested his rifle again and smoked.

Meanwhile, Willi was reading. Maryrose lay on her back, her soft gold head on a tuft of grass, her eyes closed. Jimmy had found a new amusement. Between isolated tufts of grass was a clear trickle of sand where water had coursed, probably last night in the storm. It was a miniature riverbed, about two feet wide, already bone dry from the morning's sun. And on the white sand were a dozen round shallow depressions, but irregularly spaced and of different sizes. Jimmy had a fine strong grass-stem, and, lying on his stomach, was wriggling the stem around the bottom of one of the larger depressions.

The fine sand fell continuously in avalanches, and in a moment the exquisitely regular pit was ruined.

"You clumsy idiot," said Paul. He sounded, as always in these moments with Jimmy, pained and irritated. He really could not understand how anybody could be so awkward. He grabbed the stem from Jimmy, poked it delicately at the bottom of another sand-pit, and in a second had fished out the insect which made it – a tiny anteater, but a big specimen of its kind, about the size of a large match head. This insect, toppling off Paul's grass stem onto a fresh patch of white sand, instantly jerked itself into frantic motion, and in a moment had vanished beneath the sand which heaved and sifted over it.

"There," said Paul roughly to Jimmy, handing back his stem. Paul looked embarrassed at his own crossness; Jimmy, silent and rather pale, said nothing. He took the stem and watched the heaving of the minute patch of sand.

Meanwhile we had been too absorbed to notice that two new pigeons had arrived in the trees opposite. They now began to coo, apparently without any intention of coordination, for the two streams of soft sound continued, sometimes together, sometimes not.

"They are very pretty," said Maryrose, protesting, her eyes still shut.

"Nevertheless, like your butterflies, they are doomed." And Paul raised his rifle and shot. A bird fell off a branch, this time like a stone. The other bird, startled, looked around, its sharp head turning this way and that, an eye cocked up skywards for a possible hawk that had swooped and taken off its comrade, then cocked earthwards where it apparently failed to identify the bloody object lying in the grass. For after a moment of intense waiting silence, during which the bolt of the rifle snapped, it began again to coo. And immediately Paul raised his gun and shot and it, too, fell straight to the ground. And now none of us looked at Jimmy, who had not glanced up from his observation of his insect. There was already a shallow, beautifully regular pit in the sand, at the bottom of which the invisible insect worked in tiny heaves. Apparently Jimmy had not noticed the shooting of the two pigeons. And Paul did not look at him. He merely waited, whistling very softly, frowning. And in a moment, without looking at us or at Paul, Jimmy began to flush, and then he clambered up, walked across to the trees, and came back with the two corpses.

"'We don't need a dog after all," remarked Paul. It was said before Jimmy was halfway back across the grass, yet he heard it. I should imagine that Paul had not intended him to hear, yet did not particularly care that he had. Jimmy sat down again, and we could see the very white thick flesh of his shoulders had begun to flush scarlet from the two short journeys in the sun across the bright grass. Jimmy went back to watching his insect.

There was again an intense silence. No doves could be heard cooing anywhere. Three bleeding bodies lay tumbled in the sun by a small jutting rock. The grey rough granite was patched and jewelled with lichens, rust and green and purple; and on the grass lay thick glistening drops of scarlet.

There was a smell of blood.

"Those birds will go bad," remarked Willi, who had read steadily during all this.

"They are better slightly high," said Paul.

I could see Paul's eyes hover towards Jimmy, and see Jimmy struggling with himself again, so I quickly got up and threw the limp wing-dragging corpses into the shade.

By now there was a prickling tension between us all, and Paul said: "I want a drink."

"It's an hour before the pub opens," said Maryrose.

"Well, I can only hope that the requisite number of victims will soon offer themselves, because at the stroke of opening time I shall be off. I shall leave the slaughter to someone else."

"None of us can shoot as well as you," said Maryrose.

"As you know perfectly well," said Jimmy, suddenly spiteful.

He was observing the rivulet of sand. It was now hard to tell which ant pit was the new one. Jimmy was staring at a largish pit, at the bottom of which was a minute hump – the body of the waiting monster; and a tiny black fragment of twig – the jaws of the monster. "All we need now is some ants," said Jimmy. "And some pigeons," said Paul. And, replying to Jimmy's criticism, he added: "Can I help my natural talents? The Lord gives. The Lord takes. In my case, he has given."

"Unfairly," I said. Paul gave me his charming wry appreciative smile. I smiled back. Without raising his eyes from his book, Willi cleared his throat. It was a comic sound, like bad theater, and both I and Paul burst out into one of the wild helpless fits of laughing that often took members of the group, singly, in couples, or collectively. We laughed and laughed, and Willi sat reading. But I remember now the hunched enduring set of his shoulders, and the tight painful set of his lips. I did not choose to notice it at the time.

Suddenly there was a wild shrill silken cleaving of wings and a pigeon settled fast on a branch almost above our heads. It lifted its wings to leave again at the sight of us, folded them, turned round on its branch several times, with its head cocked sideways looking down at us. Its black bright open eyes were like the round eyes of the mating insects on the track. We could see the delicate pink of its claws gripping the twig, and the sheen of sun on its wings. Paul lifted the rifle – it was almost perpendicular – shot, and the bird fell among us. Blood spattered over Jimmy's forearm. He went pale again, wiped it off, but said nothing.

"This is getting disgusting," said Willi.

"It has been from the start," said Paul composedly.

He leaned over, picked the bird off the grass and examined it. It was still alive. It hung limp, but its black eyes watched us steadily. A film rolled up over them, then with a small perceptible shake of determination it pushed death away and struggled for a moment in Paul's hands. "What shall I do?" Paul said, suddenly shrill; then, instantly recovering himself with a joke: "Do you expect me to kill the thing in cold blood?"

"Yes," said Jimmy, facing Paul and challenging him. The clumsy blood was in his cheeks again, mottling and blotching them, but he stared Paul out.

"Very well," said Paul, contemptuous, tight-lipped. He held the pigeon tenderly, having no idea how to kill it. And Jimmy waited for Paul to prove himself. Meanwhile the bird sank in a glossy welter of feathers between Paul's hands, its head sinking on its neck, trembling upright again, sinking sideways, as the pretty eyes filmed over and it struggled again and again to defeat death.

Then, saving Paul the ordeal, it was suddenly dead, and Paul flung it onto the heap of corpses.

"You are always so damned lucky about everything," said Jimmy, in a trembling, angry voice. His full carved mouth, the lips he referred to with pride as "decadent" visibly shook.

"Yes, I know," said Paul. "I know it. The Gods favor me. Because I'll admit to you, dear Jimmy, that I could not have brought myself to wring this pigeon's neck."

Jimmy turned away, suffering, to his observation of the anteaters' pits. While his attention had been with Paul, a very tiny ant, as light as a bit of fluff, had fallen over the edge of a pit and was at this moment bent double in the jaws of the monster. This drama of death was on such a small scale that the pit, the anteater and the ant could have been accommodated comfortably on a small fingernail – Maryrose's pink little fingernail for instance.

The tiny ant vanished under a film of white sand, and in a moment the jaws appeared, clean and ready for further use.

Paul ejected the case from his rifle and inserted a bullet with a sharp snap of the bolt. "We have two more to get before we satisfy Ma Boothby's minimum needs," he remarked. But the trees were empty, standing full and silent in the hot sun, all their green boughs light and graceful, very slightly moving. The butterflies were now noticeably fewer; a few dozen only danced on in the sizzling heat. The heat-waves rose like oil off the grass, the sand patches, and were strong and thick over the rocks that protruded from the grass.

"Nothing," said Paul. "Nothing happens. What tedium."

Time passed. We smoked. We waited. Maryrose lay flat, eyes closed, delectable as honey. Willi read, doggedly improving himself. He was reading *Stalin on the Colonial Question.*

"Here's another ant," said Jimmy excited. A larger ant, almost the size of the ant-eater, was hurrying in irregular dashes this way and that between grass stems. It moved in the irregular apparently spasmodic way that a hunting dog does when scenting. It fell straight over the edge of the pit, and now we were in time to see the brown shining jaws reach up and snap the ant across the middle, almost breaking it in two. A struggle. White drifts of sand down the sides of the pit. Under the sand they fought. Then stillness.

"There is something about this country," said Paul, "that will have marked me for life. When you think of the sheltered upbringing nice boys like Jimmy and I have had – our nice homes and public school and Oxford, can we be other than grateful for this education into the realities of nature red in beak and claw?"

"I'm not grateful," said Jimmy. "I hate this country."

"I adore it. I owe it everything. Never again will I be able to mouth the liberal and high-minded platitudes of my democratic education. I know better now."

Jimmy said: "I may know better, but I shall continue to mouth high-minded platitudes. The very moment I get back to England. It can't be too soon for me. Our education has prepared us above all for the long littleness of life. What else has it prepared us for? Speaking for myself, I can't wait for the long littleness to begin. When I get back – if I ever do get back that is I shall . . ."

"Hello," exclaimed Paul, "here comes another bird. No it doesn't." A pigeon cleaved towards us, saw us, and swerved off and away in mid-air, nearly settled on the other clump of trees, changed its mind and sped into the distance. A group of farm laborers were passing on the track a couple of hundred yards off. We watched them, in silence. They had been talking and laughing until they saw us, but now they, too, were silent, and went past with averted faces, as if in this way they might avert any possible evil that might come from us, the white people.

Paul said softly: "My God, my God, my God." Then his tone changed, and he said jauntily: "Looking at it objectively, with as little reference as we can manage to Comrade Willi and his ilk – Comrade Willi, I'm inviting you to consider something objectively." Willi laid down his book, prepared to show irony. "This country is larger than Spain. It contains one and a half million blacks, if one may mention them at all, and one hundred thousand whites. That, in itself, is a thought which demands two minutes silence. And what do we see? One might imagine – one would have every excuse for imagining, despite what you say, Comrade Willi, that this insignificant handful of sand on the beaches of time – not bad, that image? – unoriginal, but always apt – this million-and-a-little-over-a-half people exist in this pretty piece of God's earth solely in order to make each other miserable . . ." Here Willi picked up his book again and applied his attention to it. "Comrade Willi, let your eyes follow the print but let the ears of your soul listen. For the *facts* are – the *facts* – that there's enough food here for everyone? – enough materials for houses for everyone? – enough talent though admittedly so well hidden under bushels at the moment that nothing but the most generous eye could perceive it – enough talent, I say, to create light where now darkness exists."

"From which you deduce?" said Willi.

"I deduce nothing. I am being struck by a new . . . it's a blinding light, nothing less . . ."

"But what you say is the truth about the whole world, not just this country," said Maryrose.

"Magnificent Maryrose! Yes. My eyes are being opened to – Comrade Willi, would you not say that there is some principle at work not yet admitted to your philosophy? Some principle of destruction?"

Willi said, in exactly the tune we had all expected: "'There is no need to look any further than the philosophy of the class struggle,'" and as if he'd pressed a button, Jimmy, Paul and I burst out into one of the fits of irrepressible laughter that Willi never joined.

"I'm delighted to see," he remarked, grim-mouthed, "that good socialists – at least two of you call yourselves socialists, should find that so very humorous."

"I don't find it humorous," said Maryrose.

"You never find anything humorous," said Paul. "Do you know that you never laugh, Maryrose? Never? Whereas I, whose view of life can only be described as morbid, and increasingly morbid with every passing minute, laugh continuously? How would you account for that?"

"I have no view of life," said Maryrose, lying flat, looking like a neat soft little doll in her bright bibbed trousers and shirt. "Anyway," she added, "you weren't laughing. I listen to you a lot –" (she said this as if she were not one of us, but an outsider) "– and I've noticed that you laugh most when you're saying something terrible. Well, I don't call that laughing."

"When you were with your brother, did you laugh, Maryrose? And when you were with your lucky swain in the Cape?"

"Yes."

"Why?"

"Because we were happy," said Maryrose simply.

"Good God," said Paul in awe. "I couldn't say that. Jimmy, have you ever laughed because you were happy?"

"I've never been happy," said Jimmy.

"You, Anna?"

"Nor me."

"Willi?"

"Certainly," said Willi, stubborn, defending socialism, the happy philosophy.

"Maryrose," said Paul, "you were telling the truth. I don't believe Willi but I believe you. You are very enviable, Maryrose, in spite of everything. Do you know that?"

"Yes," said Maryrose. "Yes, I think I'm luckier than any of you. I don't see anything wrong with being happy. What's wrong with it?"

Silence. We looked at each other. Then Paul solemnly bowed towards Maryrose: "As usual," he said humbly, "We have nothing to say in reply."

Maryrose closed her eyes again. A pigeon alighted fast on a tree in the opposite clump. Paul shot and missed. "A failure," he exclaimed, mock tragic. The bird stayed where it was, surprised, looking about it, watching a leaf dislodged by Paul's bullet float down to the earth. Paul ejected his empty case, refilled at leisure, aimed, shot. The bird fell. Jimmy obstinately did not move. And Paul, before the battle of wills could end in defeat for himself, gained victory by rising and remarking: "I shall be my own retriever." And he strolled off to fetch the pigeon; and we all saw that Jimmy had to fight with himself to prevent his limbs from jumping him up and, over the grass after Paul who came back with the dead bird yawning, flinging it with the other dead birds.

"There's such a smell of blood I shall be sick," said Maryrose.

"Patience," said Paul. "Our quota is nearly reached."

"Six will be enough," said Jimmy. "Because none of us will eat this pie. Mrs. Boothby can have the lot."

"I shall certainly eat of it," said Paul. "And so will you. Do you really imagine that when that toothsome pie, filled with gravy and brown savory meat is set before you, that you will remember the tender songs of these birds so brutally cut short by the crack of doom?"

"Yes," said Maryrose.

"Yes," I said.

"Willi?" asked Paul, making an issue of it.

"Probably not," said Willi, reading.

"Women are tender," said Paul. "They will watch us eat, toying the while with Mrs. Boothby's good roast beef, making delicate little mouths of distaste, loving us all the more for our brutality."

"Like the Mashona women and the Matabele," said Jimmy.

"I like to think of those days," said Paul, settling down with his rifle at the ready, watching the trees. "So simple. Simple people killing each other for good reasons, lands, women, food. Not like us. Not like us at all. As for us – do you know what is going to happen? I will tell you. As a result of the work of fine comrades like Willi, ever-ready to devote themselves to others, or people like me, concerned only with profits, I predict that in fifty years all this fine empty country we see stretching before us filled only with butterflies and grasshoppers will be covered by semi-detached houses filled by well-clothed black workers."

"And what is the matter with that?" enquired Willi.

"It is progress," said Paul.

"Yes it is," said Willi.

"Why should they be semi-detatched houses?" enquired Jimmy, very seriously. He had moments of being serious about the socialist future. "Under a socialist government there'll be beautiful houses in their own gardens or big flats."

"My dear Jimmy!" said Paul. "What a pity you are so bored by economics. Socialist or capitalist – in either case, all this fine ground, suitable for development, will be developed at a rate possible for seriously undercapitalized countries – are you listening, Comrade Willi?"

"I am listening."

"And because a government faced with the necessity of housing a lot of unhoused people fast, whether socialist or capitalist, will choose the cheapest available houses, the best being the enemy of the better, this fair scene will be one of factories smoking into the fair blue sky, and masses of cheap identical housing. Am I right, Comrade Willi?"

"You are right."

"Well then?"

"It's not the point."

"It's my point. That is why I dwell on the simple savagery of the Matabele and the Mashona. The other is simply too hideous to contemplate. It is the reality for our time, socialist or capitalist – well, Comrade Willi?"

Willi hesitated, then said: "There will be certain outward similarities but . . ." He was interrupted by Paul and myself, then Jimmy, in a fit of laughter.

Maryrose said to Willi: "They're not laughing at what you say, but because you always say what they expect."

"I am aware of that," said Willi.

"No," said Paul, "you are wrong Maryrose. I'm also laughing at what he's saying. Because I'm horribly afraid it's not true. God forbid, I should be dogmatic about it, but I'm afraid that – as for myself, from time to time I shall fly out from England to inspect my overseas investments and peradventure I shall fly over this area, and I shall look down on smoking factories and housing estates and I shall remember these pleasant, peaceful pastoral days and . . ." A pigeon landed on the trees opposite. Another and another. Paul shot. A bird fell. He shot, the second fell. The third burst out of a bunch of leaves skywards as if it had been shot from a catapult. Jimmy got up, walked over, brought back two bloodied birds, flung them down with the others and said: "Seven. For God's sake, isn't it enough?"

"Yes," said Paul, laying aside his rifle. "And now let's make tracks fast for the pub. We shall just have time to wash the blood off before it opens."

"Look," said Jimmy. A small beetle about twice the size of the largest anteater, was approaching through the towering grass stems.

"No good," said Paul, "that is not a natural victim."

"Maybe not," said Jimmy. He twitched the beetle into the largest pit. There was a convulsion. The glossy brown jaws snapped on the beetle, the beetle jumped up, dragging the anteater halfway up the sides of the pit. The pit collapsed in a wave of white sand, and for a couple of inches all around the suffocating silent battle, the sand heaved and eddied.

"If we had ears that could hear," said Paul, "the air would be full of screams, groans, grunts and gasps. But as it is, there reigns over the sunbathed veld the silence of peace."

A cleaving of wings. A bird alighted.

"No don't," said Maryrose in pain, opening her eyes and raising herself on her elbow. But it was too late. Paul had shot; the bird fell. Before it had even hit the ground another bird had touched down, swinging lightly on a twig at the very end of a branch. Paul shot; the bird fell, this time with a cry and a fluttering of helpless wings. Paul got up, raced across the grass, picked up the dead bird and the wounded one. We saw him give the wounded struggling bird a quick determined tight-mouthed look, and wring its neck.

He came back, flung down the two corpses and said: "Nine. And that's all." He looked white and sick, and yet in spite of it, managed to give Jimmy a triumphant amused smile.

"Let's go," said Willi, shutting his book.

"Wait," said Jimmy. The sand was now unmoving. He dug into it with a fine stem and dragged out, first the body of the tiny beetle, and then the body of the ant-eater. Now we saw the jaws of the anteater were embedded in the body of the beetle. The corpse of the anteater was headless.

"The moral is," said Paul, "that none but natural enemies should engage."

"But who should decide which are natural enemies and which are not?" said Jimmy.

"Not you," said Paul. "Look how you've upset the balance of nature. There is one anteater the less. And probably hundreds of ants that should have filled its maw will now live. And there is a dead beetle, slaughtered to no purpose."

Jimmy stepped carefully over the shining round-pitted river of sand, so as not to disturb the remaining insects lying in wait at the bottom of their sand-traps. He dragged on his shirt over his sweaty reddened flesh. Maryrose got up in the way she had – obedient, patient, long-suffering, as if she had no will of her own. We all stood on the edge of the patch of shade, reluctant to plunge into the now white-hot mid-day, made dizzy and giddy by the few remaining butterflies who reeled drunk in the heat. And as we stood there, the clump of trees we had lain under sang into life. The cicadas which inhabited this grove, patiently silent these two hours waiting for us to go, burst one after another into shrill sound. And in the sister clump of trees, unnoticed by us, had arrived two pigeons who sat there cooing. Paul contemplated them, his rifle swinging. "No," said Maryrose, "Please don't."

"Why not?"

"Please Paul."

The heap of nine dead pigeons, tied together by their pink feet, dangled from Paul's free hand, dripping blood.

"It is a terrible sacrifice," said Paul gravely, "but for you, Maryrose I will refrain."

She smiled at him, not in gratitude, but in the cool reproachful way she always used for him. And he smiled back, his delightful, brown, blue-eyed face all open for her inspection. They walked off together in front, the dead birds trailing their wings over jade-colored clumps of grass.

The three of us followed.

"What a pity," remarked Jimmy, "that Maryrose disapproves so much of Paul. Because there is no doubt they are what are known as a perfectly-matched couple." He had tried the light ironic tone, and almost succeeded. Almost, not quite; his jealousy of Paul grated in his voice.

We looked: they were, those two, a perfect couple, both so light and graceful, the sun burnishing their bright hair, shining on their brown skins. And yet Maryrose strolled on without looking at Paul who gave her his whimsically appealing blue glances all in vain.

It was too hot to talk on the way back. Passing the small kopje on whose granite chunks the sun was beating, waves of dizzying heat struck at us so that we hurried past it. Everything was empty and silent, only the cicadas and a distant pigeon sang. And past the kopje we slowed and looked for the grasshoppers, and saw that the bright, clamped couples had almost disappeared. A few remained, one above another, like painted clothes-pegs with painted round black eyes. A few. And the butterflies were almost gone. One or two floated by, tired, over the sun-beaten grass.

Our heads ached with the heat. We were slightly sick with the smell of blood.

At the hotel we separated with hardly a word.

It Always Breaks Out

BY RALPH ELLISON

What a country, what a world! I don't know which was the more outrageous, the more scandalous – the burning of the Cadillac on the senator's beautiful lawn, the wild speech made by the arsonist while the beautiful machine smoked and glowed in flames, or the crowd's hysterical reaction to the weird, flamboyant sacrifice. I know only that I have neither the power nor the will to convey the incident to Monsieur Vannec. How can I, when I've been unable to frame it for myself? To hell with the inquisitive Frenchman, there is simply too much unexpected chaos involved, too many unsettling contradictions have appeared. Besides, I refuse to reveal to him that I'm so much without presence before a phenomenon of my own country. It is a matter of pride: personal, intellectual, national. And especially is this true when I consider Vannec's passionate need to define all phenomena – whether social, political or cultural – and codify them and reduce them to formulae – intricate ones – that can be displayed in the hard sparkling center of a crystal paperweight.

And speaking of paper, how should I explain the manner in which the car burning was handled by the press? How the newspapers reduced the event to a small item which stated simply that a deranged jazz musician had set fire to his flashy automobile on the senator's lawn – with all references to his wild speech and the crowd's reaction omitted? And here is the shameful part requiring an unwilling confession: I would have to tell Vannec that we, the newspapermen, members of the working press, champions of the reported fact who insist upon the absolute accessibility of the news, that we ourselves suppressed it, reduced it to insignificance by reflex and with no editorial urging whatsoever!

Or at least we tried; but despite what we did the event has had, is having, its effect. It spreads by word of mouth, it imposes itself like a bad smell carried by the wind into private homes and into private conversations. Yes, and into our private thoughts. It balloons, it changes its shape, it grows. Worse, it seeps back into consciousness despite all we do to forget it. And we, remember, are tough-minded newspapermen.

Get this: a group of us met that evening to eat and drink and chat – just as we've done once a week for quite some time. Sometimes we exchange information and discuss that part of the news which, for one reason or another, is considered untimely or unfit to print. Often, as on this occasion, we enjoy our private jokes at the expense of some public figure or incident which, in reporting, we find expedient to treat with formal propriety. But tonight our mood was light, almost gay. Or at least it seemed so at the beginning. We were delighted that at last one of the senator's butts had succeeded in answering him, if only briefly and at outrageous expense. But beneath our banter we were somewhat uneasy. The wildman Negro jazzman had made us so. Certainly there was no other reason for it – unless it was the intimate knowledge which each of us possessed of our filed accounts. Otherwise why the uneasy undertone as we relaxed there in the brightly lighted dining room with its sparkle of silver and crystal, its sheen of rich woods, its tinkle of iced glasses and buzz of friendly talk? The very paintings on the wall, scenes of early life on the then remote frontier, moody, misty scenes of peaceful life in great forest clearings, formal portraits of the nineteenth-century founders of the club – all made for a sense of security. Even Sam, our inscrutable but familiar Negro waiter, was part of a ritual. And while I don't mean to imply that the club is a great place, it is a good place indeed, and its food and drink are excellent; its atmosphere, resonant with historical associations and warmly civilized values, most relaxing.

But tonight, as I say, something was working within each of us and it was just after Sam's dark hands had served the second round of after-dinner drinks, placed clean ashtrays before us and withdrawn, that Wiggins, the economics expert, released it.

"What," he said, "do you think of the new style in conspicuous consumption?"

And there it was, right out in the open, wearing a comic disguise. We laughed explosively, not so much at his remark but at ourselves, at the quick summoning up of what lay beneath our calm.

"It was a lulu," Thompson said, "a real lulu."

"Where on earth did that fellow come from?" Wilson said.

"From Chattanooga. He rose up like a wave of heat from the Jeff Davis highway," Wilkins said. "Didn't you hear him say it?"

"I wasn't there," Wiggins said, "but when I heard of it I thought, *Thorstein Veblen, your theory has been carried to the tenth power!*"

"And in horse power," I said. "Wiggins, you always said that Veblen was the comedian of economics. Now I'm beginning to understand."

"That's right, he was an ironist, a humorist of economic theory," Wiggins said, "and all he needed to make that clear was to have had that black boy illustrate his books."

"The learned doctor would have flipped," Larkin said.

"Did you ever see anything like it, a man burning his own car before an audience?"

"He's as wild as those rich Oklahoma Indians who preferred to travel in hook-and-ladder fire trucks or brand new hearses instead of limousines," Wiggins said.

"Yes," I said, "but that was a cultural preference. The Indians were really living in a different world, but this fellow today must have been mad. Off his rocker."

"Just leave it to the senator," Wilson said. "If there's something outrageous to be brought out in people he's the man to do it."

"It'll be interesting to see what this will bring out of the insurance people," Larkin said.

"They'll be wild."

"Man, they're already rewriting their policies!"

"Well, I'll bet no one is as wild as the senator," Thompson said. "He's probably searching for laws to rewrite."

"Can you blame him, that boy tried to tie a knot in his tail."

"Yeah," McGowan said, "ole senator was up there cooking up a barbecue for his VIP guests and here comes a Nigra straight out of nowhere to prepare the hot sauce!"

"I wouldn't be too sure about how the senator is taking it," I said. "I wouldn't be surprised if he isn't sitting in his study right this minute laughing his head off."

"He's baited those people so often that he shouldn't mind when one answers back."

"The senator is an actor," I said, "nothing seems to touch him."

"He's a thick-skinned scoundrel," said Larkin, "a thick-skinned, brilliant scoundrel and a joker."

"Well, that colored fellow really tried to cap his joke. What is this country coming to? A United States senator stands on the floor of the Senate and allows himself the license of saying that so many Negro citizens are driving Cadillac cars that he suggests that the name, the trademark, be changed to the *Coon Cage Eight* – imagine! And as though that weren't scandalous enough, hardly before the news is on the air, a Negro drives an expensive Cadillac onto the senator's grounds and in rebuttal sets it afire! What on earth are we coming to?"

"The senator's a joker, the Negro is a joker, this is a nation of jokers. We aren't coming, we've arrived. Welcome to the United States of Jokeocracy."

"Hell, that was no joke, not the car. That fellow was dead serious."

"The point that interests me," Wilson said, "is that a fellow like that was willing to pay for it. He probably decided that he'd do anything to get back at the senator and this was the damnedest way he could find. If I were the senator I'd reflect on that."

"What do you mean?"

"I mean that it's possible that someone else might decide to call him, and in a more personal way. In fact, I'm surprised that he hasn't provoked someone long before today . . ."

Wilson's voice faded into his thinking and then just as the swift, barely-formed idea flashed into my own mind, Wilson looked around the table, frowning.

"Say," he said, "have we ever had a Negro assassin?"

I looked at him, open-mouthed. It was as though the words had been transferred from my mind to his. I held my breath. Past Wilson's shoulder and far across the room I could see Sam, standing with folded arms. Several pitchers of iced water and a large white crock piled high with iced squares of butter rested on the stand beside him while he glanced casually down the long sweep of the room to where a girl moved gracefully through the door. Her red hair flowed in waves to the shoulders of her white suit and she carried a large blue bag and I thought, *Hail Columbia, long may she wave.* . . . Then I heard Thompson saying,

"You mean in the *United States*?"

"That's right," Wilson said, "have we?"

"Now why on earth would you think of that," I said.

"It just struck me. I don't know. But after today maybe it's time we started thinking about such possibilities . . ."

McGowan made a cage of his fat fingers and lowered them around his drink. "What Wilson means, gentlemen, is that a Nigra who'd burn a Cadillac car would do just about anything. He means that a Nigra like that'll burn good United States currency."

We smiled. McGowan could be amusing about Negroes but we would have liked it better had he not been a Southerner. Somehow they obsessed him and he was constantly sounding off over something they did to disturb his notion of a well-ordered society. And now that I could feel him working up a disquisition on the nature and foibles of the Negro I was glad that Sam was far across the room. McGowan took a drink, sighed and smiled.

"Well, Wilson, I have to agree: that was *quite* a Nigra. But you all don't have to go into any brainstorm to analyze what that Nigra was doing. I'm here to tell you that what the Nigra was doing was running a-muck! His brain snapped, that's what happened; and far as he was concerned he was back up a tree throwing coconuts."

Across from me Wilson was still frowning, looking like a man remembering a bad dream. McGowan's humor wasn't reaching me either.

"I'm serious," Wilson said. "Has there ever been one?"

"I've been thinking about it," Larkin said. "There were McKinley, Roosevelt – Cermac that is, Huey Long – but none of the assassins were colored."

"A Nigra *assassin*," McGowan said, "Are y'all getting drunk already?"

"There might have been a few local killings with a political motive," Thompson said. "Here and there over the years some small town Southern politician might have been shot or knifed. Like that fellow down in Louisiana who made the mistake of getting into a colored man's bed and allowed himself to get caught. But you wouldn't call that political. That was sheer bad judgment and I'd have shot the bastard myself . . ."

"I say, are y'all getting drunk?" McGowan said.

"Come to think about it though," Thompson went on, "how can you tell when those people are doing something politically significant? Down home not enough of them vote and here in the North so few take a part in civic affairs that it's hard to tell what they're up to. We just don't know enough about them for all the statistics we have. We don't have, or *they* don't have, enough social forms through which we can see them with any clarity."

"*Forms?*" McGowan said, "What forms? We don't need any cotton-picking forms! Don't you Yankees recognize that everything the Nigra *does* is political? Thompson, you amaze me. You are Southern born and bred and there are three things we Southerners are supposed to know about and they're history, politics – and Nigras. And especially do we know about the political significance of the Nigra."

"Oh drop it, McGowan," Thompson said, "I'm being serious."

"No sir, I beg to differ," McGowan said, "*I'm* being serious; *you're* being Yankee frivolous. Gentlemen, will y'all grant me a few minutes?"

"Grant you?" Wilkins said. "Hell, you can't talk without making a filibuster. So go on, get it over with."

"Thank you kindly. Gentlemen, I'm going to tell you once and for all, I'm going to impress upon you once and for all, the fact that everything the Nigra does is political. I don't like to take up so sobering a matter so early in the evening but some of us here are getting too drunk too soon . . ."

"Do you mean 'everything' literally?" Wiggins said.

"I mean *everything*," McGowan said. "And especially things which you Yankees would pass over as insignificant. We can start at random. Listen: If you catch a Nigra in the wrong section of town after dark – he's being political because he knows he's got no business being there. If he brushes against a white man on the street or on a stairway, that's very political. Because every once in a while the Nigras get together and organize these 'bumping campaigns' against the white folks. They'll try to knock you off the sidewalk and break your ribs and then they'll beg your pardon as though it was an accident, when we know damn well that it was politics.

"So watch the Nigra's face. If a Nigra rolls his eyes and pokes out his mouth at you – that's downright subversive. If he puts on aristocratic airs – watch him! If he talks about moving up North, he's being political again. Because we know for a fact that the Nigras are moving North in keeping with a long-range plan to seize control of the American government. If he talks too loud on the street or talks about sending his kids up North to college in your presence, or if he buys a tractor – all this is political. Be especially wary of the Nigra who tries to buy himself a bulldozer so he can compete against white men because that is one of the most dangerous political acts of all. A Nigra like that is out to knock down Southern tradition and bury it, lock, stock and barrel. He's worse than a whole herd of carpetbaggers or seven lean years of bollweevils. Waiter," he called to Sam, "bring us another round!" and then to us, "There's absolutely nothing to dry a man out like trying to educate a bunch of Yankees."

As I watched Sam approach, I became uneasy that McGowan in his excitement would offend him. After all, I had learned during the thirties to respect the sensibilities of his people and to avoid all anti-minority stereotypes and clichés. One simply didn't laugh at unfortunates – within their hearing. But if Sam was aware of our conversation his face revealed nothing.

"Hy ya, Sam," McGowan said.

"Fine, Mr. McGowan," Sam said, and looking around the table, "Gentlemen?"

And we ordered, after which Sam slipped away.

"Let me tell y'all something else," McGowan went on. "If you catch a Nigra buying his food and clothing from the wrong dealer – or worse, if he goes to another town to trade, that's Nigra politics *pretending* to be Nigra economics. That's something for you to think about, Wiggins. If a Nigra owns more than one shotgun, rifle, or pistol, it's political. If he forgets to say 'sir' to a white man or tries to talk Yankee talk or if he drives too doggone slow or too doggone fast, or if he comes up with one of these little bug-eyed foreign cars – all these things are political and don't you forget it!"

McGowan paused. Sam was crossing the floor with a tray of drinks, which he placed before us and left.

"Come on, educate us some more," Thompson said. "Then we can talk seriously."

McGowan's eyes twinkled. "I'd be glad to. But if you think this isn't serious, study history. For instance, if a Nigra buys his woman a washing machine – watch him, he's dangerous! And if he gets her a clothes dryer and a dishwasher – put that Nigra under the jail for trying to undercut our American way of life. You all can smile if you want to but things like that are most political. In fact, there are few things in this world as political as a black Nigra woman owning her own washing machine.

"Now don't laugh about it. You Yankees must remember that the Industrial Revolution was *revolutionary*, because if y'all don't the Nigra does, and he never stops scheming to make it more so. So verily verily I say unto you Yankees: Watch the Nigra who owns more than one TV because he's getting too ambitious and that's bound to lead him into politics. What's more, if you allow the Nigra to see Indians killing white folks week after week – which is another Yankee mistake – he's apt to go bad and the next thing you know he's learning about that Nehru, Nasser, and those Mau-Maus and that's most politically unwise. It doesn't matter that the Indians are always defeated because the Nigra has the feeling deep down that *he* can win. After all, Nigras are Southern too.

"And I'll tell you something else: If his woman or his gal chillun come up wearing blonde wigs, or if they dye their kinky Nigra hair red, you might think it amusing but I know that those Nigra women are being defiantly political. On the other hand, if they *stop* straightening their hair in the old Southern darky tradition and start wearing it short and natural like those African Nigras – right there you have you a bunch of homegrown Nigras who're on the way to being hopelessly contaminated. Those Nigras are sweating and breathing politics. Call Edgar Hoover!

"Watch the papers the Nigra reads, especially if you see him subscribing to the *Wall Street Journal* or *The New York Times*. Watch him closely if he gets interested in the stock market. Because such a Nigra is power hungry and the next thing you know he'll want to vote and run for public office . . ."

"There," Wiggins said, "that's what really worries you, isn't it?"

McGowan shook his head.

"I wouldn't say that. Although I'll admit that between a Nigra making big money and getting the vote, money is the lesser evil. A Nigra millionaire – once you can stomach the idea – is a pretty safe Nigra. Because if the old saying is still true that there's nothing more timid than a million bucks, then a million *Nigra* bucks are bound to be ten times as afraid. So don't worry about the Nigra millionaire; he's just a Nigra with more money than he knows how to spend. Ever hear of one endowing a college or building a library, setting up a scientific laboratory? Hell no!"

"I'm glad to learn that there's at least *something* about the Negro which isn't political," Thompson said.

"There is, but not too much," McGowan said. "Because the Nigra is a *political* animal. He came out of Africa that way. He makes politics the same way a dirt dauber makes mud houses or a beaver builds dams. So watch his environment. If you see his woman putting up pictures on the wall – regard her with suspicion because she's liable to break out in a *rash* of politics.

"If a Nigra joins the Book-of-the-Month Club or the Great Books program – investigate him. Because when a Nigra gets hold to such deals they become more political than *Das Kapital* and the *Communist Manifesto* put together. There was a time when everybody thought that the Bible was the only book that a Nigra should be allowed to read, but now I be damned if he hasn't even made the Good Book political.

"So I counsel you to watch your educated Nigra. If he reads Bill Shakespeare, that's all right because no Nigra who ever lived would know how to apply the Bard – not even that big, stupid buck Nigra, Othello, who was so dumb that when his poor, dear, sweet little wife, Desdemona, dropped her Kotex in the wrong place and he heard about it, right away he thinks in his ignorant Nigra fashion that she's allowed somebody to tamper with her and he lets that nasty Italian bastard – what's-his-name – confuse him and agitate him into taking her life. Poor little thing. No sir, no Nigra born has ever been up to dealing with Bill Shakespeare. But if you catch you a Nigra reading that lowdown, Nigra-loving Bill Faulkner and *liking* him, there you have you a politically dangerous, integrationist Nigra!"

"Why do you specify his *liking* what he reads?" Thompson said.

"That's the kind of question for a Yankee to ask, not you; because you're suppose to know that any sensible Nigra would get scaird spitless reading what that fellow Faulkner writes. He's more dangerous to our tradition than a bulldozer.

"But now let's look into another area. You want to watch what the Nigra eats because it has been established that some Nigra foods are political while others are not. And it's a proven fact that the moment the Nigra changes his diet he gets dissatisfied and restless. So watch what he eats. Fat meat, cornbread, lima beans, ham hocks, chitterlings, watermelon, blackeyed peas, molasses, collard greens, buttermilk and clabber, neckbones and red beans and rice, hominy, both grit and lye hominy – these are traditional foods and healthy for the Nigra and *usually* – and I stress the *usually* – not political . . ."

"What about chicken," Larkin said, "you overlooked chicken."

"Chicken is no problem," McGowan said. "It's traditional and harmless in the political sense – unless, of course, a wrong-headed political Nigra is caught stealing one. And even so, there's nothing necessarily political about a Nigra stealing a chicken. In fact, down South we agree that a Nigra's suppose to steal him a chicken every now and then and the only crime involved is in his getting caught."

"But," McGowan said, holding up his hand and allowing it to slap the table, *Pow!* "*Lobster* is out!"

Wiggins sputtered over his drink. "Oh Lord," he said. "Oh Lord protect us!"

"Gentlemen, I tell you truly, lobster on a Nigra's table is political as hell. Lobster gives him false courage. It puts rocks in his Nigra jaws and wild ideas in his Nigra brain. In short, lobster, any kind of lobster, broiled, boiled, fried, fradiavalloed – serve it anyway you damn please – lobster simply messes a Nigra *up*. If the price of lobster ever hits bottom this country will have bad trouble.

"And watch the rascal if he develops a taste for T-bone steaks, Cornish hens, sweetbreads, calves liver (although pig liver is traditional and okay), parsnips, artichokes, venison, or quiche lorraine – he's been under bad influences and getting political again. Therefore it's a good idea to watch what he does with traditional foods. For instance, if he starts to baking his pigs feet in cheese cloth instead of boiling them naked in the Southern Nigra fashion – right there you have a potentially bad Nigra on your hands.

"And don't overlook the political implications of a Nigra eating too much Chinese, Japanese or Jewish food. Call the F.B.I. if you catch him buying French wines, German beer or drinks like Aquavit or Pernod. One time down in New Orleans a Nigra drank a glass of that Pernod and went straight down to the court house and cussed out the judge, a distinguished Cajun, in French! Nigras who drink such liquors have jumped the reservation and are out to ruin this nation.

"Scotch whiskey is just as bad. A Nigra doesn't even have to have heard about Bonny Prince Charlie, but let him start drinking Scotch whiskey and he swears he's George Washington's great-great-grandson and the rightful head of the United States Government. And not only that, a Nigra who switches to Scotch after being brought up on good corn and bourbon is putting on airs, has forgotten his place and is in implicit rebellion. Besides, have you ever considered what would happen to our liquor industry if all the Nigras switched to drinking Scotch? A calamity! a catastrophe!"

McGowan leaned forward, lowering his voice confidentially, his eyes intense.

"At this point I want to get on to other aspects of the subject but before I do let me remark on one of the meanest, lowdownest forms of Nigra politics I have observed, and one which I mention among a bunch of gentlemen only with the greatest reluctance. That's when a sneaky, ornery, smart-alecky Nigra stands up in a crowd of peaceful, well-meaning white folks, who've gathered together in a public place to see Justice done, and that Nigra ups and breaks wind!

"I was attending a murder trial once and just as the judge was charging the jury, some politically subversive Nigra standing way back in the rear of the courtroom – because that's *exactly* where it came from – he let loose, and gentlemen, all at once the courthouse is in an uproar. Folks are standing up protesting and complaining, ladies are fanning themselves and fainting and the flabbergasted judge is fairly beating his gavel to a frazzle ordering the windows thrown open and the courtroom cleared. It was simply what you call a *mess*. And in all that disruptive atmosphere the poor jury gets so confused that not only is the case thrown out of court but the guilty Nigra standing trial goes scot-free! And would you believe it, that nasty rascal didn't even have himself a lawyer!"

"The hell you say!" Wiggins roared.

"It's sad, gentlemen," McGowan said as we sputtered for breath, "but it's true. You simply have to be constantly alert and vigilant against Nigra politics because it can break out in a thousand forms. For instance, when you find a Nigra boy looking at these so-called 'girlie' magazines that flagrantly display naked white womanhood – which is something else you Yankees are responsible for – whip his head. Because when a Nigra starts looking at that type magazine he's long gone along the road laid down by those Japs who broke the white man's power in Asia by ordering their soldiers to sleep with every white trash whore gal they could lay their filthy yalla hands on. In the eyes of a Nigra boy all such photographs and cartoons become insidiously political . . ."

"Oh come now," someone said.

"You wonder why?" McGowan thrust forth his jaw, his eyes burning. "Because they undermine the white man's mastery, and over-expose the white woman's mystery; that's why. They show the buck Nigra everything we've been working three hundred years to keep concealed. You have to remember that those renaissance fellows had nothing on the American Nigra except power! With him even *poon* tang is a political instrument! So you think about it.

"Now Thompson here was talking about our not having any 'forms' through which we can see what the Nigra is up to politically and I've been demonstrating that he's mistaken. But he's right to the extent that the Nigra hasn't developed any forms of his own. He's just copied the white man and twisted what he copied to fit the Nigra taste. But he does have his own Nigra church, and his own Nigra religion, and the point I want to make is that he gets *political* according to his religion. Did you ever hear that explained before?"

"*I* haven't," I said.

"I know it. None of you have; so I'll go on and tell you. Baptist Nigras and Methodist Nigras and Holy Roller Nigras are okay. Even Seven Day Adventist Nigras are all right – even though they're a bit strange even to other Nigras. All these Nigra religions are okay. But you have got to watch the Nigra who changes *from* Baptist *to* Episcopalian *or* Catholic. Because that is a Nigra who has gone ambitious and turned his back on the South. And make no mistake, that Nigra isn't searching for God, no siree; he's looking for a political scantling to head-whip you with.

"And watch the young Nigra who joins up with Father Divine. It's not the same as when a poor old-fashioned Nigra who's lost in the North gets homesick for the South and joins up; the young one is out to undermine society and is probably staying up nights scheming and praying and trying to get God on the Nigra side. Same thing when a Nigra becomes a Jew – who the hell ever heard of one of our *good* Nigras joining up with the Jews? When a Nigra does that he's political, subversive, unruly and probably over-sexed – even for a Nigra!

"Now what are some of the political aspects of the Nigra here in D.C.? Well, around here things are so out of hand, mongrelized and confused that I don't know where to begin, but here are a few manifestations: Nigras visiting white folks; walking or riding along the streets with white women; visiting the Congress; hanging around Abe Lincoln's monument; visiting white churches; carrying picket signs; sending delegations to see the President; carrying briefcases with real papers in them; Nigras wearing homburg hats and chesterfield overcoats; hiring uniformed chauffeurs, especially if the chauffeur is white. All these things are political, because the Nigra who does them is dying to become a diplomat so that he can get assigned abroad from where he aims to monkey with our sovereign states rights.

"To these add those Nigras from Georgia and Mississippi who turn up wearing those African robes and turbans in an effort to break into white society and get closer to white folks. Gentlemen, there's nothing worse or more political than a Nigra who denies the United States of America because that is a Nigra who has not only turned his back on his mammy and pappy but has denied the South!

"Here are some other forms of Nigra politics which y'all have overlooked: these young buck Nigras going around wearing berets, beards and tennis shoes in the wintertime and whose britches are so doggone tight that they look like they're 'bout to bust out of them. They're not the same as the white boys who dress that way, they're politically dangerous and it's worse, in the long run, than letting a bunch of Nigras run around the Capital carrying loaded pistols. A law ought to be passed before something serious occurs.

"And be on watch for your quiet Nigra. Be very careful of the Nigra who's too quiet when other loud-mouthed Nigras – who are safe Nigras – are out sassing white folks on the street corners and in the Yankee press and over the Yankee radio and TV. Never mind the loudmouths, they're like the little fierce dogs that bark at you when you approach the big gate and then, when you walk into the yard they run to lick your hand. Throw them a bone. But keep your eye on the quiet Nigra who watches every move the white man makes and studies it, because he's probably trying to think up a theory and a strategy and tactic to subvert something . . ."

"But go back to the automobile," Wiggins said. "My father-in-law is a dealer and I think he needs instruction."

"I'm glad you reminded me," McGowan said. "Now I've told you about those little foreign cars but there's more to the political significance of Nigras and autos. Cadillacs *used* to be okay but after what that Nigra did today on Senator Sunraider's lawn, I'm not so positive. That doggone Nigra was trying to politicalize the Cadillac! Which proves again what I say about everything the Nigra does being potentially political. But once you grasp this fact you also have to watch the Nigra who doesn't want a Cadillac, because he can stand a heap of political analysis.

"And pay close attention to the Nigra who has the money to buy one but picks an Imperial instead. Likewise the Nigras who love English autos. Watch all Nigras who pick Jaguars, Humbers, and if you ever hear of one, Rolls Royces. Likewise those who go around bragging about the Nigra vote electing the president of the United States. Such Nigras are playing dirty politics even though they might not be able to vote themselves. Yes, and watch the Nigra who comes telling a white man about the Nigra's 'gross yearly income,' because there you have an arrogant, biggety Nigra who is right up in your face talking open politics and who thinks you don't recognize it. Unless of course, you're convinced that the Nigra is really trying to tell you that he knows how you and him can make some quick money. In such a case the Nigra is just trying to make a little hustle for himself, so make a deal with him and don't worry about it because that Nigra doesn't give a damn about anybody or anything except himself – while the other type is trying to intimidate you.

"Then there's the Nigra who reads the Constitution and the law books and *broods* over them. That's one of the most political types there is. And like unto him is the Nigra who scratches his behind when he talks to a white man instead of scratching his head in the traditional Southern Nigra manner – because even where the Nigra *scratches* is political!

"But gentlemen, let me hasten to say after this very brief and inadequate catalogue of Nigra political deviousness, that to my considerable knowledge no Nigra has ever even *thought* about assassinating anybody. And I'll tell y'all why: It was bred out of him years ago!"

Even as I laughed I watched the conflicting expressions moving back and forth across McGowan's broad face. It looked as though he wanted desperately to grin but like a postage stamp which had become too wet, the grin kept sliding in and out of position. And I in turn became agitated. My laughter – it was really hysteria – was painful. For I realized that McGowan was obsessed by history to the point of nightmare. He had the dark man confined in a package and this was the way he carried him everywhere, saw him in everything. But now, laughing, I realized that I envied McGowan and admitted to myself with a twinge of embarrassment, that some of the things he said were not only amusing but true. And perhaps the truth lay precisely in their being seen humorously. For McGowan said things about Negroes with absolute conviction which I dared not even think. Could it be that he was more honest than I, that his free expression of his feelings, his prejudices, made him freer than I? Could it be that his freedom to say what he felt about all that Sam the waiter symbolized actually made him freer than I? I Suddenly I despised his power to make me feel buried fears and possibilities, his power to define so much of the reality in which I lived and which I seldom bothered to think about.

And was it possible that the main object of McGowan's passion was really an idea, the idea of a non-existent past rather than a living people?

"Yes, gentlemen," McGowan was saying. "The only way to protect yourself from the Nigra is to master politics and that you Yankees have never done because y'all have never studied the Nigra."

Across the room I watched Sam, his hands held behind him, smiling as he chatted pleasantly with a white-haired old gentleman. Were there Negroes like McGowan, I wondered. And what would they say about me? How completely did I, a liberal, ex-radical, northerner, dominate Sam's sense of life, his idea of politics? Absolutely, or not at all? Was he, Sam, prevented by some piety from confronting me in a humorous manner, as my habit of mind, formed during the radical thirties, prevented me from confronting him; or did he, as some of my friends suspected, regard all whites through the streaming eyes and aching muscles of one continuous, though imperceptible and inaudible, belly laugh? *What the hell*, I thought, *is Sam's last name?*

The Will and the Way

BY SUSAN SONTAG

The story begins in a crowded place, something like a Greyhound bus station, only more refined. The main character is an intrepid young woman, of irreproachable white Protestant ancestry and even, regular construction. Her only visible fault was mirrored in her name, Miss Flatface.

Buffeted by mechanical stares, Miss Flatface decided to enter upon a career of venery. The spirits of Ben Franklin and Tom whispered hoarsely in her ears, beckoning and forbidding.

Miss Flatface lifted up her skirts. A gasp was heard from one and all. "No sex, no sex," the crowd chanted. "Who could inspire desire with that face?"

"Try me," she murmured bravely, backing against a white tile wall. They continued to taunt her, without moving.

Then Mr. Obscenity bounded into the room, wearing white knickers, a plaid shirt, and a monocle. "The trouble with you fellows," he said, leering at Miss Flatface, then dramatically ripping open her nylon blouse without bothering to undo the buttons, "is that you've got principles. Too esthetic by far, that's what's wrong with you." He gave Miss Flatface a shove for emphasis; she stared, surprised, her eyelids fluttering. "Mild as any sucking dove," he added, seizing her left breast and aiming it at the enrapt spectators.

"Hey, I'm her husband, you know," said a sturdy young fellow – Jim was his name – who separated himself from the crowd.

"Miss Flatface is only her maiden name. Back home she's plain Mrs. Jim Johnson, proud wife and mother of three, Den Mother, Vice-president of the PTA at Green Grove School – that's where our kids go – and Recording Secretary of the local League of Women Voters. She has 9 and 3/4 books of King Korn trading stamps and a 1962 Oldsmobile. Her mother – that's my mother-in-law – would be mad as hell if I let you get away with this." He paused. "If I let you get away with this – Mr. Obscenity – sir."

"That's better," said Mr. Obscenity.

"Jim," Miss Flatface called out in a cross tone. "It's no use, Jim. I've changed. I'm not coming home."

Something like a chariot, drawn by a team of two roan horses, pulled up before the frosted glass doors. Mr. Obscenity vaulted into his seat, and with a gesture that admitted of no refusal, summoned Miss Flatface to hers. Above the clattering hoofs, as they sped away, moans and giggles could be heard.

2.

Back home, Miss Flatface – formerly Mrs. Johnson – had been renowned for having the cleanest garbage on the block. But in the place to which Mr. Obscenity had spirited her, nothing seemed amenable to the laws of sanitation as she had known them. Overripe peaches were languidly let fall, half-eaten, onto the whitewashed wood floors. Sheets of pale blue legal-size paper were scrawled over with drawings of the male and female genitals, crumpled, then hurled into a corner of the room. Winestains flourished on the damask tablecloths, which were never changed. A flaking lipstick-smeared magazine photo of Marlon Brando was nailed on the inside of the closet door; the window sills remained undusted; there was barely time for Miss Flatface to brush her teeth once a day; and the condition of the bed – particularly that of the pillow, bristling with tiny feathers – was not to be believed.

From her window Miss Flatface could see the ocean, and a carousel and a roller coaster called "The Hurricane," and small figures – grouped in twos and in families – sauntering up and down the boardwalk. It was summertime, and the several greasy fans about the room carved the air without vanquishing the heat. Miss Flatface longed to bathe in the ocean, though she would not have dreamed of washing off the pungent body smells that Mr. Obscenity relished. Her craving for cotton candy was more feasible. Practically no sooner had she voiced this wish than there it lay, wrapped in newspaper, at her door. But when she was only half through, eagerly ripping off wads of the pink fuzz with her unnecessary teeth, Mr. Obscenity leaped on the bed and took her. Amid the twanging of bedsprings the slim cardboard cone, swathed with the wet sticky mess, fell unnoticed to the floor.

Sometimes people dropped in for dinner. While Mr. Obscenity presided at the end of the long oak trestle table, various swarthy figures bandied talk of Communism, free love, race mixing. Some of the women wore long gold earrings. Some of the men had pointed shoes. Miss Flatface had some notion of foreigners from movies. What she hadn't known about was their dreadful table manners, like, for instance, the way they tore off chunks of bread with their fingers. And the rich garlicky stews and foamy custards did not always agree with her. After dinner there was usually a good deal of solemn belching. Miss Flatface happily joined in.

Though sometimes unnerved, as much by the pulpy confusion of foods as by the tenor and momentum of the conversation, Miss Flatface had by now a good deal of confidence in Mr. Obscenity. He, whatever the state of his guests, was always immaculate and neatly buttoned. Her confidence was further increased by the clipboard stuffed with mimeographed papers which Mr. Obscenity often carried and frequently consulted, even at the dinner table. This augured well, thought Miss Flatface. There is some system here.

Hearty and ready for fun at the drop of a hat, that's how Miss Flatface tried to think of the guests. When lewd plaster statuettes were passed around the table, her neighbor might nudge her in the groin to express enthusiasm. Occasionally a pair of guests would sink beneath the table, which would shudder for a while until the flushed and disheveled couple re-emerged.

Observing that Mr. Obscenity seemed to wish to show her off to all his friends, Miss Flatface resolved to be as friendly as possible. One day, she hoped, there would be nothing that he might ask of her that she could not do.

"Sure is a nice little woman you got there," observed one of his black friends, a man everyone called Honest Abe. The black man flinched, flicking his cigar ash into a gold-plated diaphragm that served as an ashtray, and tilted back his chair.

"Take her," said Mr. Obscenity with a genial wave of his hand. Then he jotted something on the clipboard.

"Well, I dunno," said Honest Abe. He rubbed the fringe beard which decorated his chin, musing.

Miss Flatface wondered. Was this big black Honest Abe afraid of slim Mr. Obscenity? Or did he find her undesirable?

"Ain't much of a face."

That settled it! Tears got ready behind Miss Flatface's eyes.

"And white women ain't good for my blood. That's what the Prophet says."

"Abe!" said Mr. Obscenity, menacingly.

"Yes, Mr. Obscenity. I mean yeah, boss. I mean yes, sir."

Honest Abe hoisted his great bulk wearily from the table, dropping his napkin. A heap of breadcrumbs tumbled from his lap to the floor. "Well, little woman, let's see what you and me can do. Can't do you no more harm than it does me." He chuckled.

Miss Flatface rose eagerly. She felt the faint tingling in her stomach. The spirits of James Fenimore Cooper and Betsy Ross whispered in her ears, beckoning and forbidding. "It's my duty, isn't it?" she asked Mr. Obscenity, wishing to quell the last shreds of doubt that soiled her perfect resolution. "The national will, I mean. The national purpose. And the national presence."

"You must do what you have to do," said Mr. Obscenity coldly. "This, after all, is the American dilemma." He made a notation on his clipboard, then turned back to his guests.

Honest Abe carefully removed his maroon velvet jacket and hung it on the back of his chair, then unstrapped the transistor radio which nestled in his armpit.

So that's where the music was coming from, thought Miss Flatface.

Their union took place in a bathtub, whose hard white enamel surface had been draped with gaily-colored bath towels, blue and purple and brown and yellow, like the tent of a sheik. Over the upper portion of the towels someone had considerately, perhaps even reverently, laid the Stars and Stripes. They do smell different, Miss Flatface had the presence of mind to observe. But it's a nice strong smell. I wonder why I was so afraid of them when I went into that candy store late one night to buy a pack of Luckies, or in the movie theater balcony (I was just a kid then) when that big one sat down beside me. Seeing them in the newsreels rioting and throwing bricks in their own dingy streets, it makes you afraid. There seem to be so many of them. But, one at a time, they're not so frightening once you get really close. They deserve all the rights they can get, she concluded.

3.

As day followed night, which was followed by day, all spent in riotous pleasures, Miss Flatface sometimes wondered if she still deserved her name. But Mr. Obscenity proved a stern taskmaster. He would not allow her near a mirror. He refused to answer any questions about her appearance, her talents, or her destiny.

Never once did she think of her mother, the widow of a railroad engineer and now living in St. Louis, not even to the extent of wishing to send her a postcard. Occasionally, very occasionally, she thought of Jim and the three children. Had he sold the Oldsmobile, she wondered. He wouldn't need two cars. . . . But there was no turning back.

"You have some power," she said to Mr. Obscenity one day. "But why are people afraid of you?" The spirits of Henry Adams and Stephen Crane whispered hoarsely in her ears, beckoning and forbidding. But was it forbidden to ask questions? It shouldn't be! Not in a free country.

"I mean, how did you get Jim to let me go so easy?"

Mr. Obscenity did not reply. He was plunged deep in Miss Flatface, elementary position. He merely placed a pillow over her animated visage.

She flung off the pillow. "And Honest Abe?" she said, looking up into his calm faraway eyes. "Why was *he* afraid of you?" Still no answer. "He's bigger – I mean taller – than you."

Mr. Obscenity continued to leaf, as it were, through her body. A gale of wind, premonitory of something, had just come up. Somewhere a shutter was banging against a wall.

Miss Flatface's attention began to wander. She watched a fly sipping at a puddle of cold coffee on the nighttable. Next the label on Mr. Obscenity's new tan jodhpurs, heaped on the floor, caught her eye. Finally she wondered if Mr. Obscenity had any trouble getting listed in the telephone book.

"Pay attention," he barked, withdrawing from Miss Flatface, turning on his side, and lightly dusting her torso with sugar.

"I am."

"Don't contradict me. You aren't."

"Well, what if I do think of other things? Who says I have to think about it all the time? Doesn't thinking spoil it anyway?"

"Look," he said, "this isn't an eurhythmic exercise, you know."

"Well, I don't know what that means," she said self-righteously, "but I know it isn't supposed to be hard labor either."

"Don't play innocent with me! I don't have all these people parked here for nothing."

Above the buzzing of flies about her breasts, Miss Flatface suddenly tuned in on a chorus of raspy breathing coming from the other end of the room. In the hallway, just outside the door, four Air Force lieutenants appeared to be playing bridge.

"I didn't see them," she protested.

Mr. Obscenity grunted.

"Honest, I didn't."

"I bet you were a fussy eater when you were a kid," muttered Mr. Obscenity.

"No, really –"

Mr. Obscenity replaced the pillow. Miss Flatface resigned herself to pleasure. She would ask her questions another time.

4.

"How do you like this life?" Mr. Obscenity deigned to inquire one afternoon in a muffled voice, while nuzzling between Miss Flatface's legs.

"Gosh," she exclaimed, "I never imagined life could be like this!"

"Want to continue to live like this?" he asked.

"Sure!" Since childhood, Miss Flatface had always said "Sure!" when she wasn't. "Who'd want to live different? I can hardly imagine it," she went on, with a tremor of anxiety at this untimely chain of consecutive words.

"Ah, my dear," sighed Mr. Obscenity sitting upright amid the damp rumpled sheets and patting Miss Flatface on the thigh. "I'm afraid you've had it. Don't you know, one must never think that no other life is possible than this. All other lives are imaginable, possible, even probable."

"What have I done?" she cried, dismayed to see that he had inserted his monocle in the socket of his left eye. Mr. Obscenity never removed his monocle except when engaged in the most profound carnal inquiry.

"Unless you wish to risk your life in one of the most picturesque exploits known to man – an orgy with no holds barred – I'm going to send you on your way. With references, of course. And some cash to see you through your first week."

An orgy with no holds barred? Drugs? Instruments of torture? Perversions? Artificial phalluses three feet long? She bowed her head in thought. The spirits of William James and Fatty Arbuckle whispered hoarsely in her ears, beckoning and forbidding. Mr. Obscenity drummed an indecipherable tune on her belly with his fingertips, waiting for her to come to a decision.

She was a brave girl, but not that brave. One sought an education in order to use it. She had not left Jim to die, but to live. For Miss Flatface there was a limit, even to voluptuousness. Innocent as she might be, despite all she'd experienced, she had some sense of her own worth.

"Want to flip a coin?" said Mr. Obscenity, languidly sketching with a soft orange lipstick the details of the pudenda in the vicinity of Miss Flatface's navel.

"Don't bother. I'll go," she said.

Someone put a dime in the jukebox. "Anyone Who Had a Heart," wailed a girl, "Would Love Me." Mr. Obscenity whisked a mirror from his pocket and began preening himself. First he inspected the inside of his nostrils, then punched his midriff for signs of flabbiness. Miss Flatface had never felt so let down in all her life. Suddenly, she felt terribly, terribly alone.

5.

Yet, Miss Flatface knew she was not alone in this place. There were other young American women here, too, in the charge of other educators like Mr. Obscenity. Just possibly they might be all in the charge of Mr. Obscenity himself. Miss Flatface preferred not to think about that.

All houses by the ocean are damp. Added to the damp – for it was getting on to winter now – was the fact that the place was being painted. Workmen were constantly trooping through her room; buckets of paint, stiff abandoned brushes, rollers, cans of turpentine, and huge rough paint-encrusted ladders lay about, adding to the confusion. The place was being renovated. Miss Flatface gave way to a profound gloom.

Days went by without a glimpse of Mr. Obscenity. Miss Flatface tried to recall all she owed him. At first she supposed her tantrum was desire. It wasn't that. Not being of a grateful disposition, what Miss Flatface craved was revenge. She even had a plan. She would persuade some of the other boarders, pupils, call them what you will, to leave with her. Then Mr. Obscenity would regret the whim which had prompted him to decree her expulsion.

Who would she take? Only women, she decided. Dragging men along would make it too complicated. Miss Flatface had never thought of herself as a feminist before, certainly not when she had been Jim's wife and the mother of three. But now she felt the tug of sex loyalty. The spirits of Edith Wharton and Ethel Rosenberg whispered hoarsely in her ears, beckoning and forbidding.

Or was it that?

That very night, looking a bit slovenly in her blue flowered wraparound housecoat, she crept about the drafty corridors, listening and whenever she could watching at keyholes. Scenes of aching delight assaulted her senses. Was this the Eden she was to be deprived of? Then no one else should have it, either.

In the hall she accosted a dark-haired young lady wearing a beige trench coat over nothing else.

"You look like you can be trusted," said Miss Flatface cheerfully. "And since I'm clearing out of here – I mean I've had enough – how about coming with me? Wouldn't you like to bathe in the ocean, or ride 'The Hurricane'? You know, do whatever you want and not have to be taking down your bloomers all the time?"

Quick as a flash, the girl reached under her trench coat and pulled out a dark metal object. A gun? Miss Flatface drew back in terror. No, a camera. The girl laid the cold instrument to her eye, and rapidly snapped a number of close-ups of her astonished conpanion.

"These can be developed by morning," said the girl. "I'll send you copies, if you want 'em."

"But what for?" cried Miss Flatface, realizing that her conspiracy was not even getting off the ground.

"They're for my album." Noting Miss Flatface's uncomprehending stare, she added, "You know, my collection."

"Your collection?"

"For 1046y, Marriage & the Family," replied the girl. "A research project for my junior year. Four points."

Although mystified, Miss Flatface now grasped enough to confirm her suspicion that this place was not the haven of spontaneous misrule it might appear. How else explain this girl, a crisp secretarial type, who probably took dictation at some phenomenal speed? Miss Flatface felt like an old frump.

The girl bared her large white teeth in a smile, then glided down the corridor.

"Wait," called Miss Flatface. "I *would* like a picture. I mean, so I can see what I look like in it."

"Why not," said the girl. "Tomorrow morning. And I won't use your name. Everyone is anonymous, you know. It makes the project more scientific."

Scientific! There's an idea! Why hadn't she thought of that before? Every large institution requires great machines, and this one couldn't be different. All she had to do was to get control of that machinery. That's what a revolution is. Not simply to use force, but to seize the means of power. Miss Flatface hastened to the boiler room. The floor was flooded, piles of moldy soaked books were precariously balanced on top of orange crates, and the stench of urine was almost unbearable. But the only machinery she found was a row of television screens, each carrying a different image, topped by a single screen which repeated one or another image from the row. Below the screens was a great prickly table studded with switches and buttons and dials and levers; and before that table, manipulating the panel and sporting a set of earphones, sat a bulky figure wearing a white plastic hood.

"Mr. Obscenity," she whispered, fearing the worst, and preferring immediate censure to suspense.

Instead of turning, the figure convulsively manipulated some dials. The image on the master screen changed from a roller-skating derby to a woman, legs agape, in the last stages of childbirth. Demoted, the roller-skating derby continued, one of the images on the row below.

"Please tell me who you are. I know I shouldn't be here."

Competing with all these images, Miss Flatface feared she would never get an answer. The figure in the white hood threw a switch. A bald toothy state governor addressing a Shriners' convention was promoted from the row to the master screen, and the anguished mother-to-be seemed much calmer seen only once, next to the roller-skating derby. The political speech lasted a few moments. It was erased by the image Miss Flafface had had her eye on from the beginning, surely the most interesting, a delightful erotic scene between two women and a Nisei youth with an enormous erection.

Making an effort, Miss Flatface wrenched her glance from the master screen.

"Mr. Obscenity, I love you." This was a feckless lie.

A commercial for a new roll-on deodorant blanked out the erotic scene on the television screen. The impassive figure turned, its attention for the moment released. Miss Flatface, tremblingly, undid her blue flowered housecoat, yearning to seduce. So far so good: now she had the attention of the eyes, which were all of the hooded face she could see, quite to herself. A hand reached toward her clammy thighs. Miss Flatface noticed that the hand seemed slenderer than Mr. Obscenity's.

"Yes, yes," she cried, leaning toward the hand.

But at that very moment, the commercial ended, and the Nisei youth and the two women resumed their sport. The hooded technician's delicate hand hovered in mid-air, suspended between Miss Flatface and the instrument panel. Seconds that seemed like hours passed. Then the machine won: the hand abruptly lunged toward a dial. Humiliated, Miss Flatface wrapped the housecoat around her shivering loins, and found her way back to her room.

6.

Next morning Miss Flatface, her eyes reddened by the first weeping she had done since she left Jim, was scooped from sleep by a loud knocking.

"Laura," said the man at the door, who wore a grey chesterfield coat and a grey porkpie hat. "Laura?" he said again, turning the name into a question.

No one had ever called Miss Flatface by her first name in this place before.

"Miss Laura Flatface?"

Miss Flatface was stunned, speechless.

"Let me innerduce myself." The man handed Miss Flatface an embossed card. *Inspector Jug, Detective*, it read. *By appointment only.*

"Now let's get this straight, Laura," said the man, all ceremony seemingly concluded. He had sat down now, but hadn't removed his hat.

"Who said you could call me by my first name?" cried Miss Flatface, indignant.

"Now lookee here, Laura," said the man soothingly. "I don't mean to frighten yer" – he said yer instead of you – "but I've gotten wind of what yer up to, and it just won't wash. No ma'am, it just won't wash. Them girls stay here, and the TV sets, too, and you gotta go. That's what the boss – you know who I mean – called me in to tell yer."

Provoked by her rejection of last night, Miss Flatface decided to see if Inspector Jug was proof against her charms.

"Music, Inspector? And perhaps a little wine?"

"Don't mind if I do, ma'am."

"You can call me Laura."

Ignoring the spirits of Eddie Duchin and John Philip Sousa which whispered hoarsely in her ears, beckoning and forbidding, she put on one of the latest pop ballads, rapidly climbing to the top of the Top Forty. The voices of an androgyne quaternity and the quakings of their electric guitars resounded in a heavenly echo chamber. Miss Flatface, ever attuned to new things, was entranced. But Inspector Jug was clearly of the older generation. "Turn off that record," he howled, pulling at his tie. "How can you stand all that bawlin'?"

"I like it," said Miss Flatface sweetly, suddenly lowering herself in his lap.

"Hey, watcha –"

Just then, another knock on the door.

"God damn!" muttered Miss Flatface.

It was the dark-haired girl, good as her word, who silently proferred a small manila envelope.

Miss Flatface tore it open, then gazed with delight upon her own features. Thank God, things had not gone too far: they were not indecently protruding. Perhaps they didn't protrude even in an average way. But that a definite change had taken place – a distinctly forward, assertive movement of her face – there could not be the slightest doubt. In her glee, forgetting who else there was to embrace, she threw her arms around the dark-haired girl and kissed her.

"Who's there," called out the Inspector, who although he'd been backing off from Miss Flatface's attentions was now beginning to feel ignored. It seemed that this day he would not have his mind solely on his professional duties. "Why doncha invite yer friend in?" he said, feigning causalness. Perhaps, he thought quickly, Mr. Obscenity could use a report on this one, too.

"Okay," said the girl. "For my collection," she explained to Miss Flatface, who didn't know whether she wished to share Inspector Jug with anyone else.

"Well, well, well," said the Inspector. "What a pretty pair of ladies we have here. One a little older" – he pointed to Miss Flatface, who was gratified to be mentioned first. "One a little younger, he said, pointing to the junior student in Marriage & the Family. "One blonde" – Miss Flatface again. "And one brunette" – the girl. "One with dimpled knees" – it was Miss Flatface's knees that were being fondled; "one with knees like a tennis player" – the Inspector stroked the back of the girl's leg. "One with a mole on her –"

"Inspector Jug!"

Alas, here Inspector Jug's anatomical inventory was rudely interrupted. At the fireplace stood Mr. Obscenity, black-caped and arms extended like a great winged bat. His monocle glinted with the reflected rays of the sun, making one eye obsidian and relentless. His teeth seemed to be longer, and hair had sprouted on the palms of his hands. His face was a thing of terrible wrath. There was not a trace of mockery or compassion on it. Inspector Jug blanched, but held his ground; he did not move his hands, which rested on the buttocks of both women.

"You can't talk to me like that, Mr. Obscenity."

The girl screamed, broke away from Inspector Jug's grasp, and pulled down her skirt.

"You were my most trusted assistant, Jug," said Mr. Obscenity sternly. "And you have betrayed that trust. You know my motto: every man to his business. I know my business. And you should have known yours."

Inspector Jug had, visibly, begun to quail. Miss Flatface, feeling the hand which had grasped her buttocks so avidly now loosening its grip, becoming more tentative, even distracted in its lust, moved away. She had a faintly unpleasant sensation of coolness, also of emptiness, exactly in the place where Inspector Jug had held her.

Mr. Obscenity advanced, hands like claws.

"But Mr. Obscenity – sir –"

At these halting deferential words Miss Flatface knew the game was up. Inspector Jug couldn't brave Mr. Obscenity any more than the others. The king of the jungle, she thought, will ever be king.

"You!" called Mr. Obscenity to Miss Flatface, imperiously. "Stay where you are.

I want a word with you, as soon as I've lopped a piece off this sniveling rogue."

"Don't go, Laura," pleaded Inspector Jug. "You can clear everything up. Tell him how businesslike I was when I first came in the door. I wasn't doin' nothin' wrong. You can tell him that, Laura. Tell him! Please!"

Mr. Obscenity sank his fangs, through winter coat and all, into Inspector Jug's shoulder.

"Is there a way out of here," Miss Flatface said, addressing herself to the dark-haired girl, who crouched cowering by the door. The girl pointed, mutely. Miss Flatface heard the sound of prancing hoofs. "Consider this an escape," she announced to the two men.

"I'll get you," shouted Mr. Obscenity. "No one escapes from here. You must be expelled." Saliva streamed from the corners of his mouth.

"Me, too, Laura," shouted Inspector Jug, pressing a handkerchief to his bleeding shoulder. "I'll get yer for gettin' me in dutch with my boss. Hellion! Bitch!"

"I'm staying," said the dark-haired girl, dropping her skirt to her ankles and lifting her sweater over her head. The two men ignored her, their first act in unison. All their hot desire, tardy as the hottest desire ever is when it is not premature, was flung at the proud departing figure of Miss Flatface.

7.

She never regretted her departure-escape. Her apprenticeship was over. Strictly speaking, her chosen career of venery could only be practiced on the outside, in the world proper. It all worked out perfectly. Because the life of a woman not drawn to this profession either by breeding (remember her impeccable white Protestant descent) or by background (Jim, the three children, the League of Women Voters, the trading stamps) is a hard and lonely one, she might have faltered. As it was, she had reason to court solitude. She knew those two would not give up easily.

Pursued by Mr. Obscenity and Inspector Jug, Miss Flatface traversed the length and breadth of the United States, carrying her warm treasure between her legs. Wherever she went, she spied replicas of her former self – pale, greedy, self-denying women fortified by pop-up toasters with infrared rays and boxed sets of stainless steel steak knifes made in West Germany. Miss Flatface, penitent for her former life, traveled light. Of course, she sold herself for money. The spirits of William Jennings Bryan and Leland Stanford chided her, when she didn't get a good price.

Her mentor, Mr. Obscenity, first caught up with her in a lumber camp in the Northwest, somewhere near the Canadian border. He was not wearing his monocle or his knickers. His plaid shirt was carelessly stuffed into a pair of faded bluejeans. Miss Flatface, plying her trade in front of the town's only movie theater, did not at first recognize him. His recent exertions seemed to have aged him. He had grown a little fat, and was less well groomed.

What rang a bell was the low mocking bow he made as she ambled seductively past him.

"Come near me and I'll scream," Miss Flatface returned with surprising presence of mind.

"Don't panic. I'm not going to force you. Did I ever force you to do anything?" Miss Flatface remembered. The answer was no.

"Just come back," he said. "We'll forget everything that's happened."

"You sound like Jim," she said.

A sulky coquettish expression passed across Mr. Obscenity's features. He had decided to ignore her last remark. "I'm not as spry as I used to be," he mused aloud. "I don't know why, but I'm tired."

"I'm not," she said. "At least, not yet."

"Well, just tell me one thing. Has that rat Jug found you yet?"

Miss Flatface slowly began to realize this new, unearned power she had over Mr. Obscenity.

"Because if he does," he continued, "and you listen to him, I'll kill you both." He snarled. "Listen to me! If not for me, then for your own sake. Don't you realize he's the undoing of all that you and I have done?"

Miss Flatface considered that this was possibly so, but she wouldn't give Mr. Obscenity the satisfaction of letting him know she agreed with him.

"Well," he said, sighing, "let's get it over with. On the house, of course."

"Certainly not," said Miss Flatface with great severity. "I'm not a charitable institution."

"I was," said Mr. Obscenity.

His irony, intended to arouse sympathy, backfired. Miss Flatface laughed. Mr. Obscenity's lips became foamy, and he parted them in a sinister smile which disclosed a set of razor-sharp teeth. He advanced gruesomely, inexorably.

Miss Flatface made the sign of the cross. It didn't work. But, opportunely, a tree toppled and grazed him on the skull, leaving Miss Flatface plenty of time to slip down an alley and make her escape.

Her suppliant, Inspector Jug, first accosted her some months later while the roof of her mouth was burning from an impetuously gobbled slice of pizza-with-pepperoni. They were squeezed side by side in an all-night eatery in Times Square.

"Gee, Laura," he sighed, wheezing. "It's been a long time catching up with yer."

"I've nothing to say to you," she said, wiping her mouth with a paper napkin.

"You don't hafta say nothin' to me. Just clear me with my boss. That guy's awful mad at me."

"How's your shoulder?" asked Miss Flatface with routine sympathy.

"Poorly, Laura."

"Well, I can't help you. I've got to look after myself, think of myself first. . . . Anyway, stop passing the buck. Be a man! What do you care what he thinks? Don't you know this is a free country? You're free, So am I. And" – a little sententiously – "I intend to make use of the liberty which God and the Constitution have awarded me."

Inspector Jug looked distinctly crestfallen at this militant declaration.

"Anyway, are you on the level?" asked Miss Flatface. "I mean, is this the real reason, the only reason you've been following me around? I did get that smutty wire in New Orleans, you know. I just didn't see any reason to answer it." She ordered another slice of pizza.

"Well, little lady. . . . I reckon not. I really like yer. For yerself. You've got spunk. Guts. I sorta thought we might team up, Laura, maybe start a little agency, with you as a full partner. Lots of divorce cases, stuff like that. A lady investigator does even better than a man. How about it?"

"You mean you've been following me all over the country to make me a business proposition!" The spirits of John Brown and Dashiell Hammett whispered hoarsely in her ears, beckoning and forbidding.

"Well, I admit it ain't just that. I'm attracted to yer, I admit it. . . . Why don't we go to my hotel now and . . ."

"Look," said Miss Flatface. "I meant it when I said this was a free country. It took me a long time to find my freedom, and I'm not giving it up. At least, not until it's *my* idea, not somebody else's." And after these forceful words, she abandoned her second slice of pizza uneaten on the counter and marched out into the turbulent street.

Looking back, she saw that Inspector Jug did not follow her.

Miss Flatface's brave words to Mr. Obscenity and Inspector Jug were sincerely meant. She did love her freedom. But that did not mean she was not occasionally lonely.

Proof might be that in this period a streak of morbidity cropped out in Miss Flatface, which expressed itself in a taste for disasters. Not political disasters: while in Times Square, she rarely looked up at the news flashing by. The private, domestic ones. Between jobs, for which she used a convenient hotel on Tenth Avenue, she would buy and pore over all the scandalous weekly papers. She found irresistible such headlines as: "My Milk Killed My Nine Babies." "For My Husband's Sake I Was Blind For Forty-Two Years." "I'm Not Ashamed." "I Looked Like This Until I Had Plastic Surgery." "Cooked Alive!" "I'm A Member Of The Fourth Sex." "My In-Laws Drove Four Nails Into My Skull." "I'm Not Ugly, I'm Just Funny Looking." "They Left Me Outside For Seventeen Years." The stories, often, were less vivid than the headlines, but, no matter. From the headlines alone Miss Flatface received sufficient and, need one say, vicarious pleasure. For she'd decided that she herself was perfectly normal looking. Never did she meet the slightest reluctance from the Johns because of her flat face.

But if men generally found her attractive, she had to admit that she did not find every man equally attractive. A total sensual thrill was not always forthcoming. Yet she might flare up simply upon spotting from behind someone whom she thought at first was Mr. Obscenity, or even the insipid Inspector Jug.

Miss Flatface tried to drown her occasional discontents by keeping on the move. That way, too, she got to know this country extremely well – its enormous human resources, its majestic natural setting. From time to time she would take a vacation, travel just for the sake of traveling (this also helped to throw her mentor and her suppliant off the track), saving a little money and hitchhiking or taking a bus to the Grand Canyon or Yosemite National Park or Carlsbad Caverns. Once she spent two whole weeks in a little cabin in the Ozarks, catching up on back issues of the *Saturday Evening Post*, sleeping twelve hours a day, and occasionally yielding to the advances of George, the proprietor of the Friendly Ed Motel in the nearest town.

She knew some other work would be less strenuous than hustling. A telephone operator or a clerk at a J. C. Penny's or a waitress had it easier than she. It was not just the risk of disease but all the standing, and even worse, the walking; her feet swelled and it was hard to find attractive heels that didn't pinch her corns. But, really, she wouldn't have changed her life for any other. It had brought her a peace of mind, a vitality and an aplomb, she'd never known before. She who had often flagged in her daily tasks as a fully mechanized suburban housewife with only three children, two of them school age, now found herself always on the go, full of pep. Truly the power of sex, even though discovered late in life, is a magical one.

So great was her energy that when she first encountered both Mr. Obscenity and Inspector Jug at the same time – it was a deserted street, lined with warehouses, on the near north side of Chicago – she had the presence of mind to call the police and have them arrested for molesting her. Actually, they hadn't gotten around to that yet. Mr. Obscenity, monocled, clad in a parka, corduroy pants, and high rubber snowboots, was leading Inspector Jug by some sort of harness. That's what I call a sick relationship, she thought.

The Chicago police are not noted for their courage or their incorruptibility, but they did not seem in the least fazed by the odd-looking pair which Miss Flatface consigned to their care.

"I bet that's not the last of them," Miss Flatface reflected aloud, as she left the station, after the disreputable twosome had been booked. Mingled with anxiety, there was a wistful note in her voice.

8.
Mr. Obscenity and Inspector Jug, usually singly, rarely in tandem, accosted Miss Flatface no less than 174 times within the next five years, by telephone, telegram, and personal appearance. Often the interruption was very embarrassing, and Miss Flatface lost her composure. Gradually, however, her strongest emotion toward the pair was condescension, with a touch of alarm. Would they never give up? Didn't they know the meaning of rejection? Had they no pride?

9.
While eating in a diner just outside of Tulsa, Oklahoma, Miss Flatface finally fell in love for the first time in her life. He was a sailor, named Arthur; seated next to her at the counter, his feet twined around the bar stool, he was bulldozing his way through three hamburgers doused in ketchup and relish. Miss Flatface longed to reach out and touch his smooth healthy cheek. The spirits of Warren G. Harding and John F. Kennedy whispered hoarsely in her ears, beckoning and forbidding. For Arthur looked a little like Jim. Something in the eyes, in the shape of the head, the way the hair curled at the nape of his neck. Watch out! the Spirits cried. But he's not Jim, said Miss Flatface to herself. Nor am I I.

He's a man, that's the resemblance, observed Miss Flatface, after a few nights in Arthur's tireless arms. Of course, he isn't very interested in sexual variety. (Neither was Jim.) But who needs that, she said to herself, sternly repressing all memories of the unpredictable Mr. Obscenity. The main thing is that he loves me. And he won't sit on me – a figure of speech – as Jim did, because now I know my own mind.

She went with Arthur to San Diego, where a wedding ceremony was performed. They rented a room at the Magnolia Arms, with cooking privileges, but Miss Flatface no longer liked to cook. When Arthur was away – he regularly shipped out for weeks at a time – she lived on cans: ravioli, which she ate cold, and sardines, and spiced ham. In the morning, after going down to get the mail, she would wander over to the local Bowl; in the afternoon there was bingo. Needless to say, she was faithful to Arthur – sealing her fidelity by taking to wearing loafers and white socks, an ungainly fashion from her own high school days. And Arthur, when he returned home, was as affectionate as ever.

"Laurababy," he would shout as he burst in the door, his tanned face beaming. "Boy, did I miss my baby! Boyoboyoboy." Miss Flatface loved the boy in Arthur even more than the lover.

When she turned to his body, upon his return from a voyage, it was first to see if he had any new tattooes. That was a game between them. Arthur's forearms and biceps were already printed with colorful designs; now he made sure to get them in less likely places. He would fall on the bed squealing – he was ticklish, too; another one of his charms – as Miss Flatface examined his armpits, his navel, the folds of his groin, and all the secret zones of his body. "Just wait till I get hold of you," he would mutter with mock fierceness, between his squeals and giggles. Miss Flatface would insist on continuing to look carefully for the tattooes. This game was a lovely part of their joy. In her joy with Arthur Miss Flatface began to forget her former lives.

She had a reminder, though, after one particular evening while he was in port, and out with some of his seamen buddies. On such evenings Miss Flatface knew better than to ask to come along, but she allowed herself to question Arthur when he came home about what he did. "Aw, you know," he said this evening. "A lot of booze. And chasin' after girls – not that I'm interested in any other girl when I got my baby here at home waitin' for me. And talkin' to a couple of funny fellows at the Blue Star."

"What fellows?"

"Oh, just some guys." He laughed, and slapped his chest. "Fact is, they were the funniest two fellows you ever laid eyes on, honey. One had a monocle and some kind of crazy outfit, like he was English or something. Like one of them polo players. Real stuck up. But the other guy, the guy he was with, he was real friendly. Got me to talking about myself. I told them all about you, what a great little wife I got." He smacked his lips appreciatively, then planted them on her neck.

"Arthur," Miss Flatface cried shrilly. "You just stay away from those two men. Don't ask me to explain. Just stay away from them. Promise me! You hear?"

"Okay, okay, okay." Arthur's spirits drooped, for he was not accustomed to being yelled at by his wife. A mean thought, one of the few ever to cross his mind, came without ado to his lips. "I guess I understand. I know you got a pretty wild past –"

"Arthur!"

"Aw, I'm sorry." Kiss. "Let's forget about it. Come on, let's watch some TV and get to bed, huh?"

Throughout the night, Miss Flatface could not rid herself of the suspicion that Mr. Obscenity and Inspector Jug, at separate windows, were watching her and Arthur making love. She longed to get up and look. But she hated to alarm Arthur. She doubted – since he was groggy with beer – if his potency could have survived such an interruption.

At dawn, with Arthur curled up on one side of the bed, Miss Flatface made her way outdoors. It was as she'd suspected. Her two pursuers were nonchalantly sitting on the curb, near the bus stop.

"I thought you two hated each other," she said irritably.

"We've made up," said Inspector Jug. "Joined forces."

"Pay no attention to him," said the familiar imperious voice of Mr. Obscenity, tinged with silver mockery. "You know your place, my dear. And it's not at the side of that – boy." He spat the word out with something less than contempt. "Was it for this childish purple, red, and green Arthur that I rescued you from Jim, taught you all you know? Good God, woman, do you realize how much older you are than he? Does *he* realize it?"

"We've never talked about it," said Miss Flatface tearfully. "He loves me."

"But does he *know* you?" persisted Mr. Obscenity. "Does he know you? As I do."

"Mr. Obscenity – sir," interjected the ever apologetic Inspector Jug.

"Quiet, you moron!"

"But shouldn't we tell her the dope I've got on him? I got this whole dossier."

"What dossier?" she cried.

"Well, Laura," began Inspector Jug in a confidential tone, "yer Arthur wasn't always a sailor. Before that he was a –"

"You idiot!" screamed Mr. Obscenity, losing altogether, for the first time in Miss Flatface's knowledge, his splendid self-control. "Don't you see that's no way to get her back!"

"Oh, it doesn't matter," said Miss Flatface, growing stronger in the face of Mr. Obscenity's disarray. "You can't spoil Arthur for me. I need him. And I won't give him up."

"And when he's thirty? Do you realize what an old bag you'll be?"

"It doesn't matter," said Miss Flatface. "Let me be, both of you, I beg you. I've done my duty. I had my pleasures. Now I want to be."

Suddenly Mr. Obscenity's knickers looked wrinkled and absurd in the bright sunshine. His monocle seemed grotesquely affected. And no one, but no one, wears a hat in Southern California, least of all on a sunny early morning. Miss Flatface began to laugh.

10.

After only a few more months of second marriage, Miss Flatface, still in the flower of her womanhood, became mortally ill. It began as ptomaine poisoning, contracted just over the border, in Tijuana. As she had approached the aged vendor's cart, and even while she was chewing the tacos, a food she had never particularly liked, the spirits of Margaret Fuller and Errol Flynn screamed warnings in her ears. But she hadn't heard them. Ever responsive to the American spirit in its broader manifestations, she had never been particularly attuned to its more direct signals. Arthur, on the other hand, who never heard voices, had settled for a Pepsi.

Two weeks after she took to their Castro Convertible, sustained by the best medical care the seamen's union could provide, she became delirious. Eyeing the grieving man slumped in a chair by her side, she cried, "Jim, I didn't know that you were here!" Then, with just the slightest touch of insincerity: "It was grand of you to come!"

But it was not Jim. It was still Arthur. Faithfully, he nursed her through the endless hours of bedpans and cups of consommé and damp washcloths laid on her still far from prominent features. And although he was the one romance in her life, Miss Flatface barely acknowledged Arthur's care. In a lucid interval, between deliriums, she called for a lawyer and dictated her will. Even here, Arthur wasn't mentioned. Miss Flatface did not take into account the present at all. Her mind, as she approached death, was unexpectedly preempted by effusions of a patriotic nature, and with thoughts of her former husband and children. In the end, we all return to our beginnings.

11.

Miss Flatface's Last Will and Testament.

"To America – I salute you, especially those parts of you which are not beautiful: Doris Day, for instance, with her gross untroubled features; your new banks; your candy bars; your parking lots. I have tried always to see the best in you, and your people who while friendly and full of fun on the outside are often rather mean on the inside. But no matter. My life has been spent in the discovery of you, that is, of myself. I am what I am because I am a citizen of this country, and a votary of its way of life. Therefore, let my body be cremated and my remains scattered among the cigarette ashes next to the potatoes which lie uneaten (because you are dieting) on your dinner plates.

"To the National Association of Mental Health, to Radio Free Europe (sending beams of hope behind the Iron Curtain), to the League of Women Voters, to the NAACP (for helping speed the progress of the integration of our two great races), to the National Convention of Christians and Jews, to the Girl Scouts of America, to the Bahai Temple in Chicago, to the University of Vermont (the college of my choice) – I don't forget the TVA or the Book-of-the-Month Club, except that they don't need my help – to all the bodies which contribute to the way of life distinctly American, I would give generously, if I could I would leave ten thousand dollars to each;

"To my children, who must be grown by now, and have certainly forgotten their wayward mother – Jim Jr., Mary, and little Willums, the baby – I leave a mother's blessing, and my aquarium, which my own mother has faithfully kept for me (or so she promised) since I left home to marry your father, if the fish have not all died;

"To my former husband Jim, in the hopes that he has long since forgiven me, all my policies, fully paid up, with the Equitable Life Insurance Company;

"To Inspector Jug, my contempt, this not being intended to reflect on the honor of policemen and detectives generally;

"To Mr. Obscenity, the ingratitude he richly deserves.

"(Signed) Laura Flatface Johnson Anderson."

12.

Anderson was Arthur's last name.

At the Easy Come Easy Go Funeral Home on Las Madrinas Blvd. a crowd of mourners gathered. Arthur, flustered by the unexpected turnout, sped off unnoticed by a side door, later returning with a large carton of sugar cones and four gallons of vanilla ice cream. He loaded the cones with ice cream, three at a time, and distributed them among the guests. A photographer was circulating about. Several mourners concealed their cones when they saw their picture was being taken.

Among the mourners were to be seen a monocled figure, somewhat downcast in mien, attended by a burly man in a squashed porkpie hat. "What a waste," the man with the monocle kept muttering. "What a damned waste." When Arthur came round with a cone for the monocled man, he waved it aside haughtily, then stalked from the room. Snatching the now dripping cone from Arthur's hand, the man in the porkpie hat raced after him. "Rude bastards, aren't they?" whispered some of the mourners, relatives of Arthur's, who had never approved of his marriage but had hastened to the funeral.

In the back of the funeral parlor, a sturdy man – greying at the temples – sat alone, weeping into a large yellow handkerchief.

Just before the cremation was about to start, the weeping man lurched to the glass crypt, and grabbed Arthur by the collar.

"I'm Jim Johnson, you know. Her first husband." Then he broke down utterly. "It's hers," he said, his words broken by sobs and muffled by the handkerchief which was covering his face and to which he was referring. "Did you ever know that she loved yellow?"

"No," said Arthur sadly. Perhaps Arthur would have been a little less sad if he had known that this fondness for yellow was an item about Miss Flatface that not even Mr. Obscenity, urbane and sensually observant as he was, had known.

With a manly gesture of infinite tenderness, Arthur threw his arm around Jim. Together they both knelt in silence, as the body was consumed. Up in heaven, Miss Flatface watched approvingly. May she be pardoned if she gloated a little. It may be that none of us is ever wholly known. But who among us has been loved so well?

Runaway

BY WILLIAM STYRON

Like mine, Hark's misfortune had been that he was only a single item among a man's total capital, and this was instantly and easily disposable when the economy foundered. A Negro as fantastic as Hark could always command a lovely price. Like me, he too had been born and reared on a large plantation – his in Sussex county which borders on Southampton to the north. This plantation had been liquidated along about the same year as Turner's Mill and Hark had been bought by Joseph Travis, who at that time had not developed his wheelmaking craft but was still engaged in farming. Hark's former owners, people or monsters named Barnett, proposed to develop a new plantation down in a section of Mississippi where field labor was at that moment abundant and female house labor scarce. And so they took Hark's mother and his two sisters with them and left Hark behind, the money gained from his sale financing the rather difficult and expensive overland trip to the Delta. Poor Hark. He was devoted to his mother and his sisters – indeed he had never spent a day in his life apart from them. Thus began what was to become one of a series of bereavements; seven or eight years later he was separated forever by Travis from his wife and little son.

Hark was never (at least until I was able to bend him to my will) an obstreperous or intractable Negro, and for much of the time I knew him I lamented the fact that as with most young slaves brought up as field hands – ignorant, demoralized, cowed by overseers and black drivers, occasionally whipped – the plantation system had leached out of his great and noble body so much native courage, so much spirit and dignity, that he was left as humble as a spaniel in the face of the white man's presence and authority. Nonetheless, he contained deep within him the smoldering fire of independence; certainly through my exhortations I was later able to fan it into a terrible blaze. Certainly, too, that fire must have been burning when shortly after his sale to Travis – stunned, confused, heartsick, with no God to turn to – he decided to run away.

Hark once told me how it all happened. At the Barnett plantation, where life for the field Negroes had been harsh, the matter of running away was of continual interest and concern. All of this was talk, however, since even the stupidest and most foolhardy slave was likely to be intimidated by the prospect of stumbling across the hundreds of miles of wilderness which lay to the north, and knew also that even to attain the free states was no guarantee of refuge: many a Negro had been hustled back into slavery by covetous sharp-eyed Northern white men. It was all rather hopeless but some had tried and some had almost succeeded. One of the Barnett Negroes, a clever, older man named Hannibal, had vowed after a severe beating by the overseer to take no more. He "lit out" one spring night and after a month found himself not far from Washington, in the outskirts of the town of Alexandria, where he was taken prisoner by a suspicious citizen with a fowling piece who eventually returned Hannibal to the plantation and, presumably, collected the two hundred dollar reward. It was Hannibal (now a sort of hero to many of the slaves though to others a madman) whose advice Hark remembered when he himself became a runaway. Move in the night, sleep by day, follow the North Star, avoid main-traveled roads, avoid dogs. Hannibal's destination had been the Susquehanna River in Maryland. A Quaker missionary, a wandering, queer, distraught, wild-eyed white man (soon chased off the plantation), had managed to impart this much information to Hannibal's group of berry-pickers: after Baltimore follow close by the highway to the north, and at the Susquehanna crossing ask for the Quaker meeting house, where someone was stationed night and day to convey runaways a few miles upriver to Pennsylvania and freedom. This intelligence Hark memorized with care, particularly the all-important name of the river – rather a trick for a field hand's tongue – repeating it over and over in Hannibal's presence until he had it properly, just as he had been told: *Squash-honna, Squash-honna, Squash-honna.*

Hark had no way of knowing that Travis was at heart a more lenient master than Barnett had been. He understood only that he had been separated from all the family he had ever had and from the only home he had ever known. After a week at Travis's his misery and homesickness and his general sense of loss became insupportable. And so one summer night he decided to light out, heading for that Quaker church two hundred miles away in Maryland which Hannibal had told him about many months before. At first it was all very much a kind of lark, for stealing away from Travis was a simple matter. He had only to tiptoe out of the shed in which he was kept after Travis had gone to sleep, and with a flour sack containing some bacon and cornmeal, a jackknife, and flint for starting fires, all stolen, the entire parcel slung over his shoulder on a stick, make his way into the woods. It was easy as it could be. The woods were quiet. There he paused for an hour or so, waiting to see if by any chance Travis might discover his absence and raise an alarm, but no sound came from the house. He crept out along the edge of the trees, took to the road north and sauntered along in high spirits beneath a golden moon. The weather was balmy, he made excellent time, and the only eventful moment of that first night came when a dog ran out from a farmhouse, furiously barking, and snapped at his heels. This proved Hannibal correct in his advice about dogs, and caused Hark to resolve that in the future he would give all dwellings wide berth, even if it meant losing hours by moving to the woods. He met no one on the road and as the agreeable night passed he began to feel a tingling sense of jubilation: running away seemed to be no great undertaking after all. When dawn came he knew he had made good progress – though how far he had traveled he could not tell, lacking any notion of the size of a mile – and with the sound of roosters crowing in some distant barnyard he fell asleep on the ground in a stand of beech trees, well away from the road.

Just before noon he was aroused by the sound of dogs barking to the south, a quavering chorus of yelps and frantic howls which made him sit up in terror. Surely they were after him! His first impulse was to climb a tree but he quickly lost heart for this endeavor because of his terror of heights. Instead he crept into a blackberry thicket and peeked out at the road. Two slobbering bloodhounds followed by four men on horseback came out of the distance in a cloud of dust, the men's faces each set in a blue-eyed, grim, avenging look of outrage that made Hark certain that he was the object of their pursuit; he shivered in fright and hid his head in the blackberries but to his amazement and relief the baying and yelping diminished up the road, along with the fading clatter of hooves. After a bit all was still. Hark crouched in the blackberry patch until late afternoon. When dusk began to fall he built a fire, cooking over it a little bacon and some hoecake he made with water from a stream, and upon the onset of darkness resumed his journey north.

His difficulties about finding the way began that night and plagued him all the long hours of his flight into freedom. By notches cut with his knife on a small stick each morning, he later calculated (or it was calculated for him by someone who could count) the trip as having lasted six weeks. Hannibal had counseled two guides for the trip: the North Star, and the great plank and log turnpike leading up through Petersburg, Richmond, Washington, and Baltimore. The names of these towns Hark too had memorized approximately and in sequence, since Hannibal had pointed out that each place would serve as a milestone of one's progress; also, in the event that one got lost, such names would be useful in asking directions from some trustworthy-looking Negro along the route. By remaining close to the turnpike – although taking care to stay out of sight – one could use the road as a kind of unvarying arrow pointing north and regard each successive town as a marker of one's forward course on the journey toward the free states. The trouble with this scheme, as Hark quickly discovered, was that it made no provision for the numberless side routes and forks that branched off the turnpike and which could lead a confused stranger into all manner of weird directions, especially on a dark night. The North Star was supposed to compensate for this and Hark found it valuable, but on overcast evenings or in those patches of fog which were so frequent along swampy ground this celestial beacon was of no more use to him than the crudely painted direction signs he was unable to read. So the darkness enfolded him in its embrace and he lost the road as a guide. That second night, as for so many succeeding nights, he made no progress at all but was forced to stay in the woods until the dawn, when he began to cautiously reconnoiter and found the route – a log road in daytime busy with passing farm wagons and carts and humming with danger.

Hark had many adventures along the way. His bacon and cornmeal ran out quickly but of all his problems food was the least pressing. A runaway was forced to live off the land, and Hark, like most plantation Negroes, was a resourceful thief. Only rarely was he out of sight of some habitation or other and these places yielded up an abundance of fruit and vegetables, ducks, geese, chickens – once even a pig. Two or three times, skirting a farm or plantation, he imposed upon the hospitality of friendly Negroes, whom he would hail at twilight from the trees and who would spirit him a piece of bacon or some boiled collard greens or a pan full of grits. But his great hulking prowling form made him conspicuous. He was rightly fearful of making his presence known to anyone, black or white, and so he soon began keeping strictly to himself. He even gave up requests for simple directions of the Negroes: they seemed to grow more ignorant as he progressed north and filled his ears with such an incoherent rigmarole of disaways and dataways that he turned from them in perplexity and disgust.

Hark's spirit took wing when at sunrise, a week or so after leaving Travis's, he found himself in the wooded outskirts of what, according to Hannibal's schedule, would be Petersburg. Having never seen a town of any size or description, he was flabbergasted by the number of stores and houses and the commotion and colorful stir of people, wagons, and carriages in the streets. To pass around the town without being seen was something of a problem but he managed it that night, after sleeping most of the day in a nearby pine grove. He had to swim a small river in the early darkness, paddling with one hand and holding up his clothes and his sack in the other. But he moved without detection in a half-circle about the town and pushed on north somewhat regretfully, since he had been able to pluck from some back porch a gallon of buttermilk in a wooden cask and several excellent peach pies. That night in a wild rainstorm he got hopelessly lost and to his dismay discovered when dawn came that he had been walking due east, to God knows where. It was bleak, barren pine country, almost unpopulated, filled with lonely prospects of eroded red earth. The log road, fallen into sawdust, petered out and led nowhere. The next night Hark retraced his steps and soon had negotiated the short leg of his journey to Richmond – like Petersburg a lively community with a cedarwood bridge leading to it over a river and abustle with more black and white people than he had ever imagined existed. Indeed, from his pinewoods view down on the town he saw so many Negroes moving in and out and across the bridge – some of these doubtless free, others on passes from nearby farms – that he was almost emboldened to mingle among them and see the city, taking a chance that he might not be challenged by a suspicious white man. Prudence won out, however, and he slept through the day. He swam across the river after nightfall and stole past the dark shuttered houses as he had at Petersburg, leaving Richmond like that other town poorer by a pie or two.

And so he made his way on north through the dark nights, sometimes losing the road so completely that he was forced to backtrack for several days until he regained the route. His shoes wore out and collapsed and for two nights he walked close to the road on bare feet. Finally one morning he entered the open door of a farmhouse while its people were in the fields and made off with a pair of patent leather boots so tight that he had to cut holes for the toes. Thus shod, he pushed through the gloomy woods toward Washington. It must have been August by now and the chiggers and sweat flies and the mosquitoes were out in full swarm. Some days on Hark's pine needle bed were almost impossible for sleep. Thunderstorms rumbling out of the west drenched him and froze him and scared him half out of his wits. He lost sight of the North Star more times than he could count. Forks and turnings confused him. Moonless nights caused him to stay away from the road and lose himself in a bog or thicket where owls hooted mournfully and the water moccasins thrashed drowsily in brackish pools. On such nights Hark's misery and loneliness seemed more than he could bear. Twice he came close to being caught, the first occasion somewhere just south of Washington when, traversing the edge of a cornfield just before nightfall, he nearly stepped on a white man who happened at that moment to be defecating in the bushes. Hark ran, the man pulled up his pants, yelled and gave chase, but Hark quickly outstripped him. That night, though, he heard dogs baying as if in pursuit and for one time in his life fought down his fear of high places and spent hours perched on the limb of a big maple tree while the dogs bayed and moaned in the distance. His other close call came between what must have been Washington and Baltimore when he was shocked out of his sleep underneath a hedge to find himself in the midst of a fox hunt. The great bodies of horses hurtled over him as if in some nightmare, and their hooves spattered his face with wet stinging little buttons of earth. Crouching on his elbows and knees to protect himself, Hark thought the end had come when a red-jacketed horseman reined in his mount and asked curtly what a strange nigger was doing in such a dumb position – obtaining in reply the statement that the nigger was praying – and believed it a miracle when the man said nothing but merely galloped off in the morning mists.

He had been told that Maryland was a slave state, but one morning when he happened upon a town which could only have been Baltimore he decided to risk exposure by creeping out of the edge of the hayfield in which he had been hiding and calling, in a furtive voice, to a Negro man strolling toward the city along the log road. "*Squash-honna,*" Hark said. "Whichaway to de Squash-honna?" But the Negro, a yellow loose-limbed field hand, only gazed back at Hark as if he were crazy and continued up the road with quickening pace. Undaunted, Hark resumed the journey with growing confidence that soon it would all be over. Perhaps there were five more nights of walking when at last, early one morning, Hark was aware that he was no longer in the woods. Here in the gathering light the trees gave way to a grassy plain which seemed to slope down, ever so gently, toward a stand of cattails and marsh grass rustling in the morning breeze. The wind tasted of salt, exciting Hark and making him press forward eagerly across the savannah-like plain. He strode boldly through the marsh, ankle-deep in water and mud, and finally with pounding heart attained a glistening beach unbelievably pure and clean and thick with sand. Beyond lay the river, so wide here that Hark could barely see across it, a majestic expanse of blue water flecked with whitecaps blown up by a southerly wind. For long minutes Hark stood there marveling at the sight, watching the waves lapping at the driftwood on the shore. Fishnets hung from stakes in the water, and far out a boat with white sails bellying moved serenely toward the north – the first boat Hark had ever seen. In his patent leather boots, now split beyond recognition, he walked up the beach a short distance and presently he spied a skinny little Negro man sitting on the edge of a little rowboat drawn up against the shore. This close to freedom Hark decided that he could at last hazard a direct inquiry and so he approached the Negro confidently.

"Say, man," said Hark, remembering the question he was supposed to ask, "whar de Quakah meetin' house?"

The Negro looked at him through oval spectacles on wire rims, the only pair of glasses Hark had ever seen on a Negro. He had a friendly little monkey's face with smallpox scars all over it and a crown of grizzled hair shining with pig grease. He said nothing for quite some time, then he declared: "You is some big nigger boy. How old is you, sonny?"

"I'se nineteen," Hark replied.

"You bond or free?"

"I'se bond," said Hark. "I done run off. Whar de Quakah meetin' house?"

The Negro's eyes remained twinkling and amiable behind his spectacles. Then he said again: "You is some *big* nigger boy. What yo' name, sonny?"

"I'se called Hark. Was Hark Barnett. Now Hark Travis."

"Well, Hark," the man said, rising from his perch on the rowboat, "you jes' wait right here and I'll go see about dat meetin' house. You jes' set right here," he went on, placing a brotherly hand on Hark's arm and urging him down to a seat on the edge of the rowboat. "You has had some kind of time but now it's all over with," he said in a kindly voice. "You jes' set right there while I go see about dat meetin' house. You jes' set right there and rest yo' self and we'll take care of dat meetin' house." Then he hustled up the beach and disappeared behind a copse of small stunted trees.

Gratified and relieved to be at last so close to the end of his quest, Hark sat there on the rowboat for a long moment, contemplating the blue windy sweep of the river, more grand and awesome than anything he had ever seen in his life. Soon a lazy, pleasant drowsiness overtook him, and his eyelids became heavy, and he stretched out on the sand in the warm sun and went to sleep.

Then he heard a sudden voice and he awoke in terror to see a white man standing over him with a musket, hammer cocked, ready to shoot.

"One move and I'll blow your head off," said the white man. "Tie him up, Samson."

It was not so much that Samson, one of his own kind – the little Negro with the glasses – had betrayed him which grieved Hark in later times, although that was bad enough. It was that he had really journeyed to the ends of the earth to get nowhere. For within three days he was back with Travis (who had liberally stickered the countryside with posters); he had walked those six weeks in circles, in zig-zags, in looping spirals, never once traveling more than forty miles from home. The simple truth of the matter is that Hark, born and raised in the plantation's abyssal and aching night, had no more comprehension of the vastness of the world than a baby in a cradle. There was no way for him to know about cities, he had never seen a hamlet; and thus he may be excused for not perceiving that "Richmond" and "Washington" and "Baltimore" were in truth any of a dozen nondescript little villages of the Tidewater – Jerusalem, Drewrysville, Smithfield – and that the noble watercourse upon whose shore he stood with such trust and hope and joy was not "the Squash-honna" but that ancient mother-river of slavery, the James.

Whacking Off

BY PHILIP ROTH

Then came the years when half my waking life was spent locked behind the bathroom door, firing my wad down the toilet, or into the soiled clothes of the laundry hamper, or with a thick splat, up against the medicine chest mirror, before which I stood in my dropped drawers to see how it looked coming out. Or else I was doubled up over my flying fist, eyes closed but mouth wide open, to take that sticky sauce of buttermilk and Clorox on my own tongue and teeth – though not infrequently, in my blindness and ecstasy, I got it all in the pompadour, like a blast of Wildroot Cream Oil. Through a world of matted handkerchiefs and crumpled Kleenex and stained pajamas, I moved my raw and swollen penis, perpetually in dread of my loathsomeness being discovered by someone coming upon me just as I was dropping my load. Nonetheless, I was wholly incapable of keeping my paws from my dong once it started the climb up my belly. In the middle of a class I would raise my hand to be excused, rush to the lavatory, and with ten or fifteen savage strokes, beat off standing up into a urinal. At the Saturday afternoon movie I would leave my friends to go off to the candy machine – and wind up hiding in a distant balcony seat, where with muffled groans I would squirt my seed into the empty wrapper from a Mounds bar. On an outing of our family association, I once cored an apple, saw what it looked like, and ran into the woods to fall upon the orifice of the fruit, pretending that the cool and mealy hole was actually between the legs of that mythical girl who always called me Big Boy when she begged and wept and pleaded for a bit of what I had. "Oh, shove it in me, Big Boy," cried the cored apple that I banged silly on that picnic. "Big Boy, Big Boy, oh give me all you've got," cried the empty milk bottle that I kept hidden in our storage bin in the basement, to drive wild after school with my vaselined upright. "Come, Big Boy, come," screamed the maddened piece of liver that, in my insanity, I bought one afternoon at a butcher shop and, believe it or not, violated behind a billboard on the way to a *bar mitzvah* lesson.

It was at the end of the first year of high school – my first full year of masturbating – that I discovered on the underside of my penis, just where the shaft meets the head, a little discolored dot that has since been diagnosed as a freckle. Cancer. I had given myself *cancer*. All that pulling and pawing and tugging at my own flesh, all that friction, had given me an incurable disease! At fourteen! In bed at night the tears rolled down my cheeks: "No!" I sobbed, "I don't want to die! Please – no!" But then, because I would very shortly be a corpse anyway, I went ahead as usual and jerked off into my sock. I had taken to carrying my dirty socks into bed with me at night, so as to be able to use one as a receptacle upon retiring and the other upon awakening.

Oh, if only I could cut down to one hand-job a day, or hold the line at two, or even three! But with the horror of oblivion before me, I actually began to set new records for myself. Before meals. After meals. *During* meals. Jumping up from the dinner table, I tragically clutch my belly – diarrhea! I cry, I have been stricken with diarrhea ! – and once behind the locked bathroom door, slip over my head a pair of my sister's underwear that I have stolen from her dresser and carry rolled in a hand-kerchief in my pocket. So galvanic is the effect of those cotton panties against my tongue – so galvanic is the very *word* "panties" – not to mention all that pink against my undie-crazy eyeballs, that the trajectory of my ejaculation reaches startling new heights: leaving my joint like a rocket it makes right for the light bulb overhead, where to my wonderment and horror, it hits and it hangs. Wildly in the first moment I cover my eyes, expecting an explosion of glass, a burst of flames. Disaster, you see, disintegration, are continually on my mind. Then quietly as I can I climb the radiator and remove the sizzling gob with a wad of toilet paper. I begin a scrupu-lous search of the shower curtain, the tub, the tile floor, the four toothbrushes – God forbid ! – and just as I am about to unlock the door, imagining I have covered my tracks, my heart lurches at the sight of what is clinging like snot to the toe of my shoe. I am the Raskolnikov of jerking off – the sticky evidence is everywhere! Is it on my cuffs too, my hands, is it in my hair? All this I wonder, even as I come back to the dinner table, scowling and cranky, to snap incoherently at my father when he opens his mouth full of red jello and says, "I don't understand what you have to lock the door for. That to me is beyond my comprehension. What is this, a home or a Grand Central Station?" ". . . privacy . . . human being . . . around here *never*," I grumble at him, then push aside my dessert to scream, "I don't feel well – *will everybody leave me alone?*"

After dessert – which I eat finally because I happen to like jello, even if I detest them – after dessert I am back in the bathroom once again. I burrow through the week's laundry until I uncover one of my flat-chested sister's soiled brassieres. I string it up, a scarecrow to bring on the dreams – one shoulder strap over the knob to the bathroom door, the other on the knob to the linen closet. "Oh beat it, Big Boy, beat it to a red hot pulp" – so I am being urged by the little cups of Hannah's bra, when a rolled-up newspaper whacks angrily up against the door. "– Come on, give somebody else a crack at the bowl, will you?" my father says. "I haven't moved my bowels in a week."

I recover myself, as is my talent, with a marvelous burst of hurt feelings. "I have a terrible case of diarrhea! Doesn't that mean anything to anyone in this house?" – in the meantime not missing a single stroke – indeed quickening the tempo as my smarting, cancerous organ miraculously begins again to quiver from the inside out.

Then Hannah's brassiere *begins to move*. To swing back and forth! I close my eyes and see Lenore Blatt, who has the biggest pair in my class, running for the bus after school, her great untouchable load shifting in her blouse, oh I urge them up from their cups, and over, *Lenore Blatt's actual tits* – and realize in the same split second that my mother is vigorously shaking the knob, trying the door. Which I forgot to lock? I am caught! I am as good as dead!

"Open this door, Alex. I want you to open this door this instant."

I am not caught. And I see from what's alive in my hand that I'm not dead yet either. Beat on! "Lick me, Big Boy – lick me a good hot lick! I'm Lenore Blatt's big fat red hot brassiere!"

"Alex, I want an answer from you. Did you eat French fries after school? Is that why you're sick like this?"

"Nuhhh."

"Alex, are you in pain? Do you want me to call the doctor? Are you in pain, or aren't you? I want to know exactly where it hurts. Alex, answer me."

"Yuhhh."

"Alex, I don't want you to flush the toilet," says my mother sternly. "I want to see what you've done in there. I don't like the sound of this at all."

"And me," says my father, touched as he always was by my accomplishments – as much awe as envy, "I haven't moved my bowels in a week," just as I lurch from my perch on the toilet seat, and with the whimper of a whipped animal, deliver three drops of something barely viscous into the tiny piece of cloth where my sister, whom I hate, has laid her nipples, such as they were. It is my sixth orgasm of the day. When will I begin to come blood?

"Get in here, please, you," says my mother. "Why did you flush the toilet when I told you not to?"

"I forgot."

"What was in there that you were so fast to flush it?"

"Diarrhea."

"Was it mostly liquid or was it mostly poopie?"

"I don't look! I didn't look! Stop saying poopie to me – I'm in high school!"

"Oh, don't shout at me, Alex. I'm not the one who gave you diarrhea, I assure you. If all you ate was what you were fed at home you wouldn't have to be running to the bathroom fifty times a day. Hannah tells me what you're doing, Alex, don't think I don't know."

She's missed her underwear! Dead! Dead! I wish I were dead!

"Yeah, what do I do . . . ?"

"You go to Harold's Hot Dog and *Chazerai* Palace after school and you eat French fries with Sheldon Weiner. Don't you? Don't lie to me either. Do you or do you not stuff yourself with French fries and ketchup after school? Jack, come in here, I want you to hear this," she calls to my father.

"I'm trying to move my bowels," he shouts. "Don't I have enough trouble as it is without people screaming at me when I'm trying to move my bowels?"

"You know what your son does after school, the 'A' student here, who his own mother can't say poopie to anymore, he's such a *grown-up*? What do you think the grown-up does when nobody is watching him?"

"Can I please be left alone, please?" my father cries. "Can I have a little peace, please, so I can get something accomplished in here?"

"Just wait till your father hears what you do, Alex, in defiance of every health habit there could possibly be. Alex, answer me something. You're so smart, you know all the answers now, answer me this. How do you think Sheldon Weiner gave himself colitis? Why has that child spent half his life in hospitals?"

"Because he eats *chazerai*."

"Don't you dare make fun of me!"

"All right, how *did* he get colitis?" I scream.

"Because he eats *chazerai*! But it's not a joke! Because to him a meal is an Oh Henry bar washed down by a bottle of Pepsi. Because his breakfasts consists of, do you know what? The most important meal of the day – not according just to your mother, Alex, but according to the highest nutritionists – and do you know what that child eats?"

"A doughnut."

"A doughnut is right, Mr. Smart Guy, Mr. Adult. And *coffee*, Alex. Coffee and a doughnut and on this a thirteen-year-old *pisherkeh* with half a stomach is supposed to start a day. But you, thank God, have been brought up differently. You don't have a mother who gallavants all over town like some names I could name, shopping from morning till night. Alex, Alex, tell me, so it's not a mystery, or maybe I'm just stupid – tell me, what are you trying to do, what are you trying to prove, that you should stuff yourself with such *chazerai*, when you could come home to a poppy-seed cookie and a nice glass of milk? I want the truth from you. I wouldn't tell your father, but I must have the truth from you. Is it just French fries, or is it more? Tell me, please, what other kind of garbage you're putting into your stomach so we can get to the bottom of this diarrhea. Alex, I want a straight answer. Are you eating hamburgers out? Answer me, please, is that why you flushed the toilet? Did it have hamburger in it, is that why?"

"I told you – I don't look in the bowl when I flush it! I'm not interested like you are in other people's poopie!"

"Oh, oh, oh – fourteen years old and the mouth on you! To someone who is asking a question about *your* health, *your* welfare!" Her hurt, plus the utter incomprehensibility of the situation, causes her eyes to become heavy with tears. "Alex, why are you getting like this? Tell me please, what horrible things have we done to you all our lives that this should be our reward?" I believe the question strikes her as original. I believe she considers the question unanswerable. And worst of all, so do I. What *have* they done for me all their lives, but sacrifice? Yet that this is precisely the horrible thing is beyond my understanding – and still, Doctor, still! To this day!

I brace myself now for the whispering. I can spot the whispering coming a mile away. We are about to discuss my father's headaches.

"Alex, he didn't have a headache on him today that he could hardly see straight from it?" She looks up quickly to be sure he is still out of earshot; God forbid he should hear how critical his condition is. He might claim exaggeration. "He's not going next week for a test for a tumor?"

"He is?"

" 'Bring him in,' said the doctor, 'I'm going to give him a test for a tumor.' "

Success. I am crying. There is no good reason for me to be crying, but in this household everybody tries to get a good cry in at least once a day. My father, you must understand – as probably you do – has been going for this tumor test every month now for as long as I can remember. Why his head aches him all the time is because he is constipated all the time – why he is constipated is because ownership of his intestinal tracts is in the hands of the firm of Worry, Fear & Frustration. It is true that the doctor once said to my mother that he would give him a test for a tumor – if that would make her happy, is I believe the way that he worded it; he suggested that it would he cheaper if my father invested the money for the test in a case of milk of magnesia. That I know all this to be so does not make it any less heartbreaking to imagine my burly, overburdened father dead.

Yes, she has me where she wants me, and she knows it. I clean forget my own cancer in the grief that comes – comes now as it came then – when I think how much of life has always been beyond his comprehension, and beyond his grasp. No money, no schooling, no language, no learning. All he had to pride himself on was his dutifulness. He did not commit adultery. He did not steal. He did not beat his wife. He did not drink. He visited his mother every Sunday of her life. And he worked. For Boston and Northeastern Mutual ("The Most Benevolent Financial Institution in America") he sold insurance (or tried to) to the poorest people in all of Jersey City. He worked the lousiest district the company had, worked it like a dog. . . . So isn't this plenty to be grateful for? Isn't this a description of an admirable man? A man deserving only of sympathy and love? Am I not expecting too much, now as then? I had an uncle who played the horses and wound up in jail. To pay his debts, he fiddled with the books where he was employed as an accountant, and went to jail for a year. That kind of humiliation is something I know nothing about, I realize that. That my father was virtuous is not something that I have a right to minimize. Nevertheless, I am trying to tell the truth about what it was to be a son in that family. My emotional life is a shattered miserable thing that I must get to the bottom of, Doctor – and I am going to whine and bitch and complain all I want! Why else am I so indecisive if not because of them? Why else do I feel so boyish at the age of thirty, so temporary about myself? Why am I never a day without worries? Why do I panic so easily, weep so easily, drop into melancholy or rise into a rage at the drop of a meaningless hat? Where else but in my home did I learn such a way to respond to the simple vicissitudes of human life? What else but my past causes these insides to feel like crumbling clay twenty-four hours a day? Doctor, how deep is the damage, that's really the question? How much is lost? Why can't I be man enough to overcome this stupid, ridiculous, joke of a past!

Where were we? My father.

A person my father often held up to me as someone to emulate in life was the theatrical producer, Billy Rose. He had read in Walter Winchell that it was Billy Rose's knowledge of shorthand that had led Bernard Baruch to hire him as a secretary – consequently he plagued and pestered me throughout high school to enroll in the shorthand course. "A person who has shorthand will never have to worry. A person who has shorthand is always in demand. Why do you fight with me when this is a proven fact? Where would Billy Rose be today without his shorthand? Answer me that."

Earlier it was the piano we battled over. For a man whose house was without a phonograph or a record, he was passionate on the subjects of a musical instrument. "I don't understand why you won't take a musical instrument, this is beyond my comprehension. Your little cousin Toby can sit down at the piano and play whatever popular song you can name. All she has to do is sit down at the piano and everybody in the room is her friend. She'll never lack for friends, she'll never lack for a good time, even when she's alone. Say you'll take up piano, Alex, and I'll have one in here tomorrow morning. Alex, are you even listening to me? I am offering you a piano that could change your social life for the rest of your life!"

What he had to offer I didn't want, what I wanted he didn't have to offer. But how unusual is that? Why has it caused such grief? Doctor, what must I rid myself of, the hatred of them – or the love? I haven't begun to tell you, you see, of all I remember with pleasure – all those memories that seem somehow to be bound up with weather and the time of day, and that flash so suddenly into my mind, with such vividness, that momentarily I am not in the subway, or my apartment, or at dinner with a girl, but back then, back there. And for all that they are so gripping, they are really very simple. They are memories of practically nothing – and I have them all the time. I am standing at the kitchen window, my mother says to me, "Look outside, a real fall sky." Its is an iron-cold January day, dusk – oh these memories of dusk, of chicken fat on rye bread to tide me over to dinner, and the moon already outside the kitchen window – I have just come in with a dollar I have earned shoveling snow. "You know what you're going to have for dinner," my mother says to me, "for being such a hard-working boy? Your favorite winter meal. Lamb stew." It is night; after a Sunday in New York City, at Radio City and

Chinatown, we are driving home across the George Washington Bridge – the Holland Tunnel is, of course, the shortest route between Mott Streets and Jersey City, but I beg for the bridge, and I get it. Up front my sister counts aloud the number of supports upon which the marvelous cables rests, while in the back I fall asleep with my face against my mother's black sealskin coat. At Lakewood where we go for a weekend vacation one winter, with my parents' Sunday nights Gin Rummy Club, I sleep in one twin bed with my father, while my mother and Hannah curl up together in the other. At dawn my father is already dressed and in his hat and ear-muffs. He awakens me. "Come," he whispers, "I want to show you something. Did you know I was a waiter in Lakewood when I was sixteen years old?" Outside he points across to the beautiful silent woods. "How's that?" he says. We walk together around a silver lake. "Take good deep breaths. Take in the piney air all the way. That is the best air in the world, good winter piney air." In summer he remains in the stifling city while the three of us go off to live in a furnished room at the seashore for a month. He will join us for the last two weeks, when he has his vacation . . . however, there are nights when Jersey City is so thick with humidity, so alive with the mosquitoes that come dive-bombing in from the marshes, that at the end of his day's work he drives the sixty-five miles down the old Cheesequake – my God, the Cheesequake! – to spend the night with us in our room at Bradley Beach, where there is always a breeze through the window. Usually he arrives at seven-thirty, and dinner waits, while he unpeels the soggy city clothes in which he has been making the rounds of his debit all day, and changes into his swimsuit. I carry his towel for him as he clops down the street to the beach in his unlaced shoes. I am dressed in clean short pants and a spotless polo shirt, the salt showered off me, my hair beauti-fully parted and slicked down. There is a roughened iron rail that runs the length of the boardwalk, and I sit on the edge of it and watch while, still in his shoes, he crosses the beach below and neatly sets down his towel. He places his watch in one shoe, his eyeglasses in the other and then slowly he enters the ocean. I still to this day go into the water the way he advised. Plunge the wrists in firsts, then splash under the arms, then a handful on the face and back of the neck; ah, but slowly, slowly. This way you get to refresh yourself, meanwhile avoiding a shock to the system. Refreshed, unshocked, he turns to face me, comically waves farewell up toward where he thinks I'm standing, and drops backwards to floats with his arms outstretched in a little circle of dark velvety sea. Oh he floats so still – he works, he works so hard, and for whom if not for me? – and then at last, after turning on his belly and making with a few choppy strokes that carry him nowhere, he comes wading back into the shore, his streaming compact torso glowing from the last pure spokes of lights driving in, over my shoulder, out of stifling inland New Jersey, from which I am being spared.

And there are a lot more memories like this one, Doctor. A lot more. This is my mother and father I'm talking about.

But – but – but – let me pull myself together – there is also this vision of him coming from the bathroom, savagely kneading the back of his neck and sourly swallowing a belch. "All right, what is it that was so urgent you couldn't wait till I came out to tell me?"

"Nothing," says my mother. "It's settled."

He looks at me with disappointment. I'm what he lives for, and I know it. "What did he do?"

"What he did is over and done with, God willing. You, did you move your bowels?" she asks him.

"Of course I didn't move my bowels."

"Jack, what is it going to be with you, with those bowels?"

"They're turning into concrete, that's what it's going to be."

"Because you eat too fast."

"I don't eat too fast."

"How then, slow?"

"I eat regular."

"You eat like a pig, and somebody should tell you."

"'Oh, you got a wonderful way of expressing yourself sometimes, do you know that?"

"I'm only speaking the truth," she says. "I *patchkeh* and *patchkeh* in this kitchen, and you eat like there's a fire somewhere, bolting everything down before I even have a chance to sit, and this one – this one has decided that the food I cook isn't good enough for him. He'd rather be sick and scare the living daylights out of me."

"What did he do?"

"I don't want to upset you," she says. "Let's just forget the whole thing." But she can't, so she begins to cry. Look, she is probably not the happiest person in the world, either, you know. She was once a tall stringbean of a girl whom the boys called "Red," in high school. When I was nine and ten years old I was an addict of her high school yearbook.

> *Sophie Ginsky the boys call "Red,"*
> *She'll go far with her big brown eyes and her clever head.*

And that was my mother!

Also, she had been secretary to the track team, an office pretty much without laurels in our time, but apparently quite a post to hold in Bayonne during the First World War. So I thought, at any rate, while I turned the pages of her yearbook, and she pointed out to me her dark-haired beautiful beau, who had been the outstanding broad jumper of Hudson County, captain of the team and today, to quote Sophie, "the biggest manufacturer of mustard in New York." "And I could have married him instead of your father," she told me, and more than once. I used to wonder sometimes what that would have been like for my mamma and me, invariably when my father sometimes took us to dine out at the corner delicatessen. I look around the place and think, "We would have manufactured all this mustard." She must have had thoughts like that herself.

"He eats French fries," she says, as she sinks into a kitchen chair to weep her heart out once and for all. "He goes after school with Sheldon Weiner and stuffs himself with French fried potatoes. Jack, you tell him, I'm only his mother. Tell him what the end is going to be. Alex," she says passionately, looking to where I am edging out of the room, "*tateleh*, it begins with diarrhea, but do you know how it ends? With a sensitive stomach like yours, do you know how it finally ends? *Wearing a plastic bag to do your business in!*"

Who in the history of the world has been least able to deal with a woman's tears? My father. I am second. He says to me, "You heard your mother. Don't eat French fries with Sheldon Weiner after school."

"Or ever," she pleads.

"Or ever," my father says.

"Or hamburgers out," she pleads. "Or hamburgers out," he says.

"*Hamburgers,*" she says bitterly, just as she might say *Hitler,* "where they can put anything in the world in that they like – and he eats them. Jack, make him promise, before he gives himself a terrible *tsureh* and it's too late."

"*I promise !*" I scream, "*I promise!*" and race from the kitchen – to where? Where else?

I tear off my pants, furiously I grab that battered battering ram to freedom, my adolescent cock, even as my suffering mother begins to call to me from the other side of the bathroom door. "Now this time don't flush. Do you hear me, Alex? I have to see what's in that bowl!"

Doctor, do you understand what I was up against? My wang was all I really had that I could call my own! Oh, you should have watched her at work during polio season. She should have gotten medals from the March of Dimes. Open your mouth. Why is your throat red? Do you have a headache you're not telling me about? You're not going to any baseball game, Alex, until I see you move your neck. Is your neck stiff? Then why are you moving it that way? You ate like you were nauseous, are you nauseous? Well, you ate like you were nauseous. I don't want you drinking from that drinking fountain in that playground. If you're thirsty wait until you're home. Your throat is sore, isn't it? I can tell how you're swallowing. I think maybe what you are going to do, Mr. Joe DiMaggio The Second, is put that glove away and lie down. I am not going to allow you to go outside in this heat and run around, not with that sore throat, I'm not. I want to take your temperature. I don't like the sound of this throat business one bit. To be very frank, I am actually beside myself that you have been walking around all day with a sore throat and not telling your mother. Why did you keep this a secret? Alex, polio doesn't know from base-ball games. It only knows from iron lungs and death and crippled forever! I don't want you running around, and that's it. Or eating hamburgers out. Or mayonnaise. Or chopped liver. Or tuna. Not everybody is careful the way your mother is about spoilage, Alex. You're used to a spotless house where nothing is in the refrigerator for more than two days, where whether it is used or not it gets thrown out rather than take the risk. You don't begin to know what goes on in restaurants. Do you know why your mother when we go to the chinks will never sit facing the kitchen? Because I don't want to see what goes on back there. Alex, you must wash every-thing, is that clear? Everything. God only knows who touched it before you did.

Look, am I exaggerating to think it's practically miraculous that I'm ambulatory? The hysteria, Doctor, and the superstition! The watch-its, and the be-carefuls! You mustn't do this, you can't do that, don't don't, you're breaking an important law! *What* law? *Whose* law? They might as well have had plates in their lips and rings through their noses and painted themselves blue for all the human sense they made! Oh, and the *milchiks* and the *fleishiks* besides – all those *mishuggeneh* rules and regulations on top of their own personal craziness! Doctor, it's a family joke that when I was a tiny boy I turned from a snowstorm I was watching out the window and hopefully asked my mother, "Mamma, do we believe in winter?" Doctor, do you get what I'm saying? I was raised by Hottentots and Zulus! I could not even contemplate drinking a glass of milk with my salami sandwich without giving seri-ous offense to God Almighty. Imagine then, oh just imagine what my conscience gave me for all that jerking off! Oh, the guilt and the fears – the endlessness of our crises! Oh, the terror of life bred into my bones! What in their world was not charged with danger, dripping with germs, fraught with peril? Doctor, where was the gusto, where was the confidence and the courage? Who filled these parents of mine with such a fearful sense of life? My father, in his retirement now, has really only one subject into which he can sink his teeth, the New Jersey Turnpike. "I wouldn't go near that thing if they paid me. You have to be out of your mind to travel on that thing. It's Murder, Incorporated. It is a legalized way for people to go out and get themselves killed." And on – and on – and on! You know what he says to me three times a week on the telephone – and I'm only counting when I pick it up, not the total number of rings I get between six and ten o'clock every night. "Sell that car, will you? Will you do me a favor and sell that car so I can get a good night's sleep? Why you have to have a car in that city is beyond my comprehension. Why you want to pay for insurance and garage and upkeep, I don't even begin to under-stand. But then I don't understand yet why you even have to live by yourself over in that jungle. What do you pay those robbers for that two-by-four apartment any-way? A penny over fifty dollars a month and you're out of your mind. Why you don't move back to North Jersey is a mystery to me – why you prefer the noise and the violence and the fumes –"

And my mother, Doctor, she whispers on. *Sophie whispers on!* I go for dinner there once a month; its is a struggle requiring all my guile and cunning and strength, but I have been able over all these years still to hold it down to once a month. I get out of the elevator, see those milk bottles outside the door – and my whole gorge rises; then the door is opened and I am home: "Don't ask what kind of day I had with him yesterday." So I don't. "Alex," she says, *sotto voce*, "when he has a day like that you don't know what a difference a call from you would make. And, Alex," – even as I nod yes, yes, yes – "next week is his birthday. That mine went by last month without a card – those things don't bother me. He'll be sixty-six, Alex. That's not a baby, Alex, if you know what I mean. Send him a card. Pick up the phone. It wouldn't kill you."

Doctor, these people are incredible! These people are unbelievable! These two are the outstanding producers and packagers of guilt in our time! They render it from me like fat from a chicken! "Call, Alex. Visit, Alex. Alex, keep us informed. Don't go away again without telling us. Last time you went away you didn't tell us, your father was ready to phone the police. You know how many times a day he called and got no answer, Alex?" "Mother," I cry, "if I'm dead they'll smell the body in three days!" – "Don't talk like that!" she cries right back. "God forbid!" Oh, and now she's got the real beauty, the one that comes with age: "Alex, to pick up the phone is such a simple thing. How much longer will we be around to bother you anyway?"

Doctor Spielvogel, this is my life, my only life, and I'm living it in the middle of a Jewish joke! I am the son in the Jewish joke – only it ain't no joke! Oh Doctor, who crippled us like this? Who made us so morbid and weak? Why, why are they screaming still, "Watch out! Don't do it! Alex – no!" and why, alone on my bed in New York, why am I still hopelessly beating my meat? Doctor, what is this sickness I have? Is this the Jewish suffering I used to hear so much about? Is this what has come down to me of all that filthy persecution? Oh, my timidity! my fear! my palpitations! my sweats! Doctor, I can't stand anymore being frightened! Bless me with manhood! Make me brave, make me strong! Enough being a nice Jewish boy, publicly pleasing my parents while privately pulling my putz! Enough!

Mercier and Camier

BY SAMUEL BECKETT

The journey of Mercier and Camier is one I can tell, if I will, for I was with them all the time.

Physically it was fairly easy going, without seas or frontiers to be crossed, through regions untormented on the whole, if desolate in parts. Mercier and Camier did not remove from home, they had that great good fortune. They did not have to face, with greater or less success, outlandish ways, tongues, laws, skies, foods, in surroundings little resembling those to which first childhood, then boyhood, then manhood had inured them. The weather, though often inclement (but they knew no better), never exceeded the limits of the temperate, that is to say of what could still be borne, without danger if not without discomfort, by the average native fittingly clad and shod. With regard to money, if it did not run to first class transport or the palatial hotel, still there was enough to keep them going, to and fro, without recourse to alms. It may be said therefore that in this respect too they were fortunate, up to a point. They had to struggle, but less than many must, less perhaps than most of those who venture forth, driven by a need now clear and now obscure.

They had consulted together at length, before embarking on this journey, weighing with all the calm at their command what benefits they might hope from it, what ills apprehend, maintaining turn about the dark side and the rosy. The only certitude they gained from these debates was that of not lightly launching out, into the unknown.

Camier was first to arrive at the appointed place. That is to say that on his arrival Mercier was not there. In reality Mercier had forestalled him by a good ten minutes. Not Camier then, but Mercier, was first to arrive. He possessed himself in patience for five minutes, with his eye on the various avenues of approach open to his friend, then set out for a saunter destined to last full fifteen minutes. Meantime Camier, five minutes having passed without sight or sign of Mercier, took himself off in his turn for a little stroll. On his return to the place, fifteen minutes later, it was in vain he cast about him, and understandably so. For Mercier, after cooling his heels for a further five minutes, had wandered off again for what he pleased to call a little stretch. Camier hung around for five more minutes, then again departed, saying to himself, Perhaps I'll run into him in the street. It was at this moment that Mercier, back from his breather, which as chance this time would have it had not exceeded ten minutes, glimpsed receding in the morning mist a shape suggestive of Camier's and which was indeed none other. Unhappily it vanished as though swallowed up by the cobbles, leaving Mercier to resume his vigil. But on expiry of what is beginning to look like the regulation five minutes he abandoned it again, feeling the need of a little motion. Their joy was thus for an instant unbounded, Mercier's joy and Camier's joy, when after five and ten minutes respectively of uneasy prowl, debouching simultaneously on the square, they found themselves face to face for the first time since the evening before. The time was nine fifty in the morning.

In other words:

	Arr.	Dep.	Arr.	Dep.	Arr.	Dep.	Arr.
Mercier	9.05	9.10	9.25	9.30	9.40	9.45	9.50
Camier	9.15	9.20	9.35	9.40	9.50		

What stink of artifice.

They were still in each other's arms when the rain began to fall, with quite oriental abruptness. They made therefore with all speed to the shelter which, in the form of a pagoda, had been erected here as protection from the rain and other inclemencies, in a word from the weather. Shadowy and abounding in nooks and crannies it was a friend to lovers also and to the aged of either sex. Into this refuge, at the same instant as our heroes, bounded a dog, followed shortly by a second. Mercier and Camier, irresolute, exchanged a look. They had not finished in each other's arms and yet felt awkward about resuming. The dogs for their part were already copulating, with the utmost naturalness.

The place where they now found themselves, where they had agreed, not without pains, that they should meet, was not properly speaking a square, but rather a small public garden at the heart of a tangle of streets and lanes. It displayed the usual shrubberies, flower-beds, pools, fountains, statues, lawns and benches in strangulating profusion. It had something of the maze, irksome to perambulate, difficult of egress, for one not in its secrets. Entry was of course the simplest thing in the world. In the center, roughly, towered huge a shining copper beech, planted several centuries earlier, according to the sign rudely nailed to the bole, by a Field Marshal of France peacefully named Saint-Ruth. Hardly had he done so, in the words of the inscription, when he was struck dead by a cannon-ball, faithful to the last to the same hopeless cause, on a battlefield having little in common, from the point of view of landscape, with those on which he had won his spurs, first as brigadier, then as lieutenant, if that is the order in which spurs are won, on the battlefield. It was no doubt to this tree that the garden owed its existence, a consequence which can scarcely have occurred to the Field Marshal as on that distant day, well clear of the quincunxes, before an elegant and replete assistance, he held the frail sapling upright in the hole gorged with evening dew. But to have done with this tree and hear no more about it, from it the garden derived what little charm it still possessed, not to mention of course its name. The stifled giant's days were numbered, it would not cease henceforward to pine and rot till finally removed, bit by bit. Then for a while, in the garden mysteriously named, people would breathe more freely.

Mercier and Camier did not know the place. Hence no doubt their choice of it for their meeting. Certain things shall never be known for sure.

Through the orange panes the rain to them seemed golden and brought back memories, determined by the hazard of their excursions, to the one of Rome, of Naples to the other, mutually unavowed and with a feeling akin to shame. They should have felt the better for this glow of distant days when they were young, and warm, and loved art, and mocked marriage, and did not know each other, but they felt no whit the better.

Let us go home, said Camier.

Why? said Mercier.

It won't stop all day, said Camier.

Long or short, tis but a shower, said Mercier.

I can't stand there doing nothing, said Camier.

Then let us sit, said Mercier.

Worse still, said Camier.

Then let us walk up and down, said Mercier, yes, arm in arm let us pace to and fro. There is not much room, but there might be even less. Lay down our umbrella, there, help me off with our knapsack, so, thanks, and off we go.

Camier submitted.

Every now and then the sky lightened and the rain abated. Then they would halt before the door. This was the signal for the sky to darken again and the rain to redouble in fury.

Don't look, said Mercier.

The sound is enough, said Camier.

True, said Mercier.

After a moment of silence Mercier said:

The dogs don't trouble you?

Why does he not withdraw? said Camier

He cannot, said Mercier.

Why? said Camier.

One of nature's little gadgets, said Mercier, no doubt to make insemination double sure.

They begin astraddle, said Camier, and finish arsy-versy.

What would you do? said Mercier. The ecstasy is past, they yearn to part, to go and piss against a post or eat a morsel of shit, but cannot. So they turn their backs on each other. You'd do as much, if you were they.

Delicacy would restrain me, said Camier.

And what would you do? said Mercier.

Feign regret, said Camier, that I could not renew such pleasure incontinent.

After a moment of silence Camier said:

Let us sit us down, I feel all sucked off.

You mean sit down, said Mercier.

I mean sit us down, said Camier.

Then let us sit us down, said Mercier.

On all hands already the workers were at it again, the air waxed loud with cries of pleasure and pain and with the urbaner notes of those for whom life had exhausted its surprises, as well on the minus side as on the plus. Things too were getting ponderously under way. It was in vain the rain poured down, the whole business was starting again with apparently no less ardor than if the sky had been a cloudless blue.

You kept me waiting, said Mercier.

On the contrary, said Camier.

I arrived at nine five, said Mercier.

And I at nine fifteen, said Camier.

You see, said Mercier.

Waiting, said Camier, and keeping waiting can only be with reference to a pre-arranged terminus.

And for what hour was our appointment, according to you? said Mercier.

Nine fifteen, said Camier.

Then you are grievously mistaken, said Mercier.

Meaning? said Camier.

Will you never have done astounding me? said Mercier.

Explain yourself, said Camier.

I close my eyes and live it over again, said Mercier, your hand in mine, tears rising to my eyes and the sound of my faltering voice, So be it, tomorrow at nine. A drunken woman passed by, singing a ribald song and hitching up her skirts.

She went to your head, said Camier. He took a notebook from his pocket, turned the leaves and read: Monday 15, St. Macarius, 9.15, St. Ruth, collect umbrella at Helen's.

And what does that prove? said Mercier.

My good faith, said Camier.

True, said Mercier.

We shall never know, said Camier, at what hour we arranged to meet today, so let us drop the subject.

In all this confusion one thing alone is sure, said Mercier, and that is that we met at ten to ten, at the same time as the hands, or rather a moment later.

There is that to be thankful for, said Camier.

The rain had not yet begun, said Mercier.

The morning fervor was intact, said Camier.

Don't lose our agenda, said Mercier.

At this moment suddenly appeared from nowhere the first of a long line of maleficent beings. His uniform, sickly green in color, its place of honor rife with heroic emblems and badges, suited him down to the ground. Inspired by the example of the great Sarsfield he had risked his life without success in defense of a territory which in itself must have left him cold and considered as a symbol cannot have greatly heated him either. He carried a stick at once elegant and massive and even leaned on it from time to time. He suffered torment with his hip, the pain shot down his buttock and up his rectum deep into the bowels and even as far north as the pyloric valve, culminating as a matter of course in uretro-scrotal spasms with quasi-incessant longing to micturate. Invalided out with a grudging pension, whence the sour looks of nearly all those, male and female, with whom his duties and remnants of *bonhomie* brought him daily in contact, he sometimes felt it would have been wiser on his part, during the great upheaval, to devote his energies to the domestic skirmish, the Gaelic dialect, the fortification of his faith and the treasures of a folklore beyond compare. The bodily danger would have been less and the benefits more certain. But this thought, when he had relished all its bitterness, he would banish from his mind, as unworthy of it. His moustache, once stiff as the lip it was grown to hide, was no longer so. From time to time, when he remembered, with a blast from below of fetid breath mingled with spittle, he straightened it momentarily. Motionless at the foot of the pagoda steps, his cape agape, streaming with rain, he darted his eyes to and from, from Mercier and Camier to the dogs, from the dogs to Mercier and Camier.

Who owns that bicycle? he said.

Mercier and Camier exchanged a look.

We could have done without this, said Camier.

Shift her, said the ranger.

It may prove diverting, said Mercier.

Who owns them dogs? said the ranger.

I don't see how we can stay, said Camier.

Can it I wonder be the fillip we needed, to get us moving? said Mercier.

The ranger mounted the steps of the shelter and stood stockstill in the doorway. The air darkened immediately and turned a deeper yellow.

I think he is about to attack us, said Camier.

I leave the balls to you, as usual, said Mercier.

Dear sergeant, said Camier, what exactly can we do for you?

You see that bicycle? said the ranger.

I see nothing, said Camier. Mercier, do you see a bicycle?

Is she yours? said the ranger.

A thing we do not see, said Camier, for whose existence we have only your word, how are we to tell if it is ours, or another's?

Why would it be ours? said Mercier. Are these dogs ours? No. We see them today for the first time. And you would have it that the bicycle, assuming it exists, is ours? And yet the dogs are not ours.

Bugger the dogs, said the ranger.

But as if to give himself the lie he fell on them with stick and boot and drove them cursing from the pagoda. Tied together as they still were, by the post-coitus, their retreat was no easy matter. For the efforts they made to escape, acting equally in opposite directions, could not but annul each other. They must have greatly suffered.

He has now buggered the dogs, said Mercier.

He has driven them from the shelter, said Camier, there is no denying that, but by no means from the garden.

The rain will soon wash them loose, said Mercier. Less rut-besotted they would have thought of it themselves.

The fact is he has done them a service, said Camier.

Let us show him a little kindness, said Mercier, he's a hero of the great war. Here we were, high and dry, masturbating full pelt without fear of interruption, while he was crawling in the Flanders mud, shitting in his puttees.

Conclude nothing from those idle words, Mercier and Camier were old young.

It's an idea, said Camier.

Will you look at that clatter of decorations, said Mercier. Do you realize the gallons of diarrhea that represents?

Darkly, said Camier, as only one so costive can.

Let us suppose this alleged bicycle is ours, said Mercier. Where lies the harm?

A truce to dissembling, said Camier, it is ours.

Shift her out of here, said the ranger.

The day has dawned at last, said Camier, after years of shilly-shally, when we must go, we know not whither, perhaps never to return . . . alive. We are simply waiting for the day to lift, then full speed ahead. Try and understand.

What is more, said Mercier, we have still thought to take, before it is too late.

Thought to take? said Camier.

Those were my words, said Mercier.

I thought all thought was taken, said Camier, and all in order.

All is not, said Mercier.

Will you shift her or won't you, said the ranger.

Are you venal, said Mercier, since you are deaf to reason?

Silence.

Can you be bought off? said Mercier.

Certainly, said the ranger.

Give him a bob, said Mercier. To think our first disbursement should be a sop to bribery and extortion.

The ranger vanished with a curse.

How of a piece they all are, said Mercier.

Now he'll prowl around, said Camier.

What can that matter to us? said Mercier.

I don't like being prowled around, said Camier.

Mercier took exception to this turn. Camier maintained it. This little game soon palled. It must have been near noon.

And now, said Mercier, the time is come for us.

For us? said Camier.

Precisely, said Mercier, for us, for serious matters.

What about a bite to eat? said Camier.

Thought first, said Mercier, then sustenance.

A long debate ensued, broken by long silences in which thought took place. At such times they would sink, now Mercier, now Camier, to such depths of meditation that the voice of one, resuming its drift, was powerless to bring the other back, or passed unheard. Or they would arrive simultaneously at often contrary conclusions and simultaneously begin to state them. Nor was it rare for one to lapse into a brood before the other had concluded his exposé. And there were times they would look long at each other, unable to utter a word, their minds two blanks. It was fresh from one such daze they decided to abandon their inquiry, for the time being. The afternoon was well advanced, the rain was falling still, the short winter day was drawing to a close.

It is you have the provisions, said Mercier.

On the contrary, said Camier.

True, said Mercier.

My hunger is gone, said Camier.

One must eat, said Mercier.

I see no point, said Camier.

We have a long hard road before us still, said Mercier.

The sooner we drop the better, said Camier.

True, said Mercier.

The ranger's head appeared in the doorway. Believe it or not, only his head was to be seen. It was to say, in his quaint way, they were free to spend the night for half-a-crown.

Is thought now taken, said Camier, and all in order?

No, said Mercier.

Will all ever be? said Camier.

I believe so, said Mercier, yes, I believe, not firmly, no, but I believe, yes, the day is coming when all will be in order, at last.

That will be delightful, said Camier.

Let us hope so, said Mercier.

A long look passed between them. Camier said to himself, Even him I cannot see. A like thought agitated his *vis-à-vis*.

Two points seemed nevertheless established as a result of this consultation.

1. Mercier would set off alone, awheel, with the raincoat. Wherever he should stop for the night, at the first stage, he would get all in readiness to receive Camier. Camier would take the road as soon as the weather permitted. Camier would keep the umbrella. No mention of the sack.

2. It so chanced that Mercier, up to now, had shown himself the live wire, Camier

the dead weight. The reverse was to be expected at any moment. On the less weak let the weaker always lean, for the course to follow. They might conceivably be valiant together. That would be the day. Or the great weakness might overtake them simultaneously. Let them in this case not give way to despair, but wait with confidence for the evil moment to pass. In spite of the vagueness of these expressions they understood each other, more or less.

Not knowing what to think, said Camier, I look away.

It would seem to be lifting, said Mercier.

The sun comes out at last, said Camier, that we may admire it sink, below the horizon.

That long moment of brightness, said Mercier, with its thousand colors, always stirs my heart.

The day of toil is ended, said Camier; a kind of ink rises in the east and floods the sky.

The bell rang, announcing closing time.

I sense vague shadowy shapes, said Camier, they come and go with muffled cries.

I too have the feeling, said Mercier, we have not gone unobserved since morning.

Are we by any chance alone now? said Camier.

I see no one, said Mercier.

Let us then go together, said Camier.

They left the shelter.

The sack, said Mercier.

The umbrella, said Camier.

The raincoat, said Mercier.

It I have, said Camier.

Is there nothing else? said Mercier.

I see nothing else, said Camier.

I'll get them, said Mercier, you mind the bicycle.

It was a woman's bicycle, without free wheel unfortunately. To brake one pedaled backward.

The ranger, his bunch of keys in his hand, watched them recede. Mercier held the handlebar, Camier the saddle. The pedals rose and fell.

He cursed them on their way.

II

In the show windows the lights came on, went out, according to the show. Through the slippery streets the crowd pressed on as towards some unquestioned goal. A strange well-being, wroth and weary, filled the air. Close the eyes and not a voice is heard, only the onward panting of the feet. In this throng silence they advanced as best they could, at the edge of the sidewalk, Mercier in front, his hand on the handlebar, Camier behind, his hand on the saddle, and the bicycle slithered in the gutter by their side.

You hinder me more than you help me, said Mercier.

I'm not trying to help you, said Camier, I'm trying to help myself.

Then all is well, said Mercier.

I'm cold, said Camier.

It was indeed cold.

It is indeed cold, said Mercier.

Where do our feet think they're taking us? said Camier.

They would seem to be heading for the canal, said Mercier.

Already? said Camier.

Perhaps we shall be tempted, said Mercier, to strike out along the towpath and follow it till boredom doth ensue. Before us, beckoning us on, without our having to lift our eyes, the dying tints we love so well.

Speak for yourself, said Camier.

The very water, said Mercier, will linger livid, which is not to be despised either. And then the whim, who knows, may take us to throw ourselves in.

The little bridges slip by, said Camier, ever fewer and farther between. We pore over the locks, trying to understand. From the barges made fast to the bank waft the watermen's voices, bidding us good-night. Their day is done, they smoke a last pipe before turning in.

Every man for himself, said Mercier, and God for one and all.

The town lies far behind, said Camier. Little by little night overtakes us, blue-black. We splash through puddles left by the rain. It is no longer possible to advance. Retreat is equally out of the question.

He added, some moments later:

What are you musing on, Mercier?

On the horror of existence, confusedly, said Mercier.

What about a drink? said Camier.

I thought we had agreed to abstain, said Mercier, except in the event of accident, or indisposition. Does not that figure among our many conventions?

I don't call drink, said Camier, a quick nip to put some life in us.

They stopped at the first pub.

No bikes here, said the publican.

Perhaps after all he was a mere hireling.

And now? said Camier.

We might chain it to a lamppost, said Mercier.

That would give us more freedom, said Camier. He added, Of movement.

In the end they fell back on a railing. It came to the same.

And now? said Mercier.

Back to no bikes? said Camier.

Never! said Mercier.

Never say that, said Camier.

So they adjourned across the way.

Sitting at the bar they discoursed of this and that, brokenly, as was their custom. They spoke, fell silent, listened to each other, stopped listening, each as he fancied or as bidden from within. There were moments, minutes on end, when Camier lacked the strength to raise his glass to his mouth. Mercier was subject to the same failing. Then the less weak of the two gave the weaker to drink, inserting between his lips the rim of his glass. A press of somber shaggy bulks hemmed them about, thicker and thicker as the hour wore on. From their conversation there emerged in spite of all, among other points, the following:

1. It would be useless, nay, madness, to venture any further for the moment.
2. They need only ask Helen to put them up for the night.
3. Nothing would prevent them from setting out on the morrow, hail, rain or shine, at the crack of dawn.

4. They had nothing to reproach themselves with.

5. Did what they were looking for exist?

6. What were they looking for?

7. There was no hurry.

8. All their judgments relating to the expedition called for revision, in tranquillity.

9. Only one thing mattered: depart.

10. To hell with it all anyway.

Back in the street they linked arms. After a few hundred yards Mercier drew Camier's attention to the fact that they were not in step.

You have your gait, said Camier, I have mine.

I'm not accusing anyone, said Mercier, but it's wearing. We advance in jerks.

I'd prefer you to ask me straight out, said Camier, straight out plump and plain, either to let go your arm and move away or else to fall in with your titubations.

Camier, Camier, said Mercier, squeezing his arm.

They came to a crossroads and stopped.

Which way do we drag ourselves now? said Camier.

Our situation is no ordinary one, said Mercier, I mean in relation to Helen's home, if I know where we are. For these different ways all lead there with equal success.

Then let us turn back, said Camier.

And lose ground we can ill afford? said Mercier.

We can't stay stuck here all night, said Camier, like a couple of clots.

Let us toss our umbrella, said Mercier. It will fall in a certain way, according to laws of which we know nothing. Then all we have to do is press forward in the designated direction.

The umbrella answered, Left! It resembled a great wounded bird, a great bird of ill omen shot down by hunters and awaiting quivering the coup de grâce. The likeness was striking. Camier picked it up and hung it from his pocket.

It is not broken, I trust, said Mercier.

Here their attention was drawn to a strange figure, that of a gentleman wearing, despite the rawness of the air, a simple frock-coat and top-hat. He seemed, for the moment, to be going their way, for their view was of his rear. His hands, in a gesture coquettishly demential, held high and wide apart the skirts of his cutaway. He advanced warily, with stiff and open tread.

Do you feel like singing? said Camier.

Not to my knowledge, said Mercier.

The rain was beginning again. But had it ever ceased?

Let us make haste, said Camier.

Why do you ask me that? said Mercier.

Camier seemed in no hurry to reply. Finally he said:

I hear singing.

They halted, the better to listen.

I hear nothing, said Mercier.

And yet you have good ears, said Camier, so far as I know.

Very fair, said Mercier.

Strange, said Camier.

Do you hear it still? said Mercier.

For all the world a mixed choir, said Camier.

Perhaps it's a delusion, said Mercier.

Possibly, said Camier.

Let's run, said Mercier.

They ran some little way in the dark and wet, without meeting a soul. When they had done running Mercier deplored the nice state, soaked to the buff, in which they would arrive at Helen's, to which in reply Camier described how they would immediately strip and put their things to dry, before the fire or in the hot-cupboard with the boiler and hot water pipes.

Come to think of it, said Mercier, why didn't we use our umbrella?

Camier looked at the umbrella, now in his hand. He had placed it there so that he might run more freely.

We might have indeed, he said.

Why burden oneself with an umbrella, said Mercier, and not put it up as required?

Quite, said Camier.

Put it up now, in the name of God, said Mercier.

But Camier could not put it up.

Give it here, said Mercier.

But Mercier could not put it up either.

This was the moment chosen by the rain, acting on behalf of the universal malignity, to come down in buckets.

It's stuck, said Camier, don't strain it whatever you do.

Mercier used a nasty expression.

Meaning me? said Camier.

With both hands Mercier raised the umbrella high above his head and dashed it to the ground. He used another nasty expression. And to crown all, lifting to the sky his convulsed and streaming face, he said, As for thee, fuck thee.

Decidedly Mercier's grief, heroically contained since morning, could be no longer so.

Is it our little omniomni you are trying to abuse? said Camier. You should know better. It's he on the contrary fucks thee. Omniomni, the all-unfuckable.

Kindly leave Mrs. Mercier outside this discussion, said Mercier.

The mind has snapped, said Camier.

The first thing one noticed at Helen's was the carpet.

Will you look at that pile, said Camier.

Prime moquette, said Mercier.

Unbelievable, said Camier.

You'd think you never saw it till now, said Mercier, and you wallowing on it all these years.

I never did see it till now, said Camier, and now I can't forget it.

So one says, said Mercier.

If that evening the carpet in particular caught the eye, it was not alone in catching it, for a cockatoo caught it too. It clung shakily to its perch hung from a corner of the ceiling and dizzily rocked by conflicting swing and spin. It was wide awake, in spite of the late hour. Feebly and fitfully its breast rose and fell, faint quiverings ruffled up the down at every expiration. Every now and then the beak would gape and for what seemed whole seconds fishlike remain agape. Then the black spindle of the tongue was seen to stir. The eyes, averted from the light, filled with unspeakable bewilderment and distress, seemed all ears. Shivers of anguish rippled the plumage, blazing in ironic splendor. Beneath it, on the carpet, a great news-sheet was spread.

There's my bed and there's the couch, said Helen.

They're all yours, said Mercier. For my part I'll sleep with none.

A nice little suck-off, said Camier, not too prolonged, by all means, but nothing more.

Terminated, said Helen, the nice little suck-offs but nothing more.

I'll lie on the floor, said Mercier, and wait for dawn. Scenes and faces will unfold before my gaze, the rain on the skylight sound like claws and night rehearse its colors. The longing will take me to throw myself out of the window, but I'll master it. He repeated, in a roar, I'll master it!

Back in the street they wondered what they had done with the bicycle. The sack too had disappeared.

Did you see the polly? said Mercier.

Pretty thing, said Camier.

It groaned in the night, said Mercier.

Camier questioned this.

It will haunt me till my dying day, said Mercier.

I didn't know she had one, said Camier, what haunts me is the Kidderminster.

Nor I, said Mercier. She says she's had it for years.

She's lying of course, said Camier.

It was still raining. They took shelter in an archway, not knowing where to go.

When exactly did you notice the sack was gone? said Mercier.

This morning, said Camier, when I went to get my sulfamides.

I see no sign of the umbrella, said Mercier.

Camier inspected himself, stooping and spreading out his arms as if concerned with a button.

We must have left it at Helen's, he said.

My feeling is, said Mercier, that if we don't leave this town today we never shall. So let us think twice before we start trying to –.

He almost said recoup.

What exactly was there in the sack? said Camier.

Toilet requisites and necessaries, said Mercier.

Superfluous luxury, said Camier.

A few pairs of socks, said Mercier, and one of drawers.

God, said Camier.

Some eatables, said Mercier.

Rotten ripe for the muckheap, said Camier.

On condition we retrieve them, said Mercier.

Let us board the first express southward bound! cried Camier. He added, more soberly, And so not be tempted to get out at the nearest stop.

And why south, said Mercier, rather than north, or east, or west?

I prefer south, said Camier.

Is that sufficient ground? said Mercier.

It's the nearest terminus, said Camier.

True, said Mercier.

He went out into the street and looked up at the sky, a gray pall, look where he would.

The sky is uniformly leaden, he said, resuming his place under the arch, we'll drown like rats without the umbrella.

Camier criticized this simile.

Like rats, said Mercier.

Even if we had the umbrella, said Camier, we could not use it, for it is broken.

What fresh extravagance is this? said Mercier.

We broke it yesterday, said Camier. Your idea.

Mercier took his head between his hands. Little by little the scene came back to him. Proudly he drew himself up, to his full height.

Come, he said, regrets are vain.

We'll wear the raincoat turn and turn about, said Camier.

We'll be in the train, said Mercier, speeding south.

Through the streaming panes, said Camier, we try to number the cows, shivering pitiably in the scant shelter of the hedges. Rooks take wing, all dripping and bedraggled. But gradually the day lifts and we arrive in the brilliant sunlight of a glorious winter's afternoon. It seems like Monaco.

I don't seem to have eaten for forty-eight hours, said Mercier. And yet I am not hungry.

One must eat, said Camier. He went on to compare the stomach with the bladder.

Apropos, said Mercier, how is your cyst?

Dormant, said Camier, but under the surface mischief is brewing.

What will you do then? said Mercier.

I dread to think, said Camier.

I would just manage a cream puff, said Mercier.

Wait here, said Camier.

No no! cried Mercier. Don't leave me! Don't let us leave each other!

Camier left the archway and began to cross the street. Mercier called him back and an altercation ensued, too foolish to be recorded, so foolish was it.

Another would take umbrage, said Camier. Not I, all things considered. For I say to myself, The hour is grave and Mercier . . . well . . . he advanced towards Mercier who promptly recoiled. I was only going to embrace you, said Camier. I'll do it some other time, when you're less yourself, if I think of it.

He went out in the rain and disappeared. Alone in the archway Mercier began pacing to and fro, deep in bitter thought. It was their first separation since the morning of the day before. Raising suddenly his eyes, as from a vision no longer to be borne, he saw two children, a little boy and a little girl, standing gazing at him. They wore little black oilskins with hoods, identical, and the boy had a little satchel on his back. They held each other by the hand.

Papa! they said, with one voice or nearly.

Good evening, my children, said Mercier, get along with you now.

But they did not get along with them, no, but stood their ground, their little clasped hands lightly swinging back and forth. Finally the little girl drew hers away and advanced towards him they had addressed as papa. She stretched out her little arms towards him, as if to invite a kiss, or at least a caress. The little boy followed suit, with visible misgiving. Mercier raised his foot and dashed it against the pavement. Be off with you! he cried. He bore down on them, wildly gesturing and his face contorted. The children backed away to the sidewalk and there stood still again. Fuck off out of here! screamed Mercier. He flew at them in a fury and they took to their heels. But soon they halted and looked back. What they saw then must have impressed them strongly, for they ran on and bolted down the first side-street. As for the unfortunate Mercier, satisfied after a few minutes of fuming tenterhooks that the danger was past, he returned dripping to the archway and resumed his reflections, if not at the point where they had been interrupted, at least at one near by.

Mercier's reflections were peculiar in this, that the same swell and surge swept through them all and cast the mind away, no matter where it embarked, on the same rocks invariably. They were perhaps not so much reflections as a dark torrent of brooding where past and future merged in a single flood and closed, over a present for ever absent. Ah well.

Here, said Camier, I hope you haven't been fretting.

Mercier extracted the cake from its paper wrapping and placed it on the palm of his hand. He bent forward and down till his nose was almost touching it and the eyes not far behind. He darted towards Camier, while still in this position, a sidelong look full of mistrust.

A cream horn, said Camier, the best I could find.

Mercier, still bent double, moved forward to the verge of the archway, where the light was better, and examined the cake again.

It's full of cream, said Camier.

Mercier slowly clenched his fist and the cake gushed between his fingers. The staring eyes filled with tears. Camier advanced to get a better view. The tears flowed, overflowed, all down the furrowed cheeks and vanished in the beard. The face remained unmoved. The eyes, still streaming and no doubt blinded, seemed intent on some object stirring on the ground.

If you didn't want it, said Camier, you had better given it to a dog, or to a child.

I'm in tears, said Mercier, don't intrude.

When the flow stopped, Camier said:

Let me offer you our handkerchief.

There are days, said Mercier, one is born every minute. Then the world is full of shitty little Merciers. It's hell. Oh but to cease!

Enough, said Camier. You look like a capital S. Ninety if a day.

Would I were, said Mercier. He wiped his hand on the seat of his trousers. He said, I'll start crawling any minute.

I'm off, said Camier.

Leaving me to my fate, said Mercier. I knew it.

You know my little ways, said Camier.

No, said Mercier, but I was counting on your affection to help me serve my time.

I can help you, said Camier, I can't resurrect you.

Take me by the hand, said Mercier, and lead me far away from here. I'll trot along at your side like a little puppy dog, or a tiny tot. And the day will come –.

A terrible screech of brakes rent the air, followed by a scream and a resounding crash. Mercier and Camier made a rush (after a moment's hesitation) for the open street and were rewarded by the vision, soon hidden by a concourse of gapers, of a big fat woman writhing feebly on the ground. The disorder of her dress revealed an amazing mass of billowing underclothes, originally white in color. Her lifeblood, streaming from one or more wounds, had already reached the gutter.

Ah, said Mercier, that's what I needed, I feel a new man.

He was in fact transfigured.

Let this be a lesson to us, said Camier.

Meaning? said Mercier.

Never to despair, said Camier, or lose our faith in life.

Ah, said Mercier with relief, I was afraid you meant something else.

As they went their way an ambulance passed, speeding towards the scene of the mishap.

I beg your pardon? said Camier.

A crying shame, said Mercier.

I don't follow you, said Camier.

A six cylinder, said Mercier.

And what of it? said Camier.

And they talk about the petrol shortage, said Mercier.

There are perhaps more victims than one, said Camier.

It might be an infant child, said Mercier, for all they care.

The rain was falling gently, as from the fine rose of a watering pot. Mercier advanced with upturned face. Now and then he wiped it, with his free hand. He had not had a wash for some time.

Levitiation

BY CYNTHIA OZICK

A pair of novelists, husband and wife, gave a party. The husband was also an editor; he made his living at it. But really he was novelist. His manner was powerless; he did not seem like an editor at all. He had a nice plain pale face, likable. His name was Feingold.

For love, and also because he had always known he did not want a Jewish wife, he married a minister's daughter. Lucy too had hoped to marry out of her tradition. (These words were hers. "Out of my tradition," she said. The idea fevered him.) At the age of twelve she felt herself to belong to the people of the Bible. ("A Hebrew," she said. His heart lurched, joy rocked him.) One night from the pulpit her father read a Psalm; all at once she saw how the Psalmist meant *her*; then and there she became an Ancient Hebrew.

She had huge, intent, sliding eyes, disconcertingly luminous, and copper hair, and a grave and timid way of saying honest things.

They were shy people, and rarely gave parties.

Each had published one novel. Hers was about domestic life; he wrote about Jews.

All the roil about the State of the Novel had passed them by. In the evening after the children had been put to bed, while the portable dishwasher rattled out its smell of burning motor oil, they sat down, she at her desk, he at his, and began to write. They wrote not without puzzlements and travail; nevertheless as naturally as birds. They were devoted to accuracy, psychological realism, and earnest truthfulness; also to virtue, and even to wit. Neither one was troubled by what had happened to the novel: all those declarations about the end of Character and Story. They were serene. Sometimes, closing up their notebooks for the night, it seemed to them that they were literary friends and lovers, like George Eliot and George Henry Lewes.

In bed they would revel in quantity and murmur distrustingly of theory. "Seven pages so far this week." "Nine-and-a-half, but I had to throw out four. A wrong tack." "Because you're doing first person. First person strangles. You can't get out of their skin." And so on. The one principle they agreed on was the importance of never writing about writers. Your protagonist always has to be someone *real*, with real work-in-the-world – a bureaucrat, a banker, an architect (ah, they envied Conrad his shipmasters!) – otherwise you fall into solipsism, narcissism, tedium, lack of appeal-to-the-common-reader; who knew what other perils.

This difficulty – seizing on a concrete subject – was mainly Lucy's. Feingold's novel – the one he was writing now – was about Menachem ben Zerach, survivor of a massacre of Jews in the town of Estella in Spain in 1328. From morning to midnight he hid under a pile of corpses, until a "compassionate knight" (this was the language of the history Feingold relied on) plucked him out and took him home to tend his wounds. Menachem was then twenty; his father and mother and four younger brothers had been cut down in the terror. Six thousand Jews died in a single day in March. Feingold wrote well about how the mild winds carried the salty fragrance of fresh blood, together with the ashes of Jewish houses, into the faces of the marauders. It was nevertheless a triumphant story: at the end Menachen ben Zerach becomes a renowned scholar.

"If you're going to tell about how after he gets to be a scholar he just sits there and *writes*," Lucy protested, "then you're doing the Forbidden Thing." But Feingold said he meant to concentrate on the massacre, and especially on the life of the "compassionate knight." What had brought him to this compassion? What sort of education? What did he read? Feingold would invent a journal for the compassionate knight, and quote from it. Into this journal the compassionate knight would direct all his gifts, passions, and private opinions.

"Solipsism," Lucy said. "Your compassionate knight is only another writer. Narcissism. Tedium."

They talked often about the Forbidden Thing. After a while they began to call it the Forbidden City, because not only were they (but Lucy especially) tempted to write – solipsistically, narcissistically, tediously, and without common appeal – about writers, but, more narrowly yet, about writers in New York.

"The compassionate knight," Lucy said, "lived on the Upper West Side of Estella. He lived on the Riverside Drive, the West End Avenue, of Estella. He lived in Estella on Central Park West."

The Feingolds lived on Central Park West.

In her novel – the published one, not the one she was writing now – Lucy had described, in the first person, where they lived:

> By now I have seen quite a few of those West Side apartments. They have mysterious layouts. Rooms with doors that go nowhere – turn the knob, open: a wall. Someone is snoring behind it, in another apart- ment. They have made two and three or even four and five flats out of these palaces. The toilet bowls have antique cracks that shimmer with moisture like old green rivers. Fluted columns and fireplaces. Artur Rubinstein once paid rent here. On a gilt piano he raced a sonata by Beethoven. The sounds went spinning like mercury. Breathings all let- tered now. Editors. Critics. Books, old, old books, heavy as centuries. Shelves built into the cold fireplace; Freud on the grate, Marx on the hearth, Melville, Hawthorne, Emerson. Oh God, the weight, the weight.

Lucy felt herself to be a stylist; Feingold did not. He believed in putting one sentence after another. In his publishing house he had no influence. He was nervous about his decisions. He rejected most manuscripts because he was afraid of mistakes; every mistake lost money. It was a small house panting after profits; Feingold told Lucy that the only books his firm respected belonged to the accountants. Now and then he tried to smuggle in a novel after his own taste, and then he would be brutal to the writer. He knocked the paragraphs about until they were as sparse as his own. "God knows what you would do to mine," Lucy said; " bald man, bald prose." The horizon of Feingold's head shone. She never showed him her work. But they under- stood they were lucky in each other. They pitied every writer who was not married to a writer. Lucy said: "At least we have the same premises."

Volumes of Jewish history ran up and down their walls; they belonged to Feingold. Lucy read only one book – it was *Emma* – over and over again. Feingold did not have a "philosophical" mind. What he liked was event. Lucy liked to specu- late and ruminate. She was slightly more intelligent then Feingold. To strangers he seemed very mild. Lucy, when silent, was a tall copper statue.

They were both devoted to omniscience, but they were not acute enough to see what they meant by it. They thought of themselves as children with a puppet theater: they could make anything at all happen, speak all the lines, with gloved hands bring all the characters to shudders or leaps. They fancied themselves in love with what they called "imagination." It was not true. What they were addicted to was counterfeit pity, and this was because they were absorbed by power, and were powerless.

They lived on pity, and therefore on gossip: who had been childless for ten years, who had lost three successive jobs, who was in danger of being fired, which agent's prestige had fallen, who could not get his second novel published, who was *persona non grata* at this or that magazine, who was drinking seriously, who was a likely suicide, who was dreaming of divorce, who was secretly or flamboyantly sleeping with whom, who was being snubbed, who counted or did not count; and toward everyone in the least way victimized they appeared to feel the most immoderate tenderness. They were, besides, extremely "psychological": kind listeners, helpful, lifting hot palms they would gladly put to anyone's anguished temples. They were attracted to bitter lives.

About their own lives they had a joke: they were "secondary-level" people. Feingold had a secondary-level job with a secondary-level house. Lucy's own publisher was secondary-level; even the address was Second Avenue. The reviews of their books had been written by secondary-level reviewers. All their friends were secondary-level: not the presidents or partners of the respected firms, but copy editors and production assistants; not the glittering eagles of the intellectual organs, but the wearisome hacks of small Jewish journals; not the fiercely cold-hearted literary critics, but those wan and chattering daily reviewers of film. If they knew a playwright, he was off-off-Broadway in ambition and had not yet been produced. If they knew a painter, he lived in a loft and had exhibited only once, against a wire fence in the outdoor show at Washington Square in the spring. And this struck them as mean and unfair; they liked their friends, but other people – why not they? – were drawn into the deeper caverns of New York, among the lions.

New York! They risked their necks if they ventured out to the roadway for a loaf of bread after dark; muggers hid behind the seesaws in the playgrounds, junkies with knives hung upside down in the jungle gym. Every apartment a lit fortress; you admired the lamps and the locks, the triple locks on the caged-in windows, the double locks and the police rods on the doors, the lamps with timers set to make burglars think you were always at home. Footsteps in the corridor, the elevator's midnight grind; caution's muffled gasps. Their parents lived in Cleveland and St. Paul, and hardly ever dared to visit. All of this: grit and unsuitability (they might have owned a snowy lawn somewhere else); and no one said their names, no one had any curiosity about them, no one ever asked whether they were working on anything new. After half a year their books were remaindered for eighty-nine cents each. Anonymous mediocrities. They could not call themselves forgotten because they had never been noticed.

Lucy had a diagnosis: they were, both of them, sunk in a ghetto. Feingold persisted in his morbid investigation into Inquisitional *autos-da-fé* in this and that Iberian market place. She herself had supposed the inner life of a housebound woman – she cited *Emma* – to contain as much comedy as the cosmos. Jews and women! They were both beside the point. It was necessary to put aside pity; to look to the center; to abandon selflessness; to study power.

They drew up a list of luminaries. They invited Irving Howe, Susan Sontag, Alfred Kazin, and Leslie Fiedler. They invited Norman Podhoretz and Elizabeth Hardwick. They invited Philip Roth and Joyce Carol Oates and Norman Mailer and William Styron and Donald Barthelme and Jerzy Kosinski and Truman Capote. None of these came; all of them had unlisted numbers, or else machines that answered the telephone, or else were in Prague or Paris or out of town. Nevertheless the apartment filled up. It was a Saturday night in a chill November. Taxis whirled on patches of sleet. On the inside of the apartment door a mound of rainboots grew taller and taller. Two closets were packed tight with rain coats and fur coats; a heap of coats smelling of skunk and lamb fell tangled off a bed.

The party washed and turned like a sluggish tub; it lapped at all the walls of all the rooms. Lucy wore a long skirt, violet-colored, Feingold a lemon shirt and no tie. He looked paler than ever. The apartment had a wide center hall, itself the breadth of a room; the dining room opened off it to the left, the living room to the right. The three party-rooms shone like a triptych: it was as if you could fold them up and enclose everyone into darkness. The guests were free-standing figures in the niches of a cathedral; or else dressed-up cardboard dolls, with their drinks, and their costumes all meticulously hung with sashes and draped collars and little capes, the women's hair variously bound, the men's sprouting and spilling: fashion stalked, Feingold moped. He took in how it all flashed, manhattans and martinis, earrings and shoe-tips – he marveled, but knew it was a falsehood, even a figment. The great world was somewhere else. The conversation could fool you: how these people talked! From the conversation itself – grains of it, carried off, swallowed by new eddyings, swirl devouring swirl, every moment a permutation in the tableau of those free-standing figures or dolls, all of them afloat in a tub – from this or that hint or syllable you could imagine the whole universe in the process of ultimate comprehension. Human nature, the stars, history – the voices drummed and strummed. Lucy swam by blank-eyed, pushing a platter of mottled cheeses. Feingold seized her: "It's a waste!" She gazed back. He said, "No one's here!" Mournfully she rocked a stump of cheese; then he lost her.

He went into the living room: it was mainly empty, a few lumps on the sofa. The lumps wore business suits. The dining room was better. Something in formation: something around the big table: coffee cups shimmering to the brim, cake cut onto plates (the mock-Victorian rosebud plates from Boots' drug store in London: the year before their first boy was born Lucy and Feingold saw the Brontës' moors; Coleridge's house in Highgate; Lamb House, Rye, where Edith Wharton had tea with Henry James; Bloomsbury; the Cambridge stairs Forster had lived at the top of) – it seemed about to become a regular visit, with points of view, opinions; a discussion. The voices began to stumble; Feingold liked that, it was nearly human. But then, serving round the forks and paper napkins, he noticed the awful vivacity of their falsetto phrases: actors, theater chatter, who was directing whom, what was opening where; he hated actors. Shrill puppets. Brainless. A double row of faces around the table; gurgles of fools.

The center hall – swept clean. No one there but Lucy, lingering.

"Theater in the dining room," he said. "Junk."

"Film. I heard film."

"Film too," he conceded. "Junk. It's mobbed in there."

"Because they've got the cake. They've got all the food. The living room's got nothing."

"My God," he said, like a man choking, "do you realize *no one came*?"

The living room had – had once had – potato chips. The chips were gone, the carrot sticks eaten, of the celery sticks nothing left but threads. One olive in a dish; Feingold chopped it in two with vicious teeth. The business suits had disappeared. "It's awfully early," Lucy said; "a lot of people had to leave." "It's a cocktail party, that's what happens," Feingold said. "It isn't *exactly* a cocktail party," Lucy said. They sat down on the carpet in front of the fireless grate. "Is that a real fireplace?" someone inquired. "We never light it," Lucy said. "Do you light those candlesticks ever?" "They belonged to Jimmy's grandmother," Lucy said, "we never light them."

She crossed no-man's-land to the dining room. They were serious in there now. The subject was Chaplin's gestures.

In the living room Feingold despaired; no one asked him, he began to tell about the compassionate knight. A problem of ego, he said: compassion being super-consciousness of one's own pride. Not that he believed this; he only thought it provocative to say something original, even if a little muddled. But no one responded. Feingold looked up. "Can't you light that fire?" said a man. "All right," Feingold said. He rolled a paper log made of last Sunday's *Times* and laid a match on it. A flame as clear as a streetlight whitened the faces of the sofa-sitters. He recognized a friend of his from the Seminary – he had what Lucy called "theological" friends – and then and there, really very suddenly, Feingold wanted to talk about God. Or, if not God, then certain historical atrocities, abominations: to wit, the crime of the French nobleman Draconet, a proud Crusader, who in the spring of the year 1247 arrested all the Jews of the province of Vienne, castrated the men, and tore off the breasts of the women; some he did not mutilate, and only cut in two. It interested Feingold that Magna Carta and the Jewish badge of shame were issued in the same year, and that less than a century afterward all the Jews were driven out of England, even families who had been settled there seven or eight generations. He had a soft spot for Pope Clement IV, who absolved the Jews from responsibility for the Black Death. "The plague takes the Jews themselves," the Pope said. Feingold knew innumerable stories about forced conversions, he felt at home with these thoughts, comfortable, the chairs seemed dense with family. He wondered whether it would be appropriate – at a cocktail party, after all! – to inquire after the status of the Seminary friend's agnosticism: was it merely that God had stepped out of history, left the room for a moment, so to speak, without a pass, or was there no Creator to begin with, nothing had been created, the world was a chimera, a solipsist's delusion?

Lucy was uneasy with the friend from the Seminary; he was the one who had administered her conversion, and every encounter was like a new stage in a perpetual examination. She was glad there was no Jewish catechism. Was she a backslider? Anyhow she felt tested. Sometimes she spoke of Jesus to the children. She looked around – her great eyes wheeled – and saw that everyone in the living room was a Jew.

There were Jews in the dining room too, but the unruffled, devil-may-care kind: the humorists, the painters, film reviewers who went off to studio showings of "Screw on Screen" on the eve of the Day of Atonement. Mostly there were Gentiles in the dining room. Nearly the whole cake was gone. She took the last piece, cubed it on a paper plate, and carried it back to the living room. She blamed Feingold, he was having one of his spasms of fanaticism. Everyone normal, everyone with sense –

the humanists and humorists, for instance – would want to keep away. What was he now, after all, but one of those boring autodidacts who spew out everything they read? He was doing it for spite, because no one had come. There he was, telling about the blood-libel. Little Hugh of Lincoln. How in London, in 1279, Jews were torn to pieces by horses, on a charge of having crucified a Christian child. How in 1285 in Munich, a mob burned down a synagogue on the same pretext. At Eastertime in Mainz two years earlier. Three centuries of beatified child martyrs, some of them figments, all called "Little Saints." The Holy Niño of La-Guardia. Feingold was crazed by these tales, he drank them like a vampire. Lucy stuck a square of chocolate cake in his mouth to shut him up. Feingold was waiting for a voice. The friend from the Seminary, pragmatic, licked off his bit of cake hungrily. It was a cake sent from home, packed by his wife in a plastic bag, to make sure there was something to eat. It was a guaranteed no-lard cake. They were all ravenous. The fire crumpled out in big paper cinders.

The friend from the Seminary had brought a friend. Lucy examined him: she knew how to give catechisms of her own, she was not a novelist for nothing. She catechized and catalogued: a refugee. Fingers like long wax candles, snuffed at the nails. Black sockets: was he blind? It was hard to tell where the eyes were under that ledge of skull. Skull for a head, but such a cushioned mouth, such lips, such orderly expressive teeth. Such a bone in such a dry wrist. A nose like a saint's. The face of Jesus. He whispered. Everyone leaned over to hear. He was Feingold's voice: the voice Feingold was waiting for.

"Come to modern times," the voice urged. "Come to yesterday." Lucy was right: she could tell a refugee in an instant, even before she heard any accent. They all reminded her of her father. She put away this insight (the resemblance of Presbyterian ministers to Hitler refugees) to talk over with Feingold later: it was nicely analytical, it had enough mystery to satisfy. "Yesterday," the refugee said, "the eyes of God were shut." And Lucy saw him shut his hidden eyes in their tunnels. "Shut," he said, "like iron doors" – a voice of such nobility that Lucy thought immediately of that eerie passage in Genesis where the voice of the Lord God walks in the Garden in the cool of the day and calls to Adam, "Where are you?"

They all listened with a terrible intensity. Again Lucy looked around. It pained her how intense Jews could be, though she too was intense. But she was intense because her brain was roiling with ardor, she wooed mind-pictures, she was a novelist. *They* were intense all the time; she supposed the grocers among them were as intense as any novelist; was it because they had been Chosen, was it because they pitied themselves every breathing moment?

Pity and shock stood in all their faces.

The refugee was telling a story. "I witnessed it," he said, "I am the witness." Horror; sadism; corpses. As if – Lucy took the image from the elusive wind that was his voice in its whisper – as if hundreds and hundreds of Crucifixions were all happening at once. She visualized a hillside with multitudes of crosses, and bodies dropping down from big bloody nails. Every Jew was Jesus. That was the only way Lucy could get hold of it: otherwise it was only a movie. She had seen all the movies, the truth was she could feel nothing. That same bulldozer shoveling those same sticks of skeletons, that same little boy in a cap with twisted mouth and his hands in the air – if there had been a camera at the Crucifixion Christianity would collapse, no one would ever feel anything about it.

All the same, she listened. What he told was exactly like the movies. A gray scene, a scrubby hill, a ravine. Germans in helmets, with shining tar-black belts, wearing gloves. A ragged bundle of Jews at the lip of the ravine – an old grand-mother, a child or two, a couple in their forties. All the faces stained with grayness, the stubble on the ground stained gray, the clothes on them limp as shrouds but immobile, as if they were already under the dirt, shut off from breezes, as if they were already stone. The refugee's whisper carved them like sculptures – there they stood, a shadowy stone asterisk of Jews, you could see their nostrils, open as skulls, the stony round ears of the children, the grandmother's awful twig of a neck, the father and mother grasping the children but strangers to each other, not a touch between them, the grandmother cast out, claiming no one and not claimed, all prayerless stone gums. There they stood. For a long while the refugee's voice pinched them and held them, so that you had to look. His voice made Lucy look and look. He pierced the figures through with his whisper. Then he let the shots come. The figures never teetered, never shook: the stoniness broke all at once and they fell cleanly, like sacks, into the ravine. Immediately they were in a heap, with random limbs all tangled together. The refugee's voice like a camera brought a German boot to the edge of the ravine. The boot kicked sand. It kicked and kicked, the sand poured over the family of sacks.

Then Lucy saw the fingers of the listeners – all their fingers were stretched out.

The room began to lift. It ascended. It rose like an ark on waters. Lucy said inside her mind, "This chamber of Jews." It seemed to her that the room was levitat-ing on the little grains of the refugee's whisper. She felt herself alone at the bottom, below the floorboards, while the room floated upward, carrying Jews. Why did it not take her too? Only Jesus could take her. They were being kidnapped, these Jews, by a messenger from the land of the dead. The man had a power. Already he was in the shadow of another tale: she promised herself she would not listen, only Jesus could make her listen. The room was ascending. Above her head it grew smaller and smaller, more and more remote, it fled deeper and deeper into upwardness.

She craned after it. Wouldn't it bump into the apartment upstairs? It was like watching the underside of an elevator, all dirty and hairy, with dust-roots wagging. The black floor moved higher and higher. It was getting free of her, into loftiness, lifting Jews.

The glory of their martyrdom.

Under the rising eave Lucy had an illumination: she saw herself with the children in a little city park. A Sunday afternoon early in May. Feingold has stayed home to nap, and Lucy and the children find seats on a bench and wait for the unusual music to begin. The room is still levitating, but inside Lucy's illumination the boys are chasing birds. They run away from Lucy, they return, they leave. They surround a pigeon. They do not touch the pigeon; Lucy has forbidden it. She has read that city pigeons carry meningitis. A little boy in Red Bank, New Jersey, contracted sleeping sickness from touching a pigeon; after six years, he is still asleep. In his sleep he has grown from a child to an adolescent; puberty has come on him in his sleep, his testicles have dropped down, a benign blond beard glints mildly on his cheeks. His parents weep and weep. He is still asleep. No instruments or players are visible. A woman steps out onto a platform. She is an anthropologist from the Smithsonian Institute in Washington, D.C. She explains that there will be no "entertainment" in the usual sense; there will be no "entertainers." The players will not be artists; they will be "real peasants." They have been brought over from Messina, from Calabria. They are shepherds, goatherds. They will sing and dance and play just as they do when they come down from the hills to while away the evenings in the taverns. They will play the instruments that scare away the wolves from the flock. They will sing the songs that celebrate the Madonna of Love. A dozen men file onto the platform. They have heavy faces that do not smile. They have heavy dark skins, cratered and leathery. They have ears and noses that look like dried twisted clay. They have gold teeth. They have no teeth. Some are young; most are in their middle years. One is very old; he wears bells on his fingers. One has an instrument like a butter churn: he shoves a stick in and out of a hole in a wooden tub held under his arm, and a rattling screech spurts out of it. One blows on two slender pipes simultaneously. One has a long strap, which he rubs. One has a frame of bicycle bells; a descendant of the bells the priests used to beat in the temple of Minerva.

The anthropologist is still explaining everything. She explains the "male" instrument: three wooden knockers; the innermost one lunges up and down between the other two. The songs, she explains, are mainly erotic. The dances are suggestive.

The unusual music commences. The park has filled with Italians – greenhorns from Sicily, settled New Yorkers from Naples. An ancient people. They clap. The old man with the bells on his fingers points his dusty shoe-toes and slowly follows a circle of his own. His eyes are in trance, he squats, he ascends. The anthropologist explains that up-and-down dancing can also be found in parts of Africa. The singers wail like Arabs; the anthropologist notes that the Arab conquest covered the southernmost portion of the Italian boot for two hundred years. The whole chorus of peasants sings in a dialect of archaic Greek; the language has survived in the old songs, the anthropologist explains. The crowd is laughing and stamping. They click their fingers and sway. Lucy's boys are bored. They watch the man with the finger-bells; they watch the wooden male pump up and down. Everyone is clapping, stamping, clicking, swaying, thumping. The wailing goes on and on, faster and faster. The singers are dancers, the dancers are singers, they turn and turn, they are smiling the drugged smiles of dervishes. At home they grow flowers. They follow the sheep into the deep grass. They drink wine in the taverns at night. Calabria and Sicily in New York, sans wives, in sweat-blotched shirts and wrinkled dusty pants, gasping before strangers who have never smelled the sweetness of their village grasses!

Now the anthropologist from the Smithsonian has vanished out of Lucy's illumination. A pair of dancers seize each other. Leg winds over leg, belly into belly, each man hopping on a single free leg. Intertwined, they squat and rise, squat and rise. Old Hellenic syllables fly from them. They send out high elastic cries. They celebrate the Madonna, giver of fertility and fecundity. Lucy is glorified. She is exalted. She comprehends. Not that the musicians are peasants, not that their faces and feet and necks and wrists are blown grass and red earth. An enlightenment comes on her: she sees what is eternal: before the Madonna there was Venus; before Venus, Aphrodite; before Aphrodite, Astarte. Her womb is garden, lamb, and babe. She is the river and the waterfall. She causes grave men of business – goatherds are men of business – to cavort and to flash their gold teeth. She induces them to blow, beat, rub, shake, and scrape objects so that music will drop out of them.

Inside Lucy's illumination the dancers are seething. They are writhing. For the sake of the goddess, for the sake of the womb of the goddess, they are turning into serpents. When they grow still they are earth. They are from always to always. Nature is their pulse. Lucy sees: she understands: the gods are God. How terrible to have given up Jesus, a man like these, made of earth like these, with a pulse like these, God entering nature to become god! Jesus, no more miraculous than an ordinary goatherd; is a goatherd miracle? Is a leaf? A nut, a pit, a core, a seed, a stone? Everything is miracle! Lucy sees how she has abandoned nature, how she has lost true religion on account of the God of the Jews. The boys are on their bellies on the ground, digging it up with sticks. They dig and dig: little holes with mounds beside them. They fill them with peach pits, cherry pits, cantaloupe rinds. The Sicilians and Neapolitans pick up their baskets and purses and shopping bags and leave. The benches smell of eaten fruit, running juices, insect-mobbed. The stage is clean.

The living room has escaped altogether. It is very high and extremely small, no wider than the moon on Lucy's thumbnail. It is still sailing upward, and the voices of those on board are so faint that Lucy almost loses them. But she knows which word it is they mainly use. How long can they go on about it? How long? A morbid cud-chewing. Death and death and death. The word is less a human word than an animal's cry; a crow's. Caw caw. It belongs to storms, floods, avalanches. Acts of God. "Holocaust," someone caws dimly from above; she knows it must be Feingold. He always says this word over and over and over. History is bad for him: how little it makes him seem! Lucy decides it is possible to become jaded by atrocity. She is bored by the shootings and the gas and the camps, she is not ashamed to admit this. They are as tiresome as prayer. Repetition diminishes conviction; she is thinking of her father leading the same hymns week after week. If you said the same prayer over and over again, wouldn't your brain turn out to be no better than a prayer wheel?

In the dining room all the springs were running down. It was stale in there, a failed party. They were drinking beer or Coke or whiskey-and-water and playing with the cake crumbs on the tablecloth. There was still some cheese left on a plate, and half a bowl of salted peanuts. "The impact of Romantic Individualism," one of the humanists objected. "At the Frick?" "I never saw that." "They certainly are deliberate, you have to say that for them." Lucy, leaning abandoned against the door, tried to tune in. The relief of hearing atheists. A jacket designer who worked in Feingold's art department came in carrying a coat. Feingold had invited her because she was newly divorced; she was afraid to live alone. She was afraid of being ambushed in her basement while doing laundry. "Where's Jimmy?" the jacket designer asked. "In the other room." "Say goodbye for me, will you?" "Goodbye," Lucy said. The humanists – Lucy saw how they were all compassionate knights – stood up. A puddle from an overturned saucer was leaking onto the floor. "Oh, I'll get that," Lucy told the knights, "don't think another thought about it."

Overhead Feingold and the refugees are riding the living room. Their words are specks. All the Jews are in the air.

The Idea of Switzerland

BY WALTER ABISH

A glorious German summer.
Oh, absolutely.
Easily the most glorious summer of the past thirty-three years.
Thirty-three years? Oh, I agree.

When my father Ulrich von Hargenau was executed by a firing squad in 1944, his last words were: Long live Germany. At least, that's what I have been told by my family. He was killed in July 1944. What was the summer of 1944 like? Active. Certainly, active.

One runs little or no danger in speaking of the weather, or writing about the weather, or in repeating what others may have said on that subject. It is safe to conclude that people discussing the weather may be doing so in order to avoid a more controversial subject, one that might irritate, annoy, or even anger someone, anyone, within earshot. I am past avoiding risks. Just a few weeks after my return from Paris I narrowly avoided being killed on a deserted street by the driver of a yellow Porsche. It was a beautiful summer's day, and I was thinking of getting started on my new book, the one that is based on my stay in Paris. I am convinced that the driver of the Porsche had intended to kill or maim me for life. Yes, definitely. I was going to be put out of action. There's little risk in writing this. I did not recognize the driver, whose face I saw for only a split second. It was not an unattractive face. It was a German face, like mine. A determined and somewhat obdurate face, a face that Dürer might have taken a fancy to, and painted or sketched. Consider yourself lucky, said a passerby, after having helped me to my feet. He took it for granted that I spoke German. He also, I assume, took it for granted that it was all an accident, just as I took it for granted that it was not.

You really ought to take greater precautions, said my brother Helmut, when I mentioned the incident. And why on earth did you decide to return to Würtenburg, in the first place?

Because I was tired of hearing everyone around me speak only in French, I replied flippantly.

Well, try not to take too many risks.

The Hargenaus are not known for their humor. But then my brother might say: What's so funny about getting your head smashed in.

2.

What is my brother saying?

You should never have married Paula.

I was crazy about her.

If our father wasn't a bloody hero, and your name wasn't Hargenau, you'd be doing ten to fifteen behind bars. Maybe they'd permit you to have a typewriter, he added as an afterthought.

My brother has not yet had an opportunity to design a house of detention, as it is now called euphemistically, but he has designed a large assembly plant for Druck Electronics, an airport in München, a library and civic center in Heilbronn, another factory for Stüppen Plumbing, and at least half a dozen apartment buildings and three or four office buildings in addition to the new police station and post office in Würtenburg. He has also designed the house in the country where he and his family spend most of their weekends and their vacation each summer. I admit he works harder than I do. He works incessantly, spending at least a quarter of his work day on the phone. He never loses his temper. He is never impatient. He takes after my father.

As I was leaving my brother after spending a weekend with him and his family, he said: we must get together, you and I. We really must sit down and discuss things. I didn't have the heart to tell him that there wasn't anything left to discuss. At one time, years ago, we had our differences; now they hardly matter. I don't even remember what they were. Perhaps I had been envious of the success that he took for granted. He expected it. He was a Hargenau. He confided to me that if our father hadn't been such a complacent and self-assured aristocrat, he might have made a better conspirator. At least he was shot, instead of being left to dangle from a meat hook in front of a film crew recording the event.

Helmut rises each morning at 6:30. By 7:10 the entire family is at the table having breakfast. No one is ever late for breakfast. The children watch my brother intently. They wait for him to signal what kind of a day they can expect. He looks at his watch and purses his lips. He has two important business meetings first thing in the morning. He confides everything to Maria. She is blonde and blue-eyed like him. She faces him squarely across the table. She informs him how she intends to spend the day. Nothing is too trivial to be omitted. The children listen intently. They are seeing at first hand the life of an adult world unfold. It is a real world. Each day their father contributes something tangible to the world. Each day several buildings all over Germany rise another few feet and come closer to the completion that initially had its roots, so to speak, in his brain. By now, the entire Hargenau family knows their architectural history, backwards and forward. They know how an architect must proceed with his work by cajoling, reasoning and reassuring his uneasy and nervous clients. The children gaze into Helmut's blue eyes and are reassured. The English suit speaks for itself. At quarter to eight he's at the wheel of his car. The children admire him. His wife admires him. His secretary admires him. His colleagues admire him grudgingly. His draftsmen admire him. His clients more than admire him, they attempt to emulate his relaxed approach to anything that may come up. What they all see is a tall, blonde, blue-eyed man wearing a well-tailored English suit, preferably a plaid suit, and a solid-colored knit tie that is several shades darker than the button-down shirt. He shakes hands with a firm dry grip. He never perspires. Not even on TV with the bright floodlights focused on him. Perfectly at ease, he addresses the TV audience, the vast German audience discussing his favorite subject, architecture. The splendid history of architecture. Greece, Rome, Byzantium, a slow parade of architectural achievement culminating in the new police station in Würtenberg. Most of Würtenburg tunes in to listen to my brother, amazed at the riches he presents for their appreciation, the architectural riches in their immediate vicinity, the riches of genius. Helmut Hargenau, he's something else, they say, shaking their heads in amazement.

And his brother Ulrich?

Best not talk about him. One never knows who may be listening.

3.

On my desk is a small framed photograph of my father, taken in his study. In the background hangs a drawing by Dürer. In the lapel of his jacket is a tiny swastika. The photograph was taken in the summer of 1941, a good summer for Germany. Next to the photograph of my father is one of Paula, my former wife, Paula who calmly informed me that some of our friends had stashed a couple of cases of World War II hand grenades in the cellar. She said it quite casually, as if they were cases of champagne. I in turn admired her incredible coolness aud courage. Like my father who removed the swastika in 1942, she believed in causes, and temporary solutions.

Now that I know where she is, why don't I make an effort to get in touch with her?

Answer.

Answer immediately.

4.

A glorious summer. A glorious German summer.

Repeat.

Sometimes I feel as if the brain has become addicted to repetitions, needing to hear everything repeated once, then twice, in order to be certain that the statement is not false or misleading. I find myself repeating to myself what I intend to do next, even though I would be the first to acknowledge that repetition precludes the attainment of perfection, or, as the American philosopher Whitehead puts it: Perfection does not invite repetition.

My brain says: repeat.

The summer this year is really quite exceptional. It is almost (take note of the *almost*) perfect. Not too hot during the daytime, and not too cool at night. I may be imagining this, but the satisfied looks on the faces of the people I see daily must reflect, I am convinced, their contentedness with the weather and, in turn, with their pleasant and harmonious surroundings and, in turn, with their more or less amiable friends and relatives and in turn, with the intimate affairs that are now and then bound to occur, particularly when the person in question is not overly hampered by discontent, or some emotional disturbance, something that might impair his or her ability to judge people, and, among other things, to respond correctly to a sexual overture when it is made.

I met Paula in the Englischer Garten in Munich. I was bleeding slightly from a cut I had received when a policeman punched me in the face at the public rally in which a group of my friends and I had participated. Have you ever felt the temptation to blow up a police station, she asked me. I just laughed at the time.

You've taken leave of your senses, said Helmut in his pompous and condescending manner, when I mentioned that I intended to marry Paula. Father would have admired her guts, I said. He had a lot of guts, but little else, said Helmut, otherwise he would have headed for Switzerland. Helmut had met Paula only for several hours. What was it that he could discern in her that I failed to see?

Answer.

Answer immediately.

The characters in my books can be said to be free of emotional disturbances, free of emotional impairments. They meet here and there, in parks or public rallies and, without spending too much time analyzing their own needs, allow their brains a brief respite, as they embrace each other in bed. You're a pretty good lover, but are you able to blow up a police station, asked Paula.

What constitutes an emotional impairment?

An inner turmoil, an absence of serenity, an unresolved entanglement, self-doubt, self-hatred may be due to nothing more serious than a person's inability to appreciate the idyllic weather.

In this instance it is the perfect weather in Würtenburg and its immediate surroundings. Now, at this moment, along with the entire population of Würtenburg (approximately 125,968 according to the latest census), I am experiencing the fine weather. I am completely relaxed and have nothing but the weather on my mind. I do not expect ever to hear from Marie-Jean Filebra, or from my former wife, Paula Hargenau, the one, I assume, still in Paris, the other now free to go wherever she chooses.

Repeat.

The brain keeps persisting that it can survive on images alone.

Helmut, on meeting me at the airport on my return from Paris, promptly informed me that Paula was living in Geneva. He seemed put out when I burst into laughter, uncontrollable laughter. Geneva? What is she doing in Geneva? He smiled awkwardly, then shrugged his shoulders. I guess she's fond of the place.

Paula. In Geneva. Impossible.

Apparently I was mistaken. I still don't know what she's up to in Geneva, and have no intention of inquiring. I wouldn't want to embarrass her with my questions, my interest, or my presence. I am happy that she is free.

I am not hiding in Würtenburg. I am listed in the phone directory. If my former friends wish to locate me they can easily do so. Each morning I go out for the paper. In the afternoon, around four, I take a walk. Each morning, each afternoon, more or less at the same time. In that respect I present no problem for anyone who would wish to kill me. The man in the Porsche could give it another try.

Frequently, two or three times a week, I receive a letter from some anonymous person who appears to hate me with a greater passion and intensity than I have ever been able to hate anyone. Are all these letters written by lunatics? I could, I suppose, hand them over to the police; instead I toss them into a drawer of my desk.

Maria, my sister-in-law, calls me every three or four days. She asks me how my work is progressing. She tries to elicit from me what I am writing. Is it autobiographical? she asks.

Existence does not take place within the skin, I reply, quoting Klude.

Nonsense.

Only Maria is able to put me on the defensive by saying: nonsense.

It's true.

Repeat.

I am telling you the absolute truth.

5.

A young earnest-faced woman moved into the empty apartment on the floor above mine. I helped her carry a few heavy cartons of books to the elevator, since the doorman was on his lunch hour. Würtenburg is gradually emerging from its medieval past to which we are still so attached . . . the medieval past that is etched on so many of the faces of the people who live here. My brother and I are no exception. I gravely stare at my face in the mirror and see Germany's entire past.

A stranger, a young earnest-faced American, for instance, cannot help when visiting Würtenburg but see the world of Albrecht Dürer come to life. Dürer becomes his or her point of reference, or perhaps even guide, as he or she takes a leisurely walk down the main street past the cathedral designed by Müse-Haft Toll, with its frescoes by Alfredo Igloria Grobart and stained glass windows by Nacklewitz Jahn and then past the World War I monument on the left, a bronze riderless horse rearing up on its hind legs, the four metal tables on its granite base bearing the names of those killed in action. There are at least six Hargenau's, all officers, who died in World War I, and another half a dozen (my father's name not included) whose names are carved into the large slab of marble now standing, after a heated public debate, behind the Schottendorferkirche, a somewhat out-of-the-way part of the city, considered at the time by many as a more suitable spot for a World War II monument. After turning right at the public library it is only a five-minute brisk walk to the University where old Klude is still teaching philosophy. Or, should one say, is once again teaching philosophy after an enforced period of idleness, the result of too many reckless speeches in the thirties and early forties, speeches that dealt with the citizen's responsibilities to the New Order. Poor Klude. Once he stopped dealing with abstract theories and was able to make himself understood to one overcrowded gymnasium of students after another, the ideas he expressed were reinforced by statements such as: We have completely broken with a landless and powerless thinking. But by now Klude's former platitudinous speeches have been forgotten. His students swear by him, and his classes are always crowded. Sometimes as many as four hundred sit in a large drafty auditorium, listening attentively to Klude as he lectures on the meaning of a thing. What is a thing? he asks rhetorically. Klude is not referring to a particular thing. He is not, for instance, referring to a modern apartment building, or a metal frame window, or an English lesson, but the *thingliness* that is intrinsic to all things, regardless of their merit, their usefulness, and the degree of their perfection. I mention the latter only because the mind is so created that it habitually sets up standards of perfection for everything: for marriage and for driving, for love affairs and for garden furniture, for table tennis and for gas ovens, for faces and even for something as petty as the weather, and then, having established these standards, it sets up standards of comparison which serve, if nothing else, to confirm in our minds that a great many things are less than perfect.

6.
My brain relies on words to describe my promising future. A future filled with expectation. A future built on the words I manage to put on paper. The words in themselves would not necessarily bewilder the doorman who daily greets me with: Looks like another fine day.

Repeat.

For all I know the doorman may have been one of the squad who shot my father. It is highly unlikely. And if he had, he was under orders. If you're part of an execution squad, you can't pick the people you want to shoot. Or can you?

It is a glorious day, and I wouldn't want to be anywhere else in the world.

I am convinced that my feelings are echoed by the people now casually walking down the Hauptstrasse, stopping now and then to gaze briefly into a shopwindow, looking at the things that are on display, sometimes peering into the interior of the store to see if they can spot a familiar face, no doubt a German face, a Dürer-like face of an acquaintance or friend.

Daphne, the earnest-faced American woman, was walking back to the apartment building, her arms wrapped around a large shopping bag filled with groceries, when I ran into her. I offered to help, but she wouldn't hear of it. I then suggested that we have dinner together. She allowed a few seconds to spell out the silence of rejection. She was too busy, she explained. She was trying to put her place into some kind of order.

Well, yes, I nodded sympathetically. How about joining me for a walk this afternoon. I was afraid that I was about to burden her with the responsibility of having to reject my second invitation. But she accepted.

Why on earth should I wish to spend an hour or two together with this earnest-faced young woman. Is it because I desperately need someone to talk to, someone who does not instantaneously recognize the name Hargenau. Ulrich von Hargenau, the elder, executed after an ill-fated attempt to kill the Führer, and Ulrich Hargenau, the younger, witness for the defense in the recent conspiracy trial of the Einzig Gruppe. Why doesn't someone ask me what I think of the Einzig Gruppe.

Assholes. A bunch of assholes with hand grenades that had been stored in the cellar of the house where Paula and I lived, until we went our separate ways.

What do you really want? Paula had once asked me.
Redistribution of wealth, I said instantaneously.
No. What do you really want?
Success, I said cautiously.
No. Not success. What do you really really want?
Why not success?
You're terribly devious, did you know that.
No.
If only I knew what you really wanted I would be able to trust you, she said.
You can trust me.
No.

7.

By now I like to think that most people in Würtenburg have put me out of their minds. My somewhat inept performance in court, reported widely in all the papers and on TV and radio, has fortunately been superseded by more recent events. An earthquake in Chile, a famine in Ethiopia, a coup d'etat in Tanzania, widespread use of torture in Latin America and Greece. Once in a while, one of my wife's former friends, a fellow activist, now serving ten to twenty, or was it fifteen to thirty years for a long list of alleged crimes, including: arson, assault, kidnapping, armed robbery, and second degree murder, will go on a hunger strike and receive mention in the papers. But no one is really interested in my whereabouts. No one could possibly care what I plan to write next. I expect that a number of people familiar with my work expect to find in my next book some kind of explanation of my obviously, to them, aberrant behavior . . . an explanation that strikes me as being totally redundant. I have been led to believe that a great many of my acquaintances were convinced that I lied to the Police and in court in order to extricate Paula and myself from the mess we were in. I didn't. I merely told the truth to save our skin. It wasn't necessary to fabricate anything. I didn't have to worry about being caught telling a lie. I didn't have to worry about contradicting myself. Still, it comes to the same thing. What I had to say enabled the Ministry of Justice to convict eight people who had frequently eaten at my table and, for reasons I still cannot explain, entrusted me with their idiotic plans. After all, Ulrich von Hargenau, the elder, had died without divulging to the *Sicherheitsdienst* the names of his fellow conspirators. So why shouldn't Ulrich Hargenau, the younger, be expected to do the same. The police knew that Paula had been the chief strategist, the planner, the brain behind so many of the Einzig "wargames," just as she must have known that I, or rather our hallowed name Hargenau would pull her out of the mess.

And it did. A few hasty telephone calls, a few conferences, a few tears, a few negotiations, a few promises, and the Ministry of Justice was prepared to overlook, this once, our indiscretions. The day after the trial, the newspapers quoted Paula as saying pointedly that she and her group had been betrayed. No, she said. She would prefer not to name names. Well, she had said rather smugly when we met briefly in our house, this affair can't have hurt the sale of your books, or has it?

8.

What are you working on, my publisher asked me when we met shortly after my return to Germany. Something quite intriguing, I said. A love affair in Paris. He looked relieved. So much has already been written about your past political involvement, he commented tactfully. Still, I was under the impression that you might wish to add your . . . recollections.

Had he been about to say, your version?

I still receive a good deal of hate mail, I said after one of our customary prolonged silences.

We must have you over for dinner soon, he said politely. He had known my father quite well. It was an impossible situation, he had once told me, referring to my father. As a man of honor, he had no other option.

9.

I told the young American woman who had moved in upstairs that on my mother's side I was a distant relative of Albrecht Dürer. I said this without the slightest desire to impress her. I would not have brought up the subject had I not run into her in the university bookstore holding a book on Dürer. She greeted my statement with an appropriate skepticism, staring at me as if trying to gage my intentions. My mother's maiden name is Dürer, I explained. Her family moved to Würtenburg in 1803. At one time my family owned six drawings by Dürer, but now we are down to one. For lack of anything else to say I kept on talking about Dürer. I described one of the drawings that had been in my family's possession. It was one of his last drawings, the *Double Goblet*. As the title indicated it offered the viewer a view of the two ornate goblets, one balanced on top of the other, as well as revealing upon closer scrutiny an entirely different picture, one that disclosed an explicit sexual content.

You like that, don't you, she said, challenging me.

What? The sexual content?

No, the duality in the picture. Seeing something that others may have over-looked.

She looked startled when I said: Why are you attacking me?

Later that afternoon in a bar frequented mainly by students, she told me that she had been in Würtenburg a little over six months. Tired of sharing a place with another American student, she had looked around for an apartment and found one in the building where I was staying. To support herself she gave English lessons to young German business executives, most of whom expected to be sent by their firms to America for a year or two.

Teaching beginners must be a bore, I said sympathetically.

Oh no, she said. I enjoy it. They're all extremely eager to learn English, in addition to being so very . . . Here she paused briefly, evidently searching for the right word.

Understanding.

Understanding?

I was puzzled by the word. What did she mean. Why should her German students show understanding for anything other than the information she was imparting to them. Understanding. I think that word, more than anything else she may have said, served to arouse my curiosity. It is quite conceivable that had I not been so involved in writing about Paula Hargenau, my former wife, and Marie-Jean Filebra, my former mistress (to use an old-fashioned description), I might have paid closer attention to Daphne. From her appearance and her surname I assumed that she was of German extraction. I admit that I found her serious face, her measured and frequently humorless responses to what I said, not unattractive. I don't know why. Perhaps because she gave me the appearance of someone in need of protection, although I felt convinced that she would not permit herself to accept it, if it were offered. I had not spoken of my work to her and had no reason to believe that she knew what I did or, for that matter, who I was. She did not ask questions, and I did not offer any information. I was not in the least attracted to her sexually, and for some inexplicable reason wanted to communicate this fact to her, as if feeling the need to reassure her of my intentions, as if to indicate that she could allow herself to relax in my presence. No, that is patently untrue. At this time the burden of another intimate relationship would have been more than I could handle. If anything, I was signalling to her my own unavailability.

It was a glorious summer day. Daphne and I were seated at a sidewalk table drinking beer and observing the people passing. She mentioned that she was studying philosophy under Klude. An American studying Klude and seeing us, as only strangers can see us, with a mixture of envy and a certain disdain.

We Germans like to draw attention to our most conspicuous flaws, since the uncertainty and doubt we arouse in strangers saves us from being inundated by a deluge of uncritical admiration.

Did I say this? If I did I retract it immediately.

What does Daphne think of me?

10.

Daphne moved into the building less than three months ago. She had found her apartment the way I had, by looking at the real estate pages of the *Würtenburger Neue Zeit*. She spoke a fluent German and had no difficulty in following the lectures at the Würtenburger University, a university, incidentally, with a reputation second to none in ancient and medieval history, the history of religion, and philosophy. She had studied German in America. Why not French or Italian. I wanted to study under Klude, she admitted shyly. Was he the principal reason why she had chosen German, I asked with what must have been a look of astonishment. She laughed. No, she had been exaggerating slightly. By the time she came across the work of Klude, she had already been taking German at college. Her father, she added, had a great many friends in Germany. He had been there during the occupation. It was he who encouraged her to study German. When I inquired if he was connected to a university, she responded with a curt no.

When Daphne moved into her apartment she found an attractive armchair, a large bed, and a chest of drawers the former tenant had left behind. There may have been a few other things, but the super and the doorman always had first picking. I was surprised that they had not taken the armchair or the chest of drawers. They wouldn't have been difficult to move. I too have discarded a great many things, yet I continue to cling to so much that has clearly outlived its usefulness.

Where did you live before you moved into this building, asked Daphne.

I was deliberately vague. Oh, here and there. I chose this place because I wanted some privacy. I didn't want to run into people I knew everytime I stepped out of the front entrance. When Daphne discovered that I had been a former student of Klude she danced a little jig, which I took to be an American way of expressing enthusiasm. I wasn't a particularly successful student, I hastened to tell her. I don't believe that Professor Klude ever paid the slightest attention to me. All the same, I have sent him a copy of every book I have published. Once or twice, despite his heavy schedule, he was kind enough to send me a note thanking me for the book. He greatly looked forward to reading the work of one of his former pupils, he wrote, something I had every reason to doubt.

I didn't mention this to Daphne. I didn't want her to think of me as discontent with the notes I received from Klude. Naturally, as soon as she had discovered that I was a writer she felt impelled or obliged to buy several of my books, which is more than I can say for most of my friends and acquaintances, who expect free signed copies which they do not read. Having completed or partially completed one of my books, Daphne felt compelled to say something about the work, and, being straightforward and candid, as well as a student of philosophy, she couldn't, I recognized, simply say, I enjoyed it, and let it go at that. She had to say something that would express on her part a recognition of what I had attempted to achieve, or what she thought I had tried to achieve. Obviously she tried to like the books because she liked me, or was prepared to like me or, possibly, because she wanted to like me, but no matter how hard she tried, the work was somehow inaccessible to her. That is hardly surprising in someone who admitted that she found the exploration or probing of a relationship between two or more people as something somewhat distasteful. She felt that the writer was trespassing, and I have to admit that writing is a form of trespassing. Instead of reading on and on about the tenuousness or uncertainty of someone's feelings, she preferred to question the meaning of a thing, or the meaning of a thought, preferably raising the question in German, a foreign or at any rate adopted language that enabled her to reduce these crucial questions to pure signs, since in German the word *thing* and the word *thought* did not immediately evoke in her brain the multitudinous response it did in English, where the words, those everyday words, conjured up an entire panorama of familiar associations that blunted the preciseness needed in order to bring her philosophical investigation to a satisfactory conclusion. Could this be the reason why she came to Germany? To think in German, to question herself in a foreign language?

Has she ever slept with a German?
She must have, I tell myself.
Why this curious constraint on my part.
Answer.
Answer immediately.

11.

The police in our precinct have moved into their new quarters with a great deal of fanfare. My brother's photograph is in all the papers. All along he had been convinced that his design for the police station would be selected out of the nineteen or twenty that had been submitted. There had been a good many insinuations that he had won only because he also happened to be the son-in-law of the police chief of Würtenburg. Perhaps it did influence the jury's unanimous decision. I still recall urging him to abstain from participating for that very reason. If you win, they'll say it is because of your father-in-law. He called me naive. Christmas, he told me gleefully, he had sent the policemen at the old station a case of Piper Heitzig. Prost. Of course the newspapers did not neglect to state that the architect Hargenau was the brother of Ulrich Hargenau, the author who had admitted to being a political activist in the Einzig Gruppe. I suppose I could sue, but it would simply focus more attention on me. Attention is the last thing I need. Let Helmut get the attention.

12.

My brother takes me on a tour of the new police station. Why had I agreed to come? Immaculate corridors, large well lit offices with plate glass windows, white formica-topped desks, everything gleaming and new, and everyone, in and out of uniform, smiling broadly at us. It's like a circus. Everyone beaming their approval of my brother who is, let me not forget to add, the son-in-law of the chief of police. Helmut introduces me with a special flourish to everyone he meets. He keeps saying: This is my radical brother. Ulrich Hargenau, the writer. You may have read some of his work. To my surprise quite a number of policemen say yes. They all smile at each other as if sharing a huge joke. Any questions? my brother asks me in front of a group of senior police officers, all with glasses of champagne in their hands, all a bit red in their faces and a slight bit unsteady on their feet.

Yes. Is the young American woman on the floor above mine a radical?

I can easily find out for you, says the chief of police, smiling, feeling proud of the Hargenaus. Old, old family with a castle somewhere in East Germany. Pity that they decided to drop the von.

I return the chief of police's smile. A brief sense of camaraderie. My period of irresponsibility is past. I have become respectable again. When it came to the crunch, I did the right thing. I swallowed my medicine, and now I am back again, free to do what I want, to go where I wish.

My brother is working on another book, says my brother.

This time, be sure to make it a bestseller, says the chief of police, and they all roar with laughter.

13.

You spend an awful lot of your time sleeping, don't you? said Daphne, wrinkling her nose critically. How do you manage to get any work done?

I work late at night.

Did she look skeptical.

At the university library I looked up her father in the *International Who's Who*. Mortimer S. Hasendruck. b. Debunk, Illinois 1920. M.I.T. 1941. Dept. of Defense. 1944. Founder and President of Dust Industries. m. June G. Steinholf, 1946. s. Mark D. Hasendruck 1949. d. Daphne S. Hasendruck 1952. Address: Edea, Illinois.

What? said my brother, you mean you've never heard of Dust Industries. He seemed incredulous at my ignorance. What kind of an activist were you? Dust is one of America's largest armament manufacturers. They produced most of the advanced equipment used in Vietnam.

I guess, I said, that's why Daphne doesn't wish to speak about her father.

We must have her over for dinner, said Maria.

Sure.

14.

Today I received a note in the mail. It was brief and to the point. We know where you are. Did you expect to hide from us? Because of you Ilse, Adalbert, Jürgen, Heinz, Helga, Assif, Lerner, and Mausi are rotting in jail. Do you really expect to get off scot-free? We intend to get you. If not tomorrow then the day after, if not the day after then next week, or next month. Soon. We promise.

I didn't destroy the unsigned note. I can't bear to throw anything away. I can't even bear to discard old magazines. It is not the first note I have received. Did they really believe that I moved here to escape from them.

Sometimes I really can't understand the Germans, said Daphne. I speak the language. I read Klude, yet . . . despairingly she shook her head . . . I can't make you out. Is this the new Germany? she asked mockingly.

My brother Helmut studied architecture at M.I.T. He likes to wear button-down shirts. One day he hopes to design a sixty-storey office with an underground garage in Detroit. I guess he's the new Germany.

But what about you?

16.
In addition to killing two postal workers, the explosion of at least twelve to sixteen sticks of dynamite at the new post office designed by Helmut also totally destroyed four recently acquired sorting machines, as well as two dozen large sacks of unsorted first-class mail. Had the explosion taken place an hour earlier, a great many more people might have been killed. As it was, the damage to the building was considerable. Half an hour after the explosion, a woman called a local radio station and announced that the newly formed Seventeenth of August Liberation Group took full responsibility for the action, which had been designed to draw attention to the plight of the eight imprisoned members of the Einzig Gruppe, all sentenced to long jail terms on the seventeenth of August, one year ago. So a year had passed. I had just reached page 134 of a manuscript that was entirely based on events that had occurred since then. Until the explosion had destroyed the new post office I felt pretty confident that nothing would interrupt my work. I would go on writing the book until I was ready to submit it to my publisher, and then I would take a brief vacation, after which I would start thinking of the next book. Now I was no longer certain.

With one explosion the name Hargenau was in all the papers again. Great outrage at the senseless killings and at the mutilation of thousands of letters. Those letters would never reach their destination. Naturally there was also some speculation as to the identity of the members of the recently formed Seventeenth of August Group. My wife's name kept cropping up. She could be behind it all. But why pick on the post office? Why mutilate and destroy innocent first-class letters that may have been carrying checks to war widows and other people in need.

On the evening of the thirteenth I had dinner with Daphne in my apartment. We listened to the news. We ate sauerbraten. That's the way it reads in my diary. Dinner with Daphne. I don't keep a journal. I just jot things down in an office diary. Dinner with Daphne seemed adequate for my purposes. Explosion at post office, two dead, Seventeenth of August Group accepts responsibility. Did not call off dinner with Daphne. Watch news. Make love.

Do you still love her, Daphne asked
Who?
Paula, your wife.
What made you ask me that question?

16.
The first thing Daphne said to me the next morning when I opened my eyes was, I know nothing about you . . . absolutely nothing.

You'll find everything in my books.

Is that true?

No.

Daphne dressed in front of me and then walked to the door of my apartment.

I retain in my mind a picture of her standing at the door. Before leaving, she turned to look at me, at my possessions, at my apartment to which she now had a key. As far as I was concerned, everything was at a complete standstill, as the brain, feeding on the present, made room for Daphne, naked, legs parted, absorbing the image with the same ease as it had absorbed and incorporated the images I had formed of the explosion at the post office. The image of the explosion and my making love to Daphne were linked or connected by the date on which they had taken place, and possibly by a conviction I have always had that nothing is what it first appears to be.

17.

The following Sunday Daphne and I visited my brother Helmut and his family at their house in the country. Helmut was in a great mood. He dismissed the bombing, saying that he had never been quite satisfied with the design of the post office and secretly had always wanted another go at it. Of course, it was too bad about the two men who died, and all that mail. God knows how much of it was intended for him. Before dinner we all dutifully posed for Helmut who took our photographs on the wide terrace overlooking the dense forest in the distance where Klude spends his summer months in a small house in a clearing deep inside the wood. Helmut offered to drive Daphne to see the house the next day. Knowing that she was American he spoke at great length of his stay in America and how much he enjoyed living in Boston. He kept on about his visits to Montana and Wyoming, Arkansas and Southern California, one amusing anecdote after another, then, when she least expected it, he began to question her about herself and her family. Helmut was smiling at her as she described the town in Illinois where she had grown up, her friends, her decision to come to Germany after a year in Geneva.

Geneva? I said.

Yes, she had a number of friends in Geneva. She also gave English lessons in Geneva.

My brother interrupted her. To get back to your father.

I left the room.

Could she conceivably have met Paula?

One has so little control over the irresponsible meandering of one's brain, over the improbable connections that are activated as thoughts by impulses from the brain, although, occasionally, these remote farfetched hypothetical links have a way of coming true. Almost anything the brain can conjure up is plausible.

Daphne living in Geneva.

Daphne moving into the building where I live.

Why that particular building.

Because it had been advertised in the local paper.

But had it?

18.

On Tuesday afternoon, when I returned from the library, the doorman informed me that Daphne had moved out of her apartment during my absence. She had not given any notice and therefore was forfeiting one-months rent. Apparently a young man in a stationwagon had helped her move some of her belongings. Speechless, I looked at the doorman, then walked to the elevator. No one answered when I rang her doorbell. On Sunday she had promised me a key to her apartment. She intended to have a duplicate made that morning. Her letter to me was slipped under my door. It was addressed to Ulrich von Hargenau. It was in her handwriting, a handwriting that was still unfamiliar.

Why the von?

What was she trying to say?

Dear Ulrich,

I am returning to America, in part because I do not wish to become emotionally entangled with you at this time. I do not feel happy in a role that is so devoid of any certitude. I do not like to feel that I am depending on another person. Please feel free to take anything I have left behind in the apartment. I may continue my studies in America. I wish you had not taken me to visit your brother and his family.

Daphne.

19.

I am the first to admit that I don't know Daphne. I think I know what she thinks of Klude and of Germany in a vague sort of way. To some extent I know her taste in furniture, in music, in books, in clothes. If I know little else, it is because I failed to show much interest in her initially and did not engage her in conversations like my brother did in order to elicit from her why, precisely why she was in Germany, and what she felt about her father. That is not to say that I had ruled out ever asking her any of these questions, but until I received her letter, I had felt quite content to leave things as they were. I was content with our new relationship, content to sit back and muse over Daphne, the young earnest-faced American in Germany who never once asked me a single question regarding my dead father or my own somewhat dubious role at the Einzig trial.

20.

The doorman took a certain pleasure in telling me that Daphne had left. He had watched my face to see how I would receive the news. I turned and stiffly walked to the elevator, pressed the up button, entered the elevator, and pressed the button to the seventh floor under the stern unforgiving gaze of the doorman.

21.

I took a taxi to the airport which is on the outskirts of Würtenburg, and checked with a number of airlines if anyone by the name of Daphne Hasendruck had booked a flight to America. She had not, at least not under her own name. Wishing to be thorough, I inquired at Lufthansa if a Miss Daphne Hasendruck had booked a flight to Geneva that morning. Trying to sound as diffident as possible, I mentioned that my niece, Daphne Hasendruck, was to call me on her arrival in Geneva. Since I hadn't heard from her, I was inquiring if, in fact, she had left for Geneva. I don't think that the clerk believed my story, but she did inform me – after checking a list – that a Miss Hasendruck had taken the afternoon flight to Geneva. It was not a direct flight, but her destination was Geneva.

Did she fly there to join Paula? Or did she fly there for another reason?

My brother Helmut did his best to talk me out of flying to Geneva. Whatever it is, you don't want it. Whatever it is, you don't need it. You're free. You're in the clear. She may not know Paula, he argued. She may just be drawn to the Alps, or the abundance of chocolate.

I left for Geneva the next day. As I expected, my wife was not listed in the telephone book. I had been to Geneva several times before and without giving it much thought checked into a hotel where Paula and I had once stayed for a couple of nights. It was conveniently located near the Quai du Mont-Blanc. The first thing next day I purchased a ream of paper and a map of the city. As I rather aimlessly walked around the downtown area in the vicinity of the Jardin Anglais I kept asking myself if I was in Geneva in order to locate Daphne, or my former wife, or if I was simply collecting fresh material for my next book. On the third day I found a small decent restaurant. I also found a store where the *Würtenburger Neue Zeit* was sold. I was still in Geneva when another bomb went off in Würtenburg. This one destroyed an entire floor in the fingerprint section in the new police station. When I spoke to Helmut on the phone he, in a weary voice, suggested that I remain in Geneva for the time being, adding his cautionary: Please don't fuck up . . . do you understand what I am saying. I know it's your speciality, but try not to this time.

In my hotel room I was prepared for every eventuality. I had a ream of typewriting paper and a portable Hermes, but I couldn't write a line. My brain, my body, had stopped functioning. Everything around me seemed at a standstill. On one of my walks I had picked up Victor Segalen's *Rene Leys*. I began reading the book one afternoon in a cafe on the rue de Rhone. Somehow, it seemed to me that the narrator in the book, a Frenchman living in Peking in 1911, was contemplating an action that in many respects paralleled or, at any rate, appeared analogous to my own endeavor in Geneva. At a time when the Forbidden City was still closed to all foreigners, the Frenchman's one over-whelming desire – in order to understand what he kept referring to as the "Within" of the Chinese Empire – was to enter (penetrate would be the right term) the Imperial Palace and see what had been withheld from him all along. Clearly, in my case, the city of Geneva did not withhold anything as tangible as the Imperial Chinese Palace, some-thing one could assess from the outside. No. By drawing this somewhat specious comparison to the Frenchman in *Rene Leys* I was simply indulging in a favorite habit of mine – namely, attempting to view and place my personal affairs in a literary context, as if this would endow them with a clearer and richer meaning.

But why had Daphne left for Geneva?

22.
The day Klude died it was in all the French, Swiss, and German newspapers. Lengthy obituaries. Germany's greatest thinker since Hegel. Photographs of Klude

in his log cabin that was only a twenty-minute drive from the country house my brother had designed for himself. An entire page listing Klude's philosophical achievements. To my surprise the editors had not omitted mention of Klude's somewhat ridiculous role during the coming to power of the Nazis. Later that day, in a quarter of Geneva I didn't know, I spotted a small bookstore. I was pleased to discover that they had several of Klude's books in French and German. After some hesitation I chose *Jetzt Zum Letzten Mahl* and *Ohne Grund*, an early work written in 1936. Upon leaving the store I caught a brief but unmistakable glimpse of Daphne in the passenger seat of a passing bright yellow Porsche. I called out, shouted her name at the top of my lungs, frantically waving my hand as I ran after the car, but probably she did not see me. Hours later, when I returned to my hotel, the desk clerk handed me a note that had been left for me. It was from Paula. It simply stated: You have taken enough. Leave us alone.

Leave us alone.
Us? Us? Who is us?

23.
The interviewer arrives punctually at three. He has a foreign-sounding name which I do not catch. He is in his twenties, wearing a very worn-looking tweed jacket. I have no reason to feel distrustful of him. I've been through too many interviews. I smile at him, aware all the time of his thick spectacles, his disconcerting stare, his tape recorder dangling from one shoulder, all weapons that I wish to disarm with my cordiality and candor. From the very start the difficulty lies in trying to establish who exactly is interviewing whom. The tape recorder, set on the table, records a trite meaningless exchange. He looks around the room, recording in his brain my few visible possessions: the Hermes typewriter, a ream of paper, a small pile of books, underwear drying on a back of a chair, shoes, a guidebook. I offer him a glass of wine, but he declines. This makes it difficult for me. I could order tea or coffee, but he says that he has just eaten. He is not rude, at least not intentionally rude. I smoke, sip wine, and stare out of the window. I also inquire how he had managed to find out that I was staying in Geneva.

It's such a small city. Someone from the magazine recognized you on the street and passed on the information to me. I called a few hotels. I tried some of the more luxurious ones first and then worked my way down . . .

There are a lot of hotels in Geneva, I remark.

I was lucky.

It's very gratifying that you would wish to interview me. As I mentioned to you on the phone, I hope to have a book out at the end of the year.

Have you completed it.

No, I am just putting the finishing touches to it.

You're not using Geneva in the novel, by any chance.

I find it difficult if not impossible to write about a city I happen to be in, although Segalen, who I have just been reading, managed to write an extraordinary novel set in Peking, while staying in that city.

Segalen? Swiss?

No, French.

He jots the name down on a small yellow pad, then, avoiding my eyes, remarks that he had been informed that Paula was currently living in Geneva. Is that the reason why you are here? And have you been in touch with her?

I take a puff on my cigarette. I feel strangely lightheaded. I feel comfortably relaxed in my chair. From where I am sitting, I can see the street below. Looking down at it, I am reminded of Tanner, since it is the kind of street that frequently can be seen in his films. Tanner provided me with my first real glimpse of Switzerland.

No, I reply. My wife and I are separated. I don't even know where she is staying. I'm not even certain that she is in Geneva at this time. We have not seen each other since the Einzig trial.

Does she blame you for the excessively long sentences handed out to the Gruppe?

You'll have to ask her.

As the only writer in the Gruppe, did you ever feel tempted to keep a diary or journal during the period of time you were . . . associated with them?

Quite candidly, I see no point in discussing the Gruppe. They belong to the past. Moreover, my and Paula's decision to separate had nothing to do with the Einzig Gruppe, or the outcome of the trial. Most political trials, I have come to realize, are badly in need of some sort of scapegoat to deflect questions that try to probe a little deeper . . . This trial was no exception. What I had to say at the trial was not said under any duress, contrary to what most people seem to believe. I was never an actual participant or member of the Gruppe. True, some of them had been friends, and I helped them because they were friends. Admittedly, I got a slight kick out of helping the so-called conspirators, not because I believed for one moment in their methods or in what they were hoping to achieve, but simply because I tend to dislike bureaucrats in positions of power. I didn't mind giving them a kick in the ass.

Would you consider what happened recently in Würtenburg as a kick in the ass?

No, that was very unfortunate.

Is it a coincidence that the two public buildings recently blown up by the Seventeenth of August Group, or whatever they call themselves, had been designed by a Hargenau?

I doubt that the action was aimed at him or me. It certainly wasn't aimed at my late father, who is something of a hero in Germany.

To return to you. Do you intend to finish your book in Geneva? And why Geneva?

I hope to complete the book here. As to why Geneva. I like being a stranger in a city . . . I like being anonymous. Incidentally, Paula and I stayed in this hotel several years ago. I remember feeling pleased when I discovered that Musil had stayed here briefly upon his arrival in 1940.

What is the title of your forthcoming book.

The English Lesson.

It's not a German lesson, I see.

No. We've had enough German lessons to last us for several generations.

A number of critics have referred to the element of ambiguity that permeates much of your work. One reads your books, always feeling as if some vital piece of information is being withheld.

I'm not sure how I can respond to that. If someone withholds information, surely it is not merely for the sake of withholding information. All the same, characters, like people, frequently misread each others' intentions. In *The English Lesson* a man follows a woman who left him to Geneva.

So Geneva does play a part in your novel.

Only a minor one. Almost a negligible one.

Does he locate her?

Who?

The character in your novel.

That remains to be seen.

Why Geneva?

I picked Geneva because of the image Switzerland evokes in people. A kind of controlled neutrality, a somewhat antiseptic tranquility that I find soothing. I may also have been influenced by the films of Tanner.

But Tanner is fundamentally a politically oriented filmmaker. His films are never devoid of a political content. . . .

Well, yes. In *The English Lesson* the unexplained departure of the young American woman who supports herself in Germany by giving English lessons, hence the title, from a man ten or twelve years her senior, a man who might be labeled a political reactionary, could be viewed in a political context.

What kind of a political statement are you making in your book?

I'm sorry, my mind was on something else. What did you say?

What kind of a political statement are you making in your book?

A novel is not a process of rebellion. Just as it validates and makes acceptable forms of human conduct, it also validates and makes acceptable societal institutions.

Does that trouble you?

Not at all.

When are you planning to return to Germany?

As soon as I complete the novel. I am, you might say, searching for an appropriate conclusion. In yesterday's paper there was mention of a young woman who jumped from the fourteenth story of an office building only a few blocks from this hotel. I mention this only because in life, jumping out of a window is an end, whereas in a novel, where suicide occurs all too frequently, it becomes an explanation.

I'm terribly sorry. The interviewer looks at me apologetically. I forgot to press the record button. This has never happened to me before. Could we possibly go over the interview again. Just briefly.

Yes, why not, I reply.

An hour later, after the interviewer has left, the phone rings, and when I pick up the receiver, ready to welcome any interruption, any small diversion, anything that will keep me from sitting down and trying to write, my brother Helmut on the other end of the line, at that hour, I presume, still in his office, calmly says: I thought you might want to know that your Daphne Hasendruck is not Daphne Hasendruck.

Of course she is.

The real Daphne Hasendruck is married to the head of Dust Enterprises in Spain. They live in Madrid. They have two children. Her name, should you wish to contact her, is Daphne Wheelock.

You spoke to her?

I was just being thorough.

Then who is our Daphne?

I haven't the foggiest idea.

Did you mention this to your father-in-law?

Do you take me for an ass?

You spotted her that weekend. You saw through her. Was that the reason for all those questions?

No. I'm just thorough. I don't want you to fuck up. It takes too much of my time.

By the way, I'm sorry about the police station.

We'll patch it up. But I've been told they lost all their files, including the one on you.

This is Switzerland, I say to myself, as I set out for a stroll later that afternoon. This is the place where Musil died, where Rilke died, where Gottfried Keller lived and died, where Jean-Jacques Rousseau was born, and where Nabokov lived, as much a prisoner of the past as I am a prisoner of the present.

Geneva 1977

If on a Winter's Night a Traveler

BY ITALO CALVINO

In *a network of lines that enlace*

The first sensation this book should convey is what I feel when I hear the telephone ring; I say "should" because I doubt that written words can give even a partial idea of it: it is not enough to declare that my reaction is one of refusal, of flight from this aggressive and threatening summons, as it is also a feeling of urgency, intolerability, coercion that impels me to obey the injunction of that sound, rushing to answer even with the certainty that nothing will come of it save suffering and discomfort. Nor do I believe that instead of an attempted description of this state of the spirit, a metaphor would serve better, for example the piercing sting of an arrow that penetrates a hip's naked flesh, but this is not because one cannot employ an imaginary sensation to portray a known sensation, for though these days nobody knows the feeling of being struck by an arrow, we all believe we can easily imagine it – the sense of being helpless, without protection in the presence of something that reaches us from alien and unknown spaces: and this also applies very well to the ring of the telephone – but rather because the arrow's peremptory inexorability, without modulations, excludes all the intentions, implications, hesitations possible in the voice of someone I do not see, though even before he says anything I can already predict if not what he will say at least what my reaction to what he is about to say will be. Ideally the book would begin by giving the sense of a space occupied by my presence, because all around me there are only inert objects, including the telephone, a space that apparently cannot contain anything but me, isolated in my interior time, and then there is the interruption of the continuity of time, the space is no longer what it was before because it is occupied by the ring, and my presence is no longer what it was before because it is conditioned by the will of this object that is calling. The book would have to begin by conveying all this not only immediately but as a diffusion through space and time of these rings that lacerate the continuity of space and time and will.

Perhaps the mistake lies in establishing that at the beginning I and a telephone are in a finite space such as my house would be, whereas what I must communicate is my situation with regard to numerous telephones that ring, telephones that perhaps are not calling me, have no relation to me, but the mere fact that I can be called to a telephone suffices to make it possible or at least conceivable that I may be called by all telephones. For example when the telephone rings in a house near mine, for a moment I wonder if it is ringing in my house, a suspicion that immediately proves unfounded but which still leaves a wake since it is possible that the call might really be for me and through a wrong number or crossed wires it has gone to my neighbor, and this is all the more possible since in that house there is nobody to answer and the telephone keeps ringing, and then in the irrational logic that ringing never fails to provoke in me, I think: perhaps it is indeed for me, perhaps my neighbor is at home but does not answer because he knows, perhaps also the person calling knows he is calling a wrong number but does so deliberately to keep me in this state, knowing I cannot answer but know that I should answer.

Or else the anxiety when I have just left the house and I hear a telephone ringing which could be in my house or in another apartment and I rush back, I arrive breathless having run up the stairs and the telephone falls silent and I will never know if the call was for me.

Or else also when I am out in the streets, and I hear telephones ring in strange houses; even when I am in strange cities, in cities where my presence is unknown to anyone, even then, hearing a ring, my first thought every time for a fraction of a second is that the telephone is calling me, and in the following fraction of a second there is the relief of knowing myself excluded for the moment from every call, unattainable, safe, but this relief also lasts a mere fraction of a second, because immediately afterwards I think that it is not only that strange telephone that is ringing; many kilometers away, hundreds, thousands of kilometers, there is also the telephone in my house, which certainly at that same moment is ringing repeatedly in the deserted rooms, and again I am torn between the necessity and the impossibility of answering.

Every morning before my classes begin I do an hour of jogging, that is I put on my Olympic sweatsuit and I go out to run because I feel the need to move, because the doctors have ordered it to combat the excess weight that oppresses me, and also to relieve my nerves a little. In this place during the day if you do not go to the campus, to the library, or to audit colleagues' courses, or to the University coffee shop, you do not know where to go; therefore the only thing is to start running this way or that on the hill, among the maples and the willows, as many students do and also many colleagues. We cross on the rustling paths of leaves and sometimes we say "Hi!" to each other. Sometimes nothing, because we have to save our breath. This too is an advantage running has over other sports: everybody is on his own and is not required to answer to the others.

The hill is entirely built up and as I run I pass two-storey wooden houses with yards, all different and all similar, and every so often I hear a telephone ring. This makes me nervous; instinctively I slow down; I prick up my ears to hear if some-body answers and I become impatient when the ringing continues. Continuing my run I pass another house in which a telephone is ringing, and I think: "There is a telephone chasing me, there is somebody looking up all the numbers on Chestnut Lane in the directory and he is calling one house after the other to see if he can overtake me."

Sometimes the houses are all silent and deserted, squirrels run up the tree trunks, magpies swoop down to peck at the feed set out for them in wooden bowls. Running, I feel a vague sensation of alarm, and even before I can pick up the sound with my ear, my mind records the possibility of the ring, almost summons it up, sucks it from its own absence, and at that moment from a house comes, first muffled then gradually more distinct, the trill of the bell, whose vibrations perhaps for some time had already been caught by an antenna inside me before my hearing perceived them, and there I go rushing in an absurd frenzy, I am the prisoner of a circle in whose center there is the telephone ringing inside that house, I run without moving away, I hover without shortening my stride.

"If nobody has answered by now it means nobody is home.... But why do they keep on calling then? What are they hoping? Does a deaf man perhaps live there, and do they hope that by insisting they will make themselves heard? Perhaps a paralytic lives there, and you have to allow a great deal of time so that he can crawl to the phone. . . . Perhaps a suicide lives there, and as long as you keep calling him some hope remains of preventing his extreme act. . . ." I think perhaps I should try to make myself useful, lend a hand, help the deaf man, the paralytic, the suicide. . . . And at the same time I think – in the absurd logic at work inside me – that in doing so I could make sure the call is not by chance for me. . . .

Still running I push open the gate, enter the yard, circle the house, explore the ground behind it, dash behind the garage, to the tool shed, the dog house. Everything seems deserted, empty. Through an open window in the rear a room can be seen, in disorder, the telephone on the table, continuing to ring. The shutter slams; the window-frame is caught in the tattered curtain.

I have circled the house three times; I continue to perform the movements of jogging, raising elbows and heels, breathing with the rhythm of my run so that it is clear my intrusion is not a thief's; if they caught me at this moment I would have a hard time explaining that I came in because I heard the telephone ring. A dog barks, not here, it is the dog of another house that cannot be seen; but for a moment in me the signal "barking dog" is stronger than the "ringing telephone" and this is enough to open a passage in the circle that was holding me prisoner there, now I resume running among the trees along the street, leaving behind me the increasingly muffled ringing.

I run until there are no more houses. In a field I stop to catch my breath. I do some kneebends, some pushups, I massage the muscles of my legs so they will not get cold. I look at the time. I am late, I must go back if I do not want to keep my students waiting. All I need is for the rumor to spread that I go running through the woods when I should be teaching. . . . I fling myself onto the return road, paying no attention to anything, I will not even recognize that house, I will pass it without noticing. For that matter the house is exactly like the others in every respect, and the only way it could stand out would be if the telephone were to ring again, which is impossible. . . .

The more I turn these thoughts over in my head, as I run down-hill, the more I seem to hear that ring again, it grows more and more clear and distinct, there, I am again in sight of the house and the telephone is still ringing. I enter the garden, I go around behind the house, I run to the window. I have only to reach out to pick up the receiver. I say, breathless: "He's not here . . ." and from the receiver a voice, a bit vexed, but only a bit, because what is most striking about this voice is the coldness, the calm, says: "Now you listen to me. Marjorie is here, she'll be waking in a little while, but she's tied up and can't get away. Write down this address carefully: 115 Hillside Drive. If you come to get her, okay; otherwise there's a can of kerosene in the basement and a charge of plastic attached to a timer. In half an hour this house will go up in flames. . . ."

"But I'm not –" I begin to answer.

They have already hung up.

Now what do I do? Of course I could call the police, the fire department, on this same telephone, but how can I explain, how can I justify the fact that I, in other words how can I who have nothing to do with it have anything to do with it? I start running again, I circle the house once more, then I resume my way.

I am sorry for this Marjorie, but if she has got herself into such a jam she must be mixed up in God knows what things, and if I step forward to save her nobody will believe that I do not know her, there would be a great scandal, I am a professor at another university invited here as visiting professor, the prestige of both universities would suffer....

To be sure when a life is in the balance these considerations should take a back seat.... I slow down. I could enter any one of these houses, ask them if they will let me call the police, say first of all quite clearly that I do not know this Marjorie, I do not know any Marjorie....

To tell the truth here at the University there is a student named Marjorie, Marjorie Stubbs: I noticed her immediately among the girls attending my classes. She is a girl who you might say appealed to me a lot, too bad that the time I invited her to my house to lend her some books an embarrassing situation may have been created. It was a mistake to invite her: those were my first days of teaching, here they did not yet know the sort I am, she could misunderstand my intentions, that misunderstanding took place, an unpleasant mistunderstanding, certainly even now very hard to clarify because she has that ironic way of looking at me, and I am unable to address a word to her without stammering, the other girls also look at me with an ironic smile....

Yes, I would not want this uneasiness now reawakened in me by the name Marjorie to prevent me from intervening to help another Marjorie whose life is in danger.... Unless it is the same Marjorie.... Unless that telephone call was aimed personally at me.... A very powerful band of gangsters is keeping an eye on me, they know that every morning I go jogging along that road, maybe they have a lookout on the hill with a telescope to follow my steps, when I approach that deserted house they call on the telephone, it is me they are calling, because they know the unfortunate impression I made on Marjorie that day at my house and they are blackmailing me....

Almost without realizing it, I find myself at the entrance to the campus, still running, in jogging garb and running shoes, I did not go by my house to change and pick up my books, now what do I do? I keep on running across the campus, I meet some girls drifting over the lawn in little groups, they are my students already on their way to my class, they look at me with that ironic smile I cannot bear.

Still making running movements, I stop Lorna Clifford and I ask her: "Is Stubbs here?"

The Clifford girl blinks. "Marjorie? She hasn't shown up for two days.... Why?"

I have already run off. I leave the campus. I take Grosvenor Avenue, then Cedar Street, then Maple Road. I am completely out of breath, I am running only because I cannot feel the ground beneath my feet, or my lungs in my chest. Here is Hillside Drive. Eleven, fifteen, twenty-seven, fifty-one; thank God the numbers go fast, skipping from one decade to the next. Here is 115. The door is open, I climb the stairs I enter a room in semi-darkness. Tied on a sofa there is Marjorie, gagged. I release her. She vomits. She looks at me with contempt.

"You're a bastard," she says to me.

*　*　*

What story down there awaits its end?

Walking along the great Prospect of our city, I mentally erase the elements I have decided not to take into consideration. I pass a Ministry building, whose facade is laden with caryatids, columns, balustrades, plinths, brackets, metopes; and I feel the need to reduce it to a smooth vertical surface, a slab of opaque glass, a partition that defines space without imposing itself on one's sight. But even simplified like this, the building still oppresses me: I decide to do away with it completely; in its place a milky sky rises over the bare ground. Similarly I erase five more Ministries, three banks, and a couple of skyscraper-headquarters of big companies. The world is so complicated, tangled, and overloaded that to see into it with any clarity you must prune and prune.

In the bustle of the Prospect I keep meeting people the sight of whom, for various reasons, is unpleasant to me: my superiors, because they remind me of my inferior position; my inferiors, because I hate to feel possessed of an authority I consider petty, as petty as the envy, servility, and bitterness it inspires. I erase both categories, without any hesitation; out of the corner of my eye, I see them shrink and vanish in a faint wisp of fog.

In this operation I am careful to spare passersby, outsiders, strangers who have never bothered me; indeed, the faces of some of them, if I observe them objectively, seem worthy of sincere interest. But when a crowd of strangers is all that remains from the world surrounding me, I suddenly feel lonely and disoriented, so better to erase them as well, the whole lot, and forget it.

In a simplified world I have greater probabilities of meeting the few people I like to meet: Franziska, for example. Franziska is a friend, and when I run into her, I feel a great joy. We exchange witticisms, we laugh, we tell each other things, ordinary events, but perhaps ones we do not tell other people, and when we discuss them together, they prove interesting to both of us, and before saying goodbye, we both insist we must meet again as soon as possible. Then months pass, until we run into each other in the street, by chance: festive cries, laughter, promises to get together again soon, but neither of us ever does anything to bring about a meeting; perhaps because we know that it would no longer be the same thing. In a reduced and simplified world, now that the air has been cleared of all those pre-established situations which would make the fact of my seeing Franziska more often suggest a relationship between us somehow requiring definition, perhaps eventual marriage or, in any event, our being considered a couple, assuming a bond possibly extending to our respective families, to our forebears and descendants, to siblings and cousins, and a bond between the environment of our joint lives and our attachments in the sphere of incomes and possessions; now, having achieved the disappearance of these conditions which, all around us, silently, weighed on us and on our conversations, causing them never to last more than a few minutes, my meeting Franziska should be even more beautiful and enjoyable. So it is natural for me to try to create the circumstances most favorable to a crossing of our paths, such as the abolition of all young women wearing a pale fur like the one she wore last time, so that if I see her from a distance, I can be sure it is she, without any risk of misunderstandings or disappointments, and then the abolition of all young men who look as if they might be friends of Franziska and might conceivably be about to meet her, maybe intentionally, and delay her in pleasant conversation just when I should be the one to meet her, by chance.

I have gone into details of a personal nature, but this should not lead anyone to believe that my abolitions are inspired primarily by my own immediate, private interests; on the contrary, I try to act in the interest of the whole (and hence also my own, but indirectly). True, to begin somewhere, I made all the public buildings that occurred within my range disappear with their broad steps and columned entrances and their corridors and waiting rooms, and files and circulars and dossiers, but also with their division chiefs, their director-generals, their vice-inspectors, their acting heads, their permanent and temporary staff; but I did this because I believe their existence is damaging or superfluous to the harmony of the whole.

It is that time of day when droves of employees leave the overheated offices, button up their overcoats with their fake-fur collars, and pile into buses. I blink, and they have vanished: only some scattered passersby can be discerned, far off, in the deserted streets from which I have also scrupulously eliminated automobiles and trucks and buses. I like to see the surface of the street bare and smooth as a bowling alley.

Then I abolish barracks, guard-houses, police stations: all people in uniform vanish as if they had never existed. Perhaps I've let things get out of hand; I realize that firemen have suffered the same fate, and mail-carriers, municipal street-cleaners, and other categories which might deservedly have hoped for a different treatment; but what's done is done: no use splitting hairs. To avoid trouble, I quickly abolish fires, garbage, and also mail, which after all never brings anything but problems.

I check to make sure that hospitals, clinics, rest homes have not been left standing: to erase doctors, nurses, patients seems to me the only possible health. Then courts, with their complement of magistrates, lawyers, defendants and injured parties; prisons, with prisoners and guards inside. Then I erase the University with the entire faculty, the Academy of Sciences, Letters, and Arts, the Museum, the Library, monuments and curators, theaters, movies, televisions, newspapers. If they think respect for culture is going to stop me, they're wrong.

Then come the economic structures, which for too long a time have continued to enforce their outrageous claim to decide our lives. What do they think they are? One by one, I dissolve all shops, beginning with the ones selling prime necessities and ending with those selling superfluities, luxuries: first I clear the display windows of goods, then I erase the counters, shelves, salesgirls, cashiers, floor-walkers. The crowd of customers is momentarily bewildered, hands extended into the void, as shopping carts evaporate; then the customers themselves are also swallowed up by the vacuum. From consumer I work back to producer: I abolish all industry, light and heavy, I wipe out raw materials and sources of energy. What about agriculture? Away with that, too! And to prevent anyone from saying I want to regress towards primitive societies, I also eliminate hunting and fishing.

Nature . . . Aha! Don't think I haven't caught on: this nature business is another fine fraud: kill it! A layer of the earth's crust is all that has to remain, solid enough underfoot, and everywhere else, nothingness.

I continue my walk along the Prospect, which now cannot be distinguished from the endless plain, deserted, arid, frozen. There are no more walls, as far as the eye can see, no mountains or hills; not a river or a lake or a sea: only a flat, gray expanse of ice, as compact as basalt. Renouncing things is less difficult than people believe: it's all in getting started. Once you've succeeded in dispensing with something you thought essential, you realize you can also do without something else, then without many other things. So here I am walking along this empty surface that is the world. There is a wind grazing the ground, dragging with flurries of fine snow the last residue of the vanished world: a bunch of ripe grapes which seems just picked from the vine, an infant's woollen bootee, a well-oiled hinge, a page that seems torn from a novel written in Spanish, with a woman's name: Amaranta. Was it a few seconds ago that everything ceased to exist, or many centuries? I've already lost any feeling of time.

There, at the end of that strip of nothing which I continue to call the Prospect I see a slender form advancing, in a pale fur jacket: it's Franziska! I recognize her stride in her high boots, and the way she keeps her arms hidden in her muff, and the long striped scarf flapping after her. The cold air and the cleared terrain guarantee good visibility, but I wave my arms in vain, trying to attract her attention: she can't recognize me, we're still too far apart. I advance, hastening my steps; at least I think I'm advancing, but I lack any reference points. Now, on the line between me and Franziska, some shadows can be discerned: they are men, men in overcoats and hats. They are waiting for me. Who can they be?

When I have come close enough, I recognize them: they're the men from Section D. How is it they've remained here? What are they doing? I thought I had abolished them too when I erased the personnel of all the offices. Why have they placed themselves between me and Franziska? "Now I'll erase them!" I decide, and concentrate. Nothing doing: they're still there between us.

"Well, here you are," they greet me. "Still one of us, are you? Good for you! You gave us a real hand, all right, and now everything is clean."

"What?" I exclaim. "Were you erasing as well?"

Now I can understand my sensation that, this time, I had ventured farther than in my previous exercises of making the world around me disappear.

"But tell me something: weren't you the ones who were always talking of increment, of implementing, of expansion. . . ."

"Well? There's no contradiction. . . . Everything is contemplated in the logic of projections. . . . The line of development starts again from zero. . . . You had also realized that the situation had come to a dead end . . . was deteriorating. . . . The only thing was to help the process along . . . Tendentially, something which might seem negative in the short run, in the long run can prove an incentive. . . ."

"But I didn't mean it the way you did. . . . I had something else in mind . . . I erase in a different way . . ." I protest, and I think: if they believe they can fit me into their plans, they're wrong!

I can't wait to go into reverse, to make the things of the world exist again, one by one or all together, to set their variegated and tangible substance, like a compact wall, against the men's plans of general vacancy. I close my eyes and reopen them, sure of finding myself on the Prospect again, teeming with traffic, the street lamps lighted at this hour, and the final edition of the papers in the kiosks. But instead: nothing. The void all around us is more and more void, Franziska's form on the horizon comes forward slowly, as if she had to climb the curve of the earth's globe. Are we the only survivors? With mounting terror I begin to realize the truth: the world which I believe erased by a decision of my mind that I could revoke at any moment is truly finished.

"You have to be realistic," the officials of Section D are saying. "Just take a look round. The whole universe is . . . let's say it's in a transitional phase. . . ." And they point to the sky, where the constellations have become unrecognizable, here clotted, there rarefied, the celestial map in upheaval, stars exploding one after the other, while more stars emit a final flicker and die. "The important thing is that now, when the new ones arrive, they must find Section D in perfect working order, its cadres complete, its functional structures in operation . . ."

"But who are the new ones? What do they do? What do they want?" I ask, and on the frozen surface that separates me from Franziska I see a fine crack, spreading like a mysterious trap.

"It's too early to say. For us to say it in our terms. At present we can't even see them. But we can be sure they're there, and for that matter, we had been informed, even before, that they were about to arrive. . . . But we're here, too, and they can't help but know it, we who represent the only possible continuity with what there was before. . . . They need us. They have to turn to us, entrust to us the practical management of what remains. . . . The world will begin again the way we want it. . . ."

No, I think, the world that I would like to begin existing again around me and Franziska can't be yours; I would like to concentrate and think of a place, in every detail, a setting where I would like to be with Franziska at this moment, for example a café lined with mirrors, which reflect crystal chandeliers, and there is an orchestra playing waltzes and the strains of the violins flutter over the little marble tables and the steaming cups and the pastries with whipped cream. While outside, beyond the frosted windows, the world full of people and of things would make its presence felt: the presence of the world, friendly and hostile, things to rejoice in or to combat. . . . I think this with all my strength but by now I know my strength isn't enough to make it exist: nothingness is stronger and has occupied the whole earth.

"To work out a relationship with them won't be easy," the Section D men continue, "and we'll have to be on our toes, not make mistakes, not allow them to cut us out. We had you in mind, to win the new ones' confidence. You've proved your ability in the liquidation phase, and of all of us you're the least compromised with the old administration. You'll have to introduce yourself, explain what the Section is, how they can use it, for urgent, indispensable jobs . . . Well, you'll figure out the way to make things look best. . . ."

"I should be going then. I'll go look for them . . ." I hasten to say, because I realize that if I don't make my escape now, if I don't reach Franziska immediately and save her, in a minute it will be too late; the trap is about to be sprung. I run off before the Section D men can hold me, ask me questions, give me instructions. I advance over the frozen crust towards her. The world is reduced to a sheet of paper on which nothing can be written except abstract words, as if all concrete nouns were finished; if one could only succeed in writing the word "chair," then it would be possible to write also "spoon," "gravy," "stove," but the stylistic formula of the text prohibits it.

On the ground that separates me from Franziska I see some fissures open, some furrows, crevasses; at each moment one of my feet is about to be caught in a pitfall: these interstices widen, soon a chasm will yawn between me and Franziska, an abyss! I leap from one side to the other, and below I see no bottom, only nothingness which continues down to infinity; I run across pieces of world scattered in the void; the world is crumbling. . . . The men from Section D call me, they motion desperately for me to come back, not to risk going any farther. . . . Franziska! One more leap and I'll be with you!

She is here, she is opposite me, smiling, with that golden sparkle in her eyes, her small face a bit chapped from the cold. "Oh! It's really you! Every time I walk on the Prospect I run into you! Now don't tell me you spend all your days out strolling! Listen: I know a café here at the corner, all lined with mirrors, and there's an orchestra that plays waltzes. Will you invite me there?"

Translated from the Italian by William Weaver

One Summer's Morning, in The Village

BY AMOS OZ

All night long mist rises from the green swamp, spreading a smell of decay among our huts. Objects made of iron rust here overnight, the wooden walls are disintegrating in the clutches of the sickly vegetation, straw and hay turn black like scorched fields, mosquitoes swarm in the dank air, our rooms are full of flying insects and reptiles, and the very soil seems to bubble. Our children suffer from boils and rashes all through the summer, the old folk die from degeneration of the respiratory tract, and even the living exude a stench of death. I, who have been sent here by the Bureau for the Assistance of Underdeveloped Regions, still go out every day, towards evening, to spray the swamp water with disinfectants and to dispense carbolic acid, ointments, essential hints on hygiene, DDT, and chlorinated water to the settlers. I am still holding the fort until a replacement arrives. And in the meantime, I am pharmacist, teacher, notary, go-between, and peacemaker. Before I arrived, a few years ago, perhaps four years, though the old people stubbornly insist it was six, the District Commissioner came on a tour of inspection with his staff, and gave orders for the river to be diverted immediately so as to put an end to the malignant swamp. The Commissioner was accompanied by officers and clerks, surveyors and men of God, a legal expert, a singer, an official historian, and representatives of the various branches of the secret service. They spent a whole day here, and the Commissioner recorded his findings: dig, divert, dry out, purify, and turn over a fresh page.

Since then nothing has happened.

The old folk and the babies continue to die and the youngsters are growing older. The population, according to my cautious calculations, is declining. By the end of the century, so says the table I have drawn up, there will not be a single living soul remaining here – apart from the insects and reptiles. Large numbers of babies are born, but most of them die in infancy and their death hardly seems to stir a ripple of grief any more. The young men run away, the girls farm potatoes and wither before my eyes at the age of fifteen or twenty. Sometimes desire bursts out and inflames the whole village to nocturnal orgies by the light of bonfires of damp wood, and they all run riot, old folk and children, girls and cripples; I cannot record the details, because on nights like these I lock myself into the dispensary and put a loaded pistol under my pillow, in case they get some mad idea. But such nights are infrequent. The days are blazing hot. The work in the potato fields is apparently crushing. Some time ago, two of the gravedigger's sons joined a gang of smugglers. The two widows with their children moved in with the youngest brother, a mere lad, not yet fourteen. As for the gravedigger himself, a stubborn, silent, broad-boned man, he determined not to pass over the matter in silence. But the years are slipping past in silence. The gravedigger himself moved into the hut of his surviving son, more and more babies were born there, and no one could say which were the off-spring of the runaways and which were the youngest brother's, or which were sired by the father. In any case, most of the babies died almost as soon as they were born. Other men came and went, and also dim-witted, big-bodied girls in search of a roof, a man, a child, or food.

The Commissioner has not replied to three successive memoranda, each more strongly-worded than the last, sent to sound the alarm against the seriousness of the moral situation. I was the outraged sender of these memoranda. The years are slip-ping past in silence. Nothing happens here. Apart from the strange occurrence which I witnessed this morning, and which I shall report without comment.

In the morning the rising sun had transformed the mist from the swamp into a kind of incandescent, unclean rain. The villagers had left their huts and were prepar-ing to set out for the potato fields. Suddenly a stranger appeared at the top of the small hill which stood between us and the rising sun and began waving his arms, describing curves and circles in the air, kicking or bowing, hopping and jumping on the spot.

"Who is he," the men asked, "and what does he want here?"

"It's not one of us and it's not one of the smugglers," said the old men.

And the women said, "We've got to be careful."

While they were discussing what to do, the early morning air was suddenly full of different sounds, screeching birds, barking dogs, talking, lowing, humming of insects as large as your fist. The frogs also began to croak, the chickens tried to outdo them, and harnesses jangled. And the sounds were all distinct.

"That man," said the gravedigger's youngest son, "has been sent to break up the village and we must kill him."

"That man," said the innkeeper, "is trying to seduce the girls."

The girls shrieked, "Look he's dancing, look he's naked, look he's white like a corpse!"

And the old gravedigger said, "What is there to chatter about? The sun is up, and the white man has vanished behind the hill. Words won't help; a hot day is starting and we must go to work. Whoever can work, let him endure in silence. And who-ever cannot bear it any longer, let him die. That's that."

Passport Photograph

A veteran member of the kibbutz appears in a sepia photograph taken in Lodz some fifty years ago.

It shows a pudgy youth of seventeen, with his shirt buttoned up to the neck but without a tie. (Perhaps a compromise between respectability and pioneering ideals.) An open, slightly ingenuous face, a spoiled mouth, and a frank, direct look in the eyes. An expression which seems to be saying, "I have no complaints, and I am sure that no one has any complaints about me. I'm perfectly all right. Everything's per-fectly all right. It'll be okay."

The hair is brushed straight back, apart from a single unruly lock, suggesting a schoolboy-but-definitely-not-a-child: "You all think that I'm a simple, straightforward, likeable sort of lad, and you're not mistaken. I certainly am one of those decent chaps you can rely on, but you should know that if we're talking about, say, girls, I'm perfectly capable of getting up to a spot of mischief, and in fact I've already managed one or two japes, I'll leave it to you to guess what."

It is still possible to compare the old photograph with the man's face as it is now – wrinkled, tired, sunburnt, and windlashed, and yet, not healthy. Now, almost at the very end, all that is left of that cultured-but-pioneering smile is a disillusioned grin: "All right. That's the way it is. So be it." The hair has receded and the furrowed brow extends almost to the top of the skull. The ears, large and pendulous, have finally found their rightful place. The chin is more pointed now, and underneath it there are pockets or bags, as though this were an elderly philanderer instead of a veteran Zionist socialist and an exemplary working man.

And the concerns now: "It's all over. It's all happened. Not that it was bad or disappointing, or – heaven forbid – a bad bargain, but it's simply all over." What a terrible thing. All over. Girls. Wars. Discussions. Children. Work. Rifts and reconciliations. Grandchildren. Assignments. Victories. All over. Now the ideals have faded and the desires have grown cold, and of all the old longings, only a handful are left. A little honor. A little peace and quiet. A little affection. And, no muckraking. A little politeness please. Remember who you're talking to. Mind your manners. I haven't spoken my last word yet, and I can still cause a fair amount of unpleasantness if I decide to speak up. So, if you don't mind . . . And the astonishment: ("What?! So that's it? All over? How on earth?") And the fear, together with a tremor of despair: ("That's it. That's all. Finished. That's the way it is.")

What does this old veteran have to say to me when we are sitting over supper in the dining hall on one of those autumn evenings? First, politics: "Why do I jump around so? Carter, Shimon Peres, Gush Emunim, Kissinger, Hashomer Hatsair, perhaps I'll be good enough to listen for a moment before I give vent to hasty opinions? After all, we've been through it all before, one way or another, and it's always turned out all right in the end. It's wrong to worry so, and to spread panic. Don't get so worked up, Amos, we've been through much more problematic times in the past, and you see, we've survived, thank God. This mood will also blow over. Do you have a cigarette by any chance? No? Have you really managed to give up? Hand on your heart – have you really stopped? Truly? (A hint of Polish in the accent still.) So perhaps you'll share the secret, and tell me how it's done? These cigarettes are killing me. Literally killing me. Hey, how'd you do it? Nu? How? Wait, don't say anything, I'll tell you exactly how it's done. Wait a minute, let me finish a sentence, I'll tell you exactly and don't you interrupt."

Translated from the Hebrew by Nicholas de Lange

The Red Dwarf

BY MICHEL TOURNIER

for Jean-Pierre Rudin

When Lucien Gagnere reached the age of twenty-five he had to give up with a broken heart all hope of ever becoming any taller than the four-feet-one he had already reached eight years before. All he could do now was have recourse to special shoes whose platform soles gave him the extra four inches that elevated him from the dwarf category to that of the small man. As the years went by, his vanishing adolescence and youth left him exposed as a stunted adult who inspired mockery and scorn in the worst moments, pity in the less bad ones, but never respect or fear, in spite of the enviable position he occupied in the office of an important Paris lawyer.

His speciality was divorce and, not being able to dream of marriage for himself, he applied himself with avenging ardor to the task of destroying the marriages of other people. This was why he one day received a visit from Mrs. Edith Watson. A first marriage to an American had left this former opera singer extremely wealthy, and she had then married a lifeguard from Nice who was much younger than she. It was this second union that she now wished to dissolve and, through the numerous and confused grievances she had against her Bob, Lucien scented secrets and humiliations that more than interested him. He felt personally concerned in the wreck of this couple, even more so, perhaps, since he had had a chance to see Bob. The young man was a colossus, with a sweet, naive face – like an athletic girl, Lucien thought – a beautiful, golden pulpy fruit on the beach, designed to arouse all kinds of appetites.

Lucien prided himself on his literary talents and was most meticulous in refining the style of the insulting letters which, according to French law, couples have to exchange in order to achieve an amiable separation. This time he surpassed himself, and Bob was horrified by the vulgarity and violence of the letters which, over several months, he dictated to him and had him sign. They even included unqualified death threats.

Some time later, Lucien went to visit his client, who lived in a luxurious duplex apartment on the borders of the Bois de Boulogne, to get her signature to some documents. A spiral staircase joined the upper apartment, where Bob was still living, to the lower one, which was enhanced by a vast terrace. That was where he found Edith Watson, practically naked on a chaise longue, surrounded by refreshments. The radiance of that big, golden body, with its violent odor of woman and suntan lotion, intoxicated Lucien – and it seemed to intoxicate Edith herself, though she didn't care a fig about her visitor, and answered his questions in an absent-minded, far-off voice. The heat was stifling, and Lucien was extremely uncomfortable in his dark, thick, notary's clerk's clothes, and all the more so in that the ice-cold beer Edith had offered him on his arrival had immediately drenched him in sweat. The last straw was that it had also made him want to urinate, and he was twisting and turning like a woodlouse in the hollow of the big deck chair he had coiled up in. Finally, in a painstaking voice, he asked where the lavatory was, and Edith answered with a vague gesture toward the interior and some muttered words; the only one he could make out was "bathroom."

The room seemed immense to Lucien. It was all black marble, with a bathtub sunk into the floor. There were various nickeled appliances, spotlights, a super scale, and above all a profusion of mirrors which sent his image back to him at most unusual angles. He pissed, and then began to luxuriate in this cool spot. The bathtub, which looked like something between a pitfall, a tomb, and a snake pit, didn't attract him in the least, but he hovered around the shower basin which was surrounded by slabs of frosted glass. A whole battery of jets converged in it, and it seemed that you could spray yourself with water not only from above but also from the front, from the back, from the sides, and also vertically from below. There was a complicated set of faucets to regulate these jets.

Lucien undressed and began to switch on the various sprinklers; their direction, violence, and temperature surprised him, like aggressive practical jokes. Then he smeared himself in a light, perfumed lather which he sprayed on with an aerosol, and remained in the multiple shower for quite a while. He was enjoying himself. For the first time he saw his body as something other than a shameful, repulsive object. When he jumped out of the shower onto the rubber mat he discovered that he was immediately surrounded by a whole crowd of Luciens imitating his movements in a labyrinth of mirrors. Then they stood still and looked at one another. Their face had an indisputable air of rather majestic gravity – sovereign was the word that occurred to Lucien – with a wide, rectangular forehead, a steady, imperious gaze, a fleshy sensual mouth, and it did not even lack that slight touch of flabbiness in the lower part of the face which suggested incipient jowls of impressive nobility. After that, everything began to deteriorate, for the neck was disproportionately long, the torso as round as a ball, the legs short and bandy, like those of a gorilla, and the enormous penis cascaded in black and purple waves down to the knees.

But it was time to think of getting dressed. Lucien glanced in disgust at the dark, sweaty pile of his clothes, then he noticed a huge crimson bathrobe hanging from a chrome peg. He took it down, draped it around him until he was completely hidden within its folds, and then, with the aid of the mirrors, he devised a dignified, casual bearing. He wondered whether he should put his shoes on. This was a crucial question, for if he relinquished the four inches of his platform soles he would be confessing, and even proclaiming, to Edith Watson that he was a dwarf and not merely a small man. The discovery of an elegant pair of Turkish slippers under a stool decided him, When he made his entrance onto the terrace, the long train formed by the outsize bathrobe gave him an imperial air.

The big sunglasses concealing Edith's face made it impossible for him to see what she was thinking, and it was only her sudden immobility, when the majestic little personage appeared and with a kind of weasel leap buried himself in the depths of a canopied deck-chair, that betrayed her stupefaction. The notary's clerk had disappeared and given place to a comical, disquieting creature of overwhelming, betwitching ugliness, to a fabulous monster, whose comic aspect added a negative, acid, destructive component.

"That's Bob's bathrobe," she murmured, in order to say something, in a tone that was half protest, half simple observation.

"I can just as well do without it," Lucien replied insolently.

And, throwing off the bathrobe, he sank down onto the ground like an insect emerging from a flower, and in the same movement started climbing up Edith's chaise lounge.

Lucien was a virgin. His awareness of his infirmity had stifled the cries of his nascent puberty. He discovered love that day, and his abandon of his clerk's clothing and especially of his built-up shoes, and his acceptance of his dwarf category were in his mind inseparable from this dazzling revelation. As for Edith – who was only getting a divorce because of the inadequacy of her too-handsome husband – she was enchanted to discover that such a small, misshapen body should be so fantastically equipped, and so delightfully efficacious.

This was the beginning of a liaison whose passion was entirely physical and to which Lucien's infirmity added a slightly shameful, sophisticated piquancy for her, and a pathetic tension mixed with anguish for him. They were both agreed to throw a veil of absolute secrecy over their relationship. Apart from the fact that Edith wouldn't have had the courage to display such a strange lover to the world, he had explained to her that it was of paramount importance to her divorce for her conduct to appear irreproachable until the case came to court.

From then on, Lucien led a double life. To all appearances he was still a small man, dressed in somber clothes and built-up shoes, whom his colleagues saw every day pen-pushing at his big desk, but at certain irregular capricious hours – determined by coded telephone messages – he disappeared into the block by the Bois de Boulogne, went up to the duplex apartment to which he had a key and there, metamorphosed into an imperial dwarf, willful, swaggering, desirous, and desired, he subjected the big blonde with the sophisticated accent, whose drug he was, to the law of pleasure. His embrace sent her into ecstasies, and her love song, which usually began with guttural trills, and rapturous flourishes, extending over three octaves, always culminated in a volley of affectionate, obscene abuse. She would call her lover my bauble, my lounge lizard, my ass-scratcher, my dildo. . . . After the storm she would make him a speech from which it emerged that he was nothing but a penis with organs around it, a walking penis, and, now calling him my pendant, my lubricity belt, she pretended to be going about her business in the house while carrying him around, clinging to her flank, the way female monkeys carry their young.

He let her say and do what she liked, and, while being bounced up and down by his "dwarf-carrier" as he called her in retaliation, he would amuse himself watching her breasts wobbling above his head like a couple of tethered balloons. Yet he was terrified of losing her, and it was with anguish that he wondered whether the pleasure he gave her was great enough to make up for the satisfaction of the social life that he could not offer her. His long experience of divorce cases had taught him that women are more social beings than men, and that they can only really blossom in an atmosphere that contains plenty of human relationships. Wouldn't she one day abandon him for some prestigious – or at least presentable – lover?

A period of inexplicable silence ensued. He had been trained not to go to the Bois de Boulogne unless Edith called him. For a whole, long week, she gave no sign of life. He fretted in silence, then began to vent his feelings in violent outbursts of aggression against the office juniors. Never had the letters of rupture he dictated to his clients been so venomous. Finally he simply had to find out, and went to visit his mistress on his own initiative. He did find out, and without delay. Silently opening the door with his key, he stole into the vestibule. He heard voices. He had no difficulty in recognizing them as those of Edith and Bob, who seemed to be on the best of terms – the most affectionate of terms, even.

The blow was all the more severe in that it was totally unexpected. Had the couple become reconciled? Was there now some doubt about the divorce? This reversion made Lucien feel not only that he had been rejected by his mistress, but that he was being thrust back into his former life and frustrated of the marvelous metamorphosis that had changed his destiny. He was overwhelmed with murderous hatred, and it took a violent effort to force himself to hide under a shelf when Edith and Bob came out of the bedroom, laughing, and made for the door. When the sound of the elevator had died away, Lucien came out of his hiding place and almost automatically went over to the bathroom. He undressed, took a shower, and then, draped in Bob's big crimson bathrobe, sat down on a stool where, stock-still, he waited.

Three hours later the door banged and Edith came in alone, humming. She called out something up the inner stairway, which indicated Bob's presence on the upper floor. Suddenly, she went into the bathroom without switching on the light. Lucien had let the bathrobe slip down off his shoulders. In one bound he was on her, clutching her flank as usual, but his two hands, powerful as a bulldog's jaws, had closed around her throat. Edith staggered, then rallied, and, weighed down by her mortal burden, took a few steps into the apartment. Finally she halted, seemed to hesitate, and then collapsed. While she was in her death throes Lucien possessed her for the last time.

None of this was premeditated, and yet from then on his acts followed one another as if they were part of a long-matured plan. He dressed, and rushed back to his office. Then he returned to the apartment with the insulting, threatening letters he had dictated to Bob and put them in a drawer in Edith's dresser. Finally he went home and immediately dialed Bob's number. The telephone rang for a long time. At last a grumpy, sleepy voice answered.

"Murderer! You've strangled your wife!" was all that Lucien said, in a disguised voice. Then he repeated this accusation three times, for Bob was showing the most obtuse lack of understanding.

Two days later the papers carried this news item and went on to say that the suspect number one – the victim's husband, whose letters found at the scene of the crime left no doubt about his intentions – had taken to flight, but that his arrest was no doubt imminent.

Lucien dissimulated himself within his character of the ill-favored clerk, a suffering, mocked little man, but the memory of the superman he had become through renouncing the extra four inches his special shoes added to his height haunted him day and night. Because he had finally had the courage of his own monstrosity, he had seduced a woman. She had deceived him. He had killed her, and his rival, the husband, doubling as a ridiculous tall man, was everywhere being hunted by the police! His life was a masterpiece, and there were moments when he was overwhelmed with breathtaking joy at the thought that he only had to take his shoes off to become immediately what he really was, a man apart, superior to the gigantic riffraff, an irresistible seducer and infallible killer! All the misery of the past years was due to his having refused the fearsome choice that was his destiny. In cowardly fashion he had shrunk from crossing the Rubicon into dwarfism, as he might have hesitated at the threshold of a temple. But he had finally dared to take the step. The slight quantitative difference that he had accepted in deciding to reject his platform shoes in Edith's bathroom had brought about a radical qualitative metamorphosis. The horrible quality of dwarfism had infused him and turned him into a fabulous monster. In the grayness of the lawyer's office where he spent his days he was haunted by dreams of despotism. By chance, he had read a document about Ravensbrück and Birkenau, the Nazi concentration camps reserved for women. He saw himself as the Kommandant, the governor, controlling with his huge whip vast troops of naked, wounded women – and it was no rare event for the typists to be surprised by hearing him roar.

But the secret of his new dignity lay heavy on him. He would have liked to adopt it in the face of the whole world. He dreamed of a conspicuous, public, devastating proclamation in front of an ecstatic crowd. He went to his tailor and ordered a dark red leotard that emphasized the curves of his muscles and genitals. Back in his office he shed the livery of the little clerk, took a shower, and put on what he privately called his evening clothes, to which he added a mauve silk scarf tied tightly around his long neck, like the old style Apaches. Then, wearing moccasins with thin, pliant soles, he slipped out. He had discovered the superior comfort his height afforded him. He could pass under the lowest doorways with his head held high. He could stand upright in the smallest cars. Every seat was a spacious nest for him. The glasses and plates in bistros and restaurants offered him ogres' portions. He was surrounded by abundance in all circumstances. Soon he became aware of the colossal strength accumulated in his muscles. He quickly became known in various nightclubs where the habitués would invite him to drink with them. He would jump up and perch on a high stool at the counter, and he could stand on his hands with his short legs crossed in the air, like arms. One night, a customer who had had too much to drink insulted him. Lucien threw him onto the gound and twisted his ankle, then stood on him and started jumping up and down on his face with a rage that terrified the onlookers. The same day a prostitute offered herself to him for nothing, out of curiosity, because the sight of his strength had excited her. From then on men were afraid of the red dwarf, and women submitted to the obscure fascination emanating from him. His vision of society began to change. He was the unshakeable center of a crowd of feeble, cowardly, stilt-walkers who were unsteady on their limbs and had nothing to offer their women but the genitals of a marmoset.

But this limited renown was to be merely a prelude. One evening, in a bar in Pigalle, after he had just won a bet by tearing in half a pack of fifty-two cards, he was accosted by a man with a swarthy face and black, curly hair, whose hands were adorned with diamonds. He introduced himself: Signor Silvio d'Urbino, the owner of the Urbino Circus, whose big top was at the Port Dorée for a week. Would the red dwarf agree to join his troupe? Lucien grabbed a glass carafe, intending to smash it into smithereens on the head of the insolent fellow. Then he had second thoughts. His imagination had just shown him a vast crater in which the spectators' heads were squeezed together like granules of caviar, rising up in terraces around a harshly lit ring. From his crater a mighty, continuous, and interminable ovation burst over the head of a minuscule individual dressed in red, standing alone in the center of the ring. He accepted.

For the first months Lucien was content to liven up the interludes between the acts. He would run along the circular platform around the ring, get entangled in the apparatus, run away with shrill cries when threatened by one of the exasperated men in the ring. Finally he would allow himself to be caught in the folds of the acrobats' big mats and the men would carry him off unceremoniously, a large hump in the middle of the rolled-up sheet.

The laughter he aroused in the audience elated him rather than hurt him. It was no longer the concrete, savage, individual laughter that had terrorized him before his metamorphosis. It was a stylized, esthetic, ceremonial, collective laughter, a veritable declaration of love, expressing the deference of the female crowd to the artiste who subjugates her. And in any case, this laughter turned into applause whenever Lucien reappeared in the ring as the alchemist's lead turns into gold in the depths of his crucible.

But Lucien wearied of this petty buffoonery, which was nothing but exercises and experiments. One day his comrades saw him wriggling into something that looked like a pair of pink plastic dungarees shaped like a giant hand. A finger, ending in a nail, corresponded to his head, his two arms and his two legs. His torso was its palm, and sticking out behind was the stump of a truncated wrist. This enormous, terrifying organ revolved by supporting itself successively on each of its fingers, it sat on its wrist, it contracted when facing the spotlights, ran with nightmare speed, and even climbed up ladders and rotated around a pole or a trapeze, hanging on by one finger. The children roared with laughter, and the women had a catch in their throats at the approach of this enormous pink-fleshed spider. The press of the entire world spoke of the giant hand act.

But Lucien was still not completely satisfied by this fame. He felt there was something lacking, something was incomplete. He was waiting – not impatiently, but confidently – for something, perhaps, though more probably for someone.

The Urbino Circus had already been on tour for five months when it pitched its tents in Nice. It was to stay there a week, and then cross the frontier back to its native Italy. The evening performance of the third day had been brilliant, and the giant hand act had been a sensation. Lucien had removed his makeup and was relaxing in the luxurious mobile home he had been promoted to since his great success, when he heard a soft knock at a window. He put the light out and went over to the looped curtains framing a pallid rectangle. A tall, massive silhouette was outlined against the phosphorescent sky. Lucien half-opened the window.

"Who is it?"

"I'd like to speak to M. Gagnero."

"But who *is* it?"

"It's me, Bob."

Lucien was so overcome by emotion that he had to sit down. He knew now what he'd been waiting for, whom he had come to look for in Nice. He had been keeping a kind of rendezvous, a rendezvous with Edith Watson. He let Bob in, and the awkward mass of the water-skier immediately filled all the space of the narrow abode in which Lucien was perfectly at his ease. Once again he despised stilt-walkers, who are nowhere in their right place.

Bob explained his situation in a whisper. Ever since Edith's death he had led a hunted existence in sunbaked attics or dank cellars, fed like an animal by his mother and a friend. He was obsessed with the temptation to give himself up to the police, but just the very idea of being remanded in custody terrified him, and, worse still, there were those accursed letters of rupture, full of threats to kill her, which made his case look even blacker. But Lucien could testify that it was he who had dictated these letters to Bob for the purposes of his divorce, and that the threats they contained were fictitious – purely conventional.

Lucien fully savored his omnipotence over this giant with the girlish face. Curled up in the hollow of a nest of cushions, his only regret was that he didn't smoke – a pipe, in particular – for then, before replying, he would have taken infinite time in cleaning it, then filling it, and finally lighting it, according to all the rules of the art.

For want of a pipe, he closed his eyes and allowed himself a good minute of voluptuous, smiling, Buddhist reflection.

"The police are looking for you," he finally said. "It would be my duty to denounce you. I'll give some thought to what I can do for you. But I need proof that you have total, blind confidence in me. It's very simple, then. Go back to your hiding place. Come back tomorrow at the same time. There won't be any trap. That'll prove that you have confidence in me. Then we shall be united in a pact. You're quite free not to come back."

The next day, Bob was there.

"You can't rely on my giving evidence about the letters," Lucien told him. "But I have something better to offer you. The day after tomorrow we'll be crossing the frontier into Italy. I'll take you with me."

Bob fell on his knees in the caravan and kissed his hands.

It was child's play for Lucien to smuggle him over the frontier by hiding him in his bed. He insisted that he should stay hidden during the circus's stops at San Remo, Imperia, and Savone. He waited until Genoa to introduce him to Signor d'Urbino as a friend met by chance in the crowd, with whom he intended to stage a new act. They started work right away.

The enormous difference in their height in itself suggested several classic numbers. One such mime act was the battle of David and Goliath, to which Lucien had added a finale of his own invention. After the giant had fallen onto the ground, his conqueror blew him up with a bicycle pump. From then on he was an obese, docile, flabby pachyderm, rolling from one side of the arena to the other at the mercy of the dwarf who handled and manhandled him. He put him to various personal uses: as a pneumatic mattress to take a nap on, as a trampoline to leap up into the apparatus, as a punching bag. And the colossus was always ridiculed and trounced by his minuscule adversary. Finally Lucien perched himself astride his neck and put on an enormous overcoat that covered Bob right down to his ankles. And they perambulated in this fashion, having become a single man eight-feet-two tall, Bob blinded and obliterated by the coat, Lucien perched on high, imperious and wrathful.

It was when they reverted to the great tradition of the whiteface clown and the August that their entrance took on its definitive form and crowned Lucien's triumph. The whiteface clown, made up, titivated, wearing pumps, his calves bulging in silk stockings, had formerly had the ring to himself and dazzled the audience with his wit and elegance. But he had been foolish enough to want to find a foil, to set off his beauty and éclat, and the hilarious, vulgar August, with his tippler's face – invented for this purpose – had gradually supplanted him. Lucien extended this development by turning his over-refined partner into his thing, his whipping boy. And yet nothing was too splendid for Bob. The dwarf dressed him in a platinum wig, he added cascades of ribbons, embroidery, lace, swansdown, to his costume. Finally, carried away by the logic of his number, he imagined the grotesque marriage, to the strains of Mendelssohn's Wedding March, of this enormous girl decked out in snowy white, to the minute red toad who kept jumping up at her dress, croaking. At the end of the number he leaped up like a dog, circled his partner's waist with his short legs, and in this fashion she carried him off into the wings, to thunderous applause.

This final leap disturbed Lucien deeply, because it reminded him painfully and voluptuously of the stranglehold that had killed Edith Watson. Were not Bob and he united by their love for the former singer? Lucien used to speak of her to Bob in the evenings, and then, obsessed by her memory, he finally confused her with his companion, and as it was even more important to him to subjugate and humiliate the stilt-walkers than to take their wives away from them, it happened one night, then every night, that he climbed into the side-berth of the mobile home in which his former rival slept, and possessed him like a female.

Later, the imperial theme, first sketched out in Bob's crimson bathrobe, once again took possession of him. Nothing was more in keeping with the clown tradition than to develop the August – the name itself suggested it – into a parody of a Roman emperor. Lucien draped himself in a red tunic that left his crooked, muscular thighs naked. He wore a necklet and a crown of roses. He was no longer the August, he was Nero, gag-Nero, as he was one day called by d'Urbino, who was always on the lookout for slogans and texts for his playbills. As for Bob, he quite naturally became Agrippina. The fact that Nero had had his mother murdered, after having taken her as his first mistress seemed a good omen to Lucien (Lucius Nero) who, not having found his place among decent, everyday models, was always willing to find inspiration in the grandiose turpitudes of Antiquity. It pleased him that his life should have taken the form of a caricature of stilt-walkers' morals, highly colored and spattered with blood and sperm.

"The one thing that bothers me," he said one night as he left Bob to go back to his own little bed, "is that, whatever we do, we shall never have a child."

This thought was certainly charged with its weight of brutal cynicism, but it was nonetheless secretly inspired by a recent discovery that was to mark a new turning point in his destiny. He had noticed that while the adulation of the ordinary public had no noticeable influence on the ball of hatred that weighed hard and heavy in his breast, a warm, springlike breath did sometimes seem to reach him from the tiers, and particularly from the very top of the tiers, from the last benches hidden in the shadows of the big top. From then on he waited passionately for this breath which touched, moved, and blessed him, and tried to discover in which of the performances it manifested itself. Now it was always during the matinees, and on Thursdays rather than on Sundays, Thursday being at that time the day when children didn't go to school.

"I'd like it,', he said to d'Urbino one evening, "if once a week at least the circus refused to admit anyone over the age of twelve."

The director showed extreme surprise at this demand, but he respected the whims of those stars whose inventive genius had led to profitable and spectacular innovations.

"We could start on December 24th, Christmas Eve," the dwarf added.

The date was so close and the danger so precise that d'Urbino began to worry.

"But why, my dear Maestro, but what an idea, under the age of twelve, but what does that mean?"

Once again Lucien felt himself in the grip of his old, malevolent wrath, and he advanced menacingly on the director.

"That means that for once I shall have an audience of my own size! Can't you understand? I don't want any stilt-walkers – not a single one!"

"But, but, but," d'Urbino stammered, "if we refuse to admit adults and adolescents it'll cost us an enormous amount of money!"

Lucien's reply rooted him to the spot – Lucien who was always so prodigiously grasping.

"I'll pay!" he announced dogmatically. "We'll have the cashier work out how much you'll lose and you can deduct it from my pay.

"And in any case, for the matinee on December 24th it's very simple – I'll buy all the seats. Entrance will be free . . . for children."

This Christmas performance was to remain memorable in the history of the circus. Children flooded in from several leagues around, whole coachloads of them in some cases, because schools, reformatories, and orphanages had been notified. Some mothers who were refused entry had the idea of tying their children together so that they shouldn't get lost, and roped parties of five, six, and even seven brothers and sisters were to be seen climbing up onto the tiers.

What act the red dwarf performed that day no one will ever know because it was witnessed by no one but children, and he swore them to secrecy. At the end of the show they gave him a tremendous ovation and he, standing squarely in the sawdust on his immovable legs, his eyes closed with bliss – he allowed himself to be submerged in this storm of tenderness, this tempest of sweetness, which cleansed him of his bitterness, justified him, illuminated him. Then, children in their thousands surged into the ring, surrounded him in a tumultuous, caressing floodtide, and carried him off in triumph and in song.

Behind the red and gold curtains leading to the stables, the riders, the tamer, the Chinese conjurers, the flying trapeze artists, the Nepalese jugglers, and behind them the tall, grotesque silhouette of Agrippina, all retreated, effaced themselves, amazed by this savage hymn.

"Let him be," said d'Urbino. "He's with his own kind, he's being fêted by his own people. For the first time in his life, maybe, he is no longer alone. As for me, I have my slogan: Lucius Gag-Nero, emperor of children. I can already see my playbill: the Red Dwarf in a toga with his sword and crown, and with the crowd, the immense crowd of little people, not one of whom is a fraction of an inch taller than him! But what a matinee, my friends, what a matinee!"

Translated from the French by Barbara Wright

The Feet of a King

BY DAPHNE MERKIN

Where was my father?

My imagination, usually so busy, failed me when it came to him. I invent no one in his place, no alternate father visions, the way I do for my mother. He is too distant, or she too potent, a presence; or, more likely than either of these, he is too potent an absence. But this is something I begin to consider only years later, when I am ready to consider so predetermined a lack of choice.

It is again Friday night, but I no longer wear my sisters Lily and Rachel's outgrown velvet jumpers. My newish breasts press against the scalloped opening of an embroidered caftan, a semi-hippie style bought in the Arab market in Jerusalem. I can no longer hear the word *bush* – Moses and the burning bush; a bird in the hand is worth two in the bush – without thinking, blushingly, of my own recently sprung undergrowth. The world has turned scratchy with sexual possibility.

"Do you think he'll last?" my father asks.

My father, who inhabits the same apartment as I do, lives worlds away during the week. It is only on Shabbos that he surfaces, at the other end of the dining room table, to discuss what I think of as Current Events with someone male and powerful.

"For a while, Walter, like any politician," the guest, Mr. Hans, replies. "You and me – we could do better with one hand tied behind our backs."

Someone has been elected to high office somewhere, in Jerusalem or Paris or London or New York – it is all the same to me. None of this cares for my feelings, least of all my father. I look into my silver soup spoon, seeking the containable, the world inside me. I shift my spoon until my father's face is reflected in its curve, distorted but nonetheless there. After years of living with him, I am still looking for my father.

My father laughs, delighted by a skepticism that matches his own. "They say he's capable. Do you believe it?"

The heavy gold watch on Mr. Hans's wrist shines below his snowy white cuff. He nods his head, as though agreeing with himself in advance. "He knows how to get his way, there's no doubt about that. The financial disclosures alone would have ruined a weaker man. For the rest, wait and see is my opinion."

"He's tough, no doubt about it," my father says, taking a heap of rice from the bowl our cook Louisa holds out to him. "And I think he knows how to handle the Americans."

"Not so much rice, Valter," my mother protests, ritually. "Louisa, don't let Mr. Lehmann have too much gravy."

I cross my ankles under the table, a grumpy fifteen-year-old. Does anyone realize I have *breasts*? Why does my father ignore all the circumstantial details that other men seem intrigued by – the bracelet of green, red, and blue stones that blinks, like a headlight, on the arm of Mr. Hans's wife, or the fact that I don't look exactly the same as I did only a year ago, that my body now bears visible signs of femaleness?

"The economy can't get any worse, that's for certain," Mr. Hans says. "What do you say?" He turns to my brother Eric, who is sitting on his left, as if to solicit his opinion, and then turns back to my father.

"True," my father says. "And maybe he'll get things under control."

Lily holds out her hand in front of her like the woman in the Palmolive commercial and admires my mother's diamond ring, which she is wearing.

"It looks good on me, don't you think?"

No one listens to anyone in this family. We never have.

"It's too big," I say. "Or your fingers are too short. Or fat. Something."

The diamond, round and defined, signals blue, yellow, pink, and white in the combined glow of the candles and chandelier. Mr. Hans, who sounds to me as if he is insistently repeating himself, continues to talk to my father. My father is amorphous as the world outside my head, the world Out There.

"A good man," he says of someone Mr. Hans has proposed. "But he has no clout."

Between the two of them, they will remake the affairs of a country in which neither of them live but both have a stake in, half sentimental and half paternalistic. If I were a small foreign country, a Jewish state, would my father notice my breasts?

Mrs. Hans smiles at my mother. "Everything is so delicious," she says, although I notice she has left most of the fish salad and hasn't taken second helpings of anything.

"Don't be fooled," I want to say but don't. "My mother doesn't cook. She's not my real mother."

"Thank you," my mother says.

"What was the name of the actor who played Dobie Gillis on the 'Dobie Gillis' show?" Rachel asks.

"Maynard something," my older brother Benjamin says. "I think he killed himself."

"Really?" Rachel says. "But wasn't Maynard the name of another character on the show? Maynard G. Krebs. They always included his middle initial."

"Dwayne Hickman played Dobie Gillis," Eric says all-knowingly. "Dwayne Hickman."

"Benjamin's always making things up that he doesn't know," I say. "George Reeves is the one who killed himself."

"Everyone knows that," Benjamin says. "The guy who played Superman jumping out the window because he was afraid of heights. It's an old story, and that's not what I was talking about."

"Shut up," Eric says. "I'm trying to listen."

"Big shot," Benjamin says, snorting.

Eric flushes; "big shot" has hit the mark, reducing him to his own place on the left side of Mr. Hans, who spurns him in favor of my father.

"Pass the cookies," Lily says. "Please."

Rachel plucks a sugar cube with a pair of silver tongs from out of the bowl and puts it in her mouth, under her tongue, holding it in place until she can follow it with a bath of hot tea. I don't know where she developed this homely habit of sucking sugar while sipping tea, but whenever she does it, it is as though someone has slipped into her chair at the table. Instead of my sister – Rachel Lehmann of the glasses and brown hair – there appears in front of me the figure of an elderly Eastern European Jew. Frail and modest, he is a Jew I'm not actually acquainted with, but who is to be found in stories and novels, bent over a cup of tea at one of those large, well-lit cafeterias, Dubrow's or Famous, grasping a cube of sugar with the remnants of his teeth.

"Your children seem so marvelously close," Mrs. Hans says.

But hasn't she noticed that we are all miles apart even as we sit together at the Shabbos table? That Eric holds his tie up close and studies its pattern of polka dots as though someone has asked him for an exact count? That my youngest brother Arthur says nothing when he is here and that he disappeared from the table a while ago?

My mother smiles briefly – I think of it as her hostess smile – and says, "When they're not fighting."

"Well, they'll never be lonely," Mrs. Hans says. "So many! You must have had your hands full when they were little."

"You have children of your own?" my mother asks.

"Just two," Mrs. Hans says, as though she had secretly longed to produce a horde like my mother's. "A boy and a girl. My daughter's married."

"Oh, how nice," my mother says. "One of each."

"The lay of the land," my father is saying.

"Quite, quite," Mr. Hans says.

What Mr. and Mrs. Hans, securely enclosed in their guestdom, don't know is everything of importance.

What I have to go on are the words my father likes, words like *tough*, *clout*, and *order*. Just to think of the word *clout* makes me laugh; it sounds so much like what it's trying to be – a fist pounding on the table, a voice hollering, "Listen here, you." Although it is clear to me even when I am very young that my father has swallowed this word, like the whale swallowed Jonah, and that it now resides inside of him, I am not sure how *clout* works. For instance, do you need only to want it to have it?

❖   ❖   ❖

I am twelve years old, my tanned feet poking out from a brand-new pair of Nimrod sandals – no more than a few crisscrossed straps of brown leather – and my hair swept off my face with a headband. I am in the midst of imagining that I look very Israeli, that I have grown up on a kibbutz and am not afraid of anything, when my father, fueled by some mechanism that I can't see, decides not to wait on the long, straggly checkout line in the lobby of our hotel in Jerusalem.

"Wait a minute," he says to me.

"Where are you going?"

"I'll be right back," he says, giving me his *Jerusalem Post* to hold. "Keep an eye out for your mother. She said she'll be down soon."

He strides forward, coming down hard on the outer side of his heels, his knees locking into the joints. He goes past groups of heavywaisted women holding plastic flight bags that say TWA and EL AL and PERFECT TRAVEL, past silver-haired men in sunglasses wearing peaked sailor caps and bright, well-pressed clothes, as though the sandy, volatile Middle Eastern country they have come to see exists only as an image to be played with in their minds, a toy yacht.

"There's a line, sir. We're all waiting."

The woman who says this as my father walks by has a hairdo that looks as if it has been sprayed into immobility, and he heeds her reproach not at all. As I pretend to be caught up in the line of my Nimrod sandals, I take in the fact that my father is now signaling to someone behind the front desk and that the woman with the hairdo is agitating further.

"Arnie," she says, addressing a man wearing clothes the color of a beach ball – royal blue Bermuda shorts and a red and white checked shirt – "who does that guy think he is? There's a line here. This is a democracy!"

"Take it easy, Edith. Maybe it's an emergency."

Her husband stands several yards in front of her, and he talks to her from over his shoulder, as though it were imperative that he keep watch on the view ahead.

"This is a democracy!" the woman repeats. "We're all Americans here."

Her husband turns his head, and the two of them look back toward me. I smile at them sadly, hoping they will take me for an orphan, a young but diligent visitor, a reconnoiterer of foreign opinions – a reader of *The Jerusalem Post*.

"This is Israel," her husband says. "Wait till you get home."

I wonder what is to happen when she gets home. Is she the kind of woman who thrives on creating fusses wherever she goes, in supermarkets and movie lines? Has her husband become desperately peace-loving in the face of her willingness to take up arms? And what will she do when she discovers that my father isn't an American, after all?

"Well, I still think we should say something," she says, but she sounds pacified. "Where'd Sheila say she was going?"

"There she is now," her husband says, smiling broadly at the tall girl corning toward them. "We missed you, sweetheart."

"I just went to get a Coke. Mom, please, it's fine."

Sheila, who is very tanned and looks several years older than I do, shrugs off her mother's efforts to straighten the Peter Pan collar of her short-sleeved Villager blouse. Her mother's bangle bracelets click whenever she moves her arm, and I note enviously that Sheila is wearing a pair of elegant high-heeled sandals.

"God, their Coke is so bad! I can't wait to get home and taste real food again!"

Sheila doesn't pronounce *Coke* the way I do; she hugs the *o*, making it sound almost French: *coeuq*. Her mother seems to have completely forgotten my father's undemocratic behavior in the light of her daughter's return. She stands close to her, watching with an almost fearful affection, as though at any moment Sheila might go off again in search of another substandard refreshment.

"Daddy felt the same way about the ice cream here, didn't you, Arnie?"

"You girls," the husband says, shaking his head as though struck by his own powers of tolerance. "I can't take you anywhere."

"Don't be stupid, Daddy," Sheila says, giggling. "I *love* traveling."

I look over to the front desk, where a thickly mustached man – the same desk manager who has to be called out from some inner sanctum whenever I forget my room key – with whom my father has been in head-to-head conversation for the past ten minutes, suddenly lifts his hands, his shoulders thrust upward and elbows bent. There are dark ovals under the arms of his light blue shirt, and his gesture seems like a dramatization of defeat or frustration. But when he brings his hands back down, something has been decided, for my father pumps his hand like a victor. The deal has been decided in everyone's favor, which is conveniently his.

"Don't be stupid, Daddy, I *love* traveling." I practice saying this to myself as my father strides back toward me.

"All settled," he says.

What a wonderful purring tone it has: "Don't be stupid, Daddy. . . ." I could be –
Sally Field with her smile that stretched like a rubber band, or pert-nosed Hayley
Mills, a daughter in the movies or on TV.

❖   ❖   ❖

If I had said anything along these lines to my father, he wouldn't have known
what to make of it, there being no precedent for this sort of exchange between us. In
later years I will connect a recurring feeling of futility in myself to the recognition,
while still a little girl, that my father was not seducible – that he took me in without
being in any way stirred by the proposition that I existed. The fact that he was not in
love with Lily or Rachel, either, should have been a source of consolation, but it
wasn't.

My father is my mother's: it is that simple. What, I wonder over the years, would
it be like to have a father who is in love with *me*? Once, for his birthday, I wrote a
poem, which I read aloud. "My father is the midnight owl," it began and moved on
from there to talk of his love of bananas and how he rummaged for them late at
night.

Everyone was gathered around the dining room table at the beach house and
listened with what seemed to be an air of incredulity. Or maybe I only imagined this
response, out of my own unyielding embarrassment. My father sat in one of his
sultanlike paisley dressing gowns, Sulka's latest whorling-patterned silk. After I
finished reading the poem, he kissed my check, thrusting his lips out as though to
stamp them upon my skin, and made some mild joke. Rachel said, "How nice,
Hannah," and Eric said, "I really like it. Good stuff." So why did I end up in tears? I
went upstairs and lay down on my bed, face into the pillow. I didn't know why I
was crying so hard. I wanted my feelings to stay far away from me, to go bother
some other girl; they had no recourse in this family. If only I could have split myself
in two like Patty Duke did on her show – produce an identical cousin on whom I
could fob off my worse self. . . . After a while I went back downstairs, where everyone was eating birthday cake, and no one commented on my disappearance. My
mother passed me a piece of cake, vanilla with chocolate frosting, on a pink paper
plate, with a spoon and napkin to match. There was nothing missing that you could
see.

I imagine my father saved the piece of paper on which this poem was written, the
way he saved all our stuff – diplomas (Rachel's and Benjamin's outnumbering the
rest of ours), citations, birthday cards (Lily's being the most painstaking, with bits of
yarn and colored chalk and verses in French), a scattering of report cards. His affection displayed itself best in this sort of chronicled remove, a passion for documenta-
tion. I bet if you looked for it today, you could find it somewhere in a box or file in
his office downtown, a graying piece of blue-lined notebook paper where, in the
spotty ink from a Bic pen, my squat adolescent handwriting composed a blurred
image of a love poem.

But when I try and think of a clearer connection between myself and my father, then and now, I come up with the name of a TV show – one that eluded my actual viewing experience but that is known to me as a concept and as a name: "The Price Is Right." My father is always talking price; even when he is talking politics, he is talking price, value for your money. He reports on everything – all he has read, seen, and heard – with a succinct detachment, as though he were addressing a shareholders' meeting: "Seven up, three down. Trade today."

How, then, can I talk to him, ask for advice on my runny problems, problems that recognize no bottom line in their vast expenditures of feeling? When I knock on his study door seeking some of the lucidity I lack and that my mother keeps assuring me he can provide, he puts down his paper, folded into neat and very readable quadrants. Over the years I attempt these talks with my father, always at my mother's urging, about pending decisions– the decisions of a daughter. Should I go to summer camp? Should I travel to Europe on my own? And once, in my early twenties, in a never-to-be-repeated flurry – should I marry? Invariably these talks would become monologues, my father waxing enthusiastic about the logic – or illogic – of going to summer camp, traveling to Europe, getting married. His enthusiasm is founded on facts, statistics – the making and unmaking of corporations. (About my marriage prospect he peered at me and said, 'Just as long as you're not marrying him for his earning power." Buy me, sell me: it would be comic if I weren't the object.) I would sit on the very edge of the couch adjacent to his easy chair, silently nodding, having crawled back under cover of mute agreement into some primordial part of myself that was beyond the call of reason. When I think back on them, it seems to me that all these occasions were fraudulent from the start, insoluble – and my father believed in solutions – because they arose from a basic and fatal incapacity on my part. Behind each and every occasion that presented itself for a decision, I felt only dread, a panic about the consequentiality, the separateness, that all decision-making implied – even tiny, girlish decisions. If only I could say to my father:

"I can't move. I can never go anywhere even though I look perfectly fit because I can't leave my mother, your wife."

What I would most like to know, need to know, but don't ask is this: Am *I* value for his money? I don't think so, not at all, but can he trade me in for a more cost-efficient model? He is Pharaoh, and I am Joseph; the best I can do is to be of use, indispensable, point out that a famine is on the way and he would do well to set in supplies. My father likes people – children – who can be relied on to get things done. So it is that one winter, about the middle of January, he hits upon the perfect approximation, his form of affection.

It is the same winter I witness my cousin Beatrice screaming at the foot of the stairs and begin to have insomnia, a precursor of the pitfalls of adulthood. Come twelve, one o'clock in the morning, I can't fall asleep. Everything is keeping me awake: the library books, already overdue, I must remember to return; our nurse Lena, whom I'm afraid of; Naomi Litt, whom I want to like me but who only does so when she isn't "against" me; my mother, whom I'm afraid of; my arms, which aren't entirely smooth-skinned the way Rachel's are but are covered with a sprinkling of light brown hair, which may any day get worse and render me a full-scale freak, just like the Monkey Girl I have seen a photograph of in Benjamin's book of freaks (his favorite book after *The FBI Story*); my father, whom I'm afraid of; Lily, who is always watching me and who I wish would die instantly, clearing me from the necessity of submitting to her unfriendly, ready-to-be-jealous gaze; the geography test that I haven't studied enough for and even if I did, it wouldn't help because I still have no idea where the different states go. (No matter how many times I study the filled-in map, all visual grasp flees my mind the minute I am confronted by the blank outline in Mrs. Gordon's class with the instructions: *Fill in the fifty states.* What am I to do with Oregon and Utah and Wyoming, reduced to one unlocatable jumble, but assign them haphazard places – tucking them in around other states whose neighbors I can't remember, Florida and Louisiana?) There is every reason in the world – in my world – to be awake at midnight, but most of all there is the dull clang of my self-dislike, striking the hour of awful truth like the most discordant of clocks: Hannah Lehmann, I am as I am, wrong. If I were right, it wouldn't be possible to feel such aversion to my own skin; I would have a mother other than mine, a mother who wouldn't say, unnaturally, "Your tears don't move me," when I cry. How can I feel right unless she is all wrong, and how can she be all wrong when I long for her, loathe and desire her, and don't think I will ever cease longing?

How did my father, having no direct link with me, decipher that now was the time to prove my case, that his youngest daughter – me, Hannah – was in some slow-dawning but nonetheless genuine fashion, imperiled? Did my mother who was the usual conduit of news about "the children," good or bad, relay the symptoms of trouble? And whose idea was it to have my father, for a period of a few months, pay me a quarter every weekday evening to hang up his coat on one of the thick wooden hangers with the three initials – WLM – ornately engraved in the center? Whosoever idea, it was an inspired one: I loved my stint as my father's personal hat-check girl, greeting him at the front door and then helping him off with his heavy, single-breasted black wool overcoat. There was also a double-breasted taupe coat of cashmere, and an English raincoat. To be paid for taking my father's coat from him as he shrugged it off and for then walking several feet to hang it up in the small downstairs closet was, most clearly, to be paid for doing nothing at all – for being me. Someone – a psychiatrist my mother consulted? – must have suggested that what I needed was to feel singled out, special, loved. Although this undoubtedly was what Lily, Rachel, Benjamin, Eric, and Arthur needed, too, it was I who had begun to exhibit certain bothersome clues to a state of inner distress, small resistances in my natural functioning.

Interestingly enough, it wasn't Lily – whom I would have expected to complain about my special treatment – but Eric who was most resentful. "But she's not *doing* anything!" I could hear him say to my mother somewhere in the house when my father's key turned in the lock. "I could do the same thing even better!"

There wasn't much my mother could argue back under the circumstances, but once in a while I would hear her reply soothingly, "It's a girl's job," as though *that* had anything to do with anything.

I'm not sure why this odd ritual came to an end, but I think Eric's protests helped hasten its demise; it had been created to make me feel less overlooked, not to point up another child's similar sense of bereavement. While it lasted, though, I felt assuaged by the pretense that I worked, of an evening, at the "21" Club and that my father was a passing gentleman whose tip came about logically, as my due. Buy me, sell me – why, it made sense! The whole exchange took a matter of seconds, but it felt wonderfully clear-cut, without the web of emotion I generally spun around both my parents – that hopelessly entangling skein of anger and need and pain.

I had heard about the "21" Club to begin with from my father. His on-the-town anecdotes were one of the things I liked about him, the snatches of songs he remembered from what I took to be his *bon vivant* days at "21," the Stork Club, and the Latin Quarter. "Sam, You Made the Pants Too Long" was his favorite tune; he would break into it when he was in an especially relaxed mood – on a Friday night without any guests – sing a raucous line or two, and then fade out. "That's all I remember," he would say, smiling broadly while looking around the table, as though he had just belted out a show-stopping number and was now expecting a storm of applause. "What can you do?" he'd say. "My memory's not so good anymore. I work too hard supporting all you kids." And then he'd try it once again, braying the music, hamming up the chorus, his voice strong but not particularly lilting. There were other songs he liked – "Get Me to the Church on Time," which he tried to do like Stanley Holloway, and "Two Ladies in the Shade of the Banana Tree," which he claimed had been made popular by a twin-sister singing team with a German-sounding name, whom none of us had ever heard of.

Once, to my amazement, as if to throw out a rope from my father's raft of memories to mine, these mythical sisters actually showed up on "The Ed Sullivan Show" while I sat watching it with Rachel and Eric. This was the only TV program we were allowed to watch regularly in those years, a fitting finish to the specialness that was Sunday. Eric loved the little talking mouse, Topo Gigio; it was what he watched the show for. Topo Gigio had only to pronounce Ed Sullivan's name, "Ed-tie, pu-leez, Ed-tie," to send Eric into howls of delight. Rachel and I watched all the acts with equal and indiscriminate passion, from jugglers to ventriloquists to torch singers like Nancy Wilson. Lily disdained the show altogether, and the only times Benjamin sat through the whole thing was when Ed Sullivan announced that one of his stable of wisecracking comedians would be on, Alan King or Rodney Dangerfield or George Carlin. That evening it was just the three of us, Rachel, Eric, and me (Arthur was too young to stay up during most of the Ed Sullivan period), when suddenly there they were: blonde and buxom and very guttural, the pair swayed their ample hips in unison as they harmonized the refrain of "Two Ladies in the Shade of the Banana Tree."

I was so excited to see them in living flesh that I went around singing their hit to myself for weeks afterward, stringing out the syllables in "ban-nah-nah tree" just as they had. I think I even convinced myself for a while that these sisters had been my father's girlfriends before he met my mother – part of a distant bachelor past in which he went incessantly to nightclubs, a white silk scarf dangling from under his coat collar. In actuality, although my father married late and was by far the oldest father among the fathers I knew – grandfatherly age, in fact – he was never quite the apogee of rakishness I would have liked to believe him to have been. The female whom he escorted most often to the clubs (pocketing match-books from each, just as he always snitched hand towels from the foreign hotels he stayed in) was undoubtedly my mother, during the two years of their on-again, off-again courtship. But the reality of who my father was – or had once been – didn't much matter at these moments when he was at his ease, taking jolly part in a culture that was recognizable to me rather than recounting with great sentiment some aspect of his youth in Germany that sounded alien and intrinsically unappealing. I came closest to loving my father when he sat in his white Shabbos shirt with one button opened at the neck, tie-less, singing bits and pieces of American tunes. I could almost see him then as a harmless progenitor, safely consigned to caricature, a slightly tipsy but amiable fellow: Eliza Doolittle's father as played by Stanley Holloway in *My Fair Lady*.

What strikes me as odd in retrospect is not that there were things I liked about my father – the sandy feel of his cheeks after Shabbos, for instance, when he hadn't been able to shave for a day – but that they were highlighted so inordinately. Sitting on his lap, in my velvet jumper, I delighted in running my fingers across the grain of his grown-in bristles, his skin the texture of an emery board. When I am older and no longer invited to sit on his lap or so readily intrigued by analogous incidentals – something that looks or feels like something else, like Eric's velvet skating jacket reminding me of artichokes – there are even fewer means of contact. Throughout the years of my adolescence, I recall my father taking note of me only when I get a haircut, as though each successive one were further demonstration of the erratic nature he suspects me of harboring – the demons of Beatrice come to haunt the next generation. "I see you've cut your hair again," he says on a Tuesday night somewhere in my past. It is winter, the windowsills are bejeweled with snow. We have bumped into each other in the kitchen: my father is scavenging for a banana and I am looking for a snack, a reprieve from my schoolwork. His tone is subtly preening, as though he prides himself on his unlikely but keen visual sense: he is a man who notices haircuts.

"Yes ," I say. "Do you think it looks better than before?"

I am always trying to improve on "before"; before is never good enough. There is magic in "after," the same magic that will draw me in later years to lovers who don't like me as I am, who see in me a redoubtable object. In the land of "after," I will be unconditionally loved; I have only to find the entry to it, the inspiring aureole.

"I don't know," my father says. "I liked it longer. You look different."

"Really?" I say. "Don't you think I look better?"

My father unpeels a banana, dividing and conquering the yellow skin around the white fruit. I wonder for a moment how he would fare in a blizzard, bereft of warm clothes – I have just been lying upstairs on my bed, reading the second half of *King Lear* for an advanced English class the next day. Exposed to the elements, with Eric as his faithful Fool, would my father finally recognize he has misjudged me – his youngest daughter, pure as I am honest, his Cordelia?

"Maybe," he says, not unkindly. "Could be I'm just not used to it ."

Mirror, mirror on the wall, who's the fairest of us all? It is not Lily or Rachel I'm competing with so much as myself – a reflection that will do me justice.

"See you," I say.

These discussions with my father about my appearance, minute as they are, make me feel shy – as if I had been picked out, flooded with light.

"Hair grows," he says.

"Yeah," I say, although I have just had mine cut expressly to counteract this tendency. I am holding a glass of juice and a rocky piece of streusel cake – the buttery crumbs of its topping now gone hard as pellets – to take upstairs with me.

"Your mother starves me," my father says, eyeing my cake.

"You don't look starved," I say.

He pulls his chest up with feigned dignity and says, "Appearances are deceiving."

"Poor man," I say, giggling. My father's abiding appetite is a family joke.

"Good night," he says, shaking his head and shuffling off to his study in his slippers; his feet under his Sulka pajamas are dimpled and white, the feet of a king.

The haircut my father was having difficulty adjusting to was very short, nearly androgynous. What I've looked for in hairdressers, from the age of fifteen up, has nothing to do with their skill at improving my looks. It has to do with a quality of attentiveness, an obsession with an abstract ideal of beauty – the beauty that will insure my father's undying devotion – equal to my own. The hairdressers I go to more than once are invariably fastidious and acutely homosexual. They know nothing of my quest; they know only of my hair and what they wish to do with it, a reflection of their whimsy rather than my need. I'm not even sure some of them – those with distant fathers of their own – might not have been sympathetic to my wish had I bothered to explain it. What I desired was a haircut – like the perfectly fitting glass slipper in the Cinderella story – that would transport me from my grungy state into a condition of chosenness: I am the belle of the ball, the one who wins the hand of the father-prince.

Proust's Tea

BY NORMAN MANEA

The people crowding outside the big, heavy, wooden doors, curious about the spectacle, were perhaps themselves travelers, or their companions, or loiterers of the sort often found in train stations, but on that afternoon not one of them was allowed into the waiting room. Nor could they see what was going on inside. The windows were too high, the rectangular glass panes in the doors too dirty and clouded with steam.

The waiting room was immense; it was hard to imagine anything bringing it to life; everything got lost, swallowed up in it. Crouched over their bundles, people in rags were huddling one on top of the other in clusters from the walls all the way to the center, filling up the room. The din was unending.

Shrill and desperate voices, hoarse voices, sometimes deep moans, grew suddenly louder when the nurses came by. The white uniforms barely managed to squeeze through the tangle of legs and bodies. Hands rose up all around to grab hold of the hems, the sleeves, even the shoulders, necks, and arms of these fine ladies. People were screaming, begging, groaning, cursing. Some were crying, especially those who were too far away and had lost all hope of getting a packet of food and a cup.

Those crowded on the other side of the wood and thick glass doors would have tried in vain to guess ages and sexes from the faces on the mass of skeletons, dressed in rags tied with string, that crammed into the waiting room. The women all looked like old, wretched convicts, and children with oversized skulls popped up all around them like apocalyptic men, compressed, stunted, as if an instrument of torture had shrunk them all.

The nurses knew, of course, that there were no men in the waiting room, nor young women. Had they understood the cries and the wailing around them, they would have realized that it was this very absence that aggravated the panic: the rescued did not understand, nor did they want to accept, that they had been saved. They suspected that this was a new ruse, even more diabolical, that would undoubtedly lead to new tortures, perhaps even to the end. Why else had the men and able-bodied young women been left behind? To bring them here later, on another train? Because there hadn't been enough room? Perhaps someone had objected to piling them on top of one another?

They could have done without those big, luxurious railway cars that swayed like imperial barges . . . They wouldn't have minded traveling in carts, walking for miles and miles, so long as they'd been allowed to stay together, husbands, wives, sisters, sons and daughters, the old and the children, all of them.

Shorn like the others, her head covered by some sort of burlap hood, the woman before whom the nurse had stopped was ageless like the rest. She made no sound. She had not said a word when the person next to her had taken from her hands a piece of blanket and covered herself with it. She didn't flinch when the old woman on her left, sensing in her silence a confirmation of her own foreboding, became excited, raising her arms to the sky. Finally she lifted her head: a face shrunken, withered, old, like a Phoenician mask. But she didn't move, not even when the nurse passed by. She just kept watching, intense, like the midget resting its small yellowish head on her bare shoulder.

The air in the room quivered with heat. The continuous pulsing rumble of the mass lowered the ceiling and pulled the walls in closer. The hall had shrunk. Everything was happening close to the ground, at the height of the crowd. Only when you threw your head back and looked up did the ceiling recede, like a soaring, ever more unreachable sky. From the heights, the noise lagged, distant, weak, somewhere down below. Those who remained on the ground were deafened by it, drained by fear, oblivious to everything.

She, too, couldn't stop thinking about what might be happening on the train that never arrived. She couldn't have been allowed on board, she knew all too well that she looked like an old woman, no one would have believed that she was not yet thirty. But then she would have had no reason to want to be on the train for men and young women. Surely she too had seen how they had clung to each other without shame – my father and my cousin – the moment they left the lineup. She did not look at them, but without a doubt she had seen everything. Disciplined, she had joined her column, holding in her limp hand the hand of the midget trailing behind her. She didn't even yank at his arm as she helped him climb the high steps onto the train. She saw that the child, when he reached the top of the steps, had turned his wrinkled face toward the two who were left on the platform, sitting on the bench too close to each other. But the woman had not said a word; she sat down on the seat in the train and closed her eyes, exhausted.

Perhaps the commotion of so many confused voices coming from down below overwhelmed her, allowed her to forget, but suddenly she had turned around, pushing against the little midget's scrawny neck and dislodging him from his nest. In any event, her bony, dampish shoulder could not replace, even in the child's memory or dreams, the plump, fresh cheeks of the pillow he craved.

The hands that touched the neck and the matchstick arms of the little savage were those of the lady in the white uniform. The lady was smiling at the little midget, bending over him, the red cross on her forehead shining, coming nearer. She held out the bag of biscuits and the tin cup.

The cup was hot. The little beast's cheeks bent over the yellowish, liquid circle, into the fragrant steam. A pleasure that could not last; a pleasure one should not dare prolong, no matter what happiness one felt. An impossible pleasure, but real, because the hall was real too, and buzzing, and he heard the bag being ripped open over his head, and his hand filled with biscuits.

The boy sipped, numb with pleasure, frightened. He understood that everything was real and, therefore, that it would end; it was he, giddy with delight, who impatiently hastened its end. The cup was half emptied. He stopped drinking and looked at the stubby, fat biscuits in the palm of his hand. He began to nibble, patiently, on one of the grainy, sweet, scallop-edged shells. Only then did he feel hunger. He grabbed the bag with one hand. In the other he held the cup. He shoved a fistful of biscuits into his mouth. A little midget who inspired tenderness however ghastly he looked, and so the lady put an extra bag in his mother's hand.

"Drink the tea also. Drink, while it's still hot."

Perhaps the souls of those we've lost do indeed take refuge in inanimate objects. They remain absent until the moment they feel our presence nearby and call out to us for recognition, to free them from death. Perhaps, indeed, the past cannot be brought back on command, but is resurrected only by that strange, spontaneous sensation we feel when unexpectedly we come across the smell, the taste, the flavor of some inert accessory from the past.

But the aroma of that heavenly drink could not be reminiscent of anything; he had never experienced such pleasure. This magic potion could not, by any stretch of the imagination, be called "tea."

So it was necessary to look up toward the sky of dirty stone, where black clouds of flies swarmed, and where he expected Grandfather to appear, the only person who would have had an answer.

They had gathered, as usual, around him, everyone was holding his hot cup of greenish water infused with local herbs picked in those alien places, to which Grandfather would add, whenever he found them, acacia blossoms.

High up on the arched ceiling of the waiting room, where the light bulbs attracted billows of insects, Grandfather appeared as if on a round screen, and Grandmother, and his parents, and his aunt. They were warming their hands on the steaming cups, all of them staring at the same point high above, in front of them. Anda was there, too, of course. She took part, humble, submissive, but shameless enough, nevertheless, not to miss the tea ritual to which Grandfather summoned everybody, sometimes looking at each person a long time, letting them know that he knew everything about everybody, even about his son-in-law and this beautiful and guilty granddaughter.

Grandfather did not take his eyes off the little white cube of sugar that hung, as usual, from the ceiling lamp. They all had to stare at it intensely for some minutes before sipping the hot water. Those who remembered the taste of sugar, those, that is, who had the time, before the disaster, to accustom their palates to the sweetness of the little white lumps, gradually felt their lips become wet and sticky. The brackish green drink became sweet, good, "real tea," as Grandfather would say.

The ceremony was repeated almost every afternoon, presided over sternly yet not without a touch of humor by the old man, his unkempt beard mottled in black. He was convinced that he would return home, and he conserved as a symbol of that world, and for that world, a dirty sugar cube. While the boiling water was being poured, no one was allowed to look anywhere but in his own cup, and one waited to hear the water splash and bubble in the neighboring cup, until one by one all of them were filled. Then everyone raised his eyes toward the lamp from which a tiny parallelepiped of almost white sugar hung on a string. They had to stare at it patiently for a long time, and had to sip the tea slowly, until everyone felt his lips, tongue, mouth, his entire being refreshed, mellowed by the memory of a world they must not give up, because, Grandfather firmly believed, it had not given them up and could not do without them. The tea steamed in the cups; everyone was silent, all concentrating, as they had been told to, on a small, dirty cube of sugar that Grandfather had had the idea to save and hang up in front of them every day.

Up there, above the din in which the poor wretches tried, uselessly, to return to another life, up there, in an open space, isolated from the huge waiting room, Grandfather, confident in a return that would not come to pass, could have assured them that the magic potion was indeed proof that the world had welcomed them back. But even this strange drink did not remotely resemble "real tea."

"Dunk the biscuits in the tea. Drink it while it's hot."

"Drink while it's hot," repeated now one woman, now another.

Dunked in the tea, the plump, round biscuits had the very flavor of happiness –

had there been time for surrender, utter abandon, a dizzying fullness of feeling, the priceless gifts that only a chosen few can hope to deserve, and that some day must be returned in a miraculous exchange.

The biscuits tasted like soap, mud, rust, burnt skin, snow, leaves, rain, bones, sand, mold, wet wool, sponges, mice, rotting wood, fish, the unique flavor of hunger.

There are, then, certain gifts whose only quality and only flaw is that they cannot be exchanged for anything else. Such gifts cannot, at some later time, be recalled, repossessed, or returned.

If, later, I lost anything, it was precisely the cruelty of indifference. But only later, and with difficulty. Because, much later, I became what is called . . . a feeling being.

Translated from the Romanian by Mara Soceanu-Vamos

Weddings

A town with dusty streets lined by giant, disheveled trees. Sunlight lingered in large, well-tended courtyards. The morning rose slowly; noon hovered, indolent, over the loud, seemingly endless lunch. So many and such unusual courses, slowed down even further by a knife and fork too heavy for the boy's greediness and impatience.

Evenings came swiftly. Families lined up in rows and chairs and benches in front of low white houses, recounting stories about the war until after midnight. The silence of the crystalline sky lent their voices a strange clarity and sadness.

They hadn't moved in yet with their other relatives on the outskirts of the small town. They still lived in the center with the teachers.

Daylight burst suddenly, like an enormous orange balloon pierced by a shaft of light. Joyful young voices animated the main street. Windows flew open at the laughter and singing of the first groups that passed by. A Sunday, sort of fresh and impetuous as there hadn't been before stirred up the calm of the early morning streets. People wandered about, restless, perplexed; met, separated, sought each other out, converged.

It seemed that everyone, lured by the colors and excitement of the street, was outside. The columns of people kept getting bigger, overflowing the sidewalks, advancing in ever denser waves.

Pushed and carried by the crowd, he kept his balance by holding his cousin's hand. The small town rose on a wave of anticipation. Entire convoys, compact rows of heads bobbed toward the mark. There he would be giving his speech.

He would have liked to hurl himself into the midst of the exuberant, dancing crowd.

Walking tired him. They still knew nothing about his mission; the secret weighed on him. From all directions the wind carried the sound of loud voices, a deafening chorus. The sun filtered down in lazy rays, giving him vertigo.

His cousin dragged him along, occasionally squeezing his hand to remind him that he was still there. He understood that the boy was defending himself the way he usually did, with apathy. Efforts to make the boy tougher had failed, and finally, exhausted, he had resigned himself to the child's weakness and confusion.

Little by little, methodically, he tried to understand the boy's character. But he did not suspect how accustomed the boy was to withdrawing, as soon as he was figured out, and seeking new hiding places.

For the past month, since his acquisition of so many relatives in this unfamiliar town, the boy had been staying with his cousin, the teacher. A tender refuge, one might have thought, for from the start he cheerfully indulged the curiosity and kindness these people showed him. Soon after his arrival he had succeeded in forgetting the feeling of suffocation that had seized him at times in the past. His hosts were always ready to cheer him up, to please him with some surprise, keep him company.

Thus for almost a week they had prepared him with soothing words for the blue vitriol bath. They convinced him to associate the words "blue vitriol" – words that in fact seemed to belong to a foreign realm – with the miracle of his future growth, his becoming as big and strong as other children his age. The hypocrisy of his garrulous relatives hit him too late. Their deceitful words burned like scalding needles on his red, inflamed flesh. The water was boiling, stinging. His screams were to no avail, they held him down, determined, their tender smiles gone. Eventually, satisfied, they informed him that he was cured of his scabies.

He didn't feel the suffocation then. He felt it in the afternoon when he met with the teacher to rehearse his speech. He had learned to avoid each new trap as it was laid for him. He no longer made the mistake of believing he was secure among his own people. Aloof, indifferent, he observed the smug teacher so trusting in his own intuitions. The sessions with this cousin had turned into a game played by someone else; he no longer had reason to rebel.

Recent confrontations had taught him even more than the incident of the blue vitriol bath. At first he had let himself be deceived by the manly camaraderie – no baby-talk, no hugging – that the teacher seemed to be offering. He waited for him, happy, as in a dream. So that it seemed only natural to tell the events of his life in answer to the questions this newfound cousin kept asking him.

"Were you afraid there?"

"Yes, in the evening."

"Did they beat you?"

"Seldom. I hid from them. I wasn't scared of them."

"What scared you, then?"

"The evenings. Beautiful evenings. Fields, fields, stretching as far as the eye could see. Very beautiful evenings."

"Is that what frightened you?"

"Yes. A desert all around. Crows. I don't know. Silence. The fields went on forever. The silence too."

The cousin paused.

"I see. You were terrified by the vastness of it all. And the others?"

"They prayed, they whispered. Some cried. I was alone."

"What was the hardest thing?"

"The food."

The conversations were followed by long walks, during which the teacher found out everything he wanted to know. Sometimes he wrote things in a notebook with a shiny blue cover that he would whisk out from his shirt pocket.

"Did you ever cry?"

"When Grandfather died. He was the closest to me."

"Were there happier days too?"

"Yes, when Mara got sick the first time. They took me to Uncle's so I wouldn't catch it."

The boy paid attention to him as to an older brother; he gave him his full trust. He forgot that the others, too, had walked him to the threshold of friendship, and then suddenly had revealed their true faces. They enjoyed the sight of the extreme suffering of others, it amused them . . . He had forgotten. He didn't have the time to prepare himself and was caught unawares by his cousin's other face.

The speech sounded good; they practiced it every day. It contained everything he had told his cousin, but arranged differently; it was shorter, with new words. "Silence all around," he had said; it became "a vast Silence," no great improvement even if he didn't understand it.

Then, suddenly, the teacher became harsh, turned cold and somber like a raven.

"It's no good, it's not good at all! You've got to speak louder! If you don't nobody will hear you. Louder, louder, do you understand?"

This shouting caught him by surprise, paralyzed him. But he quickly found his voice again, hoping to appease the maniac: ". . . our brothers, in whose hands we saw a loaf of bread, when we had forgotten what bread looked like. And we say to you, let us not forget, let us not forgive, let us punish those who . . ."

"That's better. Once more now, let's hear it!"

As he grew more daring, the pitch of his voice rose too high, like a squawk. The ruler leaped in the air and landed on the table, crack!

"No, no, no! How many times do I have to tell you? You're lost in the clouds as usual. You're rushing just to get it over with! You must get the right intonation, do you understand? Enunciate, loudly . . . Come on, try it again, starting with 'our brothers, in whose hands . . .'"

Again and again the ruler hit the table in time with the desperate shouts of the little man, red with rage. The boy started again from the beginning, exhausted, with even less success.

He had to hold out his hand. The ruler came crashing down, ten times, like ice, on his fingers. The tears wouldn't come, just wouldn't, they gurgled in the depths. He held them back in time out of pity for himself. His throat was as tight as if he were being suffocated by smoke. He was splitting in two, he didn't care. Another self, detached from him, would cope with these sessions.

No one had ever struck him before. Not even the time when he had seen his father being led off at gunpoint and he had continued playing with the other children in the yard: they had called him "selfish." He didn't understand what the word meant, just felt its weight, the guilt, in his hurry to join the others, who were looking for smooth, flat pebbles to play ducks and drakes, stones that would hit the water with a smack and leap to the opposite bank of the river. Even then no one had hit him; he had never been hit until now.

The closer they got to the event, the more demanding became the rehearsals. Only the day before – since there was little hope of getting it right – his cousin had tried, with disarming stupidity, to revive their old friendship. He was joking, to show him that he could be at once young and old . . .

Now the strange hand squeezed his absent-mindedly. The teacher had neither the ability nor the sensitivity to revise and correct his earlier impressions of the boy. He would have been amazed were he aware of the calm detachment with which he was being observed. The boy had long since become skillful at shielding his feelings by retreating behind a pale mask of sleepiness. But at this particular moment he let himself go, living his experiences intensely. The teacher's presence had lost all power over him. He let himself be swept along by the frenzy of the crowd that was about to explode.

He watched the throngs in the park. Rebellious voices, festive voices. Youthful eyes, mirrors shimmering with the reflection of leaves still moist with dew. The teacher's hand seemed lifeless; he didn't catch his companion's mood.

A murmur ran through the foliage, then stillness hovered briefly over the park. But right away the railroad worker's brass band boomed a military march. A tall, very thin man with a large mustache got up on the improvised podium. He spoke of the war, of suffering in the camps, of peace, of retribution, justice, labor.

Behind the stage the small hero waited his turn. He was to speak right after the officer, before the woman. His cousin's hand, forgotten on the crown of his head, suddenly propelled him in front of the crowd.

They lifted him up and stood him up on a chair. The crowd's excitement grew. Then they abandoned him in front of the seething multitude. He was not afraid that he would forget the order of the words or the proper intonation. He was terrified that the chair might fail him, that it would overturn and pitch him forward into the pit.

They were waiting for him in total silence. He felt their eagerness. their ravenous hunger. Pulling himself together he met them head-on.

"We, who haven't known the meaning of childhood, nourished by cold and fear, under the mantle of war, we turn, today . . ."

He didn't see their veiled eyes, their tears. Applause, bravos – he rallied, haggard and drained.

Behind the podium the cousin accepted congratulations. His embarrassed face indicated that the speech had lived up to his expectations, his success was deserved. As for the little actor, he was passed from the arms of one relative to another, then to the acquaintances. The avalanche of embraces wore him out. The solicitude with which he was treated relieved him. They kept asking him, again and again, if they could get him anything, if he wanted anything, their words and gestures hesitant, as if they were afraid to hurt his feelings.

For a long while afterward the hero could still feel the crown laurels on his head. Numerous privileges that he now enjoyed reminded him of his triumph.

His cousin, the teacher, now consented to become the comrade he had been in the past. He sought other outlets for his intransigence and zeal. He thought that, surely, the boy would have forgotten the harshness with which he had treated him; after all, experiences of that sort served to build character. They started going on long evening walks again and having many conversations. Everything could be just as before.

Still, ostensibly the event was not forgotten. They recalled it at every opportunity. Indeed, they seemed to look for opportunities to bring up, and each time they found one they seemed to become more and more familiar with the great event, they even started to act proprietary toward it, with the growing conviction that it somehow belonged to them.

People would stop dead in the street to take a look at the precocious celebrity. Acquaintances, or even complete strangers, would cross from the other sidewalk and walk up to the white-haired lady:

"Excuse me, but isn't that the boy who gave the speech?"

They patted him on the head. He would feel, for an instant, as if a golden power were ennobling his shoulders. Then it would be over. He would be yelled at because he did not say hello to the tobacconist's fat wife, because his fingernails were dirty, or there he goes again, putting his hands in his pockets, he looks elsewhere, doesn't pay attention when grown-ups talk to him. . . .

Nothing upset him more than the compliments of relatives, particularly of those who lived far away and had not participated in the event, but were impressed by the mere echo of his fame.

"But my dear, why don't you come to see us? . . . I've heard . . . of course bring him over at least once. I beg you . . ."

During these visits, in houses of people he did not know, the hero was served up right after the dessert. Tears were shed and immediately forgotten in the chatter and the shouting, as each guest tried to drown out the next. Afterward coffee was served, weak and sweet.

An ever greater number of new acquaintances turned up – wives of cousins three times removed, former neighbors of the cripple who delivered seltzer water, childhood friends of deceased grandparents. People looked for each other, trying to recapture the old life, the old pleasures.

The winds of hope shook the little town during these first months of peace. They lived loudly and with excess vitality. The lust for life constantly sought reasons to break out and often did without any reason.

The parks rustled with tango rhythms. Visits, birthdays, name days, anniversaries, parties, engagements, weddings. Especially weddings. Weddings of relatives and acquaintances, of neighbors, friends, and friends of friends, innumerable weddings. They went everywhere they were invited, as if to make up for lost time and reassure themselves that they had come back alive, that they could start over again with renewed strength. The whole family went, no one was left behind, neither the old nor the children.

. . . It would be hard to say whose idea it was. Somehow, it was in the air. People kept looking for something new, exciting, something to stoke the fire, to provoke tears, laughter. Never mind who was the first to suggest it – they seized it instantly, casually. The boy went along without reacting.

He still remembered the first time he had felt as though smoke were choking him: he couldn't breathe, and then he seemed to split in two. The soldier had given him a quarter of a loaf of bread. Grandfather's and Mother's livid faces appeared in the doorway, astonished. He had returned victorious. They could hardly believe their eyes; but they forbade him ever to go near a soldier again. A part of him, the part drawn toward friendship with the soldier, was gradually torn away from him. In the following weeks, tortured by hunger, the boy often felt as though he were choking from smoke. But he became accustomed to it and learned to face it calmly.

He was jolted from his plunge into the past by the percussionist's bang on the drums. The dance stopped, the couples separated. The time for tears had come.

"Quiet everybody! Quiet, please! We have a guest of honor!"

They stood him on a chair or on a table. The wedding guests got their handkerchiefs ready. Near the door, a young man caressed his girlfriend's shoulder. When the applause broke out, he drew her closer to him.

Up on his podium, the guest of honor recited his lines. His white shirt-collar lit up his pale face, its delicate features blurred with fatigue. The stinging smoke choked him only rarely now. The split occurred painlessly. It was someone else who stood in front of him, who recited the same pathetic speech. He had become used to what was happening to him.

Applause and embraces followed. The newcomers repeated the gestures of the guests at previous parties. Those who had accompanied him to other weddings – close relatives or the habitual partygoers – were already familiar with his act, and they smiled at him conspiratorially.

He could escape the gushing and the pawing only when he finally found himself in front of a gigantic slice of wedding cake. They also brought him a small glass of wine. The musicians, he noticed, were given larger ones. It was his habit to withdraw into a corner near the orchestra.

Forgotten near the instrument cases, lost in the melodies, he would slide back into the past, among once-familiar faces: Grandfather's before the sickness struck him, as he lay his large old hand on his shoulder. . . . The doctor's in tears, standing by the bridge during that first night of plundering, after they had been attacked and dragged off the freight cars, their clothing, their rings, everything they still owned taken away from them.

Only Uncle and a very few others had been able to hold on to some money. He must have taken plenty of cash with him and hidden it so well that he still had it even after all the searches and beatings they endured. He had managed to keep the money; you could tell by the large slices of bread and jam he would buy. People would give a coat for two slices of bread, but that wouldn't worry him. From time to time, he came to them, nevertheless, to borrow money. Not much, small sums, for a few days. He never spent any of it, obviously, and he always returned it on time. But when Mara got sick they put a stop to his little game.

"What are you doing here? What are you thinking about?"

A heavy hand rested on the nape of his neck. Every now and then a reveler would discover him behind the double bass, startling him out of his trance. He would pick up the boy and hand him back to his family or drag him to the head table, forcing the bride to grant him the first dance of the evening, as a mark of respect. The groom would nod his consent.

Attempts were made to silence the crowd, but the buzzing persisted. Chairs were pushed to one side, the band blew a long fanfare. The bride strode to the center of the floor to honor the famous guest. She led him gently bending over him from time to time with a smile. The music did its part while he hurried and counted the steps, one to the left, two to the right; sometimes he would trip over the long train or the buckle and black shiny tongue of his shoe would get caught in the veil. The dance with the bride was not so much the high point of the evening as an interlude. He saw people chatting in groups, distracted, faces flushed from too much food and drink.

Occasionally his oratorical zeal was rewarded by a talk with the bride's father-in-law, who would make room next to himself at the head of the table, trying to look wise as he marveled at the hero's precocity.

But, carried away by music and drink, they soon forgot him and he returned to sit by the saxophone case. The musicians toiled conscientiously, arousing desire and spreading gaiety. The hall heated up, a haze of perspiration rose on clouds of dust.

The boy withdrew behind the percussionist; he rocked on the legs of the narrow, rickety chair and leaned his back against the wall. Frenzy mounted, they chatted and chatted, they recalled the dead and the suffering. They cried, flung money at the orchestra, clamored for horas and romantic tunes, fell into one another's arms.

Uncle had looked at Mara, ravaged by illness. He expressed sorrow for their misfortune. And then he asked them, with a certain bashfulness, to lend him some money, just for one day, just until tomorrow. Mother did not answer him; she was seething. He was her brother but he had reached bottom, she couldn't stand him any longer. She didn't answer him, not the second or the third time around, and he asked again and again in rising embarrassment. She simply looked into his eyes. Only after a while, in a tired voice, she said to him, "Sit here for a bit." Uncle stooped and, humiliated, did as he was told.

Half an hour later Uncle took him along to stay with him for two weeks, to give Mara time to recover and to avoid contagion. Uncle had behaved toward him with unusual kindness. He had succeeded in getting a blanket for the boy's exclusive use. He slept rolled up in it like a bag and no longer felt the cold floor at night. For two whole weeks he even had enough food. Uncle brought him bread, spoiled him, protected him, frowned at his wife whenever she showed resentment at the attention their guest was enjoying. But the tensions surrounding Uncle had exhausted him, and he wished that all would be over soon so that he could return home.

"Hello there, sir, why are you all by yourself? Come on, let's go see the little monkey . . ."

This time it seemed it was a bris. He shouldn't have hid from the start; it didn't last long. He knew the rituals of the various festivities, there were so many of them.

Once he woke up around midnight. His speech raced through his mind; he looked as through fog at the confusion in the room, the sour mood of the hung-over couples. He realized that his act must have been over a while ago, that it was probably the moment to approach the bride, that is, if he had executed the earlier part of the program. He stumbled sleepily to the head of the table and found himself face to face with a roly-poly grandmother in a white gown, with a flower wreath, bloated features, flour and syrup mingled into sweat running down her pasty face. This time it was not a real wedding but an anniversary, he now remembered . . . a silver wedding anniversary. Too late – the old bag had spotted him. Hastily she welcomed him, smiled at him with her big metal teeth, impatiently reached over to him with gravy-stained hands. The remains of a slice of wedding cake were melting on the dessert plate in front of her. She insisted that he eat it and offered him her lipstick-smeared spoon . . . He also saw the pickles, the chicken leftovers, the rice drenched in tomato sauce, the deep bowl of whipped cream. Swaying with nausea, he groped his way back to his corner by the orchestra and clutched tightly to his chair. They raised him onto his feet with difficulty – he had fallen suddenly in his sleep and the room was topsy-turvy, as though after an earthquake – and he had another round with the old bride. Next morning his family found him in bed at the neighbors', where he had been dropped off.

"Come, let's go, it's morning."

Other parties, other weddings. From now on everything will be different, they said, but, as though afraid of some impending calamity, they couldn't hold back. Something impelled them to recoup their energy and start all over again. The frail boy up on the chair touched them; the words of his speech bolstered their determination.

Who could tell whose idea it had been? Its promoters proved to be right; it didn't matter whose idea it had been. The young speaker lived up to expectations . . . Sometimes his speech was scheduled for the conclusion of a party, sometimes it was overlooked altogether. The hero would sneak away to the musicians' corner. He felt at ease in their company.

A new morning dawned, his legs moved unsteadily, cool air soothed his eyelids. It was as if his other self wanted to split away again, like when Uncle came to borrow money to forestall them from doing the same, or when he guiltily stretched out his hand and his cousin, the teacher, gave him a blow that felt as though it would cut off all his fingers. At parties he had always looked for his cousin, hoping to see him, at least once, mellowed by food and drink. But he never showed up. They said that the teacher was "off his rocker," he disappeared from home for days, even weeks, at a time, roaming the countryside with bands of rebels, unafraid of hunger or hardship. He had grown gaunt, emaciated, and each time he returned, they said, he could hardly wait to get going again.

The boy relived that extraordinary morning, the banners and flags, the men's lively glances, the streets dipped in gold, the festive riot in the park. He had fallen right into the bubbling, scalding applause, his skin red and swollen . . . no, no, that was another time, when they cured him with blue vitriol, held him fast so he couldn't escape. He remembered how he had drawn away from his cousin, bit by bit, when his friendship turned out to be a trap. From then on he was always on his guard.

Evening had come again. Candles and light bulbs illuminated the ballroom; the pale bride stood smiling at her father-in-law's side. His friends the musicians gave the signal: a mighty beat on the big drum, two blows with the flat of the hand on the cymbals, and the hall fell silent.

"And now, a surprise: our own young . . ."

A chair was set up in place, the audience regrouped. The soloist was lifted and placed on the pedestal.

"We, who haven't known the meaning of childhood . . ."

Afterwards – a slice of wedding cake, a small glass of wine, the horrors of the past. The nights, dragged out until dawn, flowed slowly; it took a long time for their dregs, and the thick, murky voices around him, to settle down. Then morning came. A spring day again, soft breezes blowing on tender eyes, and the boy offered the crowd his feelings, his old, choking fears. The muddy night grew thin and was washed away. Again, a delicate dawn flutters over the thick black crust of the night before. Eyes grow luminous, daylight rises, bearing life.

The sky sparkled like a new knife. Only at dawn did he feel the smoke choking him again. He reeled, dizzy with weariness and sadness.

Translated from the Romanian by Cornelia Golna

Serafim

by Tatyana Tolstoya

"Go away! Go awaaay, you lousy beast!"

Someone's dog, white, matted, disgusting, not only jumped into the elevator after Serafim, whimpered, its paws pacing the dim, clunking box racing up toward the sixteenth floor, but dared to rush to the apartment, scratching insistently at the padding of the door while Serafim struggled with the keys on the landing.

"Get out of here!"

Serafim was squeamish about nudging the warm brute with his clean foot. The dog was possessed by a frightful impatience: it drummed at the door, quickly wedged its nose to the crack and snuffed the air, drummed again, insisted, would not be disuaded.

Serafim stamped his foot and yelled – useless. He tried to trick the animal by swiftly pushing his way into the apartment, but, shuddering and wriggling like a furry snake, the filthy cur slithered in with hideous speed, rubbing against Serafim's legs in the process, and ran around the dark room, its claws clicking. Serafim squealed, grabbed a mop, overtook the dog, struck it, struck it again, kicked it out, slammed the door, and with a pounding heart collapsed against the frame. The fiend of hell quietly fluttered about on the landing, circling and rustling. It left.

His legs could still feel the revolting sensation of dog flesh slinking by. He felt nauseated.

Serafim lay against the door, calming himself down. Better now? Almost.

Leave me alone. What do you all want from me? I don't want anyone. I am separate. Higher. I descended from the starry fields to this filth, and when I've completed my earthly circle, I'll go back to where I came from. Don't touch me.

Serafim took off his coat, drank a glass of cold, clean water, lit two candles, sat down in front of the mirror and took a look at himself. Handsome. He narrowed his eyes appraisingly, threw back his head, observed from the side – excellent! That's me. Uncommonly fine! That's – me! Mind your own business, all of you. He remembered the dog. Disgusting beast. He jumped up in horror and glanced at his trousers – just as he thought – fur. Get rid of it immediately! A hot shower! He sat down at the mirror again.

. . . What a vile world. Women, children, old people, dogs . . . Yellow, heaving swill. Flesh is nauseating. The flesh of others is nauseating. Only what's mine is ravishing, pure, transparent. I am fleshless and sexless. I don't play your games. Get your muck out of here.

Serafim looked into the dark mirror. On both sides of the glass was a pure, living flame. Heavenly countenance. Candles! Heavenly countenance. But only I am permitted to admire this marvelous, inhuman sight! Turn your nasty faces away from me!

To go to work Serafim was obliged to ride the bus. He tried not to look at the swinish snouts, the camellike muzzles, the hippopotamus cheeks. People are all vile! And all of them, base, revolting, are staring at Serafim with bug eyes, grinning their grins. Yes, I am magnificent! Yes, my face shines with an unworldly light! Yes, golden curls! Snow-white wings! Angelic eyes! Part, crowd! Stand aside – Serafim goes here!

He looked in the mirror once more. Serafim's countenance swam up from the dark depths, wavering in the warm flame. A rosy glow, the reflected light of white wings behind his back. To gaze forever . . . Who are you, my beauty? Serafim sank into the divine reflection. Time to go to bed. Tomorrow would be a hard day. He blew out the flames, folded his wings together, and hung them in the soft twilight.

For the Montgolfier brothers' jubilee, the district was planning a mass flight of thirty kilometers. Serafim was also participating. He had to collect various papers: a bilirubin blood test, a general urine analysis, and a certificate of residency. "I'll fly higher than all of them," thought Serafim while the nurse drew his delicate blue blood through a tube. "Higher than the crowd, higher than the human throng, higher than their base passions. I, a child of the ether, will spread my blinding, silky snow-white wings like a million white humming birds. Oh, how magnificent my triumphant flight will be!"

He strolled leisurely along the drying spring path, carrying his curly golden head high. The quacking word ZHEK – the housing office – squatted on a brown plaque. Get the residency certificate.

He pushed open the door and entered. Two old ladies were asleep in a room without curtains furnished with rows of chairs. A middle-aged lecturer slowly read from a notebook covered with oilcloth:

"According to the absolutely apocryphal legend, god-the-father, who doesn't exist, supposedly fertilized the so-called virgin Mary by way of the non-existent holy spirit; the result of this fraudulent conception, according to the mendacious allegations of the clergymen, was the mythical figure of Christ, who is totally alien to us. These unfounded fabrications . . ."

The old ladies woke up.

"Come in, come in, Serafim!" cried the lecturer. "Today we're having an anti-Easter lecture on the evil of the so-called immaculate conception. Have a seat, it'll do you good to listen!"

Serafim looked at him coldly, slammed the door and left. I'm against any kind of conception. Fight, lecturer. Fight. Eradicate it. I'm above human beings, above their fables about vulgar gods giving birth to idiot infants in dirty cow sheds. I am pure spirit, I am Serafim!

At the store "Woodland Gifts" they had pigeons. Serafim took a pair. Simmer in a covered pot for up to an hour and a half.

The pigeons bubbled in the pot. The doorbell rang. So. It's Magda, his neighbor. She wants to get married. She visits Serafim under various pretexts, the red-headed scourge! Serafim folded his arms and began looking out the window, began to heat up. Magda sat down on the edge of the chair, her legs under it, she never knows where to put her hands. She likes Serafim. Vile thing! "Khhem . . ."

She's thinking about how to start. She glances around the kitchen.

"You're boiling a chicken?"

"Yes."

"Khhem."

Silence.

"I bought some pork too, you know, a fairly large piece, well, I mean, about three pounds, I kept looking at it, thinking, should I take it or shouldn't I, but I did;

I thought I'd bake it or something. I stood on line a long time; when I got home and unwrapped it – all fat! All fat!"

Fat is nauseating muck. The whole world of flesh - is fat. Fatty, sticky children, fatty old ladies, fatty red-headed Magda.

"Ahem. I thought, maybe, I could do some washing for you, dirty sheets or whatever. You live alone."

Go away you nauseating creature. Go away, don't soil my clean, clear, mountain spirit with your swinish hands. Go away.

She went away.

Serafim threw out the pigeons, drank a cup of clear broth. A pure, lean bird.

There. Get the results of the blood test; one last humiliation – and upward! To the stars! Serafim knew the results beforehand: no traces of filth, nothing lowly, denigrating or shameful would be detected. Not like these others!

Serafim got on the bus. People pressed in. Careful there, those are wings!

"You should take taxis," said a woman. But she looked at Serafim's luminous face – and smiled. Get away, you base thing!

He made his way to the middle. Someone touched one wing with a finger. Stung, he turned around. A small boy, hideous looking – glasses, crossed eyes, no front teeth – was looking at Serafim's luxurious, swan-like feathering. His whole body winced: the snotty freak! . . . with dirty hands!

Yes and here's the result of the blood test: aqua distillata (sic!). What did you think it would be? . . . Swine!

The day was ending. The sweaty din, sticky dirt, stench, the human swarm – everything was loaded onto wagons and carted away. The deep blue evening, brandishing a broom, nodded to Serafim as it advanced from the east. A gentle silvery sheen set in on high. On the emptying streets each black silhouette was individually underlined. Swinish snouts dared to smile at Serafim, to look into his face. "Annihilate them all," thought Serafim. "Incinerate every one of them. Yes, my face shines. Not for you! How dare you look!"

By the time he approached his building, it was completely dark. A temptingly empty bench. l'll have a breath of fresh air. And tomorrow – the flight!

He spread his wings, looked upward. The starry wheel turns slowly, slowly. Berenice's Hair, Virgo, the Herdsman, the Hunting Dogs - clean, cold, April diamonds. That was the place for Serafim. A sexless, shining body, he would glide in silvery raiment through the resonant heights, let the streaming cold of the constellations run between his fingers, dive into ethereal currents. Dling Dling! – the starry threads jingled like the strings of a harp. He would drink his fill of the clean, sparkling bubbles of the twenty-star Cup . . . And burn up the filthy earth. He'd pluck out the double, transfusing star from the Hunting Dogs constellation – the Heart of Charles . . . And he'd scorch the earth with fire.

Behind the bench, in the thick, bare bushes, something rustled, crackled, yapped – the white dog ran out, spun around, waved its tail, jumped on Serafim's lap – joyfully, joyfully, as if it had found a long lost friend. It jumped about noisily, trying to lick his face.

Serafim fell from the sky, jerked away, screamed, thrust out his arms. The dog jumped back, sat on it hind legs, tilted its head and looked at Serafim endearingly. From the sight of the affectionate muzzle and dark dog eyes, something hot and dirty rose in his chest, filled his throat. Silently, gritting his teeth, trembling, hating, Serafim moved toward the dog. It didn't understand and was overjoyed, wagged its tail, grinned, and ran to meet him. Serafim kicked at the dog's eyes with his heel, lost his footing, kicked, kicked, kicked! There we go.

He stood for awhile. The dog lay stretched out. Quiet. The stars dripped. A woman's voice called:

"Sha-arik, Sharik, Sharik! . . . Sha-aaaarinka, Sharinka, Sharinka! . . ."

"The same for you," thought Serafim. "Stamp out everyone." Trying not to make any noise with his wings, he quickly moved toward the building.

He slept badly that night. His jaw bones ached. He awoke at dawn, and felt his alarmingly changed palate with his tongue. Something was wrong. He yawned – and had difficulty opening his mouth. Everything had somehow become different. Something's in the way. It had gotten colder. He wiped his face with his hand and looked - blood: he'd cut his palm on the end of his nose. The mirror! From the white morning murk, from the oval frame someone was looking out at Serafim: a red, horny beak; a low forehead covered with blue-grey scales; from the mouth, the edges of a narrow slit, two large, long milk-white fangs. Serafim looked coldly into the frame. He ran the split tongue along the fangs. They're strong. He looked at the clock: "Off to the dentist. The private doctor. There's time before the flight."

Tap tap tap went his claws on the asphalt. Faster – tap, tap tap tap tap . . .

"The monster Serpent Gorynych!" shouted some boys. "Look there's Serpent Gorynych!"

Serafim tucked his coat tight around him, grabbed his wide black wings, and took off at a run – the bus had already rounded the corner.

Translated from the Russian by Jamey Gambrell

DATE DUE

Ill			
3411556			
10/17/99			
JUL 1 5 2008			
SEP 1 1 2014			